The
MX Book
of
New
Sherlock
Holmes
Stories

Part XXV – 2021 Annual
(1881-1888)

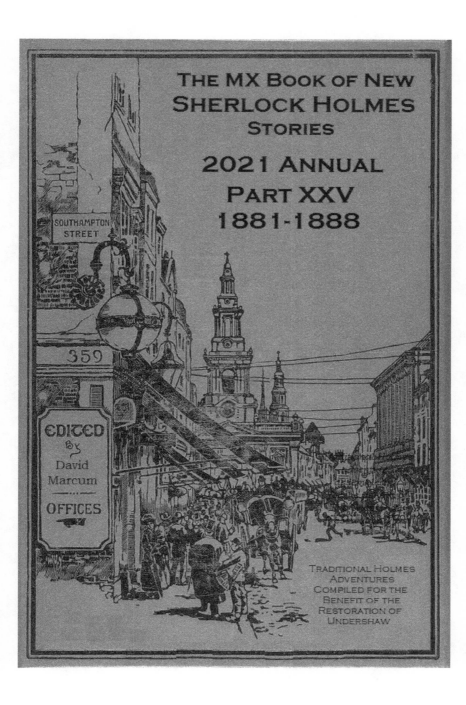

THE MX BOOK OF NEW SHERLOCK HOLMES STORIES

2021 ANNUAL
PART XXV
1881-1888

SOUTHAMPTON STREET

359

EDITED BY
David Marcum

OFFICES

TRADITIONAL HOLMES
ADVENTURES
COMPILED FOR THE
BENEFIT OF THE
RESTORATION OF
UNDERSHAW

ISBN Hardback 978-1-78705-774-6
ISBN Paperback 978-1-78705-775-3
AUK ePub ISBN 978-1-78705-776-0
AUK PDF ISBN 978-1-78705-777-7

Published in the UK by
MX Publishing
335 Princess Park Manor, Royal Drive,
London, N11 3GX
www.mxpublishing.co.uk

David Marcum can be reached at:
thepapersofsherlockholmes@gmail.com

Cover design by Brian Belanger
www.belangerbooks.com and *www.redbubble.com/people/zhahadun*

CONTENTS

Forewords

Adventures

(Continued on the next page . . . .)

(Continued on the next page . . . .)

(Continued on the next page . . . .)

**These additional Sherlock Holmes adventures
can be found in the previous volumes of**
The MX Book of New Sherlock Holmes Stories

(Continued on the next page . . . .)

(Continued on the next page . . . .)

PART V – Christmas Adventures

(Continued on the next page . . . .)

PART VI – 2017 Annual

(Continued on the next page . . . .)

The Unwelcome Client – Keith Hann
The Tempest of Lyme – David Ruffle
The Problem of the Holy Oil – David Marcum
A Scandal in Serbia – Thomas A. Turley
The Curious Case of Mr. Marconi – Jan Edwards
Mr. Holmes and Dr. Watson Learn to Fly – C. Edward Davis
Die Weisse Frau – Tim Symonds
A Case of Mistaken Identity – Daniel D. Victor

PART VII – Eliminate the Impossible: 1880-1891
Foreword – Lee Child
Foreword – Rand B. Lee
Foreword – Michael Cox
Foreword – Roger Johnson
Foreword – Melissa Farnham
Foreword – David Marcum
No Ghosts Need Apply (A Poem) – Jacquelynn Morris
The Melancholy Methodist – Mark Mower
The Curious Case of the Sweated Horse – Jan Edwards
The Adventure of the Second William Wilson – Daniel D. Victor
The Adventure of the Marchindale Stiletto – James Lovegrove
The Case of the Cursed Clock – Gayle Lange Puhl
The Tranquility of the Morning – Mike Hogan
A Ghost from Christmas Past – Thomas A. Turley
The Blank Photograph – James Moffett
The Adventure of A Rat. – Adrian Middleton
The Adventure of Vanaprastha – Hugh Ashton
The Ghost of Lincoln – Geri Schear
The Manor House Ghost – S. Subramanian
The Case of the Unquiet Grave – John Hall
The Adventure of the Mortal Combat – Jayantika Ganguly
The Last Encore of Quentin Carol – S.F. Bennett
The Case of the Petty Curses – Steven Philip Jones
The Tuttman Gallery – Jim French
The Second Life of Jabez Salt – John Linwood Grant
The Mystery of the Scarab Earrings – Thomas Fortenberry
The Adventure of the Haunted Room – Mike Chinn
The Pharaoh's Curse – Robert V. Stapleton
The Vampire of the Lyceum – Charles Veley and Anna Elliott
The Adventure of the Mind's Eye – Shane Simmons

PART VIII – Eliminate the Impossible: 1892-1905
Foreword – Lee Child
Foreword – Rand B. Lee
Foreword – Michael Cox
Foreword – Roger Johnson
Foreword – Melissa Farnham

(Continued on the next page . . . .)

Part IX – 2018 Annual (1879-1895)

(Continued on the next page . . . .)

(Continued on the next page . . . .)

The Adventure of the Silver Skull – Hugh Ashton
The Pimlico Poisoner – Matthew Simmonds
The Grosvenor Square Furniture Van – David Ruffle
The Adventure of the Paradol Chamber – Paul W. Nash
The Bishopgate Jewel Case – Mike Hogan
The Singular Tragedy of the Atkinson Brothers of Trincomalee – Craig Stephen Copland
Colonel Warburton's Madness – Gayle Lange Puhl
The Adventure at Bellingbeck Park – Deanna Baran
The Giant Rat of Sumatra – Leslie Charteris and Denis Green
       Introduction by Ian Dickerson
The Vatican Cameos – Kevin P. Thornton
The Case of the Gila Monster – Stephen Herczeg
The Bogus Laundry Affair – Robert Perret
Inspector Lestrade and the Molesey Mystery – M.A. Wilson and Richard Dean Starr

Part XII: Some Untold Cases (1894-1902)

Foreword – Lyndsay Faye
Foreword – Roger Johnson
Foreword – Melissa Grigsby
Foreword – Steve Emecz
Foreword – David Marcum
It's Always Time (*A Poem*) – "Anon."
The Shanghaied Surgeon – C.H. Dye
The Trusted Advisor – David Marcum
A Shame Harder Than Death – Thomas Fortenberry
The Adventure of the Smith-Mortimer Succession – Daniel D. Victor
A Repulsive Story and a Terrible Death – Nik Morton
The Adventure of the Dishonourable Discharge – Craig Janacek
The Adventure of the Admirable Patriot – S. Subramanian
The Abernetty Transactions – Jim French
Dr. Agar and the Dinosaur – Robert Stapleton
The Giant Rat of Sumatra – Nick Cardillo
The Adventure of the Black Plague – Paul D. Gilbert
Vigor, the Hammersmith Wonder – Mike Hogan
A Correspondence Concerning Mr. James Phillimore – Derrick Belanger
The Curious Case of the Two Coptic Patriarchs – John Linwood Grant
The Conk-Singleton Forgery Case – Mark Mower
Another Case of Identity – Jane Rubino
The Adventure of the Exalted Victim – Arthur Hall

PART XIII: 2019 Annual (1881-1890)

Foreword – Will Thomas
Foreword – Roger Johnson
Foreword – Melissa Grigsby
Foreword – Steve Emecz
Foreword – David Marcum
Inscrutable (*A Poem*) – Jacquelynn Morris

(Continued on the next page . . . .)

PART XIV: 2019 Annual (1891 -1897)

(Continued on the next page . . . .)

(Continued on the next page . . . .)

Part XVII – (1891-1898)

Part XVIII – (1899-1925)

(Continued on the next page . . . .)

Part XIX: 2020 Annual (1892-1890)

(Continued on the next page . . . .)

The Adventure of the Matched Set – Peter Coe Verbica
When the Prince First Dined at the Diogenes Club – Sean M. Wright
The Sweetenbury Safe Affair – Tim Gambrell

Part XX: 2020 Annual (1891-1897)
Foreword – John Lescroart
Foreword – Roger Johnson
Foreword – Lizzy Butler
Foreword – Steve Emecz
Foreword – David Marcum
The Sibling (A Poem) – Jacquelynn Morris
Blood and Gunpowder – Thomas A. Burns, Jr.
The Atelier of Death – Harry DeMaio
The Adventure of the Beauty Trap – Tracy Revels
A Case of Unfinished Business – Steven Philip Jones
The Case of the S.S. Bokhara – Mark Mower
The Adventure of the American Opera Singer – Deanna Baran
The Keadby Cross – David Marcum
The Adventure at Dead Man's Hole – Stephen Herczeg
The Elusive Mr. Chester – Arthur Hall
The Adventure of Old Black Duffel – Will Murray
The Blood-Spattered Bridge – Gayle Lange Puhl
The Tomorrow Man – S.F. Bennett
The Sweet Science of Bruising – Kevin P. Thornton
The Mystery of Sherlock Holmes – Christopher Todd
The Elusive Mr. Phillimore – Matthew J. Elliott
The Murders in the Maharajah's Railway Carriage – Charles Veley and Anna Elliott
The Ransomed Miracle – I.A. Watson
The Adventure of the Unkind Turn – Robert Perret
The Perplexing X'ing – Sonia Fetherston
The Case of the Short-Sighted Clown – Susan Knight

Part XXI: 2020 Annual (1898-1923)
Foreword – John Lescroart
Foreword – Roger Johnson
Foreword – Lizzy Butler
Foreword – Steve Emecz
Foreword – David Marcum
The Case of the Missing Rhyme (A Poem) – Joseph W. Svec III
The Problem of the St. Francis Parish Robbery – R.K. Radek
The Adventure of the Grand Vizier – Arthur Hall
The Mummy's Curse – DJ Tyrer
The Fractured Freemason of Fitzrovia – David L. Leal
The Bleeding Heart – Paula Hammond
The Secret Admirer – Jayantika Ganguly

(Continued on the next page . . . .)

Part XXII: Some More Untold Cases (1877-1887)

(Continued on the next page . . . .)

(Continued on the next page . . . .)

The following contributions appear in the companion volumes:
The MX Book of New Sherlock Holmes Stories
Part XXVI – 2021 Annual (1888-1897)
Part XXVII – 2021 Annual (1898-1928)

Editor's Foreword
A Series of Tales
by David Marcum

A few weeks ago, I was exchanging messages with a Sherlockian friend, and the topic of editing came up. We were discussing a new Holmes anthology which neither of us has yet read, containing stories by several authors that my friend likes and several other authors that I like (and also that I know by way of their previous participation in various anthologies that I've edited). I mentioned how it might be a little while before I would actually have time to dive into this new book, as a great deal of my free reading time nowadays is now spent editing submitted stories, which I print on 8½ x 11-inch paper and read with red pen in hand. Over the last few years, I have less time for purely recreational reading than I used to, as I currently receive around 200 traditional pastiche submissions per year for various collections that I edit, and each of those gets multiple read-throughs.

"I can't imagine," my friend, who is a noted editor himself, replied, *"wading through 200 traditional Sherlock Holmes pastiche submissions in a year. You've got my respect and sympathy for that."*

That response has stuck with me for several weeks. *Sympathy?* Why *sympathy*? Right now I'm having my Sherlockian wish come true – people send me new Sherlock Holmes adventures nearly every day. Decades ago, when I first found my way to 221b Baker Street, new stories beyond the original Canon were very few and far between. I'd be lucky to find a new pastiche *once or twice a year*. Now, in terms of new Holmes tales, we're living in the most golden part yet of the Golden Age that started when Nicholas Meyer published *The Seven-Per-Cent Solution* in 1974.

There are a lot of newer Sherlockians who don't know what it was like back then –before the internet, when one couldn't instantly research anything as soon as the idea crossed one's mind, or reach out to an author directly with praise, or to ask a question or offer a comment. One couldn't simply download something or buy a physical copy within minutes of seeing it. Back in those days, one generally didn't know about a new book or its release until it was there in front of you at the bookstore, serendipitously discovered on the shelf. And in those long-ago days, the idea that the majority of writers could write and then get their work in front of the public with any kind of ease was almost laughably impossible – akin to getting a rich man into heaven or a camel through the eye of a needle.

1

Publishing then was an elitist club with a closed door – even more than so than today, if that can be conceived. (Back then, it took so long for a new story or book to grind through the process then set in place that very few made it, and if something was picked for publication, it might be *years* before it actually physically appeared.) There were certainly a lot of potential Sherlockian authors in that era who would have brought forth Watsonian manuscripts if there had been any hope at all of them reaching the hands of the true fans. Thankfully for both writers and readers, this is a different and better time.

When I was ten years old in 1975, and obtained and read my first Holmes book, there was relatively very little out there beyond The Canon for those who wanted additional adventures. There was some scholarship, but it was generally very esoteric, and extremely difficult to locate, as most of it was published in very limited runs, which quickly vanished into private collections.

But some could be located if one was lucky. I remember when I was in high school in the early 1980's and had reason to go to the nearby University of Tennessee Library for the first time. It was then housed in a vast building that was more akin to a castle than a university building – that is to say, it was perfect. On my first trip, I happened to check the card catalog – if you don't know what that is, kids, Google it – and found that there was a whole section of Sherlockian scholarship upstairs. I was stunned and amazed.

When I navigated the Library of Congress method of cataloging and shelving – which makes no sense if you've been trained on the sensible Dewey Decimal System – I found that they had a complete run of *The Baker Street Journal*, all the way back to the first issue. There were other legendary titles that I'd only seen in mentioned in footnotes – Bell's *Baker Street Byways*, Blakeney's *Sherlock Holmes: Fact or Fiction?* and Holroyd's *Baker Street Byways*, among many others. Over the course of the next few years, I spent a goodly number of hours up there, working my way through the *Journals* and the other volumes (which I could not check out), standing at a Xerox machine and plowing through mounds of dimes to copy items from them, one page at a time. And what was I copying? *Pastiches*, of course. For those books sometimes – although quite rarely – contained a very few of them, buried amongst the scholarship, and it was worth my time and money, because *I wanted more Holmes adventures!*

It was tough then for people like me who had read through The Canon at a dead run and burst out the other end still wanting more. One option was to start in and re-read the pitifully few 60 stories again, and then again, and again, in whatever way seemed best: Straight through in the order that they were collected in book form, or jumping around randomly, as influenced by whatever tale seemed most interesting that day. (My parents gave me Baring-Gould's biography, *Sherlock Holmes of Baker Street*, early on, with its very influential chronology, but it hadn't yet occurred to me the wisdom of actually reading the stories in chronological order.)

My initial exposure to extra-Canonical adventures was first by way of the previously mentioned *The Seven-Per-Cent Solution*, followed soon after by Nicholas Meyers' much better sequel, *The West End Horror* – still one of my favorite Holmes adventures to this day. (I'll never forget the surprise ending.) I found a few others through the mid- and late 1970's – Sean Wright and Michael Hodel's *Enter the Lion*, for instance, and Michael Kurland's *The Infernal Device*, along with those reissued treasures, the Solar Pons volumes by August Derleth – and these encounters with new Holmes adventures in those days came primarily from what showed up on the drug store paperback rack. One can easily imagine how rarely something Sherlockian appeared there.

As I grew older, other methods of obtaining Sherlockian volumes became available. One could write letters to certain specialty bookstores (advertised in the back of a few mystery magazines) requesting their "catalogs" – usually nothing more than a set of poorly Xeroxed and stapled sheets. (How many Sherlockians – like me – still have those precious documents saved someplace?) There were a few dealers that put out nicer brochures and catalogs a couple of times per year – the place in California called *Sherlock's Home* and Carolyn and Joel Senter's wonderful *Classic Specialties*. And of course there was Otto Penzler's amazing *The Mysterious Bookshop* – still going strong today. My family knew that when my birthday or Christmas rolled around, I would provide them with these various catalogs, with pages suitably marked and Sherlockian items specifically requested. I imagine that Sherlockians all over the country did the same thing, and they probably learned the same lesson that I did: If you come across a Sherlockian item that you want, you'd better go ahead and get it now, because it will soon be gone, and trying to find it again later is either going to be nearly impossible or very expensive!

And so it went for several more years – Every once in a while, a traditional pastiche could survive the publishing gauntlet and appear for the hungry public in a real bookstore. Carole Nelson Douglas's definitive Irene Adler novels came along during this time, as did some anthologies by editors like Martin Greenberg and Marvin Kaye. And several small publishers offered Sherlockian titles for a while – Magico and Ian Henry, for instance. Some canny authors like Master Pasticheur Denis O. Smith self-published his initial efforts in chapbook form – and thankfully I have all of those in my collection, proving again my point to grab these things when you have the chance.

And then: *The Internet.*

The Internet changed everything in terms of Sherlockian Pastiche. (It changed everything, period, but this essay is more tightly focused on Sherlockian pastiches and publishing.) I found The Internet in the mid-1990's, when I went back to school for a second degree, this time to be a civil engineer. As an adult student, I worked full-time at night in addition to going to classes during the day, and I had lots of time to kill in between some of those. It was spent hanging out in the school's computer lab, where I received my first real exposure to The Internet. (A dial-up modem at home on a small computer that wasn't much more than a solitaire-playing machine/drink coaster combo was no help at all.)

Naturally, I spent a lot of time going down various Sherlockian rabbit holes. (My wife, a gifted reference librarian, taught me some great search tricks, and I figured out a few more on my own.) By way of the original and very useful *Sherlockian.net* (before it changed), I found links to many on-line pastiches. As am adult student, I was forced to pay certain fees to the university for things that I would never use, such as intramural sports, so I felt no guilt at taking advantage of the free printing that I was allowed in the computer lab. Thus, I was able to print hundreds – nay, *thousands!* – of traditional online pastiches that I winkled out over several years through searches into ever-more obscure places. Often one led to another, or to five more. Thankfully I did print and save them all. I still have them archived in my collection, and many of them have long-since vanished – lost Sherlockian treasures, some of which are as good or better than the Canonical stories.

At one point, I probably had a six-foot-high stack of printed Holmes stories on my desk at home, and I slowly worked my way through them, along with reading all the other Holmes volumes in my collection. (It was during these years that I was initially constructing my Holmes Chronology of both Canon and pastiche, now well over 1,000 dense pages, breaking down novels, short stories, radio and television episodes, movies and scripts, comics and unpublished manuscripts, and fan-fiction by book, chapter, page, or paragraph into year, month, day, and even hour.)

Besides printing online pastiches, I was also requesting many many obscure volumes by way of the university's interlibrary loan program, and Xeroxing them for my collection, until some future date when I could obtain the real thing – once again standing at copy machines and feeding in dime after dime. It was time and money well spent. Additionally, I was able to find many more pastiche titles for sale through The Internet than I'd ever been able to locate before using those irregular catalogs, and I started acquiring those too. My endeavors to track down as many traditional Canonical pastiches as I could was vastly aided by the late Phil Jones's online pastiche list, which allowed me to identify even more that I wanted. Thus, I built a formidable traditional pastiche collection.

And even as I was obtaining these new adventures by way of The Internet, The Internet was allowing previously suppressed and stymied Sherlockian authors, without hope, to connect with readers in ways that had never before been possible.

Who could have known that there were so many people out there who had access to some really excellent material from Watson's Tin Dispatch Box? The call to pull forth these stories might have been so strong that they would have done so no matter what, but The Internet allowed a connection between author and reader in such a new way, and with such instantaneous feedback and gratification, that it became almost addictive to keep producing stories.

The old publishing paradigm, as alluded to above, was Darwinian, with only a few survivors able to see actual publication. Often it wasn't – and isn't – fair, with material being published "professionally" that is nowhere near as good as "amateur" writings. Granted, some like Denis Smith had the gumption to produce their own pamphlet-like publications, but very few knew about them, and only a tiny number of them in the great scheme of things were ever physically produced. The Internet allowed authors – not just Sherlockians, but of any fandom – to write and publish with nearly instantaneous turnaround. And here the publishing paradigm began to shift. The old established behemoth publishing companies continued to follow the model of printing thousands of copies of the few authors' works that survived their gauntlet, with carefully calculated mathematical models to determine just how many copies had to be sold to make the thinnest margin of profit. In the meantime, copies sat on bookstore shelves, more unsold than sold, and then they rotated into remainder bins or were destroyed, like food that has gone past the expiration date.

But others had vision – like Steve Emecz of MX Publishing – who recognized the incredible value of *print-on-demand* technology, wherein an order is placed for a book, which generates that book being printed at a specialized factory where the file is already loaded. As soon as it's produced, it's then shipped, and thus into the hands of the happy reader just days later – while the author accumulates a royalty. With that simple brilliant realization, Steve Emecz managed to make the connection between the Sherlockian authors who had tales to tell and no effective way of sharing them to their benefit, and the Sherlockian readers (like me) who want more new Holmes adventures, every day.

I was aware of the MX books before I ever became involved with them. As a Holmes collector, I was thrilled when this new company showed up, and of course I started buying the books as the appeared. A few at first, then more and more as Steve perfected his system. My own first book, *The Papers of Sherlock Holmes*, was originally published in 2011 by a small Canadian press, and according to that publisher, it has yet to sell a single copy. (Curiously, I know that copies were in fact sold, because I know people that bought them. Yet I've certainly never received a single dime in royalties for that edition, although it's still available on that publisher's website.) When I saw that an excellent Sherlockian pasticheur, Gerard Kelly – who had also been with that Canadian press – had jumped to MX for a new edition of his book, I reached out to Steve Emecz (on December 13th, 2012), asking for him to forward a message to Gerard. Steve did, and Gerard and I discussed our mutual experiences with the Canadian publisher. He then advised enthusiastically that I also switch to MX. So finally, on January 11th, 2013 I formerly introduced myself by way of an email to Steve, pitching my book. That turned out to be an amazing life-changing email for me, and once again proof that if you don't ask, you'll never know. A few months later, my first book was reissued as a two-volume set (and later as a hardcover and an Audible audio book too). And there was no looking back.

I believe that MX initially began as a typical for-profit company, but Steve and his wife Sharon quickly pivoted it to become a non-profit organization, supporting several charities, including the Happy Life Children's Home in Kenya. Initially, MX was involved in saving Undershaw, one of Sir Arthur Conan Doyle's former homes, from developers who would drastically alter or destroy it. When Undershaw was saved, MX shifted to supporting the Stepping Stones School for special needs children, which is now located at Sir Arthur's former home. In addition to these charitable works, Steve has another unofficial mission: He gives Sherlockian authors who would otherwise be unable to do so the chance to have their books published. Some MX authors are quite prolific, and some of their titles are tent-poles for the broader business, while other authors just have the one story in them. Still, they are also a part of the MX family, and they've had an opportunity that wouldn't be offered by most publishers.

In 2013, the year MX re-published my first book, I made my initial Holmes Pilgrimage to London and other British locations, and I was able to meet Steve in person for the first time. It was a rainy afternoon in the bar of the Sherlock Holmes Hotel in Baker Street, where I was staying. For those who don't know, Steve is just as nice in real life as he seems when you read about him or hear him interviewed. And he's very supportive – for instance, on the occasions when I wrote and published my next two books of original material, and also when, in early 2015, I had the idea for *The MX Book of New Sherlock Holmes Stories.*

For early that year, I woke up from a dream where I'd edited a book. In spite of all the new pastiches I'd found over the past years, I wanted more – particularly to reinforce the traditional Canonical heroic Holmes, as there was too much insidious infiltration of late into pastiches of elements from a certain television show that had the word *Sherlock* in the title, but nothing else to do with Our Hero. As this show started to creep into the public consciousness, I was starting to read pastiches by people who should have known better giving Holmes a "mind palace", or indicating that he was a "high-functioning sociopath", or implying that Watson's wound was psychosomatic, or that Irene Adler was a dominatrix – all ridiculous ideas. A strong push-back was necessary.

I asked Steve about my idea for a new book of traditional Canonical adventures, and he was very supportive, so I began reaching out to some authors that I admired to see if they would be interested. I had pictured – if I was lucky – a trade paperback of maybe one- or two-dozen new stories, pleasing me but gathering little attention otherwise. Fearing failure, I overcompensated and sent invitations to every Sherlockian author that I could think of, particularly authors of books in my Holmes collection – and there were a lot of them. I also wrote to some Sherlockian friends who had never actually written a pastiche before to see if they were interested, and they we were. (I'm especially proud of recruiting first-time writers, many of whom have gone on to successfully write quite a few more pastiches since then.) Amazingly, people were interested and willing to join the party. Word spread, and more people wanted in, including many that I hadn't heard of before. This was really going to happen.

Part of what attracted these participants – besides the desire to contribute to The Great Holmes Tapestry – was the fact that early on, Steve and I had decided to direct the royalties from the project to the Stepping Stones School, and people were thrilled to be able to help in that way. Through 2015, the stories rolled in and the editing continued. Then, it was publication time. I had my second in-person meeting with Steve in October 2015, on my second Holmes Pilgrimage when I was able to return to the Holmesland for the launch of the three-volume initial set of *The MX Book of New Sherlock Holmes Stories* – for by then it had grown to over 60 new adventures, the largest collection of its kind in the world. Steve had an amazing launch party on top of one of London's skyscrapers – which just happened to hold the office where he was employed at the time. It was an amazing night, and I was able to meet a number of wonderful Sherlockian contributors in person – and my biggest regret is that I didn't get to spend more time with each of them and think to make photographs there that night.

While on that second Pilgrimage, I was able to spend some time with Sherlockian Nick Utechin, who gave me an in-depth tour of Oxford – Sherlockian points of interest and otherwise. While we ate lunch, he expressed that he wished he'd been part of the three volumes, but he'd be interested in being in the next set. *Next set . . . ?* Back home a few weeks later, I started to hear from previous contributors and the newly interested, also indicating they'd like to be in the next volumes. *Next volumes . . . ?* I'd never thought of it as anything but a one-time thing. But suddenly the future got a little brighter than it already was. *Why not another set?* Steve and I had already done the heavy lifting in setting up the previous volumes, making decisions about formats and style. We had an existing pool of contributors – Sherlockians with more stories to tell and anxious to do so. And it was for a great double cause – the Stepping Stones School, and the continued support of the true traditional Canonical Sherlock Holmes. So a week or so after I returned from Holmes Pilgrimage No. 2, the call went out for more stories, and Part IV was published in Spring 2016. There was such interest that another volume was scheduled for Fall 2016, and since then, we've published spring and fall collections every year, sometimes single volumes, but more often then not having so many stories that they run to double- or triple-volume sets. (And I'm mightily thankful that Steve is the kind of publisher who indicated that with more stories, we simply grow to more volumes, without slamming the door at a certain page count and cutting off willing authors and hungry readers from more excellent adventures.)

Since the series started, we've now produced almost 600 new Holmes adventures in 27 volumes from nearly 200 contributors around the world. And as of this writing, the donated royalties to the Stepping Stones School are somewhere over $75,000 – with no end in sight. Many of the contributors have provided enough stories that they now have enough of them accumulated to publish their own books, and there have also been a number of other Sherlockian anthologies – particularly from Belanger Books – that have started to promote the same kinds of Canonical Sherlockian tales. (I've also edited a number of those, and I think of them as MX Anthology annexes – they're set up with the same story requirements, and the same typeface and layout as the MX books, and usually submitted by the same authors. I highly recommend them.)

So when I think of my friend's comment about *Sympathy*, I'm frankly dumbfounded. Personally, I'm having the time of my life, and I expect that I'd be somewhere far outside the Sherlockian sandbox looking in if not for my initial emails to Steve Emecz in late 2012 and early 2013 and his

8

subsequent positive response. (Thanks Steve!) And beyond what these books have done for me personally, I think they provide an amazing service for others – not just the royalties for the school, or as an outlet for the authors who have tales to tell, or for the readers hungry for more of them. No, in these crazy times in which we live, there's a true *need* for Sherlock Holmes – maybe more than ever.

It's unnecessary to delve in great depth upon the calamitous events of the past few years – the COVID-19 pandemic, and the rise of fascism coupled with the need of many to race toward the cliff of stupidity. Holmes's adventures provide a much-needed escape from the idiocy of today: They show order being brought to chaos, and justice being administered to injustice. But Holmes also serves as a reminder and example of how we should be as people. For Holmes would not be a science-denier. He would not support those oppressors who would steal basic human rights from those whom they can exploit. And he would not support fascist wanna-be dictators. He would speak truth to the liars and the corrupt, and that's why he's a hero for any age.

Of course, it must be noted that Holmes the scientific supporter would have had little use for these additional Watsonian narratives of his adventures. In *The Sign of the Four*, he explains his position to Watson, when discussing the published version of *A Study in Scarlet*:

> "I glanced over it," said he. "Honestly, I cannot congratulate you upon it. Detection is, or ought to be, an exact science and should be treated in the same cold and unemotional manner. You have attempted to tinge it with romanticism, which produces much the same effect as if you worked a love-story or an elopement into the fifth proposition of Euclid."
>
> "But the romance was there," I remonstrated. "I could not tamper with the facts."
>
> "Some facts should be suppressed, or, at least, a just sense of proportion should be observed in treating them. The only point in the case which deserved mention was the curious analytical reasoning from effects to causes, by which I succeeded in unravelling it."

More pointedly, in "The Copper Beeches", Holmes says:

> "You have degraded what should have been a course of lectures into a series of tales."

9

So Holmes was a hero, but he was also capable of being wrong, as shown with this simple statement. For Watson is a hero too, taking the time and effort to bring us these heroic adventures – not just those few in the original Canon, but all the others that have been pulled from his Tin Dispatch Box in the years since, by way of those later pasticheurs who open their minds to receive them and then transcribe them for the rest of us. Now, with this latest set of *The MX Book of New Sherlock Holmes Stories*, we have 59 more of them, and they'll help brighten the current (but thankfully brightening) darkness and push back on the seemingly endless evil and willful ignorance until the next set of MX Sherlockian tales arrives. Thank heavens the paradigm shifted so that so many talented and willing people could get these *"series of tales"* to so many of us who want and need them.

* * * * *

"Of course, I could only stammer out my thanks."
– *The unhappy John Hector McFarlane,* "The Norwood Builder"

As always when one of these sets is finished, I want to first thank with all my heart my incredible wonderful wife of nearly thirty-three years, Rebecca, and our amazing son and my friend, Dan. I love you both, and you are everything to me!

During the editing of these particular volumes, I obtained employment at my dream job. When the agency where I was a federal investigator closed in the 1990's, and I was figuring out what I wanted to do with my life, we lived near a beautiful park, and as I would walk there with my son, seeing the trails and springs and streams and culverts big enough that kids were exploring them, and I realized that I was interested in infrastructure – and particularly working for that city. That led to my return to school to be a civil engineer. After a number of years working at various engineering companies, and getting my license along the way, and still wanting to work at the city, I was finally able to. That has kept me extremely busy for the last few months, which kept me from replying to emails as fast as I would have wished, so I'm very grateful to everyone who patiently waited to hear back from me about their stories.

I can never express enough gratitude for all of the contributors who have donated their time and royalties to this ongoing project. I'm constantly amazed at the incredible stories that you send, and I'm so glad to have gotten to know so many of you through this process. It's an undeniable fact that Sherlock Holmes authors are the *best* people!

The contributors of these stories have donated their royalties for this project to support the Stepping Stones School for special needs children, located at Undershaw, one of Sir Arthur Conan Doyle's former homes. As of this writing, and as mentioned above, these MX anthologies have raised over $75,000 for the school, with no end in sight, and of even more importance, they have helped raise awareness about the school all over the world. These books are making a real difference to the school, and the participation of both contributors and purchasers is most appreciated.

Next is that group that exchanges emails with me when we have the time – and time is a valuable commodity for all of us these days! As mentioned, I don't get to write back and forth with these fine people as often as I'd like, but I really enjoy catching up when we do get the chance: Derrick Belanger, Brian Belanger, Mark Mower, Denis Smith, Tom Turley, Dan Victor, and Marcia Wilson.

There is a group of special people who have stepped up and supported this and a number of other projects over and over again with a lot of contributions. They are the best and I can't express how valued they are: Hugh Ashton, Derrick Belanger, Deanna Baran, Craig Stephen Copland, Matthew Elliott, Tim Gambrell, Jayantika Ganguly, Paul Gilbert, Dick Gillman, Arthur Hall, Steve Herczeg, Paul Hiscock, Craig Janacek, Mark Mower, Will Murray, Robert Perret, Tracy Revels, Roger Riccard, Geri Schear, Brenda Seabrooke, Shane Simmons, Robert Stapleton, Kevin Thornton, I.A. Watson, and Marcy Wilson.

I also want to particularly thank the following:

- *Peter Lovesey* – I first became aware of Mr. Lovesey by way of Sergeant Cribb, hero of eight novels (and later a short story), and a set of original television episodes. I saw *Cribb* when it first appeared on PBS in 1979 – consisting of two series of filmed versions of all eight novels, as well as six original cases, as written by Lovesey and Jacqueline Lovesey. This led me to read the one Cribb volume in our house, *Invitation to a Dynamite Party* (1974), inexplicably in my dad's massive book collection – "inexplicably" because that wasn't the type of book that he read at all. (And after that he didn't own it anymore, as I took possession – and I still have it.) That one book led me to quickly acquire all the rest of them, which I read in a white heat over the next few weeks, and have re-read countless times in the years since.

11

These fifteen tales (novels, original TV episodes, and short story) make up the entire Cribb Canon, and I've desperately wished for decades for more of them. When, through the aforementioned *Internet*, I was finally able to communicate with Mr. Lovesey, I expressed as much to him, but sadly I haven't (yet) convinced him to write more adventures of that heroic Sergeant. I've also floated the idea several times of having a Holmes and Cribb share a co-adventure, as they most certainly knew one another, and Holmes would have liked and respected Cribb. Additionally, Mr. Lovesey has written several especially fine Holmes pastiches. So far no luck – but I did have an off-screen Cribb Easter-egg appearance in one of my own short stories, "The Tangled Skein at Birling Gap" in *Sherlock Holmes: Tangled Skeins*.

After Sergeant Cribb, Mr. Lovesey went on to an incredibly honored writing career, including other series featuring Peter Diamond and Bertie, the Prince of Wales. While I've tried for years to recruit him to write a Holmes story for these volumes, I'm thrilled that he's a part of them by way of his brilliant foreword – wherein I learned that he has a knowledge of Undershaw that I didn't know about.

Thank you, Peter!

- *Roger Johnson* – I'm more grateful than I can say that I know Roger. His Sherlockian knowledge is exceptional, as is the work that he does to further the cause of The Master. But even more than that, both Roger and his wonderful wife, Jean Upton, are simply the finest and best kind of people, and I'm very lucky to know both of them – even though I don't get to see them nearly as often as I'd like, and especially in these crazy days! In so many ways, Roger, I can't thank you enough, and I can't imagine these books without you.

- *Steve Emecz* – As mentioned, when I first emailed Steve from out of the blue back in late 2012 and early 2013, I was interested in MX re-publishing my previously published first book. Even then, as a guy who works to accumulate *all* traditional Sherlockian pastiches, I could see that MX (under Steve's leadership) was *the* fast-rising superstar of the Sherlockian publishing world.

12

The publication of that first book with MX was an amazing life-changing event for me, leading to writing and then editing more books, unexpected Holmes Pilgrimages to England, and these incredible anthologies. When I had the idea for these books in early 2015, I thought that it might, with any luck, be one small volume of perhaps a dozen stories. Since then they've grown and grown, and by way of them I've been able to make some incredible Sherlockian friends and play in the Holmesian Sandbox in ways that I'd never before dreamed possible.

All through it, Steve has been one of the most positive and supportive people I've ever known, letting me explore various Sherlockian projects and opening up my own personal possibilities in ways that otherwise would have never been possible. Thank you Steve for every opportunity!

- *Brian Belanger* – Brian is one of the nicest and most talented of people, and I'm very glad that I was able to meet him in person during the 2020 Sherlock Holmes Birthday Celebration in New York. (Hopefully I'll see him there again when travel resumes.) His gifts are amazing, and his skills improve and grow from project to project. He's amazingly great to work with, and once again I thank him for another incredible contribution.

- *Scott Monty and Bert Wolder, Lenny Picker, and Adrian Braddy* – I very much appreciate being interviewed by these men – respectively at *I Hear of Sherlock Everywhere (IHOSE)*, *Publishers Weekly*, and *Sherlock Holmes Magazine* – and having the opportunity to spread the word about these anthologies.

And last but certainly *not* least, **Sir Arthur Conan Doyle**: Author, doctor, adventurer, and the Founder of the Sherlockian Feast. Present in spirit, and honored by all of us here.

It was particularly unusual editing this collection through the latter half of 2020 and into 2021, as the world continued through a deadly globe-spanning pandemic. Many people ended up being stuck at home, and my first thought was that a number of them would take advantage of that newly carved-out time – although for terrible reasons – to write. However, it soon became apparent that everyone's lives were turned upside down to

13

greater or lesser degrees, and even if they had the *time* to write something, they didn't necessarily have the *heart* to do so. I was concerned that Parts XXII, XXIII, and XXIV (published Fall 2020) might not have enough stories – at least not to the level which many have come to expect and look forward to.

But as people found their footing and their spirits, the stories began to arrive, more and more of them – both for those books, and also for other Sherlockian anthologies that I've edited at the same time. And the same was true for this current set. It's been amazing, and it showed that in these dark times, people have found great comfort in writing about Holmes and Watson and those bygone days, and also that they want to share those tales with others who will find comfort as well.

For everyone who dug deep and found a way forward and is a part of this collection, and for all of you who will be reading it, thank you so much.

As always, this collection has been a labor of love by both the participants and myself. As I've explained before, once again everyone did their sincerest best to produce an anthology that truly represents why Holmes and Watson have been so popular for so long. These are just more tiny threads woven into the ongoing Great Holmes Tapestry, continuing to grow and grow, for there can *never* be enough stories about the man whom Watson described as "*the best and wisest . . . whom I have ever known.*"

David Marcum
March 4th*, 2021*
The 140th *Anniversary of Watson*
first beginning to understand why
Holmes is a hero, during the events of
A Study in Scarlet

Questions, comments, or story submissions
may be addressed to David Marcum at

thepapersofsherlockholmes@gmail.com

Foreword
by Peter Lovesey

I'm delighted to be providing a foreword for this latest collection of stories inspired by Sir Arthur Conan Doyle's great detective. By the time I was fourteen, I had devoured the entire Canon. I know this because in 1951, armed with notes I had made in the complete short stories, I went to London to visit Abbey House in Baker Street. A national effort was being made to escape the post-war gloom with a Festival of Britain, and part of the fun was a Sherlock Holmes exhibition. Between May and September, over fifty-thousand people flocked to see it.

I remember being enraptured by original manuscripts, Sidney Paget's illustrations for *The Strand*, and a selection of the many letters addressed to Holmes that were delivered to Abbey House because it was deemed by the Post Office to be the site of number 221b. The main attraction was a re-creation by Michael Weight of the great consulting detective's living room as it had looked on a given day in 1898. As I entered, I heard sound effects provided by the BBC of a barrel organ playing and the clop-clop-clop of cab horses from the street below. A cluttered interior had numerous reminders of the room's occupant: *The Daily News* open at a page reporting the death of the long-serving prime minister, William Gladstone; shelves of books and case files; a Persian slipper containing tobacco; unanswered letters jack-knifed into the fireplace; cigars in the coal-scuttle; bullet-holes in the wall; chemical apparatus; a table set for afternoon tea; and, if you looked for it, a hypodermic syringe. Holmes himself wasn't present, but his likeness was, against one of the windows, the wax bust from *The Empty House.* I believe purists protested in the press that there should not have been a deerstalker cap hanging on the back of the door with the Inverness cape, and that Holmes could never have smoked a curved pipe because the first ones in Britain were brought back after the Boer War ended in 1902, but none of this bothered me as a schoolboy. I was enchanted.

The magic stayed with me. My first attempts at crime writing nearly twenty years later were set in Victorian London. Sensibly I made my sleuth, Sergeant Cribb, an ordinary working policeman, more shrewd and dogged than brilliant. Much later, I tried a couple of short stories meant to celebrate The Master, but I'm not proud of them. The stories in this fine collection get much closer to the spirit of the originals.

15

By then I was living in Sussex, the county where the Great Detective lives on in endless retirement, but I never had the privilege of meeting him. My reason for mentioning this is that my route into London took me regularly through a notorious bottleneck in the village of Hindhead. This was before the tunnel was built that now allows traffic to by-pass the place. I would look out of my slow-moving car at a sad sight: A large, derelict building that had once been the home of Conan Doyle. He had the house built and lived there from 1897 to 1907 while writing *The Hound of the Baskervilles* and the stories in *The Strand* later collected as *The Return of Sherlock Holmes*. Undershaw had been declared a World Heritage site in 1977, but its crumbling exterior suggested nothing so grand.

What heartening news it was in 2016 that Undershaw had been completely refurbished and was opening as an alternative special needs school called Stepping Stones for children with a variety of handicaps including hemiplegia, autism, and cerebral palsy. And how fitting that the profits from all the stories in this and other volumes in the series are donated to this worthy cause.

Seventy years after I visited that exhibition, I am treated to these new adventures of Sherlock Holmes. The spell is cast again.

"Come, Watson, come!" he cried. "The game is afoot! Not a word! Into your clothes and come!"

Ten minutes later we were both in a cab and rattling through the silent streets . . . .

Peter Lovesey
November 2020

"Veritable Tales"
by Roger Johnson

Nearly seventy years ago, in the October 1953 issue of *The Baker Street Journal*, Edgar W Smith wrote: "*There is no Sherlockian worthy of his salt who has not, at least once in his life, taken Dr. Watson's pen in hand and given himself to the production of a veritable tale.*" After briefly mentioning his own two contributions to the apocrypha, he continued: "*The point is that the writing of a pastiche is compulsive and inevitable, and nothing to be ashamed of. It is a wholesome and welcome manifestation of the urge to be intimately a part of the Baker Street scene; a sublimation of the desire that is in us all to revel in the glory of the Saga, not only receptively, but creatively as well.*"

Some will disagree – I've known people who regard Holmesian pastiche with a rabid hatred that sometimes suggests actual mental disorder – but most of us, surely, realise that the Blessed Edgar expressed, far better than we could, something which we had always instinctively known even though we may not have given it much thought.

He had more to say on the subject, however, and this too may stir a thought or two that were hitherto unrecognised. "*And yet I like to think,*" he said, "*that pastiches are made to be written but not to be read. They are the stuff of dreams, the projection of our fancies, the release of our repressed desires, in which we, but not others, should be expected to take delight.*"

To sum up, then, we should all feel free to create new exploits for Holmes and Watson, but we shouldn't inflict them upon others.

Now, what sort of statement is that to make in a foreword for the latest in David Marcum's admirable series of *New Sherlock Holmes Stories* for MX Publishing? Well, Edgar Smith went on to say: "*Once in a while, when there is one superbly done, it may with some trepidation be, shared with those who understand and sympathize.*"

His standards were possibly higher and less flexible than mine. Where he required the superb (and remember that many of the sixty canonical tales don't qualify for that description) I can be satisfied with ingenuity, atmosphere, historical authenticity, wit, style . . . In short, I like a story that's neatly planned, written in good English, and written with real knowledge and love of Holmes, Watson, and Conan Doyle.

Which is to say, the sort of story that you'll find in this remarkable collection, and it makes this – and its companion volumes – the sort of book that you can confidently hand to almost any Sherlockian, with the recommendation, "This is good. I think you'll like it!"

Roger Johnson, BSI, ASH
Editor: The Sherlock Holmes Journal
February 2021

An Ongoing Legacy
for Sherlock Holmes
by Steve Emecz

Undershaw
Circa 1900

The MX Book of New Sherlock Holmes Stories has now raised over $75,000 for Stepping Stones School for children with learning disabilities, and is by far the largest Sherlock Holmes collection in the world.

Stepping Stones is located in Undershaw, the former home of Sir Arthur Conan Doyle, where he wrote many of the Sherlock Holmes stories. The fundraising has supported many projects continuing the legacy of Conan Doyle and Sherlock Holmes in the amazing building, including The Doyle Room, the school's Zoom broadcasting capability (including Sherlock themed events), The Literacy Program, and more.

In addition to Stepping Stones School, our main program that we support is the Happy Life Children's Home in Kenya. My wife Sharon and I have spent seven Christmas's with the children in Nairobi. Due to the global pandemic we didn't visit Africa this year.

It's a wonderful project that has saved the lives of over 600 babies. You can read all about the project in the second edition of the book *The Happy Life Story.*

In 2020, our *#bookstotrees* program where every book bought on our *www.mxpublishing.com* website resulted in a tree being funded at Happy Life. We reached our target of 1,000 trees in August.

In 2021, we are working on *#bookstobooks* which sees us donating 10% of the revenues from *mxpublishing.com* to fund schoolbooks and library books at Happy Life.

We've launched the Sherlock Holmes Book Club where fans can get a hardcover edition of *The MX Book of New Sherlock Holmes Stories* every month plus exclusive free books, events and competitions:

> *https://mxpublishing.com/products/sherlock-holmes-book-club-hardcover-subscription*

Our support of both of these projects is possible through the publishing of Sherlock Holmes books, which we have now been doing for thirteen years.

You can find out more information about the Stepping Stones School at:

> *www.steppingstones.org.uk*

and Happy Life at:

> *www.happylifechildrenshomes.com*

You can find out more about MX Publishing and reach out to us through our website at:

> *www.mxpublishing.com*

Steve Emecz
February 2021
Twitter: @mxpublishing

The Doyle Room at Stepping Stones, Undershaw
Partially funded through royalties from
The MX Book of New Sherlock Holmes Stories

21

A Word From
Stepping Stones
by Jacqueline Silver

Undershaw
September 9, 2016
Grand Opening of the Stepping Stones School
(Photograph courtesy of Roger Johnson)

Undershaw provided much inspiration for Sir Arthur Conan Doyle. It was the backdrop to many of his works which gained him such literary reverence. Those large south-facing windows which, in days gone by helped ease the symptoms of his wife's tuberculosis, now provide an inspirational setting for the next generation of scholars. Undershaw is seminal to the future of Stepping Stones School.

We have missed much of its magic over the past twelve months with the restrictions around the Covid-19 pandemic and the heart-breaking but necessary loss of our social interactions. However, for the most vulnerable members of our school, it has remained a safe place and we have kept our doors open for these students.

We long to return. To hear the building teeming once again with life, noise and bustle; to hear the creak of the green front door as it opens and shuts with each passing student, parent, and teacher. Undershaw has provided our school community with a sense of calm amidst the unpredictability of the outside world, this year more than ever. It did the same for Conan Doyle as he supported Louisa: An oasis amidst the tumult.

In the autumn of last year, we enjoyed a brief respite in restrictions which meant we were able to return fully. Shortly after this, we were honoured to receive a Royal Visit from Her Royal Highness the Countess of Wessex. The Countess was delighted to see such a happy and vibrant school looking ahead to the future with fresh leadership and a team of staff passionate about delivering the very best Special Educational Needs education. The students spoke proudly of their school and what it meant for them to call Undershaw home.

As we turn the year, our educational offer continues to evolve. We are wholeheartedly committed to our pursuit of raising standards for those with additional learning needs and to foster a fearless and aspirational mind-set regarding their capabilities, potential, and their futures. In our work going forward, the school is resolute in unearthing ways to *Eliminate the Impossible* for these fantastic young people.

On behalf of the students, staff, and families we support with our work here, I remain so grateful for your interest in the school. I consider us very fortunate to have such a strong and committed network of benefactors.

Jacqueline Silver
Headteacher
February 2021

"When you have eliminated the impossible,
whatever remains, however improbable,
must be the truth."

Sir Arthur Conan Doyle

"Undershaw," Hindhead. Conan Doyle's House.

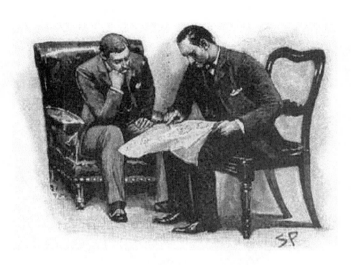

Sherlock Holmes (1854-1957) was born in Yorkshire, England, on 6 January, 1854. In the mid-1870's, he moved to 24 Montague Street, London, where he established himself as the world's first Consulting Detective. After meeting Dr. John H. Watson in early 1881, he and Watson moved to rooms at 221b Baker Street, where his reputation as the world's greatest detective grew for several decades. He was presumed to have died battling noted criminal Professor James Moriarty on 4 May, 1891, but he returned to London on 5 April, 1894, resuming his consulting practice in Baker Street. Retiring to the Sussex coast near Beachy Head in October 1903, he continued to be associated in various private and government investigations while giving the impression of being a reclusive apiarist. He was very involved in the events encompassing World War I, and to a lesser degree those of World War II. He passed away peacefully upon the cliffs above his Sussex home on his 103rd birthday, 6 January, 1957.

Dr. John Hamish Watson (1852-1929) was born in Stranraer, Scotland on 7 August, 1852. In 1878, he took his Doctor of Medicine Degree from the University of London, and later joined the army as a surgeon. Wounded at the Battle of Maiwand in Afghanistan (27 July, 1880), he returned to London late that same year. On New Year's Day, 1881, he was introduced to Sherlock Holmes in the chemical laboratory at Barts. Agreeing to share rooms with Holmes in Baker Street, Watson became invaluable to Holmes's consulting detective practice. Watson was married and widowed three times, and from the late 1880's onward, in addition to his participation in Holmes's investigations and his medical practice, he chronicled Holmes's adventures, with the assistance of his literary agent, Sir Arthur Conan Doyle, in a series of popular narratives, most of which were first published in *The Strand* magazine. Watson's later years were spent preparing a vast number of his notes of Holmes's cases for future publication. Following a final important investigation with Holmes, Watson contracted pneumonia and passed away on 24 July, 1929.

Photos of Sherlock Holmes and Dr. John H. Watson courtesy of Roger Johnson

The MX Book
of
New Sherlock Holmes Stories

Part XXV – 2021 Annual
(1881-1888)

Baskerville Hall
by Kelvin I. Jones

Once, whilst walking here,
On Dartmoor's shore,
Battling in the teeth of a grim,
Equinoctial gale,

I thought I heard him
In the storm's din,
Borne on the biting wind,
That black hell hound's
Supernatural wail.

Oft then, when dreaming,
I would hear his bone chilling,
Deadly, death rattle,
Dragging to their doom
Those who dwelt in towers
Of Gothic gloom,
And died beneath his curse
Like cattle.

Years later,
When living here
Beneath those beetling cliffs,
Wet through from a winter's squall,
We took the path
That wound through mist,
Until at last,
Chafed by the east wind's freezing blast,
We came to Baskerville Hall.

Instantly I saw this hallowed place,
This arc of dark, crenellated towers,
Glimpsed through undergrowth and ancient trees,
I saw those ruffians, garbed in wig and lace,
And the cursed Hugo,
Praying, on his knees,

That he might not die at the appointed hour.

Bone chilled, we returned home
To glass of port and roaring fire,
Whist I, like one possessed,
Leafed through crisp pages
Of my Sherlockian best,
Drinking in the Gothic gloom,
Of a tale seeped in sin, lust
And the curse of ages.

I knew then he had trodden here,
Holmes and his loyal amanuensis,
Heard, like me, the chilling growl;
Watched as it burst through the wicket gate,
Dragging men down beneath the coal - black earth,
There to await their allotted fate.

Here, beneath the towers of Baskerville Hall,
Where winds still rage like demons
By Grimpen's darkling shore,
Where lifeboats launch in the wrack and spume,
So they, who otherwise
Might perish in the sea's spitting wind
And gathering gloom,
May live once more.

There, rising to meet me,
Stands Baskerville Hall,
And by it stands the Death - Hound's face,
Curtained by a deathly pall;

Black Shuck,
The harbinger of death
And ill luck.

I smell then, its rank, malodorous breath.
I freeze, stock still with fright,
Seeing its vicious jaws,
Clamped tight,
Burning bright,
Phosphorescent green and blue,

Its eyes like blazing coals,
Red from the hexed stain of centuries.
That hellish hound,
Felled by he of the six shot Webley,
The sword stick and the cloth cap;

That grim stalker of the dark,
Its voice a weird, unearthly sound,
Its great bulk half veiled by moonlight,
Soaked through with blood and gore.

The Persian Slipper
by Brenda Seabrooke

"It's almost a hot as India," I grumbled to Holmes, sitting in his shirtsleeves, contemplating a pair of ice slivers, each in a separate cup in a small table in front of him. Smoke rose from one of them, but he made no reply.

"I say – your ice is afire. It's so hot even the ice is burning up."

We did not need even the illusion of a fire today. All of London and southeast England, as well as Europe, sweltered in this unseasonably hot July weather.

"Not quite as hot as Lahore. Last time I checked, the temperature here measured at 32-degrees Celsius."

"That doesn't sound hot enough. What is it in Fahrenheit?"

"89.8 degrees."

"That's more like it."

"The effects are the same, whatever you call it."

"It sounds hotter in Fahrenheit. I'm going out for a breath of air. Care to join me?"

He tapped a cup. "Busy."

I could see nothing but two teacups and his pocket watch. I was almost curious. "What are you doing?"

"I'm timing the melting of these two slivers of ice."

"I can see that. Why is one smoking?"

"It's chemical snow."

"Chemical?

"Yes. Haven't you heard of it?"

"I'm familiar with Thilorier's findings. It's solidified carbon dioxide, but I can't see the value of it."

"One value is it cools my hand."

"Don't waste the other sliver. Better to put it in a glass of something and sip it," I said.

"Ice in whisky? Are you mad?"

"No. Just hot."

He didn't reply as I took the stairs down to the street in search of a breeze. I didn't find one. Everything and everyone in London was drooping with the unaccustomed heat as I walked along Baker Street, first in the direction of Regent's Park, and then back. I hadn't reached Madame Tussaud's Wax Museum before the heat became unbearable and I turned around. How, I wondered, did they keep the wax from melting in this heat? I decided the museum must have a contract with someone farther north to keep it supplied with ice in times of hot weather. Perhaps that would be a good use for Holmes's chemical snow.

I collided with someone walking fast behind me. To my great surprise it was Charley Lyndley (of two y's) from my time in India. He was out of uniform and dressed for town, a solid, stalwart fellow with fair hair and bushy eyebrows over blue eyes. "Charley! Whatever are you doing in London?"

"On leave. Family problem. I heard from Bobby Shafferd you was living in Baker Street, but hang if I could remember the number. I thought I'd just walk up and down in hopes of seeing you."

As he continued to walk, I fell into step. We'd been friends in India the way one often is in foreign environs with people from the home country – casual but not close. Nevertheless, there is a connection when one has survived battles together. "You were successful. Here it is, 221b Baker."

Charley looked surprised, and I remembered that even though he looked splendid on a horse and was as brave as any of us, he never took the lead, but rather hung back. Perhaps that was something to do with his sense of direction.

"Heard you was sharing rooms with some fellow – Sherman Homes."

"Sherlock Holmes. Yes, I'm recuperating here and it seemed economical to share – not to mention the landlady's cooking. Best in London. But what brings you to my door? How long have you been a major?"

"Since Maiwand."

That didn't surprise me. Many promotions came after that battle. I unlocked the door and we took the stairs up to our rooms. He hung back on the landing.

"I'm happy to see you again, old chum, and glad you've recovered from that business at Maiwand, but it's about a family problem. Is he in?"

"He was when I left him. We're here. Come in and tell me about it. Don't mind Holmes. He's doing some kind of experiment."

I was wrong. Holmes had finished or abandoned his experiment. He sipped a glass of whisky when I introduced him to Charley. I fortified us each with a glass.

"What were the results of your experiment?" I asked as I seated Charley in the basket chair. My own chair creaked agreeably under the soft pillow and reminded me of peacock chairs in India.

"I gave it up and followed the doctor's advice. I must admit, it was most refreshing."

"You put ice in whisky?" I was aghast at the thought of iced whisky, but it was too hot for idle argument. The deed was done, though his digestion might pay the price. We'd have to wait and see. "What about the chemical snow?"

"Turned to gas."

I could have told him it would. Perverse of me not to, but I didn't want to spoil his fun. "Charley has a problem upon which he'd like to consult me."

"Indeed, Major. Pray do not even notice me."

I gave him a quick look. Was he making a joke? I'd only shared rooms with him a short time. He'd finally let me in on some of his cases, but he'd never been involved with any of mine. Should I have taken Charley to a club or even a walk in the park to avoid disturbing him?

"What is the problem?" I asked Charley, hoping I could help. I wanted to look good in my profession to Holmes, who was so good at his.

"It's about my sister. Her engagement was broken. She refuses to accept it without explanation. I'm taking her to see her fiancé to try to find out why. He was stationed on the border with the patrols in India. Missed the mess at Maiwand, returned here on leave a few months ago. My sister didn't even know. She heard it from a friend. When she wrote to him, she received a curt dictated letter under his signature breaking off the engagement. Something to do with illness."

"And the signature was no doubt his?" Holmes asked.

I gave him a look. This was my case, not his. He appeared not to notice.

"It was shaky, my sister said, but it was his. Who breaks an engagement over illness?"

"That depends on what the illness is," Holmes said.

Again I gave him a look. "Could be malaria or any number of maladies." I didn't mention the deadliest, black water fever. The poor man would already be dead from that, but if he had malaria, it could become black water, which causes red blood cells to burst and almost always kills. Or others. Dengue. Scrub typhus. Typhoid. Encephalitis. Leprosy, which would be obvious from one look. The situation could be explained by a recurring fever, but I'd never heard of an engagement broken for such a reason. Charley knew these maladies almost as well as I did. I didn't know what Holmes knew. Everything so far, I had learned.

"That's true," Charley said, "but that doesn't usually lead to a broken engagement."

"Sounds like a job for you, Watson," Holmes drawled with emphasis on *you*.

I refrained from retorting.

"Who is this former fiancé," Holmes asked, "and where does he live?"

"George Spencer-Hylton. He lives at Sundarwood in Long Mereton. He's a second son – inherited the house from his aunt, whose husband bought it for her. My sister believes he has contracted some malady, perhaps something disfiguring that he doesn't want to tell her about, in case she takes the martyr's route and marries herself to him anyway. I was hoping you could come up and try to diagnose him. You've seen as much of tropical maladies as anybody, I'd warrant."

Before I was invalided out, I had seen every known tropical disease. "I'll make arrangements."

"It is certainly cooler there than this wretched heat spilling over from the Continent," said Holmes. "I'll accompany you, even if I'm not needed." He looked as though he doubted he wouldn't be needed. Charley made no objections.

Our plans made, Charley departed to escort his sister while I prepared for traveling. Holmes left on an errand.

I packed my case with all the known remedies for tropical diseases, consisting primarily of quinine and plenty of it in powdered form, which is easier to transport. Nothing could be done for leprosy, but the disfigurement is apparent and I doubted that was the case, else it should have been mentioned by now. I packed my two best books on tropical medicine and anything else I thought that I might need, including a volume about diseases of the mind, though I doubted I would need it.

We left on the early train the next morning and, except when changing trains and eating the lunch Mrs. Hudson put up for us, our trip was uneventful – but for one incident hardly worth mentioning. A man came to the door of our compartment and rattled the knob. I looked up from my book to see a burly man with dark hair turning the handle as if to enter. He was a curious-looking fellow with a large head, and he held a box under one arm. Holmes lowered the newspaper he'd picked up in the station to have a look at the man, and to my great surprise, his upper lip now sported a full moustache, while his head was covered not by his deerstalker, but instead a derby pulled down low over his eyes. The man looked at us both, slightly longer at Holmes, and went on his way.

I inquired about his disguise.

"I'm on holiday," he said. "An escapee from the London heat wave. I wanted to look the part. And I didn't want to tell the world that Sherlock Holmes had arrived."

"Oh come now. It's not as if you're famous."

"One never knows who is connected to whom," he said and went back to his newspaper. I returned to my book and, when I next glanced at him, he sat with his head back dozing. That was fine with me. I didn't want to answer questions about my case. I returned to my studies.

Holmes opened an eye. "I suspect you will need me more than those books."

"I need to rule certain fevers out."

"I suppose the mind could be affected by fever," Holmes mused, "but for what duration?"

"We'll find out, won't we?"

He raised an eyebrow and returned to his thoughts or nap, whichever it might be.

A slight rain was falling when we reached our destination on the northern border of Gloucestershire. The cool air in Long Mereton was welcome after the heat of London and the rain refreshed me. A well-appointed coach drew up to the station. "This must be for us," I said.

"I think not," Holmes said. "Is that not your friend driving that trap headed this way?"

Indeed it was Charley, who expertly stopped in front of us just as the man we had seen on the train brushed past and spoke to the coachman, who climbed down to retrieve a large wooden box with handles on the train behind us. Holmes turned his attention to the box while I waved at Charley. The coachman set the box down to open the door for his passenger. Holmes edged closer as the man entered the coach. He stepped away as the driver lifted the box to stow inside. He closed the coach door and climbed atop.

Charley introduced us to his sister as he lifted the reins and pulled into the roadway. Recalling what Holmes had said about connections, I had decided to be Dr. Wellburn, and Holmes in his moustache and derby was Mr. Humes. I carried the bag which identified me to all as a doctor of medicine. We were a sober party as Charley drove the four-wheeled trap, pulled by a sprightly grey that required his attention. He hadn't seen Spencer-Hylton yet. Nor had his sister. "He was sleeping when we arrived and hadn't awakened when we left for the station," Miss Clarice Lyndley explained.

Before we left the outskirts of the town, the coach passed us at a fast pace. "Who is that man?" I asked Charley.

"I don't know, but he seems to be in a hurry." Charley turned the horse back into the lane, but kept it at a brisk pace.

Miss Lyndley was a pleasant young woman with bright blue eyes and pale blond hair under a dark blue bonnet, set off by her rich blue dress under a bronze cloak. "The housekeeper, Mrs. Pool, said the doctor told

41

her that George was not to have visitors. It would 'exercise his malady',"
is how she put it.

"Indeed. What else did she tell you?" I asked.

"He sits silent all day and hallucinates at night. Something about a
dancer, I think. He appears to see one – in the woods behind the back
garden."

"Is this dancer male or female?" Holmes asked.

"Female, I think. I don't know if Mrs. Pool said, but I assumed
female."

"Has anyone else seen this dancer?"

"Mrs. Pool hasn't. She seems to think it's a fever dream."

Holmes asked more questions about the household. "Mrs. Pool lives
in, but the others – the cook and the maids – live in the village."

We passed an imposing gateway which promised to lead to a large
house or perhaps castle. I inquired about it.

"No, that's Peverill Hall," Charley said. "It's owned by a man not of
these parts. He bought it just about the time George's aunt died."

Not a quarter-of-a-mile further we turned into Sundarwood, finding a
pleasant red brick Georgian style house built in 1787, according to the date
on the lintel over the front door. The surrounding park and gardens
drowsed in the late afternoon sun and birdcall filled the woods behind. "A
most pleasant place to retire," I said, doubting I could ever afford such.

Mrs. Pool was a fiftyish lady who showed us to our rooms. The house
had accommodation on the second floor for six bedchambers. Mrs. Pool
herself lived in the third floor nursery. "Got my own little suite there. We
get along, me and the major."

I refrained from saying anyone could get along with a silent
employer. We had decided earlier I would go in with Charley, who would
then leave us alone. I fetched my medical bag and he led the way to a large
room overlooking the back garden and woods.

"George, I've brought an old messmate of mine to see you," Charley
said, opening the door when his knock got no answer. "Dr. Wellburn, of
London."

The room was bright from the windows across the back. George
Spencer-Hylton sat propped in a chair, his feet on an ottoman, his legs
covered with a blanket. He wore a dark blue robe and leaned against a pile
of pillows.

Charley introduced me, but George remained staring out the window
and showed not the slightest flicker of comprehension. This did not bode
well for diagnosis. "Leave us, Charley. I need to examine him."

George accepted the thermometer into his mouth. There was no
danger of him moving for the five minutes a recording took. I made notes

42

while I waited. His eyes were clear, no redness or yellow showing. His breathing was unimpeded. He was thin but not emaciated, pale but not unduly so, considering he hadn't been out of the house in a month – maybe not even out of this room. I must get him outside in the sunlight. I took his pulse and managed to listen to his heart. His readings were in the normal range. His reflexes were perfect as they should be for a cavalry officer. I was relieved to find no indications of leprosy or any other tropical malady.

He watched me note these. "You at Maiwand?" His voice was hushed and rusty, as to be expected.

"Yes."

"Wounded?"

"I was. And you?"

I already knew his story. He had been at an outpost station too far to make it to the battlefield.

"No. Made it back to Kandahar for the siege. Got a graze on my shoulder."

"Do you mind if I check it." He had no fever, but something could have entered with the bullet.

He slid his nightclothes down and he was correct. The bullet had only grazed the top of his shoulder. The wound bore a thin clean line of a scar.

"Good stitching. Who was it? Philthorpe?"

For the first time he showed some life. "Why, yes. Do you recognize his stitching?"

"Yes. It's like telegrapher's knowing who is sending to them on the other end of the line." I didn't know. One stitch looked like another to me unless they were unduly sloppy, and in the heat of battle they often were – mine included. David Philthorpe was the first name to come to mind. He wouldn't mind me using him in the interests of a patient.

George's voice was clearer now. He made eye contact and showed memory of the events that must have caused his decline.

"I can't find any evidence of tropical disease, but I'm prescribing quinine in case something is lurking in the periphery of your innards waiting to attack. Any objections?"

"No. Malaria or worse is all I need right now."

At a drinks tray I mixed the powder with a hefty dose of whisky and found a sliver of ice floating in a silver receptacle. I added it and presented it with a flourish. "Your cure, Major."

With a little persuading and my support, he agreed to come downstairs and walk in the garden. I was careful to see that he didn't overexert himself. The change that had come over him was gratifying, but in my opinion due more to the stimulation of a fellow officer than to the quinine. Miss Lyndley was overjoyed and wanted to embrace him, but hung back in case it was too much stimulation at once. Wise lady. With the major on her brother's arm and her on the other side, they took a turn about the garden before sitting on some comfortable chairs to enjoy the air.

"I – I haven't been out in more than a month," George said.

"We'll see that you go out every day in fine weather," Miss Lyndley assured him.

I saw him looking at her hands and noticed she was wearing a ring with a square sapphire surrounded by diamonds, bought no doubt for her when he was in the East. That must be the engagement ring he told her to keep. He made no comment, but his delight in her company was evident. He acknowledged "Mr. Humes", who showed a keen interest in the roses, but heard every word of our conversation.

After a short rest following lunch, George took another turn about the garden, and by teatime, which we took outside as well, he seemed his old self according to Charley.

"You've really worked a miracle," he told me over and over.

Mrs. Pool agreed. "I was sure he was a goner."

Holmes walked some more about the grounds, spending more time on the side abutting Peverill Hall.

The quinine cure seemed so certain that I said to Holmes we could contemplate returning to London the next day.

"I believe the oppressive heat is still on," he said with one of those fleeting smiles he sometimes used as punctuation.

"Do stay another day," Charley and Miss Lyndley insisted, with George's blessing.

Another pleasant day passed much like the first, with my patient no longer needing my care. The couple were engaged again and talking about marriage in the village church.

"You have effected a miraculous cure," Charley said.

I bowed my head, pleased for once to be the solution to a case, albeit a medical one.

Within the hour all had turned to ashes. Following a delicious dinner, we were seated on the terrace at the back of the house enjoying the gloaming when, to our amazement, an apparition appeared at the edge of the trees. It seemed to glow in a mist that moved with it in the darkening woods as though lit by something other-worldly. Faint flute notes filtered through the leaves as the dancer wielded a snaky scarf.

Holmes and I leapt up, joined by Charley and Miss Lyndley. Mrs. Pool screamed and dropped the tray she was carrying.

The apparition floated sinuously in a cloud of mist in a manner familiar to me from my time in India and Afghanistan. After a stunned

44

moment, Holmes and Charley ran toward the figure, which undulated deeper into the dark woods until it disappeared. I should have followed them, but noticed my former patient slumped in his chair.

"George, what is it? What's wrong?" I felt for his pulse. He didn't look well, his jaw hung slack and his eyes had fallen back into his head.

The beat was thready, but he was alive. "Humes!" I cried, remembering barely in time to use Holmes's alias. "Charley! Come quickly. I need your help."

Mrs. Pool recovered and brought both water and a cloth to dampen for his forehead, but they weren't needed until I ascertained the cause of this turn.

"I fear he needs more than that," I said.

Charley broke off the chase and rushed to my aid. Holmes took a bit longer, as he seemed to be hunting for further indications of the apparition. When he returned, I noticed that he was pocketing some object, but assumed it was his handkerchief, which he had possibly used to wipe something. We carried George to his room and put him in bed. Miss Lyndley fluttered behind us waiting to help.

"I'm afraid there is nothing for you to do now, my dear, but fetch my case, if you will be so kind."

"Oh thank you." She sounded as if I had given her a gift. With Holmes and Charley helping, we managed to get George into his nightwear and under the covers. Mrs. Pool brought a pillow with which we elevated his feet. Through all of this, he hadn't uttered a sound nor moved. I feared a stroke or something of the heart, but hoped it was a mere faint.

I slapped his cheeks gently until Miss Lyndley brought my case. I listened to his heart. It was steady again, which was an encouraging sign, though his skin felt cold and clammy. I didn't want to raise his temperature or cool him either – not until I had more knowledge. My mind raced through other maladies I'd encountered or studied. He didn't exhibit symptoms of brain fever.

I sent Mrs. Pool to bring a physic. George's eyes fluttered before closing again. If he was having a stroke, perhaps he could swallow a few sips of willow bark infusion, known to help in such conditions.

She returned with a steaming Brown Betty wrapped in a tea towel. I had prepared the cup and filled it with the powder. A good ten minutes were needed to ensure a proper infusion. The water had cooled enough by then for him to drink. I dipped in a spoon and pushed it between his lips. He didn't choke and with another spoonful, he swallowed. Mrs. Pool and I watched for any ill effects but saw none.

"Thank you, Mrs. Pool. I am encouraged by his reaction to the tea." Indeed, George's color returned and he relaxed into a brief sleep. I stepped out with her to inform the others of the progress. "He seems to be recovering now. I'll stay the night with him."

George didn't awaken. He seemed to have fallen into a heavy sleep. I sat up with him all night, dozing occasionally, until Miss Lyndley relieved me around dawn. I had developed a headache and needed a few hours of sleep. I took two spoonfuls of the infusion and stumbled off to bed.

"Watson, this isn't like you."

"Wha – "

"Watson, wake up."

"Have they broken through the pass?" I tried to leap up at the ready, but fell back with a groan.

"Watson," it was Holmes leaning over me. "What have you taken?"

"Taken?" I pulled myself up into a half-sitting, half-leaning position. The room seemed dark and swimmy. "Wha' time issit?"

"Watson, you're in England. Clarice said you went to bed at dawn, and you slept through breakfast and luncheon, and you're about to miss tea."

I stared at him as I tried to get my bearings. I was at Sundarwood. My patient was a fellow officer from India. George something. "How is my patient?"

"In as deep a sleep as you were, if not deeper."

I swung my legs over the side of the bed. The room didn't seem to want to settle down.

"I've brought you tea. Coffee would wake you up more quickly, but tea may be better for you."

"I still have a headache." I took a sip of the hot Oolong in the cup he handed to me. My hand only shook a tiny bit. It was fortunate I wasn't at Maiwand facing the amputation of limbs or removal of bullets, though in the heat of battle such tremors tended to disappear. "I need some of that willow bark tea I made for George yesterday."

Holmes stared at me. "Did you take any this morning?"

"Well, yes I did. Two spoons full."

I almost dropped the cup as Holmes and I had the same thought. I pulled on my boots and hurried after Holmes who was already entering George's room.

"Any change?" I asked Miss Lyndley.

"No." She seemed wilted after yesterday's false improvement in her fiancé

"Has Mrs. Pool brought him anything to drink?" Holmes asked

"Just the tea you gave him yesterday. She told me to continue it every few hours if he's awake. Four, I think she said."

I reached for the pot, but Holmes beat me to it. "Is Mrs. Pool still here?"

"Yes. I told her we could do for ourselves, but she insisted on staying. Is something wrong?"

"Possibly," he said and took the pot to his room.

He soon returned, ready to go out. "I have errands in the village and need to borrow the conveyance. Since our host is not conscious, I guess you will serve in his stead, Miss Lyndley. May I?"

"I suppose so, Mr. Humes. We are affianced again after yesterday's clarity, but – "

"Let's leave it there, shall we? I feel certain when George is in his right mind, he will want to be married to you. What man wouldn't? We shall make that happen. Now, can you plan a dinner party for three days hence?"

"A dinner party? Surely not, Humes," I said.

"It's time we started driving this cart."

"Do you mean – " I started, but he interrupted.

"Certainly not, Wellborn. I mean we must be the actors in this show instead of being merely the audience."

He turned to the young lady. "Miss Lyndley, if you will consult Mrs. Pool with me, we shall start our play. I shall make a list of anything needed from the village."

He left me to mull that over as they went downstairs. Later, I glimpsed out a window the codger they must have entrusted with the invitation to be delivered to the guests. I hoped he could make it back with the replies. I watched for him, but he must have slipped by when I was attending to my sleeping patient. I refused to think of him as comatose. Not yet.

It was some time after that when I saw Holmes driving out in the trap, but I thought no more about it. Mrs. Pool brought me a tea tray. My patient seemed comfortable by the dinner hour, so I felt encouraged to go downstairs.

"Any change?" Miss Lyndley asked me as we seated ourselves.

"Sleeping naturally," I said and hoped I was right.

"Where is . . . umm . . . Humes?" Charley asked.

"I assume he is still in the village. I haven't heard him return."

"You need to check your ears, Wellburn, for I have returned with the victuals and trimmings and all things necessary for the dinner party." Holmes entered in good spirits and took his seat at the table. "Our guests are delighted and will be here at the appointed hour."

47

Mrs. Pool overheard as she brought in platters of ham and vegetables. "That do surprise me. We haven't had anything to do with village people."

"Perhaps they don't consider us villagers," Miss Lyndley said.

"Quite right," I said, as none of us were, and George was a late-comer.

"The major's sister sometimes brings her special custards," Mrs. Pool said, "to tempt his 'invalid' appetite, she says."

"And did they? Improve his appetite?" I asked.

She shook her head. "Not so's I could see, Doctor, but he did sleep a long time after."

"Tell me, Mrs. Pool, what did you put in the water you supplied for Dr. Wellburn's potion?" Holmes said with a misleading casualness.

"Just a pinch of herbs, Mr. Humes," she said as she set down a dish of creamed leeks.

"Herbs?" I sputtered.

"Where did you get them?" Miss Lyndley asked.

"From the doctor last market day." She looked from me to Holmes. "Did I do something wrong?"

"The village doctor practices at the market?" I asked with raised eyebrows. That was not done except by charlatans and fakes.

"No, sir. He weren't the village doctor. The village don't have a doctor. He weren't practicing anything. He were *consulting*."

"Practicing and consulting are very nearly the same thing." I intended to look into this. "What was his name?"

"Dr. Swami were his name. He were from that hot country where wondrous herbs grow. Patching tool and the like. An island. Tamil something."

"Close enough," Holmes said. "It was probably valerian with some opium and perhaps other mind-disordering properties. Fakirs in India and that part of the world have a number of tricks that may necessitate the use of such medicants."

Miss Lyndley gasped and Charley started to speak, but Holmes held up a hand to stop him.

Mrs. Pool looked from one of us to the other as realization dawned. "You mean it were bad for the Major?" She shrieked and threw her apron over her face to hide her sobbing. "Have I killed him?"

"No, Mrs. Pool, you haven't killed the Major," Holmes said. "Merely made him sleep – a lot, I suspect."

"For what end these herbs?" Charley asked.

"To distort one's perceptions," Holmes said.

Mrs. Pool stopped crying and wiped her eyes on her apron. I hoped she changed it before serving the remainder of the meal. "He were ever such a nice man. Didn't charge me for the second packet."

"We'll need to see these packets," I said. "It's clear something is going on here. In my experience, doctors don't give away their medicants."

"Oh, they weren't free. I paid a good tuppence for the first one, but I thought if they could help the poor Major, it were worth it."

"Quite right, Mrs. Pool," Holmes said. "Your heart was in your actions, but perhaps next time a Dr. Swami offers you a deal, you might consult a physician like Dr. Wellburn, here."

She fetched the remaining packet from the kitchen and, I noted, changed her apron. Holmes and I examined the packets of herbs. The papers into which they were folded held the scent of sandalwood, which would mask any other smell. From the looks of the herbs, we were close, if not completely accurate, in our supposition.

Poor Mrs. Pool looked like she might burst into tears again. "I made the Major sick?"

"No, no. You just gave him some deep sleep," I reassured her, hoping that I was right. We would know when he woke up if the packets caused any permanent damage.

"What did this Dr. Swami look like?" Holmes asked her.

"He were middling tall – not as tall as you," she said to him. "And not as thin." She gave him a look as if he were cheating on meals and not eating enough.

Holmes smiled, no doubt remembering nursery days. "Anything else you recall about him?"

"He had brown skin as if he worked in the sun, but without turning red. And a thin black moustache. He wore one of them high-collar coats like the clergy wear, only without a band."

Holmes nodded as if she had confirmed something.

When Miss Lyndley had left us to brandy and cigars, I voiced my disapproval of the party. "I don't see why we are having this dinner party," I said. "It seems to be an unnecessary involvement with people George doesn't even know."

"He may not know them," replied Holmes, "but I am confident they know him."

"That makes little sense," Charley said.

"I think you will find it makes a lot of sense. Have you thought about why George was seeing an Indian dancer?"

"At first I thought it was a hallucination – a memory of something in India."

"I say," said Charley, "we all saw that – that – "

49

"Yes, we did," I said. "It could have been a collective hallucination. Charley and I have been in India. It would not be too farfetched to think we were influencing each other – though I rather doubt it."

"I also rather doubt it," Holmes replied. "You forget, I saw it, too and I was not hallucinating. I haven't been to India, and I do not have hallucinations."

"Are you thinking another party is involved in these . . . spells." I couldn't think of a better word.

"That is a possibility. A very strong one. What we need is the motive. I'm already aware of the means. And I think I know what the motive is."

I waited for him to go on, but he didn't. He would say no more about the dinner, but he insisted on being the one to keep watch over George for the next two nights.

When I protested, he said, "Nonsense. You will need all your wits about you."

I wanted to ask what about his wits, but I wasn't certain how he would take that. I was grateful for some time to myself to peruse my books. Before sleep overtook me, I read about compounds which can cause hallucinations, and found them to be consistent with the effects on George.

We saw no more apparitions, and hardly saw Miss Lyndley and Mrs. Pool on the days before the dinner party, except when they put out light collations to appease our hunger. Mrs. Pool had engaged two village girls and a young man to help with the preparations. I rarely encountered Holmes, except when I took trays up for him and George, who slept on and off, Holmes reported. He slept through the days as well.

"He will not be joining us at this dinner party, I take it?"

"No" Holmes said with the gravity of a physician. "I feel confident he will soon be right, but he will not be ready to entertain guests just yet."

I was slightly irritated. After all, this was my patient. I hadn't known Holmes for very long, but I hadn't thought that he would try to take over in medical matters. "I will stay with him now," I said.

"Very well," Holmes almost smiled and I hoped he hadn't deduced what I was thinking. "I'll return in time for you to prepare yourself for the celebration."

My patient remained sleeping comfortably without the mutterings or stirrings fever could engender. Holmes, true to his word, returned an hour before the appointed time and I went to my own room to change into garments I hadn't yet worn. We hadn't brought formal dress, which guided the tone of the party. Miss Lyndley explained this to our guests in the invitation, who nevertheless came arrayed in splendor. I had buffed and

50

brushed my more casual attire, and I assumed the others had done the same. It was the best I could do.

Miss Lyndley looked sublime in turquoise silk that reminded me of the sari wraps worn by the women of India. Charley wore a more formal suit he'd borrowed from George, as they were much the same size. Holmes was the same as he'd been all day. I doubt he had given a thought to sartorial matters. In that, I was to be proven wrong.

The various guests alighted from their coach and were ushered in by Mrs. Pool. We'd forgotten to designate one of us as host since George wasn't able to be with us. I waited for Charley to take his place, but he did not. While I was still pondering what to do, I heard a voice. "I am Mr. Peverill-Smyth of Peverill Hall," a large man boomed. I recognized him as the same man who had intruded for a moment into our compartment on the train a few days before. "And this is my sister, Georgette."

The sister was a handsome high-nosed woman clad in emerald silk with real emeralds and diamonds at every possible juncture on her person. One hardly saw her features for all those dazzling jewels, but her hair was dark, though lit by the twinkle of precious stones.

Holmes had a small smile, no doubt meant to be welcoming. Only Miss Lyndley was serene. She welcomed our guests and introduced us using our false names, Dr. Wellburn and Mr. Humes.

"But where is our host? Will he not be joining us?" Peverill-Smyth asked in his deep voice. He was a big man, but his head didn't seem to fit his large blocky frame and he was half-a-head shorter than Holmes. Most curious. I wondered if some skeletal malformation had been the cause. He wore a full black beard with moustache and side-whiskers. His brows and hair were the same dark black.

"Perhaps later," Holmes murmured from behind me.

"His health has been precarious," I added, "as you know, but he is on the mend."

"So kind of you to supply him with custards in my absence," Miss Lyndley purred.

"Neighbors must look after each other," Miss Peverill-Smyth replied.

"Indeed!" her brother all but bellowed.

I gave Holmes a look of curiosity as Charley took Miss Peverill-Smyth in to dinner. Was he merely being sociable to say George might join us later? In return, he gave me an inscrutable look back as Miss Lyndley allowed Mr. Peverill-Smyth to escort her. Holmes and I followed.

Miss Lyndley and Mrs. Pool had created magic on the table, laying it with roses from the garden twined in ivy, laid down the center of the table and interspersed with candles in silver holders on the snowy damask cloth. Bert, a boy from the village outfitted in a footman's uniform with white

51

gloves was, as it turned out, Mrs. Pool's nephew. He served the dishes with hardly a mistake.

Mrs. Pool and her helpers had done us proud in the kitchen. Conversation was strangely modulated, with Peverill-Smyth's loud voice overriding anything the rest of the company said. He regaled us with tales of his diamond mines in Africa, a mahogany plantation in Honduras, and hinted of things to come. "I have a great interest in mines. For instance, Cornwall may not be the only source of precious commodities in England."

"Indeed," I said to say something, as no one else did. "Any particular type of commodity?"

"Couldn't say, couldn't say," he boomed. "This is an excellent mutton joint." He forked in a mouthful.

No one knew what to tell him. He was eating beef, not mutton. Miss Lyndley swallowed and used her napkin. "I am so glad you like it," she said. "I shall tell Cook."

Across the table, Holmes coughed into his napkin. Of all of us, he was the least likely to suffer fools and pretension, although he was kinder to the ignorant if they were less fortunate than Mr. Peverill-Smyth.

Talk turned to affairs of the Empire, with Peverill-Smyth enlightening us. "Sorry to see the end of old Disraeli. We're in the stew now with that Gladstone. He'll have beggars riding in coaches by Christmas. Mark my words."

"Now Otis, perhaps our host and friends like Mr. Gladstone," Miss Peverill-Smyth spoke up. "One should not talk thus when one doesn't know the opinions of others." She smiled around at the table. Some of us smiled back or nodded. Holmes merely coughed again. None of us enlightened her of our political leanings or opinions.

"Tell me, Miss Peverill-Smyth, do you hunt?" Miss Lyndley took a sip of her wine and candlelight caught her ring. The diamonds flashed fire. The sapphire glowed. Miss Peverill-Smyth couldn't miss seeing it.

The lady looked startled – whether at the ring or the question – though it was a common-enough query in the country.

"I think she means ride to the hounds." Charley spoke for the first time. "Fox hunting. George tells me there's an active hunt club in the valley. If you're interested, I could arrange an introduction to the master."

"I should like that, but I'll wait until Major Spencer-Hylton will be well enough to join us." She gave him an open smile. I thought her incisors looked rather long.

So that was the way the wind blew. Holmes gave me a quick look and I nodded slightly. I understood that clue. Miss Peverill-Smyth had designs on George.

Talk turned to town – meaning London, the only town that mattered in the Empire and Society in which the Peverill-Smyths seemed well-versed. I let it buzz over my head. Holmes was up to something. I could tell, though it was nothing as commonplace as raised eyebrows or a one-sided smile. He hadn't taken part in the conversation with more than a nod here and there to show he was awake, and perhaps not to give his identity away.

The long dinner finally ended with Miss Lyndley suggesting we go out to the terrace for the brandy and cigars for the men and sherry for the ladies, as it was a fine evening not to be missed. She no doubt had no desire to be alone with the shark from next door.

"It's certainly an improvement over the heat on the Continent and London," Holmes remarked, his first contribution to conviviality.

Bert served us from a little rolling cart. He had just poured a sherry for Miss Peverill-Smyth when he dropped the glass. "'Cor, looka that!" he cried.

I leaped for the glass, catching it just in time without spilling a drop and expecting to be congratulated, but no one was looking at me. Their attention was riveted to the edge of the woods at the end of the garden, where a figure gyrated – a glowing figure, an undulating wraith surrounded by mist on this clear evening. Haunting musical tones seemed to hover on the mist.

No one moved. The figure lifted a languid arm and pointed at Peverill-Smyth. His sister gave a little scream and looked like she might faint. I shoved the sherry at her and she took a gulp of it. Her brother had turned pale. He sputtered unintelligibly.

Charley pulled himself together and leaped up. "We must catch her!"

"No." Holmes put out a restraining hand. "It is best to let apparitions finish their appearances. This is obviously a repeating ghost, reliving whatever it is that turned her into one, over and over until she reaches a crescendo."

The dancer flipped the silky scarf in the direction of Peverill-Smyth, advancing toward him to the odd musical notes. Peverill-Smyth sat transfixed as if glued to his chair. His sister's face was a picture of shock, eyes wide and almost popping, her mouth open in a scream that couldn't emerge from her frozen throat. The inhabitants of Sundarwood watched them as if they were at a play in a theater.

"No! This can't be happening," Peverill-Smyth said in a gasping voice. The figure continued to undulate while gliding backward, still pointing at him with following mist until the darkness swallowed her and the last note sank down the scale and disappeared.

For a minute no one spoke, as if under a spell. I had to admit that it felt like a spell, and I had no idea what we had just witnessed – only that it wasn't the same dancer that we had seen just a few nights earlier. This one didn't move as the other one had.

"Well," Charley broke the silence, "what was that all about? She didn't point at anyone when we saw her before."

"What can it mean?" Miss Lyndley asked. "What was she trying to tell us?"

"I think it's quite clear what she meant." Holmes turned to Peverill-Smyth. "You are the man responsible for the apparition. She was not seen until you moved next door."

"How dare you!" he replied with all the indignation he could muster.

"I have no idea what you're talking about," Miss Peverill-Smyth said.

"Indeed," Holmes replied, clearly disbelieving her. "No doubt you supplied the fluting."

"Good evening all," a new voice said. We turned to see George in evening dress exit the French doors behind us.

"Did you see the dancer?" Charley asked after a moment.

"No, I'm afraid I missed this evening's performance. Perhaps it was the herbal tea prescribed by Dr. Swami," he said, looking straight at his neighbor, "or the custard offerings from Miss Peverill-Smyth, but I feel remarkably clear-headed tonight for the first time in over a month."

"What is the meaning of this – this outrage?" Peverill-Smyth said.

"I think this apparition has finished with her business here on earth," Holmes said. "Perhaps George can enlighten us further."

"There was such a dancer in the hill country province in which I was stationed, banished by the ruler. I visited her on my patrols and we became friends. She prepared refreshments for my men and we talked. She was lonely, with only one old servant for company, and a cat with blue eyes. My company had orders for Maiwand the last time I passed by. We found her little house burnt to the ground. The servant told my interpreter the ruler's men came and boarded the doors and windows and set fire to the house. It burnt to the ground, the dancer with it. I looked around for the cat, but never found any trace. The servant had waited to tell me. I asked if he had found the cat, but he'd vanished into the forest.

"We missed Maiwand, but made it to the siege at Kandahar where I was wounded. As I recovered, I tried to make sense of what had happened. Had I been lured by the dancer? For what purpose? Had she and the servant wormed information out of my men and perhaps unwittingly me? I brooded over it until I returned here, where I learned that my relatives had died – first my uncle by marriage, and then my mother's sister, who left

54

me this house. Soon after moving in, the apparition appeared – not every night, but enough to frighten me. I fell into a stupor."

"You were put into a stupor by the well-meaning Mrs. Pool," Holmes explained, "who had found a bargain cure in herbs from a Dr. Swami, who was actually Mr. Peverill-Smyth without this extra padding. And no doubt the custards as well, brought by his sister to tempt the appetite of the invalid. I suggest this will be revealed by the police." Holmes raised his voice at the last word.

"Police!" Both Peverill-Smyths jumped up and started to depart, just as a police inspector and two constables joined us.

"May I introduce Inspector Jardine," Holmes said.

The Peverill-Smyths broke into a run, but were stopped by the burly constables. The inspector then forced Peverill-Smyth to remove his coat. His torso was enveloped in a great deal of padding that would have been decidedly uncomfortable in London during the heat wave.

Mrs. Pool heard the commotion and joined us. She gasped as the neighbor was revealed to be a slim man, instead of the huge one with the normal-sized head. .

"Is this the Dr. Swami who sold you the herbal tea?" Holmes asked her.

"He doesn't have the same type of whiskers that the doctor had – " She flapped her apron at him. " – but yes, that's him. I would recognize those eyes and that voice anywhere. Shame on you drugging an ailing man!"

He ignored her.

The inspector reached out and jerked off the set of false whiskers. "Just as I thought. Ernest Batton, also known as Peverill-Smyth, and Dr. Swami, I arrest you for the illegal practice of medicine under an assumed name."

"I am a doctor," Peverill-Smyth said, drawing himself to his full height, which was not quite as tall as Holmes.

"You are not listed in the *Medical Register* under any of those names," the inspector said. "We checked. That's good enough for me and the magistrate. When we investigate, I suspect we'll find the makings of fraud."

"And perhaps the makings of murder as well," Holmes said. "Look into the deaths of the previous owners of Sundarwood."

"Good God!" the inspector said.

Peverill-Smyth didn't flinch, but I thought his face paled slightly.

"I had nothing to do with any of it!" Miss Peverill-Smyth said. She edged away from her brother. "This was all his idea."

"Shut up!" hissed Peverill-Smyth.

"She was the one that brought over custards to tempt the appetite of the invalid!" Mrs. Pool said. "After eating just a little, he slept for a whole day. I gave what was left to my nephew so's not to waste them, and he fell asleep at the table. I thought he was just lazy, or staying out too late at night. I'm sorry, Bert."

"Tha's all right Auntie. I just thought I was tired."

"Anything else, Mr. Holmes?" asked the inspector. My friend shook his head.

"Wait – " said Peverill-Smyth. "Holmes? *Sherlock Holmes?*"

Holmes smiled and nodded. "And this is my associate, Dr. John Watson."

"I know of you," said the prisoner. "You're that detective who works with Scotland Yard."

Holmes looked my way, as if to confirm that it had been a good idea for us to arrive incognito.

"This is an outrage!" Peverill-Smyth growled. "We'll see what my solicitor says about this!"

"Take them away," Inspector Jardine said, "and stay with them."

The two constables wrestled the brother and sister out, but it wasn't easy, even with the two in handcuffs.

"Wait – " Miss Peverill-Smyth interrupted. "Who was the dancer?"

George had sat down in the chair vacated by Peverill-Smyth. Now he stood up again and said, "You mean this?" He began to undulate like the dancer. "It was me."

Everyone but Holmes stared at him. "No!" Charley said. "You couldn't've done that, old man," The remaining company nodded in agreement. After all, he had been at death's door just a short time ago, but I understood now what Holmes had been doing those nights he sat with the major.

"Who made the music?" I asked.

For answer George pulled something shiny from his pocket and struck a chiming note. "Finger cymbals."

"And how did you make the fog and the costume?" I asked.

"Remember the experiment I was working on before Charley looked you up?"

"Chemical snow?"

"Correct. I obtained some from the same source that Peverill-Smyth used. I had seen the address on the box he had with him on the train the day we arrived. You recall that he opened our compartment for a moment, Watson. Surely you also noticed the label on the cardboard box he was carrying?" I had not. "I recognized it and wondered what he wanted with chemical show.

"As for decorating the costume, I found a source of fairy fire – or fox-fire – that glows in the dark on the deadfall of some of the trees in the woods and collected a sufficient amount for my purpose. I glued it onto the back of an old robe of George's from his time in hot countries. He wore it backwards after I dyed it with diluted beet juice from its original pale sand color, and I used bootblack to shape it. Watson, if you'll look inside the door, George was good enough to leave it there."

The robe lay over a chair just inside the French door. I held it up in front of me with the back side out. "Clever."

"I say," Charley exclaimed. "Dashed clever. How'd you do the fog?"

"It was chemical snow, placed in a cup with perforated paper glued over the top to allow the resulting fog to escape," Holmes explained.

"It seemed to follow the dancer," Miss Lyndley stated. "How did you make it do that?"

"The same way Peverill-Smyth or Ernest Batton did it," Holmes said.

"It was tied to his belt and dragged along," Miss Lyndley said.

"Exactly."

"How did you know it was Peverill-Smyth and not his sister?" Charley asked.

"She was the one that played the flute notes. They sounded far away because they were. Peverill-Smyth would have a better chance of escaping back to his estate than she would if something went wrong – as it nearly did the last time he appeared – and he would be less likely to be suspected of impersonating a dancer. Who would ever think a man as big as he presented himself could run fast and dance sinuously?"

"Why did he do all of this?" Charley asked.

"I talked to George's solicitor the other day. Peverill-Smyth had previously tried to buy the property from George's aunt and uncle, but they refused to sell. After his uncle's sudden death, he then tried to buy it again from his widow. When that didn't work, he tried to buy it from the estate after she died. Clearly, he wanted this property. I studied some maps and I think there are some caves deep in the wooded area. Look at the name of the house. It goes back to a time before this building was constructed. The ruins of a previous house are back in the woods that I explored. The name *'Sundarwood'*. *'Underwood'*. *'South Underwood'*. *'Under the wood'*. Perhaps an indication of caves or old mines from so long ago they've been forgotten."

"Why would caves be valuable?" Miss Lyndley asked. I noticed George's hand was on her arm.

"They could be potential mines for various ores: Iron, coal, or manganese. Peverill-Smyth bought the estate next door, either because he knew about the potential, or he discovered it after he moved in when he

57

was investigating the area. When the major came home, he thought up the scheme to marry his sister to George in order to gain control over the property and what might lie beneath it.

"First he had to break the engagement between the major and Miss Lyndley. He did that through the apparition's appearance, along with the herb packets he sold to Mrs. Pool. His sister brought over her special custards to help him, but they were no doubt laced with drugs to speed up his deterioration. At some point Miss Peverill-Smyth would worm her way in to feed the custard to the invalid herself and miraculously make him feel better through sleight of herbs or drugs until he was dependent on her. It would be easy to guide him into marriage. She might even search for a ring and pretend he'd given it to her when he was in a drug delirium and asked her to marry him. He is an honourable man and would've seen it through."

"I say," Charley repeated himself. "That is diabolical!"

Holmes smiled briefly. "These are diabolical people."

George nodded. "Indeed. It might have worked, but for your visit. Thank you, my dear Clarice for refusing to give up on me." He took her hand.

"But why did you think I wouldn't want to be with you, ill or in health? I would never abandon you."

"When I broke the engagement. I really thought I was deathly ill and only wanted to free you from a long drawn-out death."

"What I don't know is how Peverill-Smyth knew about the dancer," Charley said.

"According to my sources, it was a well-known story among the troops. Peverill-Smyth put out the word he was looking for information. What you don't know, George, is that the dancer did not die in the fire. The whole affair was part of a larger attempt to gain information about the troop movements, size, and other bits pertaining to the British Army."

"How did you find that out?" George said.

"Sources," Holmes said and would say no more. It was only years later, after learning of his brother Mycroft, that I would understand.

We lingered another day in the pleasant coolness of Sundarwood and left the next day with an invitation to the wedding.

"I'll ink it on his calendar," I said as they drove us to the station.

"What put you onto the neighbors," I asked him as we settled in our compartment for the trip to London.

"The chemical fog," he replied promptly – without explaining anything at all.

58

And that was all I ever got out of him about the case. The first thing he did back at 221b Baker Street was remove an object from his valise and nail it to the mantel on his side of the fireplace. He stuffed something into it and I smelled the pipe tobacco he was currently using.

"What have you put your tobacco in?"

"Look for yourself."

He stepped aside after filling and lighting his pipe. I beheld a large Persian slipper stuffed with black shag.

"I picked it up that first night, in the woods. It was much too large for a woman, so I knew that we were being given a show, but for what purpose? The neighbors hadn't known we were staying at Sundarwood that night. Peverill-Smyth was startled to see us there and cut his dance short. His sister saw him break it off and ran back to the house. He had a black cloak that he threw over his costume to help him disappear in the dark woods, but in his haste this slipper fell off, and he had no time to stop for it. It makes a good repository for my tobacco, don't you think?"

"It is certainly unique. I don't think I've ever heard of keeping tobacco in a shoe – Persian or English."

With Holmes, one never knew how he would address a problem. I think that I would have given the slipper a bath with carbolic soap, but perhaps he did during the nights that he and George were planning and practicing their show.

The Adventure of the
Doll Maker's Daughter
by Matthew White

In the early days of my association with Sherlock Holmes, during which I gradually recovered from my ordeal in Afghanistan, I often slept late, and it was Holmes's habit to rise early and leave our Baker Street rooms before I sat down to breakfast. Consequently, when I wasn't out searching for employment (for I had not yet established myself in practice) I often had the sitting room to myself for some hours. I remember that it was a quarter-to-ten o'clock, on the morning of September 8th, 1881, that I was sitting, smoking my after-breakfast pipe and perusing the morning paper, when Mrs. Hudson entered the sitting room desiring to consult me. I could see by her nervous, excited manner that something had badly upset her, so I urged her to take a moment to recover her composure and began to pour a measure of brandy.

"Whatever is the matter?" I asked her. "Do you feel unwell?"

"No, Doctor, but there's a wee girl downstairs shivering and shaking and frightened half to death."

"Good heavens! Who is she?"

"I don't know. She will only say that she wants to talk to Mr. Holmes."

At once I rose and collected my medical bag from its spot beside my desk.

"I'll take a look at her at once. Does she appear to be hurt?"

"I don't think so," said Mrs. Hudson as she led the way downstairs, "but she's scared and exhausted. And so dirty! I shouldn't wonder if the poor dear had walked the whole way here."

I followed Mrs. Hudson downstairs into her own sitting room. There in an armchair by the fire, wrapped in think blankets, was a little girl who could be no older than eight or nine. Her long dark hair was tangled, and the poor creature was covered in dirt. As I approached her, she looked at me like a wary animal sizing up an unknown threat. I put my bag down and knelt at her side.

"Hello, dear," I said, doing my best to sound comforting. "My name is John Watson, and I'm a doctor. I only want to help you. Do you understand?"

The little girl nodded slowly.

"What is your name?"

"Gloria," she answered in a meek little voice.

"That's a very pretty name," I said. "Are you hurt, Gloria?"

The girl extricated her left arm from the blankets and stretched it out. I could see a long cut, about three inches in length, which began at the shoulder and ran toward the elbow. I at once asked Mrs. Hudson for hot water and clean towels and opened my medical bag. At that time I was equipped only with the most basic tools of my profession, for being without a steady income I was obliged to purchase them piece by piece as I could. Happily, however, the injury was minor and needed only to be cleaned and wrapped in a carbolized bandage. Gloria was now more inclined to trust me, and disclosed several other cuts and scrapes which I similarly treated.

As I did so, Gloria asked repeatedly to speak to Sherlock Holmes, and I assured her that though he was out, he would soon be back. I tried several times to draw out the purpose of her extraordinary visit, but she refused to tell me, and I didn't force the issue, fearing that by doing so I should lose her confidence. When her injuries were suitably tended to, I took her upstairs to await Holmes in the sitting room. Mrs. Hudson brought up an ample supply of milk and biscuits which Gloria hungrily devoured.

Shortly before lunchtime, I heard the front door open and the familiar tread of my friend upon the stair. The door to the sitting room opened and Holmes, clutching a parcel wrapped in brown paper, stepped in. He looked surprised to see the little girl sitting beside the fire and wordlessly left the room the way he had come. Then I heard his bedroom door onto the landing open and close. Gloria looked to me in confusion.

"I am sure he'll be right out," I told her. When a few minutes later Holmes remained closed in his bedroom, I rose and spoke to him through the door that opened into the sitting room.

"Holmes, is everything all right?"

"I apologize, Watson. I didn't realize you would have company."

"Well, in fact, the girl's name is Gloria, and she has come to see you."

There was a moment's pause.

"To see *me*?"

"Yes. She seems to want your help."

"My help with what?"

"She won't tell me. Will you come out and talk with her?"

"Very well, very well."

The door opened, and Sherlock Holmes strode into the room and examined our young guest. I could see that, behind his weary, heavy-lidded expression, he was beginning to take a more intense interest in her. Gloria, for her part, sat looking at him with a trembling lip, as though she

61

expected him to throw her out at once. Instead, he sat down and addressed her.

"Hello, Gloria," he said in an easy, soothing way. "I am Sherlock Holmes. My friend Doctor Watson tells me that you want to talk to me. I can see you've had a hard time of it in the past ten – no, surely nine – hours. Please take as much time as you need and tell me all about it."

Gloria was as communicative toward Holmes as she had been reticent toward me. She spoke quickly, but with many repetitions and tangential details, after the manner of excited children. I will not attempt to reproduce all her words exactly, nor to recall the many questions Holmes asked in order to get out of her the details he required. Her story, worded so as to be coherent to readers, ran in this way:

Gloria Friedman (for that was her family name) lived with her father in the East End. Benjamin Friedman made a living making dolls, as well as doll clothes and doll houses. Her mother had died before Gloria was even one year old, so that her father was the only family she had ever known. The night before, the two of them had gone to bed in their rooms above Mr. Friedman's shop when Gloria heard a loud crashing sound and banging noises from below. Her father ran into her room and closed the door behind him.

"Get up, child, get up!" he hissed. "There's no time! You must get away!"

"Papa, what is happening?" Gloria asked, eyes wide with terror. "I hear men downstairs!"

"Be quiet! You must not make a sound!"

Benjamin Friedman's eyes were wide and wild, like a hunted animal's. He hastily bundled his daughter into some clothes and opened her bedroom window.

"Listen, child," he said. "No, don't cry. You must listen closely. Get help. Go to Mr. Sherlock Holmes of 221b Baker Street. Only he can help us. Do not go to the police. Go only to Mr. Holmes. You must go! Do not let anyone see you leave the house!"

Banging could be heard against the door at the top of the stairs. Gloria began to whimper, but her father put his finger to her mouth.

"You must be quiet, or they will catch you! Be brave, child, and go! Go!"

Friedman took Gloria and lowered her onto the roof of a small shed beneath the window. The window above her shut. To her left and around the corner, she could her voices coming from inside her father's shop. The shadow of a man turned the corner, and Gloria flattened herself against the roof of the shed, hoping she wouldn't be seen in the darkness. Another man followed the first, and together they went to the other side of the building, doubtless intending to prevent escape by the back door. From inside the house, she heard the door at the top of the stairs come crashing open and the sounds of shouting voices. Gloria waited a moment in case anyone else appeared before she crawled to the edge of the roof and lowered herself until she was hanging down by her hands. She let go, and fell painfully onto the hard dirt below. She gave an involuntary cry of pain.

"*Oi!* Who's that?"

One of the men at the back door turned and, seeing Gloria on the ground, called to his comrade.

"There's the girl!"

In spite of the pain, Gloria ran to where a little hole had been dug in the back fence, doubtless by some stray dog or other animal. She managed to squeeze through before the men on the other side could lay hands upon her, though not without scratching her arms and legs and pulling her hair painfully. She was now in an unused mews which ran behind the house, and she ran as quickly as her little legs could carry her down the darkest alley she could find. She could still hear the voices of her pursuers behind her. Fearing that she would be seen as she emerged into the streetlamps at the end of the alley, she dived into a shadowy ditch that ran beside the road and crawled away as noiselessly as she could.

For some time she followed the ditch, making her way over rocks and trash and listening to the heavy tread of boots passing on the street, until she could hear them no more. Gloria climbed out and ran into the next dark alley she could find. Ape-like, she went over fences and crept in shadows until she neither heard nor saw any signs of pursuit. At that moment she realized that she had no idea where she was, having been too preoccupied with escape to pay attention to where she was going. Gloria wandered the East End streets, unsure of where to go or what to do, until coming around a corner she ran headfirst into a constable on the beat, who jumped back in surprise.

"Lor' have mercy, but you gave me a fright!" exclaimed the policeman. "What's a wee girl doing out here in the night? Lost, are you?"

"Yes, sir. I'm lost, sir. I live in Baker Street," she lied, for she feared the constable would want to take her back home, "but I can't find my way home."

"Baker Street! What are you doing all the way over here, then?"

"I was visiting. Please, sir, which way is Baker Street?"

"Well, I suppose it would be . . . yes, over in that direction. But it's an awful long way for a girl to walk at night."

"Can you take me there?" Gloria asked.

The constable hesitated. At that moment, three men emerged from the fog behind his back. Gloria nearly cried out in terror, for she recognized some of the same men who had chased her from her home. Without another word, she turned her back on the astonished constable and retreated into the shadows. Over the course of many hours, and by a combination of the often-surprising cunning of clever children and helpful direction from a few kind souls, Gloria at last found her way through the cold night and the misty London morning to Baker Street.

I was so astonished by this remarkable story that I hardly knew what to say. Holmes was by this point entirely absorbed by the girl's narrative, and he asked her a number of questions, one after the other.

"I understand it may be difficult to remember things, and you may not want to think about what happened," said he in soothing tones, "but you must tell me everything if I'm to help your father. Can you do that?"

Gloria nodded resolutely.

"Very good. Now, had you ever seen any of these men before?"

Gloria's brow furrowed with the effort of concentration.

"I don't think so. But I didn't see the men that were in the house, only the ones outside."

"Did you hear anything the men inside the house said?"

Gloria nodded. "They were saying things like 'The game's up!' and 'Tell us where he is!'"

"Do you know," I interjected, "why your father didn't want you to go to the police?"

Gloria shook her head.

"Does your father have any friends?" asked Holmes gently.

The girl nodded her head. "Oh, yes. Everyone likes Father, because he makes such lovely toys and is kind to everybody."

"But does he have any special friends? Anyone who visits perhaps, or who he helped, or who helped him?"

"Well, there is Mr. DuBois. He owns our house, and he visits sometimes, but Father does not like it when he does. And there is Mrs. Cartwright. She's very nice. I have not seen her for a long time, but she helped Father get the money to set up his shop when we came to London. I was very little, but I still remember her.

"There is another man, too. I don't know his name, but he has a long black beard, and he speaks softly all the time. Father does not like for me to be about when he is there, but I have seen him."

"You have done very well," said Holmes. "Now, if you will tell us your address, Mrs. Hudson will take care of you while we go and look at your house."

Ten minutes later, Holmes and I were ensconced in a hansom, rattling away toward the East End. Gloria had been left to the kind ministrations of our landlady, whose motherly instincts had been awakened by the girl's

64

plight. Holmes didn't speak for the whole journey. He sat still, his eyes closed, his placid countenance belying the intense energy of his working mind. I knew that he couldn't be drawn out at such times, so I sat in silence also and reflected on the strange and dramatic mystery before us, trying, unsuccessfully, to use my friend's methods to imagine an explanation.

After some little time, we turned onto a dusty, narrow street. Tradesmen and women in shabby clothing paraded down either side along the old houses. Here and there, unkempt gardens broke the monotony of drab front doors. At last we alighted outside of one of these houses, better maintained than its neighbors, but still by no means pleasant to look at. A hand-painted wooden sign in the window read: *Ben Friedman's Own Handcrafted Dolls and Toys for Children of All Ages.* A collection of curious loafers were clustered about the front door, kept at bay by a helmeted constable. Holmes and I struggled through the motley crowd.

"I'm sorry, gentlemen, but this is the location of a crime. Only members of the Metropolitan Police are allowed within."

"I quite understand," said Holmes suavely. "Might I ask who is in charge here?"

"Inspector Lestrade, sir."

Holmes grinned.

"That is very fortunate. Will you please let the inspector know that Sherlock Holmes is here, and may be able to furnish him with some details about the case?"

The constable opened the door and summoned one of his fellows. The other man disappeared for a moment before returning and beckoning us inside. The crowd behind us moved forward as we did, evidently hoping that the invitation might be extended to them as well.

"Hey, back now, you lot!" said the constable at the door. "Have none of you any work to do, instead of idlin' and gawkin'? Get back!"

We passed inside the house and closed the door, leaving the flustered policeman to his unenviable task. We were in a wide room filled with shelves and low tables, many of which were turned over and their former contents smashed on the floor. Among those still intact were cunningly carved wooden animals, trains, and soldiers, beautifully painted with bright colors, as well as building bricks and other toys. In the corner, a lovely white rocking horse had survived the onslaught unscathed, but a large dollhouse had been smashed to bits. This was very delicate and must, before it was ruined, have been quite fine.

The most remarkable objects in the room, however, were the dolls, some of wood and others of porcelain, all skillfully made with delicate features and painted so as to be exceedingly lifelike. Of these there were numerous kinds, dressed in the most charmingly detailed miniature clothes. There were ladies in fine dresses with little necklaces, gentlemen in tails and top hats, policemen, soldiers, sailors, sultans, kings and queens with painted crowns, knights, magicians in pointed hats clutching tiny wands, cricketers with little bats, and more besides. I must confess that even I felt a small thrill of childlike delight as I looked at these marvelous creations, many of which, sadly, lay in broken ruins upon the floor. I felt very sorry for the poor fellow who had clearly spent so much time and effort in their creation.

At the back of the room, behind a wooden counter, was a broken door which led to a flight of stairs.

"The inspector is upstairs," said the constable who had brought us inside, and together we ascended to the first floor. At the top of the stairs, another door lay broken and splintered. We stepped lightly over its remains and followed the constable, who turned left into a room furnished only with a stove, table and chairs, a tattered sofa, and a worktable covered with bolts of cloth, spools of thread, and uncarved pieces of wood which doubtless were destined to become more dolls. These had been scattered about in disarray, and indeed the whole room had been nearly torn apart. We found Inspector Lestrade stooping over the shredded sofa. He rose as we entered, and his ferret-like face and bright, dark eyes wore a puzzled expression.

"Mr. Holmes, Dr. Watson," he said cordially extending a hand to each of us in turn. "This as strange a business as I've ever seen, so I suppose it's no wonder you're mixed up in it. But for the life of me, I can't imagine how you could know anything I don't, for it only happened last night, and I've been here since nine o'clock."

"Ah!" said Holmes with a grin. "Then after so much time, you must have learned a good deal."

"A few indications, as you would say, Mr. Holmes," said Lestrade, ignoring my friend's attempt to needle him. "But Constable Miller tells me you know something of the matter?"

"Quite so, Lestrade. Are you willing to collaborate on the case, or should I take my own line? I wouldn't wish to prejudice your own investigation."

"There's no denying you've been some small help in the past, Mr. Holmes. I think we may work together."

Briefly, Holmes and I described the morning's events and Gloria's story to Lestrade. Holmes failed to tell Lestrade that Friedman had expressly told the girl not to go to the police, and I, following my friend's lead, also made no mention of it.

"I am bound to say that agrees entirely with my own findings," said Lestrade when we had finished. "I am glad to hear the girl is safe, for I feared she'd met the same fate as her father. But why should he want her to find you? Do you know the man?"

"I assure you, I never met him," Holmes answered.

"Have you found Mr. Friedman?" I asked.

"No, not yet, Doctor," said Lestrade. "Apart from a small quantity of blood by the stove, we can find no trace of him."

Holmes at once examined the area indicated by Lestrade. There were some small drops of blood on the floor and the windowsill. He took out his lens and, crawling on his knees and elbows, meticulously looked over every inch of floor from the stove to the stairs outside the room. As he did so, he kept up a little running commentary under his breath, with an *Oh!* or an *A-ha!* escaping his lips here and there. Lestrade and I waited patiently for him to finish examining the rest of the building. When he had reached the stairs, he collected some small threads that were clinging to a shattered piece of the door. He then rose to his feet and examined a small room at the other end of the hall, which I took to be Gloria's bedroom. After spending a moment there, he returned and bent over the worktable, examining the items upon it and opening every little drawer.

"Observe the stitching!" he remarked, lifting up a little doll's jacket. "Such cunning workmanship! Mr. Friedman is certainly a very interesting fellow. What do you make of this, Lestrade?"

He pointed to some plain little pieces of scrap paper on a corner of the work table, with a lead pencil resting nearby.

"I make nothing of it, Mr. Holmes. Plainly, they are for making labels to affix to the dolls."

Holmes smiled and continued his examination of the room. He passed through a door on the far side of the room into Mr. Friedman's bedroom, which had been all but destroyed. The mattress had been flung from the bed and the chest of drawers, wardrobe, and washstand had been smashed to pieces. He looked through the piles of wreckage before returning to us and looking thoughtfully at the ruined sofa.

"I think it's clear what happened here," said Holmes. "There were at least six men here last night – Mr. Friedman and five intruders – hoping to find a clue to another man's whereabouts."

"Gloria said the men who broke in demanded to know where 'he' was," I remembered aloud.

"Exactly."

"So many?" asked Lestrade. "There is only one set of foot prints."

"One set of muddy footprints on the stairs. Yes, I saw them, but I also saw much that you did not. You must look for more than the most obvious clues if you wish to get all the facts, Lestrade. For one who knows how to read the signs, they are quite clear. One man waited by the front door, two

67

went around to the back of the house, and two forced that door and cornered Mr. Friedman here by the stove. One man was wearing a set of heavy work boots with a nail protruding from the sole. There was a struggle. I think when we find these fellows, we will see that one has quite a badly broken nose."

"Now, really – " Lestrade began, but Holmes cut him off.

"The two men subdued Friedman, perhaps by binding his hands and feet, and kept him here by the door. He would tell them nothing, so they went to work searching the house. But they couldn't find what they were looking for, and became angrier the more they looked. You see that the room becomes more and more disheveled as they get further toward the bedroom, which, in a fit of temper, they utterly ruined. The little girl's room is likewise destroyed. Then our friend with the muddy boots arrived upstairs. I think he was one of Gloria's pursuers, returning to tell his comrades of her escape. Then they left, taking Friedman with them."

Holmes gazed thoughtfully at the worktable while Lestrade busily recorded his words in a notebook.

"I have had the neighbors questioned," he said as he wrote. "No one remembers seeing anyone unfamiliar on the street last night. If anyone saw two men carrying a third away, they would surely have said so."

"Perhaps they used a cart to carry Friedman," I suggested.

"His dolls," remarked Holmes, "are very fine . . . ."

Lestrade and I stared at him in dumb puzzlement over this *non sequitur.*

"Surely you observed how each doll is almost a work of art in itself," Holmes continued. "Such a skilled craftsman could have a shop at a fashionable address, making toys for the children of the wealthiest residents of London. Why then does he toil here in obscurity?

"It does seem strange, now that I think of it," said I.

"It is unusual, no doubt," said Lestrade, who was visibly annoyed, "but I fail to see what that could possibly have to do with the matter at hand."

"Merely a thought," said Holmes. "I have a little theory I would like to put to the test. I would be obliged if the two of you would allow me to work undisturbed for twenty minutes."

Holmes disappeared downstairs. Lestrade turned to me with an amused look.

"I hope these theories of his can point us to our man," he said. "Otherwise, this is all rather a waste of time."

"Holmes's methods usually produce positive results," I said defensively.

"I won't deny he's sharp enough. But I'm a practical man, Dr. Watson, and as a practical man I work on facts, not theories."

A few minutes later Holmes came back with several different dolls of various kinds in his arms. Lestrade and I watched as Holmes sat at the work table and, taking a small knife, began to cut the clothing from the dolls.

"Mr. Holmes!" ejaculated Lestrade. "What on God's earth are you doing?"

It was Holmes's turn to look annoyed. "It is a liberty, no doubt, but as you yourself said, I have been of some help to the official force in the past, and if I have ever given you cause to feel any small confidence in my way of working, I beg you to allow me to continue with the task at hand."

"But why on earth – ?"

Holmes shot Lestrade an irritated glance, and the policeman ceased his protestations, though his small dark eyes continued to watch Holmes from beneath furrowed brows. One by one, Holmes undressed the dolls and meticulously deconstructed their tiny garments, while Lestrade and I watched. Finally, as he took apart the red jacket of a little soldier doll, he gave a cry of exaltation.

"See here, gentlemen!" he laughed as he pulled a little slip of paper out from a fold of the tiny jacket, so cunningly sewn that it had been almost invisible moments before. A short message was written upon it in pencil. Lestrade looked at Holmes in slack-jawed amazement.

"How on earth did you know?"

"I didn't know, but I thought it not unlikely. The possibility was suggested to me by those slips of paper you dismissed out of hand. If you had bothered to inspect the dolls downstairs closely, would would have seen that the labels are of stiff card paper, and written with a pen, not a pencil. This thinner, more flexible paper served a different purpose."

"It would never have occurred to me," I said.

"But this cannot help us at all!" interjected Lestrade, pointing to the message. It said:

C WILL HAVE HIM. AMELIA 9.9

Holmes, who was lighting a cigarette, furrowed his brows and closed his eyes, evidently in deep thought.

"Presumably," I said, "'*C*' is a person's initial, and the '*him*' referred to is the person whom Friedman's assailants were seeking. And that date . . . why, that's tomorrow."

"But who is Amelia?" mused Lestrade. "I'm not sure this hasn't made the whole thing more mysterious than before!"

69

Both of us looked to Holmes, who was still sitting and smoking silently.

"Well, I must return to the Yard," said Lestrade. "A constable will remain. I'll keep you appraised of any fresh developments on our end, Mr. Holmes, if you'll return the favor."

Holmes agreed wordlessly. Lestrade gave me a nod and left the room. I heard his footsteps fade as he crossed the front room downstairs and left the building. At length Holmes rose.

"I have some inquiries to make," he said, "which I could manage more quickly on my own."

He stopped for a moment to consider a framed photograph of what I took to be Gloria's father and late mother holding an infant between them. He slipped the photograph into his pocket and continued on his way.

"Be a good chap, Watson, and go back to Baker Street to look after little Gloria so that Mrs. Hudson can concentrate on her washing."

Gloria ran excitedly to meet me when I walked through the front door of 221b, but when she saw that I was alone, the poor girl burst into tears. It took some time to assure her that we had by no means given up on finding her father. After a while, she calmed down, and I took her upstairs with me. Together we sat by the fire and I listened while she spoke rapidly in the way of excited children, telling me all about her father. As afternoon deepened into evening outside, Mrs. Hudson came in and left a telegram for Holmes on the dining table. After the streets were dark and the diffuse glow of gas light shone through the swirling fog on the street below, Holmes himself appeared.

"We are getting closer to the heart of the matter," he said. "I have no doubt we shall clear it up. Ah, a telegram!"

Holmes tore upon the envelope and read the message before handing it to me with a sardonic smirk on his lips.

"Gloria, why don't you go help Mrs. Hudson with dinner?"

Gloria rose at once and went out of the room.

"Well, what do you make of it, Watson?"

"It is from Lestrade," I said. "He writes: '*Have arrested drab Amelia Cavendish in connexion with the disappearance of Ben Friedman. Cavendish known associate of gangs in the East End. Results of questioning will follow.*' Well, that was certainly quick work on his part."

"Quick, and characteristically misguided."

"You think he is on the wrong track?" I asked.

"My dear fellow, I know it," said Holmes with a laugh. "But Lestrade's error works to our advantage. This case is far too delicate to have the official police blundering about."

70

"Have your inquiries been fruitful?"

"Oh yes," Holmes said. He sat in his chair and began filling his pipe with shag. "To start with, I have learned the true identity of the mysterious Amelia."

"She isn't this drab, then?"

Holmes laughed again. "The *Amelia* in question is a ship, Watson. A ship which is scheduled to leave port tomorrow, bound for Boston."

"However did you find that out?"

"Never mind that now. For the moment, we have a more pressing concern."

"You mean '*C*'?"

"Quite so," he said. He lit his pipe and leaned back into his chair. Blue smoke began to rise above his head and the smell of strong tobacco filled the room. "You see, I'm following a chain link by link. '*C*' will lead us to the person Friedman's attackers were seeking. That person, I have no doubt, will be able to tell us who took the unfortunate doll maker, and once we know who they are and what they want, I shall be very much surprised if we cannot run them to ground."

I was about to respond to this remark when little Gloria returned.

"Mrs. Hudson says supper will be up shortly," she said seriously, like a soldier delivering crucial intelligence to her commanding officer. Holmes would say no more about the case until after dinner, when he prevailed upon Mrs. Hudson to allow Gloria to sleep downstairs in her sitting room. When we were alone once more, Holmes and I sat together smoking.

"The *Amelia* leaves tomorrow," said Holmes. "We have little time left to us, so I shall start early in the morning."

"I shall be up at the crack of dawn," said I. Holmes smiled.

"You needn't be," he said. "My first order of business will be best accomplished alone. But if all goes well, I shall need your help afterwords. Benjamin Friedman's abductors are clearly members of an organized and dangerous gang. I think you would do well to clean your revolver tonight."

That night I found sleep impossible, for I couldn't keep my unquiet mind from worrying over the day's unanswered questions. What was the meaning of messages that the doll maker had concealed? Who had taken him? Was he still alive? If, God forbid, he was dead, what would become of little Gloria?

Exhaustion must have overcome me at last, for when I woke and looked at my watch, I discovered it was nearly ten in the morning. I dressed hurriedly, but found that Holmes had already had his breakfast and, Mrs. Hudson told me, left the house "dressed ridiculously". Finding he had left no message for me, I contented myself with his previous assurances that he would call on my assistance and, after assurances of Gloria's well-being and a late breakfast, I sat down to read the paper. It was ten minutes to noon when I heard Holmes's tread upon the stairs and he entered, dressed in the shabby attire of a common loafer..

"This case, Watson!" he exclaimed, and without a word of further information darted into his room. Twenty minutes later, he emerged into the sitting room dressed in fresh clothes.

"I am sorry to have kept you waiting," he said, pouring a cup of coffee from the pot on the table. "There was no time to lose, and I could manage more quickly on my own. But now I have all the links in the chain."

"Tell me everything!" I said.

"Time presses, and we must be brief," said he. "This morning, I have been to see 'C'. It will not surprise you to learn it was none other than Mrs. Cartwright, Friedman's friend who helped set him up in business."

I nodded, though in fact until that point I had quite forgotten what Gloria had told us about her.

"The note said 'C will have him'," I recalled. "Who then is 'him'?"

"Fetch your hat and your revolver," he said. "I will explain on the way."

A few minutes later, we departed, again leaving Gloria to the care of an obliging Mrs. Hudson. Once we were ensconced in a four-wheeler as it rattled quickly through the streets, Holmes was as good as his word.

"We're going to collect Benjamin Friedman's brother, Albert Friedman," he said, peering out of the cab windows. "He appears to have offended one of the deadliest gangs in London, and they are scouring the city for him."

"Do they intend to kill him?"

"Without question. The code these gangs live by is rigid and barbarous. They will show no mercy to the man who crosses them."

"Then if I understand correctly," said I, "Albert Friedman's only hope is to escape England aboard the *Amelia*."

"Very astute of you, Watson. We shall make a logician of you yet. But if Albert escapes, Benjamin will surely suffer in his place. Indeed, he is likely to be killed in either event as punishment for shielding his brother."

"Then what are we to do?"

"We are on our way to meet representatives of the gang," Holmes answered. "There will be an exchange. Albert for Benjamin."

"Holmes!" I cried. "You cannot mean it!"

"It is a risk, to be sure, but there is no other way to guarantee Benjamin's safety."

"At the cost of his brother's life!"

"I assure you I will not allow it to come to that. Now, not another word, Watson."

Holmes tapped the roof with his stick, and the driver slowed. A man wrapped in a heavy dark coat stepped out of a house and entered the cab. Holmes moved over to accommodate him, tapped the roof again, and the cabby urged the horse forward.

The man who had joined us wore thick-rimmed spectacles and a long heavy beard under a black homburg. He nodded curtly to me, but said no word. I felt certain he was none other than Albert Friedman, come out of hiding in order to save his brother. But did he understand the risk? Though I felt sure that Holmes wouldn't have lied to him, my friend had shown himself capable of withholding details of his plans from others when it suited him. I felt the desire to ask the man directly whether he understood what was to happen, but something in the tone of Holmes's command sealed my lips. I knew from experience that Holmes always had an excellent reason for what he did, and despite my misgivings, I determined to put my faith in him. Holmes took a length of cord from his pocket and tied the man's hands together.

After a time we alighted near the place appointed for the rendezvous, a dirty, squalid street that smelled like the bowels of a sewer. Here and there piles of refuse sat like scabs on the pavement, and dirty, thin children scampered about resembling roving gangs of baboons. But for the cold London air and the English clothes on the backs of the loiterers who watched us with drooping eyelids, it might have been a scene from the faraway slums of India or Afghanistan. A cat perched on a windowsill above us surveyed the scene before indifferently turning away.

"Our meeting place is just past there," said Holmes quietly, pointing to an alley across the street. "From this point forward, Watson, it would be best if you didn't speak. Keep the revolver in your pocket, but be prepared to use it in an instant! Wait for us here, cabby."

Holmes led us down a dismal alleyway into a dirty yard surrounded by tenement houses. Waiting in the yard were three large, grim-faced men and a fourth whose hands were bound. Two of the men kept a grip on their prisoner while the third, a grim, bearded man whom I took to be the leader, stepped forward to meet us.

"Looks like him, all right," he said, regarding our prisoner, his voice soft but full of menace. "The boss has been looking for you, Albert. You might have spared yourself and your brother here some misery if you'd come back before."

The thug transferred his attention from Albert to us.

"And who are you two?"

"Our names would mean nothing to you."

73

"Let's have them, all the same."

"Surely it would be better," said Holmes in a tone that brooked no argument. "for the safety of all involved, to remain *incognito*."

The man frowned, clearly displeased with Holmes's defiant tone, but seemed unwilling to press the issue when his long-sought prize was within his reach.

"Have it your way then," he said. "Todd, hand him over."

As Benjamin Friedman was brought to us, I could see his face more clearly. He had a beard like his brother, but was taller and thinner. His face was covered in bruises, and it appeared that his nose had been broken. When Todd, a tall, dark fellow, brought him forward, I stepped forward also with Albert. It made me sick at heart to turn him over to these criminals, whatever he may have done. Benjamin, weakened by his ordeal and seeming hardly able to stand on his own, made a futile effort to grasp at Albert before he was taken away.

"I believe that concludes our business," said Holmes. "If you will excuse us, we have obligations elsewhere." Without waiting for an answer he turned back the way we had come, and I turned to follow him, allowing Benjamin use me as a prop.

We were halfway down the alley when I heard a commotion and shouting behind us. I turned around, drawing my revolver, and was astonished to see that the little yard was now full of uniformed constables, who had rushed in from every direction. Lestrade was with them, pointing a revolver at the leader while the man I had taken to be Albert Friedman had loosened his bonds and wrestled Todd to the ground. His false beard had been torn off in the scuffle.

"Don't delay, Watson. The official police force is perfectly capable of rounding up a few common thugs without our help."

Holmes lifted Friedman after him into the cab but gestured for me to remain outside. He took out his notebook and jotted some words down.

"Go back to Baker Street. Collect Gloria and bring her to this spot on the docks. The *Amelia* is berthed there. We will join you shortly, after I've taken Mr. Friedman to collect a few essentials from his home. Make haste! The ship departs in fewer than two hours."

Back at Baker Street, Gloria was overjoyed to hear that her father was safe. I bundled her up in some spare blankets and together we set off to rendezvous with Holmes and her father at the *Amelia*.

Some little time later, we arrived at the docks. I stepped out of the hansom and lifted Gloria down. Her feet had hardly left the ground when she bolted away from me. I turned and saw at once why she had run. Her father stood there, next to Holmes. He was crouched down, opening his arms wide to embrace his daughter. The sight of their happy reunion nearly brought tears to my eyes, and it seemed to me that even Holmes, in spite of his unsentimental nature, couldn't suppress a smile. Together, we escorted father and daughter to their ship, where, as it happened, the true Albert Friedman was waiting for them.

"You aren't altogether out of danger yet," Holmes told them seriously. "This gang will have contacts in Boston. It would be best for you to move from city to city for a little while, in order to throw your pursuers off the scent."

"We will," said Benjamin. "How can we ever repay you?"

"My work," said Holmes, "is its own reward."

"Goodbye," said Gloria, hugging each of us tightly in turn. "Thank you for saving my father. I hope we will still be friends, wherever we go."

"Of course we shall," said I.

"I couldn't have wished for a better conclusion to the case," said Holmes as our hansom rattled down the pavement. We were on our way back to Baker Street, and Holmes was in high spirits.

"Yes, indeed," said I. "But I confess that even now, I don't understand how we reached it. You may have all the links in the chain, but I certainly do not."

Holmes smiled.

"Right you are, Watson. I beg your pardon. Now that the business is over, I have leisure to tell you all."

"I should be obliged," said I.

"You already know," Holmes said, "how I deduced that the slips of paper Lestrade dismissed were clearly not meant to serve as labels. Thanks to my comprehensive study of past criminal cases, seven possibilities immediately occurred to me, and I considered the idea that secret messages, written on the little pieces of paper, were sewn into the dolls' clothing. Their recipient, or an intermediary, would pose as a customer and purchase the dolls containing the messages.

"If this were the case, there must be some distinguishing feature by which the intended recipient could tell the special dolls from the ordinary ones. My examination of Friedman's stock showed that, of each kind, there were always one or two with minor differences to the majority – a differently faced shape or differently colored accessory. These, as you saw, I meticulously deconstructed until – *Voila!* The message was revealed:

C WILL HAVE HIM. AMELIA 9.9

"This message, though obscure, wasn't entirely inscrutable. We now knew someone with the initial *C* was involved and had, it seemed reasonable to assume, custody of some other person of interest. But who was Amelia? It occurred to me that there must have been some reason why the name *Amelia* was spelled out, instead of being referred to by initial as *C* was. And how to interpret the date which directly followed the name? The idea of a ship occurred to me, for ships are often given female names. I made inquiries at various shipping offices to test my hypothesis, and found myself justified. The knot was unraveling, but still far from straight.

"Who was *C*? An ideal reasoner would have recalled at once that Gloria had told us of a Mrs. Cartwright who had helped her father in the past. I, frustratingly fallible, didn't recall until later that evening, when we were smoking after dinner. I rose before dawn the next morning to make inquiries into the whereabouts of this person, then returned to Baker Street for a disguise. I had determined that the best way to reach Mrs. Cartwright, in the circumstances, was to visit her *incognito*. I'm sure I gave her quite a shock, but once I had explained my errand, she was quite willing to help me, and told me all about the unhappy history of the Friedmans.

"They are originally from Austria, where they inherited their father's business making and selling fine toys. Benjamin, the eldest brother, had been taught the craft, and Albert was in charge of managing the business. But Albert fell in with bad company – criminal company, in fact – and soon took up gambling, drink, and other vices. So alarming did the state of their finances become, and so unwelcome was Albert in the town they had always called home, that Benjamin decided to leave the country for a fresh start in England. He couldn't bring himself to leave his brother behind, and so after extracting many promises from Albert as to his future good behavior, the brothers arrived in London with Gloria. They were able to set up shop with the help of Mrs. Cartwright, a childhood friend who had married an English businessman years before.

"Sadly, vice again proved to have too strong a grip on Albert. He fell into old habits, and soon became involved with a criminal organization, the full scale of which he didn't at first comprehend. After a time, he began to see what he had gotten himself into, and he tried to leave the organization. The criminal fraternity expects loyalty to the end, however, and Albert by this time knew so much that they couldn't let him go at liberty. So plans were laid to carry the family to what they hoped would be safety in America. Albert had to stay in hiding, but messages were passed back and forth, and Benjamin saved every penny he could in anticipation of the journey. The Jewish community in London is very tightly knit, and this served the Friedmans well. Fellow Jews helped shelter Albert and communicated with Benjamin by means of messages hidden in spools of thread and other supplies, and Benjamin would communicate with them as we have discovered. The gang must have known that

76

Benjamin would know his brother's whereabouts. They waited to see if he would reveal it through carelessness. When he didn't, they attempted to get the information from him directly, resulting in this very stimulating little case.

"After locating Albert through Mrs. Cartwright, I took him secretly to the *Amelia*, and then went to Lestrade. I suggested that I contact the gang and propose an exchange – Benjamin for a decoy Albert, actually a constable in disguise."

"I can't imagine he was keen on the idea," said I.

"It took some doing, but I brought him round. Lestrade kindly arranged to have the *Amelia* held at port just long enough to conceal the family on board, and now our efforts have been rewarded with success."

"So will the Friedmans be safe at last?"

"I can only hope, Watson," said Holmes. "This gang is organized, connected, and bold. Benjamin Friedman even suspected that they have agents within the Metropolitan Police, and for that reason told his daughter to avoid them. Albert himself would tell me little of the gang, but what he did say suggested a criminal network of enormous scale and influence. This isn't the first time I've suspected some larger power at work in the criminal underworld. Indeed, I have come to believe that the most dangerous gangs in London aren't disparate, but one unified organization which has a hand in half the evils that plague the city, and indeed is only one strand of a vast web which has spread over all the country, guided by a central malignant brain at the center of all."

"What brain?" I asked.

"I don't know," Holmes said, and he stared ahead as though straining to see through a veil. "Not yet."

I often wondered in the years after these events what had become of the three Friedmans upon their arrival in America. Had they assumed new names and made better, happier lives for themselves, or did the terrible arm of the criminal network which hunted them reach even across the Atlantic and find them out at last? As the years passed, however, I thought less and less of them, until eventually they passed out of my mind entirely. Then, many years later, I was sitting in my home one morning when a parcel arrived with the post. I unwrapped the paper and opened the plain wooden box to find inside two finely made little dolls. One wore a bowler and a mustache, the other was long with aquiline features and clutched a little magnifying lens in its hand. The dolls were accompanied by a note, which read:

Dear Doctor Watson,

It is with sadness that I write to inform you of the death of my father, Mr. Benjamin Friedman. Thanks to your help, he was able to establish himself here in America, and lived a good and prosperous life, though I regret to say that my Uncle Albert died of a diseased liver four years after our arrival. For many years, Father had a thriving business, which he sold some years ago, and the proceeds allowed him to live out his retirement in comfort. These dolls are the last Father ever made, and he would have sent them to you himself, had sickness not intervened. Please accept these as gifts from one who, without your aide and that of your friend Mr. Holmes, would not be here today.

Sincerely,
Gloria Goldman, née *Friedman*

Holmes scoffed when I gave him the doll which bore his likeness, but it sat on a shelf in the sitting room for many years.

The Flinders Case
by Kevin McCann

I was roused by Holmes shaking me by the shoulder with the words, "Wake up, Watson! We have a case!" I reluctantly opened my eyes to a dark bedroom and Holmes, candle in hand, smiling down at me. I sat up in bed and yawned. "What time is it?"

"Early," Holmes replied and then pointed to my bedside table. "I made you coffee. There's a hansom waiting outside, and I need you up and dressed as quickly as you can manage."

I drank the coffee as I was dressing and then went down to our sitting room, where I found Holmes (already in his hat and coat) pacing impatiently. I also noted that it was only six-forty. Holmes handed me a telegram which read:

Please come at once.

Gregson

This was followed by an address in West Hampstead.

So it was that a mere twenty minutes after being roused I was sat in the back of a hansom rattling through the still largely deserted streets of London. As well as being New Year's Day, it was also a Sunday, so the streets were even quieter than usual. Holmes was silent and in pensive mood.

It was still dark when we were met at the front gate of a suburban villa by a grim-faced Gregson. "Morning, Mr. Holmes. Doctor. Nasty one this: Slavey's dead. Mistress is missing. Page is in deep shock. It looks like an outside job, but the thing is – "

Holmes cut across him with, "We shall not speculate in advance. From the beginning, if you please, Inspector. Just the facts as you know them."

Gregson allowed himself a brief smile, produced a small notebook, and began to read. "Householder is a Mr. Bernard Flinders. Age forty-seven. Works in the City as a Senior Accountant at the City and Suburban Bank. His wife, Rebecca, aged fifty-nine." Here he paused and glanced across at Holmes (who gave him the briefest of nods) before continuing. "Slavey named Ivy. Aged about fifteen, found brutally murdered in her room. We're not sure of her exact age, Mr. Holmes, as she was a foundling. The page, Billy, aged seventeen, is still in shock."

"Is he injured in any way?"

"Superficial head wound. He claims he'd been struck down from behind, knocked cold, and then locked in the larder. His hands weren't tied though, and he managed to break free from his confinement without any difficulty. Now the thing is, Mr. Holmes, that head wound of his is no more than a graze. Shouldn't have even knocked him cold, let alone left him unconscious for a good four hours."

"Where's the boy now?"

"Seated in the kitchen with a constable keeping an eye on him."

"And Mr. Flinders?"

"In his study."

"Now let us hear Flinders' version of events."

"Claims he was surprised and overpowered by two masked men who forced him to open the safe and helped themselves to about fifty pounds in cash whilst holding his wife at gun point. Claims they then tied him up, gagged him, and took away his wife as a hostage. And there he remained until he was freed by Billy at about four this morning."

"And the ropes that held him?"

"Stroke of luck there. The boy cut the ropes, but left the knots intact."

Holmes's eyes widened with obvious pleasure. "And you have them?"

"Bagged and labelled."

"May I examine them?"

"Certainly. Shall we get out of this cold though?"

Holmes smiled. "Lead on, Inspector."

We stepped in through the front door and Gregson handed Holmes a canvas bag that had been sitting on top of a small table. Holmes took out one rope and then the other, and examined them both closely with his lens.

"Teeth marks where the knots were pulled tight." He offered the lens to Gregson who confirmed his finding. He then examined the knots themselves. "They don't seem to me to be very efficient. A child could have freed himself in moments. Any signs of a break-in?"

"Broken scullery window. Glass on the carpet, so obviously broken from the outside. However, the dust on the windowsill was undisturbed."

"So your conclusion is?"

"Nobody climbed in that way."

"And the ground outside? Any footprints?"

"None that I could see," said Gregson. "I'll need a bit more light than a bulls-eye, but the sun will be up soon enough. There was no frost in the night, but I'm not raising my hopes. I've made sure the ground's been left untouched so you can make your own examination."

"Oh, excellent Gregson! Now if you would be so kind as to lead us to the kitchen, I would very much like to hear Billy's version of events."

"But surely," I began, "we should be talking to this man Flinders first to get a fuller account of what happened."

Holmes merely smiled enigmatically. "I think we'll save him for last."

We found the page seated at the kitchen table, a blanket around his shoulders and drinking tea out of a large chipped mug, both hands curled around it. I noticed that even though the kitchen was thankfully warm – someone had obviously lit the stove – clouds of steam were rising from his tea. It was obviously scalding, yet the boy – for boy he was – continued holding onto it, seemingly oblivious to the heat. A constable was stood opposite him.

Holmes stood for a minute in the kitchen doorway, looking at the boy, who was clearly oblivious as to our presence. I knew something of his methods as a detective (and I knew enough to know I could never be his equal), and I'd already realised that they were not entirely dissimilar to those used by a good diagnostician.

The boy was thin and dressed in what was probably the only other suit of clothes he possessed, apart from a page's uniform. It was at least two sizes too big, but was clean and in a good state of repair. There was a faint smell of alcohol, and I noted a dark stain on his shirt front that suggested a spilled drink. His pupils were widely dilated, and the word "opiate" came to mind – either self-administered, or else he had been drugged.

My train of thought was interrupted by Holmes who spoke gently and quietly. "Billy, isn't it?" The boy jerked and spilled some hot tea over his hand, but again, seemed oblivious to the heat. A man can fake shock, but no one can suppress a reflex action. Evidently Holmes noted the same thing. "Doctor," he said turning to me. "Your province, I think."

I stepped forward and said, "Billy, would you put the tea down please and let me take a look at that hand?" I could see the skin was already a livid red. I turned to the constable. "Some cold water and a clean cloth."

After I'd bathed Billy's hand, reduced the lividity, and wrapped it in a clean dry cloth sprinkled in oil of lavender, I took his pulse, which was sluggish, and noted the coldness of his skin – again consistent with shock. There was grazing on one side of his face, along with a few drops of clotted blood clearly visible in his light brown hair. I cleaned the graze (noting it was superficial) whilst Holmes and the constable watched me work in silence.

81

When I was done, Holmes took my place at the kitchen table. He turned to the constable. "Could you leave us alone now, Constable – ?"

"Fawcett, Mr. Holmes. I'll be just outside if you need me. There's some tea on the pot, fresh made, if you fancy a cup."

Holmes briefly bared his top teeth in what he thought was a smile, and then turned back to the page. "Now Billy," he began, "just tell me everything that happened last night. Leave nothing out."

The boy took a sip of his tea. "Well, sir, Mr. Flinders dined alone at seven. The Mistress wasn't feeling too well, so Ivy took her up a tray."

"And who is Ivy?"

"The maid, sir."

"Who cooked the meal?"

"Mrs. Gregory. She comes in three times a day to cook main meals."

"So Mrs. Gregory doesn't live in?"

"No, sir. She's a widow woman lives in one of the cottages down by the railway line."

Holmes nodded and then produced his cigarettes. "Do you smoke, Billy?"

The boy took one with, "Yes, sir," before hastily adding, "Thank you, sir."

"So your master dined alone at – what time did you say?"

"Exactly seven, sir. He's stickler for punctuality."

"And Ivy took up a tray for your mistress at about the same time?"

"Yes, sir. Only Ivy said the Mistress was deep asleep at first, and when she did wake up – " And here he paused, clearly uncomfortable.

"Go on," said Holmes gently.

"Well, sir, Ivy said as how when she did wake up, her speech was all slurry, like she'd been at the gin. Only we both knew she was strict temperance. Me and Ivy had a bite, and then goes to collect the Master's dinner dishes at eight."

"Did he ring for you?"

"No, sir. He always dines from seven until eight exactly. Anyway, we goes to clear his dishes and he says to leave them, then gives us a shilling each and says to have the night off, but be back before midnight."

"And is he normally so open handed?"

"No, sir. He's usually tight as a duck's – He's usually a very thrifty man."

"Go on."

"Well, sir, we was delighted, what with it being New Year's Eve, so we went off to The Farmers."

"The Farmers is a local tavern?"

"Yes, sir. Anyway, we had a couple of penny nips – that's gins, sir – but we kept back most of the money. See, we had an understanding . . . ."

Suddenly, the whole facade crumbled and he collapsed in tears. I began to speak, but Holmes pressed his index finger to his lips and I fell silent. We were both struck by the immensity of his grief and sat perfectly still until his sobbing subsided. Holmes placed a hand gently on each of the boy's. "It's all right," he said quietly. "Take your time." Billy's sobbing gradually subsided, and after he'd blown his nose into a handkerchief that Holmes provided, he continued.

"The thing is, sir, everyone likes Ivy. Mrs. Gregory is teaching her how to cook so she can better herself. You know, be a cook herself one day. And Mistress is always kind to her as well. She even give her some of her old clothes she'd finished with. Like new they are."

"They're the same size?"

"Yes, sir. The Mistress is only small herself. One good gust'd blow her away." He blushed. "Sorry, sir. That must have sounded impertinent."

Holmes shook his head. "Not at all, Billy. You really are being most helpful. What time did you get home?"

"It was eleven-fifteen, sir. I heard the parish clock strike the quarter just as we got to the front gate. Master's light was still on, so I went to tell him we were back as he'd ordered, and ask if there was anything he wanted."

"In which room was he?"

"The library, sir. He spends most of his time in there."

"And where was Ivy?"

"I'd packed her off to bed, sir. She was tired and, truth to tell, just a bit tiddly. She was giggling. Told me she loved me and kissed me full on the lips. Right there in the hallway and . . . ." His voice seemed to die in mid-sentence. I glanced across at Holmes, half-expecting the usual great stone face he affected when interviewing witnesses. I could not have been wider of the mark.

"Billy," he said gently. "I know how hard this is for you, but we must go on. I need you to tell me everything while it's still fresh in your mind. I need you to be strong for Ivy's sake."

Billy nodded, swallowed hard, and then went on. "The Master was reading, and when I went in he asked if we had a good time, and then pours me a glass of port – "

I interrupted him. "I thought this was a Temperance house?"

"The Mistress don't drink, but Mr. Flinders likes a glass or two after she's gone to bed."

I glanced across at Holmes, who nodded to me, so I felt safe to continue. "How do you know that?"

83

"Ivy had seen him more than once, and so had I."

"Now think carefully," Holmes said. "Did he pour himself a glass at the same time?"

"No, sir, he already had one. 'Now the thing with port is,' he says, 'is to knock it back in one.' Well, I did my best, but I didn't much like the taste, and spilled more down my shirt front as went down my throat. Anyway, next thing, the room's going around and I'm face down on the carpet. The Master gets me to my feet and apologises for giving me such a large drink and says, 'Off to bed with you, my lad!' Now I remember going out into the hall and then something hits me from behind, and next thing I know, I'm waking up in the pantry."

"Was the door locked?"

"No, sir. It was ajar. I ran out into the kitchen and called out for Ivy, but there was no sign of her, so I grabbed a bread knife and then I ran upstairs . . . ."

"Why the knife?" I asked.

"In case there was anyone left in the house as shouldn't have been."

"Quite right," said Holmes quietly. "Please go on."

"I found the Master in his study all tied up, so I cut him loose. I probably could have untied him, but I was dizzy still, and they looked like they'd been pulled tight, so I thought it quickest way. I wanted to go and look for Ivy and check on the Mistress, but Mr. Flinders says as how I should run out into the street and fetch a cozzer – I mean a policeman – in case he was still in the house . . . ."

"You're sure he said *he* and not *them*?"

"Yes, sir. Quite sure."

"Go on."

"Anyways, I found one quick enough, and when we got back, Mr. Flinders says that Mistress has been kidnapped and . . . and . . . ."

"Nearly done Billy," Holmes said gently.

"And then he says he's been upstairs and found Ivy dead in her room . . . ." At this point he almost broke down again, and I marvelled at the strength of this lad when I saw the way he pulled himself back together and finished his account. "After that – well, after that I don't really remember much else. I just kept thinking it must be some kind of bad dream . . . ."

"One last question, Billy, and then we're done: How long did it take you to find a constable?"

"Not long at all, sir. There was one at the end of the road, and he came as soon as I shouted."

Holmes turned to me. "Watson, perhaps you'd ask the constable to step back in, and then we'll re-join Inspector Gregson. And don't worry,

Billy. I know that you're innocent, and I promise you, the guilty man will be in a police cell by the end of the week."

We found Gregson standing by the front door, and he led us around to the side of the house. It was now light enough for us to see that the broken scullery window was roughly five feet above the ground and rather small. "This, I gather, is where the alleged burglars got in?" Gregson nodded, and Holmes then stepped carefully onto the sparse grass, got down on his hands and knees, pulled out his lens, and proceeded to carefully examine the ground. After a few minutes he stood up and faced Gregson.

"Only step where I do and have a look at this." Holmes led Gregson over to the strip of grass immediately below the window, handed him his lens, and pointed to a particular spot on the ground. "What do you make of those?"

Gregson gave a long low whistle. "Ladder marks?"

Holmes shook his head. "You assume that because they're evenly spaced and, going by the depth of the indentations, have had some weight pressed down upon them. Now look here." And Holmes pointed to another spot a foot or so further back.

Gregson again examined the ground. "Two more."

"Your conclusion?"

"Looks like whoever broke the window tried two positions for the ladder before picking the right one."

"Look at the depth of the second indentations and then compare with the first."

Again Gregson examined the ground. "They look identical to me."

"Examine the shape, as well as the depth of the marks."

Gregson went from one to the other and then said, "Rectangular."

"Anything else?"

Gregson thought for a moment and then suddenly smiled. "If the ladder had been leaning at an angle, there would have been a slight slope at the end father from the wall."

"Anything else?"

"The ones nearest the wall look parallel to the ones further away!"

"They are . . . perfectly. Odd, is it not, that a burglar or burglars operating in the dark should be able to be so exact."

"They did have a three-quarter moon."

"That's true, Inspector, but this part of the outside wall is north facing and would have been in shadow." Holmes paused. "Did your men find a ladder?"

"No. They made a thorough search."

Holmes smiled broadly. "So our thieves brought their own? Carried it through the streets on New Year's Eve and nobody noticed? Now look at those indentations again, Inspector. Does their size and distribution suggest nothing to you? A kitchen chair for example?"

Gregson's mouth broadened into a grin. "Of course! That would also explain the absence of treacle, and the broken glass on the scullery window ledge."

"No tuppeny rice either, I daresay!" The words were out of my mouth before I could stop them. Gregson and Holmes both glared at me.

"Perhaps, Inspector, you could explain."

"It's an old dodge, Doctor," Gregson said. "Professionals smear the window with treacle, press a piece of thick paper onto it, and tap the paper firmly with a hammer before peeling it back and bringing the broken glass with it. That way there's very little noise and no broken glass on inside window ledges."

"So what you're saying it that someone stood on a kitchen chair, broke the scullery window, and then – "

Holmes cut across me. "Now Watson, you know that it's a capital error – "

" – To theorise in advance of the facts. Yes, I know, but can I at least speculate that it's an inside job?"

Holmes then turned to Gregson. "May we see Ivy?"

We went back into the house and up two flights of back stairs to the top floor landing. One door was open and a constable was standing in front of the entrance.

"All right, McCann, go and have a brew," Gregson said. "I know it's against regulations, but you've earned it."

The constable touched the peak of his helmet and left. Gregson turned to us. "The body and room have been left untouched. One other thing, though, before you go in: Prepare yourselves."

As Holmes stepped over the threshold, I heard him gasp. I followed him and immediately realised why. A red-haired girl of about fourteen was lying face up on the bed. Her eyes were wide open, her clothes torn, and I could see what appeared to be bite marks on the flesh. I also noted a swelling around the mouth and nose, probably the result of a blow to the face.

"Dear God, Gregson," I said. "Couldn't you at least have covered the poor girl with a blanket? Let her at least have some dignity in death?"

Holmes held up his index finger. "Not yet, Watson. Once we're done, we will cover her." He turned to Gregson. "Who found the body?"

"Well, surely that was Flinders – " I began, but Holmes silenced me with a glance.

"P.C. McCann. Flinders told him the girl was dead, but he came up here anyway to check for himself."

"Did he enter the room?"

"No, Mr. Holmes. He said he could tell at glance."

Holmes produced his lens and began a close examination of the room. Apart from the bed, there was a threadbare rug, a fireplace, and despite the cold, no fire, and no coal or scuttle. Over against one wall was a small rather battered-looking chest with all the drawers shut. The small window was closed, but the curtains were open.

Holmes turned to Gregson. "Who opened the curtains?"

"They were already that way when McCann found her."

Holmes then got down on all fours and, using his lens, began carefully examining the floor. At one point he looked up and said, "Look at these marks, Gregson. Tell me what you make of them."

The inspector got down on his knees and peered through the lens. "Drag marks," he said, and then he looked around. "Leading back to the door."

"Leading *from*, I should say. And when we put that together with the evidence of a heavy blow to the face, it indicates what?"

Gregson thought for a moment. "She opened her door to the killer, who punched her, rendering her semi-conscious. He then dragged her to the bed."

"And what do you make of this?" Holmes asked pointing under the bed.

Gregson leaned forward. "Good God, Mr. Holmes, it's a footprint! Or part of one at least."

And sure enough, there in the dust just under the bed, was a partial print of a right bare foot. Holmes produced a piece of chalk and carefully drew a wide circle around it. "Can we get this photographed? He can add it to his list."

"Certainly. I've already sent for Mr. Lawson. I know we can trust his discretion." He turned to me. "Officially we don't photograph where crimes occur, so in sending for an outsider, I'm breaking the rules, so I'd appreciate your discretion too."

Holmes turned to me. "Now tread carefully, Watson, and tell me what you make of the body." He handed me his lens. "Time and cause of death, and your thoughts on those bite marks."

I touched the girl's skin and could tell immediately that *rigor* had yet to set in. "She's been dead less than twelve hours." I glanced at my watch. It was just after eight, so that confirmed Billy's story that Ivy was still alive at midnight. I could also see a dark line around the girl's throat that was probably made by a thin cord being pulled increasingly tight. "Death by strangulation, I'd say."

"And the bite marks?"

Again using the lens, I examined the bites. I was appalled to see how deep they were and how, in places, pieces of flesh were clearly missing. The implications were clear and I found myself thanking God that given the lack of bleeding from the wounds, they were most likely *post mortem*.

They were all partials (front incisors and canines) and ragged, but there was one in the girl's upper arm that gave a perfect impression of the top four front teeth. I was about to share my discovery with Holmes and Gregson when the photographer arrived. Gregson and I stepped back onto the landing whilst Holmes carefully supervised him.

I turned to Gregson. "Our killer has all his top front teeth."

Gregson made a note, "Well spotted, Doctor. I think that just about eliminates young Billy. Most of his top teeth are gone already." He paused and then said, "And the footprint – what do you make of that?"

"Too big for the girl, so it was either left by Billy or someone else."

Holmes appeared in the doorway. "May I borrow your tape measure, Watson?"

I handed it to him and we both watched him lay it across the footprint and then step back as it was photographed. He then re-joined us as Mr. Lawson gathered together his equipment. As he stepped out of the room Holmes placed a hand gently, but firmly, on his shoulder. "Your discretion is paramount, Mr. Lawson." Lawson merely nodded. "Photographic prints to Inspector Gregson at Scotland Yard as soon as possible."

Again Lawson merely nodded and left us.

Holmes rubbed his hands together. "Once those plates are developed, we should be able to get one that's actual size. And you'd better measure the boy's foot – just to formally eliminate him. Agreed?"

"Agreed, Mr. Holmes. So, are you ready to share your conclusions yet?"

"Not quite. What steps have you taken to find our missing Mrs. Flinders?"

Gregson opened his notebook and began to read. "I plan to place men at stations and ferry terminals. Plainclothes out in all the rookeries, mainly listening. Ponds will be dragged, and I've have search parties out checking undergrowth, empty buildings, *etcetera*."

"And here?"

"The rest of the house has been searched, as have the outbuildings. We've also checked the grounds for any sign of disturbance." But that was as far as he got.

"'Scuse me, sir." It was PC McCann. "A woman's body matching the description of Mrs. Flinders has been found."

"Where?" asked Holmes.

"Less than half-a-mile away."

We took a dog cart and drove the short distance in silence. We arrived and were directed through the wayside undergrowth by one of two constables and into a small area of scrub.

And it was there that we found our victim. She was lying on her side wearing a white cotton nightdress and bed socks to match. Her hands and feet were tied, and there was a rag stuffed into her mouth. Her hair was black and tied with a red ribbon. Holmes went down in all fours and began examining the ground. He paused and looked across at Gregson. "Two clear prints – one deeper than the other, which tells us they were made by someone carrying a heavy weight and then discarding it. We shall need Mr. Lawson yet again, Inspector." Holmes then produced two lengths of string which he looped round the outside edges of boot footprints. "Plaster casts as well." Gregson nodded and stepped out of the clearing. Holmes turned to me. "Watson, would you mind?"

I knelt beside the body, noting a small tear in nightgown and some odd green stains. I glanced up at Holmes who mouthed, "Moss," took off my gloves, and touched her face with my fingertips. The skin was cold and hard as marble. I also noted dark spots on her face which I pointed out to Holmes.

"She's been suffocated," I said and suddenly the full horror of what I was seeing struck me like a thunderbolt. I'd seen death before. I'd been in Afghanistan, so one would expect that I'd become immune to horror. Such was not the case. My hands began shaking and I let fly a tirade of hate against the monster that had done this.

Holmes placed a hand gently upon my shoulder. "Steady, Watson. Your feelings do you credit, but they cloud your eyes. Look again at the body and tell me what's missing."

"Really, Holmes," I responded sharply. "And how am I supposed to tell that?"

Holmes voice remained even. "Look at her skin."

Then it struck me. There were no bite marks, no visible wounds of any kind. I looked up at Holmes. "The attack on Ivy was frenzied, but this is more – "

" – Cold blooded and cruel. Ivy was struck down and strangled. She will hardly have been conscious at all. Mrs. Flinders was probably only too well-aware of what was going to happen."

I clutched the last straw available. "How can you be so sure?"

"Examine her head. I'm sure you won't find a single wound." I did as he suggested and of course, he was right. "Now, Watson, full *rigor mortis* has set in, so what does that that tell us?"

I felt like I was going to explode. "Really, Holmes, could you be any more patronising?"

Holmes's face remained impassive. "Save your anger for our killer. Now, I repeat, what does that tell us?"

I inhaled deeply, exhaled slowly and said, "She's been dead at least twelve hours."

Holmes nodded. "Yet according to Mr. Flinders, she was alive at one o'clock this morning." He held up his left hand while using his right to count off points on his fingers. "He claims she was still alive at eleven-fifteen when Billy and Ivy returned home. He claims he was overpowered in the early hours of the morning by two masked men, forced to open his safe whilst he and his wife were held at gunpoint. He was then tied up, and his wife taken as a hostage. Therefore?"

"He's lying! By the time Billy and Ivy returned home, she was already dead and probably dumped here." I was about to stand up when I noticed that the fingers of her right hand were slightly splayed. When I looked closer I could see the edge of a button. I tried to force the fingers apart, but they were completely locked in *rigor*.

"Well-spotted, Watson," said Holmes with a chuckle. "Eighteen more hours at most and we shall be able to retrieve the evidence that may prove our case." He turned to Gregson. "Does Flinders know we've found a body?"

"Not yet, Mr. Holmes. I thought we might break it to him together."

Holmes allowed himself a brief smile. "Very well, then. Let us return to the house and meet with Mr. Flinders."

"With confirmed countenance, Mr. Holmes?"

"With very confirmed countenance, Inspector."

"One thing, Holmes," I interjected. "How did he manage to convey the body of his wife half-a-mile or so along public roads and not be seen?

Holmes smiled. "He didn't."

"You mean he had an accomplice?"

"Not at all. If you had taken just a little more note of our surroundings – " And here he paused and pointed through a gap in the undergrowth. " – you would have noted that the rear of Flinders house is clearly visible." Gregson and I both peered in the direction he was pointing and sure enough, we could make out a distant roof. "Once he had climbed over his own back garden wall, it was a short jog across an overgrown field, and then straight into the scrub . . . and there were patches of fog last night." He turned again to Gregson. "Flinders has been kept close, I trust?"

"Kept under close observation from the moment we arrived, and he hasn't been permitted to either leave the house or change his clothes."

"What was he wearing on his feet when you arrived?"

"Carpet slippers, but I've had all his outdoor boots and shoes placed together, and my man McCann has discreetly searched under beds, the backs of cupboards, and in all the waste bins for other pairs, but nothing so far."

"Excellent, Gregson. Now if you two gentlemen would like to accompany me, we shall make our way back across country – single file if you please, and only tread where I do,"

The long and the short of it was that Holmes quickly found the trail of tell-tale footprints that led us back across an overgrown field. In truth, it was fairly easy to follow, as much of the undergrowth had been trodden down. It led us straight to Flinders' back-garden wall. Holmes timed us and it had taken just a few minutes. We then moved a good yard to the left and climbed over. Holmes then led us back to the spot where Flinders had obviously climbed over.

He pointed to a spot on the wall. A small piece of white cotton material was snagged on a sharp edged piece of the stonework. Holmes produced an envelope and placed it inside. "I think we'll find this is an exact match for the tear in Mrs. Flinders' nightgown. Note also the moss is slightly smeared, which would account for the green stains on it as well." He then pointed down to the ground. There were patches of scrubby grass, but in one spot of bare earth a footprint was clearly visible. "A cast of that as well, Inspector. Now, shall we confront our grieving widower?"

We found Mr. Flinders still in his study and, after Gregson had introduced us as "two of my colleagues", Holmes suggested we adjourn to the library. "Really Gregson, hasn't this poor man suffered enough without you leaving him – " Here Holmes's voice cracked. " – in this very room with its hideous associations!" Even as he spoke, I noted his eyes sweep over the room as if memorising its exact contents and layout. Gregson looked suitably admonished as Flinders rose from his chair and led us through into his library.

The man himself was about five-foot-eight, clean-shaven, with fair hair that was neatly cut. He was about a stone overweight, and his tan-coloured eyes seemed excessively large, indicating glandular problems. There was a small scar on his right temple that vanished into his hairline.

Once we were all seated, with Flinders facing the window so the light shone on his face, Holmes, Gregson, and myself facing him. Gregson said, "I'm sorry to tell you, but we've found a body which we believe is your wife."

With a loud, "Oh God, no!" Flinders crumpled and fell forward out of his chair in an apparent faint. While Holmes watched with an air of indifference, Gregson and I rushed to catch him. As I grabbed hold of one of his arms, I noted the musculature was well-developed.

We got him back into his chair and Holmes turned to Gregson, saying, "Hot sweet tea, I think, Inspector. Best thing for shock. Don't you agree Watson?" And then, in a voice positively oozing compassion, he added, "Now, if it isn't too distressing, perhaps you could answer a few questions?"

Flinders nodded stiffly. "I'll do my best," he said quietly.

"Good man. Now in your own words, what exactly happened last night?"

Flinders then proceeded to give us his version of events. We all noted that it differed from Billy's, and I expected Holmes to latch on to these discrepancies, but to my surprise he simply let Flinders talk, unchallenged and uninterrupted.

He said that Billy had asked him for the evening off, and made no mention of the shilling apiece Billy said he'd given them. He then claimed that after Billy and Ivy had returned, he'd noted they were both the worst for drink and packed them off to bed. About half-an-hour later, two masked men had burst into his study, and one of them was holding his wife (who was gagged) at gunpoint. He was forced to open his safe, which he said contained fifty pounds that he kept for emergencies. The two men tied him to his chair, gagged him, and then left with his wife.

At this point Gregson returned with a cup of tea. With the words, "Thank you, Inspector," Holmes rose, took it, and stepped forward to hand it to Flinders. Then he seemed to stumble, pitch forward, and spill the contents down the front of Flinders' jacket. "Oh, my dear sir!" he exclaimed. "How incredibly clumsy of me!" Despite Flinders' protestations, Holmes insisted he take it off so that it could be cleaned. Then he turned to Gregson with a curt, "Perhaps you could see about a blanket."

Gregson, looking convincingly annoyed and left without a word. Holmes then turned to Flinders. "I realise this is difficult, but it's important that we get every detail while they are still fresh in your mind. Please, pray continue."

Flinders went on to claim that he'd then spent hours – "What felt like an eternity!" – in an agony of despair until he was found and freed by Billy. He added that he was far from happy with Billy and intended to give him notice in the New Year, as he was sure the boy drank and had seen him strike Ivy.

"I cannot countenance violence against a helpless young girl!"

Holmes nodded vigorously. "I agree!" He then turned to Gregson. "I think our field of enquiry has narrowed considerably, Inspector. It would seem our first instincts were correct."

"An inside job, Mr. Holmes?"

"Indeed," and here he paused smiling at Flinders. "What you have just told us confirms a suspicion that entered my mind the first time I clapped eyes on your page." He turned to Gregson again. "The page is eighteen, is he not?"

Gregson glanced at what I could see was a blank page in his notebook. "He is, Mr. Holmes.

Holmes nodded again. "Old enough to hang then, along with his two accomplices."

Flinders' face became a mask of despair. "Oh, no," he said shakily. "Surely not . . . ."

"Well, well, he may turn Queen's Evidence, of course," Holmes said rising from his chair. "Try and rest now, and later today we will have to ask you to formally identify your wife's body. Come, gentlemen," And he led us out of the room, Flinders' jacket still draped over one arm.

As soon as we were safely out of earshot, Holmes turned to Gregson. He held up the jacket and pointed. "Observe the missing button gentlemen. You also note that the other buttons are of an unusual design with the initials '*BF*', presumably standing for '*Bernard Flinders*', worked into them. Now, as Watson here will testify, I'm not usually a betting man, but I'd wager fifty guineas that the button in Mrs. Flinders hand which we shall retrieve on the morrow will be the one missing from this jacket." He then examined the inside and found a tailor's label. "Made by Cohen's – good quality material, excellent workmanship. Can I suggest a discreet visit to confirm that this jacket was made for Flinders and the buttons are unique to him?"

"I agree, Mr. Holmes, but will it be enough to convict him?"

"Not on its own perhaps," said Holmes smiling. "A clever lawyer would claim his wife had wrenched it off as she clung desperately to her beloved husband before being dragged off and done away with by some conveniently anonymous burglars. We have the bites on Ivy's body that obviously weren't inflicted by Billy, but there's nothing there which prove they were inflicted by Flinders either. We need more." He smiled briefly at Gregson and me. "*Nil desperandum*, gentlemen. We aren't finished just yet. I have a feeling that this isn't the first time he's killed."

"A guess, Holmes," I said incredulously.

"An intuition, Watson. I never guess." He turned back to Gregson. "The more evidence we amass, the better. I'm sure Flinders isn't the only man in London with these upper and lower jaw dimensions. A clever lawyer would create some shadow of a doubt which might see this particular beauty walk free."

"We also have the footprint under Ivy's bed – " I began.

"Partial footprint," Holmes corrected me, wagging his long thin forefinger. "It is suggestive, but not proof. And now a word with Billy, I think."

As we made our way through to the back of the house, I said, "There's one other thing."

"And what would that be?"

"He didn't protest that the body might not be his wife's. He didn't ask to see her, nor ask anything about where she'd been found."

Holmes smiled warmly. "Because?"

"Because he already knew she was dead."

"Exactly. Ah Billy – no, don't get up," Holmes said as Billy began rising from his chair. "We know who killed Ivy and the mistress. Are you game to help us catch the real murderer?"

Billy nodded his head, and five minutes later was led handcuffed and loudly protesting his innocence out through the front door. I glanced back and saw, just for an instant, Flinders peering out of a window.

Once we were out of sight, Gregson un-cuffed the lad and then said, "What now, Mr. Holmes?"

"Keep Flinders in the house. Post men front and rear 'for his protection'. Tell them to watch him closely and note anything he says, no matter how trivial or odd. Don't let him go anywhere unaccompanied. Tell him it's for his own safety. Find some excuse to hang onto the jacket. If he noticed the missing button, he'll be worried, and in his anxiety may make some fateful slip.

"Find some excuse to postpone identification of the body until tomorrow, and in the meantime, I suggest a further search of the house and grounds." He held up his hand to stifle Gregson's protests. "In your previous search, you looked for clues linked to the alleged break-in. You saw what had been left in plain view. Now I want you to look for what has been hidden."

Holmes then turned to Billy. "Was the safe in the study always kept locked?"

"Yes, sir. I never saw it open . . . but Ivy did, sir. Just the once, mind."

"Did she see inside?"

"Yes, sir, though only for a few moments."

"What did she see?"

"It was empty, sir."

"You're sure?"

"Certain, sir. She got a clear view before the Master looked up from the book he was reading, jumped up, threw it in the safe, and then slammed it shut."

"Did she see what he was reading?"

94

"She couldn't make out the contents, but said it was handwritten, like a commonplace book, and that there was a lock of hair lying across the top corner of the page." He paused. "She said it had a plain cover – it looked like it was made of brown leather. He was furious, and said if she ever came in again without knocking, it'd be more than her life was worth."

"When was this exactly?"

"The day before yesterday."

Holmes smiled. "Thank you, Billy." He turned to Gregson. "Find that book and we'll have our Bluebeard."

Holmes paused and then turned to Billy. "One last thing: Did he pour the port from a decanter, or a bottle?"

Billy thought for a moment, "Bottle, sir. In fact, it was the last of it."

He turned back to Gregson, "Find that empty bottle. It wasn't in his study, but there was a tantalus, and all three decanters were full, so why drink from a bottle? If you find it, have the dregs tested . . . though I suspect you'll find it has been washed."

Once we were back in Baker Street, Mrs. Hudson took charge of Billy. "He needs a mother's love right now," Holmes explained, "and Mrs. Hudson has that quality in abundance." And after that, he refused point blank to discuss the case further and spent the rest of that day smoking his clay pipe and reading Edgar Poe. I sat at my desk and began collating the notes that I would later write up as *A Study in Scarlet*.

That evening we dined at home and afterwards went to the opera. I avoided mentioning the case, as I knew that once Holmes declared a subject closed (albeit temporarily), closed it remained. I noted that he was clearly lost in his own thoughts throughout the entire performance. We returned to Baker Street late to find a note from Gregson.

As I unlocked our own tantalus and poured us both a welcome brandy (for the night was chilly), Holmes read it aloud to me:

> *Have arranged for Flinders to view body at 10:00 tomorrow at the Central Morgue. Will call for you at nine. Gregson.*

"It's a twenty-minute drive at most," Holmes chuckled. "So we'll have plenty of time to prepare the ground. And I think a telegram to Lestrade would not come amiss," before sitting down a scribbling a short note and then ringing for Mrs. Hudson.

Next morning, we arrived at the morgue at exactly nine-thirty, having been slightly delayed by an overturned coal cart just off Grosvenor Square. The body had (as per Holmes's advice) been laid out still fully clothed.

95

Her fingers (now that *rigor* had receded) opened easily, and as Holmes predicted, the button she was holding matched perfectly those found on Flinders' jacket.

"Where is Ivy?" he said, turning back to Gregson after he'd replaced the button in Mrs. Flinders palm, reclosed her fingers, and re-covered her with a sheet.

"Next door, Mr. Holmes."

"Covered?"

"Naturally."

"We'll lead our man to Ivy first, as if by mistake, and then – with no apologies – lead him here to his wife." Holmes looked around and then added, "You have the photograph of the footprint by Ivy's bed?"

Gregson was carrying a plain folder, "Right here, Mr. Holmes."

"Has he asked for the return of his jacket?"

"No . . . He told my man McCann that it had seen better days, and suggested he either throw it away or give it to a tramp."

"Hmm," was Holmes's only initial response, but then he added, "Any word from his tailor?"

"Yes," replied Gregson smiling. "The man confirms that the monogrammed buttons were made exclusively for Flinders."

He clearly had more to add, but at that moment Flinders himself came down the stairs, escorted by PC's McCann and Fawcett. .

"Ah," said Holmes in a voice oozing sympathy. "Mr. Flinders. This won't take long."

He then led the man into the alcove containing Ivy's covered corpse and pulled back the sheet. The body hadn't been washed, so small amounts of dried blood were still smeared around the edges of the bites. Flinders reacted with an incredible coolness. "That's not my wife," he said quietly. "It's Ivy."

Holmes appeared flustered and said quickly, "Oh, my dear sir, my sincere apologies. Still, as you have now seen her, perhaps you could formally confirm that this is Ivy?"

Flinders nodded curtly and then consulted his pocket-watch before adding, "May I see my wife now?"

"Certainly, sir," said Gregson and then turned to Holmes and said, "Really, Mr. Holmes, that was unforgiveable," before leading Flinders through into the adjacent alcove. Holmes and I followed silently.

Gregson pulled back the sheet. Flinders glanced and then said, "That's her."

Holmes stepped forward. "Hello," he said. "What's this?" He opened Mrs. Flinders palm and retrieved the button. "Now where have I seen a button like this before?" He turned to where Flinders' jacket was draped over the back of a chair, picked it up, and held it against one of the remaining buttons. "A perfect match. Watson, what do you think?"

Flinders had turned very pale. Holmes glared at him. "Any comment? No! Very well then. Let's see – a wax impression of your teeth will no doubt be an exact match both in size and distribution to the bite marks on the body. Any comment? No? Then we shall now turn our full attention to the footprint. Mr. Flinders, would you be good enough to remove your right boot and sock?" Flinders glared at Holmes, but did as he was told.

Gregson then placed a photograph of the partial footprint on the floor in front of Flinders' chair, next to the man's bare foot. Holmes leaned down as if for a closer look, and I heard him state, "It fits just like the glass slipper in the fairy tale."

"That's only part of a footprint.," Flinders hissed as he pulled his sock back on. "It could just have as easily been made by Billy."

"Inspector, do you have the plaster cast of the boot print found by the garden wall?"

Gregson smiled. "I do indeed." Gregson produced a plaster cast of a boot print and laid Flinders boot on top of it. "A perfect fit."

"You say this was taken by my own back garden wall?" Flinders voice oozed condescension. "I often take the air there, so I don't think my footprints in my own garden proves anything other than that."

"You admit then it's your boot print?" Holmes asked.

"Yes, of . . . course." And here Flinders hesitated, as if he already knew he'd walked into a trap.

"Capital!" Holmes chuckled. "Now the boot prints found by the body if you please."

Gregson produced the two additional plaster casts, and of course they were also a perfect match.

Flinders closed his eyes for a moment and then said, "I can't be the only man in London who wears those size boots."

"True enough," Holmes replied, "but when coupled with other evidence that we've already accumulated, the case against you builds apace." Holmes turned to Gregson. "Don't you agree, Inspector?"

"I do, Mr. Holmes. I think I've got more than enough to arrest and charge him with murder."

Flinders (still in his stocking feet) stood up, stretched out his arms before him, and said sarcastically, "Don't worry gentlemen. I'll come quietly." As he was being cuffed he turned to Holmes. "A button and a boot print – that's all you have. My lawyer will demolish you!"

Gregson instructed PC's McCann and Fawcett to hold the prisoner in the outer office until he came out. After they had gone, Gregson turned to Holmes. "He's right, of course. His feet are neither above nor below average size, and the button could have been snatched by his desperate wife as our 'burglars' dragged her away from the arms of her beloved spouse."

"Any hint as to his motive?"

"None, Mr. Holmes. We've checked his finances and found that he has close to two-thousand in the bank, whereas his wife was virtually penniless when he married her. Not only that, but the family doctor informs us that she had a weak heart and wasn't expected to live more than another year at most." He glanced at me, "Rheumatic fever as a child. One other thing though: When she was being prepared for the *post mortem*, it was discovered that she had several scars on her back that are consistent with burns from a cigar."

"So he tortured the poor woman and then, when finally tired of her, he callously murdered her." I spat out the words. "But why kill Ivy, and in such a brutal way? And why the elaborate tale? In fact, why kill either of them? His wife wasn't expected to live much longer. He didn't need her money, for she had none. I don't understand."

"Neither do I," Holmes answered. Then, after a pause, "Yet. But I think I'm on firm ground if I assert that Ivy's death was the main event. The faked robbery, the abduction and murder – they were nothing more than window dressing." He turned to Gregson, "Can I suggest that you check back through Flinders' previous history? Where he was born, his previous employment and former addresses, and from there go through the records of any unsolved murders of young women that occurred within a mile's radius of any of his former residencies. If I'm wrong, then there's no harm done. But if I'm right . . . ." His voice trailed off.

"You're guessing that he's done this before?" I asked incredulously.

"Intuition, Watson. I never guess." He turned back to Gregson, "Any luck at the house?"

Gregson shook his head, "No empty port bottle, and so far no sign of our mysterious book. We've even checked the furnace in case he tried burning it. And now, if you'll excuse me gentlemen . . . ."

After Gregson had left, Holmes sighed wearily and I suggested a return to Baker Street but he shook his head. "I need to think, Watson, and a solitary walk is just the thing."

I went straight back to Baker Street, and Holmes returned two hours later, smiling. "I think that we may have him."

He was interrupted by the sound of an urgent ringing of the doorbell at our front door, followed by a light tread on the stairs. "Lestrade, I suspect," Holmes muttered more to himself than me as the inspector walked, in carrying a leather book. His usual high colour was overlaid with a sickly pallor.

"Got your telegram, Mr. Holmes, and found it straight away," he began. "The tantalus had a false bottom, and it was under that."

Holmes smiled. "It came to me whilst I was walking. My route took me past Maskelyne's Egyptian Hall – " Here he turned to me. " – and I remembered our visit . . . and I recalled your extreme annoyance as I explained how each illusion was done – in particular the Disappearing Cabinet.

"I then remembered that Flinders gave Billy port from a bottle, which struck me as odd when he had a tantalus containing four full decanters fronted by a row of glasses. As I stood on the pavement, I visualised it, and suddenly realised that more of the stems of the glasses were visible than is usual – at last another half-inch, I'd say. Normally one can only see the bowl, and maybe a half-inch at most of the stem. This suggested that the base, which is usually flat, was somewhat deeper than is usual. The phrase 'false bottom' sprang immediately to mind."

Lestrade nodded appreciatively and said, "Cunningly made though. Even when we'd forced the restraining bar and emptied out the decanters and glasses, the base still seemed solid enough. So," and here he reddened slightly, "I examined the inside with a lens and noted some tiny amounts of flaking on the varnish at one end. The wood grain was painted in such a way as the whole thing looked solid, but I could make out a tiny gap between the base and sides, and with the help of a penknife blade, it sprang it open and I found this inside." He then held out a leather bound notebook, about the same length and breadth as a yellow-back novel.

Holmes took the proffered commonplace book and opened it. A news clipping had been pasted onto the first page. It concerned the discovery of the body of sixteen year old Alice Riley hidden in the undergrowth of some local heathland and was dated some fourteen years previously. She was described as a "natural" who had been taken into service from the Parish Orphanage, where she'd been placed by parents who'd then simply abandoned her. It transpired she'd been dismissed from her employ two days earlier for "insolence". She'd been strangled, and there was a hint that she'd been raped as well. A number of bite marks on her body initially led the police to wonder if she'd been attacked by a dog. It also stated that at this time they had no clues as to the identity of the killer.

Pasted below that was another short clipping noting the funeral of Alice Riley (buried at the expense of the Parish in an un-marked grave), and that there had been no mourners. There were no more clippings. The implication was clear.

Holmes looked up in disgust. "Was that it, Lestrade? Dead girl, but she was only a servant and a not very good one at that, so after she's buried the police simply drop their investigation!"

Lestrade coloured visibly. "Not if either myself or Inspector Gregson had been in charge!"

After a moment Holmes nodded. "Quite right, Inspector. My apologies. Shall we?"

Gummed onto the page opposite was a lock of dark red hair, tied with a short length of red ribbon. Holmes looked at it for a moment and said, "The same shade of red as Ivy's hair," before turning the page, where he found the following handwritten verse, which he read aloud:

> *Little Alice Riley walking down the street,*
> *Little Alice Riley walks on blistered feet,*
> *Little Alice Riley longs for God's true love,*
> *Little Alice Riley longs for heaven above,*
> *But little Alice Riley is just a little whore*
> *So little Alice Riley won't pass through heaven's door,*
> *Little Alice Riley, these words are your last knell*
> *Because little Alice Riley, I'm sending you to Hell.*

When he'd finished he turned to me and said, "Well, Watson, what do you make of it?"

I pondered for a moment. "The content is hateful, but there is some skill in the writing."

"Good. Anything else?"

"It's the product of a diseased and arrogant mind. The speaker, by implication, compares himself to God and, like God, decides who's fit to live and who is not."

"Excellent. Anything else?"

"Not until I've seen the other poems"

"You're guessing there'll be more?"

"Intuition, Holmes. I never guess."

He gave me the briefest of all possible smiles – what I called his lipless grin – and said, "Shall we get on?"

There were four more sections, and in each we found a similar story: A newspaper clipping, a murdered girl described as a "natural", a lock of red hair tied with red ribbon, a baffled local police, a funeral, and a vile verse. The first three were identical to the Alice Riley verse in all, but the victim's name – *Little Alice Riley* – became *Little Mary Coulson*, *Little Jenny Bailey*, and *Little Alice Peters*.

The second murder was dated exactly six months after the first. There was then a gap of three years and two more murders, a six month interval between each. At the bottom of the page there was a small clipping announcing the wedding of Mr. Bernard Flinders (businessman) to Miss Rebecca Paine (spinster of this parish). The wedding had taken place exactly seven days after his last murder. The fifth murder had taken place two years after his marriage and significantly, on his wedding anniversary.

The fifth and final girl was different. Her name was Eleanor Crane. Like the other girls she had no family, but unlike the others she was neither a "natural", nor was she destitute. She had been a pupil teacher, and was described as bright, hard-working, and much loved by her pupils. A lock of red hair, tied like all the others with red ribbon, was gummed to the page opposite.

It was also noted that her funeral expenses had been met by a Mr. Bernard Flinders, businessman and school patron. The poem was different too:

> She walks indifferent to my love
> Through life with careless ease
> And takes no more note of me
> Than the moon does of the trees.
>
> I lie asleep and dream each night
> Her hand entwined in mine,
> And dream her head upon my chest
> As our heartbeats intertwine.
>
> But then I wake each empty dawn
> Bereft of hope and life
> For I cannot have you my sweet girl
> Because I have a wife.
>
> Yet I'll hold you, first and last,
> Unfold my secret heart
> And then I'll snap your slender neck,
> Make YOU suffer for my Art.

Holmes looked up at me. "Well?"

"It's clumsy. The first verse reads like a gift, but then it becomes clichéd, as if it's been laboriously composed. The use of capitals in the final line is interesting. It's a very emphatic *you*."

"Meaning?" asked Holmes.

"Meaning that he considered he was suffering and wanted the girl to suffer in his stead."

"And first verse?"

"The moon-and-tree image in the last line is skilful. It's as if the poem was begun by one man and completed by another. And then there's the name. The others victims all had common names, but Eleanor sounds like the heroine of a novel."

"And no more real to Flinders than that –disposed of when her use was at an end."

"Thank God you stopped him, Mr. Holmes," Lestrade said quietly.

"Why wasn't he stopped sooner?" Holmes responded. "If Flinders' victims had been the daughters of Dukes, the police investigation would have been tireless. But they were only servants!" Then he walked from the room, followed by the loud slam of his bedroom door.

Lestrade broke the silence. "We have our man, and enough evidence to be sure of a conviction." He picked up Flinders vile book. "Tell Mr. Holmes he may have this once we've secured a conviction." And then he left without another word.

I spent the rest of the day playing billiards at my club with Stamford and didn't get back to Baker Street until early evening. I found Holmes slumped in his chair, scraping away on his violin. I poured myself a brandy. Holmes glanced up at me as I was adding some soda to my Napoleon. "You must surely be hungry, Watson." He took a long draw on his pipe, exhaled slowly through his arched nostrils, and added. "I don't choose to be like this you know. I do value you. It's just that now I need to be alone."

I took a sip of my brandy. "If that's what you prefer." I glanced at the brandy. "In that case, if you've no objection . . . ."

Holmes smiled and shook his head. "There's bread and cheese on the table – " And here he pointed with his pipe stem. " – courtesy of Mrs. Hudson. I myself cannot spare the energy for digestion right now, but do feel free."

I went over to the table and cut myself a slice of good strong farm cheese, buttered a hunk of bread, and said, "You usually forgo meals whilst pondering a solution, but this case is solved, so why won't you eat?"

Holmes smiled. "Is it? We know *who,* but we don't know *why.* When a man murders his sickly or unloved wife, it's usually for the insurance money." Here he picked up a telegram. "From Lestrade. It seems Mrs. Flinders life wasn't insured, so he had nothing to gain there."

He waved his pipe stem at me. "Do sit down." One may wonder why it was that, having stated he wanted to be alone, Holmes was now inviting me to sit. The fact is that Holmes wasn't quite the island that he pretended to be. He often told me that I was like a whetstone on which he could sharpen his thoughts.

He went on. "It's too easy to simply say Flinders is evil. His actions were evil, but so are the actions of a rabid hound. Does that make the dog evil?"

"But surely there's a world of a difference between a man and an animal?"

Holmes smiled again – (This really was unprecedented!) – and replied, "Not if Mr. Darwin is to be believed."

"But we are able to reason, to make moral choices – animals act purely on instinct."

"Quite right. Evil is a choice, but it is one which must be made freely, with full knowledge and consent."

"But Flinders knew exactly what he was doing. Nobody made him murder those poor girls."

"So why did he do it?"

"Are you claiming he is insane?"

"I'm not entirely sure." He paused and re-lit his pipe. "And now I really do need some time alone."

"How did you know he'd killed before?"

He picked up his violin, which he'd placed next to his chair, tucked it under his chin, and said, "That's a good and pertinent question which I must now ponder." Then began to play. It was a little shy of nine, and though I knew I wouldn't sleep yet, I picked up the brandy and glass and retired to my bedroom.

There were airs that Holmes played on his violin that ran so deep, he could hold me still, silent and mesmerised for an hour or more. Sometimes it seemed to me that as he played, all traffic noise and the sound of voices from Baker Street ceased. It was as if everyone and everything had stopped to listen.

It helped me to understand that this wasn't a man without emotions. No, this was someone whose emotions ran unusually deep – a man whose mask of apparent coldness was a shield, and all that protected him from being overwhelmed and unable to function. But no one can suppress all human sympathy permanently – No one who is normal anyway. Holmes played the violin for the same reason soldiers drink, gamble, and womanise – it is a way to forget and recover after battle.

Holmes solved crimes in his imagination. He solved them not just by *seeing* them, but by *thinking* them – By putting himself into the mind of the criminal, and thereby seeing the chain of circumstances leading to the crime's conception and execution.

But it went deeper again. Just as he could think his way into the mind of men like Flinders, so he could also imagine the pain and terror of Ivy, the tortured life of Flinders' wife, and the grief of Billy. It was his gift and it was the curse that on more than one occasion almost robbed him of his sanity.

As I lay down that night, I could still hear the faint strains of Holmes's violin. It was soothing, and I fell asleep and dreamt about my brother – dreamt about him in happier times before we were estranged.

When I came down to breakfast next morning, I found Holmes slumped in his chair, smoking his black clay pipe, a telegram clutched in his hand.

"He's confessed," Holmes said quietly and handed me the telegram.

> *Flinders made full confession, but now refuses to speak. Will call at ten.*
>
> *Gregson*

"Well at least that'll spare Billy the ordeal – "

Which was as far as I got when Holmes cut across me with, "Ah, that'll be Gregson now. Come in, Inspector."

Gregson looked tired and accepted my proffered cup of coffee, swallowing it in two swigs before sitting down heavily. He was carrying a large envelope. "A copy of his confession – very detailed and all in the third person." He glanced at me. "Any more coffee?" I poured him another cup and noted the slight tremble in his left hand that denoted extreme stress. "We showed him the book and, after admitting it was his, he refused to say another word. Then suddenly, he sends for me and gives me everything. Correct in every detail we can substantiate, but written like a work of fiction. So it is Flinders did this and Flinders did that, and once he was done – stony silence."

"Do you mean that he's catatonic?" I asked.

"No, Doctor. Just won't talk. Nods or shakes his head when offered tea and bread, but apart from that . . . ." He turned back to Holmes. "He intends to plead guilty and will offer no defence, so it should be a swift trial – three Sundays and the drop for him."

"Pity," said Holmes. "I should have liked more time to study him. You asked how I knew he'd killed before. It was an instinct – an intuition. Like the intuition of a good detective who knows when he's being lied to. He picks up instantly on inflection, tone and timbre of voice, inability to meet the eye – these are recognisable patterns of behaviour.

104

"Like a bad actor, you mean," I interrupted.

Holmes gave me a glance that said *Don't interrupt when I am being insightful* and continued. "Or a good one with a bad script." He turned back to Gregson. "Do we know anything about Flinders' background and history?"

Gregson shook his head. "Not much. Lestrade has been to the Bank where he worked. Apparently he was quiet, good at his job, punctual, and sober."

"Any sign of a will?"

"Why do we need that?"

"There's the question of property. *Cui bono.* Who benefits? Once we know that, we'll be able to discover more of his personal history. We know he committed at least seven murders, but we don't know why."

"But why do we need to know that?" I asked.

"Because there is nothing new under the sun, including this. The man's crimes seem senseless because we have no idea of the chain of events that led to him committing them."

"And I repeat," I replied rather warmly, "why do we need to know that? Flinders is evil. Simple as that."

Holmes stood. "Really, Watson! That's your reasoned conclusion? Are you familiar with the concept of cause and effect?" If you beat a dog, you either reduce it to a cowering cur, or transform it into a savage brute." And with that he turned on his heel and went into to his bedroom.

Gregson turned to me. "He does that a lot I've noticed."

I nodded. "I think I'll spend the day at my club."

I arrived back in Baker Street around seven, hoping that would be more than enough time for Holmes's temper to cool. I couldn't have been more wrong. As soon as I set foot in our sitting room, I noted that he was smoking his cherry-wood pipe – always his choice when he was spoiling for a fight – so withdrew and closed the door quietly behind me. I went back downstairs and was pondering my next course of action when I was interrupted by, "'Scuse me, Doctor."

I looked round. It was Billy. "Is Mr. Holmes all right, sir?"

"No, Billy. He's tired and needs to be left alone for a while."

"Is there anything I can do to help?"

"Yes," I said. "Get your hat and coat. You and I are going to the Music Hall."

Billy of course was quite taken aback. "But, sir," he began, "I'm below stairs."

"Oh, to blazes with that," I retorted. "One thing I discovered as an army doctor is that we all hurt the same and we all bleed the same, whether we're officers and gentlemen or other ranks. Right now I need beer, women, music, and company, so get your coat."

But Billy was adamant. "My Ivy's not even cold, so I don't feel much like living it up quite yet, so if it's all the same to you . . . sir."

His pause before the *sir* was the slap in the face I needed to bring me back to sense and reason. I took a step towards him and extended my hand. "Apologies. You're quite right of course." And after some hesitation, he took it.

This latter was followed by an awkward silence which Billy finally broke. "You hungry at all, Doctor?" Now I had eaten at my club, but I must confess that still felt empty, so I said, "Now as you mention it, I am rather sharp set."

"Right," he said. "Wait there if you please." And with the words, "It's Billy!" he knocked gently on Mrs. Hudson's door and went in.

I stood in the hall and waited. After two or three minutes, the door re-opened and he beckoned me in. Mrs. Hudson was fussing around a small deal table set out for two, and on it was a selection of cold meats, bread, cheeses, what I took to be an apple pie and a half-dozen bottles of beer. A cheery fire was glowing in the grate, and as we sat down, Mrs. Hudson resumed her rocking chair. "Are you not joining us?" I asked.

She shook her head. "No thank you, Doctor. I'll just get back to my sewing, if you don't mind,"

The silence that followed was frequently broken with comments such as, "Could you pass the salt please?" or "Are there any pickles?" or "More beer, Doctor?" I finished with a slice of apple pie and a cob of strong cheese. I noticed Billy did the same. I took a mouthful of each in turn and said, "My Mother always said that apple without cheese is like a kiss without a squeeze."

Billy nodded in vigorous agreement. "My Ivy always says tha – " and then the words died in his mouth. He was suddenly very still and seemed to be gazing at something a long way off. I'd seen that look on the faces of battle-weary soldiers. I glanced across for Mrs. Hudson, but at some point she'd slipped quietly out of the room and gone to bed.

The lamps had burned low, but I left them that way. From upstairs I could hear Holmes was playing a melancholy air. The music was faint and far away, as if it was drifting down to us from another world. Fairy music, my Grandfather would have called it.

Billy took a gulp of his beer and said, "I dreamt about her. She was standing at the end of my bed. It was night, and the curtains were open, but there must have been a full moon because everything's all bright and silver . . . She's holding this candle, only it's burning this black flame that gives off dark instead of light, so in the end, it swallows all the light in the

106

room. Then I woke up. But the thing is this. I didn't want to. I wanted to stay in the dark with her." He drained the last of his beer. "See, that's the cruel thing about ghosts. They keep coming back to remind you of what you've lost – lost forever, and can never get back."

The Sunderland Tragedies
by David Marcum

I do not recall the weather that day, the 17th of June, 1883. If asked, I'd say that it was dark, but perhaps that impression is influenced by the terrible events of the day before. While we were unaware at the time of what was happening, we would soon be involved in a peripheral matter that took precedence over all else, if only for a short while.

Holmes and I arrived in Sunderland on the 16th, located on the coast slightly southeast of Newcastle upon Tyne, looking into a question of an inheritance. What had appeared to be a simple but distasteful matter between two distrustful brothers had quickly devolved from an arrest into a serious matter of state when one of them was found to be under disreputable obligations to the German government. Holmes and I had been out all night and returned to our hotel at dawn, scraped and weary. Events had escalated quickly, and after treating our wounds, with both of us thankful that Holmes had managed to avoid a knife to the eye during an unexpected struggle, we separated in our shared sitting room and sought a few hours of sleep before the affair would recommence.

We had risen in the mid-morning, somewhat refreshed, but sore from the unexpected journey across the city on the previous night, followed by the ambush that had so nearly cost us both our lives. The miscreants were behind bars, but the job was only half-finished, and as we shared a meal that fell somewhere between breakfast and lunch, and then drank cup after cup of coffee, we discussed what must be done next to bring this seriously spiraling matter to a successful conclusion. It was then that a frantic knocking upon our sitting room door interrupted us, and Holmes rose to see who it was.

From my chair by the small dining table, somewhat behind the opened door, I couldn't observe who was facing Holmes from the hallway, but I heard a woman's tones, slightly high-pitched in an unnatural way, and breathless and hurried, as if she were restraining herself only with the greatest effort before collapsing into sobs. I stood and walked quickly to the door, uncertain as to whether my medical services would be required.

Joining my friend, I could see a woman who appeared to have dressed hurriedly. She was around thirty years of age, in expensive clothing that was unfortunately rather rumpled, reflecting her emotional state. She wore a fashionable hat, but it was cocked at an odd angle, as if it weren't properly seated on her head. She had a wedding ring, and while she seemed to be in overall good health, her color showed that she was functioning under a great stress. Her eyes, which would have been striking at normal times, were underscored by dark circles and red-rimmed from crying.

"Mr. Holmes, you must help me!" she cried as I came into view. "My daughter – he has taken her! I know it – when they didn't find her body last night amongst the dead, I knew it was him. He once threatened to take her. There were so many dead, and yet there's no sign of her. And if she wasn't killed last night, then where else could she be?"

Perhaps she would have rushed on with more of this confusing and urgent entreaty, but Holmes lifted a hand and said in a voice that surprisingly pierced her desperation and brought her up short.

"Dr. Watson and I would be happy to hear your story. Mrs. – ?"

"Barrhill. Mrs. Frank Barrhill."

Holmes nodded. "Mrs. Barrhill. Please come in. We can provide a cup of coffee, or perhaps something else to steady your nerves, and then we'll hear your story from the beginning. It's the only way to build an effective picture of what has happened, and what is required to effect a solution. No – not a word until you've settled yourself and had something to drink."

He spoke as a doctor would to a hysterical patient, and it seemed to be effective. I led her to a chair by the fireplace and asked what she would prefer. She wisely chose brandy – as I believe coffee would have been too stimulating in her condition, and she wisely indicated that waiting for tea to be requested from downstairs would take too long. Within a moment, she had the brandy in hand, and Holmes and I were seated on either side of her, in the same arrangement as if we'd been back in Baker Street before our own mantel, with the client in the basket chair between us and ready to relate an intriguing tale.

"Now," said Holmes, his voice still low and steady, infusing a calmness into the proceedings which otherwise might escalate at any moment when the woman began to tell her story. "You mentioned that they didn't find your daughter's body 'amongst the dead', and 'so many dead'. I'm afraid that Dr. Watson and I have been involved in another matter, and don't have any knowledge of what you describe. Has there been some sort of tragedy?"

The lady looked from one to another of us as if it was impossible that we could be so ignorant. It seemed that she couldn't speak. She took a sip of brandy and then whispered, "How could you not know? The . . . awfulness of it . . . ."

"I assure you, madam," said Holmes, "that we have no knowledge of any tragedy. We were out all night and – " He stopped as I rose, noticing the morning newspapers on a side table, left for us by the staff when our breakfast was served, but still untouched and unread. I recalled that the man who carried in the tray had seemed grim, but he had given no hint as to any terrible event. I stepped over and pulled the top paper from the stack. I needed to go no further than the front page – the story was emblazoned in all its terrible and graphic detail.

"My . . . *my God!*" I whispered.

"Watson?" asked Holmes, his voice rising. Beside him, Mrs. Barrhill sobbed and began to weep into a handkerchief.

The story is simply told. While Holmes and I had been dashing about, investigating the squabblings between two unadmirable brothers, we had been oblivious of the events that would tear the heart out of poor Sunderland. The previous day – the 16th of June – a pair of traveling entertainers, Mr. and Mrs. Fay, had presented their children's variety show as they had done countless times up and down the island. The Victoria Hall held over three-thousand seats, and the place was filled, mostly with children. Nearly half of them were upstairs in the gallery.

At the end of the performance, several things – all with innocent intentions – occurred, each combining to lead to disaster. It was announced that certain children with specially numbered tickets would be awarded prizes as they exited the Hall – one at a time. In order to ensure that the tickets could be inspected in an orderly manner, someone – it wasn't known who – had locked one of the stout doors at the bottom of the gallery steps so that there was a gap only wide enough for one child at a time to pass while showing his or her ticket for inspection.

In the meantime, a second set of general prizes was being distributed by the entertainers at the front of the auditorium, from the stage. The children in the gallery saw this, and – excited, ready to leave, and worried that they might miss their prize – they began to surge down the stairs, with the greater number of them pressing forward into the staircase that ended at the narrow passage beside the locked door.

It was estimated that as many as 1,100 children were in the gallery, along with just a few supervisory adults. What had seemed like a good idea by someone to keep order and allow for regimented inspection of tickets turned into a death trap.

To put it simply, 183 children were crushed or trampled to death by the slow-moving and inexorable human stampede.

Realizing what was happening, one of the building's caretakers, Frederick Graham, had valiantly tried to divert the children back upstairs. Finally he ran up another staircase to the gallery, heroically leading over six-hundred of them down a different way. At the bottom of the stairs where children were already dying, adults could not unlock or force open the door to widen the gap, and they frantically pulled child after child through the narrow remaining space and into the auditorium, even as more and more of them pressed downward on the other side. I could only imagine the screams of those trapped in the stairs as the weight from behind grew ever more steady. And then, when they could no longer scream . . . . It was found that bodies had slipped to the ground during the tragedy, to be trodden underfoot by the weight of hundreds of relentless feet above them.

Finally one heroic man was able to wrench the door at the bottom of the stairs off its hinges. I could almost imagine that I was he, sobbing as I pulled and pulled, to no avail, before giving one last desperate effort, causing the wood and metal to finally give way. But even so, that mass of people continued to overwhelm the wider door space as surely as they had the narrow gap.

I could not speak, and silently handed the newspaper to Holmes. Then I opened the other papers that had been left for us that morning, seeing much the same story. I filled a brandy glass for Holmes, and another for myself, and then refilled that of our visitor. When I'd settled myself back in my chair across from Mrs. Barrhill, I took a long swallow, holding it in my mouth and letting the burn seep slowly across the back of my throat. I closed my eyes, and kept them so until Holmes spoke, his voice tightly controlled.

"Your daughter was not among the dead."

Mrs. Barrhill shook her head. "No. I had dropped her off – it seemed safe enough, with so many children there. Betsy – my Elizabeth – is eight years old, and very wise for her years. It should have been a nice outing. I stepped down the street to do a bit of shopping, and took a cup of tea at a nearby shop. I was walking back when I saw everyone milling around outside the Hall. I started seeing the men carrying out the bodies. I thought that there might have been a fire, but there was no smoke. Some of the children were laid on the grassy verge before the men returned inside. Others were met by women – mothers like me – wailing as they recognized their children. One was crying pitifully and plucking at her little boy's coat. 'Make him breathe!' she sobbed, and the man holding him told her softly, 'He won't ever again.' The woman collapsed at his feet, and he lowered himself beside her, placing the child in her arms." Her voice drifted away as she recalled the horror if it. Her eyes rimmed with more tears

"How do you know that she hasn't been taken in by someone?" I asked, recalling her to the present. "A friend, perhaps, or another mother whom you know who led her to safety in the midst of all the chaos. Have you been home to receive word?"

"I have. I thought the same thing. When I couldn't find her among the dead, I rushed home, but she wasn't there either. When I went back out to search, I left instructions with the servants to find me, should a message arrive – but I didn't let on that Betsy is missing, or what I fear is the true reason. When my husband returns, I don't want him to know this has happened if it can be avoided.

I glanced at her wedding ring. "Your husband? He is away then."

"He is," she replied. "In South Africa. He has business interests there. That's where we met – I was traveling with my parents ten years ago when we encountered Frank in the hotel. My parents liked him very much. It was a short courtship, and we were married within a month. Soon after, we returned to England, and to his family home here in Sunderland." She recited the basic facts as if it was a story often repeated, and in doing so, she'd boiled it down to the bare bones. If there had ever been any romance to meeting and marrying her husband in a foreign land, she had long ago excised it from the telling.

"You said that 'he' has taken her," said Holmes, returning to the woman's initial statement, "a fact that I nearly lost sight of when overshadowed by this vast tragedy. Who is this 'he' to whom you refer?"

She took a deep breath and then a deeper draw on her remaining brandy. I raised an eyebrow and asked if she would care for more. She would. After it was poured, she took another breath and spoke.

"What I have to tell does not reflect well on me, gentlemen. I would never share it, except for the fact that my daughter has been taken. To get her back, I will do anything. I will share any secret, and destroy my reputation in your eyes. I only ask for your help."

We nodded.

"Before I met Frank, I loved another man – in a way that I've never felt for my husband. Altus Luckhof – It is he whom I loved . . . and he is the true father of my daughter. He's the man whom I believe has taken her.

"My late father had business interests in Cape Town during the years when I was growing up, and he often traveled there alone. But ten years ago, he decided to make a grand journey of his next trip, and to take both my mother and me along with him. I wasn't especially keen on going, but I was nineteen and had no choice in the matter, and so we set out.

"The journey was long and tedious, and I found the countryside hot and uninspiring – and nothing of what I'd been led to expect when picturing Africa. After our arrival, my father was often traveling around the countryside on business, and as soon as he would leave, my mother would take to her bed – she was always one for acquiring imaginary illnesses. Left to my own devices, it wasn't long until I became enamored

112

with Altus, one of my father's business acquaintances, and nearly two decades my senior.

"I suspect that he'd seen his opportunity while my father was away. In any case, we were very close for most of a week, and again a few days later when my father set off again in a different direction. During that time, I came to love him. I was young and innocent, and knew no better. He was tall, with black hair and a matching beard, kept short. He had an old scar on his right cheek, quite white against his sunburnt skin, which he refused to explain. He was knowledgeable and dashing, and confident and assertive. I doubt that he felt toward me anything to the level of what I experienced, but I fully expected that he'd declare publicly that we were to go forward as one instead of two as soon as my father returned. But when Father came back, Altus became more distant and formal, and then he departed, telling me vaguely that he had business to the north and would be gone for several weeks, but would try to see me again before we returned to England.

"In the meantime, father had met Frank Barrhill, a man of much the same type as him – British with extensive South African business connections, moderately wealthy, and with good prospects. Frank was about thirty then, and very . . . typical. Nothing like the dashing Altus who had won my heart.

"It was all fixed up before I knew it, and I was so full of silent private despair from the loss of Altus's company that I willingly went along with whatever was proposed, knowing by then that my parents had chosen Frank, and Altus's absence indicated his true feelings – or lack of. Frank and I were married within a couple of weeks, and the four of us – two couples, my parents and Frank and me – returned to England together soon after that. Altus never returned before we left. Frank moved us here, to his family home, and we've remained ever since.

"Our marriage has been tolerable at best, but Frank seems to expect nothing more from me than that. I was content to live the life cut out for me. We tried half-heartedly to have children, but without success. Then, nine years ago, Frank informed that one of his South African clients, in England on business, would be stopping by our house. Normally this wasn't unusual – part of Frank's success is his willingness to open our home to his business associates, in spite of this location being rather out of the way. I was expecting just another South African business-man, and nothing could have prepared me for the surprise when our visitor arrived.

"As you've likely guessed, it was Altus Luckhof. I could tell from the beginning that he wanted to keep our past meeting a secret, with neither of us letting on that we'd previously known one another. Later, when we had a chance to talk, Altus claimed that he'd had no idea that I was Frank

Barrhill's wife, and I almost believed him, but now I think that he sought out a business connection with Frank just to find me, having learned of our marriage a decade ago in Cape Town.

"Frank was oblivious to the rising and sudden rekindling of interest between Altus and myself. Suffice it to say, we . . . carried on with a physical relationship for the short time that he stayed with us – discreetly, and quite without discovery. I didn't fear that Frank would learn anything, for he was already singularly uninterested in me by that point, but I did want to avoid giving the servants anything to speak of, and I thought that Altus and I were successful. Then Altus returned to South Africa, and I soon noticed that we hadn't avoided the consequences after. Nine months after our encounters, Betsy was born. There is no doubt that she is Altus's child, but Frank still seems to have no realization of this fact, as he's never questioned it, and seems to accept Betsy in a good-natured and vague way as his own.

"Two days ago – a day before the tragedy at the Victoria – Altus suddenly reappeared, after years of not making any effort to communicate with me. Somehow he'd known that Frank would be away in South Africa, and he timed his visit to see me alone. This time, he had no interest in resuming our romance – and neither did I, for he was quite a changed man. Before, he had been dashing and mysterious and handsome, and those extra years that he'd possessed had given him a rugged and intriguing character. But he must have had a hard life since those days, and the weight of his years seemed to be resting on him like the soil of a grave. There is something ill about him now – Though tall, he is now stooped. He is gray and sunken, and tired and querulous. His black hair and beard have turned white. But none of that mattered. He'd somehow worked out that Betsy was his daughter.

"From what I could gather – from what he told me – he'd arrived several days ago and watched us, Betsy and me. He checked the official records to verify the date of her birth, and discreetly questioned our neighbors, and calculated when she was conceived. But most of all, he saw her – from a distance he said – and knew without a doubt that she was his, for she is him all over again in coloring and features and height – the way he looked a decade ago – and nothing like Frank – or much like me, for that matter, although I certainly added some aspects of my own.

"He appeared at our house two days ago – I saw him walking up the drive and knew who he was in an instant. Rather than let him be seen by the servants, I ran out and intercepted him, leading him away into a copse of trees a distance from the house. I was filled with great trepidation – I hadn't seen him since our previous tryst, and I had no idea what to expect. I was ready to be defensive, and to let him know that our previous relationship would not be renewed, and when I saw him – the wreckage that he'd become – I knew that my resolve was equal to the task. In any case, he had no interest in continuing that aspect of our association. No, he demanded to have possession of our daughter.

"There was no polite conversation. He immediately jumped to his demand – and there is no other way to describe it. 'You've had her long enough,' he growled. 'Nearly halfway to adulthood. It's my turn now.' He said it as if it were perfectly reasonable – as if my daughter would be willingly entrusted to him, and taken away from the only life she's ever known, sent away with a stranger to a strange land for the rest of her girlhood. I laughed and told him he was mad, but inside I quivered with fear, for he had the look of madness in his eyes.

"He didn't waste time with any further argument. I suppose he could see that my mind was made up. 'So be it,' he said, rising. 'There are other ways.' And with a polite nod, as if we'd never met and as if we hadn't just discussed something so monstrous, he turned and left.

"Afterward, it was almost like a dream, and I sat and tried to imagine what might happen next. I suppose I always thought that he might be back someday, to threaten exposure of Betsy's true parentage to Frank, or that he might open some sort of legal proceedings. I puzzled over various possibilities the rest of that night, going without sleep, but it honestly never occurred to me that he might do something different – that he would simply take her and vanish."

"How do you know that he was the one who took her?" asked Holmes.

"Yesterday, after the . . . after the tragedy, and when I still believed that Betsy was at the Hall, I spent much of my time hysterically going from here to there – where they were laying out the bodies, or into the building itself and back out again, or scanning all of the thousands of children wandering around outside before they drifted away or were claimed by thankful parents. All the while, the screams of anguish where the bodies were being collected, as parents identified their own lost children, both repelled me and called me back, always afraid that Betsy had been added to the rows, but needing to know if she had been.

"Finally the word came that all of them had been removed – and she wasn't there, which lifted my heart, but it also left me with even more worry, as she was nowhere to be found. I ran across an acquaintance who said that she thought Betsy had walked away with a tall white-haired old man in a dark odd-fitting suit. I instantly recognized that it was Altus, and knew what might have happened. I regretted that it hadn't occurred to me that going to the theatre would place her within his reach.

115

"I tried to think – Where could he go? How could I find them? But it was no use. I went to the police, but they had no interest in speaking with me or helping, being overwhelmed with the tragedy of dealing with the grieving families of nearly two-hundred dead children. Then, I saw your name in this morning's paper, Mr. Holmes, in connection with some arrest yesterday, and I recalled when you helped a friend of mine several years ago – Colleen Agutter – when she was staying at a hotel in Russell Square, and you were recommended to help her, since you lived just around the corner from there. She never told me what you did – only of the debt that she owes to you. She said that you believed her when no one else would."

Holmes glanced my way when Mrs. Barrhill mentioned that he'd been mentioned in the newspaper. Apparently he was displeased that our recent investigation had been reported.

When Holmes didn't speak immediately, the lady seemed to take it as reluctance to accept her case. She leaned forward, entreating, "I have nowhere else to turn. My husband is expected any day. I must have Betsy back before he returns."

"And can you offer any additional information as to where Mr. Luckhof might be found – assuming that he and your daughter haven't already departed?"

She shook her head. "I can only suspect that he would have been staying somewhere near the docks. He was always a rough man, and he could hide there. It's . . . it's a place where I wouldn't be able to follow him."

Holmes nodded. "We'll see what we can discover. Will you wait for us at your home?"

She nodded, and I asked for the address, which she provided.

"I hope to have news for you shortly. In the meantime, remain close, Mrs. Barrhill, should your daughter somehow free herself and manage to return to you."

She thanked us and rose, and yet she was still unsettled, as if she wanted to stay and talk more of her fears, while knowing that her departure would free Holmes to begin his investigation. Finally, with a nod, she left us.

As I shut the door behind her, Holmes returned my gaze with a frown. "I'm surprised that Colleen Agutter would have mentioned her little affair to Mrs. Barrhill," he said. "It was before your time, Watson. Her reputation was gravely at risk." He shifted, looking this way and that for his pipe. "Our client seemed most upset at the loss of life in the Hall yesterday."

"As anyone would be," I responded. "It's an unimaginable tragedy." As he began the process of filling and lighting the pipe, I asked, "Where do we intend to begin?"

He didn't answer for a moment, frowning into the rising smoke from the now-fuming pipe. I reached for one of the newspapers and read further of the tragedy.

One young survivor, William Codling, Jr., approximately seven years of age, explained that he was sitting in the front of the gallery when the performers began handing out toys from the stage far below. There was a great roar from the children up there when they perceived the unfairness of it all, but they were told that toys would be provided to them too, at the bottom of the stairs. He had joined the throng, and it had become tighter and tighter as he went down the steps.

He became aware that he was walking on someone who had fallen down, unseen beneath the pressed bodies. He yelled to tell someone, but no one listened. In spite of that, and the rising panic around him, he hadn't known how serious the matter was. In the midst of the screams and pleas, the people behind kept surging forward. It was only when a rumor that more toys were available back upstairs in the gallery that many turned back.

Codling recalled that the tightness of the crowd gradually loosened, and upstairs, he joined a group being led by a man to another stairwell. He soon found himself outside, reunited with his sister, who had been seated in the ground-floor of the auditorium. It was only then, as clutched him, weeping, and they wandered through the crowds and saw the dead bodies being carried out, that the true aspects of the tragedy made themselves clear.

It was then that Holmes rose to his feet. "Our options here are limited," he said. "I have no local contacts, and no Irregulars to send hither and yon for a stray fact, or to fan out like a small army, seeking Luckhof's trail. And yet, time is of the essence. The girl has been missing since yesterday. If he took her, they could already be gone – by land or sea."

"'If he took her'?" I asked. "You don't agree with Mrs. Barrhill's theory? You suspect some other explanation?"

"Let us say that I haven't accepted the explanation before us without certain reservations, until it can be adequately verified. But we'll know nothing until we make a search. I'll explore around the docks, as Mrs. Barrhill was unable to do so, and see what I turn up."

"And me?"

"I doubt that asking questions at the Hall would accomplish anything. We'll send a message to Mrs. Barrhill, asking which of her acquaintances saw the girl being led away – I should have thought to ascertain that before she left. When we have the name, we can speak with the woman and see if she recalls any further details. In the meantime, you can retrace her footsteps to the police station – although as she said, they have much more on their minds right now. Still, you might catch a sympathetic ear who knows something. I suspect that they have already become numb to worried and distraught mothers, but you can approach them with a different tone. Stay open to possibilities."

With that, he returned to his room, only to reappear in a few minutes in the guise of a dock worker. He was in a set of old rough clothes, which I knew he always packed for a journey in case they might prove necessary, but it wasn't simply those that changed him so much. He carried himself differently, and brushed his hair forward and over his eyes. He'd added some padding to his cheeks, and darkened the spaces under his eyes – more than they were already from our previous hectic day. With a nod, he was off.

While he was changing, I wrote a note to Mrs. Barrhill, asking for the name of her acquaintance who had seen Betsy led away by the white-haired man. After arranging with the hotel for its delivery, and instead of wasting valuable time sitting in our suite and waiting for a response, I set out into the streets of Sunderland.

Our hotel wasn't far from Mowbray Park, which lay alongside the Victoria Hall. I felt drawn in that direction, although Holmes had felt that making inquiries there would be a waste of time. Still, something within me had the morbid need to look upon the place.

The building itself was built like a small cathedral, rather than the theatre-like structure that I'd expected. It had tall windows – half-a-dozen of them on either side – lining the long side walls. Between each window was a protruding support column running all the way to the high terraced roof – if I knew more of architecture, I could state what the supports were called, but they seemed to be attenuated buttresses, giving strength to the towering walls. Nearby, lying nearly at the foot of the building itself, was a decorative and well-landscaped lake, with paths designed for comforting and enjoyable strolls. Now, however, there was no joy to be found there.

Many people were standing around the building, and out away from it on the pathways by the water – some talking quietly in groups of threes and fours, while others meditated in silence, heads bowed and hands folded in prayer before a spot where a number of flower arrangements had been left. Here and there would be a husband and wife, huddled together, sobbing while lingering in that place where their child had been lost. All of them kept to the pavement, leaving the various grassy verges surrounding the building empty. One could almost picture how it had looked, less than a day before, with so many dead children laid out there, and more being carried out all the while to join them, while broken parents dashed about and sought to know the truth, hoping for a better outcome before locating their children with wrenching agony. The newspapers reported that some families had lost more than one child, and in a few cases every child in the family had perished. And nearly a hundred others had been injured to one degree or another. The suffering was almost unimaginable, and I knew why no one was standing upon the grass: To do so would have been as if trodding upon and defiling a new grave.

I finally said a small prayer and turned away, making my way to the police station, but as expected, my endeavors there were unsuccessful. I found a harried and weary-looking sergeant willing to listen to my story – or as much as I wanted to provide – about a missing girl being led away during the confusion of yesterday's disaster. He understood the seriousness of the problem, but explained that they were simply too stretched just then to provide any meaningful assistance. He did offer to ask whether the officers there just then might know of anything, and I agreed. I also asked him to see if the officer who had spoken to Mrs. Barrhill the day before might be available, thinking she might have told him something useful, remembered at the time when the episode was much fresher in her mind, but forgotten a day later when she visited Holmes and me. I didn't have high hopes, and the sergeant returned in a very few minutes, saying he'd put the question to all of the officers that were currently present, and no one had any recollection of the incident, or of talking to our client. I had to accept that he had done his best, and thanked him.

Outside, I was at a loss of where to go next. It was too soon to expect a reply from Mrs. Barrhill, and Sunderland was simply too large for me to simply wander about with no plan, trusting to luck. Holmes was covering the docks. I decided to try the hotels.

Although it was something of a plan, it wasn't much better than simply wandering about, which I'd wished to avoid. I started in the area of the station and worked my way in an ever-widening exploration of the surrounding streets. At the first one I tried, there was no record of a guest called Altus Luckhof, and I was about to leave when it occurred to me that he might not have registered under his own name. I queried the desk clerk with the description given to us by Mrs. Barrhill – around fifty now, tall but stopped, white hair and beard, grayish coloring, and a white scar on his right cheek. The extra information didn't matter. The man wasn't a guest.

I had visited perhaps a dozen hotels with no success and was considering that my time might be better spent when I turned a corner and spotted Sherlock Holmes – now restored to his normal appearance. Apparently he'd been back to our hotel after what must have been a short trip to the docks. He hailed me and increased his pace. In a moment we

119

were conferring to one side of the pavement as the crowds moved past us in either direction.

"I returned to change clothes, and to see if there was a reply to your message from Mrs. Barrhill. There was not. Then, based on what I discovered, I began visiting the hotels. I take it that you're doing the same."

I nodded and related where I'd already been.

"Good. We've each been working in different directions, and haven't crossed each other's paths. Have you been asking for Luckhof by name?"

"I have, and also by description, should he have visited under an alias."

"No, he is here, and under his own name. He arrived late yesterday evening from South Africa on the *Fuwalda*."

"Yesterday evening? But Mrs. Barrhill said he visited her home *two* days ago."

"She did. However, I definitely confirmed his arrival in Sunderland after that. He has been a passenger on the *Fuwalda* all the way from Cape Town. She docked in London four days ago, but he preferred to stay on board, rather than leaving the ship and completing the journey by train. He told the captain that he is meeting a business associate here who is also returning from London, and traveling by rail would place him in Sunderland too soon – he would prefer to simply travel as he had been for the remainder of his journey. He departed the ship yesterday after they docked, but I couldn't find anyone who remembered where he went next, or who would have transported him.

"I don't understand what is going on," he continued, "but I fear that we've been deceived. We must locate Mr. Luckhof and find what he knows."

We separated and continued visiting the hotels, occasionally passing one another with simple shakes of our heads to one another, indicating a lack of success. But finally, as I was about to enter a smaller hotel on a side street, Holmes hailed me. I turned to see that he was hurrying my way.

"I located his hotel. He checked in yesterday, not long after he departed the *Fuwalda* – several hours *after* the Victoria Hall tragedy, when he was supposedly seen leading away young Betsy Barrhill. And then, an hour ago, he hired a cab to take him southwest of the city – to the address provided by our client. I spoke to the cabbie, who had just returned, and is waiting for us now."

"Is there any sign of the girl?" I asked as we walked back the way Holmes had just come.

Holmes frowned at me, as I'd clearly missed the point. "I don't believe that Luckhof has anything to do with the girl's disappearance – if

120

she's missing at all. No, there is something else happening here. We need to go to Mrs. Barrhill's as quickly as possible. I fear that there's some sort of tragedy brewing."

We were soon winding through ever-less-crowded streets and into the countryside. The cabbie informed us that our destination was no more than five miles from the city.

"You don't think that the child is missing?" I began when we were underway. "Surely Mrs. Barrhill's agitation and fear were palpable – she believes that her daughter has been taken."

"Does she? Or was she instead upset by the terrible tragedy and loss of life yesterday at Victoria Hall – as any mother would be when considering it – and did she then make use of those tears to convince us that she was also upset over her daughter's absence?"

"I don't understand," I said. "Why would she falsify such a claim? And what does Luckhof have to do with any of this?"

"I can't answer that yet. I sent a wire to Colleen Agutter, Mrs. Barrhill's friend, inquiring how much she had shared of her own situation, but there has been no reply. Likewise, I wired someone in London to provide information about Mr. Frank Barrhill, but those questions haven't had time to be answered yet either. All I can tell you is that Mrs. Barrhill has apparently lied to us about Luckhof visiting her two days ago, on the fifteenth – a day before he arrived here by ship, as verified by the crew of the *Fuwalda*, direct from South Africa by way of London – and if that portion of her tale is false, then possibly the rest of the structure is rotten as well."

I tried to see various explanations why the woman, so obviously upset, would contrive such a story, implicating a man who could not have done what she said. Holmes read my thoughts.

"If her story about Luckhof's visit to the house is a lie, as is the assumption that he led away her daughter yesterday afternoon, then one has to wonder if any of the other details so carefully and embarrassingly related – the account of her first meeting with the man a decade ago, and his subsequent visit so Sunderland a year or so later, resulting in the conception of the child – are true as well. And if not, what does she gain by creating this fiction –and by involving us?"

I nodded. I began to have a terrible suspicion what we might find at the Barrhill house, and I could see that Holmes felt the same way. I was tempted to urge the cabbie to greater speed, but we were already moving at a quick clip, and would be there soon enough.

The house was a pleasant-appearing structure, and much bigger than I would have imagined. Two stories high, and solidly built with an attractive mixture of brick and stone, it was set well-back from the road.

There was a loneliness to it, especially on that day, as there seemed to be no activity. Nothing moved, except for the lazy spiral of smoke rising from one of the chimneys standing above the rear of the house. My instincts were that something was wrong here, and I was grateful for the weight of my service revolver, which I had long-ago learned never to be without.

Instructing the cabbie to wait, we approached the door. Holmes pointed to a fresh-looking footprint, apparently made from a shoe that had stepped in a patch of earth nearby. I had accidently trod it in myself, and I put my foot down next to the print, creating a similar, though larger, duplicate.

Meanwhile, Holmes rang the bell, and again when there was no response. Finally, looking back to the indifferent cabbie who was already reading a racing sheet, Holmes put his hand forward to the doorknob. With a silent motion he turned it. The door opened, and we stepped inside as if we'd been welcomed to do so.

To one who has encountered it, the smell of burnt gunpowder, as produced from a fired gun, is unmistakable. There is nothing – burnt toast, or an extinguished candle, or burning wood or coal or oil – that quite resembles it, whether from a massive field piece in the heat of battle to a small gun in an otherwise plain room of a house. And it was that smell that we both recognized as soon as we stepped inside. The door was still open behind us, and while I withdrew my revolver from my pocket, Holmes stepped silently back outside. He was only gone for a moment, and I heard the departure of the cabbie even as he returned, pushing the door shut behind him. I didn't need to be told that Holmes had sent for the police.

We found them in a drawing room off the main hallway. Mrs. Barrhill was curled into a chair, weeping, and twisted to that she wasn't looking at the bodies stretched upon the bloodied carpet. Nearer her was the man who, based on the description we'd been provided, must be Altus Luckhof. He had a surprised expression on his face, almost comical if one had seen it displayed by an actor on the stage. But here, with his eyes glazed in death and focused on something far beyond the ceiling where they were turned, it was a tragedy instead of a comedy. A bullet wound had shattered his chest, and death must have been nearly instantaneous.

Across from him, nearer the unlit fireplace, was another man, younger than Luckhof, but still in middle age. His hair was dark, and if he'd been upright, it would likely have shown signs of needing a visit to the barber. He had a simple wedding ring upon his hand, and even in paleness of death, lividity causing the blood to settle within him, his coloring showed that he had been an active fellow, often outdoors. Now his otherwise handsome features were marred by a terrible wound in his throat, along with another centered at his heart, matching the one in the body of the white-haired man across from him.

I stepped across to the weeping woman, saying her name softly, letting her know that we were there, and asking if she could relate what had happened. She didn't seem to hear me at first, and then Holmes quietly called for me to join him.

He softly asked me to examine the bodies, and while I saw no need – both men were clearly dead – I did as he asked, and quickly understood what he had already found. Meanwhile, he continued to look around the room, observing things that were beyond my seeing, likely otherwise hidden footsteps and such, giving him a clear picture of what had happened here, and also inspecting those things which were obvious even to me: The bullet hole in the mantel, almost certainly from the shot that had first torn through the dark man's throat, and the two guns lying beside each body, dropped there after their deaths – a Swiss ordnance revolver by Luckhof, and an Enfield Mk 1 by the other.

Holmes continued to inspect the room, at one point finding a decorative quilt folded over a chair at the far side of the room. He held it up and let it open, looking at it this way and that in the light from the window. With a noise of satisfaction, he replaced it, unfolded, upon the chair. Only then did he join me at the weeping woman's side.

"Mrs. Barrhill," he said in a firm voice, louder than I would have expected, and in a rather jarring manner. "What happened?"

She had jumped when he spoke, and then for a moment made no response, other than to continue weeping. Finally, with a shuddering sigh, she pulled herself upright and placed her feet upon the floor.

"My husband came home sooner than I expected. I . . . I didn't know what to tell him. About Betsy. I hoped that you would have news soon, and also that I could send you a message to make sure that you didn't visit, giving him a chance to find out what you were doing, and why." She had rigidly kept her gaze away from the portion of the room where the two dead men rested. Now she cut her eyes that way, just for an instant, before looking back in our direction.

"He was telling me about our trip when the doorbell rang. I answered the door, and it was Altus. He pushed past me, yelling for Frank. My husband looked out and they saw one another. Altus came in here, and they argued. I tried to stop them – to stop Altus from telling him the truth – but it was too late. Almost immediately, Altus bragged that he was Betsy's father, and that he was taking her back to South Africa. He demanded money. He said that he should be compensated for missing so much of her life before. Frank roared at him. He . . . he went to his desk where he kept his gun. In the meantime, Altus pulled out a gun as well.

They circled each other for a moment, and then both fired – several times. I screamed and closed my eyes. Then it was over, and when I looked, they were both dead. I . . . I don't remember what happened after that."

Holmes nodded, and then resumed inspecting the room. He looked in the dead husband's desk, and then nodded. "There is a gun oil stain, here on the wood of this drawer. Did your husband have other guns, Mrs. Barrhill?"

She nodded. "He has a small collection. He keeps it upstairs."

"And do you have one of your own? For protection, perhaps?"

She frowned. "I do. My father taught me to shoot as a girl. But I didn't have it with me this morning."

Holmes nodded. "How long ago did this happen?"

"What? Less than an hour, I suppose. I – "

"You said that you answered the door when Mr. Luckhof arrived," Holmes asked.

Mrs. Barrhill blinked. Then, "Yes. I sent the servants away when . . . when this trouble began. I didn't want them gossiping."

"And yet, you also mentioned that the servants were instructed to notify you if any messages arrived. When did you send them away?"

She frowned, and Holmes continued. "I had the impression from our conversation just a few hours ago that they were still here. But they were gone when Mr. Luckhof arrived. How curious."

He took a step back, and her eyes followed him. I had been sitting near her, and now I stood as well. I was aware that there were a number of decorative pillows resting near the lady. I wondered if a gun from her husband's collection might be concealed beneath one of them.

"That quilt," said Holmes, nodding his head toward the one that he'd examined and refolded a few moments earlier. "It seems out of place in this room. Can you tell me why it's here?"

She didn't reply. She didn't do anything except look at Holmes with a new wariness. I noticed that her tears had dried up.

"Perhaps someone used it in here while taking a nap – although that seems most unlikely. Unfortunately, it's now somewhat ruined. It has a bloodstain on it, you see."

Still no response.

"One has to wonder why that is – folded as it was and placed in a part of the room well away from the bodies. Perhaps, however, it *was* unfolded at one point, and used to cover one of the corpses – possibly so that it wouldn't initially be noticed by another man when he arrived."

I had been correct – there was a gun under one of the pillows. And in spite of how fast she moved, her arm shooting out with the speed of a striking cobra, I was faster, having expected something along those lines.

124

A single step and my hand caught her wrist, even as she knocked aside a pillow to reveal a small but deadly American Smith and Wesson Model 10 revolver. I scooped it up with my left hand and quickly shifted back a few feet, ready in case she came after me. But she did not.

"Dead bodies are consistent," said Holmes. "Not in everything, of course. *Rigor mortis* sets in differently for different people. But two bodies that died at the same time, not very long ago, in the same location and under the same conditions, should each lose heat at the same rate. However, your husband – as Doctor Watson can verify – is markedly cooler than Mr. Luckhof. Perhaps if there was a fire lit in here, your husband's corpse would have remained warm – as warm as the other – but you overlooked that. He was killed at least several hours ago, long before Mr. Luckhof's arrival. Should you wish to step over and touch the bodies, you can see for yourself. No? Then to continue . . . .

"We know that Mr. Luckhof traveled here by cab from his hotel less than an hour ago, as the same cabbie just brought us. So he has been cooling for less than that time – that is, we can fix the time of his death to a point not long before our arrival. And your husband's skin should feel the same – but it does not.

"Discussions with the captain of the ship that brought Mr. Luckhof from South Africa, and then from London to here, revealed that the ship was running somewhat late. It was supposed to be here a couple of days ago – the day that you claim Luckhof visited you and demanded your daughter. In fact, they only docked yesterday afternoon, *after* the Victoria Hall tragedy, and *after* he was supposedly seen by your unnamed friend leading your daughter away. If you had known that fact, that he wasn't actually in Sunderland, would you have adjusted your story this morning? Probably. But you contrived it on the incorrect assumption that Luckhof was already here, and that your story of his visit to this house, and subsequent abduction of your daughter, would be accepted.

"I think we can see what happened here. Your husband arrived home from South Africa – probably today. It's certain that you knew when to expect him, contrary to your earlier vague statement that he was arriving soon. He came in, and you shot him – missing the first time, in spite of your training, and only wounding him the throat. The bullet passed through and into the mantel. A fatal shot, but not immediate. You immediately corrected the mistake and put a second bullet into his heart. There are no close neighbors, and you had sent the servants away. We'll find out from them just what pretext was given. Then you found the quilt and covered your husband's body, so that Mr. Luckhof wouldn't see him when he arrived for his pre-arranged appointment with your husband, his business associate, and was brought into this room.

125

"Did he wonder what was under the quilt before you killed him too? I expect so – it's quite visible, and there would be no mistaking what it was – but there was no need to converse with him. You had him here, in the room, and you shot him immediately – with a different gun, another from your husband's collection. I'm sure that you picked one that the servants won't readily know. Then you removed the quilt and folded it, possibly unaware that there was a blood stain, or perhaps planning to clean and remove it later.

"What next? You had the props in your play arranged and your script ready. Did you plan to run to a neighbor's house, screaming for help about the mutual shooting you'd just witnessed? Whatever you intended, it was circumvented by our arrival. You were forced to leave the quilt – so out of place in this room – folded nearby, and then you pretended to be overwhelmed by what had happened, waiting for us to discover you."

"'Pretended'?" she snapped. Her tone was sharp now, and there was no sense that she was going to deny Holmes's interpretation of events. "Why should I *pretend*? Do you think me a monster? I've just seen two men die!"

"By your hand," Holmes reminded her.

"What of it?" she countered. "My husband was an evil man – vicious and abusive. Not the sleepy ineffectual thing that I described to you this morning. Our only peace – for Betsy and me – was when he traveled. It was only getting worse – and he was turning his . . . his attentions more and more to my daughter. I . . . I would not allow that. When he left this time, I decided to find a way to be free of him."

"You could have found another option," I said. "You could have sought help."

Holmes shook his head. "She is still deceiving us. Perhaps Frank Barrhill is as bad as she claims, but there must be more to it than that. Why else craft her plan to kill another man as well? An innocent man. Isn't that correct, Mrs. Barrhill?"

She glared at him defiantly, but didn't answer.

Holmes glanced toward the dead South African. "That man has never been a big strapping fellow, dark and handsome, but now much changed. Consider his frame, Watson. And if he wasn't the man that was described to us ten years ago, then the rest of the story is suspect as well. Perhaps, Mrs. Barrhill, you did meet Altus Luckhof during your journey to South Africa. More likely you first met him when he visited here nine years ago. That can be verified, but I'd be willing to bet that he was simply a visitor who stayed here a few days while he and your husband conducted business. When word arrived that he would be returning this week for another visit, you concocted this idea of shifting the blame to him, and

126

knowing that he would be coming out here to meet with your husband upon his arrival, you sent away the servants, and then killed both of them, one by one.

"What truly impresses me is how you were able to add on extra features to your plan, based on new events. The tragedy at Victoria Hall occurred, and you saw that as way to explain how Mr. Luckhof could spirit away your daughter. You read in the newspaper that Dr. Watson and I were here on another matter and, recalling your acquaintance with Colleen Agutter and how I'd helped her, you sought me out to give credence to your story. When the bodies were found, we could explain that you'd already come to us for help. After all, you said that I believed Mrs. Agutter when no one else would – did you think that I'd show you the same courtesy?"

"But her daughter?" I asked. "Where has she been during all of this mummery?"

"Oh, I doubt if she's too far away," Holmes replied. "She's too young to be sent away on her own, and leaving her with another person would mean that someone was out there who could tell the truth when the supposed story behind these murders was reported."

At that moment, we heard the return of our cab. We would soon be joined by a sergeant and constable from a nearby station. Mrs. Barrhill remained silent while Holmes explained the situation, but began to deny the accusations, still insisting that the two men had shot each other.

"There is one more bit of evidence," Holmes said. "Make note, Sergeant, when the bodies are examined. You'll see that the cuffs of each of the dead men are clean, and that they are both right handed. Mrs. Barrhill – if you would lift your right arm?"

She did so before considering that she shouldn't. Holmes took her arm and turned it for the policemen to see. "There are a number of small burns here – from burning powder expelled by one or both of the two murder weapons when they were fired. Preserve the guns, and this shirt, gentlemen. Test firings of the weapons will confirm that such markings on the clothing are evidence of who shot the guns, and that the dead men with their unburnt shirts did not."

Mrs. Barrhill wrenched her hand down and cursed Holmes with a low and vicious stream of colorful epithets. She was still promising her revenge when she was led away.

Before they vanished into the hallway, I stopped them.

"Your daughter," I said. "You must tell us where she's hidden."

Her mouth tightened, knowing that to do so would be the first crack in personally admitting her guilt – if one didn't count the fact that she'd tried to reach for a hidden gun resting beside her just a few minutes before.

Finally, realizing that the game was lost, she seemed to sag a little and said, "She's in the attic. I told her to hide – that bad men were coming – and to stay hidden until I came for her." She looked at the sergeant. "May I go up and get her? May I see her?"

With a gruff denial from the officer, she was led outside to the cab. It was then that she broke down, her wails being apparent until they had traveled a distance from the house.

Upstairs, there was only one entrance to the attic. We climbed the stairs, calling "Betsy" in calming tones, fully aware that the girl, fearing "bad men", would be terrified of our approach. Thankfully the attic was a large open space, covering the entire top of the house, lit regularly up and down on both sides by dormer windows. The plain wooden floor was drifted with dust, and there were only a few places where odds and ends from the house were piled.

Holmes indicated a path of footprints through the dust toward a side of the attic that was more carelessly piled than the other. He whispered that he would stay by the entrance, in the center of the great space, should the child bolt. He seemed to think that I would have a more calming influence on her.

I went toward the cluttered side with its more places to hide. There were boxes and piles of clothing, slowly being ruined by dust. Furniture was scattered here and there, some broken. It was near the back that the footprints vanished, behind a range of boxes that seemed to be stacked like a wall. It was quite telling that the dust around the boxes was also disturbed, indicating that they had been recently moved. Certain that I was in the right place, I repeated the girl's name in my most winning manner and stepped around the end of the barricade –

– only to be rushed by a shrieking creature, no more than three foot high, wielding a knife! With a scream and a thrust, she was upon me. Later I would find that my coat was slashed, but thankfully no part of the blade cut me. In spite of my initial surprise, I was able to grab her thin wrist and keep a firm hold, finally forcing her to drop the blade. By then Holmes was there, and he kicked it away. Meanwhile, I held the girl close, repeating her name and telling her not to worry, we were not the bad men that she had expected. But in my heart I suspected that in a way we were. We were trying to gain her trust in this moment, but we were taking her out of this illusion of protection into a changed life – one parent dead, the other soon to be tried for a brutal and coldly planned double murder.

We carried her out of the house without going into the room where her father's corpse still lay, and over to a nearby neighbor. There Holmes privately explained the situation, obtaining agreement that the kindly residents would keep watch over the child until the return of the police, who would make other arrangements. Then we walked back to town. I heard later that distant relatives had adopted the girl – possibly out of the goodness of their hearts, or so I liked to think, but my cynicism wondered if it was also related to the fact that Frank Barrhill was much wealthier than we'd thought, and that accumulated treasure went with his young orphaned daughter – for she was such, as her mother, sentenced to a life term, had died less than a year later in prison.

We stopped by the police station to make our statements, and to inform the police where Betsy Barrhill was now located. Apparently Mrs. Barrhill was already confessing in another part of the building, and what we provided was no more than corroboration to her statement. In truth, the entire matter was very distasteful to all involved, coming as it did upon the terrible events of the day before, and while it might have been a sensation in other more normal times, it was then something that seemed to be incidental.

We concluded what remained of our business in Sunderland that afternoon in time to make the late train south. I've recorded the events for the sake of my records – especially as I cannot do so in regard to the matter which first necessitated that journey – but Holmes and I have never returned there.

The Tin Soldiers
by Paul Hiscock

By 1883, I had settled comfortably into my life in London. Between my medical duties and my investigations with Sherlock Holmes, my mind was almost constantly distracted by new mysteries and challenges. I barely thought about my previous life and the far less pleasant conditions I had endured in Afghanistan. Yet, those experiences could come flooding back in an instant as they did, in November, when I was visited by the widow of Lieutenant Colbert.

It was early afternoon when Mrs. Colbert arrived at the practice where I was acting as a *locum*. I wasn't expecting her, as there was no appointment listed. However, I did not think anything of this, as the doctor for whom I was filling in was very poor at record keeping.

"Please do take a seat, and tell me what troubles you. I can see from your clothes that you've recently lost someone – I'm guessing your husband." This was an easy deduction to make. I had sadly seen enough widows in mourning to recognise her attire instantly.

She nodded and I continued. "You seem very composed. Had you been expecting his death for some time?"

"No, Doctor, it was quite sudden, and yet, in some ways, it feels like I lost him a long time ago."

"So why have you come to see me today? Have you been experiencing trouble sleeping? It's quite common amongst the recently bereaved."

"Yes, I've been having trouble sleeping," she said, and I smiled inwardly at my correct evaluation, "and I'd appreciate it if you could help. However, I'm not really here for medical advice. I was looking for you."

I could feel that I was heading down the wrong track and felt guilty. Here was a grieving woman, in need of my help, and I was more concerned with playing guessing games.

"If I can assist you, of course I will, although I'm not sure how much help I can be if it isn't a medical matter. Have you come because you've heard that I work with Sherlock Holmes? If it's an investigation you require, you would be better approaching him directly."

"Sherlock Holmes? I'm afraid that I've never heard of him. No, you're definitely the man I need to help me. I made enquiries at the Medical Council in order to find where you were working."

I must admit that this surprised and confused me a little, but I encouraged her to continue.

"My husband was a Lieutenant in the army, and he served in Afghanistan."

"Did I meet him out there? I'm sorry. There were so many soldiers, and I'm afraid his name isn't known to me."

However, as I said this, I realised that the name did seem familiar, but not from the battlefields.

"I met a soldier in the hospital in Peshawar. Mark? Mark Colbert? Was that your husband?"

"That's right. He was wounded in action, like you."

"I was lucky," I said, as I recalled that time of my life. "The Jezail bullet which hit me ended my military service, but at least I can still lead a full life. However, Colbert lost his lower arm, did he not?"

"Yes. It was a bullet wound as well, but his became infected."

"That happened far too often. Too many wounds were left untreated for too long. I always feel guilty when I think back to that time. They needed more doctors there, not less. How many more limbs, or lives, could I have saved if I'd been able to stay there?"

"But you were injured too. Besides, you're helping people here now."

"Yes, and I'm thankful I can still use my skills to do good. But what about your husband? You said you lost him before he died. It cannot have been easy for him with his disability."

"We were lucky," Mrs. Colbert said. "My father is a factory foreman. He agreed to take my husband on in a supervisory role that he could handle, even with his disability. He had settled in well, and we were starting to rebuild our lives together, but he still slept poorly and there were times when he would just seem to go blank and not even know I was there."

I thought of the days spent in the bed next to her husband. He had been a cheerful fellow, always quick with a joke or a witty observation. Still, there is only so far a façade like that can take you, and I'd also heard him cry out in his sleep as he suffered from the nightmares we all shared.

"I'm sorry if it's indelicate to ask, but did your husband take his own life?"

"That's what the police say. He was shot in the head with his service revolver, which was found in his hand."

"You sound as if you disagree. Why? From everything you've told me, and from what I know he endured, it doesn't seem that surprising."

"I can see why people might think that, but he seemed to be in a good frame of mind recently. Still, I know he thought about death. That's the reason I'm here. He told me to seek you out."

131

"He told you to find me?"

"Yes, not long after he returned from Afghanistan. On one of his darker days, he said to me, 'Clara, if something happens to me, you should seek out Doctor Watson. He should know that I've died.'"

"That's all? Was there nothing else?"

"He told me how he'd met you, but that's all."

"I'm flattered that he thought of me, but I'm surprised that he would make a point of having you seek me out."

"I was too," said Mrs. Colbert. "He had many friends, yet he was most insistent that I should tell you myself. You clearly made a strong impression on him during your time together."

"I still haven't heard anything that rules out suicide," I said, sadly. "In fact, his request suggests that he was planning for his death and wanted to put his affairs in order. Did anything else out of the ordinary occur in the days before he died?"

"There was one other thing. The day before, he received a small package. Inside there was a note and, when he read it, he turned so pale I thought he'd seen a ghost. I don't think he realised that I had been standing there all that time, because when he saw me he immediately shut the package in his desk drawer."

"What did the note say?"

"I don't know. The next thing he did was to burn it. However, when I was going through his possessions, I found that the package was still there."

Mrs. Colbert reached into her handbag and took out a small box that had been wrapped in brown paper. She opened it slowly, and then tipped it up so as to let the contents slide gently on to my desk. As soon as she had finished, she let the package drop and sat back in her chair, as though she wanted to put as much distance as possible between its contents and herself.

I looked down at the item on my desk, expecting some strange or grotesque object, but instead all I saw was a small tin soldier.

"Why would your husband be frightened of this?" I asked. "There must be dozens of these in every toy box and nursery up and down the country. Did it have particular associations for him – maybe related to your own children?"

"We didn't have any children, Doctor. I had always hoped, but after he returned, it never seemed the right time to discuss it. However, you're wrong. It isn't like every tin soldier. Look at the arm."

I picked up the toy and examined it more closely. Sure enough, I saw that it had been damaged. Part of the right arm had been removed. The red paint had flaked away, and judging from the ragged edge of the metal, I guessed that it had been melted until it had been soft enough to tear off.

"You think the sender was referring to your husband's injury?" I asked.

"I think so, although I'm at a loss as to what it means. I've been asking all his friends about it, hoping that it might have some significance to them and that they would be able to explain what scared him so much."

I turned the disfigured toy over in my hands, looking for any mark or detail that might explain its significance, but to no avail.

"I'm sorry, Mrs. Colbert," I said. "It means nothing to me."

All this time, she had remained composed, but now she started to cry. I handed her a pocket handkerchief and she dabbed at her eyes.

"I'm sorry, Doctor Watson," she said. "I so hoped that you would know something. You were my last hope to prove that he didn't choose to commit suicide and leave me."

I took her hand and patted it gently. "There, there, my dear," I said. "I'm certain this wasn't about you. Rather, he couldn't bear living with the memories of the war. You must accept that he will be happier now he is at rest, and try to take some comfort in that."

I was quietly reading the newspaper when Holmes burst into our rooms in Baker Street.

"Watson, we have a new case."

I appreciated the distraction. The past couple of days had been quiet, and with little else to occupy my mind, my thoughts had constantly returned to Lieutenant Colbert. Like most of my comrades-in-arms, I knew the darkness of those black days when one questions the point of everything. Sadly suicide wasn't uncommon, but to leave behind a wife who clearly loved him – Lieutenant Colbert's demons must have been powerful indeed.

However, a new case with Holmes was just the thing to take my mind off such depressing thoughts.

"Lestrade wants me to take a look at a body in Wapping."

"Did he say what was notable about this poor soul?"

Wapping was an insalubrious part of town, and deaths there were all too common. There would have to be something out of the ordinary about this case for Lestrade to have become involved, and even more so for him to ask Holmes to consult.

"His message simply said that the victim didn't belong there. Shall we go and see what he meant?"

The body lay on one of the old docks by the river. The inspector hovered near it, pacing back and forth. He looked anxious, but his expression brightened when he saw us.

"Thank you for coming, Mr. Holmes. Doctor. I could really use your help with this case."

"I'm not sure why," said Holmes. "Even from here I can see that the victim was a wealthy man. He is in one of the least-desirable parts of town, and has been stabbed multiple times. It has all the hallmarks of a violent attack. Tragic, but hardly a case that requires my attention."

"Of course I could solve it," said Lestrade, "if I had time. I already know that this is Adam Danbury, the son of Lord Danbury."

"The newspaper owner?" I said.

"Quite correct, Doctor Watson, and therein lies my problem. Lord Danbury demands answers immediately, and my investigation will take time."

"You hoped that I could solve the case quickly, before your abilities are very publicly scrutinised and criticised?" said Holmes.

"It isn't my reputation, but that of the entire Detective Branch."

"Very well. I'll at least take a closer look and assess whether the case might benefit from my attention."

We walked over to the body and he knelt down next to it. The dead man's face was in a terrible state, broken and bloody.

"However did you identify him so quickly?" I asked Lestrade. "I doubt even his family would recognise him in this state."

"Luckily he was carrying these." Lestrade passed me a silver card case. On the outside was engraved the monogram *A.D.*, and inside was a small stack of calling cards belonging to the dead man.

"We also found his wallet," said Lestrade, "but the attacker emptied it before tossing it aside."

"The attack was brutal," said Holmes. "The killer kept hitting him long after he was dead. This wasn't a simple robbery. The victim and the killer knew one another. An encounter with a stranger wouldn't provoke such rage.

"The dispute may have been about money, or the money was taken to mislead us, but this wasn't a random encounter," he continued. "Besides, a professional ruffian would carry his own weapon, instead of using the victim's stick."

He pointed to a walking stick, which lay on the ground near the body. The cane was topped with a silver handle showing the initials *A.D.* and covered in blood.

"Why would he meet someone here," I asked, "or even know anyone in this part of town?"

"Excellent questions, Watson. Another would be, what is in his hand?"

The victim's left hand was curled into a tight fist, and now that Holmes had drawn our attention to it, I could see that he was holding something.

Holmes prised the fingers apart. "That's most curious," he said.

I stared at the item he held up. My shock must have been evident on my face, because Holmes had cause to ask, "Watson, are you all right?"

"It's just a child's toy," said Lestrade. "That won't help us catch his killer."

But it wasn't just any child's toy. It was a tin soldier. Identical to the one Mrs. Colbert had shown me.

Having gleaned all he could from the site of the murder, Holmes announced that we would go to question Adam Danbury's widow. Lestrade seemed relieved that Holmes had taken charge, and stayed behind to supervise the removal of the body to the morgue.

As soon as we were seated in a hansom, Holmes started to question me.

"You recognised something about the toy I found in the dead man's hand?"

"It startled me for a moment. I saw a similar toy soldier a couple of days ago, and that one too was associated with a death."

I went on to tell him about Mrs. Colbert's visit to the surgery.

"I dislike coincidences," said Holmes, when I had finished my story. "You say that the toys were identical."

He passed me the figure he had taken from Danbury's hand.

"I couldn't be sure without seeing them both again, but they are certainly very similar. Although this one seems to be undamaged."

"Look more closely," said Holmes. He turned over the small figure on my hand and pointed to its leg. A small hole, barely larger than a pin prick had been made in the metal.

"You said an arm on the other tin soldier had been removed to match your friend's injury. I would hazard a guess that this damage represents the wound that caused such a young man to carry a walking stick."

"I don't understand what he was doing there."

The Danbury family home in Chelsea was as different from the slums of Wapping as one could imagine. The widow had probably never travelled that far east.

"Where did you think your husband was yesterday?" asked Holmes.

135

"I thought he was at his club," said Mrs. Danbury. "He spent most days there. I only missed him when he didn't return home yesterday evening. We meant to attend the theatre together."

"He carried a walking stick," I said. "May I ask why he needed it?"

"That silly thing. He said it made him look distinguished. I just thought it made him look old."

"So he didn't need it?"

"He did at first, but you'd hardly notice his limp anymore."

"He had an injury to his right thigh?" said Holmes. "Maybe a bullet wound."

"How clever of you to know. Yes, he was shot in Afghanistan."

"He served in the army?" I asked.

"Yes, he was a captain."

Holmes looked at me. His face was grave. "Another coincidence," he said.

"I don't remember him, but it's possible that our paths crossed briefly."

"You were in the war too?" asked Mrs. Danbury. "A frightful business. I was so glad when they sent my husband home."

Holmes took out the tin soldier. "Do you recognise this?" he asked. "Your husband had it with him."

"Those things get everywhere. No matter how often I tell Bobby to tidy up his toys, I always find myself treading on them. My husband must have picked one of them up."

"That is probably what happened," said Holmes, but I could see that he wasn't convinced.

I slept poorly that night. I tossed and turned in my bed as I dreamt of Afghanistan. Men lay injured all over the battlefield, but they weren't wearing their proper uniforms. Instead, they wore the bright red jackets of tin soldiers. I was relieved when I finally awoke, drenched in sweat.

"Lestrade grows impatient," said Holmes, when Mrs. Hudson interrupted our breakfast to deliver a note from the inspector.

"Did you tell him about the connection to Lieutenant Colbert's supposed suicide?"

"I mentioned it, but he's is still fixated on his theory of a random attack. I sometimes wonder why he asks for my assistance, only to ignore me."

"I thought I would visit the War Office today. I'd like to take a look at the service records for both men to see if I can find a connection between them."

"A capital idea, Watson. While you do that, I'll visit Danbury's club and attempt to retrace his steps."

Holmes was less buoyant when we reconvened in Baker Street that evening.

"Danbury's trail has already grown cold," he said. "He left his club late in the afternoon, without any explanation. From there he caught a cab to Wapping, but after that I could find no trace of his movements before the discovery of his body the next morning. I hope your day was spent more fruitfully."

"It took them all morning to locate the records for both men, and aside from both serving in Afghanistan, they had very little in common. They never trained together. They never served in the same battalion. They were never even billeted in the same barracks. However, they almost met once."

"At the hospital in Peshawar," said Holmes.

"How the devil did you know that?" I asked. "It took me hours to track down that information."

"It is quite obvious. I should have seen it sooner. The connection must have been made after both men were wounded. Otherwise the killer would not have damaged the tin soldiers so specifically."

"You're correct, as usual. Captain Danbury also spent some time in Peshawar. However, by the time he arrived, Colbert had already been discharged."

"Did you meet Captain Danbury?"

"He arrived while I was still there, but my enteric fever was so severe that I wasn't capable of registering any comings or goings by then."

"So the question becomes: Who else was there? There must have been patients and medical staff that they both met, other than you."

I smiled. "For once, I've anticipated you correctly," I said. "I managed to find the hospital's admission records for that year."

"Excellent work, Watson! It would appear that my tutelage is beginning to produce results. What did those records reveal?"

"I have them here. I didn't have time to examine them before I left. It took considerable effort to persuade the archivist to let me borrow them, and only then because I suggested that lives might be at stake. Still, I have to return them first thing in the morning."

Holmes took the papers and began scanning through them at a phenomenal speed.

"There are five patients, other than yourself, whose time at the hospital intersects with both Captain Danbury and Lieutenant Colbert. Three of them died in hospital, so I believe we can discount them for now. That just leaves a Private Green and a Corporal Fleming."

137

I cast my mind back to the hospital in Peshawar. It was a time that I didn't like to think about, yet the memories surfaced easily. Suppressing them again would be the harder part.

"Green was a young lad," I said. "Too young for what happened to him. He lost his leg. They had to amputate just below the knee. He was admitted shortly before the fever claimed me. I never knew what happened to him. I'm glad that he survived."

"What about Corporal Fleming?"

"He was there when I arrived and I don't remember him leaving. He had suffered a bad head wound, which affected his movement and speech. The doctors were quite pessimistic about his prognosis, but I remember him as being surprisingly positive. His girl back home had just given birth to a child. A bit of a scandal, but he was confident that once he returned home a war hero, they would marry and everything would be fine."

"Very well. You should ask for their papers at the War Office tomorrow. Hopefully they will have current addresses for both of them. Of course, there is still the matter of medical staff, but this is an acceptable place to start."

The address listed on Private Green's discharge papers was a village in Suffolk, while Corporal Fleming was from Kent. On the strength of a coin toss, we decided to visit Fleming first and caught a train down to Chilham. Unfortunately, he wasn't at the address we had been given. The couple living there hadn't been there long, and believed that the previous resident had died. Frustrated, we adjourned to The White Horse for some lunch before returning to London.

"If Fleming is dead, that just leaves Green," I said. "Hopefully we'll have better luck when we visit him tomorrow."

"I would be interested to know how he died," said Holmes. "We might still be able to learn something from him."

"Did I hear you talking about old Fleming?"

We both looked up at the landlord, who had just come over with our food.

"Did you know him?" I asked.

The landlord laughed. "I know everyone in this village. They all come in here at one time or another. Mind you, there isn't much to say about old Fleming's passing. Died in his bed, quite peacefully."

"Oh well," I said. "Thank you for letting us know."

"Now his son – *that* was a scandal!"

"His son?"

"Yes, young David Fleming. Ran off to fight abroad, leaving young Mary Piper with child."

138

"What happened?" I asked. "Did he come back to her?"

"Tried to, but it was too late. Her dad had already married her off to make things all proper, before she had the boy. Of course, everyone still knew, but it's the look of the thing, isn't it?"

"Where is young Fleming now?" asked Holmes.

"I couldn't rightly say. His dad was already gone and he didn't have much to stay here for. He hung around for a while, moping about the place, but eventually he ran off again – nobody knew where."

"And the girl?"

"She's still around here."

Mrs. Mary Steward lived in a farmhouse not far from the village. She opened the door with a babe in her arms and pushing back a toddler with her leg in an attempt to prevent his escape from the house.

"Yes, what do you want?" she asked sharply.

"We were hoping to talk to you about David Fleming," I said.

Her expression turned fearful. "Shh! Away with you. You cannot be mentioning that name around here."

However, it was too late. A man came up behind her and pushed her to one side roughly.

"Did someone mention that wastrel boy?" said Mr. Steward. He was a large man with leathery skin and muscular arms, from working in the fields. He was also at least twenty years older than his wife.

"We're wondering if Mr. Fleming had been here recently," Holmes asked.

"He hasn't, and if he had been, I would've gotten rid of him. We don't want that old scandal raked up again."

"Hasn't he even been to visit his son?" I asked.

"He doesn't have a son. All the children here are mine and I dare you to challenge it."

"He left a long time ago," said Mrs. Steward. "Once he saw that I was happily married." Her husband glared at her, but he didn't stop her from speaking. "Went to London, I think, to try to find work. There wasn't any here for him."

"Of course not. The boy wasn't right in the head. He won't have done any better there than here."

"One last thing," said Holmes. "Does your son have any toy soldiers?"

Mr. Steward's face reddened. "Absolutely not. I won't have them in the house. Now leave, before I make you."

As we walked up the lane, back to the village, Mrs. Steward came running up behind us. When she caught up with us, she looked around to make sure nobody was watching, before she spoke.

"I'm sorry about my husband. He isn't a bad man. He just doesn't like to be reminded of the old scandal."

"It's us that should be sorry," I said. "We wouldn't have disturbed you if it wasn't important."

"You didn't risk further angering him just to tell us that, though," said Holmes.

"No. It was that last thing you asked – about the toy soldiers. The day before David left for London, he visited us. He wanted to give a present to my son."

"He gave his son a tin soldier," said Holmes.

"A box of them."

"Do you still have them?" I asked.

"I might have kept them, but my husband was there. He smashed the box on the ground, and flattened a couple of the soldiers under his boot."

"How did Fleming react?" I asked.

"He was furious. Said he'd spent the last of his money on those toys. 'Then you shouldn't have wasted your money,' my husband told him. 'Nobody wants broken soldiers here.'"

"What happened to the tin soldiers?" asked Holmes.

"David took them with him. He missed one though. I kept it."

"For your son?" I asked.

She shook her head. "I don't know why. I can't ever give it to him. Besides it's broken."

She unfolded a handkerchief and tipped out its contents into Holmes's hand. The damage wrought by Mr. Steward's boot was severe, but it was still recognisably a brother to the tin soldiers left with the two dead men.

We hurried back to the station, anxious to return to London as soon as possible.

"Fleming is obviously our man," said Holmes as we sat on the train. "We need to catch him before he kills anyone else."

"How are we going to find him?"

"He was probably living near Wapping, since he met Captain Danbury there, but if he has any sense, he'll have moved on. Still, Lestrade can arrange a search. It will give him something to do, while we check on Private Green."

"You think Fleming will go after him next?"

"I think he's in grave danger. I only hope we can get to him in time."

Private Green had returned to the village of Stutton, near Ipswich, when he was discharged from the army. Holmes was withdrawn during the train journey and I tried to read my newspaper. However, the memories of my time in Afghanistan were still preying on my mind. I had slept poorly again, and now found myself unable to concentrate on the stories of the day.

A woman opened the door at the address we'd been given. She wasn't an old woman, but the sadness in her eyes added years to her. Her black dress was far cheaper than Mrs. Colbert's, but it indicated her state of mourning just as clearly. It was obvious we had arrived too late.

"Mrs. Green," Holmes said. "We are so sorry to intrude upon your grief."

"Were you friends with my son? With my Johnny?"

"Yes, I knew Private Green. I met him in the army."

Mrs. Green smiled. "I knew you were friends Johnny's. He had so many friends. He was such a good boy. Please come in."

"Thank you. I'm Doctor Watson, and this is my friend, Mr. Holmes."

She showed us into the kitchen. There was an armchair standing to each side of the fire, and I noticed the pair of crutches beside one of them. I sat down at the dining table, where Holmes joined me.

"Can I offer you some tea?" asked Mrs. Green.

"That is very kind," I replied, "but it really isn't – "

I stopped, seeing that she was already filling the kettle.

"Yes. Thank you very much."

"I haven't met many of Johnny's friends from the army. Just you and David. Did you know David as well?"

So Fleming had been here already, as Holmes had feared.

"Why, yes I did. We were all together, for a time."

"That poor boy. He wasn't lucky like my Johnny."

"Your son lost his leg," said Holmes. "Not many people would consider that lucky."

"I guess not, but Johnny had me to come back to. Poor David didn't have anyone. Couldn't get a job neither, from what he said. Of course, we would have liked to help him, but we had so little. Still, I'm glad he came when he did."

"Why is that, Mrs. Green?" I asked, but I already knew the answer.

"It's because my Johnny died the very next day. Fell over and hit his head while I was out at the shop."

She started crying, and sat down at the table, the tea-making forgotten. I walked round to her and put my hand on her shoulder.

"We are so sorry. Maybe it would be best if we left."

"That's all right," she said, trying to dry her eyes, but I could see she was struggling to maintain her composure.

"No," I said. "We should leave you in peace."

She didn't protest again.

It was only when we were back on the train that I remembered we'd never asked if Mrs. Green had seen a tin soldier.

"It doesn't matter," said Holmes. "I don't think there is any doubt that Corporal Fleming killed Private Green."

"But why? If Fleming is down on his luck I can see why he would steal from Danbury, and it's possible that he took money from Colbert too. But the Greens had nothing worth taking."

"Nothing except for their happiness," said Holmes. "The motive here is jealousy. Corporal Fleming expected to return to a family, a home, and no doubt a job. He feels abandoned. Over time that feeling has turned into anger at anyone who achieved any measure of the happiness he thinks he deserved."

"Do you think that he'll kill again?"

"I fear that he will. I don't think he will ever be satisfied with his lot in life now."

"We should examine the hospital records again," I said. "If he met anyone else there, they're likely to be his next target. Otherwise, I'm not sure who he might kill."

"We know there was at least one other man there."

"Who? We must warn him at once."

Holmes stared at me, and after a moment I realised who he meant.

"I cannot stay shut away in here forever," I said.

It had been two days since we returned to London, and during that time Holmes hadn't allowed me to leave Baker Street once.

He stood by the window, watching the street below. "I'm certain that Fleming is coming for you, and we must be ready for him."

"He has probably fled. He knows the police are hunting for him."

"Yes. You can blame Lestrade for your confinement. If he hadn't given the newspapers Fleming's name, we would have him by now."

"I'm due at the surgery today. I will be safe enough there, surrounded by patients."

"Very well. I can see I won't be able to dissuade you. However, please take your service revolver with you, and remain vigilant."

I promised that I would, certain that nothing would happen. However, once I had left home, that certainty faded. More than once I wondered if I was being followed, and I held tightly to the revolver in my pocket during the whole journey.

It was a busy morning in the surgery, which made me almost forget about Fleming and the threat to my life. When I returned from lunch, the waiting room was just starting to fill up again. I greeted my patients cheerfully, and promised that I would see the first of them in just a few minutes.

I went into the consultation room, and hung my coat on the stand. Then I noticed that there was something standing on the blotter in the middle of the desk. As I moved closer, I recognised it as a tin soldier in a painted red uniform. I knew without looking that, if I examined it closer, there would be a tiny hole corresponding to where the bullet hit me in Afghanistan.

"They are such nice toys," said a voice from behind me. "But they are fragile. They break easily, like real soldiers." He stammered as though he was struggling to form his sentences.

I turned around and saw a man holding a gun, standing beside the door. He pushed it shut with a bang. His hair was wet and his clothes were muddy. I suspected that he'd been living on the streets for some time.

I started to reach for my revolver, before remembering I had left it in the pocket of my coat.

"We've been looking for you, Corporal Fleming," I said, trying to remain calm.

"I know. I had hoped to visit you sooner, but I wanted to speak with you privately. Your friend, Mr. Holmes, wouldn't have understood."

"Understood what?"

"What it's like to return from war. Being broken and useless."

"We aren't useless."

"No, you aren't. You were lucky. You found a nice job. You found a nice place to live. Did you ever think about the rest of us? The ones who weren't lucky?"

Had I thought about my brothers in arms from Afghanistan? I had thought about the men still fighting and suffering abroad. But the ones who made it home? Had I thought about the lives they would be coming back to?

"I'm sorry. I know you didn't receive the homecoming you had been hoping for. I wish I had been able to help you. I still wish I could help you."

"You have money. You've clearly been successful since you returned."

143

"Is that why you wrote to Colbert and Danbury? Why you visited Green? Did you ask them to give you money?"

"Colbert was like you. . He said he was my friend and wanted to help, but he thought a little money was the answer. Enough to get rid of me. I told him I wasn't looking for a handout. I wanted him to get me a job. Give a me a chance to make my own way, just like he had been given."

"So you killed him?"

"He was selfish. He refused to share his good fortune. And Danbury was even worse. Insisted we meet in the worst part of town, where none of his fancy friends would see us. He didn't offer me a penny. Just waved his cane around and threatened to beat me if I came near him again. Well, I showed him I'm not quite as useless a cripple as he supposed."

"And Green? What did he do?"

"I felt sorry for him. Sitting in that chair, barely able to walk, let alone work. Killing him was a mercy."

"He was happy. He was loved."

He seemed to hesitate and the gun dipped slightly. I almost lunged at him, but the moment wasn't long enough.

"I did the right thing," he said.

"And what are you going to do now?" I asked.

"You could give me money, or get me a job with one of your rich patients."

"Even if I could have done before, it's too late now. You're a murderer, and the police are hunting for you. I cannot change that."

"You could tell them that I'm innocent. That you and your clever friend made a mistake."

"I will not."

"Then you are just as bad as the others."

Fleming then raised his service revolver, only for it to be knocked from his hand as a figure lunged at him from behind the folding screen in the corner of the room. The gun slid across the floor towards me, and I quickly picked it up.

I pointed the weapon at Fleming, but it wasn't necessary. He was already being held in a tight grip by Holmes.

"How long have you been hiding there?" I asked. "I don't think the patients would be happy to learn that you've been eavesdropping on them."

"Never fear, Watson. Corporal Fleming's confession was the only thing that I heard. I spotted him lurking outside earlier, but was afraid that he would run if I approached him. When you went for lunch, and he failed to follow you, it was easy to deduce what he had planned. I simply hid in here just before he did."

144

"You're lucky that your friend was here," Fleming said.

"Yes, I have been lucky."

With Holmes's help, I tied Fleming to a chair using some bandages and then sent for Lestrade to come and take him away.

Even now, years later, as I write this account, I feel anxious. However, it isn't the remembrance of my close encounter with death that scares me. It wasn't my first, or the last. Rather, it's the thought of what might have been, had I not been lucky enough to have a career to resume, or to have found a home and friends in the comfort of Baker Street.

"Could I have become as bitter and angry as Corporal Fleming, if things had been different?" I asked Holmes a few days later. "Could I have become a murderer too?"

"Of course not, Watson," my friend replied. "It simply isn't in your nature."

However, I still cannot help but wonder. Holmes is an expert on a great many things, but what the madness of war can do to a man is something he will never fully understand.

The Shattered Man
by MJH Simmonds

It was a grim November morning, on the very eve of the Third Anglo-Burmese War, that brought a damp and rather miserable Inspector Lestrade to our door. Holmes was the very picture of hospitality, supplying the poor detective with warmth from both a seat directly before the fire and from a heavy tumbler of brandy. Despite the inspector's eager protestations, Holmes insisted that the policeman dry sufficiently before offering a cigar and inviting his testimony.

"One must be both calm and comfortable if one is expected to perform at his best," Holmes explained as he gestured the good inspector to begin his tale.

"Thank you, gentlemen," Lestrade began, with a slight sniffle. "It has been an extremely long and exhausting night, but I fear that this is merely the beginning of a particularly dark and difficult case."

Although Holmes had taken up his usual neutral stance – bolt upright, fingers pushed together to form an ivory arch before a stoic visage – I swear I witnessed a lone eyebrow rise by the tiniest fraction of an inch.

"I received a message, about nine o'clock last night, that a body had been pulled from the Thames. Nothing unusual there – barely a day goes by without some poor soul being fished out of its cold, dark depths. This was different though." The inspector leaned forward and took a good draught of his golden spirit. "The poor fellow had been beaten about the head so ferociously that precious little remained of his face. I have never before seen such a wantonly egregious act imparted upon a person. The victim must have been dead long before his assailant finally ceased his terrible assault."

"How ghastly," I declared. "I have seen horrific injuries inflicted by modern weapons of war, but this sounds deranged – a madman, surely."

"Or, perhaps, an attempt to disguise the identity of the victim?" Holmes's voice was quiet and thoughtful.

"That is exactly the thought that occurred to me," Lestrade responded, noticeably brightened by the meeting of minds. "However," he continued, "identifying the victim was simplicity itself. His pocketbook, monogrammed jewellery, calling cards, watch, and cufflinks left no room for doubt. The poor man's name was Tarquin Aethelbrough, a dealer in antiquities."

"From your enthusiastic demeanour," Holmes languidly commented. "I warrant that you have divined rather more about this character."

Lestrade took a long draught of warming liquor before continuing.

"Fast approaching his fiftieth year, Aethelbrough worked out of a shop on Oxford Street. However, the diminutive proportions of his premises seem to have reflected his relative level of achievement. Despite his fine attire and accoutrements, Mr. Aethelbrough was not a particularly successful businessman. He lived alone in a modest apartment on St. Anne's Street, just five minutes' walk from his place of work, and was well known in the local taverns."

"My dear friend," Holmes interjected, abruptly, "this is all very interesting, but I see little in this matter that might demand my attention."

Lestrade reddened, and I sent him a subtle calming gesture, along with an expression intended to convey my acknowledgement of Holmes's frustrating nature.

"Mr. Holmes," snapped back the inspector. "I am merely attempting to mirror your own methods and provide all possible detail. Please allow me to continue."

Holmes covered his face with his hands. "Lestrade, you are quite correct, and I beg your forgiveness," Holmes stated through his long fingers. "Pray continue your most instructive narrative."

With a slight air of triumph, the inspector returned to his tale.

"Despite his failure to prosper and rather dubious habits, this Aethelbrough appears to have been basically an honest man. He had no debts and was popular enough with the local business community. His neighbours all describe him as a polite man, one that liked a drink, but was quiet and well-behaved, even in his cups. He seems to have come from a good family, educated at Eton and Oxford, but his schooling appears to have eaten up the last of the family fortune. I managed to talk with his lawyer late last night. He confirmed he was the last of his line, the final scion of an ancient family, but one whose wealth and good fortune had long since been lost to the ages.

"An upright, if not exactly thriving, businessman," Lestrade declared, concluding with considerable passion. "A man with no identifiable enemies, beaten to a bloody pulp for no discernible reason in the very centre of London is something that we simply cannot countenance."

Holmes sat back, picked up his battered, oily, black clay, and lit it with a cedar cigar match. He drew deeply before exhaling a swirling column of thick grey smoke. The smell of spices and warm leather indicated that, for once, he had a decent Latakia mixture in his usually repugnant bowl.

"I can't imagine that it bears any significance to the case, but Aethelbrough's solicitor was good enough to provide me with a copy of his will." Lestrade lightly tossed a cream coloured envelope onto the small occasional table that held the ashtray and our glasses.

Holmes's right hand thrust out like a striking cobra. He grabbed the envelope and pulled out the single sheet of paper that lay inside. His eyes flicked swiftly across the buff-coloured sheet and, less than half of a minute after snatching the will, snapped his head upwards.

"Have you read this, Inspector?" Holmes demanded, impatiently.

"Why, of course," stuttered Lestrade, Holmes's unexpected tone causing him to knock his growing cigar ash onto the table. "He has left his entire estate to an old school friend. What of it? He had no family and no immediate or identifiable friends."

Holmes looked incredulous. His steely eyes bulged, he seemed to be fighting some internal battle. Suddenly he let out a gasp and appeared to relax.

"Apologies," Holmes smiled benevolently. "You must be far too busy in your work to have time to partake in some of my own indulgences. The beneficiary of Aethelbrough's will is listed as a Mr. James Fitzroy de La Haye. Perhaps you know him better by his current title, 'The Eighth' – and probably last – 'Duke of Wessford'."

"Good heavens!" I exclaimed. I realised then that Holmes had been alluding to his unexpected, but enthusiastic, knowledge of tawdry gossip and other lascivious affairs of questionable taste within Society.

"Do you mean the old 'Herefordshire Hermit'?" exclaimed Lestrade, his cigar now burnt down perilously close to his fingers. "'The Lonely Lord'? But why? The Duke is hardly short of a bob or two, is he? Surely, he could have left his estate to someone a little more . . . *needy*?" Lestrade scoffed. We knew well his disdain for those with unearned wealth.

By now, I had been handed the will and glanced over the text myself.

"To be fair, old chap, you have answered this question already. You stated he had no family or friends, and it says here that de La Haye was his only friend at Eton, even though he was a year above him. Despite never having seen each other again, this seems to have left a lasting impression on poor Aethelbrough. It is a rather sad tale, but somewhat touching also, I would conclude."

"Very well," Lestrade acquiesced. "However, none of this gets us any closer to identifying the poor fellow's killer or establishing any sort of motive for this terrible crime."

"Far from it," Holmes replied, most unexpectedly. "I can think of at least six different motives that would perfectly fit the crime. Sadly, I have already discounted four of these as implausible and the two remaining are

148

rapidly losing credibility. I require more data, Lestrade. We have barely laid the foundations of this case. We must now build the walls and floors."

Holmes rose and swept across the sitting room. As he rushed towards his bedroom, he raised an arm and called, "Watson, we leave in five minutes! Inspector, please feel free to stay. On our way out, I'll call upon Mrs. Hudson to send you up a fine breakfast."

We were soon in a cab, trotting towards Oxford Street. Even in the early morning hustle and-bustle, the journey took no more than fifteen minutes. We almost missed Aethelbrough's shop. There was a definite skid as the cabman pulled up sharply in response to Holmes's sharp order to halt.

I pulled myself out of the still-rocking cab and followed Holmes the few yards back to the premises of the poor victim. It was immediately clear why we had nearly passed it by – the entire frontage was not much wider than ten feet and all appeared dark and disused. The windows were black with dirt on the outside and cobweb-strewn on the inside. I could barely make out various ceramics and silver and brass contraptions lying behind the glass. This was clearly not a display of anything of any real value. It was only the presence of a constable, standing tall before the grim front door, that identified the shop as anything other than a run-down, anonymous property. The policeman nodded as we approached and moved aside without a word.

Inside the shop, things were a little better. Two large cabinets held antiques of much finer provenance and the back wall hosted a selection of tasteful watercolours and a few impressive-looking oil paintings.

"Yes, Watson, it does make perfect sense," declared Holmes. "Why tempt fate by filling your windows with valuable artefacts which could be quickly stolen with relative ease."

"Indeed," I replied, quickly recovering from Holmes's apparent display of clairvoyance in replying to my unasked question. "He kept the more valuable items out of sight from passers-by."

While Holmes disappeared into the back room, I strolled around the small shop, peering inside each display case in turn. I then examined the paintings behind the small counter. A thought began to form in my mind, and I was on the verge of calling for Holmes when he swept back into view, the faintest hint of a smile playing upon his lips.

"I say," I announced with undisguised enthusiasm, "I think I've something here."

The tall detective slowed and opened his arms, encouragingly. "Pray tell, for this case is very nearly complete. I have most all of the pieces and have real hope that we can bring cheer to the inspector before the day is out."

"Look here . . . and here." I pointed to gaps between artefacts in the cabinets. "And look at the paintings – or rather, look at the gaps between them."

Holmes stuck his face up against the glass of the cases, let out a snort, and then turned towards the wall of paintings.

"Quite right, my friend. I have one final question for the officer at the door and then we are done here."

Holmes rushed out of the diminutive store and whispered a few words to the constable standing outside. The formidable policeman nodded his confirmation and Holmes let out a cry of triumph. He bashed down his cane boyishly onto the pavement, caught it as it shot back upwards, and shouted for a cab. I demanded to know what he'd asked the constable.

"Oh, it was simply the final confirmation of what I already suspected. I asked him 'What were the contents of Aethelbrough's safe?'"

"And the answer was?"

"Exactly the same as for your 'gaps' in the inventory of the shop," he grinned. "Absolutely nothing."

"I think I am beginning to see," I replied, with more confidence than I genuinely felt. "Several pieces appear to have been removed from the cabinets and, judging from the identical patterns left in the dust, all were removed together and quite recently. It is the same story with the paintings. Although the dust is less prevalent there, it appears that at least four, perhaps five, paintings have been removed from display in the past few days."

"And when you add a recently emptied safe to this equation, it becomes most suggestive, wouldn't you say?"

Before I had time to answer, Holmes turned away from me and loudly hailed for a cab. A two-wheeler clattered to a halt before him and the lithe detective leapt aboard. With far less athleticism I joined him, and once Holmes had ordered the driver to take us back to Baker Street, I again attempted an answer to his earlier question.

"It is deeply suspicious that this man's most valuable stock appears to have been removed shortly before his murder," I suggested. "If his safe is also empty, it certainly adds a new element to this case. Do you suppose that he knew who had stolen these artefacts from him? Perhaps he confronted the villain, and this led to the poor man's terrible demise. It might also explain the extent of the injuries inflicted by the perpetrator. He might have disfigured his victim in an attempt to slow down the inevitable subsequent investigation."

"These are very good thoughts," replied Holmes unexpectedly, "and all worthy of consideration." I had just enough time to begin to feel flattered before Holmes added, "However, once duly considered, the evidence starts to point elsewhere, towards a far more egregious conspiracy, one so terrible and brilliant that it will live long in the annals of crime."

Despite Holmes's theatrical declaration, he signally refused to elaborate any further and we completed the short haul back to Baker Street in virtual silence. Lestrade had taken up Holmes's offer of breakfast but had left shortly before we returned to our rooms. Holmes immediately threw off his hat and coat and began to pull seemingly random files and volumes from his eclectic library. After throwing five or six bundles onto the couch, he seemed satisfied, gathered them together, and placed them on the small table next to his fireside chair. He stooped to both encourage the fire and pick out a grubby briar, which he filled from the Persian slipper, before finally sitting himself down, cross-legged, onto his armchair. Within seconds he was deeply engrossed in the first of his chosen volumes.

I could not help but grin as he sucked upon his unlit pipe. His face may have born a confused expression, but his mind was now far too occupied to be distracted from his work. Altruistically, I stuck a taper into the fire and held it above his pipe's grimy bowl. Holmes's only reaction to the plumes of grey smoke that now emanated from his bulldog briar, was a faint purr, somewhat redolent of a contented feline.

I called down for a light lunch and Mrs. Hudson, as always, provided us with a perfect spread of ham, cheese, and pickle. Despite several attempts at encouraging Holmes to indulge, my friend left his food untouched. Half-an-hour later, I had finished my meal and was settling down in my chair. The fire burned brightly as I lit my latest briar, an import from the Kapp Brothers of Dublin. I had only taken a few puffs before a yell from Holmes caused me to almost choke on my own draft.

"Ha!" he exclaimed. "We have him, Doctor, we have him!" Holmes thrust down the large folder that he'd been examining. It appeared to be a collection of clippings from newspapers of the most lurid kind from the past twenty years or so, the very worst of the penny press.

Holmes stepped to his writing desk and scratched out a short message onto the back of a discarded envelope. Once satisfied with the missive, he swept back through the sitting room and left the apartment. I heard his light footfalls descend the stairs, followed by barked instructions for Mrs. Hudson to hasten to the post office and dispatch his urgent telegram.

"When should we expect the inspector?" I asked casually, as Holmes returned to the sitting room. "Is it too early to bring out the brandy and cigars?"

Holmes's look of mock reproach reminded me that he was not lacking a sense of humour when he felt the occasion merited it.

151

"I've asked Lestrade to pay a visit to Wessford Hall and request an audience with the Duke himself. Shortly afterwards, I fully expect him to arrest the man responsible for this terrible crime."

To say that I was shocked would be quite the understatement. I almost choked as I coughed up tobacco smoke in surprise. A concerned Holmes slapped my back, firmly, before slumping into his armchair.

"Thank you," I gasped as I caught my breath. "What in heaven do you mean by that? Interview the Duke of Wessford? I heard that he hasn't been seen in years, and even spurns his own servants. They say he refuses to address them in person, preferring to leave notes around the house informing them of which rooms he will be visiting that day and to avoid these at all costs. But, of course, you already know all of this, don't you? I was never quite convinced of the value of those sensationalist rags that you devour each week. However, I now have a distinct feeling that I may have to change my tune."

"Lestrade will not fail. Once the inspector has decided upon a course of action, he will not be distracted, diverted, or denied. He will cling to it like a barnacle. He will speak to the Duke, face to face, and the matter will be resolved. I am quite certain."

Holmes rose and strode towards his Macassar ebony humidor.

"Lestrade will not be back until early evening, at the earliest. While we wait, I suggest we try a bowl or two of a special mixture that I've been maturing for several months."

Holmes opened his exquisite cigar box and pulled out an oilskin pouch, which he tossed, rather carelessly, towards me. Luckily, I caught it before it could unfurl and spill its precious contents over the carpet. We filled our bowls and shared a lit taper, pulled from the fire. I dragged deeply upon my briar and was rewarded with perhaps the finest taste and aroma of any pipe tobacco that I have ever smoked.

"Holmes, what on earth is this heavenly mixture?" I asked as spirals of silver smoke spun and coalesced upwards. "It's quite divine!"

"A small gesture of thanks from a grateful client," puffed Holmes, as he drew deeply upon his terrible clay churchwarden. "A tricky matter in the southern states that I was, fortunately, able to clear up via letter post and telegram alone."

We passed the following hours in friendly and fascinating conversation. Holmes even recounted two cases that were, at the time, completely unknown to me. He was in such good spirits that he happily answered any questions I posed, without protest, and even paced his recollections to allow me to easily take notes. After a simple supper, we took a glass of brandy and a brace of decent cigars. The band on my

Havana was rather loose, so I carefully pulled it off and tossed it into the fire.

"How very careless, Watson," he sniggered, an impish smile upon his lips.

"Whatever do you mean?" I sighed, knowingly.

"Have I never told you of my encounter with the Old Gryphon Club? Their evil instructions were communicated to members by secret messages, hidden on the inside of cigar bands. Once read, these were cast into the nearest fireplace. It was otherwise a straightforward case of blackmail and coercion, the work of no more than a long weekend, as I recall."

Holmes blew a column of sweetly spiced tobacco smoke upwards, knowing full well that I was unaware of this case.

Before he could elaborate on this earlier adventure, we heard the familiar ring of the doorbell, announcing the return of Scotland Yard's finest. While I was filled with anticipation as to the outcome of Lestrade's inquiries. Holmes appeared unmoved, casually sucking upon his dark corona.

The inspector's expression, as he strode into our rooms, revealed to us that his expedition had been a fruitful one. He smiled as he greeted us – head held high, chest puffed out, the very picture of confidence and success.

"Here, the night is cool. Please warm yourself before the fire," Holmes ordered with genuine concern, pulling up a chair by the fireplace before offering our happy guest brandy and a cigar.

"Mr. Holmes, I have to be honest here and admit that I very nearly ignored your telegram. Well, it seemed so far-fetched, did it not? However, your suppositions have had a modicum of success in the past, and I did recognise the logic of your theory, so I decided that I really ought to pay the Duke a visit."

"And was all as I predicted?" asked Holmes, well aware of Lestrade's subtle attempt at inveigling himself into the solution narrative.

"Oh yes," smiled the inspector. "Of course, I knew exactly how to play it once the case was clear to me."

"Well, I am certainly none the wiser," I sighed. "Can one of you please explain the matter to me?"

"I was suspicious, right from the beginning," declared Holmes, cutting across Lestrade as he was preparing to give his own account.

"The horrific beating inflicted upon the body can only have been an attempt to hide the victim's identity. However, the killer left several clues that led to a relatively straightforward identification of the corpse. This must have been deliberate – no criminal would have gone to such lengths to conceal their victim's features yet leave proof of his identity in his very pockets! This is suggestive of an alternative, and far darker, motive."

I was enthralled and my cigar ash grew long as I sat forward and waited for Holmes to continue. My colleague took a good sup of golden brandy before continuing

"The second clue was the identity of the recipient of the legacy of Mr. Aethelbrough. Why leave his entire estate to a man already vastly wealthy, one whom he had not seen for over forty years?"

"Who was also an eccentric hermit," I added, puffing on my freshly lit cigar. "And one who, in all probability, would never even notice that the bequest had ever been left to him. "

"Indeed," confirmed Holmes with a slight nod. "Aethelbrough may have had no close friends, but he was not completely without associates. He was well-known and generally respected in his neighbourhood. It seems almost perverse for him to have left his estate to a man such as Wessford."

Holmes paused, before lowering his voice.

"Unless he did no such thing," he declared, quietly.

"Come now," I sputtered. "We know he left everything to the Duke in his will. Stop being facetious."

"He did no such thing," repeated Holmes, with a casual wave of his hand, "for he never died."

He appeared to take delight in my utter befuddlement, deliberately enjoying a long draft of golden brandy before continuing.

"The scheme was quite brilliant and executed almost perfectly. If it were not for a last-minute change of plans – fuelled, I believe, entirely by greed – he would have been completely successful. Do you not see?" Holmes asked, gently. "The body was not that of Aethelbrough. It was the mortal remains of Mr. James Fitzroy de La Haye, the Eighth – and probably last – Duke of Wessford."

Holmes continued as my mouth dropped open in complete disbelief.

"For his dire scheme to succeed, Aethelbrough needed to convince the world that the body was his own. In this respect, the victim was perfect: My investigations revealed that the men were of similar age and build. James Fitzroy de la Haye may well have been famous by name, but he was a man who hadn't been seen in public for over thirty years. Impersonating such a character would not be difficult. After all, what did Aethelbrough have to do to keep up the pretence that the Duke was still alive? "

"Almost nothing." I shook my head in disbelief. "Pass a few notes and keep out of sight. Good heavens, Holmes, this might well have been the perfect crime. Impersonating someone who is never seen – there is a terrible genius at work here."

"Not a genius, sadly." Holmes sounded almost disappointed. "Aethelbrough's greed was his downfall. As you know, I already had suspicions once I had examined the body. By the time I had visited Aethelbrough's shop, I was convinced that he was somehow involved in a conspiracy. Why did he remove all of his most valuable possessions before faking his death? Surely these would pass back to him as part of his false legacy. I believe that he took these items away for two reasons: Firstly, to lower the value of his estate to avoid any death duties and, secondly, he didn't fully trust his executors and was afraid that much of his collection would vanish during probate."

"Ah, I see now," I commented. "Greed. The Duke's estate must be worth hundreds of thousands, yet Aethelbrough was trying to save himself a few hundred pounds at most."

I finally noticed the ash snake that had formed from my cigar and tapped it into the fireplace. Several questions still swirled around my head.

"That may very well be so," I declared, "but I cannot believe that you convinced our good friend the inspector to interrogate a Duke based purely upon such circumstantial evidence."

"Not at all. I provided one additional piece of information to Lestrade, one fact that would prove me to be right or wrong in a single second. However, everything hung upon Lestrade being able to meet the Duke in person."

"And that is where I excel, gentlemen," interceded the proud policeman. "Be you prince or pauper, should you be a person of interest in an investigation of mine, I will interview you. Come hell or high water, I will not rest until I have heard your testimony, given to myself, in person."

"When he was in his very early twenties," began Holmes, taking up the story, "the Duke was sent away to study at a Bavarian University. As you may know, these institutions have a long history of duelling, often for the most innocuous of reasons. The exact circumstances may never be known, but the unfortunate Duke found himself challenged to one of these contests. A proud and confident young man, he refused to yield and duly took up his sword. Sadly, for him, his opponent was as cruel as he was proficient in swordsmanship. The Duke was terribly injured, his face cut open by multiple blows, many of which were inflicted long after the duel was over as a contest. As is tradition, he was stitched up by a local doctor, but his face was left hideously scarred, an affliction that led him, first, to withdraw from public life, and then, finally, from all human contact. Thus was born the 'lost Duke of Wessford', the 'Herefordshire Hermit', the 'Lonely Lord'."

"Which explains why Lestrade had to interview him face to face, of course!" I exclaimed. "One look at the interloper would be enough to prove that it wasn't the real Duke."

"It may have taken the best part of two hours to get the blighter to talk to us, but once he appeared, I had the darbies on him in less than two minutes," Lestrade declared, grinning widely. "That wasn't the end of it though, gentlemen," he added conspiratorially.

Holmes bolted upright, his face suddenly alive and alert.

"Pray, tell us the rest."

"Well," began the inspector with considerable pride, "like yourself, I'm interested in the science of crime and the motivations and desires that lie behind such wicked actions. Therefore, I was most interested to hear what he had to say in his defence, despite my having taken him red-handed."

"Oh, yes," I agreed, "As a medical man, I would also be most interested to hear how he justified to himself such monstrous actions."

"Here's the thing, though. After the initial shock of having been caught had passed, he declared loudly that the Duke had been a willing participant in the whole scheme. He claimed that the two had recently reconnected by mail, within the past few months, insisting that, at the time, he had no knowledge of the poor Duke's misfortunes, there having had been no contact between the two since they were schoolboys. The Duke was in a terrible state. He had no heir and no prospect of siring one. His line was just a few short years from ending forever."

"Aethelbrough insisted that the plan had been instigated and planned by the Duke – he had neither the imagination nor the will to commit such an atrocity. He was quite content with his lot in life. He was not a rich man, but he made a decent enough living and lacked for nothing. It was only the promise of huge wealth and the prospect of an attractive wife that convinced him to agree to the ghastly plot."

"A wife?" asked Holmes, seriously. He appeared to be taking Aethelbrough's testimony far more seriously than I.

"Yes," replied the inspector, taking a sip of brandy. "The Duke was quite insistent on this point, according to our villain. He was to take over the Duke's position and, gradually, over a period of a few months, re-appear upon the social scene – discreetly, but visibly enough to make it known that he was now actively seeking a wife."

"The Duke is one of the richest men in the country," I commented. "There would certainly have been no shortage of suitors. But are we really expected to believe that the Duke was prepared to die so that his familial line might continue? Surely, even with his disfigurement, he could still attract a bride. None of us is naïve enough to believe that matches at this

156

rarefied level are made by anything other than convenience or opportunity. No, this is a horrific, coolly and carefully planned murder."

"Although I tend to agree with the Good Doctor," sighed Lestrade, suddenly exhibiting the effects of almost two day's continuous hard work. "It makes little difference. He arranged to meet the Duke in secret at his home, and killed him there. Then, he changed the body's clothes and returned to London, where he dumped it on the street. His explanation, even if we believed it, is no defence at all. He will hang before the year is out."

Inspector Lestrade collected his hat and coat and departed, happy that the case had come to a successful conclusion. Upon returning upstairs after seeing him out, I noticed that Holmes hadn't moved. He sat, hands held together, his fingers arched.

"You think he's telling the truth, don't you?" I asked, pouring myself a final measure of brandy.

I had filled, tamped, and lit my pipe before Holmes finally replied.

"His defence was no defence at all. Lestrade was quite right. Aethelbrough never denied killing the Duke. His testimony could never save him. So why tell a lie that doesn't improve his prospects? I'm inclined to believe his story, Watson, despite how it may appear at first. It is neither impossible nor even illogical, but it is sad and desperate – a scheme that a real friend would never contemplate. However, Aethelbrough was never a friend to the Duke."

The evening passed in sad contemplation of one life wasted through bad luck and another lost by greed.

The Hungarian Doctor
by Denis O. Smith

During the time I shared chambers in Baker Street with Mr. Sherlock Holmes, the well-known criminal investigator, our visitors came from almost every walk of life. In itself, this meant little to Holmes, for as his interest lay entirely in the problem a client might bring to him for solution, the client's particular rank or station in life was perfectly irrelevant to him, except insofar as it might affect the case. For myself, however, I must say I found this panorama of human life endlessly fascinating, not least because it was almost impossible to predict from a client's appearance or antecedents what strange tale he or she would recount.

Being a trained medical man myself, it was perhaps understandable that I should feel a heightened interest when a fellow medico called to consult my friend, and I was always fascinated to hear what others had done when they had completed their medical training. One man, I recall, had joined the Army Medical Department, as I had, although his subsequent experiences had been quite different from my own. Another had sailed for a season as surgeon on a whaling ship in the Arctic seas. Yet others had served their first years of general practice in places as far apart as Cornwall and the north of Scotland, and most of the cases they laid before Sherlock Holmes were as different from each other as their professional experience had been geographically different. Any one of a dozen such cases would make a worthy addition to this series of tales, but none was perhaps so striking in its details nor so surprising in its outcome as the strange case of Dr. Kazinczy and the bandaged man. This case may not have provided Holmes with any great opportunities for the exercise of those powers of observation and inference for which he was noted, but it nevertheless contained features which made it exceptionally memorable, especially for me, as the reader will see.

It was a cold, damp period in February 1885, the sort of weather which always made the old wound in my leg ache painfully. It was particularly bad that morning, I remember, and after breakfast I had pulled my chair closer to the fire and attempted to distract myself with the morning papers, but they contained little of interest. Holmes, meanwhile, curled up in his chair with his old mouse-coloured dressing-gown wrapped around him, had lit his pipe and pored for some time over the personal columns of *The Times*, groaning loudly with annoyance from time to time. At length, with a snort, he had cast the paper aside, sprung from his chair, and paced about the room, eventually ending up by the window, where he stood for some time, surveying the scene in the street outside.

"I believe I have some talent, Watson," said he abruptly, turning from the window.

"Of course," I replied.

"And yet, day after day, I have no work to do, nothing to which I can apply that talent. Another day as barren as the last few and I believe that, like some powerful engine which is not connected to any useful work, my racing thoughts will wrack my brain to pieces!"

I was about to make some mollifying remark, when, all at once, there came the sharp jangling of the door-bell.

"Perhaps this is a client for you," I stated in as cheery a voice as I could muster.

"I sincerely hope so," returned my companion, in a sceptical tone.

A moment later, a pleasant-faced, smartly-dressed man was shown into the room. He was, I judged, in his late thirties, and his neat black frock-coat and silk hat indicated a professional man, perhaps a doctor, a suggestion all but confirmed by the small leather bag he carried in his hand.

"Come in, come in," said Holmes, casting off his dressing-gown and pulling his chair back a little from the hearth. "Pray take a seat and tell us what we can do for you on this damp and dreary morning."

"My name," began our visitor when he had seated himself beside the fire, "is Laszlo Kazinczy. My family home, as you might guess from my name, is not in England, but in Hungary, where I trained as a physician."

"And yet," said Holmes, "you have lived here some time. Your clothes, your shoes, your hat," he explained in answer to a querying expression from the other: "They are all, I should say, of English manufacture, and although of good quality, are clearly not new. Your medical bag in particular, handsome though it is, shows signs of some years' wear. My colleague, Dr. Watson, here," he continued, nodding in my direction, "is also a medical man, and his bag regrettably shows exactly the same pattern of wear."

"You are quite correct," said Kazinczy with a smile of appreciation at Holmes's observations. "If your colleague is a medical man, he may find my account of particular interest, for it does have a medical aspect to it. But, first, I shall tell you how I came to be here. For a few years after qualifying, I worked in a large hospital in Budapest, increasing my knowledge and skill in all branches of medicine. At length I became particularly interested in the diseases and problems of the human eye, and resolved to increase my knowledge of this subject as much as I could.

"At that time, the greatest eye-expert in Europe was your Professor Whitburn, here in England, so I wrote to him, expressing my interest in his work. His response was a very friendly one. He invited me to attend a series of lectures he was about to give in London, and when I arrived here he put me up in his own house for a while. Fortunately, I was already able to speak English, although not so well as I do now. Anyway, to cut a long story short, I became very friendly with my host – who is a most generous man – and with his family, too, including his pretty daughter, Elizabeth.

"At length, Elizabeth did me the honour of consenting to be my wife. I had by then been working for some time, in a part-time capacity, as a dispensary assistant to an elderly physician, Dr. Gildersleeve, in Hackney, but saw that I should have to secure a more lucrative position if I were to support a wife. I therefore entered into correspondence with the Royal College of Surgeons to see what would be required of me if I were to practise here, and having at length satisfied the Royal College as to my qualifications and abilities, I went into partnership with Dr. Gildersleeve. His practice was certainly not the most fashionable in London, but it has kept me busy for a few years now, especially since Dr. Gildersleeve himself retired. My patients are, I must say, as varied as anyone could wish for. One minute I will be attending to the medical requirements of a well-off financial manager from the leafier parts of the northern fringe of Hackney or Stoke Newington, the next I will be consulted by a coal-heaver or street-sweeper from down Whitechapel way – and each of them brings his own unique problems to me for solution."

"Your practice sounds somewhat like my own," observed Holmes with a chuckle. "And the interesting thing, I find, is that one can never predict with any accuracy which of these very varied clients will bring an especially interesting problem. Indeed, the cases of the poorer clients are not infrequently more fascinating than those of the wealthy!"

"Absolutely," returned our visitor with a smile. "To hear you speak as you do gives me confidence that you will not simply dismiss my story as of no interest."

Holmes shook his head. "I never dismiss what a client has to tell me," he remarked in a vehement tone. "But, come! I believe we understand your circumstances now. Pray tell us what has occurred to bring you here today."

"It all happened last night," replied his client after a moment. "It was about ten minutes to six and my evening surgery-hour was almost over. I had not been especially busy, and I was tidying my consulting room and thinking about what I was shortly going to have for my supper when there came a tap at the door.

160

"'Come in!' I called, and in walked a tall, gaunt-looking man I had never seen before, wearing a heavy black overcoat. He had dark, deep-set eyes and a large, hooked nose, which gave him the appearance of a fierce bird of prey. There was a purposefulness in his tread as he came to the desk which caught my attention. I think it passed through my mind, the way such thoughts do, that, if the firmness of his step was anything to go by, there didn't seem to be much wrong with him. 'Take a seat,' I said. 'What can I do for you?'

"'It is not for me,' he replied as he sat down, 'but for the one I represent.' Although his English was perfectly good, it was delivered in an odd accent, which I could not place. I dare say I myself have an accent which native English-speakers notice but of which I am unaware, but this gentleman's accent was, I think, considerably stronger than my own.

"'I see,' said I after a moment. 'Is there some reason why the gentleman in question cannot come here himself?'

"'There are two reasons,' said he. 'In the first place, he is very ill and in some considerable pain. In the second place – ' He paused. 'I must be discreet when I speak of this, Doctor. You should know that the gentleman I serve is not from this country. In his own land he is most eminent, both an aristocrat and a scholar. He has tried to educate his fellow-countrymen, to lead them away from their old barbarity, to take their place in the modern world. But this mission has aroused the enmity of some, who are, for their own selfish reasons, opposed to his benign reforms. They call themselves The League of the Golden Ribbon, but should call themselves "The Scarlet Ribbon" for all the blood-letting they have caused.

"When his Excellency became ill, it was thought advisable that he leave the country for a time until he had recovered. This recovery has not occurred naturally, and it is feared that he needs medical assistance. Meanwhile, his enemies are looking for him all over Europe, and the latest information we have is that they are here in England. As you will perhaps now realise, his presence here in England is a secret, known only to his closest and most trusted allies. If his whereabouts were known to his enemies, his life would not be worth two farthings. He therefore instructed me to bring a doctor to examine him – a doctor, he stressed, who is as discreet and trustworthy as he is skilled in all branches of medicine. I have therefore made numerous searching inquiries, Dr. Kazinczy, and your name has been mentioned to me several times as someone who is as discreet as he is skilful.'

"'I am flattered,' I said, 'but a little surprised. I had no idea that my name was known to anyone outside my own parish. May I ask who it was that recommended me?'

161

"My visitor put his finger to his lips. 'I would rather not say,' he replied. 'You will understand, I believe, that inquiries as to the discretion of someone are themselves subject to discretion.'

"'Yes, of course,' I said. 'Can you tell me, then, something of the patient himself – his age, for instance, and general health?'

"'He is about forty-five years of age,' my visitor replied. 'He has a very strong constitution, and his health has always been first class – until, that is, his present illness.'

"'What are the symptoms of his affliction, then?'

"'The chief one is a great pain in his left side. Here,' he added, indicating with his finger-tips a place between his ribs and his waist. 'Because of this, he finds it very difficult to find a position in which he is not in pain. Even walking, which you might suppose would not be affected in any way, is so painful as to be almost impossible.'

"'I see,' I said, thinking to myself that it sounded like a kidney stone. 'Well, I will certainly go and examine him, but you must understand that I may not be able to solve his problems straight away. When would he like me to visit him?'

"'Immediately,' said my visitor in a firm tone. 'I have a cab waiting outside.'

"'Very well,' I said, 'but you must give me five minutes to get ready.' This my visitor agreed to, and I hurried upstairs to tell my wife I should be going out. I took the opportunity to fortify myself with a slice of bread and cheese. Then, packing everything I thought I might need into my bag, and picking up a volume of medical reference, I informed my visitor that I was ready. 'May I take your name?' I asked. 'Just for my records,' I added, as he seemed to hesitate.

"'You may call me Ferdinand,' said he at length.

"'Is that your first name or your last name?' I asked.

"'First name, last name – what does it matter?' said he with a shake of the head. 'From your point of view, Dr. Kazinczy, it is my only name.'

"As he shook his head, my eye was drawn to a curious scar on his upper cheek, just below his left eye, which was in the shape of a large 'X'. I had noticed it earlier, without really thinking about it, but now my gaze must have rested on it a little, for he put his hand up to it and touched it with his finger-tips. 'It is not pretty, that,' said he. 'But at least I came out of the encounter alive – the other man was not so fortunate. Put my name down, then,' he continued in an irritable tone, 'and we can be off.'

"'Very well,' said I, writing his name on one of my sheets of paper. A minute later, we were in the cab and rattling away in the darkness.

"As I watched the street-lamps passing us by, as we turned south and made our way down towards Bethnal Green, I wondered how far we should have to go, and I asked my companion.

"'That I cannot tell you,' he returned. 'Where my master is in hiding is a closely guarded secret.'

"'Oh, yes, of course,' said I quickly, fearing I had been indiscreet in asking the question. 'I understand. Well,' I added with a smile, 'I don't mind, so long as I can get back home before bed-time!'

"My companion regarded me with a cold look, and did not return my smile. '"Before bed-time,"' he repeated in a sombre tone. 'Yes, that should be possible.' After that, he lapsed once more into complete silence.

"From Bethnal Green we made our way down to Shoreditch, and so across the river, at length pulling up before London Bridge Station. Without a word, my companion opened the door, stepped from the cab, and held the door open for me to follow him. I assumed that we were about to take a train to somewhere in Kent, and hoped that it would not be too far, but, to my surprise, we passed the front of the station without pausing, and walked round the side. There, a private closed carriage stood. At our approach, a man who had been sitting on the pavement edge, smoking a pipe, sprang to his feet and pulled open the carriage door.

"In a moment we were in the carriage, whereupon, to my surprise, my companion drew the curtains and pulled down the blinds on all the windows 'It is better for you if you don't know where we are going,' said he. 'When I say 'better', I mean 'safer',' he added after a moment in a grim tone. 'Our enemies are very violent men, who would slit your throat as soon as look at you. What you do not know, you cannot be forced to divulge.'

"'I see,' I said, feeling a little unnerved at the thought of these violent, desperate men.

"After that, we did not speak again for a long time. But the silence in which we passed the journey had a surprising consequence. In the absence of conversation or any other distraction, I found myself listening with unusual attention to the noise of the traffic in the street and the sound of our carriage wheels upon the cobbles. Round a sharp right-hand corner we rattled, the carriage swaying as we turned, then round a second corner, then a third. I had almost completely lost my bearings by this time, but I felt fairly sure that we were not making our way down into Kent, as I had at first supposed, but perhaps to somewhere in the south-western suburbs. Further corners followed, this way and that, until I felt quite bewildered by all the changes of direction. But then a different sound came to my ears, which surprised me so much that I fear that my mouth fell open. I glanced at my companion and saw that he was watching me closely.

163

"'The traffic is very dense at this time of day,' I remarked, to conceal, as I hoped, what I was really thinking. For what I had heard was the distinctive sound that vehicles make when crossing one of the long bridges over the Thames. If I was right – and I felt sure that I was – then we were heading north again, back the way we had come! Clearly, these people were prepared to go to great lengths to keep their whereabouts secret and throw any pursuers off the scent.

"After several minutes of what seemed like very slow progress, we abruptly lurched forward and the horse broke into a rapid trot. Presumably, we were through the City and making our way out into the suburbs again. We then raced along with scarcely a pause, for some considerable time, our carriage swaying alarmingly at times with the great speed at which we were travelling, until at length we slowed a little, and I thought we must be reaching our destination. Where we were I had no idea, as I had no way of knowing which road we had taken north from the City, but I judged that we must be at least as far as Highbury or Dalston, and perhaps much further than that. For all I could tell, we might even be in the vicinity of my own surgery.

"My companion lifted one of the blinds a little and peered out. I could not imagine what he could see, as the night was a black one, but he evidently saw something, for as he lowered the blind again he turned to me and spoke.

"'We are almost there,' said he in a lugubrious tone. 'I must warn you not to say anything unless you are asked, Doctor. My master does not like idle chatter, and he is in such grave distress that his reaction is likely to be an irritable one.'

"'I understand,' I replied. I felt a little insulted that he should consider that I, a professional man, would engage in 'idle chatter', as he put it, but I said nothing. Perhaps, I reflected, in the country from which they came – wherever that might be – such insulting language was commonplace.

"'We have had to secure the assistance of one or two local people,' continued my companion. 'They have been sworn to secrecy as to my master's whereabouts, and have been made to understand that any loose talk could cost the lives of all of us, but other than that, they know little. The best thing for you to do is to ignore them. If you wish to request anything you need, you should do it through me.' I nodded, but that was evidently insufficient affirmation, for he fixed me with a piercing stare. 'Do you understand?' he demanded, in what I can only describe as a threatening tone.

"'Yes, certainly,' I replied. With every pronouncement my companion made, my spirits sank a little lower. I began to wonder what on earth I had let myself in for. I hope I don't sound too mean or selfish, but I confess that my sense of anticipation, the focus of my thoughts, had already shifted from the patient I was about to see to the moment when I would have done my duty as a physician and could get away from these people and go home again.

"Presently, I heard the driver call something to the horse as he reined him in, and we came to an abrupt halt.

"'We are here,' said Ferdinand, rising to his feet. 'Don't forget what I have told you!'

"I followed him from the carriage and along a narrow, muddy path. Ahead of us in the darkness, the yet-darker shape of a large house loomed up. A small lantern by the front door threw a weak, yellowy light upon the path, and it was well that it did, for there was not the tiniest speck of light from any other source in any direction. Clearly, wherever we were, we were well away from the public roads and streets of the north London suburbs.

"As we approached the lantern, I saw that it was fixed on a large, heavy-looking porch at the front of the house, the sort of porch which is a common feature of very large old houses. Within the dark recess of this porch was the front door. My companion thumped on it with his gloved fist, and after a moment it was opened a crack. 'Let us in,' commanded Ferdinand in an imperious tone, at which the door was pulled back a little and we made our way into a dimly-lit hallway. 'Dowse that light out there!' said Ferdinand. 'It's not needed now, and it gives our position away! This way, Doctor!' he continued, turning to me.

"I followed him along the hall, and up a dark, uncarpeted staircase. On the wall near the top, just where the stair took a sharp turn to the right, a small candle was flickering fitfully in a sconce, in front of an old enamelled religious picture of some sort. When we reached the landing at the top of the stairs, it was almost pitch black, but Ferdinand was evidently familiar with the layout of the house, for he pressed on without pause, and I followed him as well as I could in the darkness. Abruptly we halted, and a narrow slit of light near the floor indicated that we had reached a door.

"'My master is in here,' said he in a low tone. 'He may be asleep, for he has taken something to relieve the pain which kept him awake most of last night.'

"'Paregoric?' I asked.

"'No, that was too weak, so we got him a stronger tincture of opium.'

"'What, laudanum?'

"'Yes.'

"'I hope you are aware that laudanum is very dangerous stuff,' I said. 'There is only a small difference between an effective dose and a fatal dose.'

"'Don't you worry about that, Doctor,' said Ferdinand in a dismissive tone. 'You just concentrate on healing your patient!'

"'But I must worry about it,' I insisted. I was, I admit, irritated by his condescending manner. 'There is not much point in my solving the problem of his pain if he then kills himself with laudanum.'

"'Very well,' said Ferdinand after a moment. 'I shall keep an eye on him.' He rapped with his knuckles on the wooden panelling of the door, then pushed it open.

"The room beyond was dimly lit by two oil-lamps, both turned down very low. The air was thick and heavy with a sweet, burnt smell, which I recognized at once.

"'Someone has been smoking opium in here.' I said.

"'My master asked for it, to ease his pain.'

"'What, on top of the laudanum? He will surely kill himself, sooner rather than later, at this rate! We must open the window, and get some fresh air in here at once, or I myself shall pass out, and then I shall not be able to help him!'

"Somewhat reluctantly, it seemed, Ferdinand helped me pull down the top half of the window, and a strong gust of cold air blew into the room. There was a loud groan from behind me, and I turned to see that the man on the bed was stirring. 'I'll examine the patient now,' I said to Ferdinand. I asked him to bring one of the lamps to the bedside and turn it up. Then, just as I was bending over him, the man on the bed threw back his covers, turned my way, and began to raise himself up.

"With an involuntary cry, I stopped and took a step backwards. For a moment, I could not make out in that dim light what it was I was looking at. Where I had expected to see my patient's face, there was nothing but a grimy, featureless lump. Then, as Ferdinand brought the lamp closer, I was just able to see that the sick man's head was wound round and round with dirty-looking bandages, so that it was completely covered, and nothing could be seen of his face or his hair. From two narrow slits in the bandage, a pair of sharp eyes looked out at me, reflecting the light of the lamp.

"Abruptly, I felt Ferdinand's hand on my arm. 'You are unnerved by your patient's appearance,' he whispered, his mouth so close behind me that I could feel his breath upon my ear. 'Do not concern yourself, Doctor. He had an accident with some boiling water, and his face is covered to protect his raw skin. It is irrelevant to the malady for which he requires your aid.'

"'Who is this?' interrupted the man on the bed, in a deep, unpleasant voice.

"'It is the doctor,' responded Ferdinand. 'He has come to attend to you.'

"Without warning, the man on the bed shot out his hand and seized my arm in a vice-like grip. 'Let me see,' he said, drawing me closer to him. 'Do you know what will happen to you if you break your trust?' he demanded of me.

"I hesitated, unsure as to his meaning. 'I know that everything must be kept secret,' I responded at length. I would have said more, but at that moment he let out a loud cry of pain, released his grip on my arm, and collapsed back onto the bed.

"I signalled to Ferdinand to bring the lamp closer, and then proceeded to make a general examination of the man."

Dr. Kazinczy paused and ran his fingers through his hair. "Was any medical examination ever conducted in such strange circumstances?" said he with a shake of the head. "I felt I was living through some horrible dark nightmare from which I hoped I might soon wake up. But for the moment, I knew I must carry on. I will not weary you with the details of my examination. No doubt you are familiar with it, Dr. Watson," he continued, addressing me.

I nodded. "Familiar enough," I replied, "although I have never been called upon to do it myself since I qualified."

"Suffice it to say, then, that the result of my examination was that I was practically certain that the patient was indeed suffering from a stone, just as I had thought when I had first heard his symptoms. I gave them my opinion, and Ferdinand drew me away, as the man on the bed fell back into his opium-induced sleep. 'What should we do, then, Doctor?' he asked me in a low tone.

"'You must get him to a hospital as quickly as possible.'

"'Impossible!' he cried. 'Whatever needs to be done, must be done here, and by you!'

"I explained to him that, in such a case, surgery was always a last resort, and that however severe the pain might be at the moment, it could pass away as abruptly as it had started. I asked him how long the patient had suffered from the pain in his side.

"'About three days,' said he. 'The first day was weak pain. Yesterday and today is severe pain.'

"'Then this is not what drove him from his homeland?'

"'No. That was something else. Never mind about that. It has cleared up now. We thought it was all part of the same ailment, but perhaps it is not. What is bothering him now is what you have seen. You must do something about it.'

"I considered the matter. I was not sure that I believed anything now that this man who called himself Ferdinand was telling me. First he had said that his master had been ill for several weeks, now he was saying it

167

was a matter of a few days. Just as he had said earlier that their presence in England was a closely-guarded secret, known to no one, but had also told me that their enemies were in England, looking for them. All I really knew for certain was what I had learnt with my own eyes and my own finger-tips, that the man on the bed was suffering from a stone, probably in or near his kidney. 'Can you get a lemon?' I asked Ferdinand.

"'It may be difficult at this time of the year,' he replied dubiously. 'I will try.'

"'Get three or four,' I said. 'You must get your master to drink a glass of water every hour or two, and into every glass you must squeeze a quarter of a lemon. That is likely to do him as much good as anything I can do for him.'

"'But if that doesn't help, you must cut him open and remove the stone.'

"I shook my head. 'You need a specialist for that. You will find one in a hospital.'

"He insisted that they could not risk going to a hospital, and insisted that I must perform the operation. 'You are a qualified surgeon, are you not?' he demanded. Then he took my arm and led me out of the room, onto the dark landing. 'You must do this,' he said in a harsh tone, the sort of tone which admitted no possibility of contradiction, 'or you will surely have his Excellency's blood on your conscience forever – and perhaps the blood of all of us.'

"He took a firm grip of my elbow and propelled me forward, along the corridor and down the stair. When he spoke again, at the foot of the stair, it was in a louder, threatening tone.

"'If, for whatever selfish reason of your own, you refuse to help us, you may find your decision turns out to be an unfortunate one. In short, you may regret it. Indeed, your whole family may regret it – your wife, for instance.'

"I stopped. 'Are you threatening me?' I asked.

"'No,' said he. 'I am simply warning you, Dr. Kazinczy. The warning is for your own good. I have told you of the League of the Golden Ribbon, who would cut your throat for sixpence and think nothing of it. But there are others, too – faceless men and women who may be all around us even now, as we speak. Some of these are supposed to be on our side, but I cannot control them, and thus cannot answer for them. For your own sake, and that of your family, you must do as I ask.'

"He paused. 'I shall come for you at the same time tomorrow. Please be ready, with everything packed that you might need. Now, Simpson will show you where you can wash your hands.'

168

"As he spoke, a man materialised out of the darkness in the hall. I think he had been there all the time, but I had not seen him. 'This way,' said he, in a low, guttural voice, and I followed his grey shape along the hall in the darkness. He pushed a door open, and we passed into a plain, bare room, evidently a kitchen, illuminated by a single small lamp which stood on a wooden table in the centre of the room. 'There's the sink,' said my guide.

"I washed my hands under the cold water tap and, without speaking, the man handed me a piece of rag which was evidently meant to serve as a towel. 'Is there any hot water in the house?' I asked him, as he stood there in silence, watching me.

"He shook his head. 'No. To get hot water, we would have to light the fire here, and I was told not to, in case the smoke from the chimney gave our position away.'

"'Well, if I come again tomorrow I shall need plenty of hot water. Can you tell them?' There was a grunt of assent. 'How did the man upstairs hurt his face?' I asked as I finished drying my hands. 'I heard he scalded it.'

"'"Scalded it"?' the man repeated in a tone of surprise. 'No, there's nothing wrong with his face. Didn't they tell you? He just doesn't want anybody to see it, in case they recognise him.'

"'Yes, of course. I know all about that,' I said quickly. 'I must have just misheard something about his face.'

"'Anyway, I'm not supposed to talk to you,' said the man.

"I nodded, and held my hand up in a gesture of acceptance. 'Of course,' I said. 'I understand.' After that we did not speak again. In my own mind, however, I noted that this was yet another example of contradictory information that I had been given. It almost sounded as if the man who called himself 'Ferdinand' had just been making things up on the spur of the moment, and I began to wonder if anything at all that he had told me was really true.

"My guide led me back to the darkness of the front hall. 'Wait here,' he said, and I heard a door open and close as he disappeared into the darkness.

"I had been standing there for what I suppose was just a minute or two – although in that silent darkness it felt more like a quarter-of-an-hour – when a door opened at the side of the hall, and a figure emerged. As there was a lamp lit in the room beyond – although not a very bright one – I could see it was a young woman with dark hair. As the light was behind her, I could not make out her face very well, but I could see that she was of slim build and carried herself in an elegant sort of way. 'Hello,' I said, more from a sort of instinctive politeness than for any other reason. For a

169

moment, she stopped, and looked at me with piercing eyes and a rigid expression. Then she closed the door behind her, passed on down the hall without replying, and disappeared into the darkness. I was still thinking about her, and wondering who she was, when another door opened, further along the hall, and the man calling himself Ferdinand emerged.

"'I am sorry to keep you waiting,' said he. 'Are you ready to leave now?'

"I said I was and, without further comment, he led the way to the front door. Someone again seemed to materialise out of the darkness, who unbolted the front door and opened it for us.

"As we stepped out of the house, a very sharp, cold wind was blowing, and there were drops of rain in the air. 'Just follow close behind me,' said Ferdinand, and we set off along the muddy path. My eyes had become so accustomed to the inky darkness within the house that the darkness outside now seemed almost light by comparison, and I could see through the murk that a horse and carriage awaited us at the end of the path. Into this carriage we climbed, and away it rattled, into the night.

"Again, we rambled about for thirty or forty minutes, until I was at last discharged at the side of London Bridge Station. 'Remember,' said Ferdinand, as I stepped down onto the pavement, 'be ready with everything you will need when I call for you at six o'clock tomorrow evening. In the meantime, not a word to anyone about anything you have seen or heard this evening. Not a word – do you understand? You may be being watched, Dr. Kazinczy. And if you break your trust, we shall certainly know about it.' His voice was full of menace as he spoke these last words, and I don't mind admitting to a certain nervousness and apprehension at his threats. I certainly didn't want to risk provoking any of these people to violence."

"And yet," said Sherlock Holmes, "despite his threatening manner, and your own fears and anxieties, you have come to consult us."

"I could hardly sleep at all last night," said our visitor after a moment, "and lay awake for hours, going over and over the matter in my mind, trying to decide what to do. Eventually, I decided that, despite what Ferdinand had said to me, I must tell someone of what I had become involved in – someone, ideally, who had some familiarity with London's darkest and most mysterious happenings. I could think of no one known personally to me who might be suitable, and was for a time at a loss, until I thought of you, Mr. Holmes. Although I don't generally follow the criminal or other sensational news very closely, I have from time to time read of your involvement in fascinating investigations of all kinds, and I thought you might be the very man."

"You have done the right thing, Dr. Kazinczy. It is a remarkable account you have given us, and certainly a dark and mysterious one. Do you believe you have been followed on your way here?"

"I cannot be sure. This morning I saw a man across the street from my surgery who appeared to be watching the house, and I thought it might be one of Ferdinand's men. It is for that reason I have brought my medical bag with me, so that I can always say I was here to visit an old patient who has moved from Hackney to the West End."

Holmes nodded. "I take it from what you have told us," said he, "that you did not tell your wife about your evening's adventure."

"Only in the very broadest of terms. I did not wish to recount the matter to her in any detail, as I knew she would become so anxious about it. More than that, I knew she would do her utmost to prevent my going to see these strange, menacing people again."

"But you are determined to go?"

"I must. Quite apart from Ferdinand's threats, I don't see that I have any choice, Mr. Holmes. I may feel less than enthusiastic about Ferdinand and the others, and more than a little concerned about all their vicious and violent enemies – the League of the Golden Ribbon and the others – but, when all is said and done, I now have a patient there who has clearly been in severe pain. I have diagnosed what I believe to be the cause of that pain, but the oath I took as a medical man is worth less than nothing if I don't at least try to do something to alleviate his suffering."

"Bravo!" said Holmes with enthusiasm. "Well said!"

"Are you confident," I asked our visitor, "of performing the appropriate surgery on your patient if necessary?"

"I very much hope it doesn't come to that, Dr. Watson, but if I have to do it, then I shall."

"Your patient will need anaesthetic. Which do you favour?"

"Ether. I regard it as safer than any of the alternatives."

"I am inclined to agree with you. I have a suggestion to make, then," I said. "What I propose is that I accompany you tonight, and act as your anaesthetist."

Our visitor's features expressed surprise. "That is an extremely generous offer, Dr. Watson," said he after a moment, "but I could not possibly accept it. I feel there is danger in that house."

"No doubt, but I have faced greater danger before. You cannot both perform the surgical procedure safely and also be responsible for the anaesthetic. That is too much to ask of anyone. Nor can you with much confidence ask anyone else to do it. I, on the other hand, have considerable experience with anaesthetics. I absolutely insist on coming. Besides, if I come with you, that gives you a better excuse for calling in here today than visiting some old, mythical patient. You can tell them that you must have someone with you who is experienced in the use of anaesthetic, and that you at once thought of me, whom you met some years ago. Have you ever spent any time in Barts?"

"What, St Bartholomew's Hospital? Yes, I spent over six months there, assisting one of the best surgeons in England. That was part of what I had to do to convince the Royal Society of my fitness to practise medicine here."

"Excellent!" I cried. "That is where I did much of my initial training. When were you there?"

"About ten years ago."

"So was I. So, if anyone asks, that is where we met! I take it you have all the equipment you need? Good," I said, as he nodded his head. "Then that is settled."

Sherlock Holmes had been sitting without speaking for some time, a frown of concentration on his face.

"What do you think?" I asked.

"What I think," responded Holmes after a moment, "is that there is indeed very great danger in that house. I am very reluctant to allow you to go, Watson. On the other hand, if you don't go, I shall feel just as uneasy at Dr. Kazinczy going there alone. At least if the two of you are there together, you can, in a sense, share the danger, and each keep a watch over the other."

"What will *you* do?" I asked.

"I shall try to learn a little more about these singular people and the house they are occupying."

"I cannot think where you could possibly start," remarked Kazinczy. "It seems an impossible task."

"Come, come," said Holmes. "As a man of science, Doctor, you must appreciate that there is very little which is truly impossible to learn if a man sets his mind to it. The situation is not as hopeless as you make out. In seeking to learn new information, we must start with what we already know. You are convinced that the house you were taken to is to the north of London, rather than the south?"

"Certainly. I have no doubt we crossed the Thames after leaving London Bridge Station, and then crossed it again on the way back."

"Then that information will be my starting-point."

"But that still leaves dozens of square miles!"

"Don't let that concern you," said Holmes with a chuckle. "You will go to the old house again this evening at six o'clock, with Dr. Watson here. That is enough for you to have to think about. I must warn you again, however, that I fear there is great danger in that house. Do what you are asked to do by these people, and do not speak out of turn in any way that might anger them. Do not under any circumstances mention my name, nor this meeting we have had. Be alert the whole time and keep a watch on each other, but do not be tempted to have any private conversations with each other while you are there, for you will almost certainly be watched closely by these people."

Dr. Kazinczy gave me detailed instructions as to how to find his surgery in Hackney, and then, after a brief further discussion of the medical aspects of the matter, he took his leave. Sherlock Holmes went out shortly afterwards without saying where he was going, and I turned to my medical books to refresh my knowledge of the ailment from which Dr. Kazinczy's patient was suffering.

At four o'clock in the afternoon, I left our chambers with my medical bag in my hand. Holmes had not yet returned nor sent any message, so I had no idea where he had got to, nor whether he had managed to learn anything about the man calling himself Ferdinand and the others.

I took a Metropolitan train from Baker Street to Liverpool Street, and a Great Eastern train from there to Hackney Downs, as Kazinczy had suggested. The trains were very busy, and as I looked round the crowded platforms and packed carriages, I wondered to myself where everyone was going. From their appearance, I imagined that most of them were returning home after a day's work. I doubted if any of these hundreds of people who surrounded me were on an errand quite as strange as mine, bound for that dark and isolated house with its atmosphere of menace, inhabited by people who, according to Kazinczy's account, scarcely seemed to speak at all. I glanced again at my fellow-travellers in the railway carriage, some chatting, others immersed in their evening papers. So familiar and commonplace did it all seem, that for a moment I could scarcely believe my own memory of the account which Dr. Kazinczy had given us that morning. With a shake of the head, to try to clear my thoughts, I told myself to concentrate on the medical questions involved, and push all the other aspects of the matter to the back of my mind. Perhaps things would become clearer, perhaps they would not, but at least I could play my part as well as I was able. Then, whatever happened, I should know that I had done my best.

The directions Dr. Kazinczy had given me were very clear, so it was a simple task to find his surgery, which I reached at a quarter-to-six. The maid had clearly been told to expect me, for upon giving her my name, I was at once shown into a room at the back of the house and offered a cup of tea, which I declined.

As I sat there in silence – for the sounds from elsewhere in the house reached me only as faint murmurs – I regret to say that my mind had wandered once more from the medical aspects of my prospective journey to the people in that dark house which Dr. Kazinczy had visited the night before. Who were they? Where had they come from?

My thoughts were interrupted by the sudden opening of the door, and Kazinczy put his head in.

"If you are ready, Dr. Watson, we had best be off. Our guide is here."

"Ferdinand?"

"Yes. I have managed to convince him, with some difficulty, that I need you there this evening to administer the anaesthetic, but he wishes to see you before we leave."

I followed Kazinczy into his consulting room. A tall, thin-faced man was standing by the desk, a grim, almost menacing expression on his features. He cast a cold, calculating eye over me as I entered.

"What is your name?" said he, without preamble.

"Watson," I replied.

"Do you have experience in what you will be required to do this evening?"

"Yes."

"Where are you in practice?"

"I'm not. I was an army surgeon, but was badly wounded in Afghanistan, and was eventually pensioned off."

"Where do you live, then? I may need to get in touch with you again, so I must have your address."

I hesitated. I did not feel inclined to give my private address to this stranger just because he demanded it. On the other hand, I did not wish to arouse his suspicions in any way, or create any difficulties for Kazinczy. "221b Baker Street," I said at length.

"Baker Street is not the cheapest place to live in London," he remarked, "especially for someone getting by on a wound pension."

"That is true," I returned, "but living close to the centre of town does have its advantages. I can get to most places on foot, and thus save on travelling costs."

"Where did you qualify?" he asked abruptly, as if he had not listened to my previous response.

"Here, in London."

"And where did you meet Dr. Kazinczy?"

"At Barts – St Bartholomew's Hospital."

"I know what Barts is. What year did you meet him?"

I pretended to think for a moment, as if trying to recollect when it was. "I'm not sure," I said. "About '76 or '77, I think – nearly ten years ago."

"My problem, you see, is this, Dr. Watson: I told Dr. Kazinczy to be discreet, and tell no one what he had seen or heard last night, but he went straight off and told you about it. How do I know that you will not do the same? For all I know, you may already have done so."

"I can assure you I have told no one anything," I responded. "In any case," I added quickly, "I have nothing to tell. All I know, other than the patient's symptoms and Dr. Kazinczy's diagnosis, is that the patient is from abroad and does not wish his whereabouts to be generally known."

For a long moment, Ferdinand regarded me in perfect silence, his rigid, cold eyes fixed immovably on mine, as if he would peer into the deepest recesses of my soul. Then, without further remark, he picked up his hat from the desk and turned to the door. "We must go now," he said. "We're late as it is."

A four-wheeler was waiting for us outside, which set off at a fast clip as soon as we were aboard. The journey we took through the dark streets was exactly as Kazinczy had described to us that morning. We alighted at London Bridge Station, where a closed carriage awaited us, then set off once more. Throughout the lengthy journey which followed, neither Kazinczy nor I spoke, save only once, and that only very briefly, to discuss some technical questions concerning the anaesthetic.

This silence – on my part, at least – was because I feared that if I fell into general conversation, I might inadvertently let something slip which would reveal to Ferdinand that I had only met Kazinczy for the first time that very morning, and that had it not been for the chance of my sharing chambers with Sherlock Holmes, whom Kazinczy had come to Baker Street to consult, I should never have met him at all. What thoughts were passing in Kazinczy's mind, I could not, of course, say, but from his silence, I fancied that they were not too dissimilar from my own.

Eventually, after what seemed an absolutely interminable length of time, our carriage abruptly turned off the road into softer, quieter ground, and proceeded very slowly for some considerable distance before coming to a final halt.

"We are here, gentlemen," said Ferdinand, in a low, sepulchral voice, as he put up one of the window-blinds. The night outside was pitch black. "Follow me."

The man waiting inside the door had evidently been told to look out for us, for he opened the door as we approached along the footpath. "Any news?" demanded Ferdinand in a gruff tone, to which the other man gave a negative reply.

We followed Ferdinand into the dark hall and up the stairs, our feet clattering and echoing on the bare, uncarpeted boards.

"I think you will find that my master is in somewhat better health today," said he as we reached the landing.

"Oh?" responded Kazinczy in a tone of surprise. "You did not say anything about that when we spoke earlier, in my surgery."

"I did not wish you to make any difficulty about coming, perhaps using that as an excuse."

"You had no need to worry on that score," said Kazinczy in an indignant tone. "Once I had examined him last night and made my diagnosis, he became in a sense my patient, and I took on full responsibility for him. Whatever you had told me of him this evening, good or bad, I should still have wanted to come, to assess the matter for myself. Did you manage to get hold of any lemons for him?"

"Yes. He has been having lemon juice all day."

"Good. Let us examine him, then."

Ferdinand pushed open a door and we followed him into a dimly-lit room. Other than a bed, a small table and a single chair, the room was bare, with no carpet on the floor, and no curtain at the window. The air was thick and heavy, and it didn't surprise me that Kazinczy stepped immediately to the window and pulled it open. "You can shut it again when we've gone, if you wish," he said to Ferdinand, "but I can't conduct an examination in this atmosphere – I can hardly breathe!"

At the sound of the window's opening, the occupant of the bed stirred and raised himself up a little. I don't mind admitting that, despite being forewarned by the account Kazinczy had given us that morning, I still felt a sudden thrill of horror at the sight of this strange creature rearing up before us, seemingly covered with dirty bandages from head to foot, and with no discernible human features, like something from an evil dream. Kazinczy approached the bed, as the figure subsided once more, and began his examination. He asked several questions concerning the strength of the pain and its position, and how it compared with the pain of yesterday, but the answers were given in such a deep, gravelly whisper that it was clear he could not hear them. Ferdinand then leaned close over the bandaged figure and interpreted his responses for us. "He says the pain is lessened slightly," he related, turning to us, "but is still bad. It has also moved. It is now lower in his side."

"That is very good news," said Kazinczy, "and is what I had hoped for. It often happens after three or four days of static pain. If it is lower down today, it should be even lower tomorrow, and less painful. Surgery will almost certainly not be necessary."

176

Ferdinand regarded my companion suspiciously. "You're not using what I've told you as an excuse not to do anything, are you?" he demanded in a menacing tone.

"Of course not," returned Kazinczy dismissively. "But I thought I'd made it clear to you last night that surgery is a last resort. The operation is a difficult and dangerous one."

"What does your friend think?" demanded Ferdinand in an unpleasant tone.

"I agree with Dr. Kazinczy in every respect," I said.

Ferdinand stood in silence for a moment, his face grim. Then he opened his mouth as if to speak, but whatever he was about to say I was never to learn, for at that moment there came a terrific racket of banging and crashing from somewhere downstairs.

"What the – !" cried Ferdinand, then sprang for the door.

I turned to Kazinczy. "Have you any idea what's going on?" I asked in alarm.

"Absolutely not. The house was as quiet as the grave last night. I can't imagine what is happening."

Even as he spoke, there came a final deafening crash from downstairs, as if a door had been violently burst open. This was followed by a lot of shouting, a woman's screaming, and what sounded like a pistol shot.

"What on earth can it be?" I cried.

Kazinczy clapped his hand to his head, an expression of terror on his face. "The League of the Golden Ribbon!" he cried.

Ferdinand had yanked the door open and raced out onto the landing, but as we made to follow him, the creature on the bed behind us, no doubt roused by all the noise, lurched up again. Before I knew what was happening, he had seized my wrist in a grip like iron, his finger-nails digging deep into my flesh like the talons of some dreadful bird of prey, so that I could not move.

Kazinczy had reached the open doorway, but he got no further. He stepped back in alarm as a large figure in dark clothing abruptly appeared in the opening, barring his way. An instant later, I saw that it was a police constable. "Not so fast, you!" said he in a loud voice. Then, turning, he called out to someone further along the landing, "There's more of them in here, sir!"

A moment later, the first policeman was joined by another, in the braided uniform of an inspector. "Who are you?" he demanded of Kazinczy.

"My name is Kazinczy. I am a doctor."

"Who is he?" the inspector asked, indicating me.

"He is a medical colleague of mine. His name is Watson."

"What are you doing here?"

"Attending to this man, who is ill."

The inspector stepped forward with a frown. He had evidently not noticed our patient before. As he came closer, the bandaged man released his grip on my wrist and moved away slightly. The inspector turned up the lamp on the table, and peered closely at this strange figure. "Ah!" said he. "I believe this is who we are after!" He reached forward, and as he did so, the bandaged man at first shrank back against the wall to the side of the bed, leaning over as if reaching for something behind the bed, then, with a fierce, animal cry, sprang forward, a long-bladed butcher's knife in his hand, and launched a violent attack on the policeman.

"Oh, would you!" cried the latter, as he managed to avoid the knife, seized the man's arms, and wrestled him to the floor. "Constable! The cuffs!"

In a moment, the bandaged man was subdued, handcuffed, and led away. Then the inspector dusted himself down and turned to us. For myself, I confess I was in a state of stunned confusion at these sudden events, and, to judge by the expression on his features, so was Kazinczy.

"Do you know who any of these men are?" the inspector asked.

"No, I've no idea," I replied, as Kazinczy shook his head. "I understood that some of them were from abroad."

The inspector snorted. "Oh, did you?" he remarked with a harsh laugh. For a moment he regarded us in silence. "For all I know," he said, "you may know nothing, or you may know something. I can't tell yet, so you'll have to come along with the rest of them, until we get it all sorted out."

I picked up my medical bag and followed the others downstairs. Two lamps had been lit in the hall, and the bright light shining up the stair revealed for the first time the bare, dirty floorboards and the cracked and flaking plaster on the walls, which were festooned with filthy-looking cobwebs. The front door stood wide open, the wood cracked and splintered, and in the hall a large number of uniformed policemen were standing guard over several handcuffed prisoners. These included, I observed, the bandaged man, the man calling himself Ferdinand, and a woman I hadn't seen before. As we reached the hall, the inspector asked his men if every room in the house had been searched, and when he was satisfied there could be no one else lurking anywhere in the house, he instructed his men to take the prisoners out to the vans which were waiting outside.

"What about these two?" asked one of the constables, indicating Kazinczy and myself. "Shall I put the cuffs on 'em?"

"I don't think that will be necessary," returned the inspector, shaking his head. "I doubt they'll give us any trouble. Just put them in the van with the rest of them."

I was thus, for the only time in my life, marched to a police van and pushed inside, where I sat down with three of the most disreputable-looking individuals imaginable, watched over by four large policemen.

It was a very bumpy ride until we reached the main road, and not much better after that, but eventually, after a journey of little more than ten minutes, the van drew to a halt, the door was opened, and we stepped out into a cobbled courtyard. Through a wide doorway we were ushered, and it soon became apparent that we were in a fairly large police station, although where it might be, I had no idea.

After standing around in a reception area for several minutes, we were taken, in ones and twos into a corridor which led to the cells. Just as I was turning into this corridor, a door at the back of the main room opened, and two tall men in plain clothes entered, walking quickly and talking as they went. I stopped in surprise. The first man I recognised at once as Inspector Gregson of Scotland Yard, who had often called in at our chambers in Baker Street to consult Sherlock Holmes, but the second man, to my utter amazement, was Holmes himself. What he might be doing here – wherever we were – I could not imagine. I tried to catch his eye, and thought for a moment that I had done so, but he seemed to look right through me, as though he had not recognised me, and followed Gregson through another doorway, and so out of the room. Moments later, I found myself locked in a cell with Kazinczy.

"I have just seen Holmes," I said, "but I don't think he noticed me."

"That's a pity," Kazinczy replied. "He might have been able to get us out of here. I wonder what he's doing here, anyway."

"I haven't the faintest idea," I said. "Do you know where we are?"

Kazinczy shook his head. "We weren't in the police van for very long, so we can't be all that far from that dilapidated old house." He shivered. "It may not be very enjoyable being arrested, but I think that, on balance, I'd rather be here than there, in that gloomy old house with those menacing people."

"I'm inclined to agree," I said. "I take it you had the bandaged man and Ferdinand in your van, as they weren't in mine. I just had three other men that I'd not seen before, who spent the journey looking sulky and not saying anything."

"Yes, I had the pleasure of their company – and that of the woman, too. But you were fortunate, Dr. Watson, if your journey was a quiet one. We had a fight in the van I was in."

"Was that Ferdinand, or the one he calls his 'master'?"

179

"Neither. They were quiet enough. It was the woman. She produced a devilish-looking little knife from a pocket somewhere in her skirt and went for one of the constables with it. He had to wrestle it off her, while she was biting him and kicking him and calling him every name under the sun. I don't think I've ever heard a woman speak like that before."

I shook my head. "I wonder who she is," I said, "and what she was doing at the old house."

Thus we talked, in a desultory sort of way, for some considerable time, hearing footsteps coming and going in the corridor outside the cell, and doors being opened and closed, until at length the footsteps stopped outside our cell, a bolt was drawn back, and the door was opened. The police inspector we had seen at the old house put his head in, introduced himself as Inspector Raynor, and asked us to accompany him to his office. There he offered us a cup of tea, which we accepted. "Now," said he, "tell me exactly how you became involved with these people."

I made a gesture to Kazinczy that he should do the talking, which he did, describing to the inspector the events of the previous evening much as he had related them to us that morning in Baker Street. From time to time, the policeman made notes of what was said, and when Kazinczy's account was finished, he nodded his head.

"Well, well," said he. "I can see it has been an anxious twenty-four hours for you. I'm sorry I've had to prolong the anxiety by keeping you here, but I didn't know for certain who you were, and couldn't risk your slipping away to warn others whom we might wish to arrest in connection with this business. Fortunately, your account is precisely confirmed by what I have heard from Dudley and the others, so you are free to go. I dare say you are looking forward to your supper."

"Who is Dudley?" I asked. "And where are we now?"

"I'm sorry. I forgot that you don't really know any of these people, or what has been going on. Where you are, Doctor, is Stoke Newington Police Station. You should be able to pick up a cab in the High Street outside to take you home. As for Dudley: He's the one with the scar on his cheek, the one who told you to call him 'Ferdinand'."

"I see," said Kazinczy. "But who exactly is he, and why was he pretending to be somebody else?"

"Vivian Dudley is a criminal," said the inspector, "and one of the most vicious and violent I have ever known. You are very fortunate to come out of their clutches in one piece, I can tell you. Just as you are, by profession a doctor, so he is, by profession, a criminal. As far as I am aware, he has never done anything in his life which was not criminal. As to what he's been doing for the last few days, I'd rather not say. Our investigation is not yet concluded, and there are some others still at large

180

that we wish to question on the matter. The fewer people who know what's afoot, the less chance of the people concerned being forewarned. You will find out soon enough what it's all about."

With that less than entirely satisfying explanation, our interview was concluded, and a minute later Kazinczy and I found ourselves in a dark and deserted Stoke Newington High Street, where a cold rain was falling. But if I had thought that the evening's surprises were at an end, I was mistaken. A short distance away, a four-wheeled cab stood beside the kerb. We were walking in that direction, and I was just wondering if the cab was free, when the door was opened and, for a brief moment, someone leaned out and beckoned to us.

"Careful," I whispered to Kazinczy as we approached the cab. "It may be a crony of Dudley's, hoping to get some information from us."

As we came closer to the cab, however, the door opened again and, to my surprise, a familiar figure leaned out.

"Holmes!" I cried. "What on earth are you doing here, sitting in the dark?"

"Waiting for you," he replied in that brisk and business-like tone with which I was so familiar. "I began to fear you would never get away at all!"

"I saw you earlier with Tobias Gregson, in the police station," I said. "Why did you ignore us?"

"Get in, out of the wet," said he, pushing the door further open. "Then we can be off, and I'll explain it to you as we go."

We climbed in, thankful to be out of the rain. Holmes rapped with his knuckles on the roof of the cab, which set off at a brisk trot, then settled himself back in his seat.

"You ask me why I ignored you earlier, Watson," said he, "and the answer is, I was doing you a favour."

"What!" I cried. "It seems an odd sort of favour, I must say, to ignore two perfectly innocent men being held in a police station!"

"Nevertheless, it *is* a favour," returned my friend, leaning forward and lowering his voice slightly. "You were surrounded at the time, Watson, by a selection of the worst villains in London. These men are hardened criminals, ruthless and violent. If they had suspected for even a moment that you or Dr. Kazinczy had been responsible – even partly responsible – for their capture, they would not leave you in peace. They would come to exact their vengeance, if not now, then later – next week, next month, next year. It was therefore vital that there should be no discernible connection between you and the forces of law and order. I had therefore already decided that if I saw you I would ignore you, and I had told Gregson to do the same."

"I see," said I. "In that case, thank you for your forethought and consideration, Holmes! And forgive my short temper – it's been a trying evening!"

"Yes, thank you," echoed Kazinczy, nodding his head. "It has certainly been an odd experience! But what is this business all about, Mr. Holmes? Inspector Raynor wouldn't tell us anything, except that the real name of the man who told me to call him 'Ferdinand' is in fact Vivian Dudley."

Holmes hesitated. "I regret that any explanation will have to wait for a few days, Doctor," he replied at length. "I have promised Raynor that I shall keep the matter to myself for the moment. However, I shall write to you in a day or two, to explain some aspects of the matter, at least."

We left Kazinczy at his house, where Holmes paid off the cab. Then he and I walked on to the railway station at Hackney Downs, my friend explaining that he was breaking up the journey in this way in order to make it more difficult for anyone to follow us without being seen. There were still plenty of people about, especially at the stations, and Holmes thought it better not to speak in public of the business which had taken us to that part of town. It was therefore not until we had reached our lodgings, finished our supper, and filled our pipes as we sat before a blazing fire, that we returned once more to the case which had provided such an anxious and hair-raising twenty-four hours for Dr. Kazinczy.

"It will perhaps be simplest, Watson," my friend began, "if I tell you how it seemed to me as I listened to Dr. Kazinczy's singular account this morning. He described the man who came to his consulting rooms as tall and angular, with a large hooked nose, and – most crucially from my point of view – with a distinctive scar upon his cheek, near his left eye. Now, I do not have such an encyclopaedic knowledge of London's criminals as you sometimes credit me with, but I do try to follow the careers of the most notorious of them, and when I heard about this man's scar and his general demeanour, I at once thought of Dudley. The more we heard, the more convinced I became that this identification was indeed correct. Dudley is an odd character, Watson: He has a certain degree of intelligence and cunning – more so, certainly, than most of the men he mixes with – and might, one feels, have made a worthwhile contribution to human life, but his character is a warped one, and he seems to see his fellow human beings only as people who can be intimidated or cheated out of whatever they possess. And if they possess nothing? Why, he will intimidate or cheat them anyway, just for the pleasure of doing so. His usual method is the use or threat of violence, in the employment of which he is perfectly ruthless."

"He sounds a thoroughly unpleasant individual," I remarked.

"He is. He rules the lives of all those unfortunate enough to cross his path with a mixture of physical violence and terror. Everyone is frightened of him, and he himself is frightened of no one, save only the one man who is worse than he is – a man by the name of Muldownie – but I will come to Muldownie in a moment. If Dudley could have got what he wanted from Kazinczy simply by the application of brute force and violence, then I have little doubt that that is the method he would have employed. But as the situation clearly demanded a different approach, he fell back on his other chief talent, which is a great facility for lying. I have it from many sources that Dudley is the most accomplished and convincing liar they have ever encountered."

"Does that mean that there is no truth whatever in what he told Kazinczy last night?"

"Very little. But if I was right, and it was indeed Dudley who visited Kazinczy's surgery last night, then what, I wondered, might he be up to? For that he was up to something, I could scarcely doubt: Whenever Dudley shows his face outside his usual haunts – which is not very often – it generally spells trouble for someone.

"The first thing I considered was whether it was really just chance that Kazinczy had been chosen, out of all the medical practitioners in London, for this mysterious consultation. I have generally found that when some event appears to have happened purely by chance, it is always worth looking into the circumstances surrounding it, for you often find that what appeared at first just a matter of chance has occurred for quite specific reasons. In this instance, Dudley himself had suggested that Kazinczy had been chosen because he had a reputation for discretion, but I rather doubted that that was really the case. It sounded a little too much like the sort of flattery a man like Dudley would employ to get someone to do what he wanted. There were, I thought, at least two other more likely explanations as to why Kazinczy had been chosen, either of which – or both – might be true. In the first place, Kazinczy's practice is in the eastern quarter of London, where Dudley and most of his associates live, so it was quite possible that Kazinczy was already known to some of them as a physician who concentrated on the medical condition of his patients and did not ask too many inconvenient questions. In the second place, although Kazinczy has been resident in England for more than ten years, and speaks English fluently, he is nevertheless a foreigner by birth, and as such might be presumed to have a smaller circle of relatives and acquaintances than a native-born doctor might, and who was also unlikely to follow the intricacies of the English news very closely. If this were true, it suggested that there might have been something in the news recently of which Dudley and his associates hoped that Kazinczy had no knowledge.

183

"Now, the only really significant points to arise from Kazinczy's account concerned the whereabouts of the decayed old house in which these people were staying, and the fact that an unidentified man there was suffering from what Kazinczy had diagnosed as a kidney stone. With regard to the whereabouts of these people, it seemed likely to me that the meandering journey which our client had been taken on, both going to and returning from the old house, was not so much to throw pursuers off the trail as to prevent Kazinczy himself from learning where it was. Thanks to his alertness, however, and the mistake they made in crossing the Thames, this was not entirely successful, and, despite the lengthy detour to London Bridge Station, it seemed certain that their destination was not to the south of London, but to the north."

"Yes," I agreed. "That seemed clear enough from his account."

"Now," Holmes continued, "the man that Kazinczy spoke to in the kitchen of the old house informed him that he had been forbidden to light a fire, in case the smoke from the chimney gave away their position."

"Yes, I remember that."

"But that is strange, is it not? At this time of the year, and in this weather, every chimney in London will be puthering out smoke. That the people in the house were so concerned about it suggested to me that they were not simply keen to prevent anyone from learning that they themselves were staying there, but that anyone at all was staying there. That in turn suggested that there was something odd or distinctive about the house, for if it had been simply an ordinary empty house, what would be so surprising about someone's renting it, moving in there, and lighting as many fires as he wished? It suggested, I thought, that the house had not only been empty before these people moved in, but was known to have been so for some considerable time. It might even have been abandoned and practically derelict, possibly even half in ruins. The description Kazinczy gave us of the interior – or as much of it as he could see – as uncarpeted and almost devoid of furniture, also supported that speculation.

"All in all, it seemed to me most likely that the occupants of the house were not renting it in any normal legal way, but that it was indeed an abandoned building, which they had simply broken into. If we were to find this house, therefore, we should need to look for a dilapidated and abandoned building, and probably one which was very isolated, as our client saw no other houses nearby, nor any lights anywhere near it. This latter point, that no lights were visible anywhere about, suggested to me that the house was probably not only isolated, but stood in a very low-lying position. For it was not very late in the evening when Kazinczy first arrived there, and if the house were in an elevated position, one or two lights would surely have been visible somewhere about, on one of the

184

many roads leading to the north. Now, much of the land to the north of London is very hilly, so most of it could, I thought, be safely ruled out. My best initial conjecture was that the old house lay somewhere in the flat marshlands of the River Lea, which separates the north-eastern suburbs of London from the county of Essex."

"Your reasoning seems clear and convincing," I remarked.

"Thank you. Now, what I proposed, to try to confirm my reasoning, was to equip myself with a large-scale map of the area, borrow a pony and trap, and drive back and forth over every road and track I could find in the Lea valley until I had identified the house. Given a little time, I was confident that I could find it. First of all, though, I wanted to learn something more of what the people in the old house were really up to."

"I can't imagine what that could be," I said with a shake of the head, "nor how you could possibly have hoped to find out."

Holmes chuckled. "I agree that the whole business appeared somewhat opaque," said he. "However, the way I reasoned it was this: The bandaged man's illness was really the only significant and indisputable fact in the whole business. I wondered, therefore, if this could possibly be somehow related to the item of news which, I suspected, Dudley and the others were hoping Kazinczy had not seen in his daily paper. On the face of it, it sounded a little unlikely, I admit, but I had no other starting-point, so after our client had left us this morning, I took myself round to Scotland Yard, to see if I could learn anything there.

"Fortunately, Inspector Gregson was in his office. I have been able to do him one or two small favours in the last couple of years, so he is always willing to oblige me when I come to him for information.

"I came straight to the point. 'Do you happen to know of anyone of interest to Scotland Yard who might be suffering from a kidney stone?' I asked him.

"At this, his mouth fell open in surprise. 'Now, how in Heaven's name do you know anything about that, Mr. Holmes?' he asked in a puzzled tone. 'Of course, it was in the local papers down there, but we tried to keep it out of the big national dailies. We didn't want anyone to get in a panic about it.'

"'Who is it, then?' I asked, intrigued by his very cautious manner, and wondering why anyone's illness might cause a panic.

"'Do you know anything of Albert Muldownie?'

"I nodded. 'Before his imprisonment, he was perhaps the most brutal and ruthless criminal in London in the last twenty years, with a gang he controlled with terror. He is almost certainly a murderer, and only cheated the gallows because of the mysterious disappearance of the chief witness for the prosecution.'

185

"'That's the man,' said Gregson, 'although you forgot to mention that the jury at his trial were also seriously intimidated. We knew that for a fact, but couldn't prove it. At least we got him on a lesser charge, and he was given a fairly stiff prison sentence, which he has been serving in Dartmoor.'

"'Is he the one with the kidney stone?'

"Gregson nodded. 'Yes. Prisoners get ill sometimes, like the rest of us, and have to receive treatment. If it had been a trivial complaint, he would have been seen to in the prison's own infirmary. But as it was a more serious matter, which might have needed surgery, it was decided to send him down to the Royal Naval Hospital at Plymouth. Unfortunately, his gang somehow got wind of this, intercepted the prison van between Dartmoor and Plymouth, attacked the guards, and spirited Muldownie away. How it was arranged, how they got him away from Plymouth, and where he is now, we have no idea.'

"'I believe he may be in London,' I said.

"'You may be right. We've been keeping an eye on former members of his gang, just in case he is here, but we've learnt nothing so far. We were particularly watching Vivian Dudley, who used to be Muldownie's right-hand man, and who has taken over the gang in his absence, but he seems to have dropped out of sight altogether recently. You'll appreciate why we've tried to keep Muldownie's escape out of the papers, though. There are a lot of people in the East End who were terrified of him in the past, and if they thought he was out of prison, they'd be terrified of him all over again. Dudley is bad enough, but Muldownie was even worse. But you haven't told me how you've heard anything about it, Mr. Holmes.'

"'It's soon told,' I said, and gave him a brief account of Dr. Kazinczy's experiences last night.

"'Well, I never!' said Gregson, when I had finished my account. 'That certainly sounds like Dudley and the rest of them, and the man in the bandages must be Muldownie. They must be hoping to cure him of his kidney stone, so he can resume his previous reign of terror, perhaps in disguise and with a new name. If only we knew where that old house is!'

"'I think I do know,' I said, and described to him my reasoning as I have explained it to you, Watson. He agreed with my conclusions, but was less enthusiastic at first about my plan to drive back and forth across the marshlands until I found the house. However, I managed at length to convince him – and his superior, Superintendent Satterthwaite, who was in charge of the investigation into Muldownie's escape, and who joined our discussion – that if they flooded the Lea Valley with uniformed policeman in daylight it might only serve to give an advance warning to Dudley and the others, who might then be able to make their escape. We therefore arranged that they would assemble their men at Stoke Newington Police Station, as that was the nearest large station to the likely location of the house, I would meet them there as soon as I could, and they would then proceed, once darkness had fallen.

"As it turned out, it took me very little time to find the house in question – an abandoned, decaying old building, which stands in isolation on the Hackney Marsh. The recent carriage tracks on the lane approaching the house were as clear as day, and my suspicions were confirmed when a slight movement at one of the windows caught my eye as I drove by. I was therefore at Stoke Newington Police Station long before Satterthwaite's men were there, and spent an anxious couple of hours kicking my heels, as I waited for them. Although the policemen had agreed with my proposal to approach the house after nightfall, you will imagine that I was also keen that they got to the house before Kazinczy was obliged to commence any surgery. That they just managed, and the rest you know."

"I heard a shot as the police stormed the house," I remarked after a moment. "Do you know if anyone was hurt?"

My friend shook his head. "The woman had a pistol," he replied, "and let off a wild shot. Fortunately it didn't hit anyone, and she was quickly disarmed."

"Who is she, anyway?"

"Some connection of Muldownie's, I believe. But I gather that just as Dudley took over Muldownie's gang after his imprisonment, so he took over the woman, too."

"It makes you wonder why Dudley was so keen to get Muldownie out of Dartmoor," I observed. "Surely he'd be better off with Muldownie locked away and himself the unrivalled king of the castle."

"So you would think," said Holmes, nodding his head in agreement. "But some of the gang are known to be loyal to Muldownie, so perhaps Dudley, for all his power, felt obliged to go along with the plan. After today, all being well, the question will be a purely academic one, as these villains should all be removed from the world of honest folk for some considerable time."

That, then, is how I came to play a part – minor though it was – in the capture of some of the most violent and dangerous men in England. I made a detailed record of the matter at the time, while it was still fresh in my memory, even though I knew I should not be able to share the story while the villains involved were still alive. A couple of years later, however, we heard that the former gang-leader, Muldownie, had fallen ill again in prison, and had subsequently died. Then two or three years after that, I read with surprise in my newspaper one morning that Dudley, who had recently been granted an early release from Portland Prison on the grounds of ill health, had been shot dead the previous evening in a public house in Shadwell. No doubt his assassin – who was never apprehended – was one of the many people in the East End who had had good reason to hate him for many years. Although any unnecessary loss of life is usually regarded as a tragedy, I doubt very much that Dudley's passing elicited much sorrow in those parts of London where he was known.

As for Dr. Kazinczy, he continues to practice and flourish in Hackney, where, as far as I am aware, he lives still. I have met him once or twice since our alarming adventure together, when he has never failed to bring vividly to my mind once more the memory of that strange old dark house and the singular bandaged man.

The Black Hole of Berlin
by Robert Stapleton

Over recent years, I have accompanied my friend Mr. Sherlock Holmes on numerous ventures and investigations, but at this precise moment I craved the homely setting of our rooms in Baker Street, together with its warm fireside, Mrs. Hudson's satisfying meals, and an absorbing English newspaper.

We had journeyed together from Liverpool Street Station to Harwich, thence by overnight ferry to the Hook of Holland, and now we were on a train, in the mid-winter of early 1885, and somewhere in the middle of Germany. We were on our way to Berlin, and the winterscape outside the window made me feel depressed, even when the grey fields gave way to the dismal buildings of yet another area of urban development.

"You are bored, Watson," observed Holmes.

"I was pondering that invitation you received for us to visit the German capital city," said I. "And wondering about its purpose."

"The matter is simple enough. A representative from the Foreign Office has invited us both to join him for a meal at a certain city-center hotel there. A comfortable place I have previously heard of in the *Friedrichstrasse*."

"But the purpose remains a mystery."

"Not at all," he replied. "As you know, the West African Conference is currently being held in that city. It is being hosted by the man in charge of the New Germany – the German Chancellor himself, Otto von Bismarck. And our man is numbered among the British delegation attending that Conference. Whatever our friend has in mind in making this invitation, it unquestionably has something to do with the events taking place there at the moment."

"Then I hope it will be worth our traveling all this way."

"I'm sure the matter is serious enough to warrant our undertaking this journey. He obviously anticipates trouble, and would value my presence there."

When the train ground to a halt, I looked for some indication of where we had arrived, however temporarily.

"Hannover," said Holmes, reading my thoughts.

I groaned at the thought that we would be making no further progress in our tedious journey for several more minutes.

189

"It is clear," continued Holmes, "that you need something to distract your attention. And, unless I'm greatly mistaken, I believe that the distraction you're looking for has just stepped onto the train."

I looked out onto the platform, but could see no sign of anything or anybody unusual, apart from the normal idiosyncrasies of a German city in mid-winter: Heavily clad people standing stoically on the platform in the cold wind, notices printed in gothic script, and an official strutting along the station platform making strident announcements in an unintelligible language.

"I give the man three minutes to locate us," said Holmes, lying back and stretching his long legs out in front of him.

As I watched the station clock reach the three minute mark, I heard someone open our compartment door and step inside. I turned and was immediately astonished. The man was tall, slim, dressed in a gray suit beneath a heavy overcoat, but otherwise bearing a noteworthy appearance.

"Good afternoon, gentlemen," said our visitor, in an accent as English as any Cambridge professor. "May I join you? This train appears to be more crowded than I had imagined it might be."

Holmes waved his hand toward the empty seats beside us. "You are indeed welcome to join us," he said. As he sat down, placing beside him his valise and the document case he was holding with protective care, the newcomer unbuttoned his coat and gave a smile so broad that the white of his teeth lightened up his dark face. "My name," said the man, "is Bagamoyo."

"Swahili," noted Holmes.

"Indeed. But my baptismal name is Jonathan."

"My name is Sherlock Holmes," explained my companion, "and this is my friend and companion, Dr. John Watson."

As the train began to move away from the station, Holmes sat back and studied our new traveling companion more closely. "And now you are on your way to Berlin."

"That is easily deduced, since this train is bound for the German capital."

"Certainly, but you have just this moment joined us after changing from the train which brought you here from Paris."

"True, Mr. Holmes. I have to admit that is not so readily deduced."

Holmes laughed. "I merely noticed the ticket you have hurriedly slipped into the top pocket of your jacket. The emblem of the French railways is partially visible. But you are not French or Belgian, nor are you from those parts of Africa over which the French or King Leopold currently hold sway. Your appearance suggests rather that you are from East Africa."

"I have to admit the truth of it," said Bagamoyo. "Allow me to explain. Several years ago, I left my home village and joined the crew of a ship sailing from Mombasa with a cargo of spices. I pulled my weight, so that discrimination against me by the mixed-race crew was kept to a minimum. I ended up in London, where I settled down, earned a modest living, made the right kind of friends, and was granted British citizenship. In the meantime, I read of the adventures of white explorers as they journeyed through the continent of Africa, bringing European ideas and culture without ever considering their detrimental effects on the native peoples."

"I fail to see that this is such a crime," I said. "The intention to bring civilization, medicine, religion, and a decent standard of living to the poor people of Africa has to be a laudable ambition."

"Indeed," said Bagamoyo. "I am not opposed to European civilization, wherever appropriate. I myself have reaped the benefits of it as much as anyone. But human greed threatens to lead to exploitation of Africa and its inhabitants on an industrial scale. At present, only the coastal areas are under European sovereignty, but that will change if this current Conference has its way. The British, for example, seek political power, and access to natural resources which will benefit the people of Britain rather than the Africans. Land for settlers. Markets for the products of our industrial machinery. Yes, jobs and employment for the masses, but they must take account of the people who are living in Africa now. People who have rights to be respected, and social networks that are far too unstructured for European bureaucracy to cope with, or ever to understand."

"And now you are on your way to Berlin, with the aim of influencing those currently involved in planning the future of the African people."

He nodded. "These people represent the traders and industrialists whose eyes sparkle at the very prospect of making money from what they call the 'Dark Continent'. The so-called 'civilized' nations have been exploiting the African people for many years – selling millions of our men and women into cruel slavery, just as the Arab traders have been doing for centuries, in order to promote the lucrative trade in sugar, coffee, and cotton."

"But cultural development would surely put a stop to such corruption," I suggested.

"Theoretically, perhaps – if the people are ever allowed to exercise such power, which is doubtful. Just look at the British in India, for example."

I coughed in order to cover up my misgivings about that point of view, but the comment contained enough painful truth that I said nothing by way of reply.

"I am now acting as a representative of the African peoples who wish to present their demand that the present social and cultural life of the African peoples be respected," continued Bagamoyo, "and that no development be entered into without the full agreement of the native peoples affected. We are perhaps fighting a losing battle, but my colleague, a man called Gaston Coss, a French national himself, has spent several weeks this winter trying to explain to those present at the Berlin Conference the serious threat that their proposed activities pose to the native peoples of Africa. The trouble is that most of the delegates are more interested in gaining wealth than in spreading the message of justice, freedom, and democratic accountability among the indigenous population."

"But what can you or anybody else accomplish against such powerful adversaries?" I asked.

Bagamoyo took the case from the seat beside him, opened it up, and held up a bundle of documents. "We are preparing to do battle, Dr. Watson. I am now on my way back from Paris with documented demands for their views to be heard and respected, together with fresh and shocking documentary evidence of ill-treatment of the Africans by Europeans already operating in that continent. One would hope that such evidence will be sufficient to prick the consciences of all civilized people, including those sitting at the Berlin Conference. But be in no doubt: Unless we can rein in their ambitions, these people are planning a free-for-all across the entire continent."

We parted company with our African friend on the platform of Berlin's *Friedrichstrasse* Station and stepped out into the cold Prussian winter, made even colder by the biting wind blowing in from the Baltic. I was glad of my heavy overcoat, and the Astrakhan hat I had purchased for the journey. We made our way on foot the short distance to the hotel mentioned in our invitation – a large and austere building. There we discovered that Holmes's Foreign Office contact had pre-booked rooms for us both.

After unpacking our luggage, we returned downstairs and prepared for our evening meal. Speaking for myself, I found that the journey had confused my constitution. With Berlin on Central European time, one hour ahead of Greenwich Meantime, I found that the missing hour was later than my appetite had imagined. I felt ready for a restorative meal, and was glad when Holmes and I were called to the dining room.

We found ourselves escorted to a table laid for five. I failed to recognize the Foreign Office representative, although it was clear that Holmes knew him. The man was standing waiting for us as we approached the table. He was accompanied by two guests.

"It is good to see you again, Mr. Holmes," the official said by way of greeting.

"And you too, Sir Michael," returned my companion.

"And this must be Dr. Watson."

I smiled and shook his hand.

"Now," added Holmes, "I am intrigued to learn the exact reason for your bringing us here. You need my help, but you have so far been evasive about exactly in what way I can assist you."

"That is a matter we will deal with after dinner," replied Sir Michael. "First, allow me to introduce you to my two other guests. Monsieur Gaston Coss is a Frenchman, with a great interest in the events taking place at the Berlin Conference."

We shook hands with the Frenchman mentioned to us by Bagamoyo. He appeared affable enough, even if slightly too passionate for my taste. He was small in stature, well-dressed, and with black hair above a receding hairline. I estimated him to be in his early forties.

"We have already met your other guest," said Holmes. "Bagamoyo joined us at Hannover, and we have learned a great deal from him about the purpose of this gathering in Berlin."

Holmes was never much good at small-talk, but he appeared considerably happier when we later retired to the smoking room. When we were all seated comfortably, he took out his pipe and sat smoking attentively whilst he prepared to listen to the Frenchman and his African companion expressing their discontent about the Conference.

"You are smoking a distinctive tobacco, Monsieur Coss," Holmes observed. "I have made a study of tobaccos, and I find yours to be a singular concoction."

"These cigarettes are one of my few indulgences, Mr. Holmes," replied the Frenchman. "I have them specially blended and imported from London."

"Unique, then."

"Certainly."

"I imagine," said Holmes, turning to Sir Michael, "that you have invited us here because you anticipate some kind of trouble at the Conference. Perhaps now we may consider the matter further."

Coss, who had been itching all through dinner to speak in greater detail, leaned forward and took up the conversation. "My purpose for being here in Berlin at this time," he said, "is to attempt to bring a measure

193

of sanity to the madness of these Conference delegates. To frustrate their evil plans to colonize and exploit the entire continent of Africa."

"Is there anybody else who shares your misgivings?" I asked.

"Very few who are prepared to express their views. Certainly not the Chancellor, von Bismarck, the man who is hosting the event. It was his idea to hold this Conference here in the first place, responding to a request by the Portuguese. His clear intention is to maintain the international profile of the new Germany."

"What about the British delegation?"

"There are some here out of a matter of duty," said Coss, giving a sideways glance at our host, "but the main representative of the British government is the current Ambassador to the German Empire, Sir Edward Malet. He is here to make sure the British receive their fair share of whatever benefits might accrue from this gathering. He is hardly likely to countenance the wrecking of the Conference, or the questioning of its aims."

I could see that Coss was growing ever more agitated as he turned in his seat and faced each one of us in turn. "Gentlemen, I now have evidence, stronger than ever before, which will prove the inhuman nature of much of the European intervention in Africa, together with a plea to respect the governing structures already in place."

He pulled from beneath his jacket the very bundle of papers I had previously seen in the document case held by Jonathan Bagamoyo on the train.

"These documents, in fact."

"And how do you intend to use them?"

"I intend to confront the delegates with them. We seem to be making little progress in our countering of the aims of the Conference, but if I show these to the right people, it will challenge them as no other information can – particularly one man."

"Who is that?"

"To be fair to him, I must confront him first, and see what he has to tell me."

"The matter is pressing, then," said Holmes.

"Indeed. And do you know what these Conference delegates are doing?" asked Coss. "They are currently slicing up the map of Africa like a fruit cake. Europeans love to draw boundaries. But such thinking is alien to Africans."

With that, it was obvious that Coss was unable to restrain himself any further. He jumped to his feet, cast a challenging glance at the man from the Foreign Office, wished us all a good night, and strode from the building, followed closely by an anxious-looking Bagamoyo.

194

"You were right when you suggested I had anticipated trouble here, Mr. Holmes," our host told us as we continued to sip our brandy. "That man is stirring up a storm, and it bodes ill for the future."

After a couple more brandies, we were all ready for bed.

The following morning, after eating a hearty breakfast, we retired to the hotel lounge in order to await the unfolding of events. We imagined that our first visitor would be our Foreign Office contact, so we were surprised by the appearance instead of quite another visitor: A man of medium height, clean shaven, wearing a long black coat against the cold, and a black, broad-brimmed hat.

He stood in the doorway, removed his hat, and scanned those few of us who were present in the room. Then, identifying us as those most likely to be the ones he sought, he approached us.

"Mr. Sherlock Holmes, and Dr. Watson?"

"Indeed," returned my companion.

"I am Commissar Marius Rossmann, from Cripo – the Berlin Criminal Police. I suppose it must be the equivalent of your Scotland Yard."

"In that case, good morning, Commissar," said Holmes. "Please come and join us."

Rossmann sat down, looking decidedly uncomfortable in those luxurious surroundings.

"You must be the equivalent of our Inspector Lestrade," added Holmes, with a smile tugging at the corners of his mouth.

"You are well informed, Mr. Holmes," said the Commissar. "My superiors chose me to visit you here this morning because my English is better than that of anyone else at Alexanderplatz."

"And better than my German," commented Holmes modestly. "In that case, how may we help you, Commissar?"

"Earlier this morning, the body of a man was pulled from the River Spree."

"I am sorry to hear that. Have you managed to identify the deceased?"

"We have indeed. It is a man called Gaston Coss."

"I am shocked, but not completely surprised," said Holmes, looking at me for unnecessary endorsement. "We were talking to the man only last night, and he was telling us about the tensions which exist between himself and other delegates at the Berlin Africa Conference – one man in particular."

"That is interesting," admitted Rossmann. "Did he happen to mention who that was?"

"No."

195

I chipped in. "But now you say his body has been pulled from the river."

"Indeed."

"Then presumably the man was drowned," I concluded.

"That is the initial conclusion of the *post mortem* examination."

"Then what makes it a matter for the criminal police?" asked Holmes.

"The death is too convenient to have been a pure accident, Mr. Holmes. We have reason to believe that the deceased went out last night in order to confront another man, presumably the same one you mentioned earlier, over issues concerning the present Conference being held in our city. And now he ends up dead. It may be an accident, but my experience of investigating unexpected deaths makes me highly suspicious of this one."

On hearing this, Holmes looked up with renewed interest. "That is thought provoking, Commissar. You suggest we are looking at a homicide made to look like an accident."

"Those are my initial thoughts," said Rossmann. "As you say, Mr. Holmes, it is very thought provoking."

"Regarding the shooting: Do you have any suspects?"

"We have already made an arrest. An African."

"Bagamoyo," I exclaimed.

"That is the name he gave us."

"But on what charge?"

"None as yet. It is all purely investigative at the moment. But we have certain facts which point to the African being the killer."

"Please explain."

"Our investigations have revealed that he and the dead man were colleagues. Even perhaps friends. But late yesterday evening, neighbours heard the two men arguing loudly."

"You have had a busy night, Commissar," observed Holmes. "But how can we be of assistance?"

"We currently have Bagamoyo at the police presidium on Alexanderplatz," replied Rossmann. "He has asked specifically to speak to you both."

On our arrival at the imposing police headquarters, we were taken to a somewhat Spartan interview room where we found Bagamoyo, now in his shirt sleeves, being guarded by two uniformed policemen.

"Mr. Holmes," exclaimed the African. "It is really good to see you. These people think I killed Coss, but you know I would never do such a thing."

We sat down opposite the prisoner.

196

"Please tell us exactly what happened," said Holmes.

"When we left you last night, Coss and I went immediately back to our rented rooms. It was clear that he wanted to act without delay. He had been boiling all evening, and now he was ready to blow. He gathered the papers that I had brought and set off by cab to confront someone."

"Whom did he go to see?"

"I don't know. He didn't tell me."

"It must be the same mysterious man he mentioned last night."

"Surely. Anyway, we had an argument. I didn't want him to go, and certainly not on his own. As he was not prepared to tell me who it was, I was forced to conclude that the man he was going to see was potentially dangerous. I was afraid that Coss would be walking straight into the lion's den. I tried to dissuade him, but he was adamant. And, as it turned out, I was quite right to worry."

He paused to collect his thoughts.

Holmes nodded. "Carry on."

"I heard nothing more from Coss, and I slept badly thinking about him, until Commissar Rossmann and a couple of his colleagues knocked at my door this morning. He told me that a body had been found, and they had no doubt, from documents discovered in his pockets, that it was indeed Coss. The Commissar said they had been making inquiries among my immediate neighbours and discovered that some of those people had overheard us arguing. Rossmann considered that enough reason to bring me in for questioning."

Bagamoyo gave a sigh and looked up at my colleague.

"Now I need you to help me, Mr. Holmes. I am an innocent man and I need you to help me prove it."

Holmes stood up. "In that case, I shall do my utmost to make sure you are set free." Then, turning to Rossmann, he said, "We must examine the body. And I should like to speak to the surgeon who performed the *post mortem*."

The police morgue was an oppressive place, as cold as the weather outside, but efficient in a Prussian sort of way. The air was heavy with the smells and chemicals common in such places. Then the deceased was wheeled out for us to examine. I immediately recognized this as the man we had met on the previous evening: Gaston Coss.

The police surgeon joined us there and watched as I made my own examination of the body.

"The cause of death appears to be drowning," I concluded.

"That is quite right," said the surgeon. "I found the lungs to be sufficiently full of water as to have caused death by asphyxiation. It also seems that he had enjoyed a decent meal not long before his death."

"We can vouch for that," I answered.

"So far the evidence suggests that this was an accidental death," said Holmes, "and the only evidence linking Bagamoyo with the killing appears to be purely circumstantial – the argument between them overheard by neighbours."

"That is a matter for the police to consider, Mr. Holmes," said Rossmann, coldly.

Holmes stepped closer to the body. "And yet, look here. The skin around his mouth is slightly blue in color. A suggestion that he might have been overcome by gas prior to his drowning."

"Gas?" said Rossmann

"Oh yes."

"That confirms our initial suspicions that this is no mere accidental death."

"I'm inclined to agree with you, Commissar," said Holmes. "Judging by the evidence we've gathered so far, there may well be more to this case than at first appears."

"So," I concluded, "we have a drowning which might have been dismissed as a tragic accident, except that now the possibility of homicide has reared its ugly head. And the police are holding Bagamoyo as a suspect – a man who would not be considered a suspect if it were not for the color of his skin."

Holmes turned to Rossmann. "Do you not agree, Commissar, that the suspect you have in custody is not yet proven guilty?"

"Perhaps," replied Rossmann cautiously. "In which case, the mystery appears even deeper than ever. Do we have a homicide or not? And if we do, where might our suspicions be directed next?"

Holmes leaned closer to the corpse. "Look at his hands. The fingertips have been rubbed raw and bleeding. This man was in a desperate situation. Interesting. And look at the palms of his hands. Flakes of rust have driven deep into the skin."

"From an iron railing, perhaps," I suggested.

"Something of the sort is a distinct possibility. Both of these facts suggest he was fighting for his life."

I nodded.

"One more thing," said Holmes. "Could we see the contents of his stomach?"

Holmes gave these a careful examination, and then looked again at the body. "The man's coat has been torn, perhaps in a struggle with his assailant, or in an attempt to escape his fate."

"In which case, what sort of place was he in when he met his death?" asked the Commissar.

"That is precisely the question we need to ask."

Holmes stepped back decisively. "It's clear that two things need to be done now. Firstly, Commissar, could you please find for us the cab used by the deceased last night? I should like to speak to the driver."

"I shall put my men on to finding that information without delay," said Rossmann. "It should be a simple matter of old-fashioned police work."

"In the meantime, I should like you to show me exactly where the body was discovered."

"Very well, Mr. Holmes. Come with me."

"And my thanks to the police surgeon for his help," added Holmes as he departed.

After a short carriage ride through the streets of Berlin, we reached the banks of the River Spree, which flows through that city. The river was moving quickly, and the water high to overflowing as we followed it downstream. The carriage stopped beside the roadway in a less-congested area of the city. We alighted and followed Commissar Rossmann along a stretch of disused ground until we were standing on the muddy bank of the river.

"This is the place, Mr. Holmes," said Rossmann.

As the Commissar and I tried to keep the cold at bay, Holmes, in his accustomed manner, made a detailed investigation of the scene. "A set of cart tracks shows where police activity occurred."

Rossmann nodded.

"Another set of footprints leading in both directions must belong to the person who discovered the body."

"A local man, taking his dog out for its early morning walk."

"And where exactly was the body found?"

"Floating face-down at the margin of the river, entangled in the drooping branch of that tree."

Although the river itself was flowing swiftly, the relatively still water along the edges was beginning to show signs of forming ice on the surface.

"You were fortunate that the body wasn't swept farther downstream," said Holmes. "As it is, we might conjecture that it hadn't drifted far from where it entered the water."

"How can you say that? We are close to the edge of Berlin just here, where the river flows away from the city. He could have drifted from anywhere along its banks. The possibilities are endless, Mr. Holmes."

Holmes scanned the river more carefully. "A study of the surface of the river gives us information about the flow of water beneath. Sometimes deep, sometimes shallow, depending on the hidden currents. In this case, the middle of the river is flowing fast, but it could have picked up the body from one side of the river, conveyed it several yards downstream, and left it here. The impression might be that it has traveled a long way, but the river can be deceptive. The water flows more slowly on the outer curve of a bend such as this, often leaving behind silt or sand – or entangled bodies."

Rossmann didn't look as though he was convinced by the argument, but for the moment, he remained silent.

Holmes led the way upstream, past a number of buildings, until we returned once more to the bank of the river. Here he stopped and looked around, paying particular attention to the structures on the opposite bank.

They appeared mainly to be industrial buildings. "Tell me, Commissar," said Holmes. "That one directly opposite where we're now standing, on the far side of the river. What is that place?"

The policeman shrugged. "It's a disused warehouse, Mr. Holmes. At least, the river side of the building could be described as such. The other side of the property is an occupied dwelling. It is possible that the two buildings were built back to back, with some kind of access between them."

"Do you know who lives there now?"

Rossmann stood in silent thought for a few moments. Then he said, "I believe it is a businessman called Klaus Grimmen – an entrepreneur who is actively involved in developing trade with various lands around the world. He has a particular interest in the events taking place currently at the West Africa Conference."

"Look carefully at that building," Holmes instructed us. "What do you see?"

I was the one to answer. "A stone wall reaching from below the river level to just shy of the eves. There are several openings along this side, all boarded up."

Rossmann added, "Those openings were used in the past to transfer goods into the building, and out again."

"That could account for the iron rings along this side of the building," I said. "Mooring places for boats transporting produce to and from the warehouse."

"But do you not see it?" interjected Holmes. "At water-level."

"An opening, secured by an iron gate," I said. "A kind of portcullis."

"That could well account for the flakes of rust adhering to the hands of the deceased. If he was on the other side of that gate, he might well have been fighting for his life. Scrambling. I should very much like to take a look inside that building."

We returned to the carriage which had brought us to the riverside and found another uniformed member of the police waiting for us there.

"Commissar," the man said, "we have managed to locate the cab driver who took Monsieur Coss as a passenger last night."

"And did he tell you where he took his passenger?"

"No, sir. He refuses to say."

"Where is the man now?"

"He is waiting for us in the Alexanderplatz."

"Very well." Then, turning to Holmes and myself, he added, "Let us go and have a word with this man."

We found a hansom cab standing close to the Police Presidium. The horse was stamping and snorting, whilst the disgruntled driver was likewise stamping his feet and trying in vain to keep the bitter cold at bay. He appeared miserable, not only because of the cold weather, but also because he was losing time in making money.

A quick-fire discussion in German between Rossmann and the driver revealed the fact that on the previous evening, this cabbie had indeed collected a man from the property occupied by Coss and Bagamoyo. When asked to reveal the passenger's destination, the cabbie refused to do so. He freely admitted that he had dropped Coss off close to the address he'd been given, and the man had told him to wait. But then another man emerged from the building, paid off the cabbie, and told the man to go. He also gave him an extra gratuity of some fifty marks, to ensure that the cabbie remained quiet about the address, if asked. As a man of honor, and not wishing to offend a possible future customer, the cabbie refused to break the confidence so generously bought.

It was Holmes who provided the solution to the conundrum.

"Tell him that he has no need to break the confidence, but merely to drive me and my colleague to within a few yards of the building, and then leave us to reach the address on our own. I too shall reward him well for his assistance."

The cabbie dropped us off a couple-of-hundred yards from a building, to which he directed us. I knew at once that it was the same one that we had observed from the riverside only a few minutes previously. It appeared different from this angle, but it was undoubtedly the same place, this side being the occupied section of the property.

201

We approached the front door on foot and Holmes rang the bell.

The door opened and a face looked out. A woman's grim expression showed that she was unsympathetic toward visitors. "Yes?"

"My name is Sherlock Holmes," said my colleague, handing over his visiting card. "And this is my colleague, Dr. John Watson."

"English?"

"Yes."

"What do you want here, Englishman?"

"We're looking for a man who went missing last night – a Frenchman by the name of Coss. He is reported to have been heading in this general direction, and I was wondering if you had come across such a man."

"We do not have many visitors here," said the woman.

"May we come inside?"

"A persistent devil, aren't you, Englishman?"

"I have frequently been described as such."

The woman at the door turned away, and a few seconds later a man appeared there. He was small in stature, but bulky and muscular, with a neatly trimmed black beard, dark astute eyes, and a sardonic smirk hovering around his mouth. I could tell at once that Holmes didn't like him.

"Sherlock Holmes," he said, looking down at the visiting card. "Yes, I have heard the name. My name is Klaus Grimmen." He looked up and gave a smile which was not reflected in his eyes. "If you would like to step inside for a moment, I am sure we can quickly clear up this matter to your complete satisfaction. Then you can be on your way. I should hate to be found wasting your precious time unnecessarily."

Grimmen led us up a short flight of steps into a comfortable living room. There he turned and addressed us. "You will have to excuse me, gentlemen, but even though I have a fair knowledge of the English language, I hope I am not misunderstanding what you have to say. Now, for whom exactly is it that you are looking?"

I could see Holmes's eyes darting about the room, so I took up the conversation. "A man we met last night has gone missing, and we're looking for where he might have gone. Yours is one of several places we are hoping to visit today in our search for him. The man is a French national named Gaston Coss. We believe you might have come across him during the course of the Conference."

While Holmes walked around, stopping at one point to look at some objects upon one of the tables, Grimmen gave the impression of thinking the matter over. Then he shrugged. "I have met so many people during the Conference that I really cannot tell with any certainty whether I met this particular person or not. Perhaps there was a Frenchman – several in fact – but none of them meant much to me."

I examined Grimmen's face, but it remained impassive. Either he was telling the truth, or he was an excellent liar.

Holmes now stepped forward again. "Thank you for your time, Herr Grimmen," he said. "I'm sure we shall reach the truth soon enough. In the meantime, good day to you."

We joined Rossmann outside a moment later outside. He'd come to collect us using his own conveyance.

"Well, Mr. Holmes?" said Rossmann as soon as we were out of the biting wind.

"He denies it, of course, but Coss was certainly there. There can be no doubt about it." He held out his hand, and opened it to reveal a small cigarette stub, which he sniffed. "This is the very same tobacco that Coss was smoking when we met him last night. He told us that he had these cigarettes specially made for him, and imported them from England. Nobody else smokes this same mixture of tobacco. It is unique."

"What do you suggest we do now?" asked Rossmann.

"We need to explore that building," replied Holmes "I have to look more extensively around the place. Maybe tonight."

"In that case, you might have to do so illegally, Mr. Holmes. I'm not sure I can obtain an entry warrant before the end of the day."

"Will you come with us either way?"

"And risk my career with Cripo?"

"Or else make a name for yourself in the process."

We clattered off along the road, with the Commissar sitting beside us deep in contemplation.

Whilst at dinner, we were interrupted by the concierge, who brought Holmes a written message.

"Splendid!" cried Holmes. "Commissar Rossmann tells me that Grimmen is away from home for the evening, courtesy of Chancellor Bismarck, who has called a meeting of the Conference. It seems that the servants have been left to enjoy an evening below stairs.

"Then there is no reason for us to delay," I concluded.

"None whatsoever," said Holmes, rubbing his hands in anticipation of action. "In which case, let us be off."

Our cab dropped us within a short walk of Grimmen's house.

As we stood in the gathering darkness outside the unlit building, with Holmes adjusting his dark lantern, we were startled by the appearance of a man who stepped out from the shadows.

Commissar Marius Rossmann.

"Mr. Holmes. Dr. Watson. I'm glad you have arrived so promptly. It is very cold out here." He stamped his feet in an attempt to regain lost circulation. "Good news. I have managed to obtain the warrant we need to enter these premises in a legal fashion. It was not given readily, I can tell you, but whether with bad grace or good, we now have permission to undertake that investigation you were talking about."

"Very well," said Holmes. "Then perhaps we had better try knocking on the front door before we attempt any other method of entry."

Rossmann's knocking on the door brought no response. "To the best of my knowledge, the servants are all in there," he said, "but as they are not expecting anybody tonight. They are all probably halfway to being drunk."

We searched for another entrance, and discovered it round the corner. Using his pick-lock bundle, Holmes had the door open in seconds, and we three were inside the house.

Rossmann opened the partly-covered lantern he'd been carrying and led the way through the gloomy house. We climbed a staircase to the room where Holmes and I had met and spoken with Grimmen earlier in the day.

Using his own lantern, Holmes began a careful survey of the room. Little had changed since our previous visit. The stone floor was still covered with scattered rugs. A number of easy chairs stood around the room, whilst a table stood near a fireplace at the far end.

"This is where I found the cigarette butt left by Coss," said Holmes pointing to the ashtray on the table. "It is the dead man's signature – the evidence that he was alive and in this building at some point within the last few hours. Otherwise, it would have been removed by an assiduous housemaid."

Holmes stooped to examine the hearth and nodded to himself. "Something has been burnt here recently. Papers."

"Coss came here bearing a bundle of papers which he imagined would bring shock to whoever read them."

"If these are the papers he brought, then they are now nothing more than a bundle of black ashes."

"Certainly insufficient evidence on which to convict Grimmen of murder," Rossmann reminded us.

"Is that all we have?" I asked.

"No, Watson, that is definitely not all we have. Far from it, in fact. Can you see that curtain on the wall farthest from the window?"

"The drape stretching across a large section of the wall? Yes, I see it."

As Holmes pulled the curtain aside, I noticed that the heavy fabric hung from a thick curtain-rod, being attached to the rail above by a series of metal hoops. It opened smoothly.

"Now, what do you see?"

"A wall. A solid immovable stone wall, built of solid adamantine stone blocks, stretching across that side of the room without a break."

"The side of the house," said Rossmann.

"But examine the floor, if you will. Can you see anything significant there?"

I pushed aside one of the scattered rugs, and looked carefully at the flags that made up the solid floor. "Scratches gouged into the very stonework of the floor," I replied. "In the form of a wide arc."

"Such as may be made by any ordinary door which is habitually being opened and closed – suggesting that the wall we are looking at may not be as immovable as one might imagine."

Using the scratches as his guide, Holmes examined the wall at closer quarters. "A-ha! What have we here? Just about visible. A break in the wall, with a suggestion of massive hinges buried deep within the stonework. And, at the other end of the wall, we have an iron ring."

"Great Scott! Holmes, you're right. It is a colossal door!"

Holmes pulled the ring, but there was no movement.

Rossmann chipped in. "Look. The door has a keyhole."

"But where is the key?" I asked.

"There," said the Commissar. "Just to the right of the door. Look. A recess in the stonework, and a large iron key hanging on a hook, almost invisible in the shadows."

Holmes grasped hold of the key, inserted it into the keyhole, and turned it. The lock mechanism rotated easily, with almost no sound whatsoever. "It has been kept well oiled," he observed.

Once more, Holmes took hold of the iron ring and pulled. This time, the great stone door opened slowly outward into the room.

"It swings easily," he said. "I would imagine those hinges have been thoroughly and regularly greased, as well as the lock mechanism."

"Just as well," said Rossmann. "Otherwise we would be in danger of bringing the entire household out to see what we are doing here."

"But why would anyone bother to build such a structure?" I asked. "All we have now is another great stone wall facing us. And this one doesn't have a keyhole."

"No," said Rossmann, "but it does have an iron ring, much like the first one. This must be able to swing out the opposite way. Into whatever room or space lies beyond."

"If so, then we must be able to open it just as easily," said Holmes.

Together, we pushed on the wall. This also proved heavy, but once it was moving, the wall continued to swing, carried by its tremendous momentum, until it thudded against something in the darkness.

Holmes stepped beyond the opening and raised the lantern to reveal to our astonished gaze another long but narrow room.

"This must run beside the river," said the Commissar. "Look. Those are the high windows we saw from the far side."

We all three moved around the room, exploring the place as best we could in the dim light of our lanterns.

"Over here," said Holmes. "On the floor. What do you make of it, Watson?"

"An iron trap-door." I pulled on the protruding iron handle and found that the door swung upward and then dropped onto the floor.

We all looked down into the dark hole.

"It drops down to the level of the river," said Rossmann. "You can hear the water sloshing against the stonework."

"And it stretches deep below the level of the water," observed Holmes. "See. There are the iron railings we saw earlier, separating it off from the river."

"Maybe they could be raised or lowered by the use of this," I said, pointing to an iron wheel about eighteen inches in diameter on the wall beside me.

"That would seem logical."

"But what is this shaft?" I gasped.

"Most probably it was used to provide access to and from the river," said Holmes. "If this building was a warehouse at one time, then such access for personnel would be essential."

"But now it is disused," I pointed out.

"For that purpose, at least," said Holmes, rubbing his chin thoughtfully. "But it might have become something more sinister. An oubliette, or a dungeon, perhaps, with iron rungs attached to the sides."

Grasping his lantern, Holmes climbed into the black hole and descended into darkness.

"This is extremely interesting," came his voice from the depths.

"What have you found?" I called down to him.

"You remember I told you that Gaston Coss's coat had been torn."

"I remember."

"I have found a fragment of cloth snagged on the iron grill down here which exactly matches its color and weave."

"I would be obliged if you would bring it up with you, Mr. Holmes," said Rossmann.

"Very well. But now I think we have achieved all we came here for tonight. Perhaps the new day will reveal more."

Early the following morning, I was roused from my bed by a loud knocking upon the door of my room.

"Yes?"

"A man from Cripo is waiting for you downstairs, Dr. Watson." I recognized the voice of the concierge. "Mr. Holmes is already down there."

I looked at my watch on the bedside counter and winced at the early hour. Then, without further delay, I arose, dressed, and made my way downstairs.

There I discovered Holmes, ready for an early morning excursion, together with the Commissar and Bagamoyo.

"The game is afoot, Watson," he told me. "Commissar Rossmann has obtained a warrant for the arrest of Herr Grimmen."

"We still don't have all the proof we need," added the Commissar, "but we have sufficient to bring our suspect in for questioning."

I grabbed a roll from the breakfast room, donned my winter coat and hat, and out into the bitter winter weather. Snow was blowing in the wind as we climbed into a police carriage and set off back toward the riverside residence of Klaus Grimmen.

To Rossmann's knock, the door was opened by the same woman we had seen on the previous day, the only difference being that this time she invited us all to step inside.

"Herr Grimmen is expecting you," she told us, in a manner as cold as the weather.

"This is no real surprise," said the businessman when we joined him in his living room. "I knew that somebody had visited my home last night, whilst I was out at a pressing appointment. The servants reported that they had heard noises, and I am sure that you were the culprits."

Rossmann shrugged. "Since you were not at home, and nobody answered my knock, we considered the matter so important that we had to gain entry."

"By breaking and entering?"

"There was no breaking involved, Herr Grimmen," countered Holmes. "We had a legal warrant to enter."

Klaus Grimmen looked at Bagamoyo, and his face twisted in displeasure. "I see you have brought one of those savages with you."

"I think I am as civilized a man as you are, Grimmen," returned the African bitterly.

"Maybe more," I added.

207

"On his visit here yesterday," continued the Commissar, "Mr. Holmes asked if you had seen a missing man by the name of Coss. You said that you had not."

"That is the truth of the matter," said Grimmen aggressively.

"And yet we have reason to believe that he did come to this house, and that he was killed here shortly after he arrived."

"Are you suggesting that I am responsible for this man's death?" Grimmen held out his hands in a gesture of innocence. "Do you have any evidence at all to back up this ridiculous notion?"

"Perhaps."

"We should like to investigate the room next-door," said Sherlock Holmes.

Grimmen returned him a guarded look.

"Oh, we know about that room," added Holmes.

"It seems you were indeed extremely busy here last night," commented Grimmen.

After a painful moment of silence, during which time the hissing gas-light on the wall provided the only sound, Grimmen forced a smile. "Would you gentlemen care to see that room next door – this time in the light of day?"

We all now focused our attention on the owner of the house as, with exaggerated drama, he drew back the curtain covering the stone wall. Now, in the daylight, I could see more clearly the iron ring handle, and the keyhole beside it.

Klaus Grimmen reached up to the large iron key on its hook, and then inserted it into the keyhole. He turned the mechanism, replaced the key, and then pulled open the huge stone door.

As on our previous visit, the enormous stone wall swung easily on its hinges. Seeing it now in daylight, I was even more impressed by the ingenious mechanism.

We all stood facing the second wall, and I estimated that there would be barely a couple of inches separating the two walls of stone when they were both closed. I imagined that constructing the place must have been a massive undertaking.

Grimmen applied his full strength in order to push open this second wall-door. Once it was moving, the stone entrance swung fully open, impelled, as on the previous evening, by its own massive weight.

Our host stepped through into the second room and stood watching whilst we all filed in. Commissar Rossmann arrived first and set about examining the room that was now lit up by daylight filtering in through the high windows on one side. Next came Bagamoyo, followed by myself. I riveted my attention upon the iron trapdoor which I knew led to the flooded shaft. Holmes came in last of all, pulling the first stone door firmly shut after him but leaving the second fully open. The place felt bitterly cold.

Grimmen stood watching us all. "In years gone by, this was a warehouse, holding produce used in the wool trade. Access from the river was via an opening now sealed by those wooden slats that cover much of the riverside wall. The other main access for goods was through the house, and that was the reason for the two stone doors being constructed. To give access when required, and to assure security for those living in the house."

"Ingenious!" I exclaimed.

"Now, gentlemen, may I ask the exactly purpose of your visit here? And what is your interest in this disused warehouse in particular?"

"Monsieur Coss came here with a bundle of papers in his possession," said Rossmann.

"Papers which pointed to unjust and exploitative activities in Africa," added Bagamoyo. "And to yours in particular."

"And he left through that black hole," said Holmes, pointing to the access shaft.

"How can you possibly know all that?" demanded Grimmen. Somehow he did not appear to be surprised.

"We know that the deceased man visited you on the night of his death," continued Holmes. "The night before last. You and Coss spoke at some length. I discovered the stub of one of his cigarettes in your ashtray. So we know that he spent enough time here to smoke it. Somehow, you caused the man to drop down through to this shaft, and into the darkness below. If he was unconscious, then the water down there would have brought him back to consciousness, long enough for him to be aware of what was happening to him. We discovered that his fingernails were torn and his fingers bloodied from scrambling to try to escape. He also had flakes of rust embedded in the palms of his hands. From scrambling against the iron gate barring him from the river, and from the rusted iron rungs lining the shaft."

"The man was drowned, certainly," I continued. "And that access shaft is sufficiently full of bitterly cold river water that no one could survive for long down there. Coss would have been overcome by hypothermia and exhaustion, his hands would have been too numb to enable him to climb out, and he would have drowned within a matter of a few minutes."

"This is all pure speculation," growled Grimmen. "News reports say that the body was found outside, on the margins of the river."

"When the man was dead," said Holmes, "you then raised the iron grill separating the pipe off from the river, and allowed the water to sweep

209

the body away. Unfortunately for your plans, the body didn't travel downstream as far as you had hoped, before it was snagged on the branch of a tree."

"Utter and complete nonsense," thundered Grimmen.

"You might try to convince the world that it was indeed an accident," I pointed out. "But the evidence points to murder, and to you as the man who killed him. When the police suspected foul play, it was convenient for you that suspicion fell upon Mr. Bagamoyo here, and you did nothing to dispel that impression." All this time, Grimmen remained standing near the still-open inner stone doorway.

Bagamoyo's attitude toward the German businessman was now hardening fast into a bitter hatred, and he stepped toward him in a belligerent manner. "You swine, Grimmen!" he growled. "You may have used the river to kill my friend, but you are responsible for his death just as surely as if you had strangled him with your own bare hands. Why? Was it worth it?"

"Africa is there, waiting to be exploited by business interests among the civilized nations of Europe." Grimmen's eyes were blazing with passion. "There is nothing immoral in doing that. The continent is rife with cannibalism and barbarity."

"And you want to replace that with your own kind of barbarity. Is that it?" growled Bagamoyo. I could see that he seemed to be moving more slowly now, as though his limbs were not responding properly.

"Coss came here with similar accusations," continued Grimmen. "He made threats to derail my own plans for German commercial enterprise in Africa. So I had to kill him. You can understand that, can't you?"

"I fail to see how anybody could understand your actions," replied Holmes.

Grimmen stepped back, closer to the open stone door and, from the shadows, he brought out a sword – a sabre – and held it out threateningly toward us. "I would warn you, gentlemen, not to come any closer to me."

I could now feel something in the atmosphere causing my throat to constrict.

"Why?" demanded Rossmann. "What have you done?"

"You will already have noticed that my home is lit by manufactured gas," said Grimmen. "Unlit, that gas is a poisonous mixture of carbon monoxide and other noxious fumes. This gas is now filtering into this room through an unseen pipe above the wall. Soon you will begin to feel it starting to squeeze the life from your bodies. I shall leave you all in here as it builds up, and until it has rendered each of you unconscious. Then I shall come back, allow the gas to escape, and drop each of you in turn down into the dark and cold waters of the delivery shaft. The cold water may revive you, as it did Coss, but by then, as he found out, it will be too late to save you from drowning. Then I shall raise the grill and allow the river, which is flowing swiftly today, to take your bodies far away." He laughed. "That tree that snagged your colleague's body has now been removed. So don't trust to that to save you."

"I fail to understand," said the Commissar, who was having difficulty standing. "Why are you going to such great lengths to kill us all?"

"It was your friend Coss who is responsible," replied Grimmen. "He wanted to disrupt the Conference, and spare the people of Africa from what he considered to be unprincipled imperialism."

"Is that all?"

"Far from it. He also confronted me with evidence of my own activities, which he considered to be crimes against the human race. He threatened to bring the matter before every law-court in Europe. He might well have had me found guilty, but I couldn't run the risk of him delaying my involvement in exploiting the resources of Africa. For that reason he had to die. And for your meddling in my affairs, you too must die – perishing in the freezing waters of the River Spree. At least you will have one advantage over Coss. He had to suffocate and drown alone in total darkness."

As Holmes held Bagamoyo back from confronting the businessman, and both the policeman and the African slumped onto the floor, Grimmen grasped hold of the handle of the inner stone door and pulled it with all his strength. The huge weight of the inner stone door swung on well-oiled hinges toward its closed position, its momentum unstoppable. I noticed that, just before the door slammed shut, Grimmen stepped up confidently to the outer door, and pushed.

The two stone doors met with a gigantic slam, which shook the entire building.

"We could have stopped Grimmen," I cried out, "but now he has got away."

"I think not," said Sherlock Holmes, withdrawing a large iron key from the pocket of his coat. "I took the liberty of locking the outer door on my way in here."

As the horror of what must have happened to Grimmen began to sink in, we all stared at the closed stone doorway, each lost in his own contemplation.

"You had better go and check on our host, Watson," said Holmes softly. "Or whatever is left of him."

I did as asked, pulling open the great stone door. There I discovered the man's body in a hideous condition. The skull had been crushed, as had the ribcage and pelvis. All signs of life had been snuffed out immediately as the door had compressed the man against the cold stone bulk of its fellow. The sword lay beside him, still clutched in his lifeless hand.

"We need to make our way back to the habitable part of Grimmen's house," I told Holmes.

"Indeed." He unlocked the door. "We must close these heavy doors behind us," he said. "We have to allow the gas to escape gradually – otherwise the entire house will go up in flames."

Seized by fits of coughing, we made our way back to the safe side, where we began slowly to recover.

Holmes located and turned off the gas supply to the other room, and then opened the windows to allow in a blast of cold but refreshing air.

From my seat close to the fire, I looked up at him. "And what now?"

"The Berlin Conference will come to its inevitable conclusion on the subject of Africa," he decided.

"And this place?"

"Its fate is now out of our hands. The lawyers will have to decide about ownership, and the future of the servants employed here – unless they have made a rapid escape."

Later, when we had all recovered from our ordeal and the effects of the suffocating gas had worn off, we sat together in the warmth of our hotel lounge. "Jonathan Bagamoyo is the sort of man that the Foreign Office in London could use," said Holmes.

"And help the British take control of half of Africa? I hardly think so, Mr. Holmes," said our African friend. "I shall make my own way forward in life. My name in the Swahili language means something like 'lie down and rest', but I have plenty more to do with my life before I can think of doing such a thing."

"Commissar Rossmann," said Holmes as he lit up his pipe and sat back in contentment. "The case is now closed, and you will have the distinction of having solved the murder of Monsieur Coss."

"But I could never have done it without your help, Mr. Holmes."

"Perhaps. But the credit must go to you, Commissar. After all, I frequently assist Scotland Yard in the solving of crimes which they are unable to unravel, so why not Cripo as well? After all, I am the world's one and only private consulting detective."

The Thirteenth Step
by Keith Hann

As a man of science, my friend Sherlock Holmes usually had little patience for witchcraft, magick, and the powers unnamable. This fact inevitably surprised those who knew of his love of the grotesque and the *outré*, for surely, they asserted, such attributes were to be found in abundance in cases concerning ancient curses, fell beasts, dread sorceries, and the like. But as Holmes had once observed, the more fantastic the incident, the more it calls attention to itself, and the very point which appears to complicate a case is the one most likely to elucidate it. No incidents were more fantastic than those involving the supernatural, and thus the very oddities which so impressed the superstitious merely told the great detective precisely where to shine the light of reason. When bathed in such, most cases draped in arcane apparel were revealed to be nothing more than dull confidence games, charlatans preying upon the weak, with little of those rarified elements which engaged Holmes's higher faculties.

But there were exceptions.

Holmes and I had returned from an evening ramble just in time to meet a fine black brougham clattering to a halt in front of our dwelling. We watched as a shrewish, well-appointed gentleman of some five-and-thirty years stepped onto the pavement. Wan and drawn, with dark hollows visible through his gold-rimmed spectacles, I thought him a man in need of rest. Of course, so many who came to Holmes for help often were.

The man looked up and noticed us for the first time, blinking owlishly in evident surprise.

"How fortuitous," said he, in a precise, measured tone. "Sherlock Holmes, is it not? Might I request a moment of your time?" He handed us his card.

"Mr. Arthur Moorswaite," read Holmes. "Welcome. My condolences on the untimely death of your father."

"You read the newspapers," said Moorswaite, with no sign of distress or any other emotion, for that matter. "I would speak to you in private concerning just that."

"Certainly. Please, come up. I and my colleague here, Dr. Watson, would, I'm sure, be glad to hear you out."

We ushered our guest into our sitting room. Holmes's comment had me wracking my brain, for at first I could not recall a death of that name recently. Then I remembered: Johannes Moorswaite, prominent engineer,

213

had died in some sort of accident two weeks prior. There had been no whiff of scandal, no sign of the criminal that I recalled. I wondered if this were a matter concerning the estate. If so, our guest was to be disappointed, for Holmes left such things to the solicitors.

"Now then, Mr. Moorswaite," said Holmes, "tell us what troubles you."

"On the evening of the first of July, my father dined out with several long-time companions. They assure me that he behaved in no way unusual, reporting the evening a convivial one. When my father returned home, he retired to his study, poured himself a glass of sherry, apparently consulted a variety of tomes on the hermetic cults of seventeenth-century England, and then hanged himself."

The incongruity of this startling revelation and its manner of utterance, delivered with all the passion of one reading from an accounts-book, momentarily took the two of us aback. But Holmes recovered rapidly.

"Pardon me, Mr. Moorswaite, but the accounts of the papers all agree that it was an unfortunate accident. He fell and struck his head on his desk, if I recall correctly."

"But a tale, Mr. Holmes." His face flushed scarlet, the first sign of emotion he had yet exhibited. "I am ashamed, gentlemen, but I sought to avoid scandal, and so used our family's influence to keep the matter quiet. Your investigations must not spread news of this."

"I take it that you feel your father's death was not a natural one?"

"Oh, no, that he died by his own hand is, in my view, incontrovertible. There was no evidence of coercion or force of any kind. And his sherry was but sherry."

"Then what precisely is it that you wish me to do?" asked Holmes.

"What galls me is that I have no idea why. He was loved and cherished, hale and hearty, a man of considerable wealth. What could have caused him to risk bringing such shame upon the family?"

"You have no indication at all?" I asked.

"Well, yes, and no. My father left a note, in his unmistakable hand. I would have brought it with me, but its message was so simple as to make that unnecessary." He visibly steeled himself.

"Pray, continue, Mr. Moorswaite," said Holmes.

"'*The thirteenth step*'," he said.

"I beg your pardon," said I.

"That's it. That is all. '*The thirteenth step*'."

"I do not understand."

Moorswaite gave a snort. "You are not the first, Doctor. I haven't the slightest idea what it means. Neither do the servants. Nor did the police inspector who quietly investigated the death. I have made an exhaustive search of my father's personal effects, and spoke to any of his friends and acquaintances I felt I could question without arousing suspicion. I have tracked down distant family members." His voice rose in fury. "I have spent a week examining staircases at the establishments he frequented!" He inhaled sharply. I had the sense of a device, finely machined, pushed past narrow tolerances.

"Forgive me, gentlemen. The end result is that, two weeks after my father's death, it remains as inexplicable as it was that terrible evening I walked into his study and found him hanging from the rafters. The only thing worse than that sight, etched forever upon my mind, is the fact that I cannot explain it. And so I turn to you, Mr. Holmes."

"Were there any changes made to his will?" asked Holmes.

"No. The estate remained as it had been arranged some years prior, thus pointing to a singular culprit – myself. Much of the value was assigned to charitable causes, but the remainder was bequeathed to me."

Holmes considered a moment. "There are points of interest in the matter. With your permission, I would examine the scene in person. Perhaps we might reconvene tomorrow afternoon at your home?"

"Thank you for your consideration," said a relieved Moorswaite. "It has been a trying few weeks, and it shames me to admit that I am not up to the strain. Good evening, gentlemen."

"You rarely let your clients leave with so little data gathered," I said to Holmes after our guest's exit.

"I could see that Mr. Moorswaite was wound rather tightly. I worried that a deeper probe might have had a deleterious effect."

"I concur, and yet it will prove difficult to investigate the affair if your client cannot bear the strain."

"I would welcome your advice to that effect. Would you join me tomorrow, with a view to keeping a weather eye on our host's state of mind?"

"I would be delighted."

"Capital! Perhaps this will prove to be something more than a melancholy domestic incident."

I arrived the next afternoon as planned at a rambling Gothic townhouse. The home of the late Johannes Moorswaite appeared in no way unusual, lacking only in a certain antiquity of furnishings that told me it belonged to a family comparatively new to wealth. But when the footman opened the double doors leading into the elder Moorswaite's study, I was completely unprepared for the sight which greeted my eyes.

In most ways it was typical – a well-appointed room rich with the scents of leather and buckram, and the lingering remnants of a strange, cloying incense. The shelves groaned under the weight of books, many of evident age. But it was the end of the chamber which commanded one's attention, for against the far wall stood, on a plinth of blackest stone, a creature of legend. Upon the brawny legs and torso of a man rested the head of a mighty bull. In one extended hand it held an open tome. In the other, an overflowing cornucopia. Fully eight feet of masterfully carved marble in height, the Minotaur dominated the chamber, a remnant of a pagan age gazing upon the room's occupants with a proud, sardonic expression. Holmes stood to one side of the monster, examining it with his lens.

"Ah, Watson. Remarkable, wouldn't you say? A Ramey, I should think."

"You are correct, Mr. Holmes," said Moorswaite, leafing through a stack of papers at the room's desk. "Apparently he made several of those abominations for The Order."

"Good God, Holmes," said I. "What are we dealing with?"

"I have only just arrived myself, Watson. Mr. Moorswaite, how did your father acquire this statue?"

"He was presented with it by The Order but a few days before his death. The Order has already sent representatives to claim it, but I have dismissed them. I find the beast most disturbing, but until I settle this affair, I won't hand them a thing."

"Am I correct in supposing that matters of hermetic cults were not an unusual topic for your father?"

"Not in the least," Moorswaite replied. "Nowadays, with everything from Freemasonry to the Golden Dawn much in vogue, it isn't surprising to hear tell of someone as important as my father associated with such a society, but he was a member of The Order of Midas for some twenty-five years. His last supper was with fellow members of that Order. I can only conclude that he sought refuge in his faith before . . . making his final decision." More familiar now with his behaviours, Moorswaite's agitation was evident. Pale and continually wringing his hands, he stole glances at the rafters in a fashion which spoke clearly of being well aware he stood in the very chamber where his father had died.

Holmes had moved from the Minotaur to the books. "Curious, but by no means quaint. *De Occulta Philosophia*, *The Book of Eibon*, von Juntz's *Unaussprechlichen Kulten* – quite the treasure trove of fustian Faustianisms. It does, however, mark Johannes Moorswaite as no mere dabbler. Many of these tomes are exceedingly rare."

"I am not familiar with The Order of Midas," I said. "Who, or what, are they?"

"Father was a bitter veteran of the wars of German Unification," said Moorswaite, "and I gathered it was the atrocities he witnessed and, I think, was forced to perpetrate in the name of survival which soured him on his native land and religion both. The Order took him in soon after he landed here, and he always credited his rapid rise in society to their teachings. They are a secretive lot, and I've no truck with the ungodly, so I know little. As best I can follow, they claim to possess the secrets of the legendary King Midas, the man who was said to turn anything he touched to gold. I certainly never saw my father perform such a feat, but I must concede that he earned money with uncanny ease."

We seemed as one to turn to face the Minotaur. The sun's rays, streaming in from a skylight above, played across the creature's bestial face, causing its eyes, fashioned from some sort of dark gemstone, to sparkle wickedly.

"What so many forget is that King Midas's 'gift' was actually a curse," said Moorswaite quietly.

Our host excused himself shortly thereafter, feeling unwell. Holmes collected a series of papers and several tomes, those which the elder Moorswaite had been reading on the night of his death.

"Did you observe anything peculiar about the steps in the Moorswaite residence?" Holmes asked, as we rode in a cab back to Baker Street.

"I did not even look. When Moorswaite assured us that he had scoured his father's haunts for instances of thirteen steps, I assumed that his efforts would certainly have begun with his father's home."

"Your assumption there was correct, Watson. Nowhere were thirteen consecutive steps to be found. However, I confirmed that it was Johannes Moorswaite who designed the house, and it is interesting that every set of stairs on the property, indoors and out, consists of twelve steps."

"I fail to see how that is relevant. We know Moorswaite was a superstitious man. Isn't twelve a lucky number in some traditions?"

"Perhaps. I shall have to immerse myself in all sorts of rubbish in order to have the necessary grounds for proper deduction," Holmes lamented, patting the tomes he had borrowed. "Speaking of rubbish, I have paid little attention to mythology. Midas had nothing to do with the Minotaur, did he?"

"No," I replied. "If I remember my boyhood stories, it was Minos, not Midas, who imprisoned the monster within the Labyrinth."

"This order seems to deal in somewhat of an amateurish classical mélange. I wonder if their tenets are as muddled."

"I suspect that it will be difficult to learn much about them. For societies such as these, obfuscation of their central tenets seems, strangely enough, to be their main appeal."

"I am not surprised," said Holmes. "Reason increasingly intrudes in matters of religion and philosophy, stripping mystery from the world. For some, an existence bounded on all sides by the fathomable is a torment greater than anything Dante ever revealed."

"What is your next step, then?"

"I must learn more of Johannes Moorswaite's character and circumstances. Suicide is the most extreme of reactions, but a reaction all the same, one tending towards a reliably fixed set of causes."

"Our client has already made such inquiries."

"Indeed, but he is not a practised investigator. What he looked at he may not have seen. What he believes he saw he may not have at all. And there is certainly no guarantee that he knew the correct questions to ask or is skilled in detecting dissimulation when presented with such. Rarely can I rely upon the work of others."

"Rather a heavy burden."

He smiled. "True, but one which I can share from time to time. For instance, while I busy myself with such tedium, I would be most grateful if I could request a favour, dear Watson."

"You have but to name it."

"How do you feel about a touch of apostasy?"

For the next several days I had patients which I could not put off, but on the afternoon following, I set out with some apprehension to introduce myself to The Order of Midas.

The Order was headquartered in a neo-classical temple on Cavendish Square, the entrance flanked by winged Victories. Atop the empty necks, The Order had mounted the heads of bulls, rendering the classical lines brutish and belligerent. I climbed twelve marble steps to the entrance, and was greeted by a butler who took my name and requested my business.

"I am a friend of the late Johannes Moorswaite. I wish to speak with someone about joining your Order."

"Very good, sir. Please follow me."

I was led to a waiting room and offered refreshments. The room was richly appointed with fine tapestries, twelve in total, depicting a variety of arcane rituals whose precise purpose eluded me. Taken as a whole, they seemed to suggest an ascension of some sort, a progression from spiritual and material poverty to a higher level of existence.

"At each step, a price. At each step, gain."

I turned to see that I had been joined by a gentleman on the cusp of old age. A strong, masculine face was highlighted by a prominent, greying widow's peak, and dark, unsettling eyes. He seemed pleased to see me.

"*Chaire*, friend. I am Averill Steverson, Grand Master of The Order of Midas. Welcome to our house."

"Thank you, sir. I am Archibald Spurrell," I said, giving the name of a lieutenant with whom I had served.

"So, a friend of Johannes. A terrible loss, that was. Had you known him long?" he said, peering at me closely.

I sensed that I should not try and exaggerate my connection. The less which I claimed, the less I could be held to account for.

"Perhaps I misspoke. We were not close – more acquaintances, really. We met some years ago by chance, and struck up an occasional correspondence. But I greatly respected the man, and whenever I asked him for advice, invariably he would raise the topic of your Order."

Steverson relaxed at my words. "Johannes was quite the missionary. His advocacy was instrumental, I think, in The Order's growth these past two decades. Perhaps you will be his last success. Of what did he speak to you?"

"Oh, he told me of your pursuit of greater wisdom, of truths which our callow modern age has forgotten," I said, warming to my ruse. "He assured me that the knowledge you had preserved against the ravages of time could bring me great peace of mind, and great wealth besides. He mentioned thirteen steps – "

"I beg pardon," interrupted Steverson. "Surely you mean twelve steps."

"Oh, no, it was most certainly thirteen steps."

Steverson rose, his amiable nature replaced by a cold, unfeeling mask.

"He did no such thing. I do not know who you are, or why you have come, but you will leave, immediately."

"Please," I sputtered. "There must have been some misunderstanding."

"Get out. Now!"

I sowed a host of improvised apologies, but they fell upon barren ground, and soon realised that there was no swaying the man. I departed hastily, my face burning with embarrassment. There was nothing left but to return to Baker Street and report my failure.

There I found Holmes equally dispirited. Deep in study, he sat amidst a mountain of wigs and discarded clothing, making voluminous notes concerning the tomes borrowed from the Moorswaite household.

"Ah, Watson," he said dully. "Be wary, for you approach a man steeped in the mysteries of the ancients."

"What have you uncovered?"

"Little. Our client's insistence on concealing the true story of his father's death has necessitated a profusion of digressions, disguises, and other ruses to conduct the interviews I desire. As a Jewish haberdasher, I learned that Moorswaite's sister is having a dalliance with her gardener, while as a Latvian charity worker, I have uncovered an insurance fraud. On the whole, I have only confirmed our client's initial findings – Johannes Moorswaite was a happy man, and the bafflement at his suicide is universal. Those members of The Order which I could reach agree."

Holmes let loose a mighty sigh. "As for what the Grecians have taught me, I near uncovering the dark secrets which lead to limitless wealth. You will soon have all you could hope to gamble at the races."

"Well, you have achieved more than my own sad efforts, at any rate."

"Oh? I would welcome a reprieve from this foolishness." He began filling a pipe. "Tell me all about it."

With Holmes reclined in his chair, eyes closed, I disclosed my feeble attempts at investigation.

"You are too hard on yourself," said he, when my narrative was complete. "To be sure, I would have played the role a touch differently, but you most certainly did not fail."

Holmes was not always so charitable, and I must confess that his approval, such as it was, was a comfort.

"I have seen the elder Moorswaite's suicide note," said he, "and it indeed refers to thirteen steps. If we accept that it was the last testament of Johannes Moorswaite, it must have been significant. Now consider the reaction of Mr. Steverson. Your interview appeared to have been going rather well until you suddenly ran up against a very firm wall. Why did the mention of a thirteenth step provoke so severe a reaction? And how could he be so certain that Moorswaite had not in fact referenced such?"

"I puzzled over that very point on my way home. I think the simplest explanation is that Steverson was certain that an Order member would never reveal the existence of this step to an outsider."

"Very good, Watson. Alternately, he was certain that Moorswaite would never have made such a basic and perhaps even blasphemous doctrinal error in speaking of thirteen steps when there are only in fact twelve. In which case, the thirteenth step is a reference to something completely unknown. But Moorswaite's last words lead me to prefer your solution."

"And yet, if only The Order knows of this thirteenth step, how will you learn of it when none from The Order will speak of it? Even the dead have been more communicative."

To my surprise Holmes, with visible satisfaction, threw shut the theosophical tome he had been perusing, leaped up, and began donning his coat. "You are a veritable beacon, my friend. Good day, Watson!" He hurtled out of doors before I could ask what had occurred to him.

I did not see him again until the following morning, when I emerged into our sitting room. Clad in his dressing gown, he sat puffing away at a pipe, eyes closed. Familiar with his habits, I simply went for the morning editions and awaited events. I did not wait long.

"Finias Claybourne died a month ago," said he, not opening his eyes.

"The Irish shipping magnate? I suppose I noted such at the time. What of it?"

"Claybourne had a home here in town. He also had a mania for matters arcane."

"A member of The Order, you think?"

"I know. It was common knowledge in the City."

I was intrigued. "And how did Mr. Claybourne die? Suicide, perhaps?"

"Enteritis."

"Oh," I said, disappointed. "I had hoped for somewhat of a stronger link to the Moorswaite matter. Were the two friends?"

"I am not certain. I hope to learn more this afternoon, when I call upon his widow. Would you care to join me?"

"Surely The Order does not accept women. What might you learn from her?"

"I'm not certain. But if living members of The Order will not speak to us, perhaps the dead will, through their families and friends."

To reach the front door of Finias Claybourne's palatial former residence, we had to navigate a host of movers busily emptying the manor of its contents, which consisted of most of the British Museum, judging by appearances. The number of steps, I observed, fell into no recognizable pattern.

"Mr. Holmes," said our host, when the butler had ushered us through the sea of workmen. "Forgive the pandemonium." A stately matron swathed in mourning dress, her rich Irish lilt had survived any attempt at polishing it to meet the demands of London society.

"Not at all, madam. Thank you for granting us a moment of your time. May I ask why you are moving?"

"I loathe this city, if I may speak frankly. My husband only lived here because his firm was best operated here, and he trusted none but himself

221

to oversee it. But we never put down roots, and I'll be happy to get back to where I belong. Now, your card says that you are a detective. How marvellous. What is it you wished to speak to me of?"

"We're seeking information concerning a group to which your husband belonged: The Order of Midas."

"Ha, that foolishness? You Englishmen deride our so-called popery, and then start embracing that pagan rubbish?"

"I assure you, madam, that neither I nor my companion have any connection with The Order. I merely wish to ask of your husband's history with it."

"He'd been with them for – how long was it, Featherstone?"

"Thirty years, madam," said the butler, overseeing the move of a bedraggled stuffed dodo.

"There you have it. Thirty years. About twenty-nine too long, if you ask me. All those late-night meetings, the long trips to the country, his tiresome friends."

"Why an allowance for the one, if I may?" I asked.

"Well, they promised riches, and I must say, they delivered in that regard. My husband's business was in disastrous shape before he joined The Order, but soon thereafter made a remarkable turnaround."

"You mentioned trips to the country."

"Yes, they have a lodge up in the Lakeland. Finias would go there for the solstice and the equinox, and other times besides."

"Did he leave any mementos of The Order behind after he passed away? A library of strange tomes or the like?" inquired Holmes.

"A library?" Mrs. Claybourne laughed. "Finias was many things, most of them remarkable, but a reader he was not. The only item of note he had concerning The Order was that awful beast thing."

"A statue, perhaps?" asked Holmes, a bloodhound catching the scent.

"That it was. An enormous Minotaur, all monstrous and leering. I despised it, always felt that it was – well, if you'll pardon my foolishness – looking at me. My husband and I quarrelled fiercely over its presence here, but he utterly refused to part with it, said that it was part of the price he'd paid."

"To what?" I asked.

"I don't know. In any case, I no longer need worry about it. Hardly was Finias in the ground when I received a caller. Some oily fellow showed up at my door unannounced and said he was here to take the thing. Now, while I was glad to see the back of it, I wasn't about to give it to charity, but he produced a document stating that upon my husband's death the statue returned to The Order. It was signed by Finias, and the fellow assured me that an identical document would be found amongst my husband's papers. And so it was. I saw no point in fighting for such a monument to bad taste, and so let him have it. They carted it off at once."

"And how long did your husband possess the Minotaur, madam?"

"Oh, that would be – what do you think, Featherstone?"

"Almost ten years, madam," said he, serving as pallbearer for an Egyptian mummy.

"Yes, that sounds about right. He received it just before his promotion to the 'Inner Circle', whatever that was. 'Can't possibly tell you about it', he said, all delighted with his secrets. He seemed quite disappointed when he realised that I hadn't asked and wasn't going to, the poor dear."

"One final point, if I may. Was your husband's illness a lengthy one?"

"Oh, yes – years."

"It is interesting, I grant you, but I do not see how it helps matters," I said, ensconced in our sitting room once more. "I thought perhaps that the gift of the Minotaur and the death of its possessor were linked, but Claybourne enjoyed a long life with it."

"That in itself is useful data," rejoined Holmes. "The Minotaur is a secondary concern but is, I suspect, a symbol of The Order's grace, a sacred item which is proof – or perhaps even part-and-parcel-of-ascension – to this Inner Circle which Mrs. Claybourne mentioned."

"You believe Johannes Moorswaite was thus recently promoted to the Inner Circle, then?"

"I do, perhaps even a replacement for Mr. Claybourne. The evidence suggests that when one of The Order's senior members dies, another takes his place."

"The number of statues, then, may also mark the size of the Inner Circle's membership."

"I agree. Ramey died decades ago, and one does not go about commissioning further True Crosses, after all. We must speak to our client at once."

"How is this connected with Johannes Moorswaite's death?"

"I have but suspicions, for The Order's natural reticence – and our client's strictures – shield it from such probes as would permit a definitive answer. I hope to use our client's possession of the Minotaur, so obviously valued by The Order, to draw them into the open. From there, we may divine the secrets of the thirteenth step."

It was vague, I mused, as we rode to the Moorswaite abode, but I had watched Holmes weave the solution to a case out of more slender threads. Tireless in following a trail, his bulldog perseverance and willingness to toil solved mysteries as often as any brilliant deduction.

Our client's appearance had degenerated markedly, I saw once we were admitted. The bags under his eyes were pronounced, his skin waxen and pale. A slight palsy spoke volumes, and he made no effort to master it.

"Mr. Moorswaite," said Holmes. "Thank you for seeing us at such short notice. Tell me, do you still have the Minotaur?"

"God help me, I do. The Order has been hounding me for it, insisting that in the event of my father's death it reverts to them. But I have fought them. Oh yes, I have fought them. Privately, I must admit that in my father's papers I found a signed deed which agrees with The Order's account, but . . . ."

"Go on, sir," I prompted gently. I sensed that it would not be wise to push the man too hard.

"When that thing crossed this threshold, damnation came with it!" Moorswaite's eyes burned feverishly, and how much of it was sickness and how much of it was passion I did not know. "Whenever I would enter the study, it seemed to stare at me, eyes full of loathing. I avoided the chamber whenever I could, but too soon my father was dead. Day in and day out, as I took command of his business empire, I was forced to labour under the beast's supervision. Then the dreams began. At first it was just its eyes, glowing in the blackness, but each night the vision has grown clearer. Now, when I lay down to sleep, I find myself in my father's study. I climb onto the chair. I fasten the rope around my neck, and the beast stares at me with terrible approval. It knows what I intend, and there is no mercy there, only insistence that I finish the deed."

The poor man had obviously become obsessed with The Order's gift. Its pagan nature offended his pious sensibilities, and upon his beloved father's death his grief had settled upon this intruder as the cause of all his woes. But the toll upon his constitution was quite real, and I knew that were the case not solved soon, our client's health might be shattered permanently.

"Surely keeping the thing from The Order is not worth this," I said. "Why have you not rid yourself of it?"

"Why, because . . . ." He trailed off, his eyes glassy. I shot Holmes a look of worry, and together we eased our client into a chair.

Holmes spoke softly. "The Order will doubtless continue to press you for the statue's return, and in the long run you will certainly have to surrender it. I only ask that you hold onto it a short while longer. I believe it can – "

The butler entered, a look of apprehension upon his face. "Forgive my interruption, sir, but a Mr. Steverson is here to see you. I told him that you were indisposed, but he was absolutely insistent."

224

"Fine, send him in," said Moorswaite.

"Hold a moment!" cried Holmes. "Do you trust us to have your best interests at heart in this affair?"

Moorswaite cast about, tired, baffled. "Why, yes, I suppose – "

"Good. Then I must beg you to follow my lead. Say nothing other than to agree with what I propose."

He turned to me. "Watson, Steverson knows your face. I must ask that you conceal yourself. That closet there!"

I moved with alacrity. Fortunately, through a crack in the doors I could still witness events. Soon enough, The Order's master entered the room.

"Mr. Moorswaite," he said coolly in greeting. Turning to face Holmes, he said, "I am Averill Steverson. And you are?"

Holmes stepped forward. "Acton Pierce, solicitor. It is most fortunate that you chose to visit us at this time, for myself and my client were just discussing you. I presume that you have come about the Ramey?"

"You presume correctly, sir. I have here an affidavit, signed by the late Johannes Moorswaite, assigning ownership of the statue to our Order upon his death. I know he had a copy of his own, for I witnessed it. Your prevarication in this matter has been intolerable, sir. I must insist that you hand over the Ramey by the close of tomorrow. Failure will result in the most dire of consequences."

Holmes barked a laugh. "Your melodramatics have no place here. It is my client's position that there was no such affidavit in his father's papers, and that any which you possess is undoubtedly forged. Johannes Moorswaite was most explicit: The Ramey was to pass to his son."

Steverson paced out of sight for a moment, but when he reentered my field of view I could see plain the fury writ large upon his face.

"Mr. Moorswaite, your father was a boon companion to me these past two decades. Were he still alive, I know he would advise you, in the strongest possible terms, to keep to the pact he signed. I warn you: You cannot fathom the powers you trifle with."

Moorswaite only sat slumped in his chair, wringing his hands. If he had heard any of this, he showed no sign.

"Arthur!" shouted Steverson.

Our client's head shot up in a panic. He looked to Holmes, then to Steverson. My friend placed a hand upon Moorswaite's shoulder, and the embattled man seemed to draw upon Holmes's iron will for his own.

"I concur with my solicitor," said Moorswaite, in a reedy whisper. "His words are my own. Go."

225

"Very well," said Steverson. "I pray you change your mind, for I cannot be responsible for the results otherwise. Remember, Moorswaite – the close of tomorrow." He stormed out.

Once I heard the front door slam in the distance, I emerged from my hiding place.

"He seemed desperate, Holmes," said I. "Might he make an attempt to carry off the statue?"

My friend chuckled. "I would not credit The Order with the power to tell Aristotle from Aesop, let alone the ability to spirit an eight-foot slab of marble down a spiral staircase without detection. My worries take a baser form."

"Murder," I breathed.

"Precisely, Watson."

"You believe that The Order had my father killed?" asked Moorswaite.

"I have no reason to suppose such. But I would be remiss if I did not guard against the possibility that they did, or that they did not but in your case may reconsider. I have aided the Yard on several occasions. I believe I shall ask Inspector Lestrade for a favour. Mr. Moorswaite, would you object to a few men quietly watching the premises until, say, the end of the week?"

"Steverson specified tomorrow," said Moorswaite.

"He did, but one thing I have learned is to never take a potential criminal at their word. He may have given a false date to lower your guard. By the end of the week I hope to have the answers you desire."

"Fine, fine," said our client feebly. "I must go now. I . . . I have work to do." He began plodding up the stairs, towards his father's study.

"We shall see ourselves out," I said. "Do get some rest, sir."

Moorswaite waved apathetically in our direction and disappeared from view.

Lestrade had the men to spare, dispatching three of them to watch Moorswaite's home. The inspector promised that a constable would inform us should anything unusual occur, and thus Holmes and I were both surprised when, two days later, it was Lestrade himself who arrived upon our doorstep.

"You'd best come at once," he indicated.

"So," I said, "they managed to steal the Minotaur after all."

"No, Doctor, it is still with Moorswaite – for a little while longer at least. Your client hanged himself in the night, in the room with it."

We rode to the Moorswaite residence together, with Lestrade informing us of the tragic events of the evening prior. Moorswaite had retired to the study after supper. A servant, knocking at the door about eleven o'clock, heard no reply, but did not enter, thinking his master had simply fallen asleep at the desk. Apparently Moorswaite had grown snappish of late, and disliked being disturbed. Only in the morning did the servant risk an entrance, discovering Moorswaite hanging from the precise spot his father had employed.

"Have you observed anything unusual about the chamber?" asked Holmes.

"I've held off from a close look, for I know how particular you are about such matters. However, the servant assures me that the study looks as it did, with one exception."

"Oh?" said I.

"The statue in the room. It has been moved."

Sure enough, when we arrived and were ushered past stolid constables and weeping, pale servants, we saw that the great Minotaur now stood in the chamber's centre, facing the spot where the Moorswaite men had met their end. Terrible pangs of guilt assailed me, for we had pushed Moorswaite to keep the Minotaur when he might have broken free of its spell.

"Why move it?" I wondered aloud.

"It was not moved! It moved of its own accord!" shouted an elderly servant from the hall. "The young master was not strong enough to shift that monster. I told him it was a creature of wickedness – witchcraft! At first he agreed, held onto to it only out of spite. But he fell under its spell, and now look. Behold the price of sorcery!"

"Yes, yes, terrible," said Lestrade. "Constable, clear the hall." He returned his attention to us. "I hesitate to speak ill of the dead, but your man was barmy. Sitting up here day after day, surrounded by all this nonsense, we should be thankful he didn't sacrifice a goat in here as well."

I saw that Holmes had ignored the commotion, lost in his work. He scoured the rugs, the chairs, and the desk, looking once more over the shelves and their musty, eldritch tomes and ending with the Minotaur. The floor was deeply scuffed and gouged by years of use, so that making out a clear trail was difficult. He attempted to shift the statue from its position, but struggled to move it even a few inches. Considering how far it was from its original position, and aware as I was of Holmes' prodigious strength, I was taken aback. At last he moved to the room's centre, chin in hand, slowly pivoting, attempting to divine its secrets.

"The servants speak as one to the fellow's depression, his collapsing health, and his odd behaviours," said Lestrade. "It seems his father's death struck him quite hard. As for moving that thing, I'm sure that a fellow with a frenzied determination could have managed it, given all night. I think all

227

this mystical humbug is only distracting from what is at heart a simple matter. Regrettable, but simple all the same."

"I . . . am forced to concur," said Holmes.

Lestrade gave a start. The occasions on which Holmes agreed with his assessments were few. I think that the poor inspector had beat-to-quarters, and was startled not to have gotten his broadside. And yet, the hesitation in Holmes's reply left me unsettled.

"Well," Lestrade continued, "I have a robbery on Arlington Street which needs attending to, so if you'll forgive me, gentlemen? Sorry about the loss of your client. Good day." With a wave he departed, constables in tow.

I looked to Holmes, expecting some insight, but was disappointed when he simply left the room as well. I took one last look at the Minotaur, and shuddered at the feeling of malevolence which crept up my spine. Recalling Steverson's dire warning of unfathomable powers, I wondered anew at how the great beast had crossed that chamber.

A week later I had already consigned the case to that portion of my files dealing with lamentable failures when Holmes, only recently returned, received a visitor. A ruffled Mrs. Hudson ushered in a scruffy, dirty-faced urchin who cast a suspicious glance at me, and then moved with melodramatic caution to whisper something in Holmes's ear.

"Very good, Edward," replied Holmes. "Here's your pay. Make sure that the others get their share, for I shall be checking."

"Yes, sir!" the boy shouted, racing from the chamber with several coins and the enviable tempestuousness of youth. I heard Mrs. Hudson clucking behind him on the stairs.

"Watson, might I interest you in a countryside foray?"

"I have nothing pressing. Where are we going?"

"The Lakeland."

"What? That's practically in Scotland."

"If you recall, Mrs. Claybourne informed us that The Order has a lodge there."

On the train north, Holmes surprised me by divulging his thoughts.

"I have learned that The Order collected the Moorswaite Minotaur shortly after our client's death, only to promptly gift it to another – one Jeffrey Allington, well-to-do solicitor and dabbler in all things arcane."

"Interesting," I replied. "Does that mean that this Allington fellow is the next to be promoted, then?"

"I believe so, for recall Mrs. Claybourne's testimony that the gift of the Minotaur to her husband immediately preceded his ascension. It is a mark of favour soon to come, in addition to a signifier of status."

"And what does young Edward have to do with this?"

"I have been attempting to determine how many members The Order's Inner Circle has, and who they are. For this I have been employing the Irregulars, using them to follow individuals coming and going to their temple, then following this up with my own researches. At present I believe there are six. Edward informed me that five of them have made their way to train stations. For myself, this morning I followed Steverson, and observed him purchasing tickets to Penrith. The Order's original lodge, I have learned, is in that area, near the lake of Croneswater. They gather, Watson."

"Holmes," I said. "Our client is dead. You have no evidence of foul play in either Moorswaite case. What is this meant to accomplish?"

"Johannes Moorswaite's death vexes me."

"Not Arthur's?"

"No. His was certainly a natural one."

Recalling again the Minotaur's strange placement in the room where Arthur Moorswaite drew his last breath, I was far less certain of our client's fate, but knew that my friend would only dismiss my concerns as rank superstition.

"Having dined with members of The Order," Holmes continued, "Johannes killed himself immediately thereafter. Those present at the dinner claimed that nothing untoward occurred, but we have only their word as to such. I believe now that Johannes learned something at that last supper, something he could not bear to know, something which led him to take his own life. And I must know what that was."

"How can you hope to know what was said that night?" I asked. "No senior member of The Order will speak to us."

"True. But one thing which the Irregulars also informed me of was the fact that Allington remains at home. Whatever The Order is doing, it is without him."

"It seems unusual to be initiated from afar, but what of it?"

"If we assume that this is The Order's standard practice, then Allington will only learn of what is about to transpire after it is finished. I imagine Johannes Moorswaite was dealt with in a similar fashion. The question, then, is what transpired."

He would say no more, and we rode the rest of the long journey in silence. Alighting at the small town of Windermere, we took rooms for the evening. The contrast between the soup of London and the crisp northern air could not have been greater, and I remarked how one could see for miles in the clear, well-lit night.

"Indeed, Watson. There is a full moon tomorrow."

Holmes insisted that we remain indoors during the day, so as to avoid any chance of being spotted by members of The Order, and so it was not until the next evening that we left, taking a carriage north. Only the occasional centuries-old cottage or farmhouse, bathed in silver moonlight, spoke of human habitation, and I was astounded that one could still find such isolation in England. At a tiny village we switched to horses, riding the rest of the way to Croneswater. Surrounded by steep hillsides, the lake was a small one, choked by reeds and blooming water lilies. On its far side, wavering torchlight and strange ululations echoing across the water told us of our destination.

"What are we going to do?" I asked.

"Merely observe, Watson. If I surmise correctly, on this night of the full moon, here in their place of founding, will be Allington's initiation ritual. Should it provide no insight into Moorswaite's death, though the uncertainty will pain me evermore, I shall retire from the affair."

Creeping through the thin tree line, we moved into a position to observe the goings-on. Near the lodge was a rough pier, boats tied alongside. A small number of robed, hooded figures were clustered together in front of the pier. Towering over them was the figure of another Minotaur. This one was far cruder than the cruel masterpiece I had seen in the Moorswaite household. The gloom and distance rendered judgement difficult, but I suspected it had been formed of plaster, rather than marble.

As we closed, we heard droning, sonorous chants. The bright moon, cold and imperious in the sky, made manoeuvres dangerous, but after a hastily whispered consultation we decided that the closely-packed figures were sufficiently engrossed in their thaumaturgy to chance it. Dashing behind a nearby shed, we were able to rest within earshot.

Eventually the chanting rose to a climax, only to die off with sudden finality. As this faded into the night, a powerful, booming voice filled the void. I recognised it at once as Steverson.

"Brothers of The Order! Our circle is broken, our number incomplete. Where there is six, there should be seven. Brother Claybourne has gone to Hades, and Brother Moorswaite was a brittle reed. Guided by the ancients, we have chosen anew. Tonight we consecrate Brother Allington. Though many leagues distant, mere physical distance is no bar to the powers we unleash here tonight.

"Over the long years, each of us has ascended the twelve steps to enlightenment. But we who have been favoured know of a final step, a thirteenth step, one only crossed with the aid of others. Brother Allington has proved himself worthy, and with our sacrifice we shall guide his soul across the final threshold."

The circle parted, and to my horror I saw at their feet a young woman. Bound and gagged, she writhed desperately in an attempt to escape her bonds, but her struggles were fruitless. One of the circle moved to the Minotaur, and after some manipulation the front half of the beast swung away from the rest, revealing an inner cavity. The six forced the woman inside, strapping her firmly in place. They then swung the beast's front half closed once more, entombing her within.

"Come, my brothers," said Steverson. "Poseidon hungers." With this, the six cultists raised up the Minotaur and its monstrous cargo and lowered it into a skiff.

I heard a rustle to my side, and saw Holmes frantically searching for a sturdy branch, some sort of weapon with which we might arrest this terrible ritual. Each of us finding a suitable candidate, we bolted into the clear.

"Hold, Steverson!" my friend shouted.

The cultists whirled about, and Steverson flung his hood from his face. His wild eyes gleamed in the moonlight.

"You would profane this holy night with your presence?" He turned to his companions. "Take them!"

The hooded figures advanced upon us, cloaked in shadow, a silent, faceless menace. I felt as though we faced not men, but shades of the underworld.

Holmes, unwilling to await their pleasure, boldly leaped into their ranks. Superb with the singlestick, he wielded his branch with a fencer's grace. My efforts were more brutish. My limb was stouter, my form mere fury at the thought of the blasphemies The Order sought to perpetrate in this lonely place.

The Inner Circle may have been adept at menacing helpless women, but against our assault they soon quailed. Three having been knocked senseless, the other two begged for mercy. Steverson, seeing his fellows vanquished, raced for the craft at whose bottom lay his intended victim.

"The step must be crossed!" he cried.

He fumbled for the oars, but my friend was faster. Before Steverson could escape the pier, Holmes struck true, sending The Order's master unconscious into the dark waters. I pulled the villain clear before he drowned, and together we wrested his intended victim free of her plaster tomb.

The following day we herded our captives to Penrith, entrusting them to the local constabulary. The woman we rescued, a scullery maid from London, was shaken but unharmed, and profoundly grateful at her deliverance.

231

Back in London, we learned that "Brother Allington" professed to be completely unaware of what his fellows were enacting on his behalf. He disavowed The Order and its murderous plans, and swore he would have immediately broken from them once they informed him of the cost accompanying his promotion to the Inner Circle. Lacking any proof to the contrary, he was let alone, but something in his sly gaze and unctuous nature left me unconvinced.

In the days that followed, we learned of the shuttering of The Order's houses of worship, though to my dismay the Ramey Minotaurs passed into private hands, and I could only wonder at what malign influence they might exert, even apart from their dark masters. Steverson was never to make it to trial, for despite the strongest precautions, he was found hanged in his cell one stormy night.

One evening I found Holmes, his features troubled, consulting stacks of ancient newspapers and poring over his indices.

"What bothers you, Holmes? The Order is done for. More important, we saved a young woman's life."

"Indeed," he replied. "And we know of the terrible deed perpetrated in Johannes Moorswaite's name which caused him to end his own life. Doubtless he was told of it at his last supper, but did not react the way The Order expected. They mistook their man."

"A great tragedy, but justice has been served."

"The Order was in existence for nearly a hundred years, Watson. Its Inner Circle consisted of seven members. When one died, another took his place."

"Yes, but I still do not see – "

It was then that I did see, that I realised how many ceremonies we had not interrupted, how many offerings we had failed to prevent, how many times that final step had been taken. And I thought of that lonely lake in the idyllic English countryside and shuddered at what might lay upon its murky, weed-clogged bed.

The Missing Murderer
by Marcia Wilson

Note: This is a peculiar record. Many details that would have been useful in tracking the precise date have been blotted out of the original document. The editors do not at this time understand why Dr. Watson went through such pains to craft a case and then obfuscate its most useful elements. We assure the readers our work in transcribing the contents of Dr. Watson's Dispatch Box is ongoing, and we must believe that eventually we will come to the correct conclusion.

The Midwinter of *[Here the date is crossed out.]* had passed us in a foul mood, its latest storm leaving only long enough to circle over the North Sea and return like a bad relative. London all but shut down beneath the weight of the cold. Telegraph wires were broken repeatedly under the onslaught, and even the telephones suffered from breakage. Holmes reluctantly concluded there was little to do when simple metal could not survive. Together we shared some relief in not needing to go outside. The coal did not draw. The wind never ceased its attack against the exposed window by Holmes's chemistry table, and Mrs. Hudson dedicated herself to a never-ending delivery of hot tea. My rooms suffered a broken window against the latest winds and I was sleeping it rough on the sofa until the glazier could manage a visit.

It was hard to say who was more surprised, Holmes or myself, to hear Inspector Bradstreet from Bow Street had come to call.

"I didn't hear a thing," I confessed to Holmes.

"I believe the door-bell is frozen shut." Holmes marvelled. "Well! Send him up, Mrs. Hudson, and we shall be grateful for an extra cup." He peered out the window. "And something hot for the poor bobbies with him!"

Mr. Bradstreet was not a small man. Though I have met many who were much larger, his sheer masculine presence gave the brain the impression that there were two, perhaps three smaller men wrapped inside his coat and hat. That illusion was magnified under a woollen suit and coat lined with new flannel and policeman's blue-gloves and muffler. His cheeks were cherried from the cold and he paused to daintily brush snow crystals freezing up the ends of his black mustaches. Holmes was eternally amused at the man's astonishing delicacy against his coarse body, and I saw him cut his lips into a quick smile that he mastered into polite interest when the Bow Street Runner turned to him.

233

"Gentlemen," he nodded to us both, one at a time, and cleared his throat. "I apologise for calling you un-announced. I would prefer to give you longer notice first if I could."

"Your manners are a geologic bedrock, my good man." Holmes waved that aside. "Have a hot drink against the chill, for it shall only get worse tonight!"

"Oh, yes, that is true," he agreed and was suddenly plunged into gloom. "We've got a problem with one of the corpses in the morgue. Lestrade refuses to leave it. And in this weather!"

Holmes and I frowned at the oddness of this news. "Perhaps you could give us the facts as you know them, starting from the earliest date known?"

Bradstreet nodded and rose to stand by the fire, sipping from his cup as he did so.

"The morgue takes all sorts, as you know. A policeman's most grievous duty is finding the poor, dead from exposure. This winter has been miserable, sirs. It has been a long time since we have brought in so many corpses – man, woman, and child. With the weather and the time of year, they have been short of space all week, and Scotland Yard temporarily opened one of their annex buildings for storage. I believe you both know the one I mean. It is that gigantic brick cube against the water-facing wall? No insulation, just thick brick and plank. The weather got in through the windows and glazed it – floor, walls, and ceiling. So while it is an ice-house and worthless for anything but ice, that makes it a decent place to bring the dead until they can be moved to proper facilities.

"At 2:15 this afternoon – the bells had just gone off the quarter-hour – the wagons brought in half-a-tenement's housing. The fires had gone out in the night and . . . I needn't tell you those details. It was tragic. Lestrade and I met outside the morgue entrance by simple accident. We had both been indoors since six of the morning, and in want of some fresh air. So we were talking and sharing a cigarette, stamping the snow under our feet into ice, and watching the poor men slip and slide as they brought in the dead on their stretchers.

"'What brings you here, now?' Lestrade asked me.

"'I've a missing woman from the Northern Line. She's not right in the head, and if she wandered too far in this weather, she's frozen stiff by now. I hope I don't find her. Yourself?'"

"'I've got some – here, now!' He said this in a yell over my shoulder. I turned just in time to see a body finish tipping to the street. It was frozen in a terrible, twisty shape with its arms and legs in all directions.

"You know Lestrade as well as anyone can know 'im. Nothing gets his attention like something out of true, and he's got to pursue it to the end, or I suppose he won't sleep at night. I followed, thinking this was probably one of his daft hares, and if I didn't make him come home at a decent hour, he'd hear the rough side of his wife's frying-pan. Still, we get all kinds of poor folks frozen to death, all shapes and sizes and every which you can imagine . . . if you wanted to imagine it.

"Lestrade helped the men wrestle the dead man back on to his cart, and I tell you, I literally *saw* a thought come across him. He drew up, back straight as a surveyor's rod, and his hands fell to his hips.

"'That wasn't right,' he muttered, though if he was talking to me – I'm not sure. He draws himself up – " Bradstreet innocently indicated a height below his shoulder. " – and he said, 'Did you see that?'

"'I saw,' I said. 'But I'm not sure what.'

"And with that, Lestrade hares himself into the morgue, and what can I do but go after him?" Bradstreet suddenly shuddered, as if the memory itself had chilled him to the bone. I refreshed his teacup.

"Thank you. Well, the body was frozen solid, and they had to tie the identity-card on his wrist – the shoe and foot are all sealed together. But it said, '*Richard Roe, found at 1414 Lyons Park 7:14 A.M. PC Bee, Number-whatever-his-number-was.*' Bradstreet sighed. "The man was a mess. Clots of snow and ice-shards were all over him, and ground into his face and neck. He was frozen in a sprawled-over pose as if he died in the middle of a dancing-step or pantomime. Despite all this, we could tell he was a young man, most likely in his mid-twenties, clean-shaven with dark brown hair parted neatly to one side, eyes dark blue, pupils wide open under the frost, no gloves or hat or even a scarf. His light brown coat was summer weight, and there was a large stain where some liquid had soaked through his right side-pocket. His black stockings were thin cotton, and his shoes were better suited for indoor in a warm office, for they were thin brown calfskin. There was no necktie, and we both thought it was odd."

"As odd as everything you say," Holmes agreed. He had sunk into his favourite chair and was listening, eyes-closed, with every sign of contentment, as Bradstreet described the details.

"Surely," I offered, "this would be suspicious? A man dressed for summer?"

"How I wish I could agree," Bradstreet mourned. "But that isn't even the strangest thing a copper sees. Humans are a strange, strange herd of sheep, Doctor. He wasn't dressed for winter, but we've seen enough dead men from cold to know their brain tricks them into thinking it is much warmer than it really is."

"I have seen that for myself," I admitted. "The brain confuses the victim into believing they are perfectly warm and comfortable. That is the most dangerous level of cold-exposure, and death invariably follows unless they are rescued from their own actions and brought into a genuinely warm habitat."

"Aye. In fact, that's what the coroner is trying to say – Oh, I get ahead of myself." Bradstreet blushed in embarrassment. "Please do forgive me. Lestrade was rummaging through the man's frozen coat and pulled out a shattered gin bottle from the stained pocket. It was a nasty old thing, and broke into even more pieces in his hand! I mean, it positively shattered."

"How do you know it was a gin bottle?" Holmes wondered.

"We could still smell a bit of the fumes."

"Ah. Go on."

"We were glad of Lestrade's leather gloves. They saved him a trip to the red lamp. Lestrade was still inspecting them for splinters when the coroner came up with his little clip-board and demanded to know what we were doing.

"He's a terrible thorn in the side of us, is Mr. Brooks. You can't fault his professionalism, for he's as protective as the Good Lord himself when it comes to his charges, but he and Lestrade . . . they don't see eye-to-eye very much."

Holmes grunted. "I have not the pleasure of Mr. Godine Brooks."

"I wouldn't call it a pleasure, Mr. Holmes. Perhaps the evils of nepotism."

"Do go on."

"'What are you doing?' he screeched and tried to shoo us back. 'Get away from that poor fellow!' Lestrade, though – that's just a red flag to a bull, and he dug his heels in that frozen floor and faced him off. Mr. Brooks is about my size, so you can imagine how Lestrade felt when he seemed to think he could, ah . . . intimidate him into backing off."

"That," Holmes said drily, "makes me wish more than ever I had been there."

"Yes, well, he tried to tell Lestrade he was interferrin' with his duty to the dead. 'You can tell he died of drink and the cold. It set in his addled brain and he tried to take a walk and the drink caught him and he died in the snow. I've seen it a hundred times if I've seen it a thousand!'

"And Lestrade shot back that it was a policeman's duty to see to the living *and* the dead alike, and no one would stop him from his duty, and if he was a *real* coroner, he'd know that." Bradstreet shook his head. "The finer points of the conversation crumbled to ash at that point. Lestrade turned his back on Mr. Brooks and stuffed both his gloves into my hands. 'I'm staying here.' He announced. 'There's something strange, and if I'm going to be a fool, I'd rather be a proven a fool instead of spend the rest of my life in doubt.' With a hard eye at Mr. Brooks he added, 'Bradstreet, if you would take these to Baker and see if he can't find me another pair of gloves. These are all cut-up.'

"'In this weather!' Mr. Brooks exclaimed. 'Mr. Lestrade, that is a ridiculous risk! You'll freeze if you stay here longer than half-an-hour!'

"But he wouldn't be moved. I promised to do as he said." Bradstreet produced a pair of men's thin leather gloves, wadded and crushed into a ball. "And with that," he said solemnly, "I pass these on to you, 'Mr. Baker'."

Holmes snorted. "Someday, I expect an explanation as to who decided this would be my little *nom de guerre* among the police."

"I can't say, as it wasn't me, but most of us prefer an alias that is deathly simple. We don't like to try cleverness when we're tired and hungry."

Holmes muttered at that as he made for his chemistry table, but I could see he was pleased. With a flourish, he snapped on the adjustable lamp and carefully prized apart the gloves under its light.

We followed curiously. In concession to the terrible cold of the morgue, the gloves were still frigid. Snow and ice were not melting quickly in the warmth of the room. I could see there were lacerations on the palms and finger-pads from sharp bits of ice, and from the broken gin bottle.

"Ha!" Holmes took the tweezers and held a glove upright. A broken shard of glass fell from the inside and rattled on the marble tablet. He scowled and held the glittering chunk closer to the lamp. To me the glass seemed unusually dark. He turned and twisted it at every angle.

"Mr. Bradstreet," he said at last, "You were right to come here. Use our telephone and call the Yard. Lestrade may be in great danger."

The big man moved with a nearly unbelievable speed but just as quickly shouted back up the stairwell that the telephone-lines were still out.

"Watson, grab your coat." His lips set hard. "Your revolver too. Lestrade has taken a terrible chance, but I should not like to."

In fine weather, a man may bicycle from Baker Street to Scotland Yard in less than twenty minutes. Less than an hour on foot, and if he can travel by hansom or bus, thirty minutes. We were packed like sardines into the police-van and the weather, finally stable, did not help our travels as the winter night fell into a solid curtain of black. It kept our solid horses to a crawl. The driver trusted the discretion of the beasts, but Bradstreet fidgeted anxiously at our lack of speed.

"Tell me about Mr. Brooks." Holmes demanded. "Everything that comes to mind."

"There isn't much to tell. He's only been here two years. He started under Dr. Harper. They're cousins, I heard. He works long hours and is better with dead folks than the living."

"You implied nepotism. The cousin?"

"From what I understand, yes. Dr. Harper has doing coroner's work for us for . . . a year of Sundays, it seems. We don't really like to give anyone preferential treatment, but the coroners aren't the same as the police. If Harper was unhappy enough to leave, we'd have to struggle to find someone with his qualifications." Bradstreet groaned at the thought. "Not that Harper's happy right now. He's taken a leave of absence last week to see to some sort of family troubles. No one knows how long he'll be gone."

"He took a leave of absence for family, but Brooks did not?" I thought that odd.

"Brooks is better with the dead than with the living," Bradstreet repeated.

"Why did Brooks need help finding the job? Is he London?"

"No, he's a Crane, just like young Hopkins. Hopkins doesn't like him any more than Lestrade. Says something's odd about him." Bradstreet cleared his throat. "We don't play favourtism," he reiterated, "but when the question of hiring someone Old Harper knew . . . Hopkins offered to see if he could investigate him, to make sure nothing was untoward. He didn't find anything, though. His uncle was a bad apple, smuggling falsified liquors out of tax."

"Nothing odd about the family farm?"

Bradstreet stared at Holmes. "How did you know he had a farm? Mr. Holmes, if you know Brooks, you could tell me!"

"I don't. I am employing the facts at my disposal. What can you tell me about the family farm?"

"It's been locked into one legal battle after another, according to Hopkins. Fine old estate, orchards and sweet hay and carrots. Brooks was fighting one of his brothers awfully bitter over the title, and while they can visit the property and walk it as they please, they can't own it or share it until the legalities have settled."

Holmes grunted. "I see."

"What is it you see, Mr. Holmes?" Bradstreet finally burst.

"The glass of the gin bottle," Holmes said quietly. "Did you see it was uncommonly dark?"

"I saw it, but didn't think it unusual."

"Gin bottles are clear or tinted in various shades of green, but they are never violet in colour."

"Violet! I didn't see that!"

238

"Not everyone can see the colour. Colour perception, I regret to say, is variable enough that I dislike referring to it unless there is complete surety."

"But a violet glass . . . That would be expensive, wouldn't it?"

"No. That would be *impossible*. I cannot at this time explain to you how very impossible it would be. It is proof of murder, Bradstreet. The fumes of the gin you smelt, I fear, were a plant by the murderer. Lestrade did indeed see something amiss, but the lights in your morgue are usually too poor for a close examination."

"The morgue is a storing room, Mr. Holmes," Bradstreet reproached. "The actual examinations are done in the examination rooms, in brighter light and hygienic conditions. The annexed morgue we're heading to is even worse."

"Exactly. So why was Mr. Brooks so determined to declare drink and cold the cause of death ahead of process, in a badly lit, poorly-fortified ice-house?"

Bradstreet fumbled for an answer. "Because we were already full-up with the dead?"

"Yes, and how convenient." Holmes scowled. "I look forward to asking him a few questions of my own."

"I'll see to it you get that chance," Bradstreet rumbled. "If anything happens to one of my fellows . . . ." But he could not finish the thought and subsided. I watched his enormous hands clench like coil springs in his pockets.

Holmes pelted out the police van as soon as the horses slowed. It was quite dark now, but we managed to follow him as best as we could through the dangerously uneven lumps of snow glazed hard as stone. My leg was always weaker in bitter cold, but Bradstreet grabbed my arm, steadying me with one hand as we used our walking-sticks to good effect. I couldn't imagine a more terrible night, and yet Holmes's actions suggested we should prepare for even worse.

"You there!" he shouted to the startled constable guarding the doorway of the annex. "Is Inspector Lestrade still inside?"

The startled young man stammered. "Wh – why, no, sir. He left a good ten minutes ago."

"He did?" Holmes's pale face grew even paler. "Did you see him leave?"

The constable stared at him. "Here, now. Who are you?" he demanded hotly.

"Answer the question!" Bradstreet bellowed as he trundled up. His face was red as fire as we gasped to catch up with Holmes. "Now, Constable, or I'll have your warrant card for darts!"

"N-no, I didn't see him leave." The constable saluted. "Mr. Brooks sent me to get a fresh lantern, and when I returned, he said Lestrade had left, and not to let anyone in without permission and the key."

Holmes snarled, but nothing matched the growl from Bradstreet's throat as he shoved the constable aside and, with a single look to the lock-plate on the door, kicked it with his heel. The door-hasp snapped and juddered open.

"There's your permission and a key, Stryker." He grabbed the shocked man's lantern and lunged into the room.

It was everything I had always imagined for Dante's frozen lake of the damned. It was a cavern of ice, translucent and swollen, with shadows under the reflected light. Ice even choked the exposed windows, replacing the glass with dripping icicles that ran down the walls and corners, creating an uneven, glassy wilderness. The dead crowded this cavern, their bodies preserved in the moments of their last breath. Our own breaths smoked in the air and Holmes barked at a still figure lying on the frozen ground. It was Lestrade.

My medical instincts decided my actions. As Bradstreet and Holmes alternately shouted orders and organised a search for Brooks, I had the constables carry Lestrade to the warmer confines of the Yard. My first fear had been a killing-stroke, but the whiff of chloroform and slow pulse reassured me the little detective was far from dead. He complained of a dreadful dizziness but managed to stay awake long enough to be reassured all would be well, and promptly sank into a deeper, healthier sleep with his head propped up by a bracing draught of cold, clean air by a cracked window. Thus, he missed the humiliation of knowing his fiercest rival, Tobias Gregson, had arrived while I was using a table as a makeshift examination couch. The big man sniffed and passed around cups of his foul tea. He listened to the details as they trickled down from running policemen, Bradstreet, and occasionally Holmes. Somehow in the flurry, Brooks had gotten wind of his exposé and fled without heed or plan – the most difficult sort of man to track.

"It sounds like he owes his life to you, gentlemen," Gregson contemplated, "*and* his good Loden suit and coat. I must see about getting one of those from my own tailor. I'm sorry I laughed when I heard what he'd paid for that wool. He'll be insufferable about it once he wakes up." He shook his head in wonder. "So, if I am to understand this, Lestrade thought there was something odd about this dead man, sent Bradstreet to

240

Holmes to confirm that, but in the meantime Brooks got the jump on him, because Brooks is probably the man who killed our Richard Roe, and tried to make it look like Lestrade slipped and fell on the ice, knocked himself unconscious, and then unfortunately but completely accidentally locked himself in the morgue's annex overnight, under which circumstances he would be tragically killed?"

"That's how we understand it." PC Barrett said shyly.

"Idiot. Hitting Lestrade on the head doesn't do more than make him mad. He should have tried for his weak spot. Oh, right. He did." Gregson smirked. "And he's been fumed by dope before. He'll be right as rain in the morning . . . which is more than I can say for the poor souls who wander into his path until the headache wears off." Gregson shivered at the thought.

"Chloroform is a deadly drug," I reminded him. "One of its many toxic effects upon inhaling is a drop in body temperature. It would have hastened his death from the cold. His coat and winter suit should share the credit for keeping him alive. I don't understand why Brooks didn't hit Lestrade on the head when he was down. The floor was dangerous! Anyone would have believed he had concussed and died."

"Brooks didn't have the time." Sherlock Holmes had returned and, though he looked weary, he was smiling brightly. "He was removed enough from the police that he didn't know how long PC Stryker would be gone getting a new lamp. As soon as he sent him off for the job, he went inside and managed to get the drop on Lestrade. How he did it I'm interested to learn, as Lestrade is as suspicious as an old badger when he has his teeth in a problem."

Gregson burst out laughing. "Too right!" he agreed merrily. "Well, most of us know Lestrade doesn't do well with anesthesia. He's been that way since '83. Brooks probably slapped the pad on his face and when Ratty went down like a freight train off its metals, he imagined he killed him off." Gregson chuckled again, amused at his own thoughts. "You just wait for him to wake up. You'll know 'old badger' for certain. Brooks will be grateful for the noose."

"He'll have the chance to think it over," Holmes mused. "Brooks didn't realise the code passed between the two of you, Bradstreet. He planned for Lestrade to be discovered when the morgue was next opened – and Lestrade had passed all chance of surviving the cold. He would openly mourn his death with the rest, admit to some carelessness in not being thorough, and accept a possible dismissal in his job for his dereliction . . . but he would remind us that he had warned Lestrade of the dangers of staying here. All he would have to do is protest that Lestrade had slipped and struck himself unconscious, and he hadn't seen him in the

241

shadows. He would regretfully take the responsibility of telling PC Stryker that Lestrade had left, and unknowingly locked him to die in the tomb."

"An awful lot of trouble." Bradstreet sank into the chair Gregson left him. He took the mug of bitter tea gratefully. "Who was this man, that Brooks went through all this . . . this *effort* to hide that he murdered him?"

"I believe you'll find he matches the description of Brooks's missing brother." Holmes answered.

Even Gregson paused at that. "His own brother? Julian Brooks?" the pale man mused. His icy blue eyes were never warm, but they turned cold and barren. "That bloody farm inheritance?"

"I don't care about that," Bradstreet interrupted Gregson – an historic moment amongst the Yard. "Mr. Holmes, how did you know? Explain that gin bottle before I go mad!"

Holmes briefly related the events to the rest and picked up the thread: "The gin bottle couldn't possibly have been in use as a gin bottle. The glass turned violet under my lamp. Violet-tinted glass is an expense so exorbitant I doubt it will ever be in the common market. It is specific to the levels of manganese dioxide, an element used to render glass clearer and with less colour . . . but it ironically turns purple when exposed to the accumulative effects of sunlight's radiation.

"A gin bottle full of gin kept in storage under the sun would never keep its alcoholic properties by the time the glass turned violet. We often see violet-glass windows and window-panes in older buildings, but bottles? No. On occasion a forger will place glass in the sun in hopes of forcing that purple hue in order to convince his clients the glass is older than it truly is.

"I can only work with the facts that are given me, gentlemen, and I hope you appreciate that my theory is completely flawed until the facts are proved. But if Brooks went through the trouble of placing a dusty old gin bottle, rendered violet with age, into his dead brother's pocket, then it must have been what was on hand at the time. I suggest the usual location where such bottles are found: Old barns, chemical-sheds, and outbuildings are the best. They have the necessary exposure to the sun and are often forgotten.

"Now that the lines are restored, I managed to find Hopkins. He confirmed Bradstreet's statement that the will was a bitterly vague letter, and the brothers were actually step-brothers with little resemblance to one another. They hated each other with a passion, and the dead man, Julian Brooks, fell victim to that hate.

"You will find as I did there are small splinters of common pinewood in Julian Brooks' clothing. I believe after the murder, Godine Brooks was in a quandary. The marshlands of Cambridge are normally hospitable to hiding evidence, but with this unusual weather, everything has been frozen solid. Also, there was the commonly understood hatred between the brothers. Godine had to take the body far away. He first stuffed the gin bottle into his pocket – a stupid, irrational thing to do, and I wonder if he had thought to masque the murder as exposure to the elements even then – and then forced Julian's body into a common pinewood shipping-crate, well-padded with other objects to keep from rolling about. Julian's body froze in this unnatural position, but was safe enough as he shipped the crate to his home address in London by train.

"After receiving the crate, the cold weather was again in his favour, and the filthy conditions with its erratic illuminations, cloud cover, and the public reluctance to go outside especially during the nightly freezes, allowed him to transport the body to the Lyon Park street-corner. Several of the constables have confirmed that Brooks often did the driving for the morgue, so I suspect he used the morgue's own property for transporting. For a final touch, he poured actual gin into the pocket holding the old gin bottle, which caused the stain and further added to his little smokescreen. PC Stryker has redeemed himself for his earlier error and discovered one of the corpses brought in was missing an identification-card. I shouldn't be surprised if Brooks planned to forge another one and 'accidentally' discover it in the back of the morgue's van."

"We'll look there next." Gregson muttered. "No offense, Mr. Holmes, but your guesses are better than the facts in most books."

Holmes blinked in the shock of this rare praise and nodded roughly.

"This is all – " Bradstreet groaned. "That's a dreadful leap of faith. What if he'd been sent to some other morgue instead?"

Sherlock Holmes shrugged. "It didn't really matter, Bradstreet. The important thing is, *Dr. Harper* would not see the body. He is still indisposed, is he not?"

Bradstreet paled. "Yes. But all of this . . . ."

Gregson sighed. "Criminals aren't criminals because they are smart, Bradstreet. Haven't I told you this before?" To Holmes: "I don't mean that murderers are necessarily stupid. I mean that so much crime is done *without* planning, so it's no surprise they *over-plan* when they try to cover the consequences of their actions."

Holmes regarded Gregson with a thoughtful smile. "Do you know," he said at last, "I don't believe I've ever heard it put quite so succinctly."

"Yes, well, so long as you don't tell that hard-headed bundle of nerves." Gregson pointed at Lestrade. "We've heard him say as much . . . well, scream it, really. Usually in the faces of the new constables. My vocabulary's better."

Brooks eluded the police that season. This disappointment was almost incidental to the discoveries on the family farm. Goods were being smuggled there, including: A chest of heavy paper was found, troublingly similar in weave and weight to the paper used to draught bank-notes. This transferred the case to the Foreign Office overnight, and the final facts were years in closing. On occasion Holmes detected a faint "ripple" in the undercurrent of the country – a theft or murder that he felt was authored by the missing killer. Over time he developed the theory that killing Julian Brooks had been anything but an accident, but an opportunity exploited by an unclean brain. His distaste at failing to catch the fish in his nets was tempered, somewhat, by the knowledge that he was being just as troublesome to Brooks.

"He is not a true master – not a genius with crime." Holmes grumbled. "He is only the greatest opportunist I have ever seen! Like an old lion, if you will, turned man-eater because he cannot compete with the younger males. He wanders at random and strikes the same way, always hoping to better himself with his kills and plunder. Conversely, he is never prepared for how quickly I can recognise him and act."

A few years later, Lestrade came to call on one of his usual afternoon visits. A young bobby claimed something "felt wrong" about a seedy little gambling-dive on the waterfront. It was this and a combination of following serendipities that led to a grisly discovery: A man's dismembered body salted down and stuffed into a crumbling seawall. It was Brooks.

"But is it?" Holmes murmured after Lestrade delivered the news. He tapped his chin with his violin-bow and frowned. In the warm summer air, that bitterly cold night felt a thousand years away. "Was it ever the true Brooks at all?"

Lestrade made a face. "I cannot say. I don't know if anyone can at this point. A man who can impersonate one man may do the same with another."

"True, Lestrade. But if it is *not* the true Brooks, then there is still a very dangerous man walking the surface of the earth."

The little detective stared at my friend over the rim of his water-glass, and his dark, sly eyes never blinked.

"Almost, dare I say it, as dangerous as you, Mr. Holmes."

Dial Square
by Martin Daley

Chapter I

By my recollection, there have only been a handful of cases in my friend's illustrious career where any sort of sporting activity formed the backdrop to his investigation. Sherlock Holmes once told me that, apart from fencing and boxing, he had little interest in any form of athletic activity. As for my own sporting prowess, Rugby Football was one of my great passions in my early years. But I was recently reminded of one of only two cases, as I can remember, when Sherlock Holmes became involved in a matter relating to Association Football. I must confess that I had always considered it a rather crude form of the game – that was until Holmes received a commission to investigate a series of thefts from the munitions factory at Woolwich. As I review my notes of the case, I recall, in turn, that this would be the first of two investigations Holmes would undertake at the Woolwich Arsenal.

It was late autumn in 1886 – not a particularly pleasant time of year for myself as invariably, that wretched Jezail bullet would torment me during the damp stormy season. During the third week of November, however, the rains ceased, the fallen leaves dried, and a watery sun drew me out for an afternoon stroll.

Despite the desperately cold temperature, I enjoyed the exercise immensely and returned to our rooms looking forward to a pot of coffee by the welcoming fire. I was to be surprised and – I must confess – a little disappointed, for when I arrived, I found that we had a visitor.

"Good afternoon, Holmes – Oh, I'm sorry, I didn't realise you had company."

"Come in, my dear fellow!" replied Holmes, rising from his own chair on the other side of the hearth. "You couldn't have come at a better time. This is Mr. John Parker. May I introduce my friend and colleague, Doctor Watson."

"How do you do sir?" said a young fresh faced man, rising from the basket chair and tentatively offering a hand.

"Pleased to meet you."

"Mr. Parker called speculatively while you were out," said Holmes, "Fortunately for him, I am between cases, and he now has the opportunity to fill that gap in my schedule."

Holmes reached down into the fire with the tongs and clamped a glowing coal, with which he lit his pipe. Re-taking his seat, he smiled at our visitor. "Now Mr. Parker, tell us what brings you to Baker Street."

"Well, Mr. Holmes, I have been sent by my father, Joe Parker. He is the manager of Dial Square, which is the workshop at the munitions factory in Woolwich. I work as an assistant there. It has come to my father's attention that some boxes of ammunition have been taken from the factory, and they appear to have gone from the workshop itself."

"Why hasn't the matter been brought to the attention of the police?"

"My father is a very proud man, Mr. Holmes. He has worked at the factory all of his life. If it were to transpire that such losses had occurred under his nose, his reputation – not to mention his position – would be in jeopardy. Having heard of your great skills, he was hoping that you could look into the matter without it coming to the attention of either the police or the government."

"That may be unavoidable, I'm afraid," said Holmes. "You say it came to your father's attention. How?"

The young man fidgeted in his seat. "There was a consignment of ammunition, ready for transportation to Aldershot. When the crates came to be loaded onto the vehicle, the number of boxes didn't match the inventory."

I found Parker's manner a little odd – there was hardly any eye contact with either of us when he spoke, and he continually twisted his cap in his hands as though he was ringing a wet towel. Holmes ignored such behaviour as he continued his preliminary questioning.

"Could there have simply been a mistake on the inventory?"

"No, Mr. Holmes. The consignments go through a strict check in three parts before being released for distribution."

"So who could have had access to the crates?"

Parker fidgeted again, "That's probably the area that most concerns my father, as many people in the workshop could in theory have access to the boxes, given that they are stacked close to the main loading area."

"Does your father suspect anyone?"

"A name has been brought to his attention, but rather than accuse the man on the say-so of another and potentially cause unrest within the factory, he would like you to look into the matter, and provide him with a definitive explanation before deciding on what action to take."

"In that case," announced Holmes, rising from his chair to signify the end of the interview, "I shall be delighted to help your father with his little problem. Doctor Watson and I will meet you at the main entrance to the factory tomorrow morning at ten o'clock." He turned to me as though it was an afterthought. "That is if you're free, my dear fellow?"

"Of course," I replied.

"That's settled, then," he said as he ushered our guest towards the door. "Until tomorrow, Mr. Parker."

I watched Parker from our window as he crossed Baker Street.

"An unusual young man," I said, half to myself.

"Umm?" replied Holmes, retaking his seat and picking up the newspaper. "Yes, and an unusual circumstance. An employee who is prepared to fund an investigation from his own pocket. It should prove an interesting little problem.

At the appointed hour the following morning, Holmes and I found ourselves outside the imposing main entrance of the munitions factory. Within seconds of our arrival, our visitor from the previous day appeared.

"Good morning, Mr. Holmes. Doctor. Thank you for coming. If you would like to follow me, I'll take you to my father's office in the workshop."

He led us through several wide, hollow corridors, each separated by large timber doors, until we arrived in Dial Square, the workshop at the centre of the factory, which was to be the focus of Holmes's investigation. The workshop itself was vast. The intense heat generated by the giant forges, coupled with the deafening noise and the almost overwhelming smell of cordite, instantly transported me back to that hellish day six years earlier at Maiwand.

Young Parker kept shouting over his shoulder – presumably trying to tell us about the various processes involved in the production – but it was impossible to hear what he was saying. We followed him across the workshop floor to a set of timber stairs that led to a row of offices that were situated overlooking the operation. After having apparently arrived at our destination, Parker knocked on the door of one of the offices and entered. He closed the heavy door behind us, blocking out a lot of the noise, before he introduced us.

"Dad, this is Mr. Sherlock Holmes and his friend, Doctor Watson. Gentlemen, this is my father, Joe Parker."

The manager of the workshop got up from behind his desk, revealing his stockily built frame and, wearing an expression of intense relief, offered a large hand to greet us.

"Mr. Holmes, Dr. Watson, thank you for coming at such short notice. I think John has told you already that I wanted to be as discreet as I could be regarding this matter. I haven't told Mr. Cavendish about the thefts, and I don't want the police involved if we can help it – it would be a national scandal if it got out that ammunition was going missing from the factory."

The man was nervous about the situation and his own position. He was clearly someone who had worked hard all of his life to get the position he was in, but I had the impression that he was more used to overalls and dirty hands than the shirt and tie that he now wore. I have often seen the self-made man retain a level of insecurity when raised above his immediate circle, and I sensed this was the case with Parker.

"How long have you been the manager of the workshop`?" asked Holmes. The question took Parker by surprise. "Erm . . . five years now," he said.

"I'm sure you have nothing to worry about," replied Holmes reassuringly. "Mr. Cavendish wouldn't have appointed you to such a position and left you there for five years if he didn't have the complete faith in your abilities."

"I suppose not," said the man in reflection.

"When were the boxes of ammunition taken?"

"It was just over the weekend, probably because it was a quieter than during the week."

"And do you have any theory on who the thieves might be?"

"I do have one name that's been put to me" – Holmes's raised eyebrows prompted Parker to continue. "David Danskin, one of our engineers."

"And presumably this man was working over the weekend?"

"He was," replied the manager with some conviction.

"And why would this person steal anything from the factory?"

"We have a lot of Celtic immigrants working here. They come to London from Ireland and Scotland looking for work, and often end up in large factories like this. The theory is that Danskin and few of his friends have sympathies with those Fenian anarchists and would look to supply them with ammunition for their seditious activities."

"Where is Danskin from?"

"Fife, in Scotland."

"Hardly a hotbed of anarchism," commented Holmes, almost to himself. "How long has Danskin been with you, Mr. Parker?"

"He's only been here a year. Seems to be a very outgoing sort of a chap – makes friends easily, and can be quite influential."

"Has he caused any trouble for you in the time that he's been here?"

Parker paused and rubbed his chin in thought. "I don't suppose he has really, now you mention it."

"So why do you suspect him?"

"When we discovered the theft, his foreman told me that he'd recently heard what he thought was seditious gossip on the factory floor."

"Is the foreman on duty now? Can I speak with him?"

248

"Yes, certainly," said Parker, signalling to his son to summon the man.

Some minutes later young Parker appeared with a jolly-looking chap in his mid-thirties.

"This is Clive Irwin," said the manager. "He's been with us since he was an apprentice, and is one of our finest."

"Mr. Holmes, Dr. Watson," said Irwin, unable to disguise his enthusiasm as he wiped his hands on his overalls before offering a formal greeting. "It's a great pleasure to meet you both."

"Mr. Irwin," said Holmes, "tell about your suspicions regarding Mr. Danskin."

"Well, sir," said Irwin, looking a little embarrassed, "it isn't really for me to cast aspersions about people, but I've been hearing a bit of gossip recently on the workshop floor about these anarchists that seem to be all over the place right now. Danskin is a bit of a popular figure in the short time he's been here, and everybody seems to buzz round him as if they were bees 'round a honeypot."

Holmes smiled at the analogy. "Mr. Parker here tells me that Danskin has only been here for a year."

"Yes, that's right, sir. Decent worker, but if I were a betting man, I reckon he'll be involved somewhere along the line. He lives on the same street as me, and I regularly see lads from the workshop going in and out of the house where he stays – they all live round about themselves."

"I see," said Holmes. Holmes then paused his questioning and stared into the middle-distance, tapping his chin lightly with his cane, before announcing, "I think our Mr. Danskin is certainly worthy of interest."

Both Parker and Irwin appeared satisfied that their suspicions were justified.

"Would you like me to go and get him then, sir?" asked Irwin.

"No, that won't be necessary just yet," replied Holmes, much to the surprise of those present, "I think we should carry out just a little more investigation before we pounce."

"Very good, sir. As you wish."

"Tell me, Mr. Parker: Who supplies the coal for the workshop?"

It was such an unusual question that I even found myself a little surprised. Parker spluttered as he racked his brains.

"It's Sykes and Sons, the coal merchant at the back of Taylor's Buildings."

"They must have a large operation?"

"Yes, I suppose they do," said Parker, still coming to terms with the strange deviation in Holmes's line of questioning. "As well as the factory, they supply coal to all of the houses in the area."

"I see," said Holmes nodding slowly. Then, "Gentleman, I think this morning has been quite productive. Mr. Parker, I'm confident we will have the matter resolved in a few days, although I believe the involvement of the official authorities may be unavoidable."

"I feared as much," said the chagrined workshop manager. "At least if you can solve the matter, Mr. Holmes, it will lessen any scandal."

"I knew Mr. Holmes would help!" said Irwin, looking at me with great enthusiasm, "I told Mr. Parker here, 'If I were a betting man, Mr. Holmes is the man to sort it out.'"

Holmes also turned to me, "Watson, I need to carry out an errand. Can I trust you to look into something before you leave?" He looked across to the workshop manager. "With your permission of course, Mr. Parker?"

"Of course," repeated the bewildered Parker.

"Excellent! Watson, get me the address of Mr. Danskin and the friends Mr. Irwin suspects of being in league with him."

"John will be able to help you with that, Doctor," said Parker.

"No, I can do that, Joe," said the enthusiastic Irwin. "Perhaps John could show Mr. Holmes out?"

Parker shrugged and nodded his assent.

"Oh, and one more thing," said Holmes, turning as he reached the door, "I would like to know if there has been any change in personnel in the Accounts Office."

"Yes, there has been, as a matter of fact," said Parker, "Bob Elliot who worked in there died suddenly a couple of weeks ago – tragedy, it was. He jumped in a pond at Hampstead Heath to save a young lad and got into trouble himself. The boy escaped but poor Bob drowned. Sad business. He was replaced by a young lad in the Accounts Office – I can't remember his name now, but I'll get it for you."

"That's right, now you mention it," agreed Irwin, as he clicked his fingers in an attempt to recollect, "Got it! Elijah Watkins, they call that young lad. If I'm not mistaken, I've seen him knocking about Danskin's place an' all."

"That is also interesting. Thank you gentlemen. Watson, I will see you back in Baker Street this afternoon."

"I'll show you out, Mr. Holmes," said John Parker.

Chapter II

By the time I returned to Baker Street that afternoon, Holmes was already there, wading through some old newspapers.

"Ah, Watson, this *is* an interesting little problem," he announced as I entered our sitting room.

"I found the information you wanted," I said, "but before we go through it, I wonder if I could get Mrs. Hudson to make a sandwich?"

"Of course, my dear fellow. You must be famished! Besides, we can do nothing until tomorrow."

"What will happen then?"

"Later, Watson, later. Let us impose on our landlady first."

The ever obliging Mrs. Hudson duly arrived some minutes later with an appetising tray of sandwiches and a pot of tea.

Afterwards, I shared the names and addresses of Danskin's friends. "Danskin himself is a lodger at the home of a Mrs. Harrandon on Holgate Street. Apparently, he is also engaged to be married to his landlady's daughter – a 'real cracker', by all accounts, according to Irwin."

"Really, Watson, you're getting as bad as the factory workers for your gossip!" announced Holmes with a smile.

"I'm only relaying what I heard," I replied with a smile of my own. "And I have to say that it isn't the only bit of tittle-tattle I have returned with."

"Oh?"

"Clive Irwin gave me his theory as to why Joe Parker was trying to keep this all under his hat. It turns out that young John Parker fell in with the wrong crowd a few years ago, and at one point found himself on the wrong side of the law. Irwin told me that in an effort to get him on the straight-and-narrow, his father convinced Mr. Cavendish to take him on at the factory. Apparently Cavendish was unsure at the time, but Parker assured him that he wouldn't regret it."

"That would certainly explain why young Parker gave himself that rather non-descript title of 'assistant' when he visited us yesterday," said Holmes.

"Yes, that's what I thought. And clearly his father doesn't want to highlight the matter in case his son is somehow implicated and his own judgement is therefore called into question.

"When young Parker then escorted me out of the factory, he had his retort on Irwin by suggesting he was a bit of a 'ladies' man'. I'm not sure there is much love lost between the two."

"Perhaps," Holmes said evenly, as he lit a pipe and added with a chuckle, "they certainly seem like a happy workforce."

I showed Holmes the list I'd taken from the factory. "Apparently they are all men from the workshop who live in neighbouring streets."

Holmes referred to the piece of paper. "Argyll Road," he said, tapping the paper with the stem of his pipe. "Bunton Street, Holgate Street . . . yes I recognise these names."

"How could you possibly know these streets?" I asked.

"No matter," said Holmes infuriatingly. "You have done some fine work in my absence."

I satisfied myself with the rare compliment. "What next?" I asked.

"There isn't much we can do today," he replied, "but the matter should become clearer as the week goes on. Starting tomorrow. I propose we spend an afternoon in Rochester."

"Rochester?" I asked incredulously. "What on earth can we do there?"

"I'm sure you aren't averse to a little sporting flutter."

"No," I stammered. "But haven't we work to do on the case?"

"We will be working, my dear fellow. There is a race meeting in Rochester tomorrow that may clear the fog of our case a little."

He refused to elaborate on that comment until the following day, when we were in our carriage on the eleven-thirty from St. Pancras. As our train pulled out on that crisp autumn morning, I asked Holmes again.

"Much as I can be amused by a day's horse racing, I fail to see how it can help us with the case."

"We're going to Rochester to speak with a bookmaker who may be able to help us. You may recall that when we visited Dial Square yesterday, Parker informed us that someone in the accounts department had died tragically around two weeks ago. His name was Bob Elliot, and according to the newspaper reports of his death, as well as working at the munitions factory, he was also a bookmaker's clerk for one Isaac Hooper. It's Mr. Hooper we're going to visit."

"I see," I said, even though I didn't really see at all. Reluctant as I was to appear even more obtuse, I kept my counsel for the remainder of our journey.

The day was bright, and the fine weather had drawn out a large crowd on what was due to be the last meeting of the year. The hustle-and-bustle of such an event created an excited atmosphere, and by the time we entered the track, I was quite looking forward to the day. On the train journey, I had read up on the recent records of those competing and had made a list of horses upon which I would risk a little wager. Meanwhile, Holmes wasn't interested in the going, the form, or the crowds. As soon as we entered, he scanned the long line of bookmakers until he spotted his man.

"*Ha!*" he exclaimed with a tap of my arm and a sharp glance.

He indicated towards them with his cane and I followed him through the burgeoning, noisy crowd until we arrived at the stall under a large sign with the legend *Isaac Hooper, Turf Accountant*. A young man was marking the odds for the horses in the first race on a large chalk board, while an older man I presumed to be Mr. Hooper called out the latest prices following his tic-tacing to colleagues further along the line. Holmes finally made it to the front of the queue and the bookmaker broke off from his gesticulating.

"Two shillings on *Spanish Dancer*, please!" called Holmes above the din.

"*Two shillings on Spanish Dancer, sir!*" repeated the man for the benefit of his young colleague.

"I see you have a new clerk, Mr. Hooper," shouted Holmes. "The last time I was here, you had that chap Elliot working for you. I was so sorry to hear of his untimely demise."

The man looked at Holmes questioningly, as though trying to place him. Having decided that he didn't recognise him, and therefore accepting him at face value simply as a regular race-goer, he responded to Holmes's comment.

"He wasn't working for me by the time he met his end," he said, apparently with an air of some resentment, "I had to let him go. Fell in with the wrong crowd, he did, and in the end, he was more trouble than he was worth."

"Oh, I'm sorry to hear that," said Holmes taking his betting ticket from the man.

"Well, R.I.P, eh?" Hooper, clearly bringing the short exchange to its conclusion as the customers behind Holmes waved their money at him.

"Would you like to sit in the grandstand?" I asked as we extricated ourselves from the throng.

"No, I think I'll remain here for the afternoon. You go ahead and watch the racing."

"You mean you're not even going to watch? You've come all this way, just to ask one question?"

"Oh, I will be watching," he replied cryptically. "Watching and observing."

I knew it was futile to try and dissuade him from his course of action, so I left him to it.

It proved to be a profitable afternoon for us both. I enjoyed three winners and a second place. By the time I found Holmes again – standing next to a pillar not far from where I had left him – he wore an equally satisfied expression.

"Success?" I asked.

"Indeed," he replied with a smile. "Now, back to Baker Street."

That evening over dinner, Holmes dismissed my attempts to discuss the case in any great detail. The only thing I could get out of him was: "Tomorrow should see some significant developments. I have to go out quite early and will be away for most of the day."

"Can I be of any assistance?"

"No, it's a day for clandestine operations, and as useful as you have been so far, I'm afraid my trusted comrade will have to be patient on this occasion until I return."

I satisfied myself with Holmes's affable mood and his complimentary remarks about my contribution to the case. We spoke little more about it for the rest of the evening, and by the time I went down to our sitting room for breakfast the next morning, he had already left.

Once Mrs. Hudson cleared my dishes away, she informed me that she too was leaving to visit a friend in Islington who had fallen ill. I was therefore left alone to idle the day away. I caught up on the some reading and went out at one point for a stroll. As I wandered aimlessly around the bustling streets that encircled our lodgings, I couldn't help wondering what my friend was up to. When my absentmindedness almost caused me to be run over by a fast-moving hansom on Marylebone Road – much to the displeasure of the cabbie – I decided it was time to return home and simply wait for Holmes's reappearance. It came around four o'clock, and was one I am hardly likely to forget.

I had been dozing over the newspaper in front of the fire when I heard the front door opening. Hearing a heavy footstep on the stairs, I raised myself from my slumber As I folded my paper, the door opened.

"Good afternoon," said Holmes matter-of-factly.

I stared in disbelief at the sight. Holmes had revealed himself with his greeting, but had he not done so, it's unlikely I would have recognised him. He wore large hob-nail boots, knee-length gaiters, a longer leather smock and coalman's backing hat that reached the middle of his back. His hands and face were blackened with soot, and as he removed his hat, the almost comical sight of a perfectly clean ring around his forehead appeared.

"Holmes what have you been doing?" As soon as the question had left my lips, even I realised the absurdity of it.

"I have been on my rounds," said Holmes, continuing to lever himself out of his disguise.

At this moment, the questions that filled my mind and had been hitherto jostling for attention were set to one side as I realised that Holmes had trailed a film of soot through the room, and no doubt up the stairs.

"What about Mrs. Hudson?" I asked incredulously.

My comment seemed to take him aback as he momentarily stopped what he was doing. "Mrs. Hudson? What's wrong with Mrs. Hudson?"

"Nothing at the moment, but I'm sure that will change as soon as she sees this mess."

For the first time, Holmes looked at the floor and the trail he had left.

"Yes, I suppose I have created a little work for her," he said in a typically carefree manner.

"*A little work!* Where have you been?" I asked, returning to the matter at hand.

"I've been back to Woolwich. When I left you at the factory the other day, I visited Sykes and Sons, the coal suppliers in the area. I was told that today was the delivery day for the streets you identified when I left you. As Mr. Danskin and his confederates live in that area, it was a perfect opportunity to learn a little more about these characters. A small bribe to the working man is rarely refused, and the shift manager at Sykes and Sons was no exception. He allowed me to carry out the delivery this week and here I am – " He placed his fists in the small of his back and stretched. "A little stiff perhaps, and a bit worse for wear, but satisfied nonetheless at another productive days' work."

Before I could question him further, I heard the front door again.

"That will be Mrs. Hudson," I said in a hushed tone.

"Ah, excellent," announce Holmes, "I will impose on her to organise a bath for me."

I stood for a moment, looking at him in disbelief, before accepting that as an invitation to withdraw.

"I'll leave you to it. Enjoy your bath and we'll resume our conversation later."

I crept out of our sitting room and tip-toed up the stairs to my bedroom, just as I heard the first gasp from Mrs. Hudson in the hall below.

"*Mr. Holmes!*" I heard her cry as I closed my bedroom door quietly.

For the next two hours I remained quiet, listening to the exasperating muffled cries of the most patient landlady in London. Finally, at shortly after six o'clock, I ventured downstairs again to our sitting room. I found Holmes sitting in his chair, bathed and already changed into his night shirt and long dressing gown. His hair lay over his brow and he was staring into the fire. I glanced round the room and couldn't see a speck of soot anywhere.

"Everything all right?" I asked.

"Ah, yes. I feel much better after a nice hot bath, thank you."

"And Mrs. Hudson?"

"Mrs. Hudson? Why do you keep asking about Mrs. Hudson? Is something wrong with her?"

"Never mind," I said.

"She'll be up shortly with our dinner. I'll tell you all about my day's adventures then."

He tossed his cigarette into the fire just as our landlady entered with a tray, containing a pot of tea and two silver domes.

"Good evening," I said. "Did you enjoy your visit to your friend? I do hope she's feeling better."

"Yes, she is, Doctor. Thank you. The most upsetting part of the day was when I returned home." The latter comment was made looking at Holmes, who remained oblivious to the poor woman's lot.

"Oh dear," I said trying to sound as ignorant about the situation as possible.

Once she had left, I then returned to the subject of the case.

"So, to whom did you speak today?"

"Everyone that I wanted to. My first call was on Holgate Street to the home of Mrs. Harrandon, Danskin's landlady. When I knocked, the door was answered by a younger woman – what a pretty young thing she was."

I raised my eyebrows at such an uncharacteristic comment.

"It turned out to be Danskin's fiancée, Miss Georgina Harrandon. She was as pleasant as she was pretty, offering to make me a cup of tea on such a cold morning."

"'Go on then, Miss,' I said, 'I wouldn't say no. I'll just get the other bag.'"

"I carried two bags down the lane adjacent to the house and deposited them by the bunker in the back yard of the house.

"'I don't think you've been round here before,'" she said as she brought two mugs out of the kitchen.

"'No, I'm fairly new to this round.'"

"We chatted for a while and I offered to load the coal into the bunker. Before she could reply, a man came out into the yard – it was none other than the fellow himself, Mr. Danskin. He isn't particularly tall, but he's well-built, with jet-black hair and a matching moustache."

"'Naw, a'll dee it, pal,' he said, overhearing my offer.

"'If you like.'

"He gave his fiancé an affectionate squeeze. 'Awright 'hen?'

"'Hello, Davey. Good night was it?'

"'Aye, no bad. A'm looking forward to ma bed, mind you.'

"'Been on the night shift, I take it,' I asked.

"'Aye just at the factory round the corner,' he replied.

"'You sound as though you are a long way from home.'

"'Aye, cem down frae' Scotland last year.'

"'And how'd you find it being down here?'"

"'Aye, it's grand. The footba's good and women are nice,' he said with a smile, giving his fiancé another squeeze and a peck on the check, for which he received a playing pat on the arm.

"'*You!*' she said, laughing. 'You think more of the daft football than you do of me!'

"'Thank you for the tea, Miss,' I said draining my mug and handing in back, 'I'll bid you both a good morning.'

"Danskin certainly seems a charismatic figure. I can see how people are drawn to him. I left them both in jovial spirits and carried on with my round. I visited all of the main cast in our little play, either speaking to them personally or their respective landladies. It is quite remarkable the things you can pick up from people through seemingly meaningless, polite conversation. The trick is to never let them think their information can be of the slightest importance to you. If they think they are demonstrating their superior knowledge, or that they are simply participating in backstreet gossip, you're likely to get everything you need to know. I even called in at the Royal Oak public house where I learned that Danskin and his friends meet. The landlord was a garrulous fellow!" concluded Holmes with a laugh.

"So, it sounds like a productive day?" I asked.

"Yes, all in all," he said, as he lifted the dome from his plate.

Chapter III

The following day was slow, with not much to occupy Holmes's great mind. The last thing he'd told me the previous evening was that he was expecting a correspondence from the munitions factory that should prove to be the last piece of the puzzle. Being a Sunday, it was unlikely he would receive this vital piece of information for another twenty-four hours at least. He spent most of the morning impatiently drumming his fingers on the arm of his chair and grinding his teeth. The atmosphere of our sitting room gradually became thicker and thicker with the smoke from his strong coarse tobacco, until I could barely see him on the other side of the hearth.

"Why don't we go outside and you can clear your head?" I suggested after lunch.

Holmes snorted his contempt.

"This is doing you no good," I persisted. "You are just torturing yourself unnecessarily.

He reached for the Persian slipper once more and found it empty. Slumping back into his seat and glancing round the room, he finally relented.

"I suppose you're right. There is little else we can do on such a stagnant day as this."

Getting away from the fug of our sitting room did us both the world of good, and even Holmes's mood brightened somewhat. We walked through Hyde Park, where a group of hardy souls where sitting around the bandstand, being entertained by a military ensemble. Young couples

257

walked arm in arm and found themselves giving way on the wide pathways to the occasional carriage or cyclist who rode past. It was when Holmes saw a young man playing ball with his son that he broached the subject of the case for the first time.

"Amongst other things on my round, I discovered that our man Danskin has arranged a meeting with his confederates on Wednesday at the Royal Oak Inn."

"What do you propose to do?" I asked.

"We shall be there too. And much to Mr. Parker's chagrin, I shall be forced to invite Inspector Lestrade."

"I see. And what about the correspondence you're waiting for?"

"It should be a mere confirmation of what I believe already. Providing we receive it tomorrow, I fully expect to have the matter concluded on Wednesday."

Holmes was to have his satisfaction the following day. The young page came up to our room around eleven o'clock.

"Letter for you, Mr. Holmes."

"Thank you, Billy," replied Holmes, leaping from his chair, snatching the jack-knife from the mantelpiece, taking the letter from the silver tray, and slitting open the envelope all in one flowing movement. "*Ha!* Just as I thought."

"So you'll be reaching out to Lestrade, then?" I asked.

"I will," he said. *"Billy!"* he shouted after the boy, who was descending the stairs to resume his duties.

"Yes, sir?" answered Billy eagerly as he ran back to the landing.

Holmes was now seated at his desk scribbling two telegrams. He handed them to the page boy, "See that these are sent immediately. Then come back to me this afternoon when I'll have another letter for you to deliver."

"Right away, sir," replied to the young lad, who was already on the half turn as he took the first two notes.

"Now what?" I asked.

"We wait," said Holmes. "There's little we can do for another forty-eight hours."

He spent some time writing the third note to which he had referred, and even had the decency to explain whereas the first two, to Parker and Lestrade, asking to meet us at the Royal Oak on Wednesday. This more detailed missive was again to the policeman. This time, however, he was giving Lestrade more details about the case that would allow him to effect an arrest.

Holmes then refilled his pipe and sat contentedly by the fire. One of the many traits I've noticed in Holmes during the years we've spent together is his strange attitude towards waiting. When waiting for information that isn't forthcoming, he can be irritable and rude. But when he's simply waiting for the *denouement* of a case, he can be the polar opposite: Patient and sanguine.

So it was for the next two days. Apart from receiving replies to his two telegrams, Holmes barely moved from his chair, sitting with his eyes closed and a contented smile upon his face. Then, at the appointed hour on Wednesday, 1st December, we donned our outdoor wear once more and set off for Woolwich.

The temperature had dropped, as if to usher in the first day of the month, and as we crossed Westminster Bridge, I noticed a carpet of mist had covered the river. Big Ben struck two o'clock.

"Our munitions workers should be filling their tankards and taking their seats about now," said Holmes. "I asked Lestrade and Parker to meet us at half-past outside the inn."

Our cab gradually took us away from the activity of the capital towards the narrow, labyrinthine streets, beside which incongruously stood the largest munitions factory in the Empire. As we neared our destination, the blackened buildings – some of which were plastered with faded old newspaper advertisements – acted as supports for lines of lank washing that drooped from one side of the street to the other. We eventually arrived at the Royal Oak at twenty-five-past-two. Parker, his son, and his foreman, Irwin were already there waiting for us.

"Excellent!" Holmes said, flashing a glance to me as we alighted the cab. "Good afternoon, gentlemen!"

"Mr. Holmes. Doctor." Parker's tone was a mixture of nerves and relief that the matter was about to be resolved.

"Ah!" cried Holmes, looking down the street. "And here comes Inspector Lestrade now."

The inspector climbed down from the horse-drawn police wagon and proceeded to walk towards us with one of his uniformed officers.

"He'll need more than that," I heard the eager Irwin say to young Parker under his breath.

"Good afternoon, Inspector!" said Holmes as Lestrade approached.

"Mr. Holmes. Doctor. Gentlemen."

"Now, is everything in place?"

"I think so, Mr. Holmes. I received your correspondence, so providing what you tell me is true, there should be no difficulty."

"Excellent!" repeated Holmes.

There was then a pause in the proceedings that could only have lasted a few seconds, but somehow strangely felt longer. I looked across the street through the window of the inn and wondered how many men were in there. The same thought must have crossed the mind of Joe Parker, who asked rather nervously, "Far be it from me to tell you your business, Mr. Holmes, but won't the inspector need more than one officer and a small wagon, to round these villains up?"

"Yes, what time's the raiding party turning up?" asked Irwin with a smile of anticipation.

"Oh, we won't be going into the public house ourselves," said Holmes, casually.

We all turned as one to look at the consulting detective.

"Not going in?" repeated Parker.

"There is no need," said Holmes, himself, looking across the street at the establishment.

"I don't understand," said the manager of the workshop.

"There is no need, because the perpetrator of the thefts that have been the cause of your immeasurable discomfort is right here."

"I don't . . . ." the phrase died on Parker's lips.

"I must apologise, my dear fellow, but Watson here will tell you that I never can resist a touch of the dramatic. You see, there *has* been a conspiracy to steal ammunition from the factory – but it isn't Mr. Danskin and *his* confederates who are guilty. It was Mr. Irwin here and *his*. Or should I say, *confederate*, singular."

Everyone in turn looked at Irwin, whose expression had changed from one of smugness to one of nervous improvisation.

"What?" he bluffed unconvincingly. "What nonsense! If I were a betting man – "

"If you were a betting man, Mr. Irwin?" interrupted Holmes. "That appears to be one of your favourite phrases, is it not? But the truth of course, is that you *are* a betting man. Very fond of betting, but sadly, not very good at it."

"That's – " Irwin could offer nothing in reply.

"That's quite enough," announced Holmes. "No more lies. Inspector, I suggest you take this man away."

Lestrade nodded to his constable who handcuffed the workshop foreman and led him away towards the small wagon.

"Gentlemen," said Lestrade as he touched the brim of his hat and followed the two.

Joe Parker stood bemused, watching the prisoner being led away. "I don't understand, Mr. Holmes."

I had every sympathy with the man. Although Holmes had surely solved the case, there was almost a feeling of anti-climax about the whole thing.

"Could I make a suggestion?" asked Holmes. "Why don't we impose on our landlord opposite and I'll explain the chain of events that have brought us to this point."

The three of us agreed and crossed the street to the Royal Oak. I'd almost forgotten about the meeting of the Dial Square workers, which I thought was the purpose of our visit. We entered, and around twenty of the men were gathered in the far corner of the establishment. They were deep in their own conversation and didn't notice us enter. Holmes suggested we sit away from the men and leave them to their business, while he would share with us the series of events that led to Irwin's arrest.

Before he could, the landlord came over and asked what we would like to drink.

"Four glasses of beer if you please," said Parker. "I think this is my treat."

"Certainly, gentlemen," said the landlord. As he turned he stopped and looked at Holmes, "I'm sorry sir, but do I know you from somewhere?"

"I don't think so, landlord," said Holmes with an enigmatic smile.

"My apologies, sir," said the man turning away with a head-shake and a knitted brow. "Must have mistaken you for someone else."

"Now, Holmes," I said. "You've kept us in suspense long enough."

"Quite right," he said as he began his narrative. "When I left you the other day in the office, young John here escorted me back out of the factory. On the way, I asked if I could meet Elijah Watkins, the man who took over from Bob Elliot in the Accounts Office following his sudden demise.

"Watkins informed me that, although it appeared that the boxes of ammunition had been removed over the weekend as you suggested, Mr. Parker, it was actually part of a consignment that had been delayed for over a month. So the missing boxes had likely been stolen some weeks earlier, but the loss hadn't been discovered until the final paperwork had been signed and returned to the office. It was then that Watkins discovered the discrepancy. I asked him to go back through the records for two years to see if there were any similar discrepancies. He found no fewer than eight."

"Presumably, this was the letter you were waiting for on Monday?" I asked.

"Indeed," confirmed Holmes. "This was the final piece of information I needed in order to alert Lestrade."

"I can't believe it," said Parker, "Clive Irwin's been with us for years. I've known him since he was a young apprentice. How could he fiddle the paperwork without being found out? And why would he?"

261

"This is where the mystery deepens and becomes a little more sinister. The main instigator of this larceny wasn't actually Irwin. It was Elliot, the man who was Watkins's predecessor in the Accounts Office. His avarice and stupidity had led him to become entangled with some particularly unsavoury characters.

"Our talkative landlord here told me the other day that Elliot used to meet one such character in here on a regular basis."

"I thought you said you didn't know the landlord," asked Parker.

Holmes waved the question off as an irrelevance and continued his narrative.

"From his description of the man Elliot met, I believe him to be Grigory Yubkin. He is a Russian dissident and a key agent in the huge criminal underworld of London. He is also suspected of locating and supplying illegal arms and munitions to various anarchist groups on behalf of greater minds than his. By weaving his web around Elliot, he had the perfect channel to the factory, through which he could obtain a seemingly endless supply of munitions."

"So Elliot would falsify the records?" I said.

"But he needed someone on the workshop floor to help him conceal and despatch the boxes themselves," added Parker.

"Excellent gentlemen!" cried Holmes, "Excellent. And of course he found such an ally in our man Irwin. With the vast quantities of munitions being produced to fight our seemingly endless wars, Elliot and Irwin concentrated on small amounts, just one or two boxes that could be easily concealed and lost among the reams and reams of paperwork that go with operation."

The landlord brought over our drinks and laid them on the table in front of us, all the while peering at Holmes with a curious expression, as if he were trying to place him. He walked away again shaking his head, as my smiling friend rasped a match against the side of the box and lit a cigarette.

"When Watson and I went to the race meeting in Rochester, I spoke with Mr. Hooper, the bookmaker with whom Elliot worked as a clerk in his spare time. I had suspected that Elliot's death wasn't quite as sudden as newspaper reports would have you believe, and completely unprompted, Hooper voiced his own suspicions regarding his former clerk's demise. I believe that Elliot crossed the wrong people too often and paid for it with his life."

"But the newspaper reports said he died saving the young boy," said Parker.

"What young boy?" asked Holmes. "I found that no young boy or his family were ever identified, and there were no witnesses to the incident.

And why would Elliot be at Hampstead Heath in the first place, when it is well over ten miles from his lodgings in Woolwich? No, no, my dear fellow. The stories would have been an act of convenience and distraction – concocted by the people of influence who had Elliot removed. Elliot dies a hero, and the perpetrators of this crime and others go about their business completely unsuspected."

"So how do you think Irwin became involved?" I asked.

"While I was standing observing the crowd," resumed Holmes, "none other than our friend Irwin appeared at the stall of Mr. Hooper. As their discussion became quite animated, I moved closer to hear what was being said. Despite the hub-hub of the crowd, their raised voices told me enough of what I needed to know: Irwin had accumulated significant gambling debts. With the income from his nefarious activity with Elliot now cut off, he had resorted to asking for credit – not only from Hooper, who presumably knew him through his association with his former clerk and was now giving him summary treatment – but from the other bookmakers along the line as well."

"But it was Clive who brought the theft to my attention in the first place," said Parker, still struggling to come to terms with the apparent betrayal of his friend and colleague.

"It was actually Elijah Watkins who brought it to *his* attention," replied Holmes. "Watkins discovered Elliot's falsification of the records from a month earlier and checked with Irwin how many boxes had been dispatched. Once Irwin was struck with the realisation that the batch had been delayed and the implications of the discovery, he knew he had to act in order to divert attention away from Elliot, and ultimately himself. This is when he raised the matter with you, Mr. Parker, and planted the seed of doubt regarding the honourable Mr. Danskin over there." Holmes indicated the man in the far corner of the inn who – oblivious to our presence – appeared to be holding the attention of his colleagues.

"But why Danskin?" I asked.

"Why not?" asked Holmes, "Irwin needed someone to implicate in the crime, and Danskin was as good as anyone. He was relatively new to the factory, and Irwin was jealous of how popular he had become in such a short space of time."

"He was also jealous of his fiancé," added young John Parker, the first time he had spoken. "He often spoke of her and lucky how the Scotsman was. If *I* were a betting man, I would say he had designs on her too."

Holmes laughed at young Parker's comment before resuming. "So by removing Danskin, he would divert attention away from himself and clear the way to indulge in his other vulgar pastime."

The workshop manager then satisfied himself that Danskin couldn't possibly have been involved.

"And because Watkins discovered discrepancies going back at least two years, there is no way Danskin could have been involved, given that he has only been with us for twelve months."

"Precisely," said Holmes.

"The irony is that it was Irwin who suggested that I keep it away from a police enquiry," said Parker. "That's when I thought of you Mr. Holmes, after reading of your work."

"*Ha!* He would have been better suggesting that the police should get involved. That way he would have had a greater chance of evading capture!"

"Now I have the unenviable task of approaching Mr. Cavendish with the whole sordid affair," said the workshop manager.

"If he's the reasonable man I believe him to be," said Holmes, "I'm sure he won't apportion any blame to yourself or young John here. And besides, you aren't giving him a problem. You are clearing up a problem."

"It still leaves the issue of the missing ammunition, Holmes," I said.

"That is a much bigger issue. The network into which the munitions disappeared cannot be unravelled over a glass of beer in Woolwich. That not inconsiderable task will have to wait for another day . . . . " He raised his glass. "Let us be satisfied that we have resolved *this* little problem."

"I'll drink to that," said Parker, prompting his son and myself to follow suit.

"There is one other thing, Holmes," I asked, looking over towards the munitions workers who were still deep in conversation. "If Danskin and his friends aren't here as conspirators, what *are* they doing?

Holmes smiled.

"Something that is completely innocent and unconnected, Watson. Mr. Danskin is a keen player of Association Football – " He turned to Parker. "You're probably unaware that Mr. Parker is attempting to organise a team that will represent the workshop and the factory."

"Well, I'll be!" said the workshop manager scratching his head. "It's been a day of surprises all round."

Two weeks after our visit to the Royal Oak, I returned to Baker Street after having carried out a little Christmas shopping. I found Holmes at his chemistry table, working on some malodorous experiment.

I sat in front of the fire and leafed through the morning paper.

"Holmes," I declared, "do you remember our encounter with Mr. Danskin at Woolwich? He must have been successful in raising that team you were telling me about. Listen to this:

264

The recently formed Dial Square Football Club played its first fixture on Saturday against Eastern Wanderers. It proved a successful start for the team from the munitions factory in Woolwich, who ran out 6-0 winners in the encounter on the Isle of Dogs. The victorious team was captained by their Scottish defender, David Danskin, who works as an engineer at the factory.

"How wonderful!" I declared. "Good old Danskin!"

"Each man to his own interest, I suppose," was my friend's disinterested reply.

The Adventure of the
Deadly Tradition
by Matthew J. Elliott

T*his script has never been published in text form, and was initially performed as a radio drama on December 21, 2014. The broadcast was Episode No. 116 of* The Further Adventures of Sherlock Holmes, *one of the recurring series featured on the nationally syndicated* Imagination Theatre. *Founded by Jim French, the company produced over one-thousand multi-series episodes, including nearly one-hundred-and-forty Sherlock Holmes pastiches. In addition, Imagination Theatre also recorded the entire Holmes Canon, featured as* The Classic Adventures of Sherlock Holmes, *the only version with all episodes to have been written by the same writer, Matthew J. Elliott, and with the same two actors, John Patrick Lowrie and Lawrence Albert, portraying Holmes and Watson, respectively.*

CHARACTERS
- SHERLOCK HOLMES
- DR. JOHN H. WATSON
- INSPECTOR MacDONALD
- SIR CONSTANTINE MORGAN – 60's. Gruff, pompous old cove
- ALGERNON MORGAN – 30's. Quiet-spoken, Extremely polite
- COBB – Any age. Slightly Cockney. A manservant with a criminal past
- MAUDE – 20's. Efficient, intelligent hotel worker

SOUND EFFECT: OPENING SEQUENCE, BIG BEN

ANNOUNCER: *The Further Adventures of Sherlock Holmes* . . . Tonight: *The Adventure of the Deadly Tradition.*

MUSIC: *DANSE MACABRE*

SOUND EFFECT: QUIET LONDON STREET (BACKGROUND). THERE'S A BREEZE. HOLMES, WATSON AND MACDONALD STROLL THROUGH THE SNOW

HOLMES: And just why are we out on the streets this late on Christmas Eve, MacDonald?

MacDONALD: My notion of a present, Mr. Holmes. You don't mind, I hope?

HOLMES: Not if the gift is sufficiently imaginative.

MacDONALD: Oh, I think I can promise you both that this is something you'll never have seen before – something that's appropriate to the season.

WATSON: Those words fill me more with dread than anticipation, Inspector.

MACDONALD: The constable did his best to preserve the footprints – at least, the ones close to the body. After a few feet, they're obliterated by those of other revellers.

HOLMES: One set belongs to the victim, and the other to the murderer, since murder it plainly is. From the length of the stride, I'd say that pursued and pursuer were roughly the same height.

WATSON: And the body you mentioned . . . ?

MacDONALD: Is 'round this corner, Doctor.

WATSON: You said the crime was appropriate to the season. You don't mean the victim was dressed as Father – (HE SPOTS IT) Oh my.

SOUND EFFECT: ALL FOOTSTEPS STOP

MacDONALD: Now . . . I dare you to tell me you've seen somebody stabbed through the chest with an icicle before today, gentlemen.

HOLMES: Not unless it melted before I was called to the scene. I must congratulate you – this appears to be an intriguing adornment to the problem.

MacDONALD: We've still yet to identify him, but I didn't wish to waste any time in summoning you.

HOLMES: You were very wise, Mr. Mac. He must have snapped the icicle from over *here* . . . his pace quickens, and then he attacks.

WATSON: Robbery?

MacDONALD: It doesn't appear so, Dr. Watson. Here is his wallet – and a healthy number of notes inside, see?

HOLMES: Unless he took something other than money.

MacDONALD: What sort of robber isn't interested in money?

HOLMES: If we find him, we'll be certain to ask him. I sincerely hope you followed his footprints past this point?

MacDONALD: To the very next street, Mr. Holmes, where they simply vanish. More than likely, he hailed a cab.

WATSON: This poor chap was dressed up for some sort of social function.

MacDONALD: Of which there must be a hundred in the vicinity tonight. I have officers checking them all, but it's slow-going.

HOLMES: Would you case to estimate the dead man's age, Doctor?

WATSON: Late fifties, perhaps. Early sixties?

HOLMES: I'm inclined to agree.

MacDONALD: Is there nothing else you can tell me, sir?

HOLMES: Aside from the fact that he's a Jesuit and a clarinet-player, lately returned from India, nothing suggests itself.

WATSON: You know, in a more credulous age, these displays of apparent clairvoyance might have brought you to the stake. (TO MacDONALD) Brace yourself, Inspector – Holmes is about to be extremely clever.

HOLMES: Callus on the top knuckle of thumb indicates his fondness for the clarinet. The skin on the lower part of his face is lighter than his

268

forehead and hands. The inference is clear – he wore a beard while abroad in a hot country, and shaved it off upon his return to England.

MacDONALD: But – India?

HOLMES: The handle of his umbrella is inlaid with ivory.

WATSON: Very common in India, Inspector.

HOLMES: Finally, the cross of St. Ignatius on his watch-chain indicates his religious preferences.

MacDONALD: And what about this item next to it? Not a coin . . . Some sort of lucky charm? A depiction of three dogs – perhaps this fellow was a breeder.

HOLMES: Perhaps. Well, it's getting on, and I don't believe Watson and I can be of any particular assistance in this matter. If anything should occur to me in the morning, should we still find you on duty?

MacDONALD: Still, Mr. Holmes. The criminal pays little heed to the holidays, not even Christmas.

WATSON: A policeman's lot is not a happy one, Inspector.

HOLMES: That's a rather pithy phrase, Watson.

WATSON: Not my own, alas.

HOLMES: Ah. (TO MacDONALD) Well, we shall wish you goodnight and good hunting, Mr. Mac!

SOUND EFFECT: HOLMES AND WATSON START WALKING

WATSON: What do you have up your sleeve, Holmes? You know perfectly well what that emblem signifies!

HOLMES: Do I?

WATSON: It isn't three different dogs, it's Cerberus, the dog with three heads. That makes the dead man a member of the Herculean Society.

269

HOLMES: You astound me, Watson!

WATSON: MacDonald may not have been in London long enough to have heard of them, but I certainly have. There are only twelve members at any given time, and each one carries a disc depicting one of the Twelve Labours of Hercules.

HOLMES: Well, well.

WATSON: In fact, I believe they traditionally gather in one of the finer hotels on Christmas Eve. I can't quite remember which one . . . .

HOLMES: The Vernon. Which is where we're headed now.

WATSON: Then why did you pretend you didn't know?

HOLMES: The purchasing of appropriate Christmas gifts is one area in which I lack imagination, I'm afraid. What better present for Inspector MacDonald, then, than the identity of the murderer?

WATSON: And for me?

HOLMES: The notion that you succeeded in besting Sherlock Holmes – if only for a moment.

WATSON: I'm supposed to be grateful for that, I suppose.

HOLMES: No gratitude necessary, Watson. Look upon it simply as a token of my esteem.

WATSON: Holmes, the Herculean Society is a charitable organization. Why would someone murder one of the city's greatest philanthropists?

HOLMES: We shan't know that until we've questioned the remaining members. We're stepping close to the edge of perilously high places – We'd best watch our footing.

SOUND EFFECT: OUT

MUSIC: STING

CONSTANTINE: This is the absolute limit! We can't have non-members constantly barging in like this!

ALGERNON: Father, this is Mr. Sherlock Holmes and his colleague, Dr. Watson –

CONSTANTINE: I don't care if it's the Prime Minister and the Chancellor of the Exchequer! The society's rules are quite specific.

WATSON: We're here on police business, sir.

CONSTANTINE: Policemen, are you? Let's see your warrant cards. Come on, then. I should tell you I see Sir Charles Warren at the lodge almost every week, and if I should mention your names to him . . . .

HOLMES: I'm afraid the police commissioner holds no authority over us.

CONSTANTINE: Damn your impudence! Algernon, summon the manager!

ALGERNON: I keep trying to tell you, Father, these gentlemen are consulting detectives. They're not members of the police force at all.

CONSTANTINE: I see. You're private busybodies of some sort.

WATSON: Assisting Inspector Alec MacDonald in his investigation of the murder of a member of your society.

CONSTANTINE: What?

ALGERNON: A murder?

HOLMES: I believe there are traditionally twelve members of the Herculean Society, but I count only eleven people in the room.

CONSTANTINE: What sort of nonsense is this?

WATSON: I'm afraid it's quite true, Sir Constantine. Forgive me, you *are* Sir Constantine Morgan?

271

CONSTANTINE: Naturally.

ALGERNON: Forgive me, gentlemen, you said you were investigating a murder?

CONSTANTINE: Algernon, this is all some childish prank. Don't give them the time of day.

ALGERNON: But, Father –

CONSTANTINE: That's enough, Algernon! I've had quite enough needless disturbance for one night. (TO HOLMES AND WATSON) Gentlemen, you can either leave of your own accord, or the Vernon's staff will carry you out. It's a matter of no importance to me.

ALGERNON: I'm sorry, Mr. Holmes.

HOLMES: We've no wish to ruin your celebrations, Sir Constantine. Dr. Watson and I have the utmost respect for the work done by the society.

CONSTANTINE: The children, Mr. Holmes – the children are everything, and we must do whatever we can for them. But, once a year, we take the opportunity to – well, congratulate ourselves for all our good works.

HOLMES: And we have the utmost respect for your traditions, I assure you.

CONSTANTINE: Without tradition, where would we be? Every year, on Christmas Eve, I'd read to my chi – (HE STOPS HIMSELF FROM SAYING "CHILDREN") to Algernon here from *A Christmas Carol* by candlelight. He's a man now, of course, with a home and a life of his own, but I still keep up the tradition.

WATSON: It sounds very pleasant. But if we could just enquire –

HOLMES: Watson, we gave our word that we won't bother Sir Constantine again this evening, and we must be as good as that word. The compliments of the season to you.

CONSTANTINE: And to you, gentlemen.

WATSON: Holmes, this is absurd! A member of this society is dead, and we can't do anything because their president refuses to talk to us! We don't even know the victim's name!

SOUND EFFECT: A LARGE DOOR OPENS

HOLMES: There are always possibilities, Watson. There is one person in this hotel who can provide us with that information, and more besides.

WATSON: Such as?

SOUND EFFECT: THE DOOR CLOSES (BACKGROUND) CUTTING OUT THE BACKGROUND CHATTER

HOLMES: Someone else intruded upon the society's celebrations this evening. I'd like to know who, wouldn't you?

MUSIC: STING

MAUDE: Yes, sir, I take the coats of all the Vernon's guests.

HOLMES: Excellent! Then you'll have spoken to all the members of the Herculean Society at some point during the evening.

MAUDE: Indeed, sir.

HOLMES: Is it too much to hope that you recall their names?

MAUDE: It's something I pride myself on, sir – along with a respect for their privacy.

HOLMES: Ah.

WATSON: Perhaps . . .

SOUND EFFECT: WATSON COUNTS OUT A FEW COINS

WATSON: . . . you might care to buy yourself a Christmas present, Miss . . . ?

MAUDE: Maude, sir. Staff go by first names.

WATSON: And are staff forbidden from accepting tokens of esteem?

MAUDE: Not if the manager doesn't find out, sir.

HOLMES: Only one member of the Herculean Society has departed so far. And I've no doubt he reclaimed his coat before doing so?

MAUDE: That's right, sir. It was Mr. Hartigan.

HOLMES: A mere "Mister"?

MAUDE: There's nothing "mere" about Mr. Cecil (PRONOUNCED "SESSUL") Hartigan, sir – He was the director of the Banque Continentale here in London before he retired. Haven't seen him for quite a while.

WATSON: I have it on good authority that he's been abroad.

HOLMES: There was another visitor tonight, Maude. Someone who wasn't a Society member, but who nevertheless gained entrance to their private celebrations.

WATSON: You said that before, Holmes.

HOLMES: You remember Sir Constantine's first words upon meeting us? He complained about non-members "constantly barging in", suggesting that someone else had barged in before us. Now, if all twelve Herculeans are accounted for, who might that visitor have been? (TO MAUDE) Maude?

MAUDE: I did recognise the gentleman, sir. (SURPRISED) As a matter of fact, I think *that's* him!

WATSON: Where?

ALGERNON: (APPROACHING) Mr. Holmes?

MAUDE: I'm so sorry, Mr. Morgan! For a moment, I thought you were someone else!

ALGERNON: I want to apologise for my father's manner.

HOLMES: Think nothing of it, Mr. Morgan.

ALGERNON: He's always rather obstinate, but since he was elected president of the Society, I'm afraid he's inclined to be something of a tartar.

WATSON: It's quite understandable, Mr. Morgan, if a trifle irksome.

HOLMES: And you are a member of the society in your own right.

ALGERNON: I try to do what I think is right, Mr. Holmes. Who among us can do anything else?

HOLMES: Then perhaps you might think it right to tell us something of Cecil Hartigan?

ALGERNON: Hartigan? Yes, he went home early. Wasn't feeling quite the ticket, he said. Worried about getting a chill on his chest.

HOLMES: A fear that was entirely justified.

ALGERNON: (CONFUSED) Eh?

HOLMES: Maude, you were about to tell us the name of the gentleman who intruded upon tonight's festivities.

ALGERNON: I can tell you *that*, Mr. Holmes – it was Cobb.

HOLMES: Cobb?

ALGERNON: My father's manservant. Decent enough chap.

WATSON: Why was he here, Mr. Morgan?

ALGERNON: I've really no idea, Doctor. I spoke to him briefly, just to say hello, you know. But he came to see Father.

HOLMES: Who has hardly likely to be any more co-operative than he has been thus far. Your father's address, Mr. Morgan?

ALGERNON: Number 10 Cadogan Square. But if you'll excuse me, I really think you're barking up the wrong Christmas tree. Cobb was here a matter of minutes. I don't suppose there could be any mistake – Cecil Hartigan really is dead?

WATSON: I'm afraid so.

ALGERNON: It's almost impossible to believe! Who'd do such a thing? This was the first meeting he'd attended in years. He's been out in India. Scarcely knew a soul in England.

WATSON: Apart from the other eleven members of the Herculean Society?

HOLMES: Maude, who was the first to retrieve their coat and leave – Mr. Hartigan, or Mr. Cobb?

MAUDE: Mr. Hartigan, sir, but only by a matter of minutes . . . . (A SLIGHT HINT OF PUZZLEMENT IN THOSE LAST FEW WORDS)

WATSON: Forgive me, but you seem distracted.

MAUDE: It's a funny thing, sir . . . I didn't realize it at the time, but – I'd swear Mr. Cobb gave me the wrong cloakroom ticket. No, that can't be right. The coat, it was his, I'm certain of it.

HOLMES: Interesting. (TO ALGERNON) Mr. Morgan, we have matters to attend to. We must bid you a good evening.

ALGERNON: As you like, Mr. Holmes, but I must confess to finding this all utterly bewildering. Cobb can't possibly have anything to do with whatever happened to Cecil Hartigan. As I say, he's a decent chap.

WATSON: "Decent *enough*."

MUSIC: STING

SOUND EFFECT: A BITTER WIND BLOWS THROUGHOUT

276

COBB: Sir Constantine is not at home, sir. I'm afraid you'll have to call again.

HOLMES: We're well aware that your master is spending his Christmas Eve at the Vernon Hotel, Mr. Cobb. It *is* Mr. Cobb, isn't it?

COBB: (SUDDENLY SUSPICIOUS) Who's asking?

WATSON: May we come inside and talk?

COBB: You may not. Sir Constantine is not at home, and even if he was, I doubt he'd be at home to either one of you.

HOLMES: You have a refreshingly plain-spoken attitude for one in servitude. Perhaps you'll be so good as to answer some of my questions.

COBB: I don't see why I should.

WATSON: But equally, there's no reason why you shouldn't. You surely don't have anything to hide, Mr. Cobb?

COBB: (AFTER A BRIEF PAUSE) Make it quick – I got preparations to make.

HOLMES: You were also at the Hotel Vernon this evening, I understand?

COBB: Who told you that?

HOLMES: Mr. Algernon Morgan.

WATSON: And you were also recognized by the cloakroom attendant.

COBB: So I was at the Vernon.

HOLMES: Why?

COBB: Sir Constantine forgot his gloves – I was bringing them to him. It's a cold night, in case you hadn't noticed.

WATSON: I assure you, we've noticed. That's why we'd prefer to have this conversation next to a fireplace.

COBB: And that's why *I'd* prefer to have this conversation in the doorway.

HOLMES: Forgive me, but I find it hard to believe that, on this of all evenings, your master would have left home without a pair of gloves.

COBB: Yeah, well that's just it, y'see – he didn't. I made a mistake.

HOLMES: A mistake?

COBB: He had a pair of gloves the whole time. I went all the way out there for nothing.

WATSON: How frustrating.

HOLMES: And I imagine Sir Constantine was none too pleased at having his private celebrations invaded by a commoner.

COBB: Is that what you think of me, then?

HOLMES: It's my experience that there is no such thing as a commonplace individual.

COBB: What experience? You with the Yard?

HOLMES: Not officially. My name is Sherlock Holmes, this gentlemen is Dr. Watson. Possibly those names are familiar to you.

COBB: Possibly. I think we've spoken long enough, Mr. Holmes. I have duties to attend to. Sorry you can't stay – It's lovely and warm in here.

HOLMES: One final question: Does the name Cecil Hartigan mean anything to you?

COBB: Not a thing. Who's that, then?

HOLMES: It's of no importance. Thank you for your assistance, Mr. Collins.

COBB: The name I have is Cobb, sir.

HOLMES: Ah, yes – how foolish of me.

SOUND EFFECT: THE DOOR SLAMS SHUT

WATSON: Charming fellow, this Collins.

HOLMES: His name is Cobb, Watson, didn't you hear him insist upon it?

SOUND EFFECT: HOLMES AND WATSON BEGIN WALKING THROUGH THE SNOW

WATSON: Yes, when you mistakenly addressed him as Collins. Except that you and I know that you don't make mistakes.

HOLMES: I welcome your faith in me, old fellow.

WATSON: Christmas is the time for a show of faith, surely.

HOLMES: I only hope it's justified.

WATSON: I've never known you to doubt your own abilities, Holmes. Why are we leaving? We should have dragged him from the house and presented him to MacDonald!

HOLMES: Crack the egg prematurely, and the bird will die. Patience will catch us a falcon. Did you by any chance notice that Cobb had dust on both his index finger and the top of his head?

WATSON: Only the finger. I'm not quite tall enough to spot the other. What does it signify?

HOLMES: That's what troubles me, Watson – I've really no idea.

WATSON: It may mean nothing at all, of course.

HOLMES: Let us hope so, Watson. I'm close. I can feel it, and yet I cannot grasp it.

WATSON: And the "it" to which you refer?

279

HOLMES: The truth.

SOUND EFFECT: OUT

MacDONALD: I had a feeling you might continue with the investigation, gentlemen, in spite of what you said.

HOLMES: You're not upset, I hope, Inspector?

MacDONALD: Not a bit of it, Mr. Holmes! You've brought me some important information – plenty to be going on with over the next few weeks.

WATSON: Mr. Holmes was rather hoping that he'd be able to solve the whole matter in one night.

MacDONALD: Was he, now?

HOLMES: Even I'm permitted to think wishfully from time-to-time, Mr. Mac.

WATSON: We may at least be able to present you with the name of the likeliest suspect. I'm convinced the murderer is Sir Constantine Morgan's manservant, Cobb.

MacDONALD: Oh? And why do you believe that, Doctor?

WATSON: Three reasons: Firstly, he was at the hotel shortly before Cecil Hartigan left – very likely, he followed him and accosted him in the street. Secondly, Holmes deduced that the killer was the same height as Hartigan, which Cobb certainly is.

MacDONALD: And thirdly?

HOLMES: Holmes believes he recognised him as someone named Collins.

MacDONALD: Not a person you know socially, I imagine, Mr. Holmes.

HOLMES: You're quite correct, Inspector. In his day, Herbert Collins was quite the talented safe-cracker and jewel thief. He spent a

280

considerable amount of time behind bars in Wormwood Scrubs, after which nothing more was heard of him.

MacDONALD: And now we know why, eh? But if you'll forgive me, Dr. Watson, what we don't know is why he'd wish to murder Mr. Hartigan. Unless you have some ideas about that, as well . . . ?

HOLMES: I'm not aware of any connection between the two, or any cause for animosity. As I deduced, Hartigan was abroad until quite recently.

WATSON: But he *was* a member of the Herculean Society, of which Collins' employer, Sir Constantine Morgan, is president. Collins – or Cobb, whichever you prefer – visited him at the Vernon Hotel earlier this evening on some obviously fictitious pretext. I don't doubt that it was he who gave Collins his instructions.

MacDONALD: Then far from being a reformed character, he's an assassin in Sir Constantine's employ.

WATSON: Precisely. Of course, I don't know what reason he might have had for wanting to dispose of Cecil Hartigan, but we'll undoubtedly uncover something – blackmail, perhaps.

HOLMES: I applaud your deductive process, Doctor.

WATSON: You see, Mr. Holmes agrees with me.

HOLMES: Actually . . . .

WATSON: (SIGHS)

HOLMES: The notion of one wealthy man blackmailing another wealthy man is not without its difficulties.

WATSON: I didn't say it was definitely a case of blackmail, I merely presented it as a possibility.

HOLMES: Also, why didn't Sir Constantine give Collins his instructions before going out for the evening? Why stage this elaborate charade with the gloves?

MacDONALD: What gloves?

WATSON: It's unimportant, Inspector.

HOLMES: The fact that Collins took the first weapon to hand – an icicle – rather than bringing one with him, suggests that this was a spur-of-the-moment affair, not that he was acting out anyone's orders.

WATSON: But you do agree that Collins is the murderer?

HOLMES: I think it highly likely, Watson, yes.

MacDONALD: Unfortunately, I'll need a little more than a coincidence in height between Collins and Hartigan before I can perform an arrest.

HOLMES: (THOUGHTFUL) A coincidence in height . . . .

WATSON: Something on your mind, Holmes?

HOLMES: The wrong cloakroom ticket! And dust! A year's accumulation! Of course!

MacDONALD: I'm glad you see it, Mr. Holmes, I'm afraid I'm as much in the dark as ever.

HOLMES: Watson, before shutting the door on us, didn't Collins say he had preparations to make?

WATSON: For Christmas Day, certainly.

HOLMES: Not for Christmas Day – for later tonight! We've been looking at this from entirely the wrong direction!

MacDONALD: What does it all mean?

HOLMES: It means there is perfidy of a unique and horrifying stripe afoot here. We have to go back!

WATSON: Back to the Vernon Hotel?

HOLMES: Back to Sir Constantine's home – there's another murder yet to come. Pray we're in time to prevent it!

282

MUSIC: STING

SOUND EFFECT: HAMMERING ON A DOOR

HOLMES: (ON THE OTHER SIDE OF THE DOOR) Sir Constantine!
  Sir Constantine!

MacDONALD: (ON THE OTHER SIDE OF THE DOOR) Perhaps he's
  not yet returned, sir.

HOLMES: (ON THE OTHER SIDE OF THE DOOR) Watson, would you
  do the honours?

WATSON: (ON THE OTHER SIDE OF THE DOOR) With pleasure!

SOUND EFFECT: THE DOOR CRASHES OPEN

HOLMES: Thank you, Doctor.

SOUND EFFECT: ALL THREE ENTER THE HOUSE

MacDONALD: We don't have a warrant, Mr. Holmes!

HOLMES: Please feel free to place us under arrest, Inspector – later! In
  the meantime, put your scarf around your mouth! Whatever you do,
  don't breathe in the fumes!

SOUND EFFECT: HOLMES RUNS (OFF-MICROPHONE)

MacDONALD: Doctor, you know I have the utmost faith in Mr. Holmes,
  but are you sure that on this occasion –

WATSON: Just do as he says, Inspector!

SOUND EFFECT: (OFF-MICROPHONE) A WINDOW SMASHES.
HOLMES RETURNS TO MICROPHONE, WALKING THIS
TIME

HOLMES: (APPROACHING MICROPHONE) We must wait a few
  moments before it's completely safe. I'm afraid we were too late.
  Take a look for yourself, gentlemen.

283

MacDONALD: I take it Sir Constantine isn't dozing in that chair.

HOLMES: He's quite dead. His habit of reading *A Christmas Carol* by candlelight every Christmas Eve has been the death of him. The candle is impregnated with arsenic – the fumes did their work before he realised what was happening.

WATSON: Monstrous!

HOLMES: But ingenious, Watson. We might never have known a thing about it, were it not for the fact that Collins was forced to kill Cecil Hartigan.

MacDONALD: Collins! Where is the fellow?

HOLMES: Long gone, I fear. He was probably instructed to discover his master's body on Christmas morning, when very few officers would be in the mood to conduct a thorough investigation. But our visit a few hours ago may have frightened him off. I don't doubt that you'll catch up with him eventually, Mr. Mac, but in the meantime, you can at least arrest the person who provided him with this remarkable method of murder.

MUSIC: BRIDGE

ALGERNON: So I gave Cobb – I mean Collins, this candle which he used to kill my father. Or should I say, with which my father killed himself. You make it all seem remarkably simple.

HOLMES: I'm sure it seemed that way in the planning stages, Mr. Morgan. Tell me, were you by any chance responsible for employing Sir Constantine's manservant?

ALGERNON: I was. A few pounds in the right pockets, it wasn't difficult.

WATSON: Nor was obtaining the arsenic, I imagine.

ALGERNON: Bought it last summer – told the chemist I wanted to kill some dandelions. Actually, I had a bigger nuisance to dispose of.

284

MacDONALD: Sir Constantine was one of the most generous men in the entire country!

ALGERNON: Perhaps you didn't know him like I did.

HOLMES: Perhaps not, but we'll leave that for the moment. The method you chose to pass Collins the poisoned candle was thoroughly ingenious. When you met briefly at the Christmas celebration, you swapped cloakroom tickets. He now had the ticket for *your* coat.

MacDONALD: The one with the candle inside.

WATSON: Maude did say she thought Collins had given her the wrong ticket.

HOLMES: However, Cecil Hartigan went to collect his coat a moment earlier – and Maude gave him your coat by mistake, Mr. Morgan.

ALGERNON: My ticket was Number 9. Hartigan's was Number 6. Stupid girl looked at it the wrong way up.

MacDONALD: And so Hartigan left the Vernon wearing the coat containing the murder weapon intended for your father.

WATSON: Collins must've realised at once and determined to steal the candle back at any cost – you were right about it being an unpremeditated killing, Holmes.

HOLMES: Unlike that of Sir Constantine.

ALGERNON: You have a fearsome reputation, Mr. Holmes. You'll be pleased to know that you do not disappoint. I imagine you knew from the start.

HOLMES: If I had known, Mr. Morgan, I might have been able to foil your plan. There were certain early indications, however: The footprints in the snow told me that Hartigan and Collins were the same height. And, of course, Maude briefly mistook *you* for Collins.

MacDONALD: Three men, all the same height and build, all of whom could wear another's coat without realising. One simple mistake, and two people die.

ALGERNON: But only one of them had to. I'm genuinely sorry about Cecil. I had no idea Collins had done that.

WATSON: Then why even identify him?

ALGERNON: I didn't have much choice, Doctor, once I realised you were speaking to the cloakroom attendant. I simply had to hope he'd brazen it out when you spoke to him.

HOLMES: He certainly did that. But I noticed traces of dust on his head and finger – he'd removed a volume from the top shelf of bookcase. one that remained in place for a year at a time.

WATSON: *A Christmas Carol*. He said it was his tradition to read it by candlelight. Collins set out the book *and* the candle for him.

ALGERNON: It's not a story I really care for. I think Scrooge got off far too lightly, don't you?

WATSON: But in order to qualify as a member of the Herculean Society, you must be a very rich man in your own right. Why did you want your father's money, too?

ALGERNON: It was never about the money!

HOLMES: No, I fancy it was something rather more personal. When we spoke to Sir Constantine, he was about to mention his children, but corrected himself at the last moment. You had a brother or sister, Mr. Morgan. What became of him or her?

ALGERNON: Claudia's not dead, if that's what you're thinking. Father always found her difficult to control, and control was always his primary interest – that's why he became president of a charitable society. He saw it as a way of shaping the nation's future workforce.

WATSON: What happened to your sister?

ALGERNON: After she became pregnant – *out* of wedlock – Father arranged for her to be committed to the district lunatic asylum. He had many influential friends, you see, medical men among them. And don't ask me about the baby, because I honestly don't know what arrangements were made. We never spoke of it. He simply decided his daughter had never existed. I wasn't interested in inheriting his money, you see – just his influence.

MacDONALD: In order to reverse his decision and free your sister.

ALGERNON: You see the lengths I've had to go to? He made me do this, all of it! And for what? I don't care about myself, as far as I'm concerned, I'm already dead. But Claudia is languishing in a madhouse on the whim of a monster!

HOLMES: Dr. Watson and I are not without influence ourselves, Mr. Morgan. There's nothing we can do for you – you must face your punishment. But we can at least do what we may for your sister.

ALGERNON: Thank you, Mr. Holmes. In spite of all the advantages I've had in life, it's the only gift I've ever wanted.

MUSIC: *DANSE MACABRE*

WATSON: This is Dr. John H. Watson. I've had many more adventures with Sherlock Holmes, and I'll tell you another one . . . *when next we meet!*

MUSIC: (FADE OUT)

The Adventure of the
Fabricated Vision
by Craig Janacek

It was a late January morning in 1887 when my friend, Mr. Sherlock Holmes, was confronted by one of the most curious cases of his career to date. I had found that while Holmes possessed a rather abstract interest in certain metaphysical aspects of society and history – such as miracle plays, the Buddhism of Ceylon, or the Razor of Ockham – he was always sceptical that there was a transcendent reality beyond what is readily observable to the senses. And yet, as I look back over the course of our adventures together, the case of Mr. Henry Darnley has – for me, at least – always suggested that something nebulous remained hidden behind the veil of our limited perception. [1]

I had stopped by the well-remembered suite of rooms at Baker Street that I had shared with Holmes prior to my marriage. [2] I made a point of calling regularly, as I did not wish for us to drift apart, and I was always keen to hear details of how he was employing his extraordinary powers.

He seemed if not demonstrative – for such was not his way – at least pleased enough to see me. We sank into our respective armchairs across from the fireplace and he offered me a cigar from the coal-scuttle. So ensconced, we fell into a long conversation regarding both his various adventures in the criminal underbelly of London, as well as some of the more *outré* medical cases which had recently come through my practice, for he had long had a curiosity regarding the intersection of pathology and crime.

"This reminds me, Watson," said he, "that you may be interested in my next client."

"Oh. How so?"

Holmes glanced at his pocket-watch. "I am expecting him any minute now. He has been sent round by Lestrade, who felt that there was no criminal element at play. However, the man seemed desperate enough, and wrote that he wished to consult with me regarding an episode of madness in one of his employees."

"Well, I am hardly a psychologist, Holmes. I would much rather stitch up a man's skin and sinew than attempt to repair his broken mind."

"I too am unclear how I may be of assistance, and yet, the state of my finances are not such that I can afford to turn away a potential client –

especially if the case is too peculiar for the imagination of Scotland Yard. Ah, I think I hear him now."

At that moment, there was a loud ring at the bell, followed by the familiar steps of my former landlady. She gave a crisp knock before entering, holding before her a card upon the brass salver. Holmes motioned for me to pick it up. I did so, and I read it aloud:

Timothy Johnson, ACA [3]
Johnson, Roberts, and Company
Chartered Accountants
2 Finch Lane

Holmes nodded. "Pray ask him to step up, Mrs. Hudson."

A few minutes later, a tall, thin man of between fifty and sixty years entered the room with a diffident step. His suit was well-cut and pressed, and his cheeks were closely shaven. However, his dull grey eyes and pale face suggested a man who saw little of the sun whenever it made one of its rare appearances over the City.

Holmes introduced me as his trusted friend and indicated that the accountant should feel free to speak plainly in front of me.

Mr. Johnson nodded his head in response to these instructions. "Are you familiar, Mr. Holmes, with the affair of Sir Roger Shoemaker?"

"The alderman of Cordwainer?" replied Holmes. [4] "I have been following it in *The Times*."

"Then you are aware that Sir Roger is from an ancient and respected family. His purported misdeeds are the talk of the nation."

"Indeed. But what has this to do with your firm?"

"Sir Roger has been accused of defalcation. [5] He utilized the firm of White and Wotherspoon to keep his accounts, such that – should he be proven guilty – that venerable company is on the verge of being dragged down with him. My firm was engaged by the prosecuting lawyers to review White and Wotherspoon's accounts for evidence of malfeasance. It was a gigantic task, as there were twenty thick ledgers to be examined and checked, and the lawyers gave us less than three weeks to evaluate them all in time for the trial – which was scheduled for the 21st of this month."

"Ah yes, I recall reading that it has been postponed?"

"Indeed. But only for three days, and that was two days ago. We are running out of time to prove our case. Tomorrow afternoon, if I am unable to supply proof of Sir Roger's guilt, the case for the prosecution will collapse."

Holmes shrugged. "I fail to see how I may be of help."

"You see, Mr. Holmes, I had originally considered utilizing a team of accountants upon this task. However, I worried that the ledgers might be so convoluted that – where a group of individuals might miss a pattern of clues – a single man might be able to see the forest for the trees, if you will excuse the metaphor. I asked myself who was on track to become a junior partner? Who was my most reliable and hard-working man? I could only conclude that Henry Darnley was the fellow I needed. I left this vital bit of business entirely in his hands, confident that he would justify my choice."

"And did he?"

"That is the precise question, Mr. Holmes. At first, I had no doubts. He was at the office every day from ten to five, and then a second sitting from about eight in the evening to one in the morning. I have often thought that Mr. Darnley has accountancy seeped into his marrow."

"A queer obsession," I noted.

He looked over at me. "Ours is perhaps not the most glamourous occupation, Doctor. We are not the type to go running after villains and throwing them in chains, or sewing up a man who is bleeding to death. And yet there is drama in an accountant's life. When we find ourselves in the still early hours, while all the world sleeps, hunting through column after column for those missing figures which will turn a respected alderman into a felon – well, you will hopefully understand that it is not such a prosaic profession after all."

Johnson turned back to Holmes and continued his account. "I spoke to Mr. Darnley on the 4th of January. It was a Tuesday, and I could tell that he had worked upon the case throughout the weekend, without pause. And I could see by the light in his eyes that he was onto something – and that no heavy game hunter ever got a finer thrill when first he caught sight of the trail of his quarry, even if the jungle through which Darnley had to follow Sir Roger's tracks before he got his kill was made up of twenty thick ledgers, rather than a tangle of trees and vines. Hard work – but rare sport, too, in a way!"

Holmes waved his hand. "The colourful metaphors are strictly unnecessary, Mr. Johnson. Just the facts will do. Pray continue."

"Well," said the man, looking somewhat put out, "I checked in with Darnley regularly, and he appeared to be making good progress upon the stack of twenty ledgers. He told me on the 6th of January that he had completed three of them. While the rascal Shoemaker had covered his tracks well, Darnley was convinced that he could pick them up for all that. By the 17th, the lawyers began to clamour for their material, as the trial was but four days away, and Darnley had finished reviewing only three-quarters of the ledgers. He promised to do the rest in a forced march, but noted that he already had enough evidence to give the lawyers, and anything else would be to spare. Darnley said that he had Shoemaker fast on a hundred counts, and that he expected that he would get a large share of the credit when the judge realized Shoemakers's true nature – a slippery, cunning rascal. Darnley claimed to have proof of false trading accounts, false balance-sheets, dividends drawn from capital, losses written down as profits, suppression of working expenses, manipulation of petty cash – a fine record!"

"And has something happened to Mr. Darnley?"

"You are most perspicacious, Mr. Holmes. In fact, three nights ago, Mr. Darnley collapsed in his home, slumped in his chair over the final ledger. He was found by his housekeeper, who summoned his physician. Mr. Darnley is, at this moment, residing in Dr. Andrew Sinclair's private hospital, raving about visions of the past." [6]

"A tragic tale of over-work, Mr. Johnson, but I fail to see your problem," said Holmes. "Darnley is alive. He may not be fit to testify directly, but his notes have not vanished, have they?"

"No," said Johnson shaking his head. "His figures are in the solicitor's possession, even as we speak. However, like Pepys before him, Darnley utilized a form of brachygraphy that we have been largely unable to decipher. [7] And even if we could, his notes are not in such a form that would be admissible in court. Darnley must himself testify regarding the nature of Shoemaker's crimes, or the case for the prosecution is likely to be thrown out. But I can ill afford to put a madman before the court. We would be the laughingstock of the City. So, I ask you, Mr. Holmes – is Mr. Darnley fit to stand before a judge? Is his evidence against Shoemaker accurate, or yet another a fantasy?"

Holmes furrowed his brow. "This seems like the work for another accountant."

"There is no time for that!" cried Johnson. "We need an answer by tomorrow, and an accountant would take weeks."

"Then a psychologist. What does Dr. Sinclair say?"

"That is unclear. When I spoke to the doctor, he seemed uncertain if Mr. Darnley was simply overstrained, or if he experienced an actual vision from the past. If it is the former, then I may feel confident in his work, for that was what broke him. However, if Darnley is seeing visions, I cannot allow the barrister for the defence – Sir Kenneth Bailey of Inner Temple – to examine him. Sir Kenneth is far too sharp – he would ferret out that Darnley has been in the hospital, and would probe and inquire until all comes out. Then we would be ruined. I simply cannot take the risk. I would rather say that we found nothing in the ledgers of White and Wotherspoon that would implicate Sir Roger than destroy the future of the firm."

Holmes was eventually persuaded to look into Mr. Johnson's case, which meant a trip to question the invalided Mr. Darnley. Dr. Sinclair's hospital was located off Shoreditch, so Holmes engaged a hansom cab to take us along the New Road, veering right at Angel to follow City Road.

The hospital was a small affair, with under twenty beds, but to my professional eye it looked to be smartly-run and clean. Nurses scurried about busily, and the patients appeared to be well cared-for.

We were soon shown into the office of Dr. Sinclair, where we found him seated behind his desk. This was littered with a precarious pile of medical notebooks, as well as several musty volumes – which looked to be historical records rather than professional texts. However, a mere glance at the man was sufficient for me to recognize a fellow man of science. He was rather past sixty, with a mane of flowing white hair. His face was square, his jaw strong, and piercing blue eyes shone under a thatched brow.

Holmes introduced us and the reason for our visit. At first, Dr. Sinclair seemed somewhat reluctant to discuss the particulars of his patient. However, when Holmes explained that Mr. Darnley's professional reputation was at stake, the physician relented.

"Very well," said Sinclair, reaching for his notebook and flipping through it. "Ah, yes, here we go. Mr. Darnley first came to see me on the 6th of January. He complained, not of a pain *per se*, but only a sort of fullness of the head with an occasional mist over the eyes. He thought perhaps some bromide, or chloral, or something of the kind might do him good." [8]

"Ah!" said Holmes, with interest. "And did you prescribe such an agent?"

Dr. Sinclair shook his head. "I did not. I could tell that he was nervous and highly-strung, and told him that drugs would not help him. Instead, I prescribed rest."

"And what was Mr. Darnley's response to your prescription?" asked Holmes.

"I am afraid that he did not take it well."

"How so?"

"If I recall correctly, I believe that he called me an 'ass', and a 'foolish spouter of perfect nonsense'. He said that rest was out of the question, and that I might as well shout to a man who has a pack of wolves at his heels that what he wants is absolute quiet."

"A vivid image," said Holmes.

"Yes, well, that is hardly the most vivid image that Mr. Darnley has seen this month."

"What do you mean?"

Instead of answering, Dr. Sinclair continued his tale. "Mr. Darnley returned to see me three days later. He was under considerable pressure, and I believe that he originally had little intention of seeing me again. And yet he felt that he had to, for a queer experience drove him to me. All in all, he is a curious psycho-physiological study."

"What was the peculiar experience?" asked Holmes. "You spoke of an image?"

"Yes, or perhaps I should say a vision, to be more precise. You see, Mr. Darnley has developed a mania of sorts regarding an old silver-framed mirror in his room. Now, if you are familiar with accountants, Mr. Holmes, you will know that they are a precise sort, and Darnley is no exception. He kept an exact record of his symptoms and sensations. I have been studying these notes, and they are interesting in themselves, and also because now – when I try to get him to speak of what he saw in the mirror – the visions all seem blurred and unreal, like some queer dream betwixt sleeping and waking."

"And what precisely did he see?"

"Upon the first occasion – which appeared as he was working at his desk – it was the vague outline of a woman's head, her eyes filled with a passionate emotion."

"It sounds as if he had dropped asleep over his figures," said Holmes, "and that his experience was nothing more than a dream."

Dr. Sinclair smiled. "I see that you are a sceptic, Mr. Holmes. Well, there is no doubt that is one possible explanation, and I suggested as such to Mr. Darnley. However, he responded that – and I quote – 'As a matter of fact, I was never more vividly awake in my life.' Still, I persisted in arguing this hypothesis with him, and told him that it was a subjective impression – a chimera of the nerves – begotten by worry and insomnia. I am not certain that he believed me, and he left my office an unsatisfied man."

"And your diagnosis?"

"It was plain that he was overly straining his nerves, risking a complete breakdown, even endangering his sanity. He was on the verge of a full-blown brain fever."

I concurred with Dr. Sinclair's judgment, and said as much.

Holmes nodded. "What happened next?"

"Well, I was most concerned for him, so two days later – on the evening of the 11th of January – I went 'round to Darnley's house – he lives at Clerkenwell Close across from St. James's – in order to ensure that he was well."

"And was he?"

"Hardly. He gave me a smile at the door, but one that looked as if his nerves would break over it. When I asked how he was doing, Darnley said that he had determined that the mirror was a sort of barometer which marked his brain-pressure, for each night, he would reach out and rub it before going back to work. He then observed that would cloud up before he reached the end of his task."

"He sounds quite unstable," I interjected.

"Indeed. Darnley was obsessed with that silver mirror, so I agreed to have a look at it. It was a highly polished affair, for all its age. He pointed out that something was scribbled in crabbed old characters upon the metal-work at the back. I examined this with a lens, but could make nothing of it. '*Sanc. X. Pal.*' was my final reading of it, but that did not bring us any farther. I advised him to put it away into another room. However, he only laughed, saying something to the effect that after all, whatever he may see in it is – by my own account – only a symptom."

Holmes nodded gravely. "For a madman, he is most perceptive. It is in the cause that the danger lies – not the visions."

Dr. Sinclair frowned. "What cause?"

"That remains to be determined," said Holmes. "Pray continue."

"I went 'round again on the morning of the 14th, and Darnley seemed somewhat improved. He reported that on the 12th, he had made good progress on the ledgers which had so consumed his time and thoughts. Therefore, he could afford to follow my advice to drop work for a day. It was quite evident that the visions depended entirely upon his nervous state, for he reported that he had sat in front of the mirror for an hour the night before, with no result whatever. His soothing day had chased them away. However, he had plainly not fully abandoned his obsession with the mirror. He had examined it the prior evening under a good light, and besides the mysterious inscription '*Sanc. X. Pal.*', he was able to discern some signs of heraldic marks, very faintly visible upon the silver."

"Ah, additional marks," said Holmes, with interest. "Could you recognise them?"

"They are plainly very ancient, as they are almost obliterated. So far as I could make out, the symbols are three spear-heads, two above and one below. Some sort of armorial bearings. Mr. Darnley agreed with my identification. I admit, Mr. Holmes, that his case deeply interested me. I cross-questioned him closely on the details of his vision, for I was torn in two by conflicting desires – the one that my patient should lose his symptoms, the other that the medium – for so I began to regard him – should solve this mystery of the past. I advised continued rest, but could not oppose him too violently when Darnley declared that he felt perfectly well again. He said that he intended that nothing else should stop him until his task was finished, so such a thing as rest was completely out of the question until the ten remaining ledgers had been checked."

"And how did he end up here?"

"Well, as he was adamant about continuing his excessive work and was refusing my advice, I stopped visiting him. I regret that decision now, of course, for I might have prevented his complete collapse. But he eventually broke under the intolerable strain. He had worked himself to the limit. I was called in and had him brought here for the rest that he so desperately needed. After his collapse, he was insensible for the first two days, and only began to speak intelligibly last evening."

"Surely it is unusual for a man to suffer an attack of brain-fever solely from an immoderate amount of work?" said Holmes. "In my experience, it is usually a traumatic event that precipitates such a frenzy."

"I concur, Mr. Holmes, and in this case, I believe that there was something beyond work alone which brought low Mr. Darnley."

"Yes? What was it that drove him over the edge?"

Dr. Sinclair smiled wryly. "You will not believe me if I told you. You should hear it from Darnley himself. Come, let us see if he is awake."

Sinclair rose and picked up both his notebook on Darnley's case, as well as two of the old volumes from his desk. He led us out into the main corridor, and we made our way along the passage's whitewashed walls and umber-coloured doors. We climbed a stone staircase, and stopped in front of one of the propped-open doors.

The doctor rapped with his free hand, and a pale face looked up from the bed. "Mr. Darnley, how are you doing this afternoon?"

Darnley was a small man, nearing only thirty years of age, yet with thinning brown hair and thick glasses. He wore the provided white garments – so that everyone would know his place in the hospital – and from beneath these gowns, I noted his skin appeared rather rashy. When he spoke, his voice had a trace of a Scottish inflection. "Ah, Dr. Sinclair, it is good to see you, sir!" he cried. "My figures must be out by a certain date. Unless they are so, I shall lose the chance of my lifetime, so how on earth am I to rest? I'll take a week or so after the trial."

"You are resting now, Mr. Darnley," said the doctor, gently.

"Nonsense!" the little man cried. "Stop work? It's absurd to ask such a thing. It's like a long-distance race. You feel queer at first and your heart thumps and your lungs pant, but if you have only the pluck to keep on, you get your second wind. I'll stick to my work and wait for my second wind. If it never comes – all the same, I'll stick to my work. Two ledgers are done, and I am well on in the third."

"According to Mr. Johnson, you have completed rather more than that, Mr. Darnley," said Sinclair.

"Have I?" said Darnley, looking confused. "That is good. Still there is more work to be done. Well, I'll stand the strain and I'll take the risk, and so long as I can sit in my chair and move a pen, I'll follow the old sinner's slot." [9]

"I have brought two visitors who are interested in your case," said the doctor.

"Your employer, Mr. Johnson, sent us," Holmes explained. "I am Sherlock Holmes, and this is my associate, Dr. John Watson."

"I assure you, gentlemen, that Dr. Sinclair has done all that is possible. If only I had listened to him sooner, I would not even be in this predicament. Please thank Mr. Johnson for his kindness, but I shall not require your services."

"Mr. Darnley," said Holmes, gently, "we are not here to assume Dr. Sinclair's duty. Rather, we have come to ask you about Sir Roger Shoemaker."

The man began to chuckle to himself. "Ah, I see. You know, I saw the fat fellow once at a City dinner, his red face glowing above a white napkin. He looked disdainfully at the little pale man sitting at the end of the table, believing that I could be neither a help nor a threat to his schemes. He would have been pale too if he could have seen the task that would be mine. Good Lord! Well, I will have at it, and if human brain and nerve can stand the strain, I'll win out at the other side."

"Your work is already done, Mr. Darnley," said Holmes. "The ledgers are complete and your notes in the hands of the prosecuting lawyers."

"Are they?" Darnley cried, shaking his head. "Yes, I remember now. Well then, the hunt is over. I must say that I am glad to be done with those endless figures."

"I am most interested in your mirror, sir."

"My mirror, you say? Perhaps it would have been wiser after all if I had packed away the mirror. I had an extraordinary experience with it. And yet I find it so interesting, so fascinating, that even now I think that I will keep it in its place. Still, I wonder what on earth is the meaning of all that I have seen?"

"Perhaps if you tell us of what you viewed in the mirror, while it is still fresh in your mind?" suggested Holmes.

The little man nodded. "Of course. The mirror is so situated, you understand, that as I sit at the table I can usually see nothing in it but the reflection of the red window curtains. I will – from time to time – reach out and adjust it. But a queer thing happened a few nights back. I had been working for some hours, very much against the grain, with continual bouts of that mistiness of which I had complained to Dr. Sinclair. Again and again, I had to stop and clear my eyes. Well, on one of these occasions I chanced to look at the mirror. It had the oddest appearance. The red curtains which should have been reflected in it were no longer there, but the glass seemed to be clouded and steamy, not on the surface – which glittered like steel – but deep down in the very grain of it. This opacity, when I stared hard at it, appeared to slowly rotate this way and that, until it was a thick white cloud swirling in heavy wreaths. So real and solid was it, and so reasonable was I, that I remember turning, with the idea that the curtains were on fire. But everything was deadly still in the room – no sound save the ticking of the clock, no movement save the slow gyration of that strange woolly cloud deep in the heart of the old mirror."

"Only clouds?" asked Holmes. "I thought you had perhaps seen people?"

"Not at first. But then, as I looked, the mist, or smoke, or cloud, or whatever one may call it, seemed to coalesce and solidify at two points quite close together, and I was aware, with a thrill of interest rather than of fear, that these were two eyes looking out into the room. A vague outline of a head I could see – a woman's by the hair, but this was very shadowy. Only the eyes were quite distinct. Such eyes – dark, luminous – filled with some passionate emotion – fury or horror, I could not say which. Never have I seen eyes which were so full of intense, vivid life. They were not fixed upon me, but stared out into the room. As I sat erect, I passed my hand over my brow, and made a strong conscious effort to pull myself together. The dim head then faded into the general opacity, the mirror slowly cleared, and there were the red curtains once again."

"Fascinating," said Holmes. "Why do you think you saw this particular shape? And who is the woman?"

"The very questions I asked myself, sir!" cried Darnley. "And I wondered what was the dreadful emotion that I read in those magnificent brown eyes? I can only say that they came between me and my work. For the first time, the following morn I had done less than the daily tally which I had marked out. Perhaps that is why I had no abnormal sensations that second night."

"But they returned again?"

"Oh yes, Mr. Holmes, and each time more vivid and distinct than the last. The next time, I suppose it was about one in the morning, and I was closing my books in preparation for staggering off to bed, when I saw her there in front of me. Nothing had appeared in the mirror all evening. I would even reach out and rub it, as if it were the bottle of a genie in the Arabian Nights – to no avail. But then everything changed. The stage of mistiness and development must have passed unobserved, and there she was in all her beauty and passion and distress, as clear-cut as if she were really in the flesh before me. The figure was small, but very distinct – so much so that every feature, and every detail of dress, are stamped in my memory. She was seated on the extreme left of the mirror. A sort of shadowy figure crouched down beside her – I could dimly discern that it was a man. Behind them it was cloudy, in which I saw vague figures – figures which moved. It was not a mere picture upon which I looked, I tell you. It was a scene in life, an actual episode. She crouched and quivered. The man beside her cowered down. The vague figures made abrupt movements and gestures. All my fears were swallowed up in my interest. It was maddening to see so much and not to see more."

"Can you describe the woman?" asked Holmes.

"To the smallest point. She was very beautiful and quite young – not more than five-and-twenty, I should judge. Her hair was of a very rich brown, with a warm chestnut shade fining into gold at the edges. A little flat-pointed cap came to an angle in front, and was made of lace edged with pearls. Her forehead was high, too high perhaps for perfect beauty – but one would not have it otherwise, as it gives a touch of power and strength to what would otherwise be a softly feminine face. The brows are most delicately curved over heavy eyelids, and then came those wonderful eyes – so large, so dark, so full of over-mastering emotion, of rage and horror, contending with a pride of self-control that holds her from sheer frenzy! The cheeks were pale, the lips white with agony, the chin and throat most exquisitely rounded. She sat and leaned forward in the chair, straining and rigid, cataleptic with horror. The dress was black velvet, a jewel gleaming like a flame in the breast, and a golden crucifix smouldered in the shadow of a fold. This is the lady whose image still lives in the old silver mirror."

"Amazing!" interjected Dr. Sinclair. "What dire deed could it be which has left its impress there, so that now, in another age, if the spirit of a man be but worn down to it, he may be conscious of its presence?"

"Hmm, perhaps," said Holmes. "Was there anything else?" he asked Darnley.

"Ah, yes," cried Darnley, "there was one other detail. On the left side of the skirt of the black dress was, as I thought at first, a shapeless bunch of white ribbon. Then, as I looked more intently or as the vision defined itself more clearly, I perceived what it actually was. It was the hand of a man, clenched and knotted in agony, which held on with a convulsive grasp to the fold of the dress. The rest of the crouching figure was a mere vague outline, but that strenuous hand shone clear on the dark background, with a sinister suggestion of tragedy in its frantic clutch. The man was frightened – horribly frightened. That I could clearly discern. What had terrified him so? Why did he grip the woman's dress? I believed that the answer lay amongst those moving figures in the background. They had

298

brought danger both to him and to her. The interest of the thing fascinated me. I thought no more of its relation to my own nerves. I stared and stared as if in a theatre. But I could get no farther. The mist thinned. There were tumultuous movements in which all the figures were vaguely concerned. Then the mirror was clear once more that evening."

"But the vision returned a final time?" asked Holmes.

"Indeed. It was on the 20th of January, I believe. That day, I spent some twenty or thirty minutes carefully positioning the mirror in order to optimize my viewing of it, and then returned to my work. That night, the mirror in its silver frame was like a stage, brilliantly lit, in which a drama was in progress. There was no longer any mist. The oppression of my nerves had wrought this amazing clarity. Every feature, every movement, was as clear-cut as in life. To think that I, a tired accountant, the most prosaic of mankind, with the account-books of a swindling bankrupt before me, should be chosen of all the human race to look upon such a scene!"

"So it was the same scene as before?"

"It was the same scene and the same figures, Mr. Holmes, but the drama had advanced a stage. The tall young man was holding the woman in his arms. She strained away from him and looked up at him with loathing in her face. They had torn the crouching man away from his hold upon the skirt of her dress. A dozen of them were round him – savage men, bearded men. They hacked at him with knives. All seemed to strike him together. Their arms rose and fell. The blood did not flow from him – it squirted. His red dress was dabbled in it. He threw himself this way and that, purple upon crimson, like an over-ripe plum. Still they hacked, and still the jets shot from him. It was horrible – horrible! They dragged him kicking to the door. The woman looked over her shoulder at him and her mouth gaped. I heard nothing, but I knew that she was screaming. And then, whether it was this nerve-racking vision before me, or whether – my task finished – all the overwork of the past weeks came in one crushing weight upon me, the room danced round me, the floor seemed to sink away beneath my feet, and I remembered no more."

"And that was the last time you have looked into the mirror?"

"It was. To be honest, I am not certain that I have the strength to do so again. The visions are too much for my nerves. And yet, I wonder whether I shall ever penetrate what they all mean?"

"As you may have heard, Mr. Holmes," said Dr. Sinclair, "Mr. Darnley's landlady found him early the following morning, stretched senseless before the silver mirror."

"I knew nothing myself until yesterday mid-day, when I awoke in the deep peace of the doctor's nursing home," said Darnley.

"And you have listened to this story before, Dr. Sinclair?" asked Holmes.

"Oh yes, Mr. Darnley told it to me last night. At first, I would not allow him to speak of such matters, for I did not wish to bring about a recurrence of his brain-fever. But he seems to be making progress, so I attended with an absorbed interest."

"And what do you make of it?"

"You don't identify this with any well-known scene in history?" he asked, with suspicion in his voice.

Holmes assured him that he knew nothing of history, and I confirmed that this was one of his limits, along with his rather narrow knowledge of astronomy and politics.

"Well, you share that trait with Mr. Darnley here," said Dr. Sinclair, chuckling. "What of you, Dr. Watson?"

I rubbed my moustache. "I admit that there is something familiar about it, but I cannot put my finger on it."

"Well, I suppose that I may forgive you, for we are talking about an episode that transpired over three-hundred years ago. Have none of you any idea from whence that mirror came and to whom it once belonged?" Sinclair continued.

"Have you?" I asked, for he spoke with meaning.

"It's incredible," said Sinclair, "and yet how else can one explain it? The scenes which Mr. Darnley described before suggested it, but now it has gone beyond all range of coincidence. This morning, I consulted some pertinent tomes, and made various notes about what I have found." He stepped forward and placed the two musty volumes upon Darnley's bed. "These you may consult at your leisure," he continued. "I also have some notes here which you can confirm. There is not a doubt that what you have seen, Mr. Darnley, is the murder of David Rizzio by the Scottish nobles in the presence of Mary, which occurred in March 1566. [10] Your description of the woman is accurate. The high forehead and heavy eyelids combined with great beauty could hardly apply to another woman. The tall young man was her husband, Henry Stuart, also known as Lord Darnley." [11]

The accountant's brow rose in amazement. "What a coincidence!"

"Ah, but your tongue has a trace of Glaswegian accent," said Holmes. "Surely you have some Scottish blood?"

"Of course. My father hails from a small village outside of Glasgow – and I was born there, before we moved to London when I was a boy of ten."

"There is more," said Dr. Sinclair. "Rizzio, says the chronicle, 'was dressed in a loose dressing-gown of furred damask, with hose of russet velvet.' With one hand he clutched Mary's gown, with the other he held a dagger. Your fierce, hollow-eyed man must have been Lord Ruthven, who was new-risen from a bed of sickness. [12] Every detail is exact."

"But why to me?" asked Darnley, in bewilderment. "Why of all the human race did they appear to me?"

"Because you were in the fit mental state to receive the impression," said Dr. Sinclair. "And because you chanced to own the mirror which gave the impression."

"The mirror! You think, then, that it was Mary's mirror – that it stood in the room where the deed was done?"

"I am convinced that it was Mary's mirror," continued Dr. Sinclair. "She had been Queen of France. [13] Her personal property would be stamped with the Royal arms. What we took to be three spear-heads were really the lilies of France."

"And the inscription?"

"Ah yes! '*Sanc. X. Pal.*' You can expand it into *Sanctae Crucis Palatium*. Someone has made a note upon the mirror as to whence it came. It was the Palace of the Holy Cross."

"Holyrood!" cried Darnley. [14]

"Exactly. Your mirror came from Holyrood," concluded the doctor. "You have had one very singular experience, and have escaped. I trust that you will never put yourself into the way of having such another."

"Fascinating," said Darnley, drawing the top volume into his lap, and beginning to flip through the pages, each time licking his index finger.

Holmes had been silent during this exchange. "You have indeed had a singular experience, Mr. Darnley, and I echo Dr. Sinclair's advice. I have but one final question for you, sir. Where did you acquire the silver mirror?" he asked.

Darnley considered this for a moment. "It was given to me by an old friend from school who had a taste for antiquities, and he – as I happen to know – picked it up at a sale. I believe that he had no notion where it originally came from."

"Your friend's name?"

"Patrick Rootes."

"And his address?"

"12 Devonshire Square."

"Very good," said Holmes, turning to the physician. "Dr. Sinclair, I trust that you agree that Mr. Darnley has recovered to the degree necessary to testify in tomorrow's trial of Sir Roger Shoemaker?"

"Yes, I suppose that would be safe enough, as long as he comes back here afterwards to recuperate after the strain of a deposition. We have more work to do to prevent a recurrence of his brain-fever. I certainly do not think he is ready to gaze into the mirror again."

"On that, I wholeheartedly agree with you," said Holmes. "In fact, Mr. Darnley, if I may be so bold, may I suggest that you donate it. The British Museum would be glad to have it, and your credit from the doubtlessly successful impending prosecution of the Shoemaker case will be even further compounded."

"So you intend to recommend to Mr. Johnson that Darnley be allowed to testify?" I asked as we departed the hospital.

Holmes pursed his lips. "A difficult question, Watson. On the one hand, we can plainly see that the man is not yet fully himself again. However, his ultimate mental collapse did not begin immediately. Therefore, any findings from the initial ledgers are, at least, likely valid."

"And the later ledgers? What if those contain the critical details that implicate Sir Roger?"

"Indeed. This is why we must determine how far we may trust Mr. Darnley's sanity."

"What then is our next course of action?"

"A visit to Mr. Darnley's house. I should very much like to see this silver mirror for myself."

"For what purpose?"

"Are you not curious, Watson, to see if the visions may be re-created?"

I frowned and peered at him. "Are you serious, Holmes?"

The corner of his mouth curled up. "We shall see."

As it was almost two miles between Dr. Sinclair's hospital and the abode of Mr. Darnley, Holmes waved down a passing hansom. That conveyance swiftly rattled down Old Street and deposited us at our destination a quarter-of-an-hour later. Darnley's apartment was situated in a plain brick building, its staring façade lit by the harsh glare and tawdry luminosity of the public house across from it.

A thought occurred to me. "I do say, Holmes – unless I missed it, you neglected to borrow Mr. Darnley's key."

He smiled and removed several skeleton keys from his coat pocket. "As you know, Watson, the opening of locks is a particular hobby of mine. Unless Mr. Darnley has equipped his door with a particularly sophisticated lock, it should prove to be only a matter of minutes before I have it open."

Obscured in a convenient archway from the probing eyes of any passing constables, Holmes was true to his word. We were soon inside Mr. Darnley's house, with Holmes leading the way along the dark passage, ducking his head into each door as we went. He soon found the room that he was seeking. "Hallo, Watson! This *is* a rather impressive thing!"

I followed him into the chamber that – judging by the paper-strewn desk – Darnley utilized as a study. In the corner of the room, turned in such a way as to primarily display the red window curtains across from it, was the silver mirror. It was large – three feet across and two feet high – and leaned against the back of a side-table to the left of the desk. The frame was flat, about three inches across and was plainly very old. The glass part projected with a bevelled edge, and had the magnificent reflecting power that is only – as it seems to me – to be found in very old mirrors. There was a feeling of perspective when you look into it such as no modern glass could ever give.

I said as much to Holmes, and he merely shook his head. "You see what you want to believe, Watson."

"What do you mean?"

"Your brain equates – at a level likely even below your perception – that something this old must be expensive and therefore of high quality."

I bristled slightly at this charge. "So you do not think it is a splendid piece?"

He shrugged. "It is a mirror."

"Not at all. If Dr. Sinclair's theory is correct, it is a direct channel to the past."

"Yes, well, let us explore that hypothesis further. If you will do me the favour, Watson, of sitting at Mr. Darnley's desk and gazing into the mirror – no, do not touch it, leave it just as is – I will inspect the marks to confirm Dr. Sinclair's impressions."

I did as he requested and stared into the silver mirror for a span of some twenty minutes. However, try as I might, the mirror remained just that. No swirling clouds or beautiful women appeared in it.

Meanwhile, Holmes was engaged in inspecting the back of the mirror with his large magnifying glass. After this task was complete, he used a stray rag to polish the edge of the frame. He finally straightened his back and turned to me. "I perceive that you have had no visions, Watson," said he.

"No," I admitted. "And from this, you conclude that Mr. Darnley is mad."

He shook his head. "Not at all. In fact, from what I have seen here, I am quite convinced by Mr. Darnley's story. He has undoubtedly had a vision of the murder of David Rizzio in front of Mary, Queen of Scots."

Despite my cry of astonishment at this pronouncement, Holmes would speak no more of it. Instead, he merely smiled diffidently. "There are still a few loose ends. However, I believe that I may just provide a valuable service to Mr. Johnson tomorrow morning. The remaining tasks are fairly trivial. Therefore, may I suggest that you return to your wife, for your dinner will soon be cold. However, should you be interested in learning the final details, pray come round Baker Street in the morning. Say, at quarter-to-ten."

Knowing that I was more likely to squeeze water from a stone than a secret from Sherlock Holmes when he was in one of his dramatic moods, I followed his advice to the letter. When I arrived at Baker Street at the appointed time the following morn, I was surprised to find both Mr. Johnson and Inspector Lestrade sitting upon the settee. The apartment was much as I left it, though a new odour filled the air, and several of the retorts on Holmes's chemical bench appeared to have been recently utilized.

Holmes waved me to my old armchair. "Do not fear, Watson. I haven't shared with our guests anything beyond what we learned at Dr. Sinclair's hospital. However, the impending *dénouement* requires the presence of one more individual. Ah, I think I hear him now."

A knock upon the door was soon followed by the appearance of a dashing young fellow, whose clean-shaven face was marked by a bright, smiling expression. His suit appeared new and somewhat showy, while his black shoes gleamed.

"Mr. Patrick Rootes of 12 Devonshire Square?" asked Holmes, using the name of Mr. Darnley's friend.

"That's right," said Rootes.

"Pray have a seat, sir," said Holmes, guiding the guest to the basket chair.

"I have come as you asked, Mr. Holmes," said Rootes, settling into his seat, "but am unsure of how I may be of assistance?"

"All in good time, Mr. Rootes. We are gathered here today to help Mr. Henry Darnley recover his lost sanity. This is Mr. Timothy Johnson, Mr. Darnley's employer, and the other gentleman is Inspector Lestrade of Scotland Yard. Now, would you be so kind as to tell us of your relationship with him?"

The man shrugged. "We have been acquaintances since our schooldays."

"Just acquaintances?" asked Holmes. "Mr. Darnley described you as a friend."

"Well, just so. Friends then," Rootes nodded.

"And Mr. Darnley noted that you have a passion for antiquities."

"That is correct."

"Does Mr. Darnley share your interest?"

"No, I would not say that. Henry cares mainly about numbers. All else is rather unimportant to him."

"Why then did you gift him a valuable antique silver mirror?"

The man pursed his lips. "Well, let me think. Ah yes, I recall now. I had gone round to his place before the holidays and noted that it was severely lacking in décor. A few days later, I found the mirror at a broker's in Tottenham Court Road for sixty shillings – you will never believe the sorts of odd treasures that old Rosenberg has in his shop – and immediately thought of Henry. I figured it would brighten up his office, and brought it round with my belated compliments of the season."

"A most generous gift," said Holmes. "I have examined the mirror and believe it to be early seventeenth-century."

"Mid-sixteenth, more likely," said Rootes.

"Indeed," said Holmes with a smile. He then turned to me. "I would value your professional opinion, Watson. What do you make of Mr. Darnley and his visions?"

I considered this question. "Well, there are many medical reasons for such mis-firings of the temporal lobe. [15] Certain forms of mania – such as Hecker's Hebephrenia – are accompanied by distinct hallucinations. [16] Even the aura that proceeds an epileptic's fit can sometimes be mistaken for a vision."

"You speak of the permanent organic causes," said Holmes. "But there are more temporary kinds, are there not."

"Such as higher visions?"

"Ah, do you refer to the supernatural, Watson?"

"I suppose you might call them such," said I. "These would include the visions seen by William Blake or Joan of Arc. I believe that Dr. Sinclair is of the opinion that Mr. Darnley's images fall into this category."

Holmes shook his head. "Let us set aside the illusions of madness and of ergotism. [17] No, I speak of the ingestion or inhalation of certain substances, such as the fungal spores which once drove poor Professor Sidney to his fatal actions." [18]

"Do you think that Mr. Darnley is addicted to the use of some narcotic?"

"While I note that the visions of Darnley and Mr. Coleridge have much in common," said Holmes, "he does not have the wasted look of a habitual opium user. [19] No, I have an alternate hypothesis in mind." He turned back to Rootes. "You said that you met Henry Darnley at school. Would that perchance be accountancy school?"

"Yes. That is correct."

"Would you be so kind as to inform Inspector Lestrade where it is that you work, Mr. Rootes?"

The man's eyes darted towards the policeman. "In the city. Old Broad Street."

"At Gresham Chambers, if your landlady is to be believed," said Holmes.

"Yes," said Rootes, his voice strained.

Holmes smiled broadly, like a cat with a canary. "And what firm precisely?"

The man licked his lips and hesitated.

However, Mr. Johnson suddenly jumped up from his chair. "White and Wotherspoon have their offices in Gresham Chambers!"

"What is all this?" said Lestrade, a perplexed furrow in his brow.

"Three weeks ago, Lestrade, Mr. Darnley was tasked by Mr. Johnson here," said Holmes, "with an inspection of the ledgers of White and Wotherspoon to determine if that venerable firm was complicit in the embezzlement carried out by Sir Roger Shoemaker. It is a rather odd coincidence – is it not? – that one of White and Wotherspoon's employees should happen to call upon Mr. Darnley at this precarious time?"

"A man cannot call upon his friend at holiday time?" cried Rootes, springing to his feet. "Is the giving of gifts now against the law?"

"No," said Holmes, spinning about and pointing one of his long, thin fingers at Rootes. "But surely the poisoning of one's friend is a matter for Scotland Yard."

"Poison!" exclaimed the inspector. "Who is dead?"

"Not all poisons are lethal, Lestrade," said Holmes. "The one in question is rarely fatal, for such an event would hardly further the cause of White and Wotherspoon. Should Mr. Darnley have suddenly died in mysterious circumstances, it would have been simple enough for the prosecution to request an extension to the date of the trial. However, if Mr. Darnley was found to have gone mad, then all of his work would be cast into question. Only the most lenient of magistrates would permit any additional delay for Mr. Johnson's firm to repeat their investigation of the ledgers due to such an unusual situation. I inquired as to who was presiding over Sir Roger's trial, and I assure you that Sir James Hannen is not the most indulgent of judges."

"That is a grave accusation, Mr. Holmes," said Rootes. "You can be certain that you will hear from my solicitor about such libellous claims. However, I have no need to stand here and listen to any more of this nonsense." He moved to the door, but Holmes slid into his way. The man turned to Lestrade and held out his arms in a pleading manner. "This amateur has no official capacity to detain me, Inspector. If he resists my departure with force, will you permit such an assault upon my person?"

Lestrade appeared troubled and shook his head. "This is all rather circumstantial, Mr. Holmes. What proof do you have?"

"I am getting to that, Lestrade" said Holmes. "If you would each do me the favour of resuming your seats, I shall make all clear."

Lestrade nodded slowly, as if mentally calculating the number of past situations in which Holmes had provided him with the correct solution to a case. "I suggest, Mr. Rootes," said the inspector, finally, "that you do as he says. Let us hear him out. If there is no proof, you have my word that you shall be detained no longer."

"And if I choose not to listen any longer?" asked Rootes.

"Then I am afraid that you will listen in chains," said Lestrade, slowly pulling a pair of steel cuffs from his pocket and dangling them menacingly.

The man silently glared at the inspector, but took his seat. The others followed in turn, save only Holmes.

"As I was saying," resumed Holmes, pacing about the room. "Mr. Henry Darnley has slowly and gradually been poisoned with bromine, a substance that – when it builds up in the system – leads to irritability, hallucinations, and eventually stupor."

"Bromism!" I exclaimed. "Yes, I noted that Mr. Darnley has a rash, which may be seen in individuals who have consumed an excess of bromine."

"Ha!" cried Rootes. "And how precisely did I poison Henry? I have not even laid eyes upon him this year!"

"That is where you were exceptionally clever, Mr. Rootes. You are a most unfortunate individual. If Mr. Johnson had not asked me to investigate, I daresay that you would have gotten away with it." He turned to me. "Did you notice, Watson, that when Mr. Darnley turned the pages of the history book given to him by Dr. Sinclair that he always first licked his index finger?"

I considered this for a moment. "Yes, I believe he did."

"Such a habit is something that is deeply ingrained. You are either a person does it or you are not. Darnley likely developed such a routine during his schooldays, a fact that did not go unnoticed by his old acquaintance here, Mr. Rootes. And when Rootes eventually found himself in a situation where needed to discredit the reputation of his supposed friend, he ingeniously decided to employ this habit of Mr. Darnley's as the means by which the bromine was ingested Whenever Darnley would touch or manipulate the position of the mirror, some of the bromine was transferred to his fingers, and from there to his tongue."

"That is a very fancy theory, Mr. Holmes," said Lestrade, a hint of doubt creeping into his voice. "Can you prove it?"

"Sadly, there is no method by which to prove that Mr. Darnley has bromine in his body. However, we may test the mirror itself. [20] And I have done so. Yesterday, Watson and I inspected the mirror and I took various swabs from its surface." He waved towards his chemical bench. "The results are conclusive. The mirror in Mr. Darnley's home office has been generously coated with potassium bromide. You may have these experiments repeated, should you wish, Lestrade. However, I assure you that the results shall not vary."

"So what?" said Rootes, with a sneer. "If there was bromide on that mirror, it was either there when I purchased it, or Henry put it on himself."

Holmes reached into his pocket and pulled out a stack of receipts. "Why then, Mr. Rootes, did you purchase a quart of potassium bromide from no less than six chemists in the vicinity of your home in the two days after you acquired the mirror?" Holmes turned to Lestrade and handed him the papers. "You may send a man round to Mr. Rosenberg's shop and Mr. Darnley's home, Lestrade. However, I strongly doubt that you will find a supply of potassium bromide at either locale. If you choose to do so, I trust that you will – in the interim – at least detain Mr. Rootes. We do not want him making a run for the coast."

Once the steel cuffs clicked onto his wrists, Rootes broke down and confessed. The rival accountant admitted that he had perpetuated the bromine poisoning of Mr. Henry Darnley on behalf of his employers, who threatened him with a loss of employment on the one hand, and proffered a generous bonus on the other. As Lestrade hauled him away, Rootes was wailing about how he never intended to harm Darnley, and how his friend was still alive and recovering his wits, so no harm was really done. "How much time could I get?" was the last thing I heard him cry.

As I followed the case of Sir Roger Shoemaker in the newspapers over the next few weeks, I learned the answer was one year in Exeter Gaol – Rootes' term having been reduced for his statement blaming his actions upon the orders of his former employers at White and Wotherspoon. That venerable firm collapsed under the combined weight of Rootes' testimony and the evidence unearthed in their ledgers by the work of Mr. Henry Darnley. In turn, both Mr. White and Mr. Wotherspoon agreed to testify against Sir Roger in exchange for lower sentences of their own. For his crime of defalcation, Judge Sir James Hannen sentenced Sir Roger to fifteen years, though he hung himself after just five days.

A few weeks later, I called upon Holmes on my way back from my rounds. He was seated in his armchair, droning away upon a new violin, no recognized tune arising from those notes. At my arrival, he set down the violin, and welcomed me to my old chair. Eventually, our talk turned to the case of Mr. Henry Darnley.

"I suppose I shall always wonder, Holmes, whether Mr. Darnley saw a true vision."

He stared at me in concern. "What do you mean, Watson? Patrick Rootes confessed to poisoning the man. It was merely a drug-induced hallucination."

"Surely you will admit, Holmes, that his visions were curiously precise? In my experience, those images that appear during such intoxications are rarely so accurate. Even Dr. Sinclair was amazed. Could this not be a remarkable synchronicity between the centuries – Henry Stuart, Lord Darnley, calling forward to plain old Henry Darnley, the accountant, through the medium of the mirror once belonging to his wife Mary, Queen of Scots?"

"I will admit, Watson, only to Patrick Rootes' cunning. You see, there is a major impediment to your theory of psychic connections."

"Which is?"

"That was not the mirror of Mary, Queen of Scots."

"What!" I cried. "But the inscription! Holyrood! The lilies of France!"

Holmes shook his head. "I went round to see Mr. Rosenberg at his shop in Tottenham Court Road. The broker was most friendly, and showed me his ledger where the purchase of the mirror by Mr. Rootes was documented. Rosenberg is a most thorough individual, and the bill of sale plainly states: '*One silver-framed mirror, mid-sixteenth century, three feet across and two feet high, bevelled edge, unmarked.*'"

"Unmarked!"

"Yes, Watson. Mr. Rootes added those marks himself. Surely it is too great a coincidence that the actual mirror of Mary, Queen of Scots, would come into the possession of a man who shared the name of her murderous husband? Rootes took note of his friend's unique surname and employed the legend of David Rizzio's murder to play upon Darnley's somewhat limited imagination. He knew that Darnley was a rather thorough gentleman, and would carefully inspect his new piece of décor, especially after the effects of the bromine began to take effect. Rootes counted upon Darnley deciphering the marks and making the link to the ancient legend. From there, Darnley's future bromine-induced visions took a predictable route."

"But Darnley denied knowing the legend of Rizzio," I protested.

"He may have forgotten it, but as a Scotsman, he undoubtedly learned it as a child. It was there, stowed deeply in the box-room of his brain, ready to be unearthed when the moment was right."

"So there was nothing spiritual about it?" said I, disappointedly.

"Surely life is fantastic enough, Watson, and does not require the existence of even stranger things," said he, with a laugh, as he placed his violin to his chin.

309

I nodded my farewell, and as I descended the steps, I listened to the long-drawn, haunting notes of the Berlioz Symphony wash over me. Perhaps Holmes was right, I thought. Perhaps life was fantastic enough. For whom could have predicted that a simple former army surgeon would have such adventures as others could only dream? And yet, I will always wonder about the amazing clarity of Mr. Henry Darnley's visions – undoubtedly induced by bromine as they were – and whether some trace of them came from a place beyond the edge of the unknown.

NOTES

1. The astute reader will recognize many aspects of this case correspond with a story called *The Silver Mirror*, published in *The Strand Magazine* in August 1908 by Sir Arthur Conan Doyle, Watson's first literary editor. It is unclear why Conan Doyle did not submit it in its original form, but felt compelled to remove all mention of Holmes and instead publish it solely as the purported report of Mr. Darnley's strange experience.

2. Dr. Watson did not meet and wed Mary Morstan until 1888, so this is plainly a reference to his first wife, whom he married in (approximately) the autumn of 1886.

3. The post-nominal *"ACA"* indicates that Mr. Johnson is a member of the Institute of Chartered Accountants in England and Wales, established by Royal Charter in 1880.

4. An alderman is a member of a county or borough council, next in status to the Mayor. Cordwainer is one of the twenty-five ancient wards of the City of London, named for the professional shoemakers whose guildhall is located in that area.

5. "Defalcation" is a crime in which there is misappropriation of funds by a person entrusted with its charge.

6. Private hospitals were established in the nineteenth century by a doctor or group of physicians for the care of paying patients. They employed trained nurses, and were considered cleaner, less crowded, and more respectable than the "voluntary" hospitals that served patients free of charge and that ran solely upon voluntary contributions.

7. *Brachygraphy* is a synonym for stenography, or the process of writing in shorthand – the abbreviated symbolic writing method that increases speed and brevity of writing. Several different systems existed in England, starting from 1588, and the art was popularized by Samuel Pepys, who used it for his *Diary* (1825).

8. Bromine-based compounds, especially the salt-form potassium bromide, were commonly used as sedative and headache remedies in the nineteenth and early twentieth centuries, until evidence began to emerge that long-term consumption can lead to neurologic symptoms. Chloral hydrate was another widely-used sedative and hypnotic after its discovery in 1832. It fell out of favour due to its addictive nature and the identification of safer agents.

9. The word "slot" is here used in the archaic sense of *"trail"*, as in a *"slot-hound"*. The term eventually evolved into the word *"sleuth-hound"*, from which the modern *"sleuth"* derives.

10. David Rizzio (c.1533-1566) was an Italian courtier and singer from Turin. He travelled to Scotland with the ambassador from the Duke of Savoy, where he ingratiated himself with the Queen's musicians, eventually rising to the post of her secretary. Rumours whispered that he became her lover and was the true father of her son, the future James VI of Scotland and James I of England (1566-1625).

11. Henry Stuart (1545-1567), Lord Darnley, was the first cousin and second husband of Mary, Queen of Scots. He was later murdered, likely by James Hepburn (c.1534-1578), the Earl of Bothwell, who wed Mary a few months later.

12. Patrick Ruthven (c.1520-1566) was a Scottish nobleman who led the conspiracy of Protestant lords – likely at the behest of Lord Darnley – who murdered David Rizzio at Holyrood Palace, partly out of concerns for the Catholic courtier's influence over the queen.

13. Mary Stuart (1542-1587) had wed the fourteen year-old Francis II, then Dauphin of France, in 1558. Francis ascended to the throne in July 1559 upon the death of his father, Henry II. Francis died seventeen months later, likely from invasive mastoiditis. The throne passed to his younger brother, Charles IX, and Mary returned to Scotland.

14. The Palace of Holyroodhouse is the official residence of the British monarch in Scotland, located at the downhill eastern end of the Royal Mile in Edinburgh. Built from 1671-1678 to serve as the principal residence for the Kings and Queens of Scots, it derives its name from the now-ruined Holyrood Abbey situated on its grounds, which once contained a fragment of the supposed "True Cross".

15. Diseases of the temporal lobe, including epileptic foci and tumours, can lead to auditory and visual hallucinations.

16. Mania, now referring to a state of elevated arousal and emotional lability, had a broader sense in the past. Ewald Hecker (1843-1909) was a German psychiatrist who coined the term "hebephrenia" to describe the adolescent onset of what would later (in 1908) be termed schizophrenia, the modern word for an affliction characterized by hallucinations, delusions, and disorganized thinking.

17. Ergotism, a poisoning by the ergot fungus in rye, can lead to psychosis and is one theory advanced for Joan of Arc's supposed "visions".

18. The story of Professor Sidney is not reported in The Canon.

19. Samuel Taylor Coleridge (1772-1834) was addicted to opium for most of his life, and he reported that his great work, *Kubla Khan, or a Vision in a Dream,* was written immediately after emerging from the drug's influence.

20. Although rarely used since bromine agents were withdrawn from general use, bromine is radiopaque and can be seen on an abdominal radiograph. However, Wilhelm Röntgen did not discover the utility of his so-called "X-rays" for such purposes until 1895.

The Adventure of the
Murdered Maharajah
by Hugh Ashton

*"The whole question of the Netherland-Sumatra Company
and of the colossal schemes of Baron Maupertuis . . . ."*

It was one of those cold days in the early English Spring that remind us
that Winter has not yet completely departed. A light rain fell as I gazed out
of the window at the passers-by in Baker Street.

"I do not think he will return to his wife," Holmes suddenly remarked
to me.

"Who on earth are you referring to?" I asked, completely nonplussed
by this statement, uttered completely at random, as it seemed to me.

"The cab-driver on the opposite of the road, talking to the flower
girl."

"She is remarkably pretty," I observed.

"I bow to your superior judgement in these matters," Holmes smiled.

I must suppose that I blushed a little at his words. "But how, in the
name of goodness, can you make such an observation about the marital
history of a complete stranger?" I asked him.

"Ah, but Jeffreys is far from being a complete stranger to me. He is
by way of being a cousin of some sort to Wiggins, whom you have met in
his capacity as the leader of the Baker Street Irregulars, and came
recommended to me by that young gentleman as a discreet and resourceful
driver should I ever have need of the same."

"I take it you followed the recommendation, then?"

"I did, and I have not had cause to regret it. His sole fault is that he
will insist on talking – not at critical junctures in an investigation, mark
you – but at times when he considers that I will enjoy his monologues. I
am now in possession of more information regarding the home life of Mr.
Arnold Jeffreys than I have ever considered necessary. However, his skill
at following the vehicles of others, and at avoiding notice while so doing
is, in my experience, unequalled by any jarvey in the metropolis."

"And he has an eye for the ladies, I take it – provided that their name
is not Mrs. Jeffreys?"

"Indeed that is the case. That particular flower girl seems to have
caught his eye for longer than most. From the little I have seen of her, she
would appear to be well-suited to him."

313

I laughed. "Holmes, I take it that you are not thinking of taking up the profession of marriage-broker to the lower classes?"

"By no means. I am currently engaged on an investigation that would not bode well for my future were it to go awry."

"The client is well-known?"

"Very much so. One who holds a high position, and whose influence on others is considerable."

"And you fear that your art will desert you in this case?"

Holmes sighed. "My dear Watson, painting is an art, music is an art, but my profession is a science."

"Very well," I smiled. "And may I suppose that those against whom you set yourself are also followers of a scientific profession?"

"By no means," he contradicted me. "Among those few whom we may term 'professional criminals', given that most crimes are committed almost by accident, there are those who seem to regard the business of breaking the law as somewhat of an art. In this instance, I would quote the example of a certain young man who is on the rise in his profession. I currently see him as the fourth smartest man in London. He is no stranger to imagination and daring." I knew that Holmes would place himself in the first three, but refrained from enquiry regarding the other two. "Then," he continued, "there are those who would regard it as a science. We need merely examine the records of those who have taught at our universities, or those engaged in the professions – including yours, Watson – for such examples."

He paused, as if uncertain as to whether to continue. "There is a third category?" I asked.

"There is indeed, and it is this category that is perhaps the most dangerous of all. These are the criminals who regard their deeds simply as a business. Such a one is the man known to the *cognoscenti* as The Deptford Assassin. Even I do not know his true name, but I do know that this man takes money in exchange for taking the life of one named by the payer. He is said to be without emotion, to work swiftly and efficiently, taking no pleasure in others' sufferings, and only finding satisfaction in a job well done, as he views matters. He sees these transactions as no more than a way of making a living."

I shuddered. "This does indeed appear to be as cold-blooded a criminal as one can imagine."

"Another such is Baron Maupertuis, but in his case, his business is the dissemination of lies and deception leading to his financial enrichment at the expense of others. There is, I will grant him, a certain artistry in some of his deceptions, but this appears to be merely a product of his ingenuity, rather than an example of art for art's sake. And it is he against whom I am presently set."

"He is set to defraud your client?"

"Indeed that is his intention. He is a most persuasive man, albeit that he usually works at least two removes from his victims, employing others to act as his intermediaries. The whole business is diabolically organised, and even with the expenses he is forced to meet in order to pay his associates, I estimate he brings in a cool two- or three-hundred-thousand-pounds-per-annum for himself."

"What is his story?" I could not help enquiring.

By way of answer, Holmes fixed me with his steady gaze. "Watson, I have come to rely on you in many cases. May I entreat you to assist me in this case? No," and he held up a hand to prevent my speaking. "Do not answer hastily or glibly, but hear me out. This is not a simple matter of tracing footprints to discover a thief or a murderer. It will present danger to those involved – Maupertuis is known to be utterly ruthless on occasion, and the number of police agents who have met untimely ends while investigating his affairs is now in the dozens. To trap Maupertuis and silence him is not the work of one or two men, but there is no one that I would sooner have at my side than you, my trusted friend."

"Can you doubt that I will be with you on this?" I asked.

"I confess that I was expecting an answer along those lines," Holmes said to me. "Thank you. It is good to have my faithful Watson by my side." I was touched by the warmth of his tones, which were seldom, if ever, heard by others, and which belied his reputation as a cold, calculating, machine-like character, devoted only to his work and a few obscure hobby-horses and pastimes. He continued, "I should inform you now that I am working alongside the official forces on this occasion. I believe you are acquainted with Inspector Gregson, whom I believe to be one of the most intelligent and resourceful officers currently employed by the police."

"That is good," I replied. I had met Gregson in the past, and had a very favourable opinion of the man.

"As it happens, I was on my way to the Yard to discuss the case with him. Will you accompany me?"

"With pleasure," I told him. Within ten minutes we were on our way.

Inspector Tobias Gregson welcomed us into his office, and we sat facing him across his desk, which was piled high with papers and files.

"Maupertuis," he sighed. "Baron Gérard Louis-Philippe de Maupertuis, if you wish to refer to him by his full name, Doctor," he added to me. "Baron of some piffling little town in Western Germany, which formed part of France until the war of 1870. He was made Baron for his services to Germany following the war, although he is Belgian by birth."

"A man of many allegiances, then?" I suggested.

"Many, and none, I fear," Gregson answered me. "He appears to be entirely without scruples, or loyalty to any, except himself."

"His associates would attest to that," Holmes agreed. "There are those who are in charge of criminal organisations – the Professor springs to mind, eh, Gregson?" The police inspector nodded, and Holmes continued. "Such men, and the leaders of Italian gangs, such as the Neapolitan Camorra and the Sicilian Mafia, will take care of their subordinates should they be unfortunate enough to be taken by the authorities, providing legal assistance and so on."

"Not to mention outright subversion of the police and the judicial system through bribery," added Gregson.

"The same is true of many American gangs," Holmes went on. "However, Maupertuis, as I mentioned to you earlier, Watson, sees his dealings purely in a business light. The rewards for his followers are generous if they succeed, but if they fail – that is, if they fall into the hands of the law – they are 'written off the books', to use an expression employed in business."

"Indeed, if they fail in their primary task, that of procuring money for the Baron, they are thrown to the wolves, as it were," Gregson added. "The Baron does not tolerate failure within his organization. I should also mention that the same ruthlessness applies to those with whom he finds himself in competition, as well as those with whom he finds himself in opposition. I would advise you, Doctor, as I have advised Mr. Holmes here, to go about your business armed. I do not say this to alarm you, but simply to advise you that I see it as a necessary precaution in this instance."

"You are implying that Baron Maupertuis or his henchmen may resort to violence?"

"It is more than an implication – it is a virtual guarantee," Gregson said, shaking his head. "In the usual run of things, I would have more than a little hesitation in allowing amateurs to take part in this business, but I have sufficient knowledge of Mr. Holmes's experience and skills, and those of you, Doctor Watson, to be as confident, or even more so, in your ability to set yourselves against the Baron, as I would of two of my own men."

"That is a most gratifying thing to hear," I said to him.

"Now, to the practicalities of the business," Holmes said. "Where, in your opinion, Inspector, do you feel we should start our investigations?"

"The Baron himself is rumoured to be in Recife in Brazil. According to my sources, he has plans to create a monopoly in the coffee trade of that country. If he succeeds, those who buy the coffee in the belief that they are making their purchases from many sources, will have no idea that they are in fact making their purchases from different aspects of the same many-headed Hydra."

Holmes chuckled. "I had not seen you as being one to turn such a poetic phrase, Inspector," he laughed.

"We all have our hidden depths," Gregson replied, amused. "However, it isn't that which is of immediate concern. We have reports – and do not enquire at present from where they have come – that the Baron, prior to moving on to his coffee scheme, has set in motion the wheels of the most elaborate and by most estimates the largest swindle yet recorded." He paused, as if for effect. "He has it in mind to sell an island to which he has no rights."

"A small one?" I hazarded.

"By no means," Gregson told us. He was smiling broadly. "The island in question is one of the Dutch East Indies – that of Sumatra."

"If I recall correctly," Holmes said, "that island has twice the area of England, Wales, and Scotland combined."

"To a rough approximation, that is correct. I can provide you with the exact figures if you wish," Gregson answered.

Holmes waved a negligent hand. "I don't feel them to be necessary at present. But as you say, this island is currently owned by the Netherlands. How can Maupertuis present himself as the owner?"

"Maybe I misled you a little in my description," Gregson apologised. "The agents of Maupertuis do not claim that he owns it. Rather, they claim to be acting for the Dutch government, which wishes to sell the island – or to be more precise, shares in the island's wealth, to a private consortium of some of the world's richest men. The money so raised, so they say, is to be used to fund Dutch naval expansion. When they talk to the French, naturally, the ships so purchased will be used to defend the Netherlands against the Germans, and when they approach German millionaires, they refer to the Gallic menace."

"And the Dutch government has been unable to act against these agents?"

"As you can imagine, the whole affair is presented as being one of great secrecy. It is emphasised to the prospective buyers that the business is a closely guarded secret, even at the highest levels of the Dutch government. It is represented to them that this is a personal initiative of the Dutch Royal Family. Since those being approached are typically those who have made their money through trade, it is considered unlikely that they will ever come into contact with royalty."

I smiled. "Maupertuis would appear to know his fish well, and how to bait his hook."

"And how successful have these approaches been so far?"

"We know of at least one Frenchman who is rumoured to have purchased some thirty million francs' worth of shares. A Bavarian industrialist has purchased at least as many, and there are rumours that some American steel and railway magnates have been persuaded to take part."

"But as yet, no Englishmen?" Holmes enquired.

"No, nor Scotchmen or Welshmen or Irishmen for that matter," smiled Gregson. "However, we are aware that one of the Baron's men is currently in London, attempting to take money from someone who is generally reckoned to possess one of the largest personal fortunes in the world. That man being – "

" – the Maharajah of Rajipur, who is currently visiting London with his entourage," I broke in.

"Indeed so," Gregson said in some surprise. "You are familiar with the gentleman?"

"I once had the honour of treating one of his wives for a minor ailment. Though I never conversed with His Highness at any length, I did observe him at close quarters on more than one occasion, and we exchanged greetings."

Holmes laughed. "You never cease to amaze me, Watson. Why you will persist in chronicling my poor exploits, when you appear to have led a life of excitement and adventure, I do not know."

"I have had enough adventure and excitement for one life," I answered him, unconsciously rubbing the shoulder where a Jezail bullet had left its mark. "I have no wish to relive it."

"Even so," Gregson remarked, "this is a more than fortunate coincidence. If you think it possible to renew your acquaintance with His Highness, your help in preventing him from making the supposed investment will be invaluable."

"And meanwhile, I take it," Holmes added, "I will be following Maupertuis' agent, with a view to securing a lead to the man himself, and luring him to a place where he may be taken?"

"Indeed so," said Gregson. "You are ahead of me, as always, Mr. Holmes, and it is a pleasure to be working with you. Now, with your permission, I would like to introduce to you a M. Pierre Lejeune, who is a member of the French *Sûreté*, and who has been on the trail of Maupertuis for a number of years now. He has come to London to offer his assistance in this matter."

M. Lejeune, who was ushered into the office some minutes later by Gregson, was a middle-aged man with little of the apparent alertness which marks our British detectives.

However, Holmes greeted him with apparent pleasure, speaking in his rapid and fluent French. After a few exchanges in this language, during which Lejeune observed the expressions of bemusement on Gregson' and my faces, he spoke in competent, albeit heavily accented, English.

"My apologies, gentlemen," he told us. "I was unaware that the private detective whom I had been informed by the good inspector here was retained on this case was the famous Sherlock Holmes." He made a bow in the direction of my friend, which was returned. "And you," turning to me, "must be the equally famous Doctor John Watson." We shook hands.

"And for myself," Holmes replied, "I am more than happy to make the acquaintance of M. Lejeune, who covered himself with such distinction in the Abbeville double murder case."

The little French detective gave a start. "But you know of this case, Mr. Holmes?"

"Naturally. I had come to the same conclusion as yourself, based on my reading of the newspaper accounts, but your capture of the postman was masterly, and may serve as an excellent lesson to all engaged in our profession."

"I am flattered and honoured," the other replied. "But now, let us talk about Maupertuis, and the danger he represents to your country and to mine, and to Europe as a whole. Has the inspector informed you of the latest fraud he is perpetrating, that of the Netherland-Sumatra Company? He has? Excellent. Now let me tell you of the Frenchman and the German who have fallen prey to his wiles. In Germany, it is Graf Friedrich von Heissen who has invested in this swindle. In France, it is M. Thierry de Lantis. Do these names mean anything to you gentlemen?"

I confessed that both these were unfamiliar to me, but Holmes spoke up.

"Both men are owners of large industrial enterprises engaged in the manufacture of arms. If I recall correctly, da Lantis owns a large shipbuilding company on the French Atlantic coast specialising in the production of light naval vessels. The von Heissen factory is noted for its naval guns."

"You are well-informed, Mr. Holmes."

"It is my business to be so," my friend smiled.

"Contrary to his usual practice, Maupertuis has not demanded cash as payment for the fraudulent Sumatra shares that he is offering."

"What, then?"

"He has taken shares in these gentlemen's companies in lieu of cash. The paper value of these shares is less than the supposed value of the fraudulent shares he is offering."

I frowned. "This seems like a very strange way of conducting business," I said.

"Ah, but wait until you have heard the whole story, my friend," Lejeune told me, wagging his finger in my direction. "For some months prior to this, Maupertuis had been buying shares through proxies. As a result of his latest acquisitions, he now holds a controlling interest in these companies, though the supposed owners are unaware of this fact. And to what end? you may be asking yourselves," he added, with a typically Gallic shrug.

"It can only be that he wishes to build his own fleet of warships!" I exclaimed, "Ridiculous though the idea may seem."

"Indeed, Doctor, that is the conclusion which we in Paris have also reached."

"But he cannot put a navy to sea," I objected. "And to what end? He cannot pit himself against the great powers of Europe or the Americas."

"Nor would he wish to," replied the Frenchman. "The goals of Baron Maupertuis have never been territorial, but rather financial."

"Piracy?" suggested Holmes. "A small fleet of fast but powerfully armed gunboats, acting as cruisers, and operating in remote areas of the globe, changing their base of operations at regular intervals, to attack rich merchant ships or even passenger steamers, holding the crew and passengers for ransom. Alternatively, he could simply hold the shipping lines of the world to account, letting them know that if they pay a certain sum of money to an agent, their ships and cargos will not be attacked. In any event, the possession of a fleet of small warships, specialised for the purpose of raiding the commerce of nations, would spell disaster to the world's economies."

"I think you have the correct solution, Mr. Holmes. At least, that is what many on the Quai d'Orsay believe."

"Such an enterprise would require a significant sum of money to implement," remarked Gregson. "Even with control of the arms factories that you have mentioned, he is unlikely to be able to maintain a fleet of warships."

"Hence his approach to your Maharajah here in London," Lejeune told us. "Maupertuis is playing a very long game. You have heard from Gregson here that he is in Brazil?"

"For the purpose of making a 'corner' in the coffee market," I said.

"That may be one of his motives, but I can assure you that it is far from being the sole motive, or even the major one. We have good reason to believe that he is setting up a chain of coaling stations along the eastern seaboard of the Americas, with the most northerly being in the Caribbean, though we are unsure of the exact location, and the most southerly in southern Brazil. From there, he can potentially control much of the trans-Atlantic trade. He already owns, quite legally, several cargo vessels which might be used as colliers, allowing any armed piracy vessels to stay at sea for longer than would otherwise be the case."

"Even given all that you have said, monsieur," I objected, "and I have no doubt you and your colleagues are correct in their surmises, I find it hard to believe that a man can take on the might of the navies of the world. The Royal Navy is one of the most powerful military forces ever known, as you are no doubt well aware – "

" – all too aware, I fear, Doctor." He grimaced slightly.

"Forgive me. I was about to add that the navy of France runs a close second, and of course neither the German nor the American navies can be said to be negligible."

"Doctor, your pride and confidence in your navy and that of others may be a little misplaced here. Notwithstanding Trafalgar and the other notable victories of your naval forces, many of them at the expense of my country, piracy is a difficult matter to counter with any effectiveness. I know you have served with the army, Doctor Watson, but I take it you have never served on a ship? No? Then you may not be aware that it is possible to sail for weeks, even months at a time without coming into contact with another vessel. And if the hunted vessel is taking precautions to hide herself, well . . . ." He spread his hands. "You may forget any hope of discovering her."

Holmes had been listening to this exchange, and broke in. "How much money does Maupertuis currently have at his disposal for the construction of this pirate fleet?"

"In terms of his possessions, he has more than enough to match the fleet of a smaller European nation – Denmark, for example. We are aware that he has a liking for works of art, some of which have been acquired legally through dealers, and some, we are convinced, are the results of thefts from galleries, though whether these thefts have been originated by him or not we are unsure. If these were ever to find their way onto the market, there is no doubt that he would have many millions of francs to his name. However, that hardly seems likely, especially in the case of the stolen artworks.

"In terms of ready cash, however, we are reasonably confident that he does not possess much at present. Many of his reserves were spent in building up shareholdings, not only in the companies that I mentioned earlier, but also in chemical works and producers of ammunition, *etcetera*.

In this way, though, he has provided himself with the potential of a nation when it comes to the availability of weaponry."

"And the potential is there? I see," Holmes mused. "It would seem that our task here in London is to prevent his man from acquiring the cash that would allow him to set up his little scheme."

"Precisely, Mr. Holmes. And should he fail here in London, as we sincerely hope he will, we must prevent him from attempting the same feat elsewhere, whether it be Rome, Constantinople, Moscow, Buenos Aires, or New York."

"And there is no time to lose," Gregson added. "The first intended victim is the Maharajah of Rajipur, as I said, who is currently staying at the Cosmopolitan Hotel. His plans are to remain in London for the Jubilee later this year, but we believe he will be joined here in the coming months by a number of other Indian princes. If he is persuaded to subscribe to the Baron's swindles, we can be sure that his example will be followed by many others of his compatriots. If, on the other hand, he can be convinced that this is indeed a swindle, he may well be the cause of preventing others of his country from giving their money to this scheme."

"And the name of the Baron's agent who will approach him?"

"Alas, that is unknown to us," explained Lejeune. "We know him only as 'Number 17'."

"I take it you have intercepted a written communication?" said Holmes.

"Precisely. All we know is that Number 17 is currently in London, and his duties are first to approach our friend at the Cosmopolitan, and to encourage him, once his money has been successfully taken from him, to persuade his Indian peers to disgorge their wealth in the Baron's direction."

"Was this letter written in French or English?"

"Neither. It was in the Italian language, and we have reason to believe that it was written by an Italian."

"So we are searching for a resident of London whose first language is Italian, but who also possesses sufficient fluency in English to persuade an Indian prince to part with a considerable sum of money?" I laughed. "Why, there must be several hundred such, in the guise of waiters, servants, barbers, and the like."

"Hardly so," replied Holmes. "In the first place, we can hardly imagine that His Highness will deign to listen to a financial scheme presented to him by a barber or a waiter. No, such a man would be of such a standing as to inspire confidence in His Highness. In the second place, why should we assume that the transaction will take place in English? Would not the Maharajah be more receptive to a proposal couched in his

322

own language, Hindustani or Urdu? We may well be searching for a man in the Italian Embassy, possibly of noble birth, whose background includes time spent in India."

"These thoughts had not occurred to us," Lejeune remarked, "and it may very well be that you are correct in both these points."

"Gregson," Holmes addressed the police inspector, "would it be possible for you to provide a list of all the Italian diplomats currently in London?"

"I will have it sent to Baker Street at the earliest possible opportunity."

"My thanks. Very well," said Holmes, rising. "Monsieur Lejeune, you will be in London for some time?"

"A matter of a few weeks only, alas, I regret."

"I would be delighted to see you at Baker Street for dinner some evening, should you find yourself at a loose end," Holmes invited him.

"I accept with the greatest of pleasure."

"There is no time like the present," Holmes said to me as we walked away from Scotland Yard. "We should visit His Highness as soon as possible. Do you think that he will recognise you?"

"It is possible, I suppose," I answered. "However, you should bear in mind that our last brief meeting was several years ago, and in somewhat different surroundings."

"At any rate, there is a connection on which we can build," Holmes said. "We must use that for all that it is worth."

"Do you seriously believe those stories of Lejeune regarding Maupertuis' plans to set up and deploy a pirate fleet? It all sounds so fantastical to me that I find it almost impossible to believe."

"I share your scepticism to some extent, but from what I hear and know of the Baron, there are few limits to his ambition. It may be, of course, that he is not altogether sane, even though he is intelligent, and his lack of judgement has caused him to take this path. However, I have faith in Lejeune and his organisation, and I believe that, unlikely as this scheme may sound, it's probably true to say that Maupertuis is pursuing it. Furthermore, given what we have heard, it is, sadly, more than feasible – it is practicable to a man of the Baron's resources, and could well be implemented sooner than we wish."

These words of my companion gave me pause for thought as we made our way through the London streets towards the luxurious hotel in which we were to meet Maupertuis' intended quarry. On arrival, Holmes presented his card to the concierge, with whom he appeared to be on familiar terms, and requested that a message be sent to His Highness, expressing Holmes's desire to meet him.

The answer arrived in a few minutes on a handwritten slip of paper, informing us that His Highness would be delighted to meet the famous detective and his friend, the accounts of whom he had read in the newspapers had generated the most keen interest, and inviting us to make our way to his suite.

On entering the room to which we were guided by a hotel porter, I was struck dumbfounded. The Maharajah of my memory was a portly elderly man whose English was less than perfect. The man who smilingly stepped forward and introduced himself as the Maharajah of Rajipur in response to our introductions was a trim figure of a young man with a luxuriant moustache, who spoke fluent English with a distinct Oxford accent. My surprise must have shown on my face.

"Doctor Watson? Is something the matter?" he asked, with an air of some concern.

"No, it is nothing. I merely remember meeting a rather different figure some years ago when I treated the wife of the Maharajah of Rajipur," I stammered.

"I believe you will have made the acquaintance of my father, then," the young man told me, "who passed away some two years ago, upon which I inherited the title, and indeed, the princely state of Rajipur. I flatter myself that in the short time that I have held my position, Rajipur has prospered thanks to a series of reforms I have initiated. One of these reforms," he said, turning to Sherlock Holmes, "is the establishment of a force of detectives to solve crimes. Should you ever be inclined, Mr. Holmes, to undertake the journey, I would be more than willing to recompense you handsomely for any instruction you cared to provide to my detectives."

"A most generous offer, indeed," replied Holmes, "and certainly one that I will bear in mind for the future."

"But I am sure that you did not make this visit merely for the sake of idle chit-chat. Pray, sit. And may I offer you some refreshment? A brandy-and-soda for you gentlemen? I generally partake of one at this time of day."

Holmes and I assented, and the Maharajah clapped his hands, giving orders to a turbaned bearer who entered from what was presumably the bedroom in answer to the summons.

"Excellent, your Highness," said Holmes on tasting his drink.

"Please, no more of 'your Highness'," protested the Indian. "Pray call me 'Jaimie'. It is not too far from my Indian name of Jaimal, and I became accustomed to it in my time at Balliol."

"We come to you on a rather delicate financial matter," Holmes said to him. "No," holding up a hand, "neither Doctor Watson nor I wish to borrow money from you or to take money from you in any way or under any pretext. Rather, I would ask you a few questions, if I may, and I would advise you that it will be in your best interests if you answer them as completely and sincerely as is possible."

"You intrigue me," smiled the young monarch.

"Thank you. First of all, may I ask about the finances of Rajipur? You mentioned that you had instituted several reforms, and in my limited experience of such things, changes like this cost money."

The Indian made a face. "You are correct, Mr. Holmes. Provision for my subjects in their old age, and other such changes to the society that I have instituted, impose a strain on the state's coffers. I am unwilling to raise taxes, though my efforts to eliminate corruption have increased the annual amount paid to the treasury, while decreasing that paid to the collectors themselves."

"And your personal fortune? Forgive me for my impertinence in asking, but these things are relevant."

"It is not my personal fortune – it is that of my family. Of my father, my grandfather, and those who came before him, and it is as much the fortune of my as yet unborn children and their children as it is of my ancestors. I may not diminish it, though I may increase it."

"And has anyone recently proposed to you a means of increasing it?"

"Why, yes. Only two days ago, a Signor Pietro Andretti visited me here in this very room, and laid before me a way in which, although my family's wealth would be temporarily diminished, the loss would soon be recouped by the profits that would pour in from this investment."

"May I hazard a guess at the nature of the investment?" Holmes asked. On receiving an affirmative nod, he continued. "This Signor Andretti informed you that he was acting on behalf of the Royal Family of the Netherlands who control the Dutch East Indies, specifically the island known as Sumatra. They are floating the island as a company, to be known as the Netherland-Sumatra Company, and you are invited to subscribe to shares in this company, which will pay handsome dividends, even from the start of the investment."

"You have it to a 'T', Mr. Holmes."

"And your answer to him?"

"I asked for a few days to consider the proposition. The amount that he suggested that I invest in this venture was considerable – somewhere above one-million pounds sterling. It is not a matter to be undertaken lightly, you understand."

"Indeed not," said Holmes. "May I ask you for a description of this Signor Andretti?"

"Certainly. He is what one might term a "thick-set" man. Not as tall as Doctor Watson here, and with a mass of black curly hair. A waxed moustache, turned up at the ends, otherwise clean-shaven. A somewhat flattened nose which looked as though it might have been broken at some time in the past. Well-dressed in a way that would not invite notice."

"You would definitely believe him to be Italian?" I asked.

"As far as I understand a typical Italian to appear, yes, though such stereotyping of races and nationalities seems to me to be a somewhat valueless exercise."

I blushed somewhat at this subtle rebuke.

"And one more question, if I may?" Holmes asked him. "Was there any suggestion of, shall we say, a 'commission' to be paid to you in the event that any other of your fellow Indian rulers were to make a similar investment, based on your recommendation?"

The young Maharajah flushed slightly. "Nothing definite was agreed in that area, but there were certain hints dropped that this might be the case."

"I feared that might be so."

"You advise against the investment?"

"I do more than advise you, Your Highness." Holmes's use of the title added some force to his words. "I urge you in the strongest possible terms to have nothing more with this Signor Andretti or the organisation that he claims to represent. You are an intelligent man, Your Highness. May acquaint you with some of the facts as I have been given them?"

"Very well." There was clear disappointment in the young man's words, presumably at the prospect of the proceeds of what had seemed like a profitable and welcome investment disappearing from his life.

Holmes proceeded to give a detailed account of what we had been told by Lejeune and Gregson, with the Maharajah listening in horrified fascination.

"I believe you, Mr. Holmes, though I find it hard to do so. This Signor Andretti produced such convincing proofs of his veracity that I would not credit what you have just told me had they come from another. See here." He crossed to a table that stood by the window and brought over some papers for Holmes's inspection. My friend took them and examined several through one of the high-powered lenses that he always carried with him.

"These are excellently done," he pronounced. "This signature here would deceive anyone who did not possess intimate knowledge of the handwriting of the Dutch monarchy. See here, the shape of the '*e*', and the tail of the '*p*'."

"And you have such knowledge?" the young man enquired.

"A case on which I was engaged a few years ago," Holmes replied negligently. "There is also the question of the paper. I find it hard to believe that the Royal Household has changed from the use of natively produced paper from Rotterdam to this product from Turin. One or two other details are suggestive, but to my mind, the points I have just mentioned are proof positive that these documents are forgeries."

"And your advice?"

"To refuse to see this Andretti in the future, and, should any of your compatriots report to you any dealings with him, or with anyone representing this supposed organisation, to refer them to me immediately. From what I have told you, I am sure that you understand."

"Indeed so. Indeed, I am due to receive Andretti later today. Should I cancel the meeting, do you think?"

"As long as you are firm and persistent in your refusal of any offers he may make to you, I would think that there is little to be gained by cancelling the meeting."

"I thank you for the advice and the warning, and for your honesty and courage in informing me. Too often I am told the things that it is believed I want to hear, rather than what I should hear. My invitation to you should you ever decide to visit India is as open to you as it ever was. Good day to you, Mr. Holmes. Doctor."

We made our farewells and left the hotel. As we walked along the street, Holmes spoke to me, though without turning his head.

"Watson, do you think you could manage to trip and stumble over that paving-stone a few yards ahead of us? Do not ask why, but simply do it."

"Of course," I answered him, and suited my actions to the words. As I recovered my footing, Holmes was at my elbow, assisting me to regain my balance, and we continued on our way.

"Excellently done, Watson," he told me. "Thanks to you, I was able to get a clearer view of the ruffian who has followed us from the hotel than I have been able to achieve from the reflections in the shop windows."

"We are being followed? By one of Maupertuis' men?"

"Indeed we are being followed, and I have little doubt as to the accuracy of your guess concerning the identity of the rogue's employer. I don't recall having seen him in the past, and he has a distinctly Mediterranean cast to his features. However, I believe it's time to put him behind us." He hailed a cab, and we set off for Baker Street, Holmes confirming that we had left our follower standing helplessly on the pavement, unable to follow.

Once we had returned to Baker Street, we discovered waiting for us the list promised by Gregson of those at the Italian Embassy. Hardly to our surprise, the name of Andretti was not among them.

Though our quarry's name didn't appear in the list supplied by Gregson, Holmes appeared undaunted. He took down the scrapbooks that formed his Index and started to peruse them.

"It is possible," he said, after some fifteen minutes' study of these materials, "that Maupertuis has engaged some of the criminal elements of Italy to assist him. They are not all, by any stretch of the imagination, violent illiterate hooligans, though the leaders may employ men of that description to carry out their bidding. This 'Andretti' may be a leader of the Camorra or Mafia, hired to put us off the track. The description we were given doesn't give us many clues." He lit his pipe and smoked for a few minutes in silence.

"I have sometimes thought," he said, "of a device that could be of value to the police. Have you ever considered how difficult it is to describe a face? Unless a person has a clear feature that is out of the ordinary, or a deformity, a description is difficult. And yet, presented with a range of images of noses, say, I am certain that most witnesses could choose a nose that corresponded to the face they had seen. And if not noses, why not eyes, mouth, chin, ears, and hair? It would be a mighty work to undertake, to be sure, but I'm convinced it would bring positive results. In the meantime, however, we cannot examine the face of every Italian in London, in the hope that we will find our man that way."

"That is very true," I said. "However, is it not possible that at the Italian Embassy there is an official with links to the Italian police force who might be of assistance?"

"An eminently reasonable suggestion," Holmes said. "My compliments. I regret to inform you, however, that I had formed the same idea myself not ten minutes before." He smiled at my crestfallen face. "But it is no less valuable for all that." He glanced at his watch. "However, I fear that we will have to wait until tomorrow before we can produce any sign of life at 25 Queen's Gate. In the meantime, I may profitably spend my time on the case of the Amersham jewels, whose simple solution still appears to elude the Berkshire police force, despite the hints I've dropped in my letters to the local paper. I think the time has come for me to spell out the whole solution in full, and present it as a letter to be delivered through Lestrade or some other of the Scotland Yarders. Heigh-ho."

The next morning saw Holmes up bright and early, penning his missive on the Amersham jewel case to Lestrade at Scotland Yard. Following breakfast, he and I set out together for the Italian Embassy in Queen's Gate, where we planned to determine the true identity of the man who had called himself Pietro Andretti.

On arrival at the Embassy, Holmes asked for the Italian Legal Attaché by name, and we were immediately shown into that official's office.

"My dear Signor Holmes," the diplomat exclaimed, rising from his seat and embracing Holmes warmly. "And your friend. Doctor Watson, may I assume?" I was spared the intimacy of an embrace, Signor Rabello contenting himself with a warm handshake. "Coffee for you gentlemen? I was about to order some for myself?"

We accepted with pleasure, and am Embassy servant entered in response to the bell.

"Now, what can I do for you?" Rabello asked Holmes. "I know that you are a busy man, and you would not come here purely for a social visit and chit-chat, as you English say."

"But it is always a pleasure to chit-chat with you, Signor," protested Holmes. "However, on this occasion, it is indeed a matter of business that brings me here."

"A-ha! Some mystery, perhaps?"

"Indeed so. May I ask you if you have any knowledge of the doings of some of the criminal organisations of Italy in this country? For example, the Mafia of Sicily, or the Camorra of Naples, or the equivalents in Rome or Milan?

The other shrugged. "There are some of these men here, yes. We know they are here, but as long as they break no laws here, there is little we can do about it. If we became aware that they had broken English law, then I suppose that we would inform Scotland Yard of this, but so far that eventuality has not transpired."

"Then perhaps you would tell me if a man such as this is currently in the country?" Holmes asked, giving a description of the fellow who had proposed the Sumatra deal to the Maharajah of Rajpur. As he proceeded, I believed that I saw a flicker of recognition in the eyes of the other, but it might well have been an error of perception on my part.

"I am sorry, but that face and that name have no meaning for me. If you like, I can send a cable to headquarters in Rome and discover if they have any records relating to this person."

"That would be most helpful. Thank you."

Holmes and Rabello exchanged a few more words on other matters before we took our leave and rose to go. Once outside the Embassy, Holmes looked around him before letting out a low whistle.

"I am saddened to see my friend in the clutches of those men," he said softly.

"Rabello?"

"Indeed. He knows that man Andretti. I could see it in his face, and I could see the fear in his face as he believed I was going to press him further. Naturally, I expect nothing from the office in Rome, even if he makes the promised enquiry, which I very much doubt he will."

We walked on in silence, broken only by Holmes's monotonous whistling of some tune that I had previously heard him scraping on his fiddle.

Our progress was suddenly arrested by a police constable standing in our path.

"Excuse me, sir, but are you Mr. Sherlock Holmes?"

"I am," replied my friend.

"Then I must request you and this gentleman here to come with me to the nearest police station," he informed us gravely. "If you will come quietly, there is no need for any fuss or bother."

Holmes held out his hands in front of him. "You wish to apply the 'darbies', Constable?"

"That won't be necessary, sir."

We walked in front of the constable a matter of a few hundred yards to the nearest police station, where the sergeant immediately recognised my friend.

"Sorry about this, Mr. Holmes, but Inspector Gregson from the Yard has been looking for you, and didn't know where you was to be found, so he asked us all to go looking for you."

"That's all right, Latimer," replied Sherlock Holmes. "No harm done, and Watson here was only a little embarrassed."

In truth, I had been more than a little embarrassed, but I deemed it best to hold my peace at this juncture.

"Fancy you remembering my name, sir," said the sergeant, wonderingly.

"One never forgets a man who does his work well," Holmes answered him.

"Well, be that as it may, sir, our orders from Inspector Gregson was to get you to the Cosmopolitan Hotel as soon as possible."

"Why? What has happened?" I asked.

The sergeant shook his head. "It wouldn't be for me to tell you, sir, even if I knew, which I don't," he smiled. "I'm sure you will find out soon enough."

Once seated in the hansom that had been ordered for us, Holmes turned to me. "I fear the worst," he said in low tones.

I did not enquire further, but we sat in silence until we arrived at the hotel. Gregson was waiting for us on the steps leading to the entrance.

"It is a bad business, Mr. Holmes," he warned us.

"What is the matter?" I exclaimed.

"See for yourselves," Gregson said to us, leading the way to the apartments where we had met the Maharajah the previous day. A uniformed constable was stationed outside the door, and saluted Gregson as we approached.

"See for yourselves," Gregson repeated, flinging open the door with a certain flourish.

On the carpet, beside a small escritoire, in a pool of blood which had spread out from the centre, lay the body of a man, face downwards, dressed in the same clothes in which we had seen the Maharajah dressed on the previous day.

"Death appears to have been instantaneous," Gregson informed us. "A stab to the heart from under the ribs, using a long narrow blade, according to the surgeon who examined the body."

"A blade such as a stiletto, as used by Italian criminals?" Holmes suggested.

"Precisely so. I believe we are thinking along similar lines," Gregson answered.

"I am sorry for His Highness," I said. "He seemed to me to have the welfare of his people at heart."

"And he still does," came a voice from behind me.

I turned, and to my amazement, beheld the man to whom we had been speaking the day before.

"I am sorry for Ibraham, my servant," he said, indicating the body. "I would invite you to examine the face, and you will instantly see where the confusion has arisen."

I turned the body over and beheld a face that, while in many ways similar to that of the Maharajah, was nonetheless not the same. They eyes were open with a kind of horror in their expression. Clearly, though, the body was not that of the Maharajah. I closed the staring eyes, and returned my attention to true Maharajah.

"Let me explain the facts as they occurred to me," continued our host, if I may term him such. "After you had left me, Mr. Holmes, I got to thinking. I confess that not all my reading at Oxford was that which I had been assigned by my tutors, but I developed a taste for sensational literature, including stories in which Italian criminal gangs carried out their foul deeds.

"As we agreed, however, I admitted Andretti, who arrived some two hours after you left me. He was all smiles, expecting, I believe, a

331

substantial cheque to be paid to him as a deposit on the investment he was persuading me to make. Without giving precise reasons, though, I told him that I was now unprepared to make the investment, and politely invited him to leave.

"Mr. Holmes, he was furious. I have hardly ever seen a man in the grip of a greater passion. He swore that I had given my word that I would pay him the money he was demanding. I angrily refuted this, and told him to his face that he lied. At this, he then reached inside his coat, as if for a weapon – "

"Did you see such a weapon?" Holmes asked him.

"I did not. My servants, Ibraham here, and Abdul, who also function as body-guards, were also in the room at the time. They observed Andretti's move, and immediately leaped upon him, pinioning his arms to his side. I ordered them to remove him from my presence, and they did so, he spitting what I take to be Italian curses at me.

"Just before the door was shut, he thrust his face, contorted with rage, towards me, and spoke in English. 'You will pay for this!' he told me. Once he had been removed from the room, I rang the bell for the porter and gave him strict instructions that Andretti was not to be admitted again, no matter what seeming proof of my welcome he might produce.

"Ibraham was far from satisfied, however. 'Highness,' he said to me, 'allow me to wear the clothes you are currently wearing, and to sit with my back to the door here at this desk. I fear that whatever orders you have just given regarding Andretti, he or one of his men will undoubtedly attempt to reach you for the purpose of killing you. Better for our people if I am the one who dies, rather than you.

"Reluctantly, I agreed to this proposal. I did not seriously expect that an attempt would be made on my life, but I waited, as Ibraham had suggested to me, in the bedroom through that door there. I remembered the tales I had read about Italian gangs, and I was ashamed of myself for having agreed to place my faithful servant in a position of danger. Indeed, I was about to enter this room and order him back to his duties, when I heard a knock on the outer door, and a voice announcing that the hotel was providing fresh towels."

"One moment," Holmes interrupted. "You say you saw nothing?"

"I was in this room, as I told you. The door between here and the sitting room was closed."

"And the voice? That of a man, or of a woman?"

"It was a deep man's voice, unmistakably. Furthermore, it was speaking with an accent which was not English. It may be merely my fancy, but I believed it to be Italian, even before what then took place.

"I heard Abdul opening the door, after he had instructed Ibraham to stay where he was. This was swiftly followed by a strangled scream, and the sound as of a chair being knocked over . . . ." Wordlessly, Gregson indicated the overturned chair next to the body. "And another sound – a gasp followed by a horrible kind of bubbling."

Here the Maharajah appeared to be overcome with emotion. It was hard for me to remember that although this young man was the ruler of several million souls, and the possessor of considerable presence and intelligence, he was still a young man, not long from University.

"I was petrified, Mr. Holmes. I cast about me for a weapon, but could see nothing, save the razor on the washstand, but before I could reach it, I heard the door to the hallway open once more. I dashed to the connecting door and opened it, only to find my servants lying in their blood on the floor, and the back of a dark coat vanishing down the corridor. It was hopeless, I realised, to attempt to follow him, or even to call the hotel staff – he would have vanished long before any assistance could arrive. I bent to Abdul – "

"Where is he?" Holmes asked.

"He is in the hospital," Gregson told us. "He is wounded, but expected to survive."

"Ibraham, as you can see for yourselves, was not so fortunate, Having ascertained the state of things, I rang for the hotel staff, who arrived, and immediately notified the police."

"I had given strict instructions that in the event of any disturbance of any kind at this hotel, whether or not it concerned His Highness, I was to be immediately informed," Gregson said. "Accordingly, I was on the scene very soon after the incident."

"I would say within twenty minutes," the Maharajah commented. "Remarkably prompt."

"You were expecting something of this nature to occur, then?" Holmes asked Gregson.

"Not at all. However, His Highness is a most important guest, and with the link to the Baron's scheme that we had uncovered, I felt it best that I should be involved at as early a stage as possible should anything untoward occur."

"And you have nothing to add regarding the description of the man who did this?" Holmes asked.

"I saw nothing, as I told you."

"Very well. Gregson, I take it the body here has not been moved?"

"I may have moved him slightly when I ascertained that life was extinct," confessed the Indian. "But otherwise, he is in the position that I discovered him." Again, he appeared ready to break down.

333

Suddenly, Holmes gave a sharp cry. "A-ha!" he exclaimed. "See here!" He pointed to the dead man's right hand, in which a light gunmetal chain was grasped. He gently opened the fingers and extracted the chain, to which was attached a crudely stamped small medal, seemingly made of pewter or some similar material. "If I'm not mistaken, this is a representation of the Black Madonna of Naples." He turned the medal over and examined the other side. "Interesting," he remarked, passing it to Gregson.

"Indeed. With a Neapolitan connection such as you believe to be present here, we may well suspect that the Camorra has a hand in this. And if these prove to be the murderer's initials on the back, why we have him!"

Holmes had continued his examination of the body, with a careful examination of the hands and the lower arms. "See here," he remarked. He pulled up the sleeves of the corpse's jacket and shirt. "This is interesting, is it not?" He indicated, on both wrists, marks as of a tight bracelet or armband, which had been removed.

"Interesting, yes," agreed Gregson. "If we can catch the assailant, no doubt we will find the stolen items – the bracelet or whatever it may be that these Indians wear – in his possession. I believe with a little help from the Italian Embassy, we will have the killer in our power in a very short time from now."

"I'm sorry to tell you that such assistance is unlikely to be forthcoming," Holmes told Gregson. He informed the policeman of our fruitless quest earlier at the Italian Embassy.

"That is most disappointing," said Gregson.

"Never fear," said Holmes. "All is not yet lost. I have other sources of information on these subjects. Our native home-grown criminals resent the intrusion of foreigners on their turf, and I may be able to use my contacts in those areas to discover more about our killer, and maybe even the mysterious Signor Andretti. The killer, I believe, may well be the man who followed Watson and me last night. In any event, it's possible that the staff of the hotel can provide us with a description of the man, if he entered the hotel through the usual route."

"Very well," said Gregson. "I take it you have seen all you need?"

"Almost," said Holmes. He picked up the dead man's other hand. "See here," he told us, displaying a shred of cloth. "I would lay odds that this once formed part of the killer's clothing, possibly his jacket. And look!" he exclaimed. "A button. Once we obtain some sort of description, and we find a man who conforms to that description, we can easily prove or disprove his presence at this scene."

"I believe there is a book of recipes, including one for jugged hare, that begins with the words '*First catch your hare*'," smiled Gregson.

"Oh, we will catch him right enough, never fear," said Holmes. "And if we're lucky, he'll lead us to bigger game than a hare."

"Andretti?" I asked.

"Indeed, and possibly even to the Baron himself."

"Then let us have the body taken up, and we should inform His Highness of what we know. I'll have a further guard set on the door," said Gregson.

"However," added Holmes, "for now, it may be useful to give the impression to the attackers that the attempt on His Highness' life was successful."

"I agree," the policeman answered him. "Given the rank of the supposed victim, a little secrecy in these matters may be expected, in any case." He gave the necessary orders to the constable at the door for the removal of the body.

"Watson," Holmes ordered me. "Take His Highness elsewhere, and if you have anything about you that will help to calm his nerves, pray administer it. Inspector, I may require your assistance."

I gently led the Maharajah into the next room and attempted to explain the situation.

"This is a hard thing for me to take in," he said. "Ibraham had been a companion since childhood, and even accompanied me to Oxford to serve me there. Such a man becomes much more than a servant – more than a friend, even. It is as if a piece of me has been cut out and discarded. I feel that I should leave London as soon as possible in order to make provision for his family – two wives and three small children. They will be cared for, you may be sure, as if they were my own."

I couldn't help but feel for this young prince, who appeared completely sincere in his grief for the loss of his retainer.

"I am counting on you and Mr. Holmes to avenge this death," he told me with the greatest solemnity. "Swear to me that you will do so."

"I swear," I told him, "on behalf of myself and Mr. Holmes, that as far as it is in our power, this crime will not go unpunished."

"Thank you," he said. "Now leave me to my grief." It was a regal dismissal. But first I administered a small dose of a sedative, having observed a bottle of a patent mixture by side of the bed. I guessed that it had been prescribed by an Indian doctor, given the indication on the label. Once he had swallowed a few drops of the tincture, dissolved in a glass of water, His Highness appeared calmer, and acceded to my suggestion that he lie on the bed and repose himself. Immediately he did so, he appeared to fall into a deep sleep, occasioned, I guessed, by the recent expenditure of nervous energy as much as from the effects of the drug.

I passed as silently as I could into the other room and closed the connecting door behind me. Holmes looked up from his kneeling position beside the Indian's body.

"How is he?" he asked me.

I described my actions and His Highness's current state. Holmes said nothing, but nodded and went back to his work, quietly talking to Gregson as he did so.

"Rum beggars, some of those Indians," Gregson said later, as we descended the stairs to the entrance lobby of the hotel after I had explained what had transpired. "But he's got a good heart, it seems, that one."

On approaching the concierge, Holmes enquired which of the staff had been on duty at the time when the murder had taken place, and they were brought to us.

One of the porters, an elderly man, claimed to have seen a man whose appearance suggested that he might have been the murderer.

"Sort of foreign-like, he was," he told us. "Dark skin, curly hair, and short. He'd only come up to my shoulder, I reckon, and I'm not that tall, as you can see for yourselves, gentlemen. I noticed how short he was when he walked past that potted palm over there."

"Excellent," said Holmes. "Anything else that you observed about him?"

"Now you come to mention it, sir, there was something else. One of his feet – let me think now – yes, it was his left foot, was dragging a bit, as if he had something wrong with his leg. And did I say about his hair and his moustache? Wild hair, you'd have to say. Black and curly. And a moustache on him that a Guardsman would be proud of."

"You are obviously a keen observer," Holmes said to him. "Did you speak to him?"

"I did, sir. 'Where are you off to, then?' I asked him. He didn't look like one of our guests, see, so I didn't see the need to be that polite to him, like I would to a guest."

"Quite so. And what was his answer?"

"Well, he just looked at me, with a sort of hard look, and told me he had a package for His Highness. I didn't need to ask who he meant, because at the moment we only have one Highness staying here. We'll have a lot more come the Jubilee, of course, but right now, just the one."

"And he showed you the package?"

"He did that, sir. Small, wrapped in brown paper, it was. So I let him through and watched him go up the stairs."

"And when he came down?"

336

"Now you come to mention it, sir, I never saw him come down or go out of the door. That's bit queer, isn't it, sir?"

"Perhaps the doorman might be able to inform you of that, Mr. Holmes," the concierge suggested.

"Perhaps," Holmes replied, "but I doubt it."

His prediction of having seen the man enter the hotel, though his attention at the time was taken up with welcoming another guest, and he had no memory whatsoever of seeing him leave.

"Probably slipped out of the back entrance," Gregson said.

"I'm sure you are correct," Holmes told him, and thanked the hotel staff of the hotel for their assistance.

"One more thing," Holmes asked the concierge. "Who would have been on duty in the doorway and in the hall yesterday evening?"

However, on questioning those members of the hotel staff regarding the man who called himself Andretti, and who had been reported by the Maharajah as having visited him the previous evening following our departure, we also drew a blank. None admitted to having seen a man such as had been described to us having visited the hotel at that time, though a porter and a doorman claimed to have seen him on the previous day, the porter actually having shown him to the Maharajah's suite.

"If he was aware that we were on his tail," Gregson remarked, "it's likely that he wouldn't wish to be seen here."

"If indeed he did visit the hotel at that time," said Holmes, enigmatically, but did not expand on this. "There is no doubt in my mind," he told Gregson, "that the man whom we believe killed the Indian servant is the one whom I observed following us last night, and who is, if the evidence of the medal found in the dead man's hand is to be believed, a member of the Camorra."

"I believe you should be concerned, Mr. Holmes, and you too, Doctor. Allow me to post some of my constables outside your lodgings to protect you against this man."

Holmes laughed. "I am indeed concerned, Inspector, but my main concern is that this man may *not* trouble to visit us. He may believe that London is too dangerous for him, knowing that we are involved in the business, and he may either lie low, or, as I believe more likely, he will attempt to slip out of the country."

"I will have the ports watched," Gregson said.

As it turned out, Holmes's prediction was correct. Following Gregson' prompt action in alerting the port authorities, a man corresponding to the description that we had been given was apprehended at Newhaven, attempting to board a ferry to Dieppe. His papers gave his name as Antonio Betteroni, and he was described as a cobbler and a native of Naples. He claimed that he had been visiting his brother, and gave an address in Whitechapel as proof of his veracity.

He was immediately arrested on suspicion of having killed the Maharajah's servant and brought by Gregson to London for questioning. Holmes was present at the interview, and I was also allowed to attend.

Gregson wasted no time on preliminaries. "Your attempt to kill the Maharajah failed," were his opening words.

If this had been an effort by Gregson to trick the other into some sort of admission of guilt, it failed. There was little reaction.

"Come, now," Holmes told him. "We know that you speak English well enough to explain your presence in this country to the port authorities in Newhaven. Have you no answer to give the inspector here?"

"I do not know what you are talking about," came the sullen answer.

"Very well, then," said Holmes. "You are acquainted with the Cosmopolitan Hotel?"

The Italian spread his hands. "I, a simple cobbler, should know about one of the most famous hotels in London?" He realised what he had just told us, and attempted to rectify his error. "What I mean to say is that naturally I have heard the name. But to be acquainted with it? You imagine that I can afford to sleep between silk sheets? To drink champagne for breakfast? You are a little *pazzo* – crazy, Signor, if you believe that."

"The sheets at the hotel are linen, not silk," Holmes told him. "And I would expect a rough red to be more to your taste than champagne. I was not asking you if you had stayed there. I was asking if you were acquainted with it. Do you, for instance, know where it is located?"

"I could not draw you a map, but yes, I know."

"And do you know where Baker Street is located?"

A look of fear came into the other's eyes. "I know the name, yes."

Holmes glanced at Gregson, who nodded almost imperceptibly, whereupon Holmes withdrew from an inner pocket the medal that had been discovered in the dead man's hand. "Is this yours?" he enquired in an almost casual tone.

The Italian's hand flew to his throat, before seemingly remembering that the medal was no longer in his possession. "What . . . what is it, Signor?" he stammered, much of his previous bluster now gone.

"I think you know very well what it is," Holmes said to him. "Your initials are *A.B.*, are they not? The same initials that I see on the back of this medal." The other nodded. "It is not conclusive proof of your guilt, I agree, but it is strongly suggestive, is it not?"

"Where did you find it?"

"In the hand of the man you killed," Gregson said drily.

"You said to me just now that I killed nobody, Mr. Policeman," protested Betteroni.

"I said nothing of the sort," said Gregson. "I simply said that your attempt to kill the Maharajah had been a failure."

"*Dio!*" the Italian exclaimed. "I cannot understand what you mean here!"

"What the Inspector is telling you is that you killed the wrong man. The man whom you left dead on the floor of the room at the Cosmopolitan Hotel was not the man you intended to kill."

"Then who was he?" came the answer. Immediately, Betteroni clapped a hand over his mouth. "What I meant to say was – "

"So you are aware of the murder at the Cosmopolitan?" Gregson asked.

"Naturally. It was in the newspapers," said the Italian.

Holmes shook his head. "I'm sorry to tell you that there has been no mention at all of the incident in the press. So where did you hear about it? Did a friend inform you of it?"

The Italian shook his head slowly. "I suppose you have me. Yes, I killed the Maharajah of Rajipur."

"I must warn you," Gregson told him, "that anything you say may be used in evidence at your trial. Do you understand?"

"I do."

"Did you kill at the orders of one Pietro Andretti?"

"At the orders of another. I do not know his name."

Holmes repeated the description of the man that we had been given by the Maharajah.

"That is he," said the other, "but I swear to you that I do not know his name or where he is to be found."

"How did you come to meet him?"

"A note pushed under the door of the room where I lodge, while I was at work."

"Your trade and place of work?" asked Gregson.

"I am a waiter. I have no permanent place of work, but I assist at hotels when there is a banquet or some other big occasion where extra hands are needed."

"And I may take it that you have sometimes worked at the Cosmopolitan Hotel?" Holmes asked.

"I have."

"Then no doubt that would explain how you were seen entering the hotel, but not exiting. You entered through the front as a visitor in search of a guest, and you left from the back as a waiter, unremarked among the many hotel servants."

"My hat is off to you, Mr. Holmes."

"And you followed me and Dr. Watson back to Baker Street?"

"I did. I was told that you were investigating the doings of the man who hired me, whom you call Andretti, and I was asked to discover how easy it would be to remove you from the investigation."

I was chilled at these words, realising how close Holmes and I had come to death at the hands of this assassin. Holmes for his part appeared almost sanguine. "Very good, then," he said. "Perhaps you will tell us more of the events surrounding the death of the man you believe to be the Maharajah."

"Oh, you think you are so clever, Mr. Holmes, with your 'the man you believe to be'. But yes, I will tell you of these events. The man who hired me – let us use the name 'Andretti', since that is the name you have, and I have no name – approached me a week ago, leaving a letter under my door. He told me that he was here to do a particular piece of business – to collect money from an Indian prince which was owing to his employer in Naples."

"How had he heard of you?" asked Gregson.

"My name is as famous in my circles," answered the Italian, "as that of Mr. Holmes is in his. To be sure, I do not seek publicity in the newspapers, nor do I have a Doctor Watson to record my doings, but when I have completed a job for one of my clients, it will usually be on the front page of the newspapers."

I was somewhat taken aback by the fact that this murderer appeared to show no remorse for his actions, but rather seemed to take pride in his foul deeds.

"Yesterday I accompanied him to the hotel and waited outside while he conducted whatever business was to be done. As he came out, he described you and Doctor Watson here, and told me to follow you to your lodgings."

"Can you describe his mood?"

"He was in an excellent mood. Happy, almost to the point of madness, I would say."

"How did you report back to him once you had followed us to Baker Street?"

"I did not. I was to wait for instructions. They came under my door. I was to go to the hotel, see myself up to the Maharajah's suite, and there to do him to death as swiftly and silently as possible. I was admitted by one of his servants, whom I felled silently with a blow from my dagger. The Maharajah was sitting at a desk with his back to me. He did not hear me approach, and I reached around and stabbed him through the heart, under the ribs. He fell to the floor, and I left the room."

340

"There was no one else in the room? No one attempted to stop you?"

The other spread his hands. "Who would have stopped me? The Maharajah was dying – I stooped to check his pulse, and his hands grasped feebly at my throat. At that time, I did not notice that the medal you hold there was missing. I then left the room, entered a linen room, and took off my overcoat, revealing the uniform of a waiter. You will find the overcoat at the bottom of a linen basket – that is, if one of the hotel servants has not already taken it for himself."

"And then?"

"I had been ordered by this 'Andretti' to leave England as soon as I had completed my work. I was told that I would be paid when I returned to Naples. And that, gentlemen, is where you found me – preparing to leave the country."

"Is there anything else you wish to say?"

"I wish an advocate."

"Do you have one in mind?"

"Signor Rabello at the Embassy."

Holmes and I exchanged glances.

"I will see what can be done," Gregson told him. "Though you had far better to plead guilty and maybe earn yourself a long sentence on the Moor rather than the hangman's rope." His words seemed to have no effect on the other, who sat stolidly until two constables answered Gregson' summons and took him to the cells.

"My word," said Gregson to us when the door had closed behind the prisoner. "What are we to make of all this?"

"That the murderer confesses to killing a man, but he claims to have murdered a man with whom we have just been talking? That his statements entirely contradict what we were told by His Highness?"

"Indeed, the confession that he made to us just now would be torn to shreds by any competent lawyer, when set against the word of the Maharajah of Rajipur," said Gregson.

"I do not think that you will be able to present the word of His Highness as evidence."

"Why on earth not?"

"Because His Highness is dead."

Both Gregson and I started to our feet in amazement. "Holmes," I ejaculated, "What in heaven's name do you mean? We were talking to him!"

"Were we indeed? I wonder."

"You agree that the man to whom we talked earlier today, and the man with whom we spoke yesterday are the same man, do you not?"

"Indeed I do."

"And yesterday we spoke with His Highness, and ergo, we spoke to the same man – that is, the Maharajah of Rajipur?"

"An entirely logical conclusion, my dear Watson, but you are basing your argument on a false premise."

"That being?"

"That we spoke with His Highness yesterday."

I was dumbfounded. "Then with whom did we speak?"

"My guess is that it was with the servant Ibraham, who we were informed today had been killed defending his master."

"Then where was His Highness when we talked yesterday?"

"I believe he was in the bedroom, sedated and bound, and probably gagged intro the bargain. You mentioned that there was a bottle of some Indian sedative medicine near the bed?" I nodded. "You recall that the dead man's eyes were open when we turned over the body to examine the face?"

"I do," I shuddered.

"The pupils were like pinpricks, surely evidence of opium or some such substance having been administered. I would also draw your attention to the marks on the dead man's wrists. They were not the marks of bangles, or arm-bands or of any kind of jewellery. It was clear that these marks were the result of the arms being bound at the wrists."

"I will take your word for it," I said, and Gregson nodded.

"And I take it that neither of you remarked the state of the hands? Tut. The hands, my dear Inspector, can tell you more about their owner than the face ever will. These were hands that had never laboured for a living. The palms were soft, and it was unlikely that they had ever held any tool more effective than a cricket bat. The nails were smooth and polished, delicately manicured. These were not the hands of a servant, but of the master of a servant."

My mind was reeling with what Holmes had just told is. "But," I objected, "the man to whom we talked spoke excellent English, and talked about his time at Balliol."

"Remember what we were told today by the man, in his character of the Maharajah," Holmes reminded me. "He said that his servant had been his companion since he was a boy, and had even accompanied him to Oxford. Given that the man is as intelligent as the master – and there is no reason why this should not be the case – and given the continued intimacy of the relationship over many years, I think it is more than likely that the servant should acquire linguistic skills at least equal to that of His Highness."

342

"So we were speaking to a servant yesterday, when we believed we were talking to the Maharajah himself?" Gregson asked. "I can hardly credit it."

"I believe that part of the deception lies in the fact that the actors in this little game are not English. Should an English butler decide to impersonate his titled master, we could easily detect the difference. There are those little things that mark a servant as being of a different class. But when we are faced with a society and rules which are not ours, then can we rely on our instincts to distinguish the imposter from the real thing?"

"What do you consider was the sequence of events?" Gregson asked after a pause. "Whose initiative is this, do you feel?"

"My feeling is that one of the servants was aware that vast wealth had been promised to those who would invest in the Baron's scheme. Now, we have no way now of knowing what the actual relations were between the Maharajah and his servants. Perhaps the matter was discussed between them, or perhaps one of the servants in some way acquired and read a letter which pledged investment in the scheme, but the end result is the same.

"Again, we don't know the precise thinking behind all these actions, but I think it would be reasonable for us to assume that the servants conspired for one of them to impersonate His Highness. My feeling is that they wished to acquire this wealth for themselves. In any event, I think we may take it that Andretti, when he first met the Indians, did not speak to the man to whom he believed he was speaking. Rather, he was speaking to one of the servants, who promised to invest the money, which had been promised earlier by the Maharajah. I believe this to have been the case."

"And where was the Maharajah at that point?" asked Gregson.

"Why, as I said just now, he was sedated, and possibly bound and gagged, in the bedroom. Meanwhile, the servant Ibraham was dressed in his clothes, and was happily informing Andretti that the deal was forthcoming. He was still in this character when we came to visit. I'm sure that much of what we were told was the truth – with regard to His Highness' time at Oxford, for example. It may even be that His Highness was proposing to make this investment for the good of the people of his state, but we cannot be sure of that.

"In any event, it's certain that the Maharajah couldn't be allowed to live following this impersonation. The servants no doubt were reluctant to perform the deed themselves, given their long association with him, and possibly a personal oath that they had sworn. It is impossible for us to know with any certainty. I have long held that the ways of the Oriental mind are not for us to understand. In any event, Andretti was informed by the servants that it was for him to ensure the demise of the Maharajah. Accordingly, the man Betteroni was dispatched to eliminate their master,

343

who was dressed in his own clothes, drugged, and placed in the chair by the desk as a sacrificial victim. A fight was staged in which one of the servants was slightly wounded, in order to give some verisimilitude to the story, and the body of the Maharajah was then presented to us as that of one of the servants."

"If you're correct, Mr. Holmes, we must secure these servants immediately and confront them with all of this!" exclaimed Gregson.

Holmes shook his head. "I fear we'll be too late. I'm certain that they will have flown the coop. If you were to search among the Lascars in the docks, there might be a chance, albeit a faint one, of discovering them, but I think we can assume that we will never more hear of them."

"And the Maharajah himself?" asked Gregson. "Do we play along with the deception and simply regard him as missing, or do we accept the corpse as his?"

"I believe," said Holmes, after a moment's reflection, "that our best course of action will be to publicly accept what we were originally told, and identify the corpse as that of the servant who gave his life to save his master. We can give out that, as a result of this failed attempt on his life, His Highness has left the hotel, and is now in a secluded location prior to his return to India, which will be made incognito."

"That would seem to fit the bill," I said. "But what are the next steps in this case?"

"Why, we must discover how much money the Baron has received from this source. If, as I fear, the funds are of a sufficient magnitude for him to begin the construction of his fleet of pirate gunboats, then our attentions must be turned overseas."

"To the German shipyards, and French steelworks?" I suggested.

"Indeed. Also to the financial institutions that Maupertuis uses to move his ill-gotten gains from one location to another."

"But cannot we – by which I mean the British government – alert the French and German authorities as to the Baron's intentions, and thereby make them the cause of frustrating his plans?" I enquired.

It was Gregson who answered, shaking his head. "In the usual way of things, Doctor Watson," he replied, "that would be how such a case would be handled, were it one simply of murder, or even embezzlement or theft. But in this case, questions of national defence come into play. Both the manufactories where Maupertuis now has a controlling interest are of vital importance to the nations in which they are situated. Alerting the governments of these countries would be seen as a ploy by Great Britain to weaken their defences. No, I fear that we must work outside government circles in order to frustrate the designs of the Baron."

It transpired that Sherlock Holmes was correct in his assumption regarding the Indians. We made our way to the Cosmopolitan Hotel instantly following the conversation recorded above.

We were informed by the manager that the Maharajah and his retinue had left the hotel about an hour previously, and had left no forwarding address. Although the porter remembered the number of the cab which had carried them from the hotel, and the driver was subsequently interviewed by Gregson, it transpired that they had been taken to Liverpool Street Station. Further enquiries there produced no memories of the Indians, and as Holmes remarked, any further attempt to trace them would be unnecessarily time-consuming.

My friend's attention therefore turned to the Continent, where Maupertuis was now operating.

"The devil of it is," he said to me, "that we have no idea how much money he has raised so far. The shares in the von Heissen and the de Lantis enterprises are a matter of public record, of course, but I'm hoping that Lejeune will be able to provide us with more information regarding the amount of ready cash now available. I also have hopes that the Pinkerton Agency in New York can provide us with a little more information regarding the American side of the matter.

"But for now," he continued, "I feel I must take myself abroad."

"Do you wish me to accompany you?" I asked him.

"The offer of your assistance is greatly appreciated, as always, but at this stage of the case, I would prefer you to remain in London. Rest assured, though, that should I require your assistance, I'll telegraph you immediately. And on the subject of money, I may inform you in the strictest of confidence that all our expenses will be met by Her Majesty's Government."

I couldn't help but feel a certain stab of disappointment at his words, though I recognised that it would almost certainly be necessary for the success of Holmes's operations that there was someone in London on whom he could rely absolutely, and it was with some satisfaction that it was I who had been selected for that role.

"However," Holmes went on, "it will be necessary for me to make a few enquiries in the City before I set off, and it would ease my task considerably were you to assist me in this matter."

The next few days saw us visiting stockbrokers in a vain attempt to discover any dealings in stocks and shares where the hand of Maupertuis could be traced. Not only did it appear that the shares of the Netherland-Sumatra Company had never been traded in London, but the very name of the company appeared to be unknown to the gentlemen of the City whom we visited.

"It was Lejeune who informed us of this Netherland-Sumatra business, was it not?" I asked Holmes one evening following a day of fruitless tramping in and out of offices. "Can we be sure that the information with which he provided us is correct?"

"I have known of Lejeune's work for some time," he answered me. "He has the reputation of being a most meticulous researcher – perhaps a little lacking in imagination, which is unusual for a member of the Gallic race, who are, as you know, prone to a certain amount of exaggeration, but that is all too common in the official detective forces. I believe that the facts as he related them to us are essentially true. It is merely that the shares in the company are not offered openly, but the deals are conducted in secrecy, given the ostensible and the true nature of the business."

In the end, Holmes was forced to leave for France without being in full possession of the true state of affairs, one which vexed him somewhat, and which proved to be somewhat of a handicap in his subsequent endeavours.

The God of War
by Hal Glatzer

Mr. Sherlock Holmes was a patriotic subject of Queen Victoria, but he was not by nature deferential to royal or titled persons from any country, including our own, because he was never awed by rank. The people he most admired were those who, like himself, gained authority by merit, not inheritance. When someone, be it prince or peasant, brought him a puzzle to solve, he accepted it only if it appealed to his curiosity.

In the years that Holmes and I shared a flat in Baker Street, I often heard him disparage noblemen and titled aristocrats for bringing him "trivial" problems. And once, in my presence, he turned down a commission from an archbishop.

A contrary example, however, of taking on a royal client, occurred in June of 1887. It was a month particularly memorable for being filled with celebrations, all across the Empire, in honor of Victoria's fifty years on the throne.

Holmes's patriotism was second-nature, but his manner of expressing it was unpredictable, much like the man himself. He did not hang colorful bunting from the windows, and he was not inclined to join parades with waving flags and shouting crowds. He expressed devotion to the Queen in a more subtle and generous way. For the Golden Jubilee, as it was called, the Royal Mint had issued a commemorative half-sovereign in gold. Holmes purchased ten pounds' worth – a score of coins – and gave most of them to his young "Irregulars", the urchins who spy for him, to help their families enjoy the great occasion.

One morning during the busiest week of the Jubilee, just before nine o'clock, Holmes glanced out the window and announced, "Alas, Watson, we shall be interviewing a visitor with royal connections."

It had been a week of unusually warm weather – even for London in the early summer – and the Fahrenheit thermometer on our window ledge had already reached 81. I looked past it, down into the street, and indeed, a carriage sporting a very regal crest stood in front of our steps.

We heard footsteps on the stairs. When our landlady Mrs. Hudson knocked, Holmes called, "Come in," and turned to face the door. "A Mister . . . Dominis to see you," she said, squinting at the name on his card. She gestured for him to enter, gave Holmes the calling-card, and then left us, closing the door behind her.

"'*John Owen Dominis*'," Holmes read aloud, then looked up at him. He was a tall and hefty middle-aged man, formal not only in dress but in posture – very pale of face, with brown hair, and a slightly darker full beard that came down well past his collar. "You have come halfway around the world. From the Sandwich Islands, I perceive."

"We prefer to say 'the Hawaiian Islands.' But how did you know from where I've come?"

"You arrived with livery, in a carriage belonging to the British royal household, but you are not a member of our Queen's family. There is, however, a charm depending from the watch-chain between your waistcoat pockets. It is carved from what is almost certainly whalebone, in a stylized way to suggest a fish-hook. That, I believe, is a signifier of Polynesian chiefs. It was reported in *The Times* a few days ago that a royal delegation has come to London from the Kingdom of Hawaii to attend the Queen's Golden Jubilee. But as you are fair-skinned, you are not likely to be, even distantly, a relation in line for a Hawaiian kingship, and because it was reported that your queen is here representing her husband the king, who remains in Hawaii, it follows that you must be the consort of the other royal lady in your delegation. You are married to the princess who is your king's sister."

"You are right." He took a deep breath. "My wife is Her Royal Highness the Crown Princess Liliʻuokalani, sister to His Majesty Kalakaua, and sister-in-law to Queen Kapiolani. [1] We need your help."

"You may speak freely. This is my excellent friend and colleague, Dr. John Watson, who is the soul of discretion."

"A pleasure, sir." We nodded acknowledgements.

Holmes gave him a half-smile, waved him into taking our basket chair, and eased himself into a sprawl on the sofa across from it. I sat in my desk-chair, took up a pencil, and opened my notebook to a blank page.

"Mr. Holmes, thank you for seeing me without an appointment. I asked . . . a certain gentleman in Queen Victoria's household . . . whom I should consult about a problem that has arisen during our sojourn here. He immediately urged me to . . . see you."

Dominis was not a well man. Shortness of breath may connote a lung ailment, but heart trouble seemed more likely for a man with an otherwise robust frame.

"A carriage was placed at my disposal," he continued, "to convey me here . . . in hopes that you might best comprehend and . . . with luck, resolve a most unfortunate situation. My wife is being . . . blackmailed."

"Are there letters from some youthful indiscretion," I asked, "that would damage her reputation if they were made public? Mr. Holmes has resolved several such cases."

348

"No, no, Dr. Watson. Perhaps blackmail was . . . not the right word."

"Indeed, not," said Holmes. "I think it unlikely that the Crown Princess of Hawaii should be threatened, here in England, by the society parasites who prey upon women in our upper classes. More likely, this is some affair of *state*."

"That is so, Mr. Holmes." He took a handkerchief from an inside pocket of his morning-coat and dabbed perspiration from his high forehead. As if to confirm my impression of his ill health, he lifted a small brown-glass bottle from another pocket, uncorked it, and took a sip. After sitting still for a moment, he gave a little shrug of apology and spoke more slowly, so he could pause for breath between whole sentences.

"You may not be acquainted with the history of our kingdom, but it bears deeply upon our present difficulty. May I bring you up to date?"

Holmes signaled assent with a palms-up gesture, but then half-closed his eyes, as he often did, to the surprise and discomfort of his clients – not from *ennui*, but concentration.

"Our islands," Dominis explained, "were for centuries a Polynesian kingdom, before they were – you would say 'discovered'. We say 'encountered' – by white men in the seventeen-seventies and eighties. In the decades that have followed, Hawaii has become a modern nation: A constitutional monarchy with a king and a legislature. But our legislature is increasingly under the sway of influential men who call themselves the Reform Party, and who continuously raise strong objections to His Majesty Kalakaua's policies regarding trade and the administration of the Islands."

Holmes's eyes flicked open. "Are these men native Hawaiian chiefs, like members of our House of Lords?"

"No sir. They are mostly white men. Several were born of marriage between Hawaiians and Americans, but most are the sons and grandsons of merchants and missionaries who came earlier in this century from the United States. A few are recent arrivals who have had themselves naturalized. All, no matter their racial heritage, are full citizens of the Kingdom. But what they have in common is that they represent commercial interests, particularly the planters and plantations of sugar cane. And they all favor a close and ever-closer alliance with the United States. They are also, and rather vehemently, prejudiced against Chinese merchants who, in Hawaii, have long been our entrepreneurs: Importers, shopkeepers, tradesmen, and so on."

"I gather, then, that your problem involves this Reform Party," Holmes said. "Are any of its members here with you in London?"

"None of them came on the ship with us from Honolulu to San Francisco, nor in our railway carriages across the continent. But on the

349

Atlantic crossing, we met three American businessmen who acknowledged ties to the Reform Party, and who were *en route* to London, as we were. One is from San Francisco, one from Indianapolis, and the third from Chicago. Like most Americans, these men are anti-royalists – not the sort who would kowtow before kings and queens. It seems strange to us that they would come here to celebrate Victoria's long reign. And of course, they have not been invited to the official Jubilee events, which we have been attending. But we did see them at a small reception last evening that was given by a former American Secretary of State. We fear that they are here to undermine our sovereign kingdom in some way."

"I hope you will not consider me impolite, Mr. Dominis," I said, "but isn't it possible that these men came here simply in pursuit of their commercial interests? Even if they do not revere our Queen, they may very well enjoy themselves in London this week, in the general spirit of merry-making."

A little smile peeked through his whiskers. "I think not. Most of the Reform Party's members, possibly reflecting their missionary heritage, are men of ill-humour. They frown on merry-making – at least as it is practiced by His Majesty Kalakaua. Our royal court is rather informal, compared to those of Europe, and our king is a very – " A wider smile flickered briefly. " – *sociable* man, fond of congenial company. He enjoys his libations. He has built a palace in the latest style, with telephone instruments and electric lamps. He employs a large brass band. One of our newspapers calls him our '*Merrie Monarch*'. His *joie de vivre* has made him well-loved by the vast majority of the people – especially the native Hawaiians. The Reformers, however, consider his expenditures frivolous and his gaiety beneath contempt."

Holmes opened his eyes and stared at our visitor. "Why give me all this history? You might as well lecture on astronomy or philosophy. It has no connection with my work in criminal investigation."

"My apologies, Mr. Holmes. But I felt obliged to provide the background to the problem at hand, which concerns opium."

Now he had engaged my friend! Holmes shifted on the sofa into a more nearly upright posture.

"His Majesty Kalakaua retains many royal prerogatives, one of which is the granting of licenses for the importation, distribution, and sale of opium. This is a very lucrative trade, as you British are keenly aware."

Indeed, we are. The late James Matheson, and his predeceased partner William Jardine, grew fabulously wealthy by growing opium in India and then creating a market for it in China. The British government and her armed forces waged several small wars in support of that market, which overcame China's resistance to trading with the West. Millions of Chinese

350

people are now enslaved to opium, thanks to the firm of Jardine Matheson." [2]

"Mr. Dominis," said Holmes, "I am indifferent to politics. And I have no particular objection to opium. I feel it makes addicts only of men whose will is too weak to resist its lure."

I suppressed the urge to laugh aloud at the words "no particular objection". I had once seen him smoke it – though sometimes he took it in the form of morphine, which he injected intravenously when he was bored, or when he needed a counteracting depressant from over-indulgence in the stimulant cocaine. As a medical man, the unprescribed use of these drugs is abhorrent to me, but I have never been able to persuade Holmes to refrain.

"There are a few opium addicts in Hawaii, chiefly among the mendicants," our visitor went on, "but it is not addiction that has caused the problem which brings me to your door. The greatest portion of the opium that comes to Hawaii is sold legitimately, for medicine. Pharmacists – you call them 'chemists' – make alcohol tinctures, such as laudanum, which are much in demand, not only for surgical operations, but for soothing the pains of childbirth and quieting the cries of colicky babies. There is practically no household in Hawaii that does not have an opiate medication on its shelves. Hence the importation. Wholesale and retail transactions of opium are significant contributors to our economy.

"To come to the point, we received an invitation by messenger, yesterday morning, from the senior American agent for Jardine Matheson. His name is Henry Dunn. He requested us to come to his suite at the Walsingham House Hotel, and there he asked my wife to persuade her brother the king to grant Jardine Matheson the exclusive license to import opium to Hawaii. In return for this, he proffered a gift of considerable value. It was done in private, of course, but if it were known to the Hawaiian nation, it would be construed as a bribe."

"Surely," said Holmes, "you do not need me to counsel you on this matter. Refrain from telling anyone, and decline the gift."

"If only that were possible!"

"Why is it not?"

"A photographer was present – also American, by the way – so there is a photograph of my wife standing beside Mr. Dunn, with his gift between them. We had no choice but to accept it. And to be frank, we want to keep it."

I piped up, "What is this gift?"

"It is a statuette, carved in wood, and decorated with colorful bird feathers."

"*Feathers?*" I could not suppress a laugh.

"Yes. The statue represents the ancient Hawaiian war god, Kukailimoku – more simply called Ku. [3] In the centuries before the Europeans and Americans came, sculptures like these were venerated in ceremonies. The missionaries, however, construed them as idols. As Christianity spread, and adherents to the old religion passed away, nearly all of these statuettes were destroyed, mainly by fire. A few survive today, only because they were removed from Hawaii, either by scholars of Polynesian culture or by collectors who regard them as works of art by primitive people. There is a Ku in the Imperial Museum in Berlin and another in the Peabody, in Boston. This particular statuette is one of two that were brought here by a Royal Navy captain in 1825. One is in the British Museum while the other has, since 1863, resided in the London office of Jardine Matheson. Naturally, Lydia wants to . . . excuse me, that is her given name and it is what I call her at home. She became Lili'uokalani upon her brother David's ascent to the throne. At any rate, she wants to bring the Ku back with us to Honolulu. Our friend Charles Bishop is building a museum of Hawaiian history and culture, so we want David – Kalakaua – to donate the Ku to the new museum in a great public ceremony. That would increase the king's popular appeal. It would also embolden the native Hawaiian and royalist parties in the legislature. They do not always agree with one another, so this would unite them when voting against the Reform Party. However, to achieve these good outcomes, the king would have to grant Jardine Matheson the opium license."

Holmes reached for his tobacco and pipe. "You must forgive me, Mr. Dominis, but I don't see a problem here, nor any evidence of coercion by Mr. Dunn. In Britain, some royal licenses are famously bought and sold. A condiment maker may pay an annual fee to call itself '*Purveyor to the Crown*'. If the Kingdom of Hawaii is, as you say, a steady customer for opium from Asia, why should your king not grant the transactional license to the very *experienced* firm of Jardine Matheson?"

Dominis sighed. "That is something which . . . it would be better for the Crown Princess to address. If you will accompany me to the Midland Grand Hotel, you may have an audience with her."

"Please go on ahead. Dr. Watson and I shall come later. First, we shall visit Mr. Dunn at his hotel."

"I understand." He rose, but needed a moment to steady himself, and sip once again from his little bottle, before taking his hat from the rack and leaving.

352

We rode by hansom to Walsingham House, the tallest hotel in Mayfair. From the reception desk, we were taken up to the sixth floor, the highest, in a hydraulic lift.

Dunn's suite may well have been the hotel's most costly. Its windows commanded a sweeping view over the entire neighborhood, with Hyde Park, Green Park, and Buckingham Palace beyond. The paintings, carpeting, and furniture in the sitting room rivaled those in the finest clubs I have ever seen. There was ornate marquetry in the wainscot, and an enormous fireplace with a broad marble mantel. Jardine Matheson evidently didn't spare any expense housing its American agent.

After an exchange of *cartes-de-visite*, we sat in soft leather armchairs, but declined his offer of sherry.

As Americans are wont to do, given their congenital disregard for *politesse*, he came straight to the point. "I know of your reputation, Mr. Holmes. I assume that Mr. Dominis called on you this morning, and that that is why you are here."

"You are correct."

"As it happens, however, the opium license for Hawaii may have already been awarded. The king has a longtime friend in Honolulu, a merchant Chinaman named Ah Kee, who is prepared to bribe him for it, with thousands of dollars in cash. However, Mrs. Dominis – the princess – doesn't know that."

"But you do?"

"Yes. Another Chinese merchant, with whom we do some business with in Honolulu, brought a rumor of it to our San Francisco office yesterday. They telegraphed it to New York and from there, by way of the Atlantic cable, it came to our main office here in London. It takes a week for a ship to reach California from Hawaii, so the bribe may well have been made already – and accepted. But if it has, the news has not yet reached the Hawaiians in London. So my company might still have a shot at getting the license. We had one of those feathered statues in our headquarters, so I suggested we present it to Mrs. Dominis, *quid pro quo.*"

"How can you be sure." I asked, "that word of that bribe hasn't reached the Hawaiian delegation here?"

"If Mr. Dominis didn't tell you, then he doesn't know. In any case, I think the statue ought to go back to Hawaii, and my superiors have told me the company doesn't need it. The British Museum has one of its own. So this one might as well return to the people who created it, and Mrs. Dominis surely agrees. Which is why she took it with her when she left here."

Holmes had been listening with all ten fingers making a little tent in front of his face. "Considering how you decline to use her royal name and title, why," he finally asked, "did you offer to help the princess and the king in this way?"

"Mr. Holmes, I'm an American. I have no love for royalty, not even for good-natured, broad-minded monarchs like Kalakaua. But the truth is, if the Reformers ran Hawaii and the license were theirs to offer, they would never give it to Jardine Matheson. They'd go with some American outfit, most likely a pharmaceutical company that would package and stamp their brand on the opium. So this may be my company's last chance to do business in Hawaii."

Holmes made no sign of agreement. Instead, he said, "Suppose the Chinese merchant's bribe *were* offered and accepted. The king could publicly say that, yes, money was paid. But it is an estimated payment of the revenue tax for . . . what? The first year? Two years?"

"Perhaps. But I've met 'His Merrie Majesty'. He enjoys the good life, all right, and he likes being seen as a man-of-the-people. But he's not foolish. He wouldn't want it known that he took a bribe. Look – I'm a company man. My first loyalty is to my firm. When you do business as we do, all over the world, you have to trade fairly with everybody. Jardine Matheson represents the very highest quality opium grown anywhere on earth, and we want to sell our product in every part of every country. The customer could be a king, a president, a duke, a mayor, an alderman – we don't care. Our counterpart in business is whoever signs the contract. In this case, with my deal, everybody wins. Jardine Matheson gets the license. The bird-catcher goes home with the princess. And the king looks like a hero, instead of a crook."

In a hansom on our way to the Midland Grand Hotel, I turned to Holmes and said, "I'm confused. Why did Mr. Dominis think we could help him take the statue without trading it for the license?"

Holmes shrugged and settled back in his seat.

I nudged his arm. "Holmes?"

"My apologies, Watson. I have dealt far too much with international intrigues already, this year. My work on behalf of the Netherland Sumatra Company, bringing Baron Maupertuis to justice, left me totally exhausted. I had to recuperate for two weeks in Lyon!"

"You were, certainly, in poor condition when I found you there."

"I couldn't have returned to London without your help."

"It is my greatest pleasure to do so in any way I can."

"Well, this problem the Hawaiians have brought me – you could certainly have handled it yourself."

"Really?"

"I had expected it to be focused on opium! Seriously, Watson: Does a bribe in a tiny kingdom on the other side of the world really require my attention? I ought not to have taken this case, but it's too late to decline now. We must see where it leads."

We arrived at the *porte cochere* of the Midland Grand, which has St. Pancras Station behind it and King's Cross station across the road from it. When we announced ourselves at the desk, the host told a young man in staff uniform to show us to the Royal Suite. We strode up a grand staircase for two short flights and into a well-lit hallway, where our guide rapped on an ornately carved oaken door.

"Thank Heaven you have come!" Mr. Dominis called before we had even crossed the threshold. "Our Ku is gone!"

From reading *Grimm's Fairy Tales*, or Scott's historical romances, one may imagine that a princess is young, supple, fair of complexion, endowed with long golden tresses, and given to swooning. The Crown Princess Lili'uokalani was none of these. Though shorter than her husband and Holmes, she was as tall as me – taller than most English women. Several newspaper accounts had described her color as "dusky", but she was not black like an African. Her skin's hue was a medium-brown, like that of a violin. Her hair, however, was quite dark and thick. She wore it drawn up, high on her head, and secured with a very large tortoise-shell comb. Wearing a pale green silk gown, and a necklace of large, identical pearls, she cut a very grand, matronly figure, sallying her large frame toward us with a dancer's grace.

Holmes and I were formally introduced and drawn into the suite. Its furnishings were every bit as luxurious as those in Mr. Dunn's hotel but, where his resembled a Pall Mall gentleman's club, the Royal Suite of the Midland Grand was furnished like a Belgravia town house, with chairs and sofas in the style of Louis XVI, wainscot trimmed with gold leaf, tall portraits of monarchs on the walls, and fine china and knickknacks behind glass in vitrine cabinets.

The princess settled into one side of a sofa, after which her husband sat on the opposite side, and we took seats in wing-back chairs across from them. She poured tea out of a silver service on the low, carved mahogany table between us.

"I want you to recover the Ku," she said, evidently disinclined to make small-talk. "John, give them the photograph. That is the image which Mr. Dunn had taken of us yesterday. As you can see, the Ku is about a yard high. It is the stylized image of our ancient war god in a taut, crouching posture, as though about to leap onto an opponent. The facial expression is a bellicose grin, showing great teeth. If the picture could have been made with true colours, you would see that the dark feathers are red, and the lighter feathers yellow."

"Those are the colors of the Hawaiian nobility," Dominis put in. "The feathers come from two of the rarest of our country's jungle fowl."

The princess gave her husband a look very like that employed by wives everywhere when they resent being interrupted. Then she went on, "Rather surprisingly, the box in which it was carried here was not taken."

"Indeed. Show me."

Dominis rose and we followed him into the bedchamber, where a mahogany armoire stood. He opened its doors and brought out a rosewood box about four feet long, three wide, and two deep, with shiny brass hinges. While he held it, Holmes peered with his magnifying lens at all the outside edges, the latch, and each hinge.

"How much does the statue weigh?"

Dominis looked at his wife. "Mr. Dunn told us it weighed sixty-two pounds."

"That's right, John. He said sixty-two."

"Watson, take the box from Mr. Dominis. What do you estimate it weighs?"

To assay its heft, I dandled it, as one might a baby. "Could be two stone or a little more. Twenty-eight? Thirty pounds, maybe? Rosewood is very dense."

I expected Holmes to open the box, but instead he knelt on the floor and examined, through his lens, all of the carpeting in front of the armoire. Then he gestured for me to set down the box. He unfastened the latch, opened and then half-closed the box, and re-opened it, letting the lid rest open, all the way back, before examining the interior.

There was a heap of kapok fibre inside the box that must have been packed around the statuette to cushion it. Holmes removed it, a little at a time, giving attention to almost every clump and strand before letting them fall to the floor. When the box had been emptied he peered inside it, his lens almost touching every board, seam and corner.

"There are no traces of feathers. There must have been some additional protection," he said. "Was it wrapped in fabric of some kind?"

"Yes. A hemp-cloth sack, like a sailor's duffel bag, with hempen twine threaded through the opening, and tied at the top with two overhand knots."

"Mr. Dunn returned it to the sack and tied it up himself."

I could not resist asking, "Did you actually see the statue go into the box? Could it have been closed and latched without the statue inside?"

"No, Dr. Watson. We saw it tied up in the sack and set into the box, and the box closed up tight, before we brought it here."

Holmes nodded. "Did anyone else handle the box *en route*?"

"Certainly!" said the princess, with a stern look that reminded us: Royals do not carry their own baggage. "It was heavy. Two porters at Mr. Dunn's were needed to carry it to our cab. When we arrived here, two of this hotel's porters brought it upstairs for us, and placed it in the armoire."

"When did you notice that the box was empty?"

"Not until I returned from seeing you this morning," Dominis said. "I opened the armoire to hang up my coat, and Lydia – excuse me, my dear – Her Highness asked me to see if standing the box upright had caused the packing material to shift. As soon as I took hold of the box, I wondered why it seemed to weigh so much less than before."

"We opened it, of course," said the princess, "and after recovering from the shock of finding the Ku gone, we replaced the box in the armoire."

"You did not sift through the kapok with your fingers, or – ?"

"Certainly not. It was obvious the Ku was missing. We found the box just as you found it, Mr. Holmes."

We were following them back to the sitting room when there was a knock at the door. Lili'uokalani called, "Enter!"

A young Hawaiian woman opened the door and curtseyed to the Princess. "Queen Kapiolani wishes to know if you are receiving."

The princess exchanged glances with her husband before saying, "Yes."

The youngster, evidently a lady-in-waiting, turned aside, and after a moment Kapiolani entered. She was shorter and a little darker than Lili'uokalani, and even more elegantly attired. Perhaps because she moved slowly and with more deliberation, she seemed much older. [4] Behind her came a large Hawaiian man in a morning suit with a double-breasted waistcoat.

We resumed our seats when the queen settled into a wing chair. She said something in Hawaiian. Dominis responded the same way, and then introduced her to Holmes and me by name. Lili'uokalani had an exchange with her in Hawaiian, but I recognized the words *Westminster* and *Buckingham.*

Turning to us, Lili'uokalani said, "I have told her that you are here to confirm our arrangements for the official Jubilee celebration at Westminster Abbey tomorrow, and the banquet to follow at Buckingham Palace."

Kapiolani addressed us in Hawaiian, which Lili'uokalani translated, "Queen Kapiolani asks if you will be present also?"

"Please tell her," said Holmes, "that we are not invited to such occasions. We are not peers of the realm. We are merely our Queen's factotums."

The princess translated, whereupon Kapiolani gave us a little nod and said "Good afternoon." Then she rose, turned, and walked out the way she had come, trailed by her lady-in-waiting.

Her male companion stayed, however, while we resumed our seats and closed the door behind her. He was taller than all of us, and very thick in the chest and stomach. His hair was black, flecked with gray and cut close to his head, much the way that a soldier's hair is trimmed to accommodate the helmet. He walked closer, but did not sit down, and he stared at us through large brown eyes under thick brows.

Lili'uokalani said, "This is Joseph Iuakea. [5]

He gave a curt nod and said, "When I am in uniform, I serve as Colonel of the Guard to the royal family. Thank you for your assistance." Like the princess, he had an accent unlike any I had ever heard, but his command of the English language was similarly excellent.

"The colonel is a longtime friend of my wife and her brother," Dominis added. "Because the king sent us here without any of the soldiers who would normally protect Their Majesties at home, he delegated Colonel Iuakea to be our guard."

Holmes looked toward the door. "I had hoped to interview the queen."

"You would need us to serve as interpreters," said the princess. "Kapiolani does not speak English. Only Hawaiian."

"Really?" I wondered. "No English? In this day and age?"

Dominis waited a few seconds. "It is her affectation. She knows the formalities, of course – hello, good bye, please and thank you, I'm honored to meet you, and so forth – but she feels she does not need to know more."

"She devotes her energies," said the colonel, "to improving our people's health, by founding hospitals and clinics, and – "

"But," the princess interrupted, "she has no influence beyond her husband's ear, and not always there. Her role in government is entirely ceremonial. So I did not tell her why you are really here."

"I would have told her!" declared the colonel. "John, you did not see me this morning, but I was nearby when you asked the Prince of Wales to suggest someone to consult about resolving the opium license problem."

"My apologies, Joseph. Clearly, we must take you deeper into our confidence."

The princess nodded agreement. "There has been a new and unfortunate development."

Dominis took a minute or so to summarize what had transpired in our flat. He added that we had also spoken with Dunn, and he ended by revealing that the Ku was missing.

Iuakea snorted. "Stolen?"

"Apparently."

I asked, "Did either of you leave this suite between the time you placed the box in the armoire yesterday, and this morning when you found it empty?"

"Of course!" said the princess, with another look of rebuke. "We are obliged to attend various functions every day. Last evening there was a small reception hosted by Mr. James Blaine, the former United States' Secretary of State. The queen, my husband, myself, and the colonel were his guests."

"Just the five of you were present?"

"No. In fact, we were surprised to see that three American men of business were also invited: A Mr. Williams, a Mr. Sexton, and a Mr. Fallsworth. They are the men I told you about this morning, whom we'd met on the ship from New York to Liverpool."

"A photographer was there as well. Remember?" Dominis said. "The same man who had taken our picture at Mr. Dunn's hotel. Apparently, he is very popular with Americans in London. He told us he also served on Mr. Blaine's staff, as the official photographer for the Department of State, when Blaine was Secretary."

"May I see the photographs from the reception?"

"My apologies, Mr. Holmes," said the colonel. "I insisted that no photographs be taken. So he left, taking his camera with him, before we sat down at the table." Turning to the princess, with furrowed brows, he said, "I am still concerned. Why did you not tell Kapiolani of the theft? You told her, yesterday, about accepting the Ku from Jardine Matheson."

The princess responded, "There is no reason to involve her in this new problem until it is resolved. I do not want her to complicate our efforts to recover it."

"But she is your queen!"

"She is my sister-in-law. More to the point, I am heir to the throne, and she is not. So I shall act on the king's behalf, as I see fit, until we return."

"You have always been unkind to her, Lydia."

"Oh, Joseph, she is so frustrating! She imagines, despite all evidence to the contrary, that Hawaii will somehow turn back into the traditional monarchy that it was in our youth. She encourages my brother in his desire to unite all of the Pacific kingdoms into a confederation, with himself as head-of-state! That way, our international statecraft could be conducted in Hawaiian. Not English, mind you. Not even French!"

There was a silent moment, which ended when Holmes asked the princess, "Did you send your husband to me this morning in hopes I could help you take home the statue without giving the license to Jardine Matheson?

"Yes. I would prefer that the license be granted to someone from Hawaii."

"A native Hawaiian?"

"Ideally, yes. Our people need *entrée* to more commercial opportunities."

"Colonel," Holmes asked, "did you know where the statue of the war god was being kept?"

He nodded, then pointed. "He was in that armoire."

"Was it there before you left for the reception?"

"I assume so. But I did not actually see him inside."

"You saw the box it came in?"

Iuakea closed his eyes and took a deep breath, in and out. When he opened his eyes, he spoke slowly. "Ku is not an *it*, Mr. Holmes. Kukailimoku was the guiding deity of our first modern king, Kamehameha the Great. [6] He was inspired by Ku to conquer all the islands of Hawaii and unite them into one kingdom, at the beginning of this century. We are Christians now. But for those of us who are native Hawaiians, Ku is not an artifact of wood and feathers. He is an eternal connection to our ancestors' realm of belief and worship. He may not make us warriors again, but he is central to our history, and our nation's glory."

"I am sure that is so," said Holmes, "but at the moment, we mortals must find your living god's tangible incarnation, so that it – excuse me – so that *he* can return to his rightful place among your people. So I ask you again: Did you see the box?"

"Yes."

"Was it opened after it came here?"

"If so, I was not present."

Holmes nodded, then looked around. "Tell me more about that reception you attended last night."

Dominis replied, "It was in a semi-private room off the lobby of the Great Northern Hotel, beside King's Cross Station. It is so close that we walked."

"How long were you away?"

"We left here just before seven o'clock," said Iuakea. "Supper was served at nine, and we returned here about half-past eleven."

Holmes turned to the princess. "Did any hotel staff come in during the evening, while you were away?"

"They must have done. As we departed, two maids were in the corridor, a few doors along, collecting laundry in a cart. When we returned, our bed-clothes had been turned down. And the shades in the bedchamber windows had been drawn."

"Did you enter this sitting room during the night?"

Dominis shook his head. "We had no need. We did not come into this room until around eight o'clock this morning, when breakfast was to be delivered."

"This is a calamity," said the princess. "By taking the Ku from Mr. Dunn, I committed myself to . . . well, to attempt, at any rate, to persuade my brother to award the opium license to Jardine Matheson. I felt compromised, but surely the Ku must return to Hawaii. Even Mr. Dunn thinks so. But someone evidently intends to sabotage the agreement."

"They could make that photograph public," said her husband, "proving you had accepted his offer. If it then transpired that the Ku had disappeared, they could slander the royal family as careless and unsuited to rule, for having lost it."

"Or worse," said the colonel, "they could declare that Lydia must have sold it to pay her brother David's debts."

"That would be a terrible embarrassment," she said, "and perhaps even fatal to his reign. I cannot return to Hawaii without the Ku."

"It would be best," said Iuakea, "if this affair were not made known to anyone other than ourselves – with the exception, however, of including Her Majesty Kapiolani."

"Please, Joseph," said Dominis. "That is Lydia's decision."

"You would keep her ignorant of something so important?"

The woman glared at him. "We shall tell her of the theft. But only when we, and the Ku, are on a ship bound for home."

"Assuming," Iuakea snarled, "that we get him back."

It was a short walk to the Great Northern Hotel. From the clerk at the reception desk, we learned that Secretary Blaine had been staying there almost a month. Holmes asked if any other Americans happened to be registered. Indeed, these included the three of whom Dominis had told us: Charles Sexton of Chicago, Stephen Fallsworth of San Francisco, and Claude Williams of Indianapolis.

By observing keys in the pigeonholes behind the reception desk, the host determined that Fallsworth and Williams were out, but that Sexton was in. We asked the clerk to telephone him and say we wished to see him.

A porter escorted us past a dining hall with lunch service in progress, a smoking lounge with half-a-dozen leather armchairs, and a small paneled room that was probably where Secretary Blaine's private dinner-party had been held. Today, however, straight-back chairs stood in half-a-dozen rows, and the walls were hung with black crepe, for what was likely to be a funeral or memorial ceremony later in the day. It seemed unusual for such an event to be held in a hotel, and I said so to the porter as we mounted the stairs.

"Yes, sir," he replied. "As I understand it, there was a problem at the location originally scheduled, but this saloon was available."

On the next landing, the porter led us down the hall and announced us through the door.

Charles Sexton was about fifty, short and paunchy, flush of face, prone to squinting, and bald save for a wispy white fringe, much like a monk's tonsure.

"We are inquiring about the reception you attended, last evening," said Holmes, "which was given by your former Secretary of State."

"Please come in and sit, gentlemen," he said. "Would you care for whisky?"

"No, thank you," said Holmes.

Sexton had a room, not a suite, but it had three chairs, and the décor included some rather nice touches: Flocked wallpaper, a four-poster bed with silk curtains, and on the washstand a large basin and ewer of gleaming blue-and-white Delftware.

He nodded as we sat. "That party, huh? Was there more trouble afterward?"

Holmes took hold of this new thread at once. "Considering the aftermath, we would like to know about the trouble itself. How did it begin?"

"Well, uh, we were all pretty chummy at the start. Secretary Blaine, Claude Williams, and I made small-talk with the Hawaiians as soon as they arrived. Steve Fallsworth came in a little later, but he got into the spirit right away, and wound up buttonholing their colonel about a deep-water harbor project in Honolulu. Fallsworth's in shipping."

"So, there were no problems at first?"

"That's right, Doctor. The trouble started with the toasts after supper. I proposed a toast to our president, Grover Cleveland, and we all drank to him. Mr. Dominis – d'you know who he is?"

"Yes," Holmes said. "Were you previously acquainted with the other Americans?"

"We met on the ship. Claude told us that he knew Secretary Blaine, and that he was staying at the Great Northern, so if we checked in here too,

362

we'd have a good chance of meeting him. Well, it's not every day you can get chummy with somebody that high up in the world. With his connections, he might be able to help me in my business – help my company back home in Chicago. We're international brokers for American hemp products.. And I'm sure the other men felt the same way. Sure enough, when Secretary Blaine learned that we'd met the Hawaiian delegation on the ship, he invited us to his party last night."

"A singular honor, surely."

"That's right, Doctor. I saw it as an opportunity to maybe get the Hawaiians to import more rope and cloth. Anyhow, when we finished eating, Mr. Dominis proposed a toast to his absent king. Secretary Blaine, being a diplomat and all, stood up, raised his glass and said 'To King Kalakaua!' I did the same, and so did the Hawaiian colonel, and Steve Fallsworth. The queen and the princess remained seated, of course, but raised their glasses and drank the toast with us. But Claude – Mr. Williams – did not join in. He did something that embarrassed the rest of us. It was downright unkind. Claude stood, lifted his glass, and said, 'To the United States of America, and her Manifest Destiny.' Well, as you may imagine, the royal contingent was not inclined to join in *that* toast! You know about Manifest Destiny, don't you?"

I nodded, but Holmes shook his head and waved his hand in dismissal. He has long been convinced that politics, especially international politics, are irrelevant to his work.

"It's the idea," Sexton explained anyway, and with a hearty pride, "that the United States is divinely inspired to keep expanding to the west. We added territory past the Mississippi River, then past the Rocky Mountains. And it's our God-given destiny to go further, beyond California and into the Pacific, to capture some islands and make them territories. I'm all for it. But I don't bring up the subject when I'm not in the States. My firm does some business in the Pacific – everybody needs rope! – So I was sent around to a bunch of those islands a few years ago, and I can tell you: The Hawaiians, especially their chiefs, are worried about Manifest Destiny. They're convinced that we are actually planning to do that – send Navy gunboats out to Honolulu and take over."

I asked, "Is that likely?"

"The people I do business with in Hawaii would like us to do it. Secretary Blaine thinks we should do it! He told us so before the Hawaiians showed up. But it won't matter to me if we do or don't. I'm just a hemp-broker from Chicago – a middle-man between the American producers of rope and fibre, and the countries that import them."

"What is Mr. Williams's business?" Holmes asked.

"That was a lucky coincidence, meeting him on the ship. Claude's a high-flying drummer, one of the top salesmen for a pharmaceutical company in Indianapolis, Indiana – Eli Lilly, it's called. They make quinine for malaria, which is what Claude sells. Anyhow, like I said, I represent rope and fibre, but my brokerage also has men who handle the oils and medicinal extracts from hemp flowers. So I promised I'd introduce them to Claude, when we get back to America."

"Why did you come to London for the Queen's Jubilee?"

He chuckled. "I didn't even know about it until I got here! I'd been to a hemp-growers' convention in Baltimore, and my next appointment was in Berlin, but not until July. I'd never been to England, so I figured to spend a week here seeing the sights before heading over to Germany. With all this hoopla for the Queen, it's been a lot of fun."

"Are your fellow Americans having fun, too?"

"Maybe. I don't know. They – Well! Look who's here, now."

The hallway door had opened and a tall, fair-haired man entered. He wore a bespoke tweed suit – a Norfolk-style jacket with knickerbocker trousers – and carried a leather dispatch case.

Sexton pointed. "Meet Stephen Fallsworth. His room's just across the hall. Steve, this is Mr. Holmes and Dr. Watson. They're Englishmen, and they're asking about that little kerfuffle last night. Seems Claude may have created an international incident."

"Happy to meet you, gentlemen. Sorry I'm late, Charlie. There are so many people in town for this Jubilee thing! My cab driver had to fight the traffic all the way. Would you mind if I wait in here for a few minutes? That cute little Irish maid is doing my room again. She got the wrong idea, yesterday, when I was watching her make the bed. I don't want her complaining to the management." He set his leather case down on the credenza beside the whisky and glasses and said, "Mind if I help myself?" as he reached for the decanter.

Holmes sprang up from his chair. "Please excuse me, gentlemen. I must send a wire. Mr. Sexton, do you happen to know where the hotel's telegraph desk is located?"

"I do. I had to wire Berlin yesterday. It's in a little alcove off the lobby, to the right as you go downstairs."

"Thank you. Watson, carry on, would you? I'll return in a moment." Holmes whisked himself out.

"Well, well," said Fallsworth, taking a sip and looking straight at me. "The Queen sent a doctor to check up on us! What's the matter? Does she think Americans are sick, just because we don't have the best manners?"

"Oh, no. Nothing like that. Please, tell me about last night. What happened after Mr. Williams made his . . . undiplomatic toast?"

364

Fallsworth exhaled a loud *whoosh* through pursed lips. "I don't like having to apologize on his behalf. I'm an American, and proud of it, but I don't brag about it when I'm over here. Claude, he's a patriot, too, but he just can't keep it to himself when he should. He made the rest of us look like bad apples. Made *me* look bad. And if I look bad, so does my company."

"What is your business, exactly?"

"I'm with a new outfit, the Matson Navigation Company. Just started five years ago. We haul Hawaiian sugar to a refinery in California. But I would never throw that Manifest Destiny stuff into the faces of the most important, highest-ranking ladies in Hawaii. In my business – in anybody's business, really – if you want to make the best deals, you have to be nice to people. You've got to be like-able."

Holmes appeared at the door. There was either a smile or a smirk on his lips but it disappeared quickly as he resumed his seat and said, "My apologies, Mr. Fallsworth. I gather, from what Mr. Sexton told us earlier, that you have business interests in Hawaii."

"Shipping."

"Yes. I wonder: Are any of your business associates connected with Hawaii's so-called Reform Party?"

"Oh, sure. But which party do you mean?"

"Is there more than one?"

He grinned. "There are two factions. The sugar barons are the biggest dogs in the pack, and they're keen to get America to take over the islands. Their word for it is 'annexation'. If that happened – if Hawaii became an American territory – they could get Congress to slap a protective tariff on sugar coming from everywhere else in the world, making it more expensive than Hawaiian sugar. And that would give the Hawaii planters a big advantage in the American market."

"What do you think about Manifest Destiny?"

"I don't think much about it, Doctor. My friends and I in the Reform party, we're . . . neutral on the question of annexation. We don't exactly oppose it, but we feel that things are going along just fine for us the way they are. Let me tell you, Hawaii is a very easy place to do business. The taxes are not oppressive. The people are law-abiding. They don't have race-riots, like in Malaya. Or labor troubles, like America's got. The king enjoys palling around when he's off-duty – drinking, playing cards, making music."

"Is he," I said with a smile, 'like-able'?"

"He is *very* 'like-able'. By me and my friends, anyway. That said, there are some native bigwigs and Chinese merchants in Honolulu who the king has to keep happy. So, okay, they get some of the government contracts that maybe otherwise would go to American businessmen. If American companies had only Americans to deal with, we might take a few bucks more out of Hawaii than we do now. But if you want my opinion, everything could just keep going the way it is, with everybody getting a fair shake. Before dinner, before Claude stirred up trouble last night, I was talking to the princess and her husband, and their – what is he? Their *bodyguard*? Anyhow, I told them just what I'm telling you now. As long as Kalakaua treats us right, my company will treat *him* right."

We took our leave but Holmes stopped at the reception desk, asking to be connected by telephone with Mr. Blaine. "It has come to our attention," he said, "that the royal delegation from Hawaii was upset last evening by remarks made at your table, in your presence, by one of your countrymen. May we speak with you about it?"

Blaine, having served in a high government post, assumed that we had come in some official capacity, charged with reconciling two of Britain's allies with one another, because he immediately said, "Yes. Of course. I would like to help smooth those ruffled feathers. Please come up to my suite."

Holmes always skipped over the columns by foreign correspondents in *The Times*. But I always read them, so I knew who Blaine was, and I thought it expedient to tell Holmes while we were on our way up the stairs. Blaine had been Secretary of State for one year, 1881, under President James Garfield. When Garfield was assassinated, [7] his successor, Rutherford Hayes, replaced Blaine with another man. Blaine was politically ambitious and stood for election himself in 1884, hoping to become president, but he was narrowly defeated by Grover Cleveland.

Blaine greeted us at his door, in the formal attire worn by diplomats all over the world. He was in his late fifties, and his hair and spade-shaped beard were entirely gray, giving him an elder-statesman's mien of sagacity.

The suite was large and comfortably furnished in the modern style, but its windows were the draw. They overlooked the enormous arched train sheds of Kings Cross and the trackage beyond – a commanding view of British railway engineering at its best. No longer representing the American government, Blaine may well have had to pay for his London accommodations with private funds, or from his own pocket, but he surely intended the view from this suite to impress his visitors.

He gave us very firm handshakes, and then gestured for us to sit down. When we'd done so, he proffered a box of cigars, which we accepted.

When our smokes were lit, he said, "I have heard of you, Mr. Holmes. You are famous in this country. So obviously, you have been retained in some official capacity, charged with reconciling two of Britain's allies with one another."

Holmes did not disabuse him of this misconception. Instead, he asked, "What, in your own words, transpired last evening?"

Blaine fitted a tapered cheroot into an amber holder and lit it with a safety match. "You must know that Hawaiians are very 'tetchy' about America's interest in the Pacific."

"What is the American intention toward Hawaii?"

"Free trade. That's what my country has always stood for, beginning a hundred-and-eleven years ago, when we declared our independence from your country. Nothing personal, you understand."

"What Mr. Williams said in his toast," I prompted him, "wasn't 'free trade' but 'Manifest Destiny'. Was that not a taunt?"

"I think his purpose was less to insult the Hawaiians, and more to curry favor with me."

"Had you ever met him before last night?"

"No. We have some mutual friends in the pharmaceutical industries, but . . . from what the other two men said, I gathered that Williams had claimed he knew me. I chose not to contradict that. It seemed a harmless exaggeration. I'm often consulted by my fellow Americans to help them in pursuit of their commercial interests."

"Were you previously acquainted with the queen and the princess?"

"No. But I did once meet Kalakaua. Six years ago. I was Secretary of State when he visited Washington on his voyage around the world. Naturally, I wanted to meet his wife and his sister. And since we're all here for the Jubilee, I held a small reception in their honor."

"Did you know the other Americans?"

"Mr. Sexton was the stranger. I had met Stephen Fallsworth. William Matson, the founder of the Matson Line, introduced us about a year ago."

Holmes nodded. "How strongly do you think Mr. Williams's toast might have aggravated tensions between the United States and the Kingdom of Hawaii?"

Blaine drew deeply from his cheroot and exhaled slowly before responding. "Clearly it did not calm the waters, but neither was it a *casus belli*. I believe that America is destined to expand across the Pacific, and everyone knows that I advocate annexing the Hawaiian Islands. I was replaced as Secretary of State because, among other reasons, President Hayes did *not* wish to make Hawaii a territory. Nor, I might add, does President Cleveland. He favors keeping the monarchy as our trading-partner."

"What if a president were elected who agreed with you?"

He leaned forward. "It could happen. But annexation would have to be done without bloodshed, or we would be condemned for it by every other great nation. We have no desire to dominate the Hawaiian people, but we hope to persuade them that they will have a brighter future under the American umbrella. We can save them from subjugation as a colony by Spain or France or Germany – "

"Or England?"

"Yes, Dr. Watson. England too. We have a doctrine, promulgated by President Monroe more than sixty years ago, that the United States will actively resist any attempt by a European power to exert its influence on the nations of the Western Hemisphere."

"Hawaii is somewhat *west* of the Western Hemisphere," I said.

"Point taken, Doctor." Blaine forced a smile. "But Kalakaua faces a difficult question: How can he sustain Hawaii as an independent country? The reality is that, to survive in the modern world, one must either be a powerful nation or live under the protection of a powerful nation. For Hawaii, the former is impossible, so the latter is Hawaii's only recourse, and I believe its protector should be the United States. To be that, we would need a naval base there, so we would like to lease a sheltered lagoon near Honolulu. We would widen and dredge the opening to the sea, and construct a modern naval coaling station."

"Will the king grant the United States such a lease?"

"It was my intention to engage the queen and the princess on the merits of that proposal last evening. Unfortunately, Mr. Williams made his injudicious toast before I had a chance to explain all the advantages that Hawaii would enjoy as an American territory. Now he has prejudiced them against me."

"Would it help your cause," Holmes asked, "if the monarchy were to be . . . shall we say '*discredited*' in some way?"

Blaine took a long pull on his cheroot, half-closing his eyes when he exhaled. "Kalakaua is well liked, but he is . . . unrealistic. He believes that he ought to be, in so many words, King of the Pacific. He desires that the rulers of Fiji and Samoa join him in a confederation that will resist the efforts of Europe and America to control the ocean. But none of them has any military capability – no navy to speak of – with which to support or enforce such resistance. Hawaii is the largest and most prosperous of those island nations, but it is only barely able to feed its own people. If any of the great powers were to set up a naval blockade and prevent ships from trading with Hawaii, its economy would collapse in less than a year and its monarch would fall with it, so I would prefer that Kalakaua accept the

368

reality of the international forces ranged against him, abdicate, and let us annex the islands."

He had parried Holmes's question. "If he abdicated," I said, "his sister, Lili'uokalani, would become queen. We have met her. I doubt that *she* would willingly abdicate."

"Quite right, Dr. Watson. Only some evidence of . . . shall we say 'gross misconduct' would embarrass her or her brother to such an extent as to compel them to relinquish the throne."

Holmes leaned forward. "Even so, she does not strike me as the sort of woman to meekly acquiesce. On the contrary, she is rather headstrong."

"Indeed she is! She would be a more formidable antagonist to the United States than her fun-loving, spendthrift brother. She is, in many ways, more intelligent than Kalakaua, and undoubtedly sees her country's vulnerability more clearly than he does. I was hoping, by meeting with her in person, that I could prevail upon her to persuade her brother to accept the inevitable. Isn't it obvious that, all over the world, kingdoms are in decline? They will not survive much beyond the end of this century. The age of monarchy has passed."

He looked at his pocket-watch. "I'm sorry, Gentlemen. You will have to excuse me now. I have a visitor coming in a few minutes. He is a diplomat with whom I worked closely when I was Secretary of State. Only last week, his young daughter died of consumption. Her funeral will be held at six this evening, here in the hotel." Stubbing his cheroot into an ashtray and giving a little sigh, he explained. "It was supposed to be held in their home, but the streets in their neighborhood were expectedly closed today for a big Jubilee celebration. Fortunately, this hotel has a saloon available, and I paid the rent on it. It's the least I can do for my friend, at such short notice." He sighed again. "There has always been more to diplomacy than treaties and international intercourse. There must be, underneath it all, collegiality and friendship."

We took our leave. It was already past three o'clock. When we were downstairs, Holmes said we would not need to interview the feckless Claude Williams, so we could return to Baker Street. While I waited outside for a cab to be summoned, Holmes had a private conversation with one of the porters.

"It is astounding how much information one may obtain in return for a shiny new half-sovereign," said Holmes, in the hansom.

"To help him celebrate the Jubilee?"

"Of course." He smiled.

"And . . . ?" I waited. But Holmes sank into one of his deeply thoughtful moods. Absent an emergency, I do not interrupt them.

369

Arriving at our flat, we found that our thermometer's mercury now hovered between eighty-eight and ninety Fahrenheit degrees. When Mrs. Hudson learned we hadn't had luncheon, she brought us a cold joint of mutton with condiments, and steins of beer.

"How do you suppose the statue was removed from the princess's bedchamber?" I asked Holmes.

"It was quite easily accomplished when the royal delegation left for Secretary Blaine's reception."

"And . . . do you know who took it?"

"Of course. Don't you?

"No!"

Holmes sighed. "How long have we known each other, Watson? Over six years, isn't it?"

"Yes,:

"And you have often come along, in the course of pursuing the little problems that are brought to me. You see everything that I see, but you fail to reason from what you see. What was the most salient characteristic of the hemp merchant – the short, balding Mr. Sexton?"

"He . . . squints."

"Very good! And what else is there about his eyes?"

I thought back, picturing his face in my mind. "Now that you mention it, his pupils are quite small. Oh, my word! They are pin-points. He uses opium!"

"You see how easy it is?"

"I don't understand. Did he take the statue?"

"No, no. He is innocent of that. I was merely testing your powers of observation. You did well, but you had to be prompted."

"Thank you. I suppose."

"Did anyone else today exhibit that signifier of opium consumption?"

Again, I tried to visualize our interviews. "None that I recall."

"What do you make of the little bottle from which Dominis needed to sip?"

"He is obviously ill. I'm sure it was medicine, but not laudanum. His eyes were normal. Most likely the bottle holds digitalis, for a weak heart."

"Excellent! What of the other Americans? Are they opium-eaters?"

"I think not."

"Was there anything about them that struck you as suspicious?"

"Such as . . . ?"

"Did you notice Fallsworth's trousers?"

"The shipping agent? His trousers were . . . tweed knickerbockers, matching his jacket. What about them?"

"There were fragments of Kapok fibre on the knees."

"I didn't notice."

"Evidently. There were also fibres of kapok on the carpet in the princess's room. I was, therefore, alert to the possibility that someone might have knelt in them. But neither Dominus nor the colonel had done so, whereas Fallsworth obviously had. He placed the box on the floor before opening it, and when he knelt down to remove the statue some of the packing material fell onto the carpet."

"Why not take box and all?"

"Too heavy. The statue weighs four-stone-six. But with the box, as Dominis said, two porters were needed to carry it."

"Why would he do this? Act against the royal family? He said he is happy with the way his shipping line does business with the king. And that he, personally, is neutral on the question of annexation."

"A man who is neutral may need only a little push to come down on one side or the other. Recall that he also said that his company would earn more money from Hawaii if they could work only with Americans. In any case, I found the statue in his room."

"Oh. So that's where you went."

"Yes. The maid was there, as he said. I told her Fallsworth had asked me to fetch his dispatch case, and she continued to do her work while I searched the room. Sexton had mentioned that Fallsworth came late to the reception. Obviously, stealing the Ku and then dressing for dinner is what delayed him. On his bedside table I saw a copy of the photograph we were shown this morning. And the statue was in a blanket-chest, still secured in its hempen duffel bag."

"How could Fallsworth have carried it, unseen, from the Midland Grand, around the corner and across the street to the Great Northern?"

"I gave the maid one of the Jubilee half-sovereigns and asked whether she had found an extra bedsheet there yesterday. She said that she had, and was surprised to find it bore the laundry-mark of the Midland Grand. Evidently Fallsworth had wrapped the effigy in a sheet he stole from the laundry cart in the corridor outside the Hawaiians' Royal Suite. We may assume that he slung it over his shoulder like a bundle to be laundered, and carried it into the Great Northern through the tradesmen's entrance."

I laughed aloud. "Then let us go steal it back!"

"Alas, we are now known to the hotel staff. If we carried something out that we hadn't brought in with us, we could be questioned."

I pondered the problem for a moment. "Ah! We could do as you did to reveal where Irene Adler hid that photograph of her with the King of Bohemia. We will create a danger from which it must be saved. He will grab it and run outside with it, where we can–"

"No, Watson. Fallsworth does not appear to be a man easily frightened or gulled."

"Then, what do you propose to do?"

"I propose to smoke a pipe – perhaps more than one – of some excellent Balkan tobacco."

I was reviewing my note pages when, to my amazement, Holmes did not finish even his first pipe-full. He leapt from his chair and said, "You have a black suit. Get into it right away."

By the time I came down from my room, dressed as he had asked, Holmes was wearing his own black suit. From the shelf above the hall-tree he grabbed our collapsible opera-hats. Down the stairs we went, out onto the street and, with a wave of his hand to hail it, into a cab. "The Great Northern Hotel, and hurry!"

"Why?" I finally managed to ask.

"We are going to steal back the statue."

"But you said we would be seen."

"And so we shall!"

When the cab pulled up to the hotel, Holmes put on his hat. I did the same, and he advised, "Pull it down as far as you can. Lower your gaze and, whatever you do, do not smile. Follow me."

Holmes set a slow pace, past the reception desk, the dining hall, and the smoking lounge, and stopped at the large public room with its black-crepe hangings. The rows of straight-back chairs were filled, and a man wearing a black armband stood before the mourners reading aloud from *The Book of Common Prayer*. Beside him was a small coffin on a catafalque. Holmes motioned me to step in and stand alongside him in the aisle behind the last row of chairs.

The service continued for ten minutes or so. Another man, and then a woman, delivered short eulogies for the girl who had perished at the tender age of twelve. The last to speak was Secretary Blaine, who praised the courage of the girl's parents in confronting the unbearable loss of a child. Finally, the mourners stood and sang "Rock of Ages, Cleft for Me".

Two men who had been standing on the far side of the room walked to the front. Holmes tugged my sleeve, and we fell into step with them. They looked at us with questioning gazes, but said nothing as we joined them in taking hold of the coffin, lifting it off its catafalque, and hoisting it onto our shoulders.

They led the way out of the room, not through the lobby but through a side-door of the hotel, to the semicircular driveway of the tradesmen's entrance. A hearse stood in readiness.

As we loaded in the coffin, one of the men finally said, with an American accent, "Who are you?" and then to the other man, "Claude, do you know these fellas?"

"Ah," said Holmes to the second man, "You must be Mr. Williams. Sorry we were late. We work for Secretary Blaine. He asked us to ride along to the rendezvous. After the switch, we will take the coffin on to the churchyard. There's so much traffic, with all the celebrations for the Queen's Jubilee. If it becomes necessary, we can walk in front of the hearse to clear the way."

The first man squinted at Holmes. "Blaine never told *us* about anything – "

"You are welcome to go back inside, to confirm it with him."

"We'll do that. Come on, Claude."

As soon as they'd gone, we sprang up onto the driver's bench. Holmes flicked the reins, and the two black horses began to walk, then trot, bearing the hearse out of the driveway and into the Euston Road. We turned south into Judd Street and were soon out of sight from the hotel. When we reached Brunswick Square Gardens, Holmes reined in the horses and we leapt down. I unlatched the hearse's door, and we climbed inside.

"I hope you're right," I said.

"I am certain."

The tiny bell jingled as we lifted the coffin lid, but no child lay inside. Nestled within the white silk padding was a heavy, hempen sack.

Kukailimoku stood on the low table in the Hawaiians' hotel suite. Even to my Western sensibility, this was a compelling icon. The colors of the feathers shone vividly in the gaslight. The white half-shell eyes, with black pearls for pupils, commanded one's attention. And the wide, hideous grin, replete with sharks' teeth, seemed to be shouting a battle-yell at anyone who might contemplate making war against the Hawaiians.

"We most heartily thank you, Mr. Holmes, for recovering our Ku," the princess declared.

"What is your fee for services rendered?" asked Dominis. "We have funds on deposit with the Bank of England. I shall write you a draft."

"You owe me no fee," Holmes said. "But I will accept a pound as reimbursement for my expenses, which were two half-sovereigns."

Incredulity was manifest on their faces, but Holmes waved it away with a smile. "This has been a most singular adventure, utterly different from the mundane problems which so often come to me. And in the general spirit of royal celebrations this month, I am pleased to have prevented what could have been a terrible injustice."

"You have our sincere thanks."

"Thanks are also owing to your Colonel Iuakea, who provided invaluable assistance at a crucial juncture."

The colonel smiled, while the queen's lady-in-waiting translated all this for Kapiolani, who then spoke for a moment.

Lili'uokalani translated: "On behalf of His Majesty Kalakaua, the Queen extends an official invitation to you and Dr. Watson to visit the Kingdom of Hawaii, as their guests."

"Thank you, Your Majesty," I said.

"Yes, thank you," Holmes added. Then he turned to face Lili'uokalani and Dominis. "Now then, you will want to notify Mr. Dunn. Tell him that you are taking your war god back to Hawaii. I believe he made his offer in good faith, and that you should likewise treat it fairly. But you may want to mention that his American photographer evidently made an extra print for Secretary Blaine, who gave it to Stephen Fallsworth when he recruited him to his scheme. Colonel: I assume you recognize the 'pallbearers'?"

"Yes, Mr. Holmes. One was indeed Williams. The other was the American photographer. They remembered me as well, and tried to stop you from taking the hearse. But I held them by their collars until you had driven away."

"Thank you for taking swift and decisive action."

"I don't understand," said Dominis to Iuakea. "How did you come to be there, at that moment?"

"I was doing as Mr. Holmes requested."

"After Dr. Watson and I interviewed Secretary Blaine, I asked a porter to take a note to the colonel, in the Midland Grand."

Iuakea nodded. "Mr. Holmes asked me to station myself beside the tradesmen's entrance to the Great Northern, and intercept Mr. Fallsworth if I should see him carrying a bundle. I waited and waited for him, but he did not appear. That surprised me. But I could not desert my post. I felt that Mr. Holmes would want me to stay on the spot, and be alert to anything suspicious that might arise there."

Lili'uokalani touched his arm. "Thank you, Joseph."

Holmes leaned back in his chair with a smile of satisfaction. "The omnipresence of a photographer at crucial moments these past two days was not likely to be coincidental. We learned that he had worked in Washington for Secretary Blaine, and that, here in London, he was frequently employed by resident and visiting Americans. His sympathies were therefore more likely to be in America's favor than that of the Hawaiians.

"Of the three Americans whom you met aboard ship, only Sexton seemed apolitical. Fallsworth and Williams were well up on the situation

374

confronting your kingdom, and therefore more likely to be engaged than to be mere observers. Once I had established that Fallsworth stole the statue from your suite—"

"What? How?" That was Dominis.

Holmes looked at me. So I said, "Bits of kapok were stuck on his trousers' knees."

"What remained," Holmes went on, "was to prevent him from spiriting your statue away. It seemed likely, from the way Blaine dodged certain questions I posed to him, that he suspected I was aware of the theft. So it was also likely that he would contact Fallsworth as soon as we departed, and tell him to remove it surreptitiously from the hotel. If he had done that, of course, we would never have been able to trace its whereabouts. That's why I asked the Colonel to step across the road from the Midland Grand, and to position himself at the tradesmen's door of the Great Northern. That was the most logical and therefore most likely portal for Fallsworth and the statue to make their exit.

"I must admit I was feeling rather proud of myself for having done that. Watson and I returned to Baker Street, where I fully expected that a note or a wire from the colonel would be waiting."

"Mr. Holmes's note asked me to let him know as soon as I had made the apprehension."

"But no such news arrived. An hour passed, and then another, with no news from the colonel. Surely Blaine and Fallsworth needed to act quickly. So, why had they not?

"I was forced to consider other ways by which the statue could be removed. We had been told that a saloon was rented for a funeral. And Blaine himself told us he'd paid the rent. He couched it as a gesture of friendship, but I realized – almost too late – that such a great distraction provided him with a perfect way to conceal the statue and remove it from the hotel. The porter I talked with had said that, when the coffin was delivered, Blaine had signed for its receipt and taken possession. I didn't have time to send another note to the colonel. I had to take immediate action."

Iuakea nodded. "As soon as I recognized the four pallbearers emerging with the coffin, and heard their short conversation, it was clear to me that I should detain Williams and the photographer, while Mr. Holmes and Dr. Watson made off with the hearse. What the Americans intended to do with our Ku, we can only speculate."

Holmes paused, so I felt comfortable in saying, "I think they had two objectives." Holmes smiled, so I continued, and turned to the women. "Losing your god of war – being seen to have lost it – would be, as you told us, a terrible blow to the prestige of the royal family, and would greatly benefit the opposition. Moreover, the king would have no reason to grant Jardine Matheson the opium license. And that I think, was the other objective: to create an opportunity for the license to go to an American competitor, most likely the pharmaceutical firm that Mr. Williams works for."

Dominis sighed. "It is too late for them. And for Jardine Matheson as well. A cablegram arrived this afternoon. It says that Kalakaua has accepted seventy-one thousand dollars from a Chinatown merchant called Ah Kee, in exchange for which he has awarded Ah Kee the exclusive opium license for Hawaii."

Colonel Iuakea shook his head. "There is no other way to construe that, except as a bribe. More than likely, by now, the Honolulu newspapers have printed the story, and turned public sentiment against His Majesty."

Holmes nodded. "Such things cannot be concealed forever."

"It will not go well for the kingdom," said Dominis. "The Reformers will use the embarrassment over Ah Kee's bribe as a cudgel to force Kalakaua to grant them more power in the government. The best we can hope for is that, by making a great ceremony of bringing the Ku to Mr. Bishop's new museum, we can restore at least some of the people's good will toward their king."

Kapiolani's lady-in-waiting had been translating for her all along, in whispers. Finally, the queen spoke, and Lili'uokalani translated:

"Her Majesty says that, when the scandal has died down, she will counsel Kalakaua to travel to the United States and negotiate a treaty with President Cleveland. She wants that treaty to ensure that America regards Hawaii as a sovereign nation, and that the Americans will respect us, as such, forever."

The others smiled and nodded assent, but I could tell from their faces that they doubted such a treaty could, or would, ever be made.

Postscript

Six years have passed since these events transpired. It is 1893, and I have now produced a coherent tale from my notes. But I must also record that, after Queen Victoria's Jubilee, things did not go well for the Hawaiian nation.

The scandal of the seventy-one-thousand-dollar bribe hung over the king, even after his wife and sister had returned to Hawaii from London. Kalakaua's donation of the Ku, and its prominent display in what is now called the Bishop Museum, did take some of the sting out of the situation.

But the most ardent of the Reformers had gained the upper hand, and the scandal convinced the legislature's neutrals to join their side. They forced Kalakaua to accept a new constitution which they drafted to increase their own power and diminish his. They also forced him to grant the Americans a long-term lease for a naval base in the lagoon that they now call Pearl Harbor.

At the end of 1891, Kalakaua sailed to California, expecting to travel on to Washington and fulfill Kapiolani's desire for negotiating a treaty respecting Hawaiian sovereignty. But he took ill suddenly and died in San Francisco. John Owen Dominis had died earlier that year, leaving his wife not only without a husband but without her closest and most trusted advisor when she ascended to the throne.

As Queen, Lili'uokalani was immediately constrained by what her supporters called the "bayonet constitution" that had been forced on Kalakaua. She drafted a new constitution that would restore much of her authority, and sought support from the royalist legislators, but the Reformers did not want to lose their grip on the country. Backed by an armed contingent of American Marines that surrounded the palace, they demanded her abdication, and to avoid a civil war, she stepped down. The Reformers thereupon proclaimed Hawaii to be a republic, and made one of their party's stalwarts its president.

As I write this, Lili'uokalani herself is in Washington to ask President Cleveland, and friendly senators, to disavow the republic and restore her monarchy.

No one knows what the future holds for that Pacific – in both senses of the word – country. But it is certain that Kukailimoku will never again summon the Hawaiians to make war.

NOTES

1. I am well aware that my fellow Britons have difficulty pronouncing names in foreign tongues. So before I set out to write my account of this adventure, I obtained the assistance of a native gentleman of Hawaii to proofread my spelling and suggest phonetic pronunciations. The Crown Princess Lili'uokalani is called 'Lee-LEE-you-oh-kah-LAH-nee," King Kalakaua is "KAH-LAH-kah-oo-ah", and the Queen, Kapiolani, is "KAH-pee-oh-LAH-nee".

2. As a physician, and a veteran of our Afghan campaigns, I appreciate the analgesic power of opiate medicines for treating wounded men. But I have also seen firsthand the pernicious effect of addiction to those same medicines. And contrary to the view of most British subjects, I consider my country's complicity in foisting opium on China to be a black mark against us, since we have otherwise exerted a civilizing influence around the world.

3. "KOO-kah-ee-lee-MOH-koo"

4. They were not, I later learned, far apart in age. In June of 1887, Lili'uokalani was 49, and Kapiolani 53.

5. "EE-oo-ah-KAY-ah.

6. "kah-MAY-hah-MAY-hah"

7. Two U.S. presidents were shot to death by their own countrymen in less than twenty years! It is no wonder most Europeans are convinced that Americans have an unhealthy affection for firearms, and that they are all too quick on the trigger.

The Atkinson Brothers
Of Trincomalee
by Stephen Gaspar

In the reminiscence of cases involving my friend Sherlock Holmes, I have endeavoured to portray those abilities of observation and analysis for which he has become well-known. "You have seen, but you have not observed," he would sometimes tell me. Holmes had trained himself to closely observe a man's fingernails, coat-sleeves, shirt-cuffs, boots, and trouser-knees. Tattoos, watches, and bootlaces told their own histories. No detail seemed to escape his notice and no detail appeared trivial. The study of foot-steps, tobacco ash, and bicycle tires were of immense help to him in his work. He elevated deduction to an exact science, cold and emotionless.

The majority of the cases I have recorded portray Holmes's successes, rather than his failures. By his own admission he was bested four times, including once by a woman while in the service of the King of Bohemia. He unfortunately failed to protect the life of John Openshaw, nor did Holmes catch his killers. In the case of Grant Monroe and his wife, Holmes drew the wrong conclusion. Though Holmes broke a secret code and caught the killer, he was unable to save the life of his client, Hilton Cubitt. In the cases of Victor Hatherley and Mr. Milas, the criminals escaped. Some cases didn't allow Holmes's powers of logic and deductive reasoning to be utilized. And yet there were other cases where the London consultant could not bring cases to a satisfying conclusion.

One such instance I had not intended to record, for it was one of those affairs where all my friend's skills and abilities were practically useless, and which he admitted later that the case was beyond his ken. But thinking over the incredible drama that unfolded in Baker Street, I decided to record it for the public, as it contains aspects it that make it absolutely unique and inexplicable. And whereas it's true that my friend was often drawn to the unusual, the bizarre, and even the grotesque, I believe that sometimes these cases somehow mysteriously sought out Sherlock Holmes.

It was mid-November, and my wife and I had just finished breakfast when we heard the sharp clang of the bell. The maid shortly brought me a telegram from Holmes and it ran in this way: "*Note well the article in today's paper regarding the murder of Harold Atkinson. This case may interest you.*" I handed the telegram to my wife and picked up the morning paper. I found the article with the lurid headline, *London Businessman Found Murdered*. The story ran thus:

> *Late last evening local businessman Harold Atkinson, of Atkinson Bros. on Wigmore Street, was found fatally stabbed to death in his home in Grosvenor Square. The perpetrator of the crime, a brown-skinned man with no identification, was also found dead at the scene, fatally wounded by the gun still clutched in the hand of Harold Atkinson. Police suspect the unidentified foreigner had broken into Atkinson's home to rob him. Atkinson must have come upon the man, who stabbed the owner of the home before he himself was shot by Atkinson. Readers will remember that Atkinson's partner and brother, Walter Atkinson, was found dead of apparent suicide just two weeks ago.*

I finished reading the article, not at all surprised that this tragedy would be of interest to Holmes, but wondering how, if at all, he was connected to these deaths.

"Are you going to pay a call on your friend?" my wife asked me.

"Not this morning," I replied, as I had a very busy day ahead of me.

The entire matter left my mind as I focused on my work, but by the evening, after my last call, I found myself a block away from my old residence in Baker Street. Despite my fatigue, I decided to make the short detour that took me to the place where I had shared so many interesting and sometimes extraordinary cases with my friend, Sherlock Holmes.

Upon knocking at Number 221, I was greeted by Mrs. Hudson, who appeared genuinely happy to see me again. We spoke for a bit then she indicated that I should go right upstairs. Ascending the steps, the melodious sounds of the violin filled the stairwell. I gave a soft rap upon the door and opened it. The music stopped and Holmes turned to see me.

"My dear Watson, how good of you to come," he said, setting down his instrument and with long strides came across the room to greet me. We shook hands warmly and he motioned me to my old chair.

"Sit down, old fellow, for you look tired," he said. "It cannot be easy having an unruly child under your care."

"And how do you know that?" I asked, slightly amazed.

"Those small teeth marks on the back of your right hand did not come from an adult. Luckily the bite didn't break the skin."

I rubbed my hand, remembering the bite.

"And how is Mrs. Watson?" he asked. "Well, I trust."

"She is very well, and sends her best."

"Splendid. Would you care for a cigar, or there is tobacco in the Persian slipper. Perhaps a drink – you look like you could use one."

It wasn't often I had seen Holmes in such a gracious mood. It told me he was at work again, or perhaps he was glad to have someone in his rooms to talk with.

"Why don't you tell me about this Atkinson story," I said, once I was settled into my old chair with a Cuban cigar in one hand and a whisky-and-soda in the other.

"I assume you read of his murder in the paper," Holmes said.

"Yes, I recall the simple facts stated there. I assume he was your client."

"Not Harold Atkinson, but his brother Neville. The man came to see me just two days ago. Perhaps I should tell the tale from the beginning.

"A few days ago, I received a note from a man who wished to consult with me and that he would come for two o'clock. He arrived at two precisely, a well-dressed young man who couldn't be over five-and-twenty. He is good-looking, and I deduced by his physical appearance and face, deeply browned by the sun, that he had spent most of his life in a tropical climate, from his handshake that he was familiar with hard physical labour, and from the way he spoke that he'd received a good education. He has a colonial accent which I couldn't place, but I decided that he'd spent most or all of his life in some warm southern country. I could also tell from his demeanor that he wished to consult with me regarding something quite serious, for he appeared sombre with worry. He spoke well, but lowly, as if he carried a troubling weight about him. He said his name was Neville Atkinson, and had come to discuss his brother, Harold.

"Harold Atkinson was the owner of Atkinson Brothers, a thriving mercantile store in Wigmore Street. The business was originally started by Harold and his other brother Walter, who died only two weeks ago, of apparent suicide. Walter's life, unfortunately, had been marred by tragedy, as his wife and child were killed in a railway accident in the summer of '84. Do you remember the Bullhouse Bridge accident? That was the one. Their untimely deaths attributed, most thought, to Walter taking his own life.

"Neville said he was very concerned about his only surviving brother, Harold, who, according to Neville, had been acting very strangely of late. Neville attributed his brother's behaviour to the loss of their brother Walter. 'But it is more than that, Mr. Holmes, I'm certain of it,' said the young man urgently. 'There appears to be some dark malevolence hanging about my brother. He is sorely troubled and anxious. Recently, Harold seems suspicious of everyone – even of me sometimes. This behaviour is

381

not so different from what I observed of my brother Walter, shortly before he took his life.'

"'I'm going to need more of your history to get a clear picture on your problem,' I told him. 'Would you be willing to give me a complete understanding of the facts?'

"'Where shall I begin?' he asked.

"'Anywhere you like,' I said.

"He breathed a heavy sigh. 'My brothers and I grew up in the coastal town of Trincomalee on the northeast coast of Ceylon,' he said. 'Trincomalee is like a paradise and has one of the best harbours in the world. Our father, Thomas Atkinson, left England and went to Ceylon as a young man to carve out a life for himself. He landed in Trincomalee just when there began a systematic cultivation of the hill country. He hired workers to help him clear the land, and he started a coffee plantation. He survived the cholera outbreak in 1846, and through family friends a wife was sent to him in 1850. Our mother bore him four sons, all healthy, strapping lads who grew up in the sunshine, exploring the rocky promontories that surrounded the bay, swimming in the ocean, running up and down the endless white sand beaches, and climbing the leaning palm trees along the coast. Our father taught us to work hard on our plantation, but we were always ready for a bit of adventure. We all received our education on the west side of the island in Colombo. When I was away at school, I received word that our oldest brother Chester was killed by an elephant while on a hunting party. He would be the first of the Atkinson brothers to die tragically, Mr. Holmes. Arriving home for Chester's funeral, I was shocked to find out my two remaining brothers, Harold and Walter, had left Ceylon not long before, under mysterious circumstances.'

"'When exactly did your brothers leave the island?' I asked him.

"'That's just the point,' he told me, shaking his head with confusion. 'My parents were very close-mouthed about the entire matter, and wouldn't speak of it. I found this most strange and inexplicable, and I could find no reason for my brothers' absence or my parents' secrecy. At one point my mother implored me not to speak of it or inquire any further.

"'When I completed my schooling, I returned home and began to notice some disquieting behaviour on the plantation. Some of our workers were Sinhalese, but mostly Tamils. I had always gotten along well with the workers. I had grown up working alongside them, but now I began to garner strange looks from some of the men. Some of them would ask about my brothers – where were they, and had I heard from them. Being totally ignorant of any facts, I remained mute.

"'Tragedy struck our family again in November of 1883. I was away from the plantation, and Trincomalee was hit by a terrible monsoon that

382

took the lives of my mother and father. On my return home, I was wracked with grief when I saw their bodies laid out in the caskets that the workers had made by hand. It was only a day or two later that I was grew suspicious of their deaths.'

"'And what did you suspect?' I asked him.

"'The majority of deaths from a monsoon are due to drowning by flood or mudslide, but there was no evidence of either. In my mind, Mr. Holmes, the manner of my parents' death continues to be suspicious. They may have even been murdered!'

"Neville Atkinson had said these words in the gravest manner," Holmes explained. "He was totally sincere and spoke rationally. When I asked whom he suspected may have murdered his parents, he shied away from the question, as if he feared the answer.

"'Imagine my shock and surprise, Mr. Holmes,' he continued, 'when three months after my parents' death, I received a letter with a postmark from England. I suspected it was from a relative of my father or mother, but it was actually from my brothers, Harold and Walter. They had heard through discrete connections about the death of our parents. In the letter, my brothers strongly advised that I should sell the plantation and come and join them in England. The letter intimated that it wasn't safe for me to stay in Ceylon, and that my life was in danger if I didn't leave. The strange missive ended with an urgent plea that I tell no one anything regarding the letter, and that I was to burn it after I read it. I wasn't to reply, but was to make arrangements to leave Ceylon as soon as was humanly possible. The letter also stressed that I was to travel in secret, telling no one I was leaving, and I was to go to Paris.

"'As remarkably puzzling as the message read, I sold the planation very quickly and boarded the first available ship west. I passed through the Suez Canal, into the Mediterranean, and then onto France. Once in Paris, I instantly checked into the Grand Hotel du Louvre under the name of Mr. Blackburn as instructed, and then waited until I received word. This lasted two full days, before there was a knock on my door. Expecting to see at least one of my brothers, I was instead surprised to find a strange man standing outside my hotel door. He was a short, stout Frenchman who said, in his passable English, that he had come to take me to my brothers in London, and that we were to leave immediately. I packed hurriedly and we boarded a train to Calais where we crossed the Channel to Dieppe, then continued on to London. By the time we arrived at our destination, a house in Grosvenor Square, it was dark. The small Frenchman, who had accompanied me from Paris, led me up to the door and knocked. Then he simply turned and walked away. The door opened and standing there were my two brothers, whom I hadn't laid eyes on in over two years. They were both now bearded, but there was no disguising them. We embraced, but somehow it wasn't a totally joyful reunion, for it was marred by the memory of our parents' deaths, and the mysterious circumstances of my coming to London.

"'I was to find out that this was my brother Harold's house. It was very nice from what I could see of it, for there were few lights. I was taken to a room where we sat and talked. Though I pressed them about their strange disappearance from Trincomalee a few years before, neither was willing to discuss it. When I asked about all the secrecy in meeting them, they said it was for the benefit of all three of us, and that this level of secrecy must be maintained.

"'My brothers proceeded to tell me of their success here in London, and that they wished for me to join them in the mercantile business that they had started. They had high hopes and spoke of expanding one day soon, as the business was growing. Harold and Walter spent hours trying to convince me, and, of course I accepted, though I didn't feel totally sanguine about the entire affair, for it was obvious there was something they held back.

"'I told them I had sold the plantation, lock, stock and barrel, and let it be known I was relocating across the island in Colombo. Many of the coffee plantations were experiencing coffee rust which damages the plants, and I'd used that as an excuse to sell. My brothers thought that was a wise and clever thing to have done, being that none of us would ever return to Ceylon. Again I pressed them why this was, but they wouldn't say, only that we would all be happy together in the homeland of our parents. I also told them that they were entitled to their share of our parents' estate, but they would have none of it. I told them I wanted to begin a side business and bring in goods from Ceylon. They thought this a very good idea, save for one thing: Harold and Walter insisted that any dealings with Ceylon should be done using an assumed name. I told them I would, if they wished it, and again I asked them why I needed to take such a precaution. Again they refused to give me an adequate response.

"'Settling into life in London was vastly different to the country of my birth. I hadn't seen a city like London and, whereas it held certain attractions, I couldn't help but miss my home in Trincomalee with its swaying palm trees, the miles of white beaches, and the forests and hills teeming with wildlife. It seemed that I had willingly left paradise for reasons that I didn't fully understand.

"'My brother Harold proposed that I live with him in his house in Grosvenor Square, as he wasn't married with a family like our brother Walter. And so I soon adapted to life in this great city. I began my business importing goods from Ceylon – tea and coffee, sugar and cinnamon,

384

potatoes and coconut oil. My brothers gave me business advice and sold some of the imported goods in their store. Atkinson Brothers was creating a name for itself in London, and we planned on opening other stores. We were together again, as a family should be, and some of the dark shadows of the past were beginning to fade, but unfortunately tragedy struck again. Our brother Walter lost his family in the Bullhouse Bridge rail accident in July of 1884. Walter was almost inconsolable, and it was everything Harlod and I could do to keep him from going mad with grief. We Atkinsons, Mr. Holmes, have had our share of sorrow.

"'What I am going to tell you now, Mr. Holmes, is something that is a part of this mystery, but I haven't been able to get to the heart of it. My brothers had a special bond between them, of which I was not included. They were close in age and I not so much, but I believe it was more than that.

"'Soon after my arrival in London, I noticed my brothers took to speaking together more often in private. At first I allowed them their privacy, but as I began to suspect that their conversations might affect me and our business, I took to listening from another room.

"'One time I overheard Walter plead with Harold to 'Give it back! Just give it back!' though I don't know to what he was referring. I believe Walter said this in more than one conversation, and both times Harold refused the plea. Another time Walter spoke of being watched. Though he couldn't prove it, he was certain someone was following him and watching him. He once uttered that it felt like the hand of doom was closing its grip upon him. Then, less than two weeks ago, our brother Walter took his own life.

"'Neither Harold nor I told the police of Walter's suspicions, and the police ruled it a suicide brought on by grief over the loss of his family.'

"'What do you think, Mr. Atkinson?" I asked him. 'Do you believe your brother took his own life?'

"'I may have thought so at first, Mr. Holmes, but now I'm not sure.'

"'What has occurred to cause you to change your mind?'

"Neville Atkinson hung his head as if deep in thought, then looked up at me, quite forlorn. 'Because, Mr. Holmes,' he said. 'My brother Harold now believes that he too is being watched and followed. He told me that more than once he's seen a brown man watching his house from across the street. He claims he has seen the same man in different parts of the city. Harold is now exhibiting some of the same nervous traits, the same feelings of persecution and dread, as Walter had before he died. But Harold is more combative. "If they want me, let them come!" he says angrily, in fits of rage. He has let me know that he is armed and not afraid, though I believe it is all bravado.'

"He abruptly ended his narrative, and looked at me expectantly. Truly, my dear Watson, I did not know what to make of his strange story, and I told him so.

"'I came to you, Mr. Holmes, for your counsel and advice," he said. 'I need to help my brother. I cannot afford to lose him too!'

"'Surely it is obvious your brother isn't being straightforward and honest with you, Mr. Atkinson. You must discover this secret he is keeping from you. It appears obvious that something momentous took place in Ceylon. This strange, dark man, if he does exist, is probably from there. But what does he want? Why would he kill your brother?'

"Young Atkinson and I spoke a little more, and then he rose, thanked me and left. Two days later his brother was dead."

Holmes paused and I stood to stretch my legs. I walked to the window. It had now grown dark on the streets of London, and the streetlamps were being lit. The mention of Ceylon had made me think of my service in India and Afghanistan. It all felt so far away, not only geographically, but in terms of time as well. It was a different world over there, far removed from England and normality. My mind drifted and I privately reminisced about the 5th Northumberland Fusiliers and the 66th Berkshires. At the Battle of Maiwand we were outnumbered almost ten to one, but unlike Henry V at the Battle of Agincourt, we were not victorious. We lost many good men that hot July day. I barely escaped with my life.

Holmes had also risen from his chair. He stood by the mantel, stuffing his pipe thoughtfully.

"I am glad you were not among the Last Eleven, my dear Watson, or we should never have had the opportunity to meet one another," Holmes said.

"Yes," I said. "I was now just thinking . . . I say Holmes, how did you know I was thinking of Afghanistan?"

Holmes smiled. "It is gratifying to know that I can still surprise you. You are surprised, aren't you?"

"Yes, of course. But how could you know what I was thinking?"

"While looking out the window I saw you donned a thoughtful, melancholy look. Your gaze stole to the wall where your Gurkha and Kukri, weapons you brought back from the east, used to hang. You were thinking of your military service. You then touched the wound you received at Maiwand. Your eyes watered slightly and you thought of the loss of your comrades that day, and very likely recalled the Last Eleven who made their valiant last stand."

"You are entirely right, of course," I said. "But let us return to the Atkinson case. How did you decide that Harold Atkinson had been murdered – the newspaper?"

Holmes shook his head. "I was sent a telegram late last night to come to the Atkinson house in Westminster. Inspector Gregson was in charge of the case and already on the scene when I arrived. He allowed me to view the murder tableau. From the positioning of the bodies and locations of the wounds, I was able to reconstruct the murder. The intruder, very likely the brown-skinned man Harold Atkinson that had seen previously, was able to gain entry and was confronted by the owner of the house, who had been working at his desk in his study. Harold Atkinson was armed with a Webley revolver. The intruder, armed only with a knife, stabbed Atkinson, who in turn shot the man. They both died of their wounds. Neville Atkinson, sleeping in his room, heard the gunshot and hurried downstairs. He found his brother, mortally wounded, lying on the floor. He knelt down close and found him upon the verge of death. According to Neville Atkinson, his brother looked at him and said something about being 'safe', which the younger Atkinson took to mean that he was safe now, or would be safe. Grief-stricken, Neville could not be certain precisely what his brother's dying words were, or exactly what they meant, for he was overcome with anguish. His brother died in his arms, and a short time later he sent for the police – and for me."

"A most strange set of circumstances," I said.

"Most foul, strange, and unnatural."

"Do you have any clue what it is all about?"

"The knife used in the murder may give us some clue," Holmes said. "It is a singular dagger, with markings on the blade and carvings in the handle. It is a weapon that you yourself might recognize. It was a *pihkā-kaetta*."

"It means '*billhook knife*'", I responded. "It is used by the Sinhalese. Whatever this bad business is, it has its roots in Ceylon."

"So I see it," said Holmes. "Something dramatic took place there while Neville Atkinson was away at school. His two brothers did something, or said something that put their lives in such danger, that they felt the need to flee their home and that entire part of the world. Despite Harold Atkinson's last words, I do not believe young Mr. Neville is safe."

Just then, as if on cue, the door opened and there in the aperture stood a young man. He stood for a moment in the shadow. Holmes and I sprang from our seats.

"Neville Atkinson," I heard Holmes whisper.

Though it was a cool November evening, the man wore no overcoat and no hat. He carried in his hand a small leather grip no bigger than my doctor's bag. Holmes crossed the room and addressed him.

"Do come in, Mr. Atkinson. May I take your case?" Holmes reached for the bag, but Atkinson clutched it closer to him. Holmes took the man by the arm and walked him to a chair. The man sat mechanically, saying not a word. Holmes went to the sideboard, poured some whisky-and-water into a glass, and handed it to the young man, who took and held it. "Drink," Holmes urged. Slowly Atkinson raised the glass to his lip and drank. Holmes took it from him and set it down.

By the light of the lamp on the table, I could study Neville Atkinson a bit closer. He was a handsome fellow, with dark features made even darker by his mood. His brown eyes were heavily lidded, as if he hadn't slept for days, and it appeared he had paid little attention to his toilet and dress. All the time he didn't let go of the small leather grip which he now kept in his lap.

Holmes introduced us, but the man barely acknowledged my presence.

"Harold told me what occurred in Ceylon," the man said. His voice was low and he spoke slowly as if he were half asleep. "Last night – an hour or so before he died."

"When did he tell you?" Holmes asked.

"Last night I pressed him and he finally acquiesced."

"Are you willing to tell us?"

The young man nodded. "What I relate to you gentlemen now is from the tale told to me by my brother just last night, shortly before his death.

"When we were boys, we sometimes took time off from working on the plantation, and would spend our afternoons on the beaches of Trincomalee. We would climb the leaning palm trees, swim in the ocean, and explore Kona-ma-malai, a rocky cliff that drops four-hundred feet into the sea. A permanent resident of the beach was Old Cuthbert, a reprobate who claimed he fought in the Crimean War. Mostly he would tell war stories to anyone foolish enough to give him a few rupees, and for free he would regale us boys with tales of the Dutch and Portuguese influence on Ceylon. He told tall tales of untold wealth hidden in the deep forests.

"While I was away at school, Harold and Walter took to seeing Old Cuthbert again. They gave him the attention he craved, and sometimes shared a bottle with him. They asked him about all the stories he told us when we were children. Were any of these stories true? Cuthbert looked at them insulted. 'They were all true!' he said. What about the hidden treasure in the forest? Again he looked affronted. 'Give me paper and a pencil!' he demanded. These were given to him and Cuthbert proceeded to draw them a map. 'Beginning with the Mahaweli Ganga that empties into the Bay of Bengal, follow the river as it winds its way south. After about two or three days of paddling, begin to look for a tall rock angled at its peak that rises on the right bank.' From there they were to leave their boat and head west into the interior. After a few days they would see another rock formation, this one much larger rising in the forest. A tall rock promontory in the middle of a jungle forest with a human face carved on two sides. Atop the rock is an ancient temple containing treasures of untold wealth. My brothers looked doubtful. Cuthbert's face grew oppressively sombre. 'It's there, laddies – I've seen it!' he whispered. Why hadn't Cuthbert or anyone else taken the treasure, they asked him. The old man donned a countenance of fear and dread. 'Because it's cursed!" he said.

"My brothers thought little more of his story, but as days went by, they started to plan a boat trip up the Mahaweli Ganga. They rented a wooden canoe and stocked it with food and supplies. Harold and Walter told our parents they would be gone for a few days on a river excursion. They paddled up the Mahaweli, often signaling to native boats on the river. After a day they saw no one, and as they headed further into the interior, they began to feel alone save for the magpies, drongos, and ducks that flew overhead. Tree ferns, jak trees, and orchids lined the riverbanks. They had to be mindful of viperous snakes such as the pala polonga hanging from low-hanging branches. From the dense forest came the haunting cries of peafowl, and the trumpeting blasts of elephants.

"For three days they paddled up the winding river, keeping close watch on the right bank. Finally, rising above the treeline they saw it, a tall rock with a slanted peak. They steered the craft to the shore and packed their gear on their backs. It became an arduous hike through the forests of ebony, satinwood, and teak. Traversing westward for almost an entire day, as they were instructed, but found nothing but jungle forest. They considered turning back but it was late in the day, and decided to move forward until night and make camp. In the morning they would decide what to do. Exhausted, they bedded down by their small campfire. Harold couldn't sleep, for he had such dreams of discovering long lost wealth that it was repugnant to him to return home empty-handed. He lay on his back looking up at the stars in the night sky. He turned to lie on his side, facing the fire. Stealthily a leopard had wandered into their camp. It stood still, ten feet away from him. They stared at one another for a long moment. The man wondered what the big jungle cat would do. The leopard wondered what the man would do. Then without any provocation, the lithe creature stole from the camp as quietly as it came in.

"In the morning, my two brothers rose from their bedrolls, stood, and stretched as the first rays of the sun cast shadows on their camp. They looked about. It had been quite dark when they arrived at this spot, and they had far to venture for firewood. Now Walter stood mute, staring up past his brother. Harold turned and followed his gaze. There, standing tall, was a rock promontory with what looked like a human face carved into it, just like the one that Old Cuthbert had described.

"The rock jutted out of the earth and must have stood over five-hundred feet high. According to Cuthbert, an ancient temple stood atop the rock. Fortunately, my brothers had prepared for this eventuality and they broke out their climbing gear and great lengths of rope. Much of the rock's surface was smooth, worn by countless centuries of wind and rain, so climbing would be difficult. They were, of course, determined, and clefts and handholds were found, and with great persistence the healthy young men ascended little by little until they came to the top.

"Disappointment lay heavily on their faces when they discovered that the temple at the top of the promontory lay bare and empty. They looked at one another as if to say, 'What do we do now?' Harold was driven to cursing and threatening Old Cuthbert's life. Walter remained calm, choosing to explore the very edges of the hilltop. He looked around to the surrounding areas and down the rock-face. Then he called out to Harold and motioned over to where he stood on the very edge. Harold stormed over to him, and Walter pointed down the east face of the promontory. There, about thirty feet from the top, was what looked like an opening, which was hidden from below, but now could be seen. If it were a cave, then perhaps the treasure lay hidden within.

"The two brothers gathered up their rope, and it was determined that Harold would be lowered down, while Walter anchored him. Harold edged his way down the sheer rock face. The morning sun beat down on him, as his muscles strained. He lowered himself onto the mouth of the cave that stuck out only a few inches. Relieved to be on solid footing again, he called out to Walter. He then stepped into the cave, wide but with a low ceiling, causing him to stoop. Morning sunlight entered the opening, and he stepped toward the rear of the cave, where a crude altar had been carved out of solid rock. He wondered how old this primitive temple was. What ancient race had first set foot in it?

"At the foot of the altar lay an intricately carved box or chest made of satinwood and ebony. Nervously and with heightened anticipation, Harold opened the lid to reveal its contents. There, his wide eyes beheld an incredible assortment of precious stones: Glimmering purple sapphires and amethysts, sparkling blue topazes, and blood-red rubies. Surely this was a king's ransom, perhaps all collected over centuries from the gem fields of Ceylon. Harold ran his hands caressingly over the stones. He wanted to cry out in triumph, but thought better of it, as this was a sacred place, and he didn't wish to bring down the wrath of an ancient pagan god.

"He carried the chest to the mouth of the cave and the gems gleamed brilliantly in the morning sun. He closed the lid, secured the box to the rope, and called for Walter to haul it up, which he did. While he waited, Harold went back into the cave to see if he had missed anything. There at the back of the altar, sitting in a niche cut out of the cave wall, was a figure. He hadn't noticed it before as it sat in the shadows. Harold drew the figure out and held it in his hands. It was the figure of a woman's head, her eyes closed, her thick lips poised in a slight smile. An ornate crown encircled the head. It too, Harold thought, was ancient, but what made it truly remarkable was that it was made of solid gold. It was somewhat bigger than a man's fist. As he stared at it, it seemed to stare back, and Harold Atkinson was enamoured with it. He hid it in his canvas satchel worn around his neck. The climb to the crest seemed effortless, as he felt buoyed and filled with energy, and when he stood atop the mount, the two brothers embraced and laughed at the treasure chest.

"As much as they wished to stand high above the ground and celebrate, they climbed down with their newfound riches. Upon reaching the ground, they broke camp, packed up only what they needed, and began the trek west for the river. They moved faster on the way back. Reaching the Mahaweli Ganga, they loaded their craft and were just about to shove off when Harold stopped and looked intently at his brother.

"'What is it?" Walter asked.

"'We can't go back to Trincomalee,' Harold said, ominously. 'We can't remain in Ceylon. We cannot explain these jewels. We cannot sell them in this country. Someone will know. Someone will figure it out and discover what we've done.'

"Walter was about to argue this point, but then instantly saw the logic behind the reasoning. 'What should we do?' he asked. Harold looked upriver and said they should head southwest until they reached Colombo and take the first ocean-going vessel. They didn't consider where they should go until the long cross-country journey from one river to another, until finally the Kelani Ganga brought them to the city. Once there, they took the first oceangoing ship out that was bound for Europe.

"Arriving there, they decided to sell some of the gems in different cities before deciding to settle in our parents' mother country of England. Harold kept the golden statue secret from Walter, who only learned about it two years later. They used their ill-gotten gains to start a business, but Harold never sold the golden idol. That he would keep locked up in his home.

"Harold told me all this the night before he was killed. He never revealed to me where he kept the golden statue, but I figured it out."

"How?" Holmes asked.

Neville Atkinson looked at my friend for an intense moment. "His dying words."

Holmes nodded. "Safe."

"Harold kept a safe in his room. I didn't know the combination, but I spent the entire evening trying numbers. Finally, I used our mother's birthday. I opened the safe, and along with documents and money, there it was." He reached into the grip that sat on his lap. From inside he extracted a magnificent golden idol. "I believe this is the source of the tragic death of my entire family. None of the deaths were accidents. My family was killed because my two brothers stole the idol and the precious gems."

"Are you speaking of a curse, Mr. Atkinson?" Holmes asked.

"Not precisely. I believe human agents killed each one of my family. After Harold and Walter fled Ceylon, word soon got out. Some primitive network of communication was set in motion, and word spread. Somehow, they knew their temple had been plundered, and by who. My family was questioned, but they knew nothing. They killed my brother Chester first. He was killed on a hunt, but he was the hunted. Then they killed my parents during the monsoon. They might have killed me if I hadn't fled Ceylon when I did. The rail accident that killed my brother's family may have been an accident, I don't know, but I don't believe that Walter hanged himself. It has all been done discreetly, without clues or witnesses. Only in my brother Harold's death was the murderer discovered. But you don't know Ceylon, gentlemen. It is an ancient place whose history and customs and religions stretch back countless centuries. This hill-top temple is older than Buddhism or Hinduism. This ancient sect is perhaps countless thousands of years old. I know that they will never rest until they retrieve what is theirs."

"What do you plan to do now?" I asked him.

"I'm going to take this back to Ceylon – not because I fear for my life, for I believe life holds nothing for me now. I'm going to return the idol because it doesn't belong to anyone but them, some ancient order, some unknown sect. The brig *Eastern Star* sets out for Ceylon in two days. I plan to be on it with this." He indicated the idol, which he put back in his bag.

"Goodnight, gentlemen," he said. He shook our hands weakly, as if his strength was waning. "Thank you, Mr. Holmes."

"I only wish I could have been more help," Holmes said. "Mr. Atkinson, I would appreciate it if you would write and let us know how things turn out."

"Yes, of course," he uttered, and he left us.

The two of us remained silent for many minutes. Holmes picked up his pipe and recharged it.

"A strange and bizarre tale," I finally said, breaking the silence. "How do you explain it all?"

"More things in heaven and earth," he said.

"What was that?"

"My dear fellow, have I not said that life is infinitely stranger than anything the mind of man can invent. I have made a career of finding out things that others cannot fathom. But this? What am I to make of this? The world of London is my milieu, the study of the criminal classes my *métier*. But how do I explain this? There would appear to be more than simply a human factor here. But what? How do I make sense of it all? There must be an answer, there must! Truly, I find it difficult to admit that I'm baffled – it is beyond my ken."

I could see that Holmes was rather upset, and I attempted to give him some solace.

"It would be the height of arrogance to think we can know or come to understand everything. It's a large world with different ways. We believe we live in a modern, civilized society, and to some extent we do. But there are things in this world beyond our hope of understanding. I have been to the East. It is a different world out there, a world of wonder and awe. Ceylon is an ancient country. Who knows what past cultures existed there? Perhaps the Atkinson brothers delved into something they had no right to disturb. Perhaps it was their greed that set unknown forces in motion, and they paid the price for their actions. We should all be aware that our actions, either for good or evil, have consequences in this world. Who is to say what is just?"

Holmes looked at me and smiled. "Why, Watson, you are a philosopher."

"No," I said, "just a tired doctor who needs to go home to sleep."

"Perhaps there will always be things unknown to us," Holmes said resignedly.

"Good night, Holmes," I said, rising from my chair.

"Good night, my friend."

That night I slept soundly and did not dream of Ceylon, or ancient treasure, or strange deaths. In the morning, the story told by Neville Atkinson seemed like a dream that becomes more unclear as days pass. Admittedly, I had forgotten the entire matter until three or four weeks later when I was sitting with my wife at breakfast. There was a pull at the bell, followed shortly with the maid bringing me a telegram. It was from Sherlock Holmes. Its cryptic message was brief: "*The fate of the* Eastern Star". I searched my memory and recalled that the *Eastern Star* was the ship Neville Atkinson was to take to Ceylon.

I picked up *The Morning Post* and quickly scanned the news items. There, on one of the inside pages was this story:

It is with sadness that we report that the Eastern Star, *a full-rigged brig bound for Ceylon, sank in the Arabian Sea. No reports have yet come in to verify under what circumstances the tragedy occurred. At this time, we are unable to print any details, except that there were no survivors.*

The Switched String
by Chris Chan

"There are some intriguing potential crimes in the newspaper, Holmes."

I had expected him to reply with a nonplussed "*Potential* crimes? What do you mean by that?" Instead, he remained completely focused on playing his violin. I cleared my throat a couple of times, trying to catch his attention, but he continued to play a complex and fast-paced piece for the next three minutes. When he finally lowered his bow with a flourish, he turned to me and said, "Indeed. I counted no less than sixteen likely crimes that might take place in the coming week."

I had only discovered three, but I was reluctant to reveal this fact. "There's a new exhibition of Vermeer paintings at a local gallery," I replied, "which might lead to a potential theft. I see there's a report of a gang of anarchists that are targeting prominent manor houses for arson. And there's that ambassador from Eastern Europe who is making a speech tomorrow. He's considered very controversial, and there are rumors that he's been targeted for an assassination."

"Quite right. Of course, you've overlooked how a construction project might provide cover for robbing a local bank, and the wedding announcement for a terminally ill duke to a woman forty years his junior. His nephew, who is currently the heir to the title, certainly has a motive to see his uncle pass before he can sire a son. A seemingly benevolent charity that on closer examination appears to be a confidence scheme . . . ." Holmes continued for several minutes, leaving me feeling like I'd been out in the sun for far too long. No one has a better premonition of impending crime than he.

Once he finished his lengthy list of potential lawbreaking, there was a twinkle in his eye that forewarned me that he was about to issue a challenge that I had little chance of passing. "If you'll allow me to change the subject, did you notice anything amiss with my violin playing just now?"

I thought for a moment. "I don't believe so. You sounded just like you normally do."

"Nothing amiss or discordant?"

"I said that your playing sounded normal to me."

"Hmm. I suppose that I have an advantage on you, as I was able to use not just my hearing abilities to identify the problem, but my powers of sight as well. Observe the '*A*' string here."

"What of it?"

"Examine it, dear fellow. What differentiates it from the other strings?"

At first I saw nothing, but then Holmes tilted the violin very slightly, allowing the light to reflect off of the strings. "That '*A*' string . . . it's a slightly different color from the others, isn't it?"

"It is indeed! What else?"

I took the violin from him and scrutinized it more thoroughly. "It's rather hard to tell using just my vision, but doesn't that string look a tiny bit thinner that the others?"

"Most certainly, my friend! Also – " Holmes extended a finger and tapped the string in question. "If you will use your sense of touch, you will note that it is decidedly less supple than the other strings." I ran my fingers lightly over the strings and confirmed that this was indeed the case.

"My ears are not so trained and musical as yours are. How does the quality of this string compare to the others?"

"It is decidedly inferior. The pitch is off, and any note played in this string lacks resonance. It is a cheap string, the kind no one with any appreciation for music or pride in performance would use. Young children might use strings like this when they are learning how to play for the first time, when they need to learn technique."

"Then you would never place a string like this on your violin."

"It would be akin to slapping Stradivarius across the face."

"Then how did it get there?"

"Ah! That is the question I've been asking myself for the last several minutes."

"What are your theories?"

"The first question centers around opportunity. Who had the chance to defile my instrument in this manner? I know that I had nothing to do with it. The violin's strings were perfectly fine yesterday. We have had no clients visiting our rooms in the past twenty-four hours. There is only one other man with access to this violin. His motive? Perhaps he wished to play some sort of practical joke, or perhaps he sought to provide me with an unexpected and irresistible puzzle?"

There was a twinkle in Holmes's eye, but I felt no merriment whatsoever. "I can assure you that I had nothing to do with changing the string on your violin."

"Are you certain of that?"

"I am not in the habit of damaging musical instruments in my sleep."

"No, you are not. I realized that you had nothing to do with this as soon as I saw your facial expressions when I queried you about the string. But if you are not responsible, then that means that someone else must have done this. So who had the opportunity? Could someone have crept into our rooms while we slept? It's possible. I didn't lock my violin away, and door locks can be picked."

"It would have had to be an outsider. Mrs. Hudson would never do anything like this."

"I agree, but I think we should question her. Remember, we went out to dinner at Simpson's last night. We were gone for over two hours, so it's possible that someone could have crept inside without our knowledge – but that means that someone would have had to come inside without Mrs. Hudson observing him as well."

Holmes summoned her, and she confirmed his conclusion that she knew nothing about what had happened to his violin. When asked if anybody had been inside 221b while we were gone, she replied in the negative.

"At least, not as far as I know," she added. "I wasn't here all evening. Around half-past-seven, a neighbor down the street came to me for help. Someone had smashed two of her windows and she needed help cleaning up the shattered glass in her living room."

"How far away was this?" Holmes looked interested.

"Just three houses down, sir. Mrs. Ardor's been a friend of mine for years, but I don't think that you know her."

"Did you find any stones or bricks in the house? If I could examine them . . . ."

"We found nothing like that, Mr. Holmes."

Disappointed, he muttered, "Perhaps they struck the windows with a cane or something like that so as to leave fewer clues behind." Raising his voice, he asked, "Can you describe Mrs. Ardor?"

"About my age, sir, though her eyesight isn't good, and her rheumatism means it's difficult for her to sweep up a mess. That's why she needed to call on me for assistance. I also helped her cover up the broken windows with some cloths, as a glazier couldn't come until the morning. Luckily it was a warm night."

"Does she have any other friends nearby?"

"Not to my knowledge. She doesn't get out much, and she's on a very limited income, living off her late husband's pension. She didn't have enough to cover the cost of replacing the glass, so I had to lend her a wee bit of my housekeeping money to pay the bill."

"So if someone damaged her home, she would almost certainly come to you for assistance," Holmes mused. "When did you return?"

"Not for over an hour. Perhaps twenty minutes to nine."

"Seventy minutes. More than enough time to perform this act of vandalism."

"Not really vandalism, is it?" I questioned. "After all, it's easily fixed."

"Yes, and once again, the question is 'Why?' What could be gained by this? Why go to the trouble of damaging our neighbor's home just to lure Mrs. Hudson away? If this was a practical joke, why arrange it in a way that no one could see my reaction save you, Watson?"

"It's not like you were planning to perform at the Royal Albert Hall."

"Exactly. I can see no other acts of disruption around our rooms. This is such a tiny thing . . . ."

After a few minutes of silence, I asked, "Whatever happened to the original string?"

"An excellent question. It had no particular value. No one would have any reason to steal it."

The three of us searched our rooms for the missing string. The hunt only lasted for three minutes before Mrs. Hudson discovered it in the wastepaper basket.

"Hmm!" Holmes studied the string, which had been coiled up into a little ring. "It's been cut. Too damaged to restring. Yet as it was left behind, then the goal was to affect the violin rather than gain access to the string itself."

"If someone had theft in mind, why not take the whole violin?" I asked. "After all, it's quite valuable, even if you did purchase it for a fraction of what it's worth."

"Precisely." Holmes picked up his violin and examined it further. "I wondered if someone tried to hide something inside the holes, but I can see nothing, and light shaking provides no sounds. No, I don't believe that someone removed the string in order to facilitate the insertion of some unknown object into this violin." Holmes gently laid down his instrument and then began examining the lock to the door. "There are some new scratches – faint but clear. I think it's reasonable to conclude that someone skilled at picking locks was here. And . . . ." He hurried downstairs and examined the front door. "Yes, there are similar marks around the keyhole," he reported when he returned. "We can now confirm that someone was here last night while we were all away, and that someone has a good deal of training in housebreaking. An amateur would have left clearer traces of his entrance – as well as of his exit when he re-locked the door, for that matter."

"Unfortunately, we know absolutely nothing about him."

"Not quite. We know that he has large, nimble hands, is probably reasonably young and healthy, is musically inclined, and is carrying a handkerchief with cream-colored smears on it."

I balked at asking the question Holmes wished me to ask, "How could you possibly know that?" before succumbing to the inevitable and inquiring.

"Remember the original string we found in the wastepaper basket? Most likely he wrapped it around his finger several times to form the ring we found. Given the size of the circlet, he must have rather large hands. Yet they must be quick and nimble, given the dexterity needed to pick some high-quality locks and restring an instrument. Obviously no arthritis has set in yet.

"Additionally, he had to have smashed our neighbor's windows and hurried away sufficiently swiftly so as not to be noticed by other people on the street, again indicating a younger man in athletic condition. He was able to unstring and restring my violin without much difficulty. While the replacement string is of a markedly inferior grade, I couldn't have attached it to my instrument better myself. It takes practice to develop this skill, especially when one considers that under the best circumstances, one should not have to replace violin strings too frequently."

"So he's both a trained lockpicker and a violinist?"

"We can proceed under that assumption."

"And the stained handkerchief?"

"The smears are violin polish. I applied a thin coating of it before dinner last night when I had finished playing. I noticed no finger-marks or other signs of disturbance to the veneer before I began playing. Tying a string to a violin is difficult enough with bare hands, it is far more challenging when gloves are worn. The culprit almost certainly touched this instrument with bare hands, and then wiped it down, almost certainly with a handkerchief, thereby removing both any finger-marks and most of the new polish as well. I shall need to polish it again. I rather resent having my possessions handled by an intruder."

I had almost forgotten that Mrs. Hudson was still there when she asked, "Are you sure that the violin is the only item that was touched, Mr. Holmes?"

"My initial cursory examination of our rooms has revealed nothing out of order, but it's quite possible that something equally subtle has occurred." With that, the three of us began a closer, more detailed examination of our possessions. Mrs. Hudson carefully flipped through every book on the shelves, checking for torn-out pages or scribbled messages. I scrutinized our furniture and found nothing amiss. Holmes was the most active of all of us, darting from corner to corner, sniffing his laboratory equipment, pulling each cigar out of the coal-scuttle and examining it, rifling through his files, shaking out the curtains, and otherwise darting around with remarkable energy.

Fifteen minutes into our search, there was a knock at the front door. Mrs. Hudson went down, and a young man handed her a telegram. When she returned and tried to give it to Holmes, he tossed it onto a side table without even glancing at it and continued to hold his pipe-tobacco up to the light, sifting it through his fingers.

Hours passed, and I eventually became convinced that we had confirmed that every carpet fiber and floor nail was exactly where it should be. Mrs. Hudson was compelled to go to bed shortly after midnight, and I reached the point of total exhaustion a bit before three in the morning. Holmes showed no signs of weariness, and continued to give our rooms the fullest possible scrutiny. He pored through his massive index, checking to see if any of his records were added to, altered, or removed. He sifted through every article of clothing he owned, including his substantial collection of disguises, examining everything minutely for added or removed buttons, items sewn into the lining, holes, or stains. All of his chemistry supplies were tested to make sure that they hadn't been tainted, as was his stage makeup. Even mementos from previous cases were checked from every angle under a magnifying glass to see if they had been damaged in any way. Naturally, this painstaking search took a very long time, and several hours later, when Mrs. Hudson brought in breakfast, I realized that he hadn't slept at all that night.

"Did you discover anything?"

"Nothing. I had wondered if an inferior cigarette might have been slipped into a box, or if a bottle of one of my chemistry supplies had been emptied and refilled with flour, but as far as I can tell, the violin string is the only item that is amiss."

"And you're quite sure that there's no one who would perform this sort of practical joke on you?"

"In all the time that you've known me, have you ever suspected that I'm the sort of person who cavorts with merry pranksters?"

"But what possible motive could anybody have for this?"

"Are you doubting that it happened?"

"No. I know that somebody replaced your violin string. I saw the false string. The original was rolled up and deposited in the wastepaper basket. That is undeniable. It wasn't you. I had nothing to do with it, and Mrs. Hudson would never had done anything like that in a thousand years. But the chain of events, while I do not doubt it happened, still beggars belief. Think about it: Someone waits until we have left 221b. That person then breaks our neighbor's windows and runs away. The vandal knew that our neighbor would walk to 221b and ask Mrs. Hudson for help cleaning up the broken glass, knowing that she'd be gone for the better part of an hour. The culprit hides in a place where he can watch our neighbor walk to 221, and soon after Mrs. Hudson leaves, he rushes to the front door and carefully unlocks it, being able to do so sufficiently quickly to not draw any attention."

I paused and reflected for a moment. "It's surprising that no one saw a strange man picking the lock of the front door."

"Not really. It was dark at that time, and it was a chilly night. Few people would have been idling around the street, watching the area. Additionally, I often enter and exit our home at all hours of the day and night, wearing all sorts of disguises. A strange man fumbling at the lock is not such a rare occurrence."

"Fair enough. Then the villain hurries upstairs, picks the lock to our rooms, locates your violin, removes one string, replaces it with an inferior string, and hurries out of 221b, locking the doors behind him as he goes. He then disappears into the night, having achieved his only objective." After a deep breath, I concluded. "Do you agree that is an accurate summation of events?"

He tented his fingers and leaned back in his chair. "I believe that it was accurate until your final sentence."

"Are you saying he didn't disappear into the night?" A wave of horror swept over me. "Do you believe that he's still here, hidden somewhere in the building?"

"What? No, that is not what I mean, and that isn't the portion of the sentence that I found suspect. I meant the five words, 'having achieved his only objective'."

"Is there something we missed?"

"The intruder didn't want the string itself. That is proven by the fact that it was tossed in the wastepaper basket. In any event, the string has no intrinsic value. Just because it was used on a Stradivarius doesn't make it any more valuable than any ordinary fiddle string. I certainly didn't plan to audition for a position in an orchestra. No public embarrassment or any direct negative consequence could come to me from this. And we have agreed that a practical joke becomes less amusing to the prankster when the person initiating the supposed humor isn't there to witness the results. Which raises one distinct possibility: The purpose of substituting a string was to generate an indirect consequence."

"But what sort of indirect consequence could result from switching a violin string?"

"What did happen?"

"We wasted hours searching our rooms."

"Precisely! From the moment I noticed how my instrument has been defiled, I have obsessed over who might have done this and what the goal of this stunt might have been. I have been focused on this string at the expense of everything else. If I'm correct in my deductions, then that means that this entire charade was meant as a distraction – a bagatelle that would demand my full attention. Something that would keep me away from something more important – like one of the potential crimes in the newspaper we discussed earlier!"

It took me a moment of reflection, and then everything made sense. "You mean that someone was planning a major crime, became afraid that you would become involved, and created this subtle, mystifying distraction?"

"Doesn't that make perfect sense to you?"

"I cannot say that it does."

"Consider that a clever criminal is in the process of planning a major crime. The villain in question is aware of my existence, and for reasons that I'll theorize about later, believes that it is probable that I'll be called into the case – either immediately after the crime occurs, or perhaps right before it occurs, in an attempt to prevent it. Do you see a flaw in my logic?"

"After all we've been through together, you should know how unlikely such an occurrence might be."

"My blushes, Watson. Therefore, if my involvement isn't wanted in this theoretical crime, then the perpetrator must find a way to prevent my investigation. Open threats wouldn't work. Such aggression would only serve to make me more determined to insert myself into the case. If I cannot be *bullied*, then perhaps I can be *distracted*. The only way to keep me away from a very important case is to provide me with an irresistible problem. Perhaps the person in question attempted to come up with an impossible murder or some other baffling crime. Maybe this individual's powers of creativity weren't up to the task, or perhaps this plotter feared that the mystery wouldn't be interesting enough to attract me, or that I might solve the case too quickly. Perhaps after much thinking, the criminal at the heart of this mystery realized that the best way to catch my attention was to personalize the problem he created for me. Instead of planning an additional complex crime solely for the purposes of distracting me, why not derail me with a simple question?"

"Why would someone change out one of your violin strings?"

"Precisely. It is reminiscent of Lewis Carroll's famous riddle in *Alice's Adventures in Wonderland*: How is a raven like a writing desk?" Holmes paused for a few moments, and I pondered before admitting defeat.

"There is no answer. Carroll deliberately proposed a riddle for which he didn't have a solution. Of course, over the years readers have proposed their own solutions, such as 'they both produce notes', 'they both have inky quills', and my personal favorite, 'Edgar Allan Poe wrote on both'. But the point is that when Carroll wrote that riddle, it was designed to go unanswered. So it is with the violin string substitution. There is no rhyme or reason for the action *in itself*. It is the *consequence* of the switch that is of paramount importance. The person involved might have put pepper in my tobacco, or gold sovereigns in my dressing-gown pockets, or even left an actual wild goose in my bedroom for me to chase. The point is that I was meant to become obsessed with this ridiculous, pointless charade, and my opponent triumphed spectacularly. Full marks to him."

"But who would do such a thing? Who would not only plot a terrible crime, but go through all of this rigmarole just to prevent you from getting involved?"

"Once we find the crime, my dear fellow, we will have our answer. We haven't had any potential clients knocking on our door, have we? Could the solution to this puzzle have been turned away?"

"No one has been to 221b since that boy delivered that telegram – " Scarcely had the words escaped my lips than Holmes leapt up, sprinted across the room, and retrieved the missive. "It is from a Baron Culmond, a man who has worked with the Government on many previous occasions. It seems that he is hosting that Eastern European ambassador you mentioned yesterday. He's concerned for the diplomat's safety, and if I am correct, he has every right to be."

In less than a minute, Holmes, who was disheveled from the previous night's escapade, had thrown on a coat and had summoned a hansom cab. As we drove away from Baker Street, I asked him, "But you can't be certain that this is *the* crime you think you were distracted from, can you?"

"No, but seeing as how no one else has tried to hire me lately, and given the importance of this ambassador, it is by far the most likely option. The ambassador in question here is pivotal to resolving a trade dispute between England and his home country. If he were to die on British soil, then the negotiations would fall apart, and someone who was well-positioned in the business world could conceivably make hundreds of thousands of pounds from the resulting economic chaos."

A half-hour later, we arrived at Baron Culmond's home, and after some very terse words with the butler, the Baron met us in the hall. "Mr. Holmes. You never responded to my telegram, so I assumed that you had no interest in my worries."

"I apologize, sir. I was caught up in a very clever scheme orchestrated by the man who I believe is planning to assassinate the ambassador at any moment."

After a few words of shock and concern, the Baron led us into the ballroom where the ambassador was addressing an audience of about fifty guests. Holmes scanned the room, and after about seven seconds, he spun around and sprinted out the door. I hurried after him, but I was so far behind that I could barely hear my friend declare, "He's outside, Watson! He's in the oak tree!"

When I finally caught up with Holmes, he was crouched behind a shrub in the courtyard. He placed a finger over his lips and then pointed upwards. I could see a shadowy figure sprawled out on a very thick branch halfway up the tallest tree, pointing a rifle at the window. Holmes's eyes darted around the ground before discovering a rock the size of his fist, and upon grabbing it, he hurled it upwards at the gunman, striking him on the head. The man and his rifle hurtled to the ground with an unsettling thud.

"Is he alive?"

After a brief examination I nodded. "He's unconscious, and I suspect one arm and both legs are broken, but he ought to survive."

"He shall live long enough to be tried and convicted," Holmes declared, and he was right. We summoned the authorities, who carried the gunman away on a stretcher, managing to do so without disturbing the guests inside the house.

Upon learning of our actions, the Baron and the ambassador were both effusive in their thanks. The agents of both governments decided to speed up their negotiations, and a deal was struck and signed shortly after midnight. The ambassador returned home the following day without incident.

Holmes and I returned to Baker Street as soon as the treaty was signed. "There's just one unanswered question."

"Oh? What's that?"

"Who was behind all of this? Who not only planned the death of the ambassador in order to profit from the resulting chaos, but who knew that you would be involved, and that you would be distracted by a little adjustment to your violin? Who would break our neighbor's windows, knowing that Mrs. Hudson would be called away to help?"

Holmes sighed. "You ought to know the answer to that, Watson. Only one criminal in all of England knows my character so well, realizes the danger I pose to him, and could position himself to turn international upheaval into a small fortune. I suppose I should be grateful that he only sought to distract me instead of killing me. I have no strength to discuss

404

my nemesis now, as I am spent, and haven't slept in over forty hours. If you will excuse me, my good fellow . . . ."

And with that, he staggered into his bedroom for some well-deserved rest.

The Case of the
Secret Samaritan
by Jane Rubino

It has long been a rule of mine, when debating which of Sherlock Holmes's cases to lay before the public, that preference should be given to those that offer a touch of the dramatic, so dear to my friend's heart, above those that merely recount some commonplace crime, devoid of singularity or surprise.

One such matter came to us on the last Friday in March of '88, and while our Baker Street address has been the site of many singular entrances, no entrance, I think, took my friend quite by surprise as that of Miss Violet Musgrove.

Holmes had been without a case of any importance since the affair of John Douglas, and the dark epilogue to the matter, and the weeks of idleness that followed left my friend in that state of irritable melancholy which had him particularly susceptible to the lure of the cocaine bottle. And so it was with great relief when, late on that Friday morning, I heard a ring at the bell, the murmur of voices below, and our landlady's step upon the stair.

Mrs. Hudson entered, bearing a card upon a salver.

Holmes snatched it eagerly. "Miss Violet Musgrove," he muttered. "Well, ask this lady to step up, Mrs. Hudson."

"She is not alone – another lady attends her."

"Then ask both ladies to step up."

A moment passed, and then we heard the rustle of skirts upon the stair, and two ladies, one young, one middle-aged, entered the room. The elder of the two possessed the upright posture and resolute features that bespoke a woman of intelligence and strong character, but it was her young companion, a girl of no more than nineteen or twenty, whom we knew instinctively to be Miss Violet Musgrove. She was a tall, slim brunette, dressed in a simple traveling costume of pale blue, with a velvet tam perched upon her dark curls, and a small, drawstring bag of matching velvet suspended from her wrist. But we were not struck as much by the young woman's extraordinary beauty, nor by her air of maturity and composure, as by the steel-rimmed, blue-tinted spectacles that concealed her eyes, and the gloved hand that hand rested upon her companion's sleeve, which pronounced her to be blind.

"Mr. Holmes?" said she.

406

"I am Sherlock Holmes. My friend and colleague, Doctor Watson, is in the room as well. I hope that you have no objection to his presence."

"Oh, no! Allow me to present Miss Mary Elder of St. Lucy's, whom I mentioned to you in my letters. From your voice, I think there are ten paces between us?"

"Twelve," corrected her companion, whereupon Miss Musgrove advanced, her steps uniform and steady, while her lips silently counted out twelve paces. Holmes glanced at me, and then turned his attention to the girl whose extended hand did not seek that of my friend, but instead reached toward his face, whereupon she ran her fingers across the line of his brow, down his jaw, and 'round his chin. "Your features are good – noble – though not as poetic as I imagined," she said, and then, to my friend's very great surprise, she embraced him and kissed his cheek. "I have tried to respect your wishes, sir, but we sail in three days' time, and however this journey may end for me, I felt that mere letters had not expressed how grateful I am for all you have done. I *knew* that I must tell you so in person."

"Violet, dear," said Miss Elder. "You embarrass Mr. Holmes."

Indeed, the expression upon my friend's face was one of amused embarrassment. Gently, he detached the lady's arms from around his neck, as Miss Elder stepped forward, cupped her hand under the blind girl's elbow, and guided her toward the settee. "I will have you know, sir," said she, as they sat, "that it was my opinion to leave matters as you wished, but Violet can be somewhat headstrong, and I have learned that when she sets her mind to something, it is best to give way, and she refused to depart before she had thanked you in person, and so here we are in London when we ought to be in Liverpool."

"My dear Miss Musgrove, it is generally at the conclusion of a matter rather than in advance of it that I receive thanks," said Holmes. "I am bound to say, that I'm not aware of anything I have done to deserve yours."

"Mr. Holmes, I know from your letters that you are modest – "

"I am not one who ranks modesty highly," Holmes interrupted. "And I place ignorance well below it, and yet, I must confess to utter ignorance when you allude to letters and offer thanks. Your name is not at all familiar to me, I cannot recall a Musgrove from any of my cases, and I'm certain that we have never met."

Miss Elder sighed and gave a sort of shrug as if to declare that there was no point in disputing the matter further. "Then we can only apologize for the intrusion and wish you a good morning," said she. "Come, Violet. Mr. Holmes is a very busy man, and we must not take up any more of his time."

Miss Musgrove's sightless gaze fixed upon Holmes for a moment, and at last, she gave a sigh of resignation and laid her hand upon her companion's sleeve. "Yes, you're right," she said. "It was a fool's errand."

"No, no!" Holmes cried, as the ladies made a motion to rise. "You bring a curious puzzle to my door, so let us see it through. "You speak of Saint Lucy's?"

"St. Lucy's Institute for Blind Girls at Farnham," said Miss Elder. "I have taught there for twenty years."

"And you mention that you sail in three days – where do you go?"

"To Boston," replied Miss Musgrove. "As I wrote in my last letter."

"You say that we have corresponded?"

"Yes – for nearly seven years," the girl maintained.

Holmes looked from Miss Musgrove to her companion, and then gave a bewildered shake of his head. "Miss Musgrove, my correspondence is extensive, and so it is possible that the occasional letter may be lost or mislaid, but not seven years' worth, I assure you – not without my having a hint that something was amiss."

"Then how do you explain this?" The girl probed the contents of the small bag at her wrist and at last drew out a square white envelope and extended it in the vicinity of my friend. "It is your reply to my last letter."

Holmes reached for the envelope and for his lens. "'*Miss Violet Musgrove, St. Lucy's School for Blind Girls, Farnham*'," he muttered, as he studied the object. "London postmark. Hmm! And you have received other letters, you say? Seven years' worth?"

"Yes."

"And you wrote to me at this address?"

"No, I did as you asked. When you first wrote to me, you said that you received a great deal of correspondence, and that if I wished to reply, there would be less chance of my letters being mislaid if I addressed them to Mister S. Holmes at the Upper Baker Street Post Office, to be held until called for."

"Indeed?" Holmes drew two sheets of paper from the envelope.

My dear Violet, [he read aloud]

You must not thank me! What better use could I have for my own good fortune than to share it with such a fine, courageous girl! As for what you ask – perhaps one day we shall meet, but for now, let us leave things as they are. Be brave! Do not give up hope, do not think of anything but what is before you, and be assured that if all that is needed for your journey to be a

success are the prayers of your humble servant, then its
success is certain.

Holmes passed the letter to me and took up the second sheet. "And what is this? A poem?"

"Yes – you always sent a poem."

Holmes read aloud:

> *There dreams repose, – so fair*
> *So frail that but to sigh*
> *Their names upon the air*
> *Would force them die.*
> *These give, like violets hid*
> *A perfume to the mind*
> *Give light, as once they did*
> *To poet blind!*

The girl recited the last lines in unison, and then said, "Miss Elder read them to me, the letters and the poems, after – after I was no longer able."

"Though Violet can read Moon Type," declared Miss Elder. "In fact, she has become so proficient that she is able to teach it to some of our other pupils who, like herself, lost their sight after they had learned to read."

"So these letters always had some lines of verse enclosed?"

"Yes, always." She patted the small drawstring bag. "I know them all by heart."

"You have them with you?"

"I would not travel without them. They are my good luck charms."

"May I see them?"

She again reached into her bag and drew out a packet bound with ribbon. Holmes leafed through the papers, muttering, "'*Violet, sweet Violet, thine eyes are full of tears*' – Hmm! Emerson, I think. And this – '*A violet by a mossy stone, half hidden from the eye*' – That is Wordsworth. '*Where oxlips and the nodding violet grows.*' Shakespeare. And yet, Miss Musgrove, you did not find me to be poetic!"

"Appearances may be deceiving," she replied, with a hint of a smile.

"You were certainly deceived. But whether you are the object of someone's benevolence or the victim of some misguided hoax, I cannot say."

"Yet, how is it, Holmes," I asked, "that this fellow singles out Miss Musgrove for his benevolence or sport?"

"A theory must be built upon facts, and I am afraid that a brief letter and a packet of verses make for a very poor foundation. But the matter interests me, Miss Musgrove. Perhaps if I knew something of your history, I might be better able to assist you."

It was Miss Elder who spoke up. "I am afraid, as far as Violet's earliest history is concerned, the details are somewhat vague, and I cannot vouch for their relevance or even for their accuracy."

"I will be glad of any details, whether you think them relevant or not," said Holmes. "Perhaps what appears vague to you will be less so to me."

"I suppose you are right. I was told that Violet's parents had been living in India – there was some claim that her mother had been a teacher of music – and that it was the anticipation of Violet's arrival which persuaded them to return to England. Her mother sailed on the *Lahore*, which left Bombay in late '67, but it does not appear that her father was among the passengers. Perhaps he meant settle some business matters, and follow after.

"In the course of the voyage, Violet came into the world – somewhat sooner than anticipated – and her mother left it. A few of the lady passengers tended her, and an elderly clergyman baptized her, christening her 'Violet Musgrove', which was said to be her mother's name. When no relations or friends of Mrs. Musgrove came to meet the *Lahore* upon its arrival, the clergyman arranged for Violet to be taken to the Alexandra Orphanage for Infants, where she remained for four years, and afterward was placed at the School for Indigent Orphans at Guildford."

"And what efforts were made to locate Miss Musgrove's father?"

"I have no idea. This all occurred many years before I came into the picture. Indeed, what I have just told you was passed down to me third-hand, so to speak, from the matrons at the orphan school."

"But Miss Musgrove is no longer at the orphan school."

"No. For nearly six years, she has been at St. Lucy's."

"Nearly six years," Holmes muttered. "And I must conclude that the onset of Miss Musgrove's affliction was the reason for the change?"

"Yes."

"Pray, continue."

"The orphan school is not ten miles from St. Lucy's, and our staff and theirs are well acquainted with one another. In fact, I had seen Violet many times, for the orphan school has a first-rate choir, and I often went to hear them sing. Violet has been blessed with an extraordinary voice. There had been talk of raising funds to have her sent to town, so that she might compete for a musical scholarship one day. Alas," the woman sighed, "when Violet was brought to town, it was for a very different reason."

410

"Miss Musgrove had begun to experience problems with her eyesight."

"Yes, Mr. Holmes. When Violet began to suffer headaches and episodes of dimming and blurred vision, the headmistress of the orphan school came to me for advice. Violet was brought to a local optician, but he found nothing which might explain her symptoms, and suggested that she be taken to an ophthalmologist in town – Doctor Sadler, on Harley Street. The headmistress asked if I might accompany Violet– she thought that, as a teacher of the blind, I would be better able to discuss the case with him than one of her matrons could. The school provided a small fund for our hotel – Ashley's on Henrietta Street – and the consulting fee."

Holmes sat back in his chair, his fingertips pressed together. "Pray, continue."

"We traveled to town, and Doctor Sadler examined Violet, but her early symptoms had been so irregular that he could offer no definitive opinion – although," she interjected, with a glance toward the girl, "his look and his tone were so very grave, that I suspected even then that he anticipated the worst. Nevertheless, he said that a number of conditions might account for Violet's complaint – a childhood injury, or a tumor, or neuritis, or even simple eye strain. He even raised the possibility of hysteria, anxiety brought on by talk of auditions and scholarships. He suggested that we might consult with a neurologist while we were in town, and said that he would like to see Violet again in a year, or sooner, if her symptoms advanced."

"And did you consult with a neurologist?"

"Yes, as it happens we did. Our stay was to be for two days only – our funds did not allow for more, or for an additional doctor's fee. I was willing to draw upon my own resources, but when we returned from Doctor Sadler's, the hotel clerk handed Violet a small parcel that had been left at the desk in our absence."

"And what did it contain?"

"Five sovereigns and tickets to the opera."

"Indeed! You are fond of the opera, Miss Musgrove?"

"I had never been, but I love music and I had read that Miss DeReszke was to sing *Aida* – "

"Ah, yes. April of '81, as I recall. And who sent the parcel?"

Miss Elder shook her head. "I don't know. I asked the clerk at the hotel desk, but he could tell me only that it had been delivered by a hired messenger."

"Had you mentioned to anyone at the hotel, even in passing, that you would like to go to the opera, Miss Musgrove?"

411

"Only to Miss Elder. It was the day of my appointment with Doctor Sadler. The hotel clerk was writing out directions to the doctor's office for Miss Elder and I was wandering around the lobby – there were so many people! – and I saw a messenger deliver an envelope to a lady, and heard her say that they were tickets to the opera, and I told Miss Elder that it had always been a dream of mine to go to the opera one day."

"Clearly, your remark was overheard by some benevolent person who arranged for that parcel to be waiting upon your return. And you recognized no one at the hotel?"

"No one at all, Mr. Holmes," replied Miss Elder. "But there were a great many guests and the hotel staff was quite large, and there were always messengers and delivery-men about, and on that first visit, there was also some sort of gathering or conference – for training nurses, I believe."

"And so Miss Musgrove's remark could have been overheard by any of the guests or staff or delivery-men or messengers or congregating nurses?"

"Yes."

"And thanks to one of them, you had the funds to prolong your visit, which allowed you to consult with a neurologist and enjoy the opera. And this correspondence – when did that begin?"

Again, it was Miss Elder who replied. "A month after our return, a letter and a small parcel arrived, addressed to Miss Violet Musgrove at St. Lucy's School, Farnham."

"Not 'St. Lucy's School for Blind Girls at Farnham'?'"

"No, and I thought it rather odd, because later the letters did write out the entire address."

"When you registered at the hotel, you wrote down only '*St. Lucy's School, Farnham*'?"

"Why . . . yes."

"Then clearly that is where this mysterious benefactor first made note of your address, and assumed that Miss Musgrave's address and yours were the same. It was only some time after the correspondence began that this benevolent person learned of the school's entire name. You say there was also a parcel – was that first letter enclosed in it?"

"No, the letter was mailed separately."

"And, what did this parcel contain?"

"Five sovereigns," said Miss Musgrove.

"And the letter's contents?"

"You wrote," said Miss Musgrove, still persuaded that Holmes had been her correspondent, "that life was often unkind, but we must bear up and always be glad for any opportunity to make amends, and that you

412

hoped I would accept a small gift of pocket money and would be grateful for a word now and then as to how I got on, so long as I didn't waste my ink on expressions of thanks. And that if I had leave to reply, I was to address my letter, as I have told you, to '*Mister S. Holmes*' at the post office. And there was a postscript – two lines of verse."

"Can you recall them?"

"'*Though winter's set, the violet, Shall come back with the spring.*'"

"Hmm! And this was in the spring of '81. Did you mention to anyone that the doctor advised you to return in a year?"

"Certainly, Violet and I spoke of it," said Miss Elder. "And I may have said something to one of the clerks – not about Violet's condition, merely how comfortable and convenient the hotel was, and that we would likely stay there again the following year – and he said that it was always best to reserve a room as far in advance as possible, especially during the spring holiday."

"And you replied to this letter?"

"Yes – I asked the matron's leave to – " The girl smiled. " – to waste a bit of ink on thanks."

"A matron at the orphan school?"

"Yes."

"But not long after, you were enrolled at St. Lucy's."

"On my recommendation," said Miss Elder. "As I said, Doctor Sadler was not sanguine, and in the event – well, I have always said that if you prepare for all possibilities, you will not be unprepared for the worst one."

"Quite so. And a correspondence was allowed to continue?"

"Yes. I saw no harm in it. There was nothing improper – a few kind words of encouragement, a few lines of poetry – and four times a year, Violet was sent a packet with five sovereigns. Three came to her at the school, and the fourth was always waiting at the hotel desk when we traveled to town."

"Twenty pounds a year!" I exclaimed.

"Yes."

"And you have no clue as to this kind benefactor's identity?"

Miss Elder shook her head.

"Pray, continue."

"Violet's condition grew worse – quite gradually at first, and then more rapidly, and finally its cause was determined to be a tumor that had grown to the point where it pressed upon the optic nerve. Violet's sight was now all but gone. Doctor Sadler informed us that an operation was possible, but it would mean the removal of an eye. Perhaps both."

The girl gave a slight shudder.

"And then, when we visited Doctor Sadler last spring – Violet had decided that she must submit to this operation – Doctor Sadler informed us that he had read of a new procedure in the medical journals, one that might not only preserve the eyes, but possibly restore Violet's sight. But there are very few surgeons who perform this operation, and the best of them was in Boston. It is a risk, of course, but Violet has been a true soldier throughout her ordeal, and was willing to go forward. Only one obstacle stood in the way."

"Money," said Holmes.

"Yes. We were told that we would need no less than five-hundred pounds to meet the cost of travel and medical expenses, and there would be at least six months' convalescence in America before Violet could return home. We had thought of applying to some charitable societies, and then, nearly three months ago, not long after the new year, an attorney – Mister Graham was his name – wrote to us stating that he represented a certain party – Violet's benefactor, I have no doubt – who wished to advance eight-hundred pounds for Violet's operation and expenses."

"Eight-hundred pounds!" Holmes and I cried in unison and looked at one another in amazement.

Our expressions seemed to bring home to Miss Elder that Holmes had not been feigning ignorance – that, indeed, he was not Miss Musgrove's benefactor.

Holmes was silent for several minutes. "You leave in three days. Do you stay in town until then?"

"We are at Ashley's Hotel, but we must be in Liverpool on Sunday night, and sail on Monday morning."

"And this benefactor has no notion that you have come to town to seek him out?"

"None at all," said Miss Elder.

"Well then, let us do this: I would like for you to leave your papers with me – I will see to it that they are returned to you before you depart, and in the meantime, I will do my best to locate your Good Samaritan. But, if I am successful, Miss Musgrove, and yet this person insists upon remaining anonymous, how am I to proceed?"

"Leave it be, then. I will know, at least, that I have tried my best," the girl replied. "Only, I beg you, Mr. Holmes, to express my thanks, as earnestly as you can."

"You have my word."

The ladies rose, and Miss Musgrave extended her hand in Holmes direction. He shook it, and escorted them to the door.

"Well, Watson, what do you make of that!" he cried as he crossed the room and dropped back into his chair.

414

"What a very secretive and generous fellow you are!"

Holmes chuckled and then turned his attention to the packet of verses. "The girl is an interesting study," he muttered. "It is rare to find such resolve in one so young. Have a look at these and tell me what you think."

I looked over the pages that he tossed to me. "'*I may be lovelier than the violet flower*', '*Violets in the chilly spring*', '*and the violet blue, glowing like a woman's eye*.' If she had not been little more than a child when the business began, I might say that these were sent by a secret admirer."

"And if they had not been written by a woman, I might agree with you."

"A woman!"

"A woman," Holmes repeated. "Sentimental, honorable, somewhere in middle-age, and with a passable English education."

"You might be describing Mrs. Hudson!"

"Our good landlady is certainly a sympathetic, upright, generous creature, but a gift of eight-hundred pounds is well beyond her means, I think."

"Perhaps she won at the Derby." I looked over the papers once more. "You're certain, Holmes, that the writer is a woman?"

"The hand hasn't the firmness of a writer who is male or young, and it hasn't frailty of age. And those exclamation marks – men are far more sparing, but there you have one, two, three in the first few lines. The verses are suggestive, as well. You have Emerson and Shakespeare, but then you have the sort of mawkish drivel that you will not see outside of a ladies' magazine."

"And the education?"

"The uniformity of the lettering, the short, precise bars upon the letter '*T*'. That is sound, orthodox, day-school penmanship."

"And the generosity – that much is obvious – but you said she was honorable."

"Note that she did not slip her letter into those packets – a device that is frowned upon by the post office, but which is often done to save the cost of posting a letter separately. She is too scrupulous to cheat the post office of a few pennies."

"She does not scruple to call herself '*Mister S. Holmes*'. Perhaps she knows you."

"Or knows my name, at least. Seven years ago, my career was in an earlier stage, but one or two of my cases may have earned me a drop of printer's ink. I confess," Holmes added, gravely, "that I have scruples of my own when it comes to drawing this person out of the shadows. It is one thing to bring a crime to light so that the injured party may be made whole,

415

so far as that is possible. But Miss Musgrove has not been injured – quite the reverse, in fact. Am I justified in exposing an individual who has done no harm and whose only wish is for anonymity?"

"And yet, think of what harm may come from refusing to act," I said. "I know a little about the surgery Miss Musgrove spoke of. The risk cannot be underestimated – She is a young, healthy girl, but if she does not survive, her benefactor may forever regret that she had not taken advantage of the opportunity to meet the object of her generosity."

"A fair point," he conceded. "I will concentrate my efforts on locating our 'S. Holmes' and decide how I am to proceed afterward."

"Can you do so before they sail?"

"I can but try."

I handed the papers back to Holmes. "One detail of Miss Musgrove's account puzzles me."

"Only one?" he said, with a smile.

"This woman may set down 'S. Holmes' as her signature, but how does she retrieve the letters? Surely, the conditions of *poste restante* would make it impossible."

"Difficult, not impossible. You will recall that Windibank had poor Miss Sutherland address her letters to Hosmer Angel at the Leadenhall Street Post Office, to be left 'til called for. The fact that it tests the regulation book does not mean that it cannot be done."

"Then surely a clerk at the Upper Baker Street branch office can tell you who came for the letters."

"Perhaps, if it were a matter of seven days or seven weeks, but are talking about a period of seven years, Watson. There are thousands of clerks scattered among the scores of London post offices, and when you consider the possibility of transfers, promotions, and departures over the course of a half-dozen years, it is unlikely that our fair benefactor has been served by the same clerk often enough to be remembered. And that assumes that she did not resort to disguise or employ an imposter."

"Well, you do know when the business began, so it must all have begun with Miss Musgrove's first visit to town. Her mysterious benefactor saw her at the hotel, left a gift for her at the desk, discovered – from the clerk, possibly – that she was to make annual visits to town. That is why one of those quarterly gifts of five sovereigns was always waiting for her at the hotel. Perhaps one of the employees at Ashley's Hotel may be of some help to you."

Holmes shook his head. "I daresay that, over the course of many years, a hotel's staff has seen as many changes as that of an active post office. And, again, this person may have employed – But wait! – Recall what Miss Elder said? That it was a – Yes!" He cried, and then strode over to his desk, dashed off a note, and rang for the page-boy. "Recall, Watson, what Miss Elder had been told," Holmes resumed when the boy had left. "That it was a hired messenger who delivered that first parcel. I daresay, the same expedient was used afterward. Such a liaison may serve us better than an employee at a busy post office or crowded hotel."

"But there are scores of hired messengers in London."

"Yes, but I can lay my hands on a particularly well-informed one, a fellow who knows every railway station, receiving office, restaurant, bank, omnibus route, and hotel."

"A commissionaire!" I cried. "Our old friend, Peterson!"

"Yes, Peterson. With only three days' time, an additional pair of sharp eyes and active feet will be invaluable."

Some time later, Holmes said, "Ah, that is his step I hear now. I confess to some surprise that he is still with the corps."

It wasn't long before the commissionaire appeared in our doorway.

"Step in, Peterson!" Holmes greeted. "I was just telling Watson here that I had expected to hear of your resignation, and yet you are still at your old post, I see."

"I hope that you do not think the worst of me for it, Mr. Holmes, after you had all of Lady Morcar's reward come to me."

"It was you who found the Carbuncle, Peterson."

"Well, to be frank, it was *Mrs.* Peterson, and we both had some unease about it, for nothing was given back to her Ladyship but what was hers in the first place."

"Well, well, sometimes the most charitable course is to allow others to be generous," said Holmes as he waved the man into a chair. "And so, the post is the same?"

"Wimpole at Wigmore, among the best. A clear six-bob-six a day, and as my old injury gives me little grief and I am yet on the fair side of fifty, I hope to remain there many years more. Even a fellow who collects a thousand-pound reward must do something with himself, and to be frank, I know no fatigue but that of idleness, as they say."

"Have you time for a small commission?"

"Yes, indeed."

"It is somewhat outside of your sphere, Peterson. It is more in my line."

"Detective work, is it?" The commissionaire rubbed his hands together briskly at the thought of taking part in one of my friend's adventures.

"I am attempting to locate a woman," said Holmes, "but I do not have a name, and what I do have are more inference and conjecture than data."

Peterson nodded, and drew out a pocket-book and pencil.

"This lady," Holmes continued, "would be somewhere in middle age, most probably single, or widowed perhaps, reasonably well-educated, well-to-do, and may have some small reputation for open-handedness. She has a fair knowledge of London – your quarter, in particular – though she may be a visitor rather than a resident, one who is often in town at this time of year."

"London is quite popular at Easter time, Mr. Holmes, filled with all sorts, even those from abroad."

"I think the odds are against her being a foreigner. When she is in town, she will likely reside at a respectable lodging house or a modest hotel, and she will often employ messengers – discreet, reliable ones, such as yourself and your brother commissionaires for very trivial errands: Delivering small parcels, fetching letters from the post office, making sundry purchases."

Peterson, who had been scribbling as Holmes spoke, scratched his head with the end of his pencil, then adjusted his cap. "Why would a lady who knows her way about not save her shillings and see to these matters herself?"

"She may be an invalid, or reclusive, or may have matters of business that allow her no time for errands."

"But you say she is well off. Hasn't she servants to fetch and carry?"

Holmes shrugged his shoulders. "Women are secretive by nature, and in practice. Commissionaires have a reputation for discretion, which a servant does not always enjoy. I daresay your brothers in the corps can offer up a few candidates?"

"Or a great many."

"Too many are better than none."

Peterson tapped his pencil against his pocket-book. "Well, sir, I might give you one or two straight off, but they do not exactly fit into the frame."

"The frame can be adjusted."

"The Countess of Rufton comes to mind, but only because she summoned me just this morning. She is neither a spinster nor a widow, but she is middle-aged and learned and well-set in life. She and her daughter always pass a few days in town at Easter-time, and generally put up at Ashley's or Durrant's."

"Modest accommodations for the wife and only child of the Earl of Rufton."

"Well, they have no house in town, and to be frank, she is a pious sort and not given to show. This afternoon, her Ladyship and Lady Frances may be found at the Good Friday services at St. Albans, and will stay on after to serve meals to the poor. Tomorrow, they visit the Home for Lost and Starving Dogs, and will likely take one or two poor creatures home with them, as they do every year."

"And what was your commission for the lady?"

"Lady Rufton and Lady Frances pledge to a number of charities, and when they are in town, they often have commissionaires deliver their donations, so as to avoid the fuss and to-do of being thanked. I was just carrying the last of them when you summoned me."

"Indeed? Would you have any objection to showing it?"

The commissionaire drew a square blue envelope from his breast and handed it to Holmes. "Hmm! The Dumb Friends League!" Holmes studied the object for a few seconds and then handed it back to Peterson. "Her Ladyship's devotion to animals does her credit. Any other prospects?"

"Well, there is Miss Armitage, who is a single lady, near middle-age, I suppose, and quite clever. She is the private nurse to a solicitor from Eastbourne, though she acts as secretary and companion as well. She manages all of his correspondence and sees to his errands, and even accompanies him to the opera and concerts and such when he is in town."

"How often does he come to town?"

"Two or three times a year."

"Why does he require a private nurse?"

"He had been with a London firm, but a hard case of rheumatism put him into an invalid wheel-chair, and he was advised to lessen his professional doings and take himself to Eastbourne for a more agreeable climate. Now he comes to London only to visit a Harley Street specialist."

"And to take in the opera and concerts and such," Holmes added.

Peterson nodded.

"I would not call a private nurse a lady of means," I said.

"Well, she is no countess, Doctor, but she lives and boards handsomely at Mr. Graham's expense and her salary, I have heard, is a hundred a year."

"'Graham', you say?" Holmes raised his eyebrows. "And are Mr. Graham and Miss Armitage in London now?"

"Yes, at the Langham."

"Mr. Graham is not as modest in his choice of accommodations as Lady Rufton, then?"

"Well, he must have the lifts now, because of his chair."

"Quite so. Well, well, you have been very helpful, Peterson. I will begin my own researches and send you off to carry out Lady Rufton's charge and to quiz your fellow commissionaires. And as time is of the essence," Holmes added, as he reached into his pocket, "I must ask you to wire me of any prospects as you hear of them. Do not wait – "

419

"No, no, Mr. Holmes!" cried Peterson, waving off my friend's attempt at payment. "I am a thousand pounds in your debt already."

"Then allow me to be generous toward your fellow commissionaires," replied Holmes as he pressed the handful of silver into the fellow's palm.

"I suppose I must let the reign of genuine charity commence, as they say." With a nod to us both, Peterson pocketed the coins and bade us good-day, but had no sooner reached the door than he turned back.

"To be frank, Mr. Holmes, one other woman comes to mind, only because she is well set, for all the good money may do her, and clever as a fox, and knows the lay of London as I know the palm of my hand, for she is a Londoner of long-standing. She calls herself 'Missus', though I have never seen nor heard of the 'Mister', nor know anyone who has, and I would not call her middle-aged unless she means to live as long as Moses, for she will not see sixty again. But that is the way," he added with a sigh. "The good die before their time and it seems the wicked go on forever."

"And who is this woman?"

"Mary Jeffries," he said, heavily.

"Mrs. Jeffries!" I cried. "But she is still at Holloway, surely."

"You do not keep up with the times, Watson," said Holmes. "It was decided, very discreetly, to waive the remainder of Mrs. Jeffries' sentence – six months without labor, as I recall – and allow her to return to her lair. But Peterson, I would not say that she has any reputation for generosity, unless it is charity to indulge man's most base nature."

"To be frank, I believe she has given up her trade."

Holmes's frown expressed his doubt. "But surely you have no dealings with Mrs. Jeffries. Thurloe Place is not within your post."

"Well, sir, the other commissionaires will have nothing to do with her, but her commissions are not improper – no more than posting letters or making some small purchase. I oblige her more out of pity and cannot bring myself to take her coin, for Mrs. Peterson says who knows but if she meets with a Christian now and again, she may have a change of heart – though, with respect to Mrs. Peterson's way of thinking, I have no expectations. But if it is a recluse you look for, she is certainly that."

"Well, that is all for now, Peterson, I will send you off to your researches, and begin my own."

"Very well, sir."

"You told him nothing of Miss Musgrove," I remarked, when the commissionaire had gone.

"If Peterson allowed her name to slip out in the course of his inquiries, he might frighten off the very woman we seek. No, no," he added, as he reached for his hat and stick. "It is best that I keep my own counsel for now, and call upon the two prospects Peterson has given us. Will you come?"

"Of course. But you say 'two prospects'? You exclude Mrs. Jeffries, I take it."

"No, Lady Rufton. The hand that addressed the envelope she gave to Peterson and the one that penned Miss Musgrove's poems were not the same."

"The envelope's address may have been written by a servant or secretary."

"Perhaps. But we cannot call on her Ladyship now in any case. It is just past noon, and if I recall aright, the Good Friday services at St. Alban's have begun and carry on for three hours, and then she and her daughter go to their charity work after. No, we shall try the solicitor, Graham, first. It is probable – highly probable, I think – that he may be the same Mister Graham who delivered that eight-hundred pounds to Miss Musgrove."

At the Langham Hotel, Holmes sent up his card, and in short order we were directed to Mr. Graham's suite. Waiting for us in the corridor was a tall, formidable-looking woman who stood like a sentinel guarding the door of her master's domain.

"Mr. Sherlock Holmes?" she looked from one of us to the other and then her steel gray eyes settled on Holmes. "I am Miss Armitage. What is the nature of your business with Mr. Graham?"

"It is business that I prefer not to conduct through an intermediary, nor to discuss in a hallway."

The lady hesitated a moment, then seemed to accept that she faced an opponent as daunting as herself, and said only, "Bear in mind that Mr. Graham's health will not stand much strain," before she conducted us into the handsome sitting room of her employer's suite.

Mr. Graham was a gentleman of fifty or thereabouts, whose ruddy complexion and animated features contrasted with the gnarled hands that protruded from the blankets draped around his shoulders and laid across his lap.

Miss Armitage made the introductions and then took her post at the gentleman's side, laying a protective hand upon his shoulder.

"I have heard of you, of course, Mr. Holmes, by way of Doctor Watson's pen – that story last Christmas about the man avenging his lost love. Reading – that is, reading which is not connected with the uninspired prose of the law – is one of the few pleasures I have in my present state."

"And concerts, so I hear," replied Holmes.

"Concerts, opera, yes. But you did not come to discuss music, I think."

"No, it is a matter of law, after a fashion," replied my friend. "I see that you are still active in the trade. On that table at the door are a number of letters to be posted, too great a number to be merely personal correspondence."

"Yes, my ailment has not called halt to my practice altogether. I have the advantage of a very able clerk, you see." He smiled and reached up to pat the nurse's hand. "So what is the legal matter that brings you here, Mr. Holmes?"

"I have a client – a young lady named Musgrove – who has, for some years, been the object of an anonymous benefactor's generosity. This person has lately provided Miss Musgrove, through a liaison, with funds for a medical treatment that would otherwise have been far beyond her means. It is my understanding that you were that liaison, Mr. Graham. Miss Musgrove sails to the United States in a matter of days and, before she goes, she is most anxious to meet the kind and generous person to whom she is indebted."

"Miss Musgrove is in no one's debt, Mr. Holmes. My client would not wish her to think so. And I must abide by that client's wish for anonymity. I hope," he added, "that you don't ask me to give preference to your client over mine."

"Surely there can be no harm in it. Miss Musgrove asks for nothing, only to thank one who has provided not only this extraordinary gift, but all that have preceded it for some years."

"There is harm, Mr. Holmes, in breaking faith with my client. It would not only be unprofessional, but dishonorable. Be assured, sir, and assure this young lady, that my client neither needs nor wishes for thanks."

Holmes shrugged his shoulders. "Very well. In that case, Miss Musgrove asks that, should you see this generous person again, you will at least express her profound gratitude."

"That, I can promise to do."

Holmes bade the invalid a good day, and Miss Armitage ushered us to the door. As she did so, Holmes's stick slipped from his hands in such a way as to knock the tray of letters to the floor. He immediately apologized for his clumsiness and stooped down to repair the mishap and return the tray to the table.

"It was well done," I said as we stepped onto the street. "You got a good look at the addresses on those letters. Did you recognize a name that might be Graham's anonymous client?"

"Not one, but I did not expect to. It was a look at the handwriting that I was after. You saw his hands – I daresay he cannot hold a pen. It is the watchful Miss Armitage who writes and addresses his correspondence, and the writing on those envelopes bore no resemblance at all to that upon

Miss Musgrove's papers. Graham may have been the intermediary for Miss Musgrove's benefactor, but it was not his nurse who transcribed those letters and poems. And so, we go on to a far more unsavory candidate."

"Mary Jeffries," said Holmes, as we settled in a cab, "may well be the worst woman in London. There are others who trade in debauchery and vice, but those who exploit the young – " Holmes shook his head. "Only think, Watson, what would have become of Miss Musgrove, an orphan without relations, and one whose affliction made her especially vulnerable, if she had fallen into the hands of such a person."

"Six months was far less than Madam Jeffries deserved," I muttered. "And to release her beforehand? The law showed more compassion for her than she ever did toward her victims."

"Oh, she was not released out of compassion. I daresay. She was set free for the same reason that allowed her to enjoy liberty as long as she has."

"She threatened to expose former clients. Prominent ones."

Holmes gave a grim nod.

Mrs. Jeffries' address was within a crowded, bustling district which included museums and cricket grounds and Kensington Station, and yet, as we stepped down from our cab, I noted that the pavement in front of her home was deserted, for pedestrians would cross the street rather than pass by the narrow, whitewashed residence set behind a high iron gate.

Our ring was answered promptly, and the footman admitted us to the entry hall and took Holmes's card and then vanished, leaving us for several minutes before he reappeared and said, "This way, if you please," leading us up a thickly carpeted stair and along a corridor to a chamber at the back of the house.

Though it was midday, the heavy draperies were drawn so that the room would have been thrown into utter darkness but for the scant illumination from a shaded lamp. I was able to make out a large, carved writing-desk, two walls of book-shelves, and sumptuous furnishings that spoke to an excess which was on the verge of vulgarity.

"Mr. Holmes."

The address came from a figure who sat well out of the lamplight, so that we could only make out a spare, gowned silhouette in an armchair beside the hearth.

"Madam. Thank you for seeing us."

"I had expected that we would meet well before today – *quite* expected it when I heard that our friend Count Von Kramm had called on you. But that matter was an entanglement of a different sort, I understand. Some common intrigue with an opera singer. So, how may I help you?"

"I have a client, a young lady whom an anonymous benefactor has made the object of considerable generosity. This benefactor is not unlike yourself. She is somewhat well-to-do – "

"I am very wealthy," she corrected.

"Reclusive."

"Cautious."

"Educated."

"Enterprising."

"With some knowledge of London."

"I think few know London better, Mr. Holmes."

"Its public places – railway stations, concert halls, hotels, and the like."

"Public places are where you pick up the daintiest flora. Your young lady is not here, if that is the purpose of your call."

"It is not. Every spring, for seven years, the young lady has come to London, and when she arrives at her hotel, a packet of five sovereigns is waiting, a gift of this anonymous benefactor."

"My dear Mr. Holmes! Surely you don't look to me? Is my character so little known? I do not give five pounds *to* young girls, it is what I give *for* them. Oh, dear. Your friend does not know whether to be appalled, or to hope that *this* lady," she laid a hand on her breast, "doth protest too much, and I may indeed be your fairy godmother. Perhaps he thinks that I hold out some hope of redemption and seek, when queasy conscience has its qualms, to lull the painful malady with alms. I am afraid that to be so would require me to have a conscience, an inconvenience that I have – thankfully – been spared."

I could scarcely see Holmes face through the shadows, but his grave silence suggested that he had been profoundly struck by the lady's remark, and for reasons that were not obvious to me.

Rather abruptly, he rose and said, "I think you have answered my question, madam."

The lady likewise rose and stepped forward to ring for the footman. As she did so, I saw two alert dark eyes set in a hideous mask of a thick face powder, a thin gash of carmined lips set in a pitiless smile. "I am sorry to have disappointed you."

"On the contrary, madam. I do not often meet one who so thoroughly lives up to her reputation."

With that, Holmes gave a nod and strode out without waiting for the footman.

He sprang into a hansom and sat with his chin sunk upon his breast, a rueful smile upon his lips. "I am bound to say, Watson, that you are sharing a cab with one of the greatest fools in all of London, a fellow whose brain has gone soft, and who has dispensed with the last few wits God gave him."

"It could be worse, I suppose. We could be at sea."

"Oh, I have been that, I daresay. It is what comes of going so long without brain-work."

When we arrived at our address, he fairly leaped from the cab and darted into the house, and when I entered our rooms, I found him scribbling a pair of notes that he handed to the page-boy, who gave him one in return.

"What an industrious fellow Peterson is!" Holmes chuckled as his eyes ran over the sheet. "It has been scarcely two hours and already he has turned up a dozen candidates."

Then, tossing the paper aside, he began to rummage through the rows of volumes on his shelves. "You have nothing pressing, I trust? I will want an accomplice."

"I am at your service," I said, "but what is my role? It is clear that you have seen or heard something that has escaped me."

"On the contrary," he replied, as he snatched a volume and began to leaf through its pages. "You have seen and heard all that I have. My error was in drawing the wrong conclusion from what I have seen, which set me off, like an addled hound, upon the wrong scent. I must credit both of our afternoon visits with setting me right. We shall have a few guests in a short while, and your role is simply to follow my lead. A little improvisation will be called for, but I trust you will know what to say."

I shrugged my shoulders and dropped into a chair while Holmes continued to leaf through the pages of a book.

"Ha!" and cried at last, and jabbed his finger upon a passage as we heard once again, a pull at our bell, the murmur of feminine voices, and the brush of skirts upon our stair.

"We came as soon as we received your note, Mr. Holmes," said Miss Elder, as my friend ushered that lady and Miss Musgrove into the room.

"You have found him!" cried the girl. "Is he here?"

"No, no, only Doctor Watson and I are here, but I have every hope that I may soon produce your benevolent friend. For the present," Holmes instructed, as he threw open his bedroom door, "I must ask you to be so good as to step in here. Further, out of sight, if you please, Miss Elder, and I must ask you and Miss Musgrove to be absolutely silent. I will leave the door ajar just a bit. Now – " he continued, as he returned to his chair and took up his volume once more, "we wait upon one more guest."

A moment later, there was a ring at the bell, and the sound of a brisk step upon the stair, and our friend the commissionaire entered the room.

"Ah, Peterson," Holmes greeted, his eyes on the page of his book. "Good of you to come."

"You had my note, sir?"

"Yes, yes. Quite a list! Commendable. We shall discuss that presently, but just now you have found the good doctor and myself in the middle of a dispute. I cannot locate the passage, Watson, but I am certain that I am right!"

I had sense enough to know that I was to say, "I am sure that you are not," and hoped that I did not look as baffled as I felt.

"A half-crown says that you are wrong! It begins, '*True charity, a plant divinely nursed; Fed by the love from which it rose at first . . . .*'" Holmes began to tear through the pages of the volume. "I know that the next line begins with '*Lives*' – I am sorry to keep you waiting, Peterson – I am certain that I am right."

"And I am certain that you are wrong," I said. "It is not '*Lives*'."

"I say that it is!"

Peterson looked from Holmes to me. "Begging your pardon, Mr. Holmes, but to be frank, the word is '*thrives*', not '*lives*'. '*Thrives against hope, and in the rudest scene, Storms but enliven its unfading green.*'"

"I told you so!" I cried.

Holmes clapped the book shut, laid it aside and rose. "Peterson, I think you are right! I would never have imagined you to be so poetic. But then, looks are often deceiving, are they not? As I am certain," he added, with a nod beyond the commissionaire's shoulder, "the young lady behind you would agree."

Peterson whirled about to face a trembling Miss Musgrove, who stood with one hand upon the door jamb while the other clung to Miss Elder's sleeve.

The commissionaire gasped and staggered back a step or two, and then looked from Holmes, to me, and again to the ladies.

"I know you, sir," said Miss Elder. "You are one of the hired messengers I have often seen at our hotel."

"Peterson, allow me to present Miss Mary Elder, of St. Lucy's School for Blind Girls at Farnham. The young lady, I think you know."

The commissionaire paled, and then his cheeks flushed, and he tugged off his cap, and twisting it in his hands, he looked from Holmes to the girl. "Mr. Holmes," he stammered. "Mr. Holmes . . . ."

The girl released Miss Elder's arm and, hands outstretched, took a few tottering steps in the commissionaire's direction. At last Peterson tossed his cap aside and took her hands in his and drew her close and held her in his arms. Miss Musgrove reached up and probed his face with her fingers as she had done with Holmes. "It is you!" she said. "I don't need

426

eyes to know that it's you!" And then the poor girl burst into a passionate fit of sobbing.

"Let us have none of that." Peterson's voice choked and he fumbled for a handkerchief and pressed it into her hand. "None of that, now. You mustn't – my poor girl – don't cry! How like your mother you are! The very picture of her!"

"I think," said Holmes, "that Doctor Watson must excuse ourselves. There are matters that you may wish to discuss with Miss Musgrove in private."

"No, no." The commissionaire kissed the girl's forehead, and then said, "What you have done – it is for the best. There has been too much secrecy as it is. It is time to put an end to it."

Holmes held a chair for Miss Elder while Peterson carefully guided the girl toward the settee. He took one of her hands between his, and began his tale. "When I was a very young man, I went into the army and was with the thirty-third regiment in India when I met Violet Musgrove. As with many young ladies who are alone in the world, she decided to try for a bit of adventure, and so took a post as choir mistress at a school for girls in Bombay. It was in the spring of '67 at a ball given by the governor of Bombay that we met, and I do believe I fell in love from the moment I laid eyes upon her, and I was the happiest fellow in all the world when she made it clear to me that she returned the feeling, and said 'Yes' to being Mrs. Peterson. We settled it between us that we would marry at Christmas-time, but perhaps we ought to have wed straight off as we were not – well, we were young and, to be frank, we were not as prudent as we ought to have been. And then, the orders came down – Napier was to organize a rescue of the European hostages held at Magdala by the Emperor Tewodros, and in October of that year, my regiment set out."

"You were part of the Abyssinian Campaign, Peterson?" I asked.

The commissionaire nodded. "Napier was an excellent choice to lead the expedition, for he was an engineer and so there was no obstacle he could not think his way around. I hoped that his skill would make for a swift campaign and have me back to the altar by Christmas-time, but it is no easy thing to transport fifteen-thousand men and their mounts, to say nothing of the camels and elephants – Contrary beasts, the both of them! – from Bombay to the fortress at Magdala, and it was not until April that we reached our destination. We needed no more than three days to rout the Abyssinian legions and set the hostages free, and with only two of our own lost, and not more than twenty injured. But alas! – I was among the wounded and not fit to be returned to Bombay until June. There, I found her note telling me that the condition in which she found herself made it desirable for her to return to England, and indeed, I was told that she had

427

sailed the previous December, and that word had since come back that on the voyage, she had born a child and both had perished."

Miss Musgrove gasped, and Miss Elder slipped a handkerchief from her sleeve and dabbed at her eyes.

"It was the end of me for some time. I resigned from the regiment with a wound pension and found my way to London and the Corps, and was laid low with the scarlet fever that went around in '71. It was a very kind young nurse who brought me through it, and when I recovered my health we began to keep company . . . ."

"And she is the present Mrs. Peterson," said Holmes.

Peterson nodded. "I was very frank with her about my former attachment, and we set ourselves toward the future, never imagining what had survived of my past. And then one afternoon, in early 1881, I had been sent to fetch some opera tickets for one of the guests at Ashley's Hotel and I had no sooner placed them in her hand than I heard a sweet voice, singing, and saw a young girl exploring the lobby as if she had never seen such a place in all her life. And then I heard you," he gave a nod toward Miss Elder, "call out 'Violet, come, we will be late,' and the girl hurried to this lady's side, and turned around so that I saw her full in the face and got such a shock that I am surprised I did not faint dead away. I drew near enough to hear the girl express a wish to go to the opera, and for Miss Elder to reply that every penny of their stay in London had been accounted for and there was nothing left over for amusement. When they had gone, I gave a shilling for a peek at the register and saw Miss Mary Elder from St. Lucy's School at Farnham and Miss Violet Musgrove."

"And so you recognized the name, and saw to it that Miss Musgrove had her amusement and something left over," said Holmes. "What did you do next?"

"Well, that night I told Mrs. Peterson, of course – a fellow does best not to keep such matters from his wife. I said that unless my eyes betrayed me, I had come upon my own daughter that very afternoon when all these years I had supposed her to be dead. Mrs. Peterson was of the opinion that I should make myself known to Violet straight away, but I said that the girl has gone thirteen years without a father and might not wish to have one now. Mrs. Peterson said that I had done right to leave presents for the girl, but that it was our duty to do more, that as we were comfortable, and had a little laid aside, we must see to it that my child was comfortable as well, and so it was settled between us that we must send Violet pocket money from time to time."

"But, as you were reluctant to introduce yourself to Miss Musgrove, you decided to begin with correspondence. Letters written by Mrs.

Peterson. It was why I fell into the error of looking for a woman. Those verses that Miss Musgrove showed me were written in a woman's hand."

"Yes, sir, it was Mrs. Peterson who wrote the letters. She has more of a way with words, and then there is the hand, you see." He held up one ungloved hand which bore traces of an old wound. "These poor fingers can scratch out a signature well enough, but they make a clumsy business of more than a line or two of writing."

I knew from Holmes's pensive nod that he was thinking of Miss Armitage, who managed the correspondence for an employer who could not hold a pen.

"It was my notion to add a bit of poetry," Peterson continued. "I am quite fond of poetry, though you might not think so to look at me. I left the choosing to Mrs. Peterson, and it was her notion to seek out verses about violets. A tribute to you," he said to the girl. "And to your mother as well, poor girl! When I returned to Bombay, she was gone and all that was left of her were the few books of verse she had given me, all dog's-eared and underlined in her hand. I have them still if you should ever – " He pressed the girl's hand to his lips. "When your eyes are well again, you will read them yourself."

"In her letters to you, Miss Musgrove wrote nothing of the seriousness of her condition?"

"Nothing at all. I wrote to a blind school, but her letters spoke of nothing more than eye strain and headaches, and when she came to town to visit the doctor, she seemed able enough, but of course, I often got no more than a glimpse of her. And then, on their last visit to town, I saw Violet in the hotel lobby, sitting so quiet and still, she who had once wandered around, singing. And then Miss Elder approached and spoke and held out her arm and the way my poor girl laid her hand upon it . . . ."

"You offered fetch us a cab," said Miss Elder. "And would not take a sixpence."

Peterson nodded. "In the letters that followed, Violet wrote that her problem was more serious than she had let on, but that it might be made right with an operation, and that Miss Elder hoped to persuade a few charities to provide the funds for it. Well, Mrs. Peterson and I put our heads together to think what we might do. There was our little nest egg, and we made a vow not to give each other gifts at Christmas, and Mrs. Peterson said she might find employment in a shop or go back to nursing, and yet we could not see our way to half what was needed. Still, Mrs. Peterson said we must not give up hope, that the Lord would provide, and proposed that we might see what we could get for our wedding rings, as we would still be every bit as married whether we wore them or not. And then, of all things, Lady Morcar's blue stone pops out of the Christmas goose. When

429

Mr. Holmes, here, insisted that all the reward should all come to me, Mrs. Peterson just laughed and said it was proof that the Lord will provide, and what a good joke it was that His provision came by way of the larder. So now it was only a matter of how to get the funds to Violet. I had often aided a solicitor from Eastbourne when he is in town – "

"Mr. Graham," said Holmes.

"He is a good honest fellow who heard me out and agreed to act the go-between and wouldn't take a penny. Mr. Graham proposed that I advance eight-hundred for Violet's American expenses, and keep two-hundred back in the event there were some needs to be met when she returned home. And now, Mr. Holmes, I have told all. And I am very sorry, Violet, that I have not been a father when you most needed one, but as Mrs. Peterson says, we must not dwell upon the past, but be grateful that I am now able to make amends."

The girl laid her head upon his shoulder and reached up to pat his cheek. "Let us have none of that," she said as she dabbed away a tear.

"I must say, Mr. Holmes," declared Miss Elder, "that when we intruded upon you this morning, you gave us little hope that Violet's Good Samaritan could be found at all, and yet within hours you have produced both a patron and a parent. Your reputation does not do you justice."

"Well, well, some credit must be given to a very able assistant."

"Yes," said the lady. "Doctor Watson."

"No. William Cowper."

Holmes regarded our four puzzled expressions with a smile. "All of Miss Musgrove's letters were accompanied by verses. Our benefactor, therefore, was fond of poetry. Now this – " Holmes reached for the book he had laid aside. " – is a volume of Cowper's work. He has fallen out of vogue with all but true lovers of poetry. Earlier today, Peterson, you quoted Cowper when you remarked that you knew of no fatigue but idleness – a sentiment with which I concur, incidentally. And when I insisted, over your protests, upon paying for your researches, you called upon him once more when you said that we must let the reign of genuine charity commence. That is, in fact, from his poem entitled 'Charity'. And then, as fate would have it, a certain woman – *not* a charitable one, I'm bound to say – happened to quote from that very same work. You remember, Watson. '*Some seek, when queasy conscience has its qualms, To lull the painful malady with alms.*'"

I nodded. "I remember that you seemed particularly struck by the remark."

"The lady called to mind that I had already heard Cowper quoted twice that morning, and by one who answered to nearly all that I had deduced from Miss Musgrove's account – middle-aged, generous, honorable, poetic, though not – as I had wrongly concluded – a woman. Now, gifts of twenty pounds-per-annum would be well within his means, though he would be hard-pressed to come up with the five-hundred needed for Miss Musgrove's medical expense. And yet, he does – and not five-hundred, in fact, but *eight*-hundred. Not immediately, however. Not for some months, in fact."

"He has come into money," concluded Miss Elder.

Holmes nodded. "In his last letter to Miss Musgrove, our Good Samaritan writes that he could do no better with his own good fortune than to use it for her benefit. What is the source of this good fortune? Not the Derby, I think," Holmes said, with a sly look at me. "And not theft, certainly. A person who is too scrupulous to slip a letter into a packet and cheat the post office is no thief. So what is left: An inheritance or a reward. But I have just one question, Peterson. The alias. How did you happen to choose '*S. Holmes*'?"

"That came about a fortnight or so after I first saw Violet – before Mrs. Peterson had sent off the first letter. It hadn't been long before that when you and Doctor Watson took up lodgings here, and you had me carry some boxes and dispatch a wire or two, if you recall. And it struck me that, as I did not wish to come forward, '*Holmes*' would do well for an alias, as it is quite common – there must be thousands of Holmes-es about, but '*Sherlock*' was more irregular, and so I thought it best just to take the initial. And then, of course, as time passed, I could not come forward if I wished to, for you began to make a name for yourself, Mr. Holmes. Violet would suppose that her patron was a famous detective. How could I have her know that I was only a commissionaire?"

The girl threw her arms around his neck. "I would rather be a commissionaire's daughter than a king's!"

"I will do all in my power to make certain you always think so," said Peterson. "But now, we must go – we have given Mr. Holmes too much trouble as it is, and it is near tea time. You and Miss Elder must come with me to meet Mrs. Peterson. She has been impatient to know you for so long, I think it is well past time we put her at ease."

Peterson rose and held out his arm to the girl as he had seen Miss Elder do, and Miss Musgrove laid one hand upon his sleeve and extended the other in Holmes's direction. As Holmes took her hand and bade her farewell, it seemed to me that there was a tone of voice, and expression on his face that he rarely betrayed, a hint of emotion that did not often make its way to the aloof and rational exterior. But in the time it took me to escort our guests downstairs and return to the sitting room, he was his cold and impassive self once more.

431

"I am certain, Watson," he said, as he reached for his pipe, "that it will add a touch of humor to your account of this matter when you relate how my erroneous conclusion about the sex of our Good Samaritan led me to send off the very party I was seeking to search of her. Indeed, whenever I risk becoming too confident in my powers, I have no doubt that you will find occasion to introduce Peterson's name to the conversation, or utter the phrase 'wild goose chase'."

NOTES

The verse quoted in the poem read by Holmes is from nineteenth-century poet, Bryan Waller Proctor, who wrote under the pseudonym Barry Cornwall.

The phrase "Moon Type" was a system of writing and reading for the blind, developed by William Moon in the 1840's. It was said to have some advantage over Braille for those, who like Moon, lost their sight as adults.

The Abyssinian Campaign of 1868 was one of the most ambitious and dramatic nineteenth-century military missions conducted by the British, and Robert Napier, later Baron Napier of Magdala, was one of the most revered military figures.

On the other end of the spectrum was the infamous Mary Jeffries, a notorious nineteenth-century sex trafficker whose houses of ill repute catered to the social and political elite.

The Bishopsgate Jewel Case
by Stephen Gaspar

It was early in April 1888, and Holmes and I were sitting in our rooms in Baker Street. He was in his chair, smoking and reviewing some of his recent cases, while I was reading the afternoon paper.

"You really shouldn't read them, Watson, if they disturb you so," Holmes said.

"Whatever do you mean?" I responded, totally perplexed.

"When I see you shaking your head while making '*Tsk!*' sounds with your tongue and uttering disdainful moans and groans – all of them totally oblivious to your conscious mind, I'm sure. I know you're lamenting over the awful state of disreputable behaviour exhibited in our great city and recorded there in the daily rag."

He was of course correct. I read aloud some of the more lurid items from the newspaper. These included a robbery in Kensington, a murder of a woman in Whitechapel, a jewel theft in Bishopsgate, and a stabbing in Lambeth.

"What could possibly drive some men to do such things?" I asked. It was a rhetorical question, born more of frustration and derision rather than a legitimate query, but Sherlock Holmes regarded it genuinely and responded in his own inimitable fashion.

"*Possunt, quia posse videntur,*" Holmes said. "I personally would list the causes of crime thus: Greed, jealousy, fear, revenge, mental disease or defect, the mere thrill of the act, and thus as an addiction. Is that six or seven? Aristotle once listed the seven causes for all human actions: Chance, nature, compulsion, habit, reason, passion, and desire. And speaking of the number seven, there are, of course the Seven Deadly Sins that Dante portrayed so brilliantly: Pride, greed, lust, envy, gluttony, wrath, and sloth. I would suggest most of those can lead to crime, but not all. I could hardly imagine anyone who is slothful, yet can find the energy to burgle a house, or a glutton successfully escaping the clutches of the police by running down an alleyway while eating a sandwich."

Holmes continued his lecture unwavering, citing recent cases.

"The fate of Victor Savage is a prime example of what can happen when one trucks with evil. Young Grice-Paterson vowed revenge and he himself fell prey to that same violence. The Camberwell poisoning case was very rare, possessing both a degree of elegance and the savage. The

434

Bert Stephens affair was quite arcane with elements of grandeur and simplicity."

The detective spoke for nearly three-quarters of an hour on the subject of crime before he was interrupted by a knock at the door. Holmes opened it to find the tall, stout figure of Inspector Bradstreet of Scotland Yard. He took Bradstreet's right hand as ushered the man inside. The detective's face didn't brighten, but kept the same dour expression as when he stood in the doorway.

"My dear Bradstreet, come in and sit," Holmes said good-naturedly. "Let us hear all about the jewel robbery in Bishopsgate."

Bradstreet looked shocked. "How could you know about that, Mr. Holmes? I only got on the case this morning!"

In answer, Holmes plucked the newspaper from my hands. "There is already a story in the afternoon paper. Other than the fact that there were jewels stolen and you were called in, the story is sparse in facts. Perhaps," Holmes said as he sat in his chair and motioned Bradstreet to take the seat opposite, "you can tell us the story from the beginning."

With a heavy sigh, Bradstreet sat and began his tale. Holmes closed his eyes, and a slight smile touched his thin lips.

"Last night, Lady Catherine Wilkinson, of Bishopsgate, attended a formal dinner at the home of Lord and Lady Hampstead. Lady Wilkinson decided to wear her gold-and-emerald necklace, a gift from her late husband, Lord Henry Wilkinson, reported to be worth in excess of four-thousand pounds.

"Lady Wilkinson's escort for the evening was Sir Gerald Baldstroke, who is looked upon in disrepute by high society. Some regard him as something of a bounder. It was a very nice evening, according to Lady Wilkinson. Sir Gerald escorted her home in a carriage, walked her to her door, and bid her goodnight. Her Ladyship was let in by her maid, who followed her mistress to her room, but was soon dismissed.

"The maid couldn't swear she saw her mistress wearing her emerald necklace when she came in, as her Ladyship kept her wrap pulled tightly around her throat. Lady Wilkinson definitely remembers taking off the necklace and placing it in its case that sat upon her vanity in her room. When her Ladyship woke in the morning, the necklace was missing. She looked in the case and among her items on her vanity, but it wasn't there. She called her maid and had her look through her things, but the maid couldn't find it. Lady Wilkinson then called for the police and I was dispatched. In the meantime, her brother, Colin Baxter, arrived at the home to visit. He's a rather handsome man, about thirty years of age and ten years younger than his sister. He was told about the missing jewel necklace and he agreed to join in the search, seeing that she was very much upset.

"I arrived at Bishopsgate with some constables and had two of them search the house while another two remained outside searching the nearby grounds, just in case someone inside took the necklace and decided to chuck it out a window to be retrieved at a later date.

"The household normally consists of Lady Wilkinson, her maid, her butler, a cook, and the cook's daughter, who helps with the cooking and other household chores. Her Ladyship vouches for their integrity, claiming that she trusts them all implicitly. Despite that, they were all questioned by me and none were permitted to leave the house. They were all searched, including her Ladyship's brother, who joined us after coming from the kitchen. Both Baxter and his sister initially objected to such treatment. 'But he wasn't even in the house when the necklace went missing!' objected Lady Wilkinson. 'That's right, I wasn't,' Colin Baxter agreed. I told them both it was procedure, and the sooner we got it done, the sooner I could move on. Baxter reluctantly agreed at the behest of his sister, who was still very upset. 'Could you just do it for me, dear?' she said. I had the man remove his coat, which I searched, turn out his pockets, and even remove his shoes, but no necklace. 'If you want to know what I think,' Baxter said, with a degree of contempt, 'you should be questioning that bloke Baldstroke. He was with my sister last evening. If someone stole that emerald necklace, it was he.'

"Just then there was a shout from one of my men stationed outside. I raced out to see. A constable told me it was Constable Maikens who let out a cry and chased after someone. In a moment, Maikens returned alone and said that he'd seen a man outside a window of the house talking to a woman whom he took to be the maid. The woman had leaned out the window and handed something to the man. Maikens called out and startled them. The maid closed the window and the man bolted away across the garden and through the gate. Maikens pursued the fleeing man, but he got away.

"I went back inside and told her Ladyship that I needed to question the maid, whose name is Edith Foche. I asked her who it was she was speaking to at the window, and what she had given him before he ran away. She tried to bluster out of it, claiming ignorance of the entire affair, but I told her she'd been seen by one of my men and her best option was to be completely honest for the sake of herself, her position, and her mistress. 'It's all right, Edith,' her Ladyship said, soothingly. 'You can trust the Inspector. Please tell him what you know.'

Edith Foche was hesitant, but the truth is the man at the window is her fiancé, which she had been keeping secret from Lady Wilkinson for several weeks now. What she handed him was a love note whose contents she felt no obligation to reveal. She reiterated that she had always

436

remained loyal to her Ladyship and, save for the fact she had kept her engagement secret, she would never think of betraying her. The young woman was nearly in tears, and she was dismissed.

"I spoke to the butler next. His name is Perkins. He's about sixty years of age and had been in the service of Lord Wilkinson even before his marriage. He too, professed his loyalty and was personally distressed at the missing necklace, as it had been a gift from his Lordship, whom he served faithfully and missed very much.

"Perkins hadn't seen Lady Wilkinson return that evening, so he wasn't able to say if she indeed was wearing her necklace, but he did see her out earlier and observed that she was indeed adorned with it. Perkins was too readily willing to give his opinion of Sir Gerald Baldstroke, whom he regards as a 'rogue and peasant slave', and not a gentleman by any means. Perkins said he wouldn't be surprised if it was discovered that Sir Gerald had somehow pilfered the necklace.

"Next I spoke with the cook, Mrs. Dowdy, and her young daughter Emma, a pretty girl of sixteen, but a little slow-witted. They didn't see Lady Wilkinson leave that evening and were in bed when she returned. Neither seemed to know Sir Gerald Baldstroke, and therefore have no opinion of him. They both professed that the maid Edith Foche is a very nice young woman, hard-working and honest. The morning the robbery was discovered, they were both busy in the kitchen and heard the news from Lady Wilkinson's brother, Colin Baxter, who visited the house semi-regularly.

"'He asked me if he might have some breakfast, as he hadn't eaten,' Emma said, blushing. From the way she spoke, I believe young Emma has a crush on Mr. Baxter.

"Those are the bare facts of the case, Mr. Holmes. I haven't found the missing jewels, and was of the mind that you might wish to look into the affair – come with me to Bishopsgate and see things for yourself."

Holmes remained silent for a moment. He then opened his eyes and stood up rather quickly.

"I trust you have a cab waiting," he said to Bradstreet, who nodded. "Then give us a moment, and Watson and I will be ready shortly.

We were soon rattling down the streets of London, and Bradstreet told us of his further investigation into the Bishopsgate jewel case.

"I paid a visit to Lord and Lady Hampstead, whose dinner party Lady Wilkinson had attended the night before. They are a fine stately couple who were distressed to hear of the loss of the necklace. Yes, they said, Lady Wilkinson did wear her necklace that night and was wearing it when she left with Sir Gerald Baldstroke. When asked what they thought of Sir Gerald, they both hesitated, and then said they hadn't invited him, but he was Lady Wilkinson's escort for the evening. My impression was that the Hampsteads didn't think highly of him.

"I then went to Sir Gerald's residence to question him, but found him not at home. I left a constable there with instructions that upon his return, my man was to ask that he accompany him to Lady Wilkinson's regarding something of the highest urgency. If Sir Gerald refused, my officer was to watch the house and follow him if he left.

"I also sent a man to question Edith Foche's fiancé, but he has yet to be found."

"It would seem that you are taking all the proper and prudent steps," said Holmes.

"Now we come to a very strange development," Bradstreet continued. "When her Ladyship's brother, Mr. Baxter, left Bishopsgate, I had him followed, just in case. According to the officer, Baxter didn't take a cab, but instead walked to his residence in James Street. To be precise, it isn't his own residence, but instead he's staying with a married couple in their home, a Mr. and Mrs. Grayson. On approaching the house, Baxter was quickly set upon by a man who threw vitriol into his face! The attacker yelled something at Baxter and then ran away. Baxter brought his hands to his face, cried out in agony, and ran into the street, where he was then run over by a heavy wagon! By the time the constable reached Baxter, he was unconscious. He's is in hospital now, and may not recover."

"What else have you found out regarding Baxter?" Holmes asked.

"Very little, I'm afraid, save for the fact that the man is practically destitute. The Grayson's told me he's stopped paying rent for his room. He has asked them for money, which they refused to provide. It's known that he owes a good deal about the city."

"So you're thinking is – " Holmes began.

Bradstreet nodded. "The vitriol was a warning sent by an illegal money lender. You can't collect from a dead man, so they didn't mean that Baxter should die, but that looks like how it may turn out."

"Inspector, your man didn't happen to search Baxter as he lay on the street, did he?"

"Actually, he did, Mr. Holmes. I can attest that Baxter didn't have the necklace on his person when he left Bishopsgate, and he didn't have it on him when he was attacked."

"So we can assume for now that the theft of the jewels and the attack on Baxter aren't related," Holmes uttered as he mused over the problem.

"It wouldn't appear so," the Scotland Yard man agreed.

We arrived at Lady Catherine Wilkinson's home in Bishopsgate, a somewhat large, stately, two-story structure, with lawn and garden enclosed by a wall.

438

As we stepped out of the cab, a constable ran up to Bradstreet, gave a brief salute, and said, "Inspector Jones is here, sir."

"Jones?" Bradstreet repeated the name. "What could he want?" He turned to us. "This way, gentleman."

Bradstreet led us toward the front door that was already being opened by the butler. We passed through the tiled hall to a sitting room. There was a middle-age woman, whom I took to be Lady Catherine Wilkinson, sitting in a chair listening to a man that stood close by. She was a pretty woman in her forties who seemed desperate to hang on to her youth. The man standing by her turned at our approach and regarded us suspiciously with keen, beady eyes. He was stout and portly, dressed in a grey suit of clothes.

"Bradstreet," he said, focusing his gaze on the younger Scotland Yard man.

"Inspector Jones," Bradstreet greeted him. "I'm surprised to see you here."

"Yes, well, the Yard decided a more senior man was needed. I'm taking over the case."

"You're . . . you're taking over the case?" Bradstreet said, clearly dismayed. "I don't believe that is necessary, Inspector."

"You can stay on and see how things are done," Jones said, condescendingly.

"See here, Inspector," Bradstreet said, barely holding his anger in check. "I have things well in hand."

"You do, eh?" said the other detective, his thick, puffy face growing red. "Do you have a suspect then?"

"I have several leads I'm following."

"I have one, and he is our man."

"And who is that?"

"Sir Gerald Baldstroke. He accompanied her Ladyship last evening, and she doesn't believe she had the necklace when she came into this house."

Bradstreet looked aghast. He turned imploring eyes upon the woman. "Lady Wilkinson, you told me emphatically that you *did* have the necklace when you came home last night."

Lady Wilkinson looked at Bradstreet and shrugged her shoulders in a hopeless, resigned manner. "I know I told you that, Inspector, and I am sorry, but after speaking with Inspector Jones, I cannot swear for certain I did have the necklace. It was quite late and I was very tired. Perhaps in the morning I was simply recalling another time I removed my necklace and placed it in the case."

"There you are," Jones said triumphantly. "Baldstroke is our man. I heard that you gave orders to have him brought here. You were right to do that, at least."

"Lady Wilkinson," Bradstreet said, taking a tender tone. "I have some bad news. Your brother was attacked outside his rooms, and is currently in hospital."

The woman put her hand to her throat and her breath came fast. "Colin – oh dear God, Colin!" She called for her maid, who arrived quickly. "Edith, my smelling salts! I left them by my bedside." The maid quickly vanished.

I stepped forward to offer what assistance I could. I told Lady Wilkinson that I was a doctor, and asked if I could do something for her. She replied that she needed her smelling salts. In the interim, Holmes had stepped over to the side table where sat a carafe of water. He poured a glass, gave it to me, and I encouraged the lady to drink. She did so, and I suggested that she lay her head back on the chair.

"And what are these two doing here?" asked Jones, haughtily.

"They are here at my request."

"Your *request*?" Jones repeated, his chubby face breaking into a wide grin. "Are you that desperate, Bradstreet, that you need to get advice from outside the Yard? You stick close to me, and I'll show you how to catch the thief."

"Where is that girl with my smelling salts?" Lady Wilkinson asked, perturbed.

After a few long minutes the maid came into the room carrying a small bottle.

"Oh, there you are, Edith," Lady Wilkinson said. "What kept you?"

"It wasn't by your bedside table, your Ladyship," the maid said, both apologetic and frustrated. She gave the bottle to Lady Wilkinson, who clutched it to her bosom comfortingly.

Just then a constable came to the door. He hesitated, as if not knowing which inspector to address. "Sir Gerald Baldstroke has just arrived, sir," he announced, not looking at either of his superiors.

"Ah, splendid," Jones said, with a grin.

"Sir Gerald is here?" Lady Wilkinson said. She drew in a deep breath, smoothed her dress, and patted her hair. "Have him come in, won't you?"

"I'm sorry, Lady Wilkinson," Jones said, in his sweetest of voices. "I must have a few words with Sir Gerald first. You understand, I'm sure. Afterward . . . ." He didn't finish, as he suspected he would be leading Sir Gerald away in irons. "If you'll excuse me, Lady Wilkinson." Jones gave a brief bow and left the room.

Bradstreet, Holmes, and I did likewise.

Sir Gerald Baldstroke was standing with a constable in the hall. He was a distinguished-looking man about fifty years of age, with streaks of gray in his dark hair, heavy brows over deep-set blue eyes, and a well-trimmed moustache above a wide, thin-lipped mouth. He stood tall and fashionably dressed.

Jones introduced himself and informed Sir Gerald that he was investigating the robbery of Lady Wilkinson's necklace.

The man appeared startled and dismayed. "Lady Wilkinson must be very upset," he said. "May I see her?"

"Yes, I am certain you wish to see her," said Jones. The detective did have the ability to put people at ease. "I just need to ask you a few questions first."

"Of course, Inspector," Sir Gerald said. "Whatever I can do to help."

"First of all, Sir Gerald . . . ." Jones began, then looked at us and said, "Perhaps we can speak privately in here." He ushered Sir Gerald into an adjoining room. Standing in the doorway he said to Bradstreet. "Are you coming?"

We all stepped forward and Jones held a staying hand. "This is official police business. Only Inspector Bradstreet."

Bradstreet looked at us apologetically and went into the room. The door shut.

"What do you think of that?" I asked. "Imagine being called out to consult on a case, then being deprived of even hearing what a witness may have to say." I thought my friend would be insulted, but he remained perfectly calm.

"Perhaps we may find some other way to occupy our time."

Just then the door opened to the sitting room that we had occupied moments before and the maid came out. Holmes instantly approached her.

"Excuse me – you are Miss Foche, aren't you?" Holmes asked her. She nodded hesitantly. "My name is Sherlock Holmes, and this is my friend and associate, Dr. Watson." The young woman curtsied. "We only wish to ask you a few questions about the missing necklace." She nodded again. "When you went to fetch the smelling salts for your mistress, you didn't find them where she said. Is that at all typical of Lady Wilkinson?"

"Why, bless me, sir," she replied, "I wouldn't wish to speak against my mistress."

"Of course not," said Holmes, in an understanding and disarming tone. "But do you think she may have misplaced her necklace?"

"If anyone could misplace something, Mr. Holmes, I'm certain my mistress could. She has often has misplaced things, but we all searched the house completely and it wasn't to be found. If she returned last night wearing it, then it must have been stolen."

441

"Yes, I see your point," Holmes said. "*If* she wore it home last night," he repeated. "It's my understanding that you cannot say for certain if Lady Wilkinson was wearing her necklace when she returned last night."

"That is true, sir."

"The inspectors are presently questioning Sir Gerald Baldstroke about what he may know," Holmes said. "What's your impression of Sir Gerald?"

"Sir?"

"Do you think Sir Gerald could have stolen the necklace?"

"I cannot say, sir. Her Ladyship is fond of him. He is handsome. I couldn't imagine Sir Gerald doing such a thing."

Just then the butler came into the hall. He stopped to look at the maid and cleared his throat audibly.

The maid blushed, looked down, and said, "You will excuse me, sirs." And she hurried away.

Holmes turned to the butler and addressed him. "Mr. Parker, isn't it?" he asked him.

"Yes, sir."

We approached the older man, who regarded us with little interest. His head was balding, and he stood with a slight stoop.

"Parker, what do you think of Sir Gerald? Do you think he stole Lady Wilkinson's necklace?"

"I wouldn't be surprised, sir."

"You don't think he is a man of upstanding character?"

Parker made a disapproving sound. "Ever since the death of Lord Wilkinson, it seems her Ladyship is inundated by these types. Her own brother is another. Two of a kind, if you ask me."

"You are referring to Mr. Colin Baxter?"

"I don't see how her Ladyship came to have such a brother," Parker said with scorn. "Always coming to see her for this or that, but mainly for money. I'm sure that's why he came to see her today. If the necklace hadn't gone missing before he stepped in the house, I would suspect him. Be that as it may, I kept an eye on him. I usually do when he's here. When he saw me watching him, he came up to me, brazen-like, and said he was going to the kitchen for breakfast. I followed to make sure that was where he was going."

"Did you see him after he'd been in the kitchen?" Holmes asked.

"I was there when the young inspector searched him," Parker said, with a smirk. "He objected to being searched, but he agreed. Soon after that, the man left. Good riddance, that's what I thought."

"Thank you, Parker," said Holmes. "Which way to the kitchen?"

The butler pointed out the way and discreetly followed us until we entered it.

Our trespass was marked by the cook, Mrs. Dowdy, and her teenage daughter, Emma, who obviously regarded us as intruders into their personal little province.

"What a wonderful place!" Holmes exclaimed to them. "You know, I believe the kitchen is the heart of every home, and this one is absolutely splendid."

The girl smiled, but Mrs. Dowdy wasn't so easily won over. "What can I do for you gentlemen?" she asked blandly.

Holmes introduced us and explained we had been brought in by the official police force regarding the robbery of Lady Wilkinson's necklace.

"We wouldn't know anything about that, sirs, as that has nothing to do with us or our work."

"Oh, please, I'm not accusing either of you of having anything to do with it," Holmes said, earnestly. "I'm certain there have been a lot of comings and goings. The house is simply abuzz with people. No one has come in to bother you, I hope."

"Other than you two, the police were in here looking for the necklace" said the cook, distraught at the remembrance of her sanctum being invaded by strangers. "What a mess they made – disturbing my pots, emptying the cupboards, looking in the oven."

"When was that?" Holmes asked.

"I'd say just before noon."

"Did you see anyone perhaps earlier in the morning?"

The cook shook her head.

"Mr. Colin Baxter, perhaps?

The cook's daughter hesitantly spoke up.

"Mr. Baxter did come in this morning, sir," she said, and I believe she blushed when she said it.

"He did?" the cook said.

"Yes, mum. He asked me to prepare him something to eat."

"Well, he has a nerve, that one."

"It was no trouble, mum."

The mother made a disapproving sound.

"And what did you prepare for Mr. Baxter?" Holmes asked, smiling.

"Ham and eggs, sir."

"And what did you two talk about? Did he mention the missing necklace?"

"No, sir. We didn't hear about that until later."

"Did Mr. Baxter say anything at all?"

443

"Yes, sir," she said, smiling shyly. "He said how much he liked my cooking."

"Your daughter is a good cook, then?" Holmes asked Mrs. Dowdy.

"She's coming along, sir. Emma just needs to keep her head straight about measurements."

"My measuring is fine," young Emma protested.

"Sometimes you mix them up," her mother told her. "Then there was the time you put salt in the pie instead of sugar."

"But Mr. Baxter likes her cooking," Holmes prompted.

"He was just being kind, I'm sure," Mrs. Dowdy said.

"He was not!" Emma declared, her feelings being hurt. "Mr. Baxter does think I'm a good cook. After he ate, he asked me for a loaf of my bread, didn't he?"

"Bread?" Holmes repeated.

"Yes sir," said Emma, who was wiping a tear from her eyes. "I had some loaves ready for the oven and Mr. Baxter asked me to send one to him when they was done. He even marked the one he wanted by putting raisins on top. 'This is the one I want, Emma,' he said. 'The one with raisins.'"

"And did you give it to him?" asked Holmes.

"Not personally sir, as he said he had to go and couldn't wait. He told me his address and asked if I could send it. When it was pulled from the oven, I wrapped it nice and neat and gave it to a boy who sometimes does little chores about the yard. I wrote the address on a card and gave it to him to deliver."

"And did he deliver it?"

"I suppose so, sir."

"And what is Mr. Colin Baxter's address?" Holmes asked.

The girl went to answer, then stopped to think. Her brows knotted and she frowned.

"I'm afraid I've already forgotten," she said, apologetically. "Is it – ? No, I can't be certain of the number, but I'm sure it's on John Street."

"Thank you, both," said Holmes with a grin. "We'll let you get back to your work now."

We left the kitchen and we saw Inspector Athelney Jones and an officer leading Sir Gerald Baldstroke out the door. Bradstreet approached us.

"He's arrested Sir Gerald," Bradstreet announced with a heavy sigh. "The man denies the charges, of course."

"And do you also suspect Baldstroke?" Holmes asked him.

Bradstreet shook his head. "I don't think so. When I spoke with Lady Wilkinson, she told me she returned with the necklace and remembers removing it. Jones was somehow able to convince her she hadn't."

"It fits his theory that Sir Gerald stole it," Holmes said. "Lady Wilkinson's mind is a bit scattered, and Jones was able to confuse her enough to change her story."

Just then a constable entered holding the arm of another man.

"What's this, Maikens?" Bradstreet asked.

"Mr. Nat Taylor," the constable said. "This here's the man who ran from the house after receiving something from the maid."

"She's my fiancé!" Nat Taylor said, heatedly. "It was only a note. A personal note."

Young Mr. Taylor was dark-haired and red-faced, presumably from the fact his simple explanation wasn't sufficient to keep him from being arrested. He was dressed something a bit better than a common loafer with a cloth cap, worn coat, pants, and boots. A faded red cravat was tied about his neck.

"Well, we'll see about that," Bradstreet told him. "Constable, take Mr. Taylor into that room and I'll question him there."

Maikens led the man away and Bradstreet turned to Holmes. "Would you care to be present during his questioning?"

"Do you truly believe this man Taylor had anything to do with the theft of the jewels?" Holmes asked. The doubt in his face and words were evident.

Bradstreet looked slightly abashed. "I just can't let Jones get the better of me, Mr. Holmes. He's already made an arrest. I have to do something. Taylor is my only lead. I'm sorry." With that, Bradstreet turned and went into the room where awaited his suspect.

We stood there staring at the door that Bradstreet had just closed.

"What are we to do?" I asked my friend.

Wordlessly he turned and faced the sitting room door, which was also closed. Then he strode to it, rapped upon it gently, waited for a response, and then entered. I followed.

Lady Wilkinson sat in the same chair as when we left her. She still clutched the smelling salts bottle and looked at us questioningly. "Yes?"

"Please excuse our intrusion, Lady Wilkinson," Holmes said. "We only wished to see if you were well, and if you needed anything."

"No, thank you," she replied. "I have my servants to tend to me."

"We also wish you to know that we're intent on recovering your jewel necklace," Holmes told her.

"Thank you."

"You certainly have suffered much – with the theft of your property, and then your brother the unfortunate victim of a brutal attack."

"Poor Colin," the lady said, bringing the back of her hand to her forehead. "He has certainly had his share of misfortune."

"Yes," said Holmes. "He paid a visit to you just this morning, I believe."

"Yes. I was very upset over the loss of my necklace. Colin helped me look for it, but to no avail. He even got down on his hands and knees. At one point, I thought he found it. He called out to me, but when I returned to my boudoir, he told me he had no luck. It was then the police arrived. I'd called them before Colin's arrival."

"Yes, a pity. Lady Wilkinson, do you have your brother's address?"

"Yes, why?"

"We had heard he is staying with someone, and we only wish to inform them of your brother's most unfortunate condition."

"That is very kind of you. He is staying with a kind couple named Grayson. I don't know them, but they're friends of Colin. The address is 143 James Street. I believe it's near Oxford Street."

"Are you certain it isn't John Street?" Holmes asked.

The lady almost looked indignant. "I am quite certain it is 143 James Street.

"Thank you, Lady Wilkinson," Holmes said, consolingly. "We hope to have good news for you very soon."

With that, we left the lady and the house. Once outside, Holmes breathed in deeply and a smile played on his lips.

"Not a very complicated little problem," he said, with a hint of hubris.

"You mean that you've solved it?" I asked.

"You saw and heard everything I did. Are you saying you cannot follow my line of reasoning?"

"You appear to put some importance in the unfortunate Colin Baxter, but I cannot see how he has anything to do with the theft, as he didn't arrive at Bishopsgate until *after* the theft."

"Is that how you see it?"

"He was even searched by Bradstreet."

"Yes, he was.

"He didn't walk out with any jewels," I said, "and none were found on him after he was attacked."

"Cab!" Holmes called out.

We got in and Holmes said to me, "Give him our destination, won't you, Watson."

I studied my friend's face for several seconds, then I called out, "143 James Street, cabbie."

446

We arrived and alighted on the pavement. The homes on the street were modest, not half as opulent as the one we had just left in Bishopsgate. Holmes used his stick and knocked upon the door.

The door was opened by a pleasant middle-aged woman who greeted us with a smile.

"Mrs. Grayson?" Holmes asked.

"Yes, I'm Mrs. Grayson."

"My name is Sherlock Holmes, and this is my associate, Dr. Watson. I'm afraid we have bad news regarding your boarder, Mr. Colin Baxter. He's been the victim of a terrible attack and is in hospital."

The woman brought her hands to her face that displayed total shock.

"Good gracious, is he badly hurt?"

"I am afraid so."

"Are you his doctor?" she asked me.

"No," I said. "I haven't had the opportunity to see him."

"Mrs. Grayson," Holmes said to her, "I need to ask you about the delivery you received today."

"Delivery? We have received no delivery today," she said, slightly confused.

"It was addressed to Mr. Baxter at this address," Holmes said. "It would have been delivered this morning by a young lad."

"I'm sorry, gentleman, but I've been home all day, and there has been no delivery."

Holmes looked crestfallen and confused. "Well, then, we must take our leave," he told the woman solemnly.

We stepped back into our cab and Holmes gave the driver our Baker Street address. The detective sat silently, his chin sunk upon his chest, deep in thought. Then, after several minutes, he raised his head with a start and an exclamation.

"Of course!" he said, and called for the cabbie to stop. He got out and told me to proceed to Scotland Yard and make sure that Jones and Bradstreet would be at Bishopsgate when he returned

"Wait for me there!" he said, and started down the street.

"Holmes!" I called out to him. "What are you going to do?"

"I am going to find a bake shop!"

By the time I located Jones and Bradstreet and convinced them to come back with me to the house in Bishopsgate, more than an hour-and-a-half had elapsed. We were greeted at the door by the butler and escorted us to the sitting room, where I was surprised to find Holmes already waiting for us. Also in the room was Lady Wilkinson.

It was obvious to me by Holmes's verbose and friendly manner that he'd brought this case to a successful conclusion, though I couldn't see how. By contradiction, the official detectives appeared dour and defeated. Lady Wilkinson still clutched her smelling salts and appeared sorely troubled.

"Thank you all for coming," Holmes said. "What we hope to do is untangle this affair and uncover exactly what has happened here in this house. *Omnia causa fiunt*. For this we must look to causes and inferences and effects."

And for the next quarter-of-an-hour, Holmes gave a talk on this subject and how – when inferring the cause of something – one must use reason to the conclusion that something is the cause of something else. The identification of the cause of a phenomenon is established by a time-order relationship, with the cause preceding the effect and then eliminating the plausible alternate causes. Time in this case, he said, is important, and we must look at the sequence of time. Using these, one may form a theory or theories that are then put to the test.

"Mr. Holmes," Jones said, forcefully and with a degree of impatience. "I didn't come here to be lectured by some private consultant."

"Inspector, I was hoping you would see the benefit of how this may assist you in the future in your police work," Holmes said with less ire, but still with force. "But since you see no practical purpose, we will dispense with the 'lecture' and move on to the theft of the jewel necklace."

"Do you know who stole my necklace?" Lady Wilkinson asked, pleadingly.

"Yes, dear madam, I do," said Holmes. "And it was you yourself who gave me an important clue."

"I did?" Lady Wilkinson seemed both amazed and pleased with herself.

"Yes, you did," Holmes said, and addressed everyone present. "Two arrests were made in this house today. One was Mr. Nat Taylor, fiancé to Lady Wilkinson's maid, Edith Foche. He was arrested because he was seen accepting something from the maid. Tell me, Inspector Bradstreet, has Taylor confessed?"

"No."

"Was the necklace found on his person or in his home?"

"No."

"Does Taylor still profess his innocence?"

"Yes."

"That is because he is."

"It's my intention to release Taylor, Mr. Holmes."

"Very good," Holmes said and turned to Jones.

"Mr. Jones, you arrested Sir Gerald Baldstroke for the theft of the necklace. Do you still suspect him?"

448

"Yes, I do," Jones said defiantly.

"Even though the man professes his innocence and the necklace wasn't found on his person or in his home."

"I'll find it. Don't you worry yourself, Mr. Theorist."

"I wish you good luck."

"Mr. Holmes, please," Lady Wilkinson said.

"Very well. When you woke this morning, you noticed your necklace was missing from where you left it. Even though Inspector Jones convinced you that you didn't come home wearing the necklace that night, I believe you did. It was late. You removed the necklace quite casually, and as you most likely were more interested in going to bed, you didn't take notice of exactly where you laid it. In the morning, thinking you placed the necklace in the case, you looked for it there, but it was not. You looked around and couldn't find it. But to be honest, you have misplaced things before, haven't you, Lady Wilkinson?"

The woman looked abashed. "I may have misplaced some item once or twice."

"It was soon after that you began looking for your necklace that your brother, Mr. Baxter, arrived, probably to ask you for money. He is in the habit of asking you for money, isn't he?"

She nodded.

"But before he could ask, you told him of your dilemma, and he agreed to help you look. You probably told him you saw it last on your vanity and that is where he searched. He was down on his hands and knees and knew if he found it, you would wish to reward him. His efforts were successful. He found your necklace, probably on the floor, beneath the vanity. He called out to you to show you, but as soon as he called, the devil showed him how he could keep the necklace which was worth far more than he wished to ask. He simply pocketed it and when you came to answer his call, he said he couldn't find it."

"But I searched Colin Baxter, Mr. Holmes," Bradstreet protested. "The man didn't have the necklace on his person, and he didn't have it when he was attacked."

"That is where we need to observe time," said Holmes. "You searched him *after* he returned from breakfast."

"Did he eat the necklace?" Bradstreet asked.

"Of course not," said Holmes. "Baxter knew the police were swarming the house and grounds. He couldn't keep it on his person. He wandered into the kitchen where the cook's daughter was preparing to put her bread doughs in the oven. Behind her back, Baxter slipped the necklace into a dough that sat upon the table. He then topped the dough with raisins to cover the spot and to mark the one he wanted. He complimented the girl

449

in the kitchen and told her he liked her cooking. Then he asked her to bake the raisin bread especially for him and have it sent to the address he gave her. She found the boy who does chores about the house to deliver it."

"But Holmes," I interjected, "I was with you when you went to the house on James Street, and no delivery was made there."

"That did stump me for a bit," Holmes admitted. "But recall that the girl in the kitchen and how her mother told us that her daughter mixed up measurements, and once added salt to a pie instead of sugar. It struck me that a girl like that just might mix up an address. Do you remember how she said it was on John Street, when it was actually James Street?"

"What did you do then, Mr. Holmes?" Lady Wilkinson asked.

"I went to a bakery, bought a fresh loaf of bread, and started knocking on doors along James Street. I knew I just might have to also knock on every door on John Street as well, but luck was with me and at Number 134, I found the house that had received a loaf of bread from a young boy. I saw the address card. The cook's daughter had accidentally transposed the last two digits. My arrival at the house was fortuitous, for they were just about to cut into the bread. I explained it had mistakenly been delivered to the wrong address and that if they would give it to me I would gladly exchange it for a fresh loaf. They saw no reason to refuse and they handed it over."

"You have it?" I asked.

Holmes bent down and by his feet was a small carpet bag. From the bag he took out a small bundle wrapped in a checkered cloth and tied with a blue bow. He undid the bow and removed the cloth to reveal a golden-brown loaf of bread with raisins on top.

"Are you saying the necklace is in there?" Jones asked, incredulously.

"If it isn't, I shall eat the entire loaf," Holmes said, then quite dramatically he ripped it open to reveal the emerald-and-gold necklace. He held it up triumphantly, and then presented it to Lady Wilkinson.

"Well, I'll be jiggered," Jones uttered.

"Mr. Holmes, this is fantastic!" Bradstreet exclaimed with a grin.

"Excellent, Holmes, excellent!" I congratulated him.

Lady Wilkinson looked from her necklace to Holmes and said, "Mr. Holmes, I don't know how I can thank you."

"There is no need, my dear madam," Holmes said, magnanimously. "I'm pleased I was able to aid your Ladyship."

Athelney Jones walked up to Sherlock Holmes. Some of his bluster had now dissipated. He licked his thick lips and his mouth moved, twitching and puckering. "Mr. Sherlock Holmes," he said.

Holmes regarded Jones casually. "Inspector Jones, I won't keep you from going to Scotland Yard where you and Inspector Bradstreet are anxious to return and release your prisoners."

Jones bowed his head slightly and walked out of the room.

Holmes and I were back in Baker Street by eight o'clock that evening.

"I must congratulate you again, Holmes, on a fine piece of detective work," I said.

"Thank you, my dear fellow, but it was only a piece of very simple reasoning," he said, stuffing his pipe. "Just this morning we were speaking of human action, sin, and the root of crime, but in detection we must look at the human nature of not only the criminal, but of any and all that are involved. Most didn't suspect Colin Baxter because they believed he arrived after the supposed theft. They were mistaken. Learning more about Lady Wilkinson, we saw that she is prone to misplacing things and not remembering exactly where she leaves them. From her mother, we learned the young Emma Dowdy sometimes mixes things up in her mind. She also possesses a girlish affection for Colin Baxter and wouldn't suspect him of any wrongdoing. Bradstreet and Jones were so anxious to make an arrest that they closed their minds to other theories and possibilities."

He lit his pipe and stood staring out the window and onto the endless rooftops that stretched out before him.

"What now?" I asked. "Dinner, perhaps?"

"*Mox nox*. Light thickens and the heavens draw their shades of night over the city," he said, thoughtfully. "What evil will prowl through the streets of London this night, I wonder? I suppose we'll find out in the morning."

Some may have observed that I have occasionally rounded off some of my narratives somewhat abruptly, omitting those final details which the curious might expect and find consoling. So as to not leave any threads hanging, I write this as an epilogue from a short handwritten note attached to my manuscript dealing with this case.

Mr. Colin Baxter did recover from his injuries, and though his speech was affected, he was able to identify the man who threw the vitriol, and the man who had hired him to carry out the attack. As it turned out, Bradstreet was correct. The attack on Colin Baxter was ordered by an illegal money lender named Larson to whom Baxter owed a great sum of money. It is ironic indeed that, had Baxter not been attacked on the street and subsequently hit by a mortified but innocent cabbie, he might have been able to discover just where the raisin bread had been delivered and would have had more than enough to pay his debt.

Despite having stolen from his sister, Lady Catherine Wilkinson, in a show of forgiveness and fidelity, moved her brother into her house to fully recuperate from his injuries. I can only trust that all the valuables in the house have been locked away and that the butler, Parker, is keeping a close eye on Mr. Colin.

About the Contributors

The following contributors appear in this volume:
The MX Book of New Sherlock Holmes Stories
Part XXV – 2021 Annual (1881-1887)

Hugh Ashton was born in the U.K., and moved to Japan in 1988, where he remained until 2016, living with his wife Yoshiko in the historic city of Kamakura, a little to the south of Yokohama. He and Yoshiko have now moved to Lichfield, a small cathedral city in the Midlands of the U.K., the birthplace of Samuel Johnson, and one-time home of Erasmus Darwin. In the past, he has worked in the technology and financial services industries, which have provided him with material for some of his books set in the 21st century. He currently works as a writer: Novelist, freelance editor, and copywriter, (his work for large Japanese corporations has appeared in international business journals), and journalist, as well as producing industry reports on various aspects of the financial services industry. However, his lifelong interest in Sherlock Holmes has developed into an acclaimed series of adventures featuring the world's most famous detective, written in the style of the originals. In addition to these, he has also published historical and alternate historical novels, short stories, and thrillers. Together with artist Andy Boerger, he has produced the *Sherlock Ferret* series of stories for children, featuring the world's cutest detective.

Brian Belanger is a publisher, editor, illustrator, author, and graphic designer. In 2015, he co-founded Belanger Books along with his brother, author Derrick Belanger. He designs the covers for every Belanger Books release, and his illustrations have appeared in the MacDougall Twins with Sherlock Holmes series, as well as *Dragonella, Scones and Bones on Baker Street*, and *Sherlock Holmes: A Three-Pipe Problem*. Brian has published a number of Sherlock Holmes anthologies, as well as new editions of August Derleth's classic Solar Pons mysteries. Since 2016, Brian has written and designed letters for the *Dear Holmes* series, and illustrated a comic book for indie band The Moonlight Initiative. In 2019, Brian received his investiture in the PSI as "Sir Ronald Duveen". Find him online at *www.belangerbooks.com*, *www.zhahadun.wixsite.com/221b*, and *www.redbubble.com/people/zhahadun*

Chris Chan is a writer, educator, and historian. He works as a researcher and "International Goodwill Ambassador" for Agatha Christie Ltd. His true crime articles, reviews, and short fiction have appeared (or will soon appear) in *The Strand*, *The Wisconsin Magazine of History*, *Mystery Weekly*, *Gilbert!*, *Nerd HQ*, Akashic Books' *Mondays are Murder* web series, *The Baker Street Journal*, and *Sherlock Holmes Mystery Magazine*. His latest book is *Sherlock and Irene: The Secret Truth Behind "A Scandal in Bohemia"*.

Martin Daley was born in Carlisle, Cumbria in 1964. He cites Doyle's Holmes and Watson as his favourite literary characters, who continue to inspire his own detective writing. His fiction and non-fiction books include a Holmes pastiche set predominantly in his home city in 1903. In the adventure, he introduced his own detective, Inspector Cornelius Armstrong, who has subsequently had some of his own cases published by MX Publishing. For more information visit *www.martindaley.co.uk*

Sir Arthur Conan Doyle (1859-1930) *Holmes Chronicler Emeritus*. If not for him, this anthology would not exist. Author, physician, patriot, sportsman, spiritualist, husband and father, and advocate for the oppressed. He is remembered and honored for the purposes of this collection by being the man who introduced Sherlock Holmes to the world. Through fifty-six Holmes short stories, four novels, and additional Apocryphal entries, Doyle revolutionized mystery stories and also greatly influenced and improved police forensic methods and techniques for the betterment of all. *Steel True Blade Straight.*

Steve Emecz's main field is technology, in which he has been working for about twenty years. Steve is a regular trade show speaker on the subject of eCommerce, and his tech career has taken him to more than fifty countries – so he's no stranger to planes and airports. He wrote two novels (one a bestseller) in the 1990's, and a screenplay in 2001. Shortly after, he set up MX Publishing, specialising in NLP books. In 2008, MX published its first Sherlock Holmes book, and MX has gone on to become the largest specialist Holmes publisher in the world. MX is a social enterprise and supports three main causes. The first is Happy Life, a children's rescue project in Nairobi, Kenya, where he and his wife, Sharon, spend every Christmas at the rescue centre in Kasarani. In 2014, they wrote a short book about the project, *The Happy Life Story.* The second is the Stepping Stones School, of which Steve is a patron. Stepping Stones is located at Undershaw, Sir Arthur Conan Doyle's former home. Steve has been a mentor for the World Food Programme for the last several years, supporting their innovation bootcamps and giving 1-2-1 mentoring to several projects.

Matthew J. Elliott is the author of *Big Trouble in Mother Russia* (2016), the official sequel to the cult movie *Big Trouble in Little China, Lost in Time and Space: An Unofficial Guide to the Uncharted Journeys of Doctor Who* (2014), *Sherlock Holmes on the Air* (2012), *Sherlock Holmes in Pursuit* (2013), *The Immortals: An Unauthorized Guide to* Sherlock *and* Elementary (2013), and *The Throne Eternal* (2014). His articles, fiction, and reviews have appeared in the magazines *Scarlet Street, Total DVD, SHERLOCK,* and *Sherlock Holmes Mystery Magazine,* and the collections *The Game's Afoot, Curious Incidents 2, Gaslight Grimoire, The Mammoth Book of Best British Crime 8,* and *The MX Book of New Sherlock Holmes Stories – Part III: 1896-1929.* He has scripted over 260 radio plays, including episodes of *Doctor Who, The Further Adventures of Sherlock Holmes, The Twilight Zone, The New Adventures of Mickey Spillane's Mike Hammer, Fangoria's Dreadtime Stories,* and award-winning adaptations of *The Hound of the Baskervilles* and *The War of the Worlds.* He is the only radio dramatist to adapt all sixty original stories from The Canon for the series *The Classic Adventures of Sherlock Holmes.* Matthew is a writer and performer on *RiffTrax.com,* the online comedy experience from the creators of cult sci-fi TV series *Mystery Science Theater 3000* (*MST3K* to the initiated). He's also written a few comic books.

Mark A. Gagen BSI is co-founder of Wessex Press, sponsor of the popular *From Gillette to Brett* conferences, and publisher of *The Sherlock Holmes Reference Library* and many other fine Sherlockian titles. A life-long Holmes enthusiast, he is a member of *The Baker Street Irregulars* and *The Illustrious Clients of Indianapolis.* A graphic artist by profession, his work is often seen on the covers of *The Baker Street Journal* and various BSI books.

Stephen Gaspar is a writer of historical detective fiction. He has written two Sherlock Holmes books: *The Canadian Adventures of Sherlock Holmes* and *Cold-Hearted Murder.* Some of his detectives are a Roman Tribune, a medieval monk, and a Templar knight. He was born and lives in Windsor, Ontario, Canada.

Hal Glatzer is the author of the Katy Green historical mystery series, set in musical milieux just before World War II. He has written and produced audio/radio plays, scripted and produced the Charlie Chan mystery *The House Without a Key* on stage, and adapted "The Adventure of the Devil's Foot" into a stage and video play called *Sherlock Holmes & The Volcano Horror*, set on the Island of Hawaii, where he has lived for twenty-five of the past fifty years. See more at: *www.halglatzer.com*

John Atkinson Grimshaw (1836-1893) was born in Leeds, England. His amazing paintings, usually featuring twilight or night scenes illuminated by gas-lamps or moonlight, are easily recognizable, and are often used on the covers of books about The Great Detective to set the mood, as shadowy figures move in the distance through misty mysterious settings and over rain-slicked streets.

Keith Hann is a Canadian Ph.D. student, slaving away in the realm of military and diplomatic history. To dodge dissertation deadlines, he enjoys pulp fiction, trash cinema, and crafting the occasional Holmes piece, one of which has appeared in *Ellery Queen's Mystery Magazine*.

Paul Hiscock is an author of crime, fantasy, and science fiction tales. His short stories have appeared in several anthologies and include a seventeenth century whodunnit, a science fiction western, and a steampunk Sherlock Holmes story. Paul lives with his family in Kent, England, and spends his days chasing a toddler with more energy than the Duracell Bunny. He mainly does his writing in coffee shops with members of the local NaNoWriMo group, or in the middle of the night when his family has gone to sleep. Consequently, his stories tend to be fuelled by large amounts of black coffee. You can find out more about his writing at *www.detectivesanddragons.uk.*

In the year 1998 **Craig Janacek** took his degree of Doctor of Medicine at Vanderbilt University, and proceeded to Stanford to go through the training prescribed for pediatricians in practice. Having completed his studies there, he was duly attached to the University of California, San Francisco as Associate Professor. The author of over seventy medical monographs upon a variety of obscure lesions, his travel-worn and battered tin dispatch-box is crammed with papers, nearly all of which are records of his fictional works. To date, these have been published solely in electronic format, including two non-Holmes novels (*The Oxford Deception* and *The Anger of Achilles Peterson*), the trio of holiday adventures collected as *The Midwinter Mysteries of Sherlock Holmes*, the Holmes story collections *The First of Criminals, The Assassination of Sherlock Holmes, The Treasury of Sherlock Holmes, Light in the Darkness, The Gathering Gloom, The Travels of Sherlock Holmes*, and the Watsonian novels *The Isle of Devils* and *The Gate of Gold*. Craig Janacek is a *nom de plume*.

Roger Johnson BSI, ASH is a retired librarian, now working as a volunteer assistant at the Essex Police Museum. In his spare time, he is commissioning editor of *The Sherlock Holmes Journal*, an occasional lecturer, and a frequent contributor to *The Writings about the Writings*. His sole work of Holmesian pastiche was published in 1997 in Mike Ashley's anthology *The Mammoth Book of New Sherlock Holmes Adventures*, and he has the greatest respect for the many authors who have contributed new tales to the present mighty trilogy. Like his wife, Jean Upton, he is a member of both *The Baker Street Irregulars* and *The Adventuresses of Sherlock Holmes.*

Kelvin I. Jones is the author of six books about Sherlock Holmes and the definitive biography of Conan Doyle as a spiritualist, *Conan Doyle and The Spirits*. A member of *The Sherlock Holmes Society of London*, he has published numerous short occult and ghost stories in British anthologies over the last thirty years. His work has appeared on BBC Radio, and in 1984 he won the Mason Hall Literary Award for his poem cycle about the survivors of Hiroshima and Nagasaki, recently reprinted as "Omega". (Oakmagic Publications) A one-time teacher of creative writing at the University of East Anglia, he is also the author of four crime novels featuring his ex-met sleuth John Bottrell, who first appeared in *Stone Dead*. He has over fifty titles on Kindle, and is also the author of several novellas and short story collections featuring a Norwich based detective, DCI Ketch, an intrepid sleuth who investigates East Anglian murder cases. He also published a series of short stories about an Edwardian psychic detective, Dr. John Carter (*Carter's Occult Casebook*). Ramsey Campbell, the British horror writer, and Francis King, the renowned novelist, have both compared his supernatural stories to those of M. R. James. He has also published children's fiction, namely *Odin's Eye*, and, in collaboration with his wife Debbie, *The Dark Entry*. Since 1995, he has been the proprietor of Oakmagic Publications, publishers of British folklore and of his fiction titles. He lives in Norfolk. (See www.oakmagicpublications.co.uk)

Peter Lovesey is the author of the Peter Diamond mysteries, well known for their use of surprise, strong characters and hard-to-crack puzzles. He was awarded the Cartier Diamond Dagger in 2000, the *Grand Prix de Litterature Policiere*, the Anthony, the Ellery Queen Readers' Award, and is Grand Master of the Swedish Academy of Detection. He has been a full-time author since 1975, and was formerly in further education. Earlier series include the Sergeant Cribb mysteries seen on TV and the Bertie, Prince of Wales novels. Peter and his wife Jax, have a son, Phil, also a teacher and mystery writer, and a daughter Kathy, who was a Vice-President of J.P.Morgan-Chase, and now lives with her family in Greenwich, Ct. Peter currently lives in Chichester, England. His website at *www.peterlovesey.com* gives fuller details of his life and books. "Try him. You'll love him," wrote the doyen of the mystery world, Otto Penzler, in *The New York Sun*.

David Marcum plays *The Game* with deadly seriousness. He first discovered Sherlock Holmes in 1975 at the age of ten, and since that time, he has collected, read, and chronologicized literally thousands of traditional Holmes pastiches in the form of novels, short stories, radio and television episodes, movies and scripts, comics, fan-fiction, and unpublished manuscripts. He is the author of nearly eighty Sherlockian pastiches, some published in anthologies and magazines such as *The Strand*, and others collected in his own books, *The Papers of Sherlock Holmes*, *Sherlock Holmes and A Quantity of Debt*, and *Sherlock Holmes – Tangled Skeins*. He has almost sixty books, including several dozen traditional Sherlockian anthologies, such as the ongoing series *The MX Book of New Sherlock Holmes Stories*, which he created in 2015. This collection is now up to 27 volumes, with more in preparation. He was responsible for bringing back August Derleth's Solar Pons for a new generation, first with his collection of authorized Pons stories, *The Papers of Solar Pons*, and then by editing the reissued authorized versions of the original Pons books, and then volumes of new Pons adventures. He has done the same for the adventures of Dr. Thorndyke, and has plans for similar projects in the future. He has contributed numerous essays to various publications, and is a member of a number of Sherlockian groups and Scions. His irregular Sherlockian blog, *A Seventeen Step Program*, addresses various topics related to his favorite book friends (as his son used to call them when he was small), and can be found at *http://17stepprogram.blogspot.com/* He is a licensed Civil Engineer, living in Tennessee with his wife and son. Since the age of nineteen, he has worn a deerstalker as his regular-and-only hat. In 2013, he and his deerstalker were finally able make his first trip-of-a-lifetime Holmes Pilgrimage to England, with return Pilgrimages in 2015 and 2016, where you may have spotted him. If you ever run into him and his deerstalker out and about, feel free to say hello!

Kevin Patrick McCann has published eight collections of poems for adults, one for children (*Diary of a Shapeshifter*, Beul Aithris), a book of ghost stories (*It's Gone Dark*, The Otherside Books), *Teach Yourself Self-Publishing* (Hodder) co-written with the playwright Tom Green, and *Ov* (Beul Aithris Publications) a fantasy novel for children.

Sidney Paget (1860-1908), a few of whose illustrations are used within this anthology, was born in London, and like his two older brothers, became a famed illustrator and painter. He completed over three-hundred-and-fifty drawings for the Sherlock Holmes stories that were first published in *The Strand* magazine, defining Holmes's image forever after in the public mind.

Jane Rubino is the author of *A Jersey Shore* mystery series, featuring a Jane Austen-loving amateur sleuth and a Sherlock Holmes-quoting detective, *Knight Errant, Lady Vernon and Her Daughter*, (a novel-length adaptation of Jane Austen's novella *Lady Susan*, co-authored with her daughter Caitlen Rubino-Bradway, *What Would Austen Do?*, also co-authored with her daughter, a short story in the anthology *Jane Austen Made Me Do It, The Rucastles' Pawn, The Copper Beeches from Violet Turner's POV*, and, of course, there's the Sherlockian novel in the drawer – who doesn't have one? Jane lives on a barrier island at the New Jersey shore.

Brenda Seabrooke's stories have been published in a number of reviews, journals, and anthologies. She has received grants from the National Endowment for the Arts and Emerson College's Robbie Macauley Award. She is the author of twenty-three books for young readers including *Scones and Bones on Baker Street: Sherlock's (maybe!) Dog and the Dirt Dilemma*, and *The Rascal in the Castle: Sherlock's (possible!) Dog and the Queen's Revenge*. Brenda states: "*It was fun to write from Dr. Watson's point of view and not have to worry about fleas, smelly pits, ralphing, or scratching at inopportune times.*"

Jacqueline Silver is the Headteacher of Stepping Stones School. She has developed her career from her early days as an accomplished Drama teacher and has a strong background in school leadership. She has always had a passion for creating nurturing and positive school environments for mixed ability children. Her recent career history has seen her spearhead pastoral care provision at a number of schools where she has also been resolute in her vision for safeguarding, particularly of the most vulnerable children in our society. Since her appointment as Headteacher of Stepping Stones School, she can realise her prime personal focus for improving the employability of young people with learning needs. Quality of life, independence, and positive engagement with society are linchpins of Jacqueline's vision for the future. Stepping Stones will flourish under her leadership.

Matthew Simmonds hails from Bedford, in the South East of England, and has been a confirmed devotee of Sir Arthur Conan Doyle's most famous creation since first watching Jeremy Brett's incomparable portrayal of the world's first consulting detective, on a Tuesday evening in April, 1984, while curled up on the sofa with his father. He has written numerous short stories, and his first novel, *Sherlock Holmes: The Adventure of The Pigtail Twist*, was published in 2018. A sequel is nearly complete, which he hopes to publish in the near future. Matthew currently co-owns Harrison & Simmonds, the fifth-generation family business, a renowned County tobacconist, pipe, and gift shop on Bedford High Street.

Denis O. Smith's first published story of Sherlock Holmes and Doctor Watson, "The Adventure of The Purple Hand", appeared in 1982. Since then, numerous other such accounts have been published in magazines and anthologies both in the U.K. and the U.S. In the 1990's, four volumes of his stories were published under the general title of *The Chronicles of Sherlock Holmes*, and, more recently his stories have been collected as *The Lost Chronicles of Sherlock Holmes* (2014), *The Lost Chronicles of Sherlock Holmes Volume II* (2016), *The Further Chronicles of Sherlock Holmes* (201). He also wrote a Holmes novel, *The Riddle of Foxwood Grange* (2017). Born in Yorkshire, in the north of England, Denis Smith has lived and worked in various parts of the country, including London, and has now been resident in Norfolk for many years. His interests range widely, but apart from his dedication to the career of Sherlock Holmes, he has a passion for historical mysteries of all kinds, the railways of Britain and the history of London

Robert V. Stapleton was born and brought up in Leeds, Yorkshire, England, and studied at Durham University. After working in various parts of the country as an Anglican parish priest, he is now retired and lives with his wife in North Yorkshire. As a member of his local writing group, he now has time to develop his other life as a writer of adventure stories. He has recently had a number of short stories published, and he is hoping to have a couple of completed novels published at some time in the future.

Matthew White is an up-and-coming author from Richmond, Virginia in the USA. He has been a passionate devotee of Sherlock Holmes since childhood. He can be reached at *matthewwhite.writer@gmail.com*

Marcia Wilson is a freelance researcher and illustrator who likes to work in a style compatible for the color blind and visually impaired. She is Canon-centric, and her first MX offering, *You Buy Bones*, uses the point-of-view of Scotland Yard to show the unique talents of Dr. Watson. This continued with the publication of *Test of the Professionals: The Adventure of the Flying Blue Pidgeon* and *The Peaceful Night Poisonings*. She can be contacted at: *gravelgirty.deviantart.com*

*The following contributors appear
in the companion volumes:*
The MX Book of New Sherlock Holmes Stories
Part XXVI – 2021 Annual (1888-1897)
Part XXVII – 2021 Annual (1898-1927)

Ian Ableson is an ecologist by training and a writer by choice. When not reading or writing, he can reliably be found scowling at a clipboard while ankle-deep in a marsh somewhere in Michigan. His love for the stories of Arthur Conan Doyle started when his grandfather gave him a copy of *The Original Illustrated Sherlock Holmes* when he was in high school, and he's proud to have been able to contribute to the continuation of the tales of Sherlock Holmes and Dr. Watson.

Leslie Charteris was born in Singapore on May 12th, 1907. With his mother and brother, he moved to England in 1919 and attended Rossall School in Lancashire before moving on to Cambridge University to study law. His studies there came to a halt when a publisher accepted his first novel. His third one, entitled *Meet the Tiger*, was written when he was twenty years old and published in September 1928. It introduced the world to Simon Templar, *aka* The Saint. He continued to write about The Saint until 1983 when the last book, *Salvage for The Saint*, was published. The books, which have been translated into over thirty languages, number nearly a hundred and have sold over forty-million copies around the world. They've inspired, to date, fifteen feature films, three television series, ten radio series, and a comic strip that was written by Charteris and syndicated around the world for over a decade. He enjoyed travelling, but settled for long periods in Hollywood, Florida, and finally in Surrey, England. He was awarded the Cartier Diamond Dagger by the *Crime Writers' Association* in 1992, in recognition of a lifetime of achievement. He died the following year.

Craig Stephen Copland confesses that he discovered Sherlock Holmes when, sometime in the muddled early 1960's, he pinched his older brother's copy of the immortal stories and was forever afterward thoroughly hooked. He is very grateful to his high school English teachers in Toronto who inculcated in him a love of literature and writing, and even inspired him to be an English major at the University of Toronto. There he was blessed to sit at the feet of both Northrup Frye and Marshall McLuhan, and other great literary professors, who led him to believe that he was called to be a high school English teacher. It was his good fortune to come to his pecuniary senses, abandon that goal, and pursue a varied professional career that took him to over one-hundred countries and endless adventures. He considers himself to have been and to continue to be one of the luckiest men on God's good earth. A few years back he took a step in the direction of Sherlockian studies and joined the *Sherlock Holmes Society of Canada* – also known as *The Toronto Bootmakers*. In May of 2014, this esteemed group of scholars announced a contest for the writing of a new Sherlock Holmes mystery. Although he had never tried his hand at fiction before, Craig entered and was pleasantly surprised to be selected as one of the winners. Having enjoyed the experience, he decided to write more of the same, and is now on a mission to write a new Sherlock Holmes mystery that is related to and inspired by each of the sixty stories in the original Canon. He currently lives and writes in Toronto and Dubai, and looks forward to finally settling down when he turns ninety.

John William Davis is a retired US Army counterintelligence officer, civil servant, and linguist. He was commissioned from Washington University in St. Louis as an artillery officer in the 101st Air Assault Division. Thereafter, he went into counterintelligence and served some thirty-seven years. A linguist, Mr. Davis learned foreign languages in each country he served. After the Cold War and its bitter aftermath, he wrote *Rainy Street Stories, Reflections on Secret Wars, Terrorism, and Espionage*. He wanted to write about not only true events themselves, but also the moral and ethical aspects of the secret world. With the publication of *Around the Corner*, Davis expanded his reflections on conflicted human nature to our present day traumas of fear, and causes for hope. A dedicated Sherlockian, he's contributed to telling the story of the Great Detective in retirement.

Harry DeMaio is a *nom de plume* of Harry B. DeMaio, successful author of several books on Information Security and Business Networks, as well as the fourteen-volume *Casebooks of Octavius Bear*. He is also a published author for Belanger Books and the MX Sherlock Holmes series edited by David Marcum. A retired business executive, former consultant, information security specialist, private pilot, disk jockey, and graduate school adjunct professor, he whiles away his time traveling and writing preposterous books, articles and stories. He has appeared on many radio and TV shows and is an accomplished, frequent public speaker. Former New York City natives, he and his extremely patient and helpful wife, Virginia, live in Cincinnati (and several other parallel universes.) They have two sons, living in Scottsdale, Arizona and Cortlandt Manor, New York, both of whom are quite successful and quite normal, thus putting the lie to the theory that insanity is hereditary. His books are available on Amazon, Barnes and Noble, directly from MX Publishing and at other fine bookstores. His e-mail is *hdemaio@zoomtown.com* You can also find him on Facebook. His website is *www.octaviusbearslair.com*

Ian Dickerson was just nine years old when he discovered The Saint. Shortly after that, he discovered Sherlock Holmes. The Saint won, for a while anyway. He struck up a friendship with The Saint's creator, Leslie Charteris, and his family. With their permission, he spent six weeks studying the Leslie Charteris collection at Boston University and went on to write, direct, and produce documentaries on the making of *The Saint* and *Return of The Saint,* which have been released on DVD. He oversaw the recent reprints of almost fifty of the original Saint books in both the US and UK, and was a co-producer on the 2017 TV movie of *The Saint*. When he discovered that Charteris had written Sherlock Holmes stories as well – well, there was the excuse he needed to revisit The Canon. He's consequently written and edited three books on Holmes' radio adventures. For the sake of what little sanity he has, Ian has also written about a wide range of subjects, none of which come with a halo, including talking mashed potatoes, Lord Grade, and satellite links. Ian lives in Hampshire with his wife and two children. And an awful lot of books by Leslie Charteris. Not quite so many by Conan Doyle, though.

Tim Gambrell lives in Exeter, Devon, with his wife, two young sons, three cats, and now only four chickens. He has previously contributed stories to *The MX Book of New Sherlock Holmes Stories,* and also to *Sherlock Holmes and Dr Watson: The Early Adventures* and *Sherlock Holmes and The Occult Detectives,* also from Belanger Books. Outside of the world of Holmes, Tim has written extensively for Doctor Who spin-off ranges. His books include two linked novels from Candy Jar Books: *Lethbridge-Stewart: The Laughing Gnome – Lucy Wilson & The Bledoe Cadets,* and *The Lucy Wilson Mysteries: The Brigadier and The Bledoe Cadets* (both 2019), and *Lethbridge-Stewart: Bloodlines – An Ordinary Man* (Candy Jar, 2020, written with Andy Frankham-Allen). He's also written a novella, *The Way of The Bry'hunee* (2019) for the Erimem range from Thebes Publishing. Tim's short fiction includes stories in *Lethbridge-Stewart: The HAVOC Files 3* (Candy Jar, 2017, revised edition 2020), *Bernice Summerfield: True Stories* (Big Finish, 2017) and *Relics . . . An Anthology* (Red Ted Books, 2018), plus a number of charity anthologies.

James Gelter is a director and playwright living in Brattleboro, VT. His produced written works for the stage include adaptations of *Frankenstein* and *A Christmas Carol,* several children's plays for the New England Youth Theatre, as well as seven outdoor plays co-written with his wife, Jessica, in their *Forest of Mystery* series. In 2018, he founded The Baker Street Readers, a group of performers that present dramatic readings of Arthur Conan Doyle's original Canon of Sherlock Holmes stories, featuring Gelter as Holmes, his longtime collaborator Tony Grobe as Dr. Watson, and a rotating list of guests. When the COVID-19 pandemic stopped their live performances, Gelter transformed the show into The Baker Street Readers Podcast. Some episodes are available for free on Apple Podcasts and Stitcher, with many more available to patrons at *patreon.com/bakerstreetreaders*.

Dick Gillman is an English writer and acrylic artist living in Brittany, France with his wife Alex, Truffle, their Black Labrador, and Jean-Claude, their Breton cat. During his retirement from teaching, he has written over twenty Sherlock Holmes short stories which are published as both e-books and paperbacks. His initial contribution to the superb MX

Sherlock Holmes collection, published in October 2015, was entitled "The Man on Westminster Bridge" and had the privilege of being chosen as the anchor story in *The MX Book of New Sherlock Holmes Stories – Part II (1890-1895)*.

Denis Green was born in London, England in April 1905. He grew up mostly in London's Savoy Theatre where his father, Richard Green, was a principal in many Gilbert and Sullivan productions, A Flying Officer with RAF until 1924, he then spent four years managing a tea estate in North India before making his stage debut in *Hamlet* with Leslie Howard in 1928. He made his first visit to America in 1931 and established a respectable stage career before appearing in films – including minor roles in the first two Rathbone and Bruce Holmes films – and developing a career in front of and behind the microphone during the golden age of radio. Green and Leslie Charteris met in 1938 and struck up a lifelong friendship. Always busy, be it on stage, radio, film or television, Green passed away at the age of fifty in New York.

In real life, **Anthony Gurney** lectures in Computer Science at a university in Scotland where he lives with his wife and children. The first books that he bought for himself were a two volume hardback collection of the Holmes Short Stories and the Long Stories for 10p each at a church jumble sale. It was the start of a lifelong affair.

Arthur Hall was born in Aston, Birmingham, UK, in 1944. He discovered his interest in writing during his schooldays, along with a love of fictional adventure and suspense. His first novel, *Sole Contact*, was an espionage story about an ultra-secret government department known as "Sector Three", and was followed, to date, by three sequels. Other works include six Sherlock Holmes novels, *The Demon of the Dusk*, *The One Hundred Percent Society*, *The Secret Assassin*, *The Phantom Killer*, *In Pursuit of the Dead*, and *The Justice Master*, as well as two collections of Holmes *Further Little-Known Cases of Sherlock* Holmes, and *Tales from the Annals of Sherlock Holmes.* He has also written other short stories and a modern detective novel. He lives in the West Midlands, United Kingdom.

Stephen Herczeg is an IT Geek, writer, actor, and film-maker based in Canberra Australia. He has been writing for over twenty years and has completed a couple of dodgy novels, sixteen feature-length screenplays, and numerous short stories and scripts. Stephen was very successful in 2017's International Horror Hotel screenplay competition, with his scripts *TITAN* winning the Sci-Fi category and *Dark are the Woods* placing second in the horror category. His three-volume short story collection, *The Curious Cases of Sherlock Holmes*, will be published in 2021. His work has featured in *Sproutlings – A Compendium of Little Fictions* from Hunter Anthologies, the *Hells Bells* Christmas horror anthology published by the Australasian Horror Writers Association, and the *Below the Stairs*, *Trickster's Treats*, *Shades of Santa*, *Behind the Mask*, and *Beyond the Infinite* anthologies from *OzHorror.Con*, *The Body Horror Book*, *Anemone Enemy*, and *Petrified Punks* from Oscillate Wildly Press, and *Sherlock Holmes In the Realms of H.G. Wells* and *Sherlock Holmes: Adventures Beyond the Canon* from Belanger Books.

Mike Hogan writes mostly historical novels and short stories, many set in Victorian London and featuring Sherlock Holmes and Doctor Watson. He read the Conan Doyle stories at school with great enjoyment, but hadn't thought much about Sherlock Holmes until, having missed the Granada/Jeremy Brett TV series when it was originally shown in the eighties, he came across a box set of videos in a street market and was hooked on Holmes again. He started writing Sherlock Holmes pastiches several years ago, having great fun re-imagining situations for the Conan Doyle characters to act in. The relationship between Holmes and Watson fascinates him as one of the great literary friendships. (He's also a huge admirer of Patrick O'Brian's Aubrey-Maturin novels). Like Captain Aubrey and Doctor Maturin, Holmes and Watson are an odd couple, differing in almost every facet of their characters, but sharing a common sense of decency and a common humanity. Living with Sherlock Holmes can't have been easy, and Mike enjoys adding a stronger vein of "pawky humour" into the Conan Doyle mix, even letting Watson have the second-to-last word on occasions. His books include *Sherlock Holmes and the Scottish Question, The Gory Season – Sherlock Holmes, Jack the Ripper and the Thames Torso Murders*, and the *Sherlock Holmes & Young Winston 1887 Trilogy* (*The Deadwood Stage, The Jubilee Plot*, and *The Giant Moles*), He has also written the following short story collections: *Sherlock Holmes: Murder at the Savoy and Other Stories, Sherlock Holmes: The Skull of Kohada Koheiji and Other Stories*, and *Sherlock Holmes: Murder on the Brighton Line and Other Stories*, among others. *www.mikehoganbooks.com*

Jeremy Branton Holstein first discovered Sherlock Holmes at age five when he became convinced that the Hound of the Baskervilles lived in his bedroom closet. A life-long enthusiast of radio dramas, Jeremy is currently the lead dramatist and director for the Post Meridian Radio Players adaptations of Sherlock Holmes, where he has adapted *The Hound of the Baskervilles, The Sign of Four*, and "Jack the Harlot Killer" (retitled "The Whitechapel Murders") from William S. Baring-Gould's *Sherlock Holmes of Baker Street* for the company. Jeremy has also written Sherlock Holmes scripts for Jim French's *Imagination Theatre*. He lives with his wife and daughter in the Boston, MA area.

Naching T. Kassa is a wife, mother, and writer. She's created short stories, novellas, poems, and co-created three children. She lives in Eastern Washington State with her husband, Dan Kassa. Naching is a member of the *Horror Writers Association*, Head of Publishing and Interviewer for *HorrorAddicts.net*, and an assistant and staff writer for Still Water Bay at Crystal Lake Publishing. She has been a Sherlockian since the age of ten and is a member of *The Sound of the Baskervilles*. You can find her work on Amazon. *https://www.amazon.com/Naching-T-Kassa/e/B005ZGHTI0*

Susan Knight's newest novel from MX publishing, *Mrs. Hudson Goes to Ireland*, is a follow-up to her well-received collection of stories, *Mrs. Hudson Investigates* of 2019. She is the author of two other non-Sherlockian story collections, as well as three novels, a book of non-fiction, and several plays, and has won several prizes for her writing. She lives in Dublin where she teaches Creative Writing. Her next Mrs. Hudson novel is already a gleam in her eye.

John Lawrence served for thirty-eight years as a staff member in the U.S. House of Representatives, the last eight as Chief of Staff to Speaker Nancy Pelosi (2005-2013). He has been a Visiting Professor at the University of California's Washington Center since 2013. He is the author of *The Class of '74: Congress After Watergate and the Roots of Partisanship* (2018), and has a Ph.D. in history from the University of California (Berkeley).

Kevin Patrick McCann *also has a poem in Part XXVI*

David Marcum *also has stories in Parts XXVI and XXVII*

Adrian Middleton is a Staffordshire-born independent publisher. The son of a real-world detective, he is a former civil servant and policy adviser who now writes and edits science fiction, fantasy, and a popular series of steampunked Sherlock Holmes stories.

James Moffett is a Masters graduate in Professional Writing, with a specialisation in novel and non-fiction writing. He also has an extensive background in media studies. James began developing a passion for writing when contributing to his University's student magazine. His interest in the literary character of Sherlock Holmes was deep-rooted in his youth. He released his first publication of eight interconnected short stories titled *The Trials of Sherlock Holmes* in 2017, along with a contribution to *The MX Book of New Sherlock Holmes Stories - Part VII: Eliminate The Impossible: 1880-1891*, with a short story entitled "The Blank Photograph".

Mark Mower is a crime writer and historian whose passion for tales about Sherlock Holmes and Dr. Watson began at the age of twelve, when he watched an early black-and-white film featuring the unrivalled screen pairing of Basil Rathbone and Nigel Bruce. Hastily seeking out the original stories of Sir Arthur Conan Doyle, and continually searching for further film and television adaptations, his has been a lifelong obsession. Now a member of the Crime Writers' Association, The Sherlock Holmes Society of London, and The Solar Pons Society of London, he has written numerous crime books. Mark has contributed to over 20 Holmes anthologies, including 13 parts of *The MX Book of New Sherlock Holmes Stories*, *The Book of Extraordinary New Sherlock Holmes Stories* (Mango Publishing) and *Sherlock Holmes – Before Baker Street* (Belanger Books). His own books include *A Farewell to Baker Street, Sherlock Holmes: The Baker Street Case-Files*, and *Sherlock Holmes: The Baker Street Legacy*, and *Sherlock Holmes: The Baker Street Epilogue* (all with MX Publishing).

Will Murray has been writing about popular culture since 1973, principally on the subjects of comic books, pulp magazine heroes, and film. As a fiction writer, he's the author of over 70 novels featuring characters as diverse as Nick Fury and Remo Williams. With the late Steve Ditko, he created the Unbeatable Squirrel Girl for Marvel Comics. Murray has written numerous short stories, many on Lovecraftian themes. Currently, he writes The Wild Adventures of Doc Savage for Altus Press. His acclaimed Doc Savage novel, *Skull Island*, pits the pioneer superhero against the legendary King Kong. This was followed by *King Kong vs. Tarzan* and two Doc Savage novels guest-starring The Shadow, and *Tarzan, Conqueror of Mars*, a crossover with John Carter of Mars. He is the author of the short story collecdtion *The Wild Adventures of Sherlock Holmes. www.adventuresinbronze.com* is his website.

Tracy J. Revels, a Sherlockian from the age of eleven, is a professor of history at Wofford College in Spartanburg, South Carolina. She is a member of *The Survivors of the Gloria Scott* and *The Studious Scarlets Society*, and is a past recipient of the Beacon Society Award. Almost every semester, she teaches a class that covers The Canon, either to college students or to senior citizens. She is also the author of three supernatural Sherlockian pastiches with MX (*Shadowfall, Shadowblood*, and *Shadowwraith*), and a regular contributor to her scion's newsletter. She also has some notoriety as an author of very silly skits: For proof, see "The Adventure of the Adversarial Adventuress" and "Occupy Baker Street" on YouTube. When not studying Sherlock, she can be found researching the history of her native state, and has written books on Florida in the Civil War and on the development of Florida's tourism industry.

Roger Riccard of Los Angeles, California, U.S.A., is a descendant of the Roses of Kilravock in Highland Scotland. He is the author of two previous Sherlock Holmes novels, *The Case of the Poisoned Lilly* and *The Case of the Twain Papers*, a series of short stories in two volumes, *Sherlock Holmes: Adventures for the Twelve Days of Christmas* and *Further Adventures for the Twelve Days of Christmas*, and the ongoing series *A Sherlock Holmes Alphabet of Cases*, all of which are published by Baker Street Studios. He has another novel and a non-fiction Holmes reference work in various stages of completion. He became a Sherlock Holmes enthusiast as a teenager (many, many years ago), and, like all fans of The Great Detective, yearned for more stories after reading The Canon over and over. It was the Granada Television performances of Jeremy Brett and Edward Hardwicke, and the encouragement of his wife, Rosilyn, that at last inspired him to write his own Holmes adventures, using the Granada actor portrayals as his guide. He has been called "The best pastiche writer since Val Andrews" by the *Sherlockian E-Times*.

Geri Schear is a novelist and short story writer. Her work has been published in literary journals in the U.S. and Ireland. Her first novel, *A Biased Judgement: The Diaries of Sherlock Holmes 1897* was released to critical acclaim in 2014. The sequel, *Sherlock Holmes and the Other Woman* was published in 2015, and *Return to Reichenbach* in 2016. She lives in Kells, Ireland.

Frank Schildiner is a martial arts instructor at Amorosi's Mixed Martial Arts in New Jersey. He is the writer of the novels, *The Quest of Frankenstein, The Triumph of Frankenstein, Napoleon's Vampire Hunters, The Devil Plague of Naples, The Klaus Protocol*, and *Irma Vep and The Great Brain of Mars*. Frank is a regular contributor to the fictional series *Tales of the Shadowmen* and has been published in *From Bayou to Abyss: Examining John Constantine, Hellblazer, The Joy of Joe, The New Adventures of Thunder Jim Wade, Secret Agent X* Volumes 3, 4, 5, and 6, *The Lone Ranger and Tonto: Frontier Justice*, and *The Avenger: The Justice Files*. He resides in New Jersey with his wife Gail, who is his top supporter, and two cats who are indifferent on the subject.

Joseph W. Svec III is retired from Oceanography, Satellite Test Engineering, and college teaching. He has lived on a forty-foot cruising sailboat, on a ranch in the Sierra Nevada Foothills, in a country rose-garden cottage, and currently lives in the shadow of a castle with his childhood sweetheart and several long coated German shepherds. He enjoys writing, gardening, creating dioramas, world travel, and enjoying time with his sweetheart.

Kevin P. Thornton is a seven-time Arthur Ellis Award Nominee. He is a former director of the local Heritage Society and Library, and he has been a soldier in Africa, a contractor for the Canadian Military in Afghanistan, a newspaper and magazine columnist, a Director of both the *Crime Writers of Canada* and the *Writers' Guild of Alberta*, a founding member of *Northword Literary Magazine*, and is either a current or former member of *The Mystery Writers of America, The Crime Writers Association, The Calgary Crime Writers, The International Thriller Writers, The International Association of Crime Writers, The Keys* – a Catholic Writers group founded by Monsignor Knox and G.K. Chesterton – as well as, somewhat inexplicably, *The Mesdames of Mayhem* and *Sisters in Crime*. If you ask, he will join. Born in Kenya, Kevin has lived or worked in South Africa, Dubai, England, Afghanistan, New Zealand, Ontario, and now Northern Alberta. He lives on his wits and his wit, and is doing better than expected. He is not one to willingly split infinitives, and while never pedantic, is on occasion known to be ever so slightly punctilious.

466

Stephen Toft is a homelessness worker and writer who lives in Lancaster, UK with his wife and their children. He has published three collections of poetry, and has recently began writing crime stories.

Thomas A. (Tom) Turley has been "hooked on Holmes" since finishing *The Hound of the Baskervilles* at about the age of twelve. However, his interest in Sherlockian pastiches didn't take off until he wrote one. *Sherlock Holmes and the Adventure of the Tainted Canister* (2014) is available as an e-book and an audiobook from MX Publishing. It also appeared in *The Art of Sherlock Holmes – USA Edition 1.* In 2017, two of Tom's stories, "A Scandal in Serbia" and "A Ghost from Christmas Past" were published in Parts VI and VII of this anthology. "Ghost" was also included in *The Art of Sherlock Holmes – West Palm Beach Edition.* Meanwhile, Tom is finishing a collection of historical pastiches entitled *Sherlock Holmes and the Crowned Heads of Europe,* to be published in 2021 The first story, "Sherlock Holmes and the Case of the Dying Emperor" (2018) is available from MX Publishing as a separate e-book. Set in the brief reign of Emperor Frederick III (1888), it inaugurates Sherlock Holmes's espionage campaign against the German Empire, which ended only in August 1914 with "His Last Bow". When completed, *Sherlock Holmes and the Crowned Heads of Europe* will also include "A Scandal in Serbia" and two additional historical tales. Although he has a Ph.D. in British history, Tom spent most of his professional career as an archivist with the State of Alabama. He and his wife Paula (an aspiring science fiction novelist) live in Montgomery, Alabama. Interested readers may contact Tom through MX Publishing or his Goodreads author's page.

DJ Tyrer is the person behind Atlantean Publishing, was placed second in the Writing Magazine "Local Reporter" competition, and has been widely published in anthologies and magazines around the world, such as *Disturbance* (Laurel Highlands), *Mysteries of Suspense* (Zimbell House), *History and Mystery, Oh My!* (Mystery & Horror LLC), and *Love 'Em, Shoot 'Em* (Wolfsinger), and issues of *Awesome Tales,* and in addition, has a novella available in paperback and on the Kindle, *The Yellow House* (Dunhams Manor) and a comic horror e-novelette, *A Trip to the Middle of the World,* available from Alban Lake through Infinite Realms Bookstore.
His website is: *https://djtyrer.blogspot.co.uk/*
The Atlantean Publishing website is at *https://atlanteanpublishing.wordpress.com/*

Peter Coe Verbica grew up on a commercial cattle ranch in Northern California, where he learned the value of a strong work ethic. He works for the Wealth Management Group of a global investment bank, and is an Adjunct Professor in the Economics Department at SJSU. He is the author of numerous books, including *Left at the Gate and Other Poems, Hard-Won Cowboy Wisdom (Not Necessarily in Order of Importance), A Key to the Grove and Other Poems,* and two volumes of *The Missing Tales of Sherlock Holmes* (as Compiled by Peter Coe Verbica, JD). Mr. Verbica obtained a JD from Santa Clara University School of Law, an MS from Massachusetts Institute of Technology, and a BA in English from Santa Clara University. He is the co-inventor on a number of patents, has served as a Managing Member of three venture capital firms, and the CFO of one of the portfolio companies. He is an unabashed advocate of cowboy culture and enjoys creative writing, hiking, and tennis. He is married with four daughters. For more information, or to contact the author, please go to *www.hardwoncowboywisdom.com*

Margaret Walsh was born Auckland, New Zealand and now lives in Melbourne, Australia. She is the author of *Sherlock Holmes and the Molly-Boy Murders, Sherlock Holmes and the Case of the Perplexed Politician,* and *Sherlock Holmes and the Case of the*

London Dock Deaths, all published by MX Publishing. Margaret has been a devotee of Sherlock Holmes since childhood and has had several Holmesian related essays printed in anthologies, and is a member of the online society *Doyle's Rotary Coffin*. She has an ongoing love affair with the city of London. When she's not working or planning trips to London. Margaret can be found frequenting the many and varied bookshops of Melbourne.

I.A. Watson, great-grand-nephew of Dr. John H. Watson, has been intrigued by the notorious "black sheep" of the family since childhood, and was fascinated to inherit from his grandmother a number of unedited manuscripts removed circa 1956 from a rather larger collection reposing at Lloyds Bank Ltd (which acquired Cox & Co Bank in 1923). Upon discovering the published corpus of accounts regarding the detective Sherlock Holmes from which a censorious upbringing had shielded him, he felt obliged to allow an interested public access to these additional memoranda, and is gradually undertaking the task of transcribing them for admirers of Mr. Holmes and Dr. Watson's works. In the meantime, I.A. Watson continues to pen other books, the latest of which is *The Incunabulum of Sherlock Holmes*. A full list of his seventy or so published works are available at: *http://www.chillwater.org.uk/writing/iawatsonhome.htm*

Marcia Wilson *also has stories in Parts XXVI and XXVII*

The MX Book of New Sherlock Holmes Stories
Edited by David Marcum
(MX Publishing, 2015-   )

"This is the finest volume of Sherlockian fiction I have ever read, and I have read, literally, thousands." – Philip K. Jones

"Beyond Impressive . . . This is a splendid venture for a great cause!
– Roger Johnson, Editor, *The Sherlock Holmes Journal,*
The Sherlock Holmes Society of London

Part I: 1881-1889
Part II: 1890-1895
Part III: 1896-1929
Part IV: 2016 Annual
Part V: Christmas Adventures
Part VI: 2017 Annual
Part VII: Eliminate the Impossible (1880-1891)
Part VIII – Eliminate the Impossible (1892-1905)
Part IX – 2018 Annual (1879-1895)
Part X – 2018 Annual (1896-1916)
Part XI – Some Untold Cases (1880-1891)
Part XII – Some Untold Cases (1894-1902)
Part XIII – 2019 Annual (1881-1890)
Part XIV – 2019 Annual (1891-1897)
Part XV – 2019 Annual (1898-1917)
Part XVI – Whatever Remains . . . Must be the Truth (1881-1890)
Part XVII – Whatever Remains . . . Must be the Truth (1891-1898)
Part XVIII – Whatever Remains . . . Must be the Truth (1898-1925)
Part XIX – 2020 Annual (1882-1890)
Part XX – 2020 Annual (1891-1897)
Part XXI – 2020 Annual (1898-1923)
Part XXII – Some More Untold Cases (1877-1887)
Part XXIII – Some More Untold Cases (1888-1894)
Part XXIV – Some More Untold Cases (1895-1903)
Part XXV – 2021 Annual (1881-1888)
Part XXVI – 2021 Annual (1889-1897)
Part XXVII – 2021 Annual (1898-1928)

<u>In Preparation</u>
Part XXVIII – More Christmas Adventures

. . . and more to come!

The MX Book of New Sherlock Holmes Stories
Edited by David Marcum
(MX Publishing, 2015-)

Publishers Weekly says:

Part VI: *The traditional pastiche is alive and well . . . .*

Part VII: *Sherlockians eager for faithful-to-the-canon plots and characters will be delighted.*

Part VIII: *The imagination of the contributors in coming up with variations on the volume's theme is matched by their ingenious resolutions.*

Part IX: *The 18 stories . . . will satisfy fans of Conan Doyle's originals. Sherlockians will rejoice that more volumes are on the way.*

Part X: *. . . new Sherlock Holmes adventures of consistently high quality.*

Part XI: *. . . an essential volume for Sherlock Holmes fans.*

Part XII: *. . . continues to amaze with the number of high-quality pastiches.*

Part XIII: *. . . Amazingly, Marcum has found 22 superb pastiches . . . This is more catnip for fans of stories faithful to Conan Doyle's original*

Part XIV: *. . . this standout anthology of 21 short stories written in the spirit of Conan Doyle's originals.*

Part XV: *Stories pitting Sherlock Holmes against seemingly supernatural phenomena highlight Marcum's 15th anthology of superior short pastiches.*

Part XVI: *Marcum has once again done fans of Conan Doyle's originals a service.*

Part XVII: *This is yet another impressive array of new but traditional Holmes stories.*

Part XVIII: *Sherlockians will again be grateful to Marcum and MX for high-quality new Holmes tales.*

Part XIX: *Inventive plots and intriguing explorations of aspects of Dr. Watson's life and beliefs lift the 24 pastiches in Marcum's impressive 19th Sherlock Holmes anthology*

Part XX: *Marcum's reserve of high-quality new Holmes exploits seems endless.*

Part XXI: *This is another must-have for Sherlockians.*

Part XXII: *Marcum's superlative 22nd Sherlock Holmes pastiche anthology features 21 short stories that successfully emulate the spirit of Conan Doyle's originals while expanding on the canon's tantalizing references to mysteries Dr. Watson never got around to chronicling.*

Part XXIII: *Marcum's well of talented authors able to mimic the feel of The Canon seems bottomless.*

Part XXIV: *Marcum's expertise at selecting high-quality pastiches remains impressive.*

The MX Book of New Sherlock Holmes Stories

Edited by David Marcum

(MX Publishing, 2015-   )

MX Publishing

MX Publishing is the world's largest specialist Sherlock Holmes publisher, with several hundred titles and over a hundred authors creating the latest in Sherlock Holmes fiction and non-fiction.

From traditional short stories and novels to travel guides and quiz books, MX Publishing caters to all Holmes fans.

The collection includes leading titles such as *Benedict Cumberbatch In Transition* and *The Norwood Author*, which won the 2011 *Tony Howlett Award* (Sherlock Holmes Book of the Year).

MX Publishing also has one of the largest communities of Holmes fans on *Facebook*, with regular contributions from dozens of authors.

www.mxpublishing.co.uk (UK) and *www.mxpublishing.com* (USA)

CPSIA information can be obtained
at www.ICGtesting.com
Printed in the USA
BVHW031643240521
607999BV00012B/2474/J